KNIGHTS

OF THE

ECLIPSE

GRAHAM RIVERS

First printing, 2025.
Cover Art and Interior art by Etheric Tales and etheric Designs

www.ChroniclesOfEvermore.com/

ISBN-13: 979-8-218-81532-5
Library of Congress Control Number: 2025923905

DEDICATION

To:
My parents, Bob and Patricia Kirk, my sister (Kerry)
& nieces (Elice and Brooklyn)

My Furbots:
Charlie, Dorothy Rose, & Blanche Sofia
The Baddest Cats to Have Ever Catted

Thomas Murphy

Acknowledgments

Dad: You read this beast of a series, struggling through a tablet just to read my books. You will never know how much that meant to me when no one else dared to put in that effort to explore this world.

Mom: you have always supported in the unseen ways with a word here and there or through a simple act of kindness that buoyed me through this journey.

Robert L. Bacon: You have been essential in this trial by fire. This book series would not have gone near as far as it has without your continued belief and guidance in seeing this project come into realization. Balance be, ever, always, and forevermore.

Caryn Gross-Devincenti and the West Boynton Beach Library Writers' Group: Yours and everyone's infinite patience, kindness, and well of information put me on the path toward publishing. If not for this wonderful group of men and women, I never would have met Rob or succeeded in this endeavour. I owe all of you so much gratitude.

Etheric Tales and Etheric Designs: I cannot credit this company enough with their diligent work and professionalism throughout the cover art and interior art process. They were prompt, fantastic to work with from start to finish, and their artwork is absolutely gorgeous. You can find them at this website: https://etherictales.com/etheric-designs/

Kari Holloway: Thank you so much for taking on formatting this monster. It means the world. You can find her at KH Formatting.

Friends & Coworkers: Some of you are as much a part of this journey as anyone else. You have heard me discuss this series to the hells and back, and deserve acknowledgement for listening to me nattering on about this obsession.

Thomas Murphy: a long time ago, I read a chapter to you and I will never forget the awe and joy in your face when you realized some of what you said to me about life ended up in this book. The words: 'You put me in a book. I'm in a book' lives on in one of these characters and forever will. You are greatly missed and never forgotten by the people who had the honor and fortune of meeting you.

Foreword

I grew up reading legends and myths and fell in love with folklore, fables, and the tales of time immemorial. Eventually, I realized that I could not see myself in any of the heroes or villains. The beauty of the Knights of the Roundtable was everyone was equal while sitting at that table. No matter how different, each voice at the table held as much weight as that of a king or other noble. King Arthur and his knights and ladies were a diverse bunch from all walks of life and came from as far as Persia, Africa, and Europe. Over time, their stories were forgotten in favour of other characters. Their stories were no less important than those who have become the frontrunners of Arthurian legend.

This series is meant to remember and bring to light the faces of such forgotten legends as Bors, Morien, Palamedes, Safir, Segwarides, Constantine, Dagonet, and so many others. It is also meant to bring to life a love for the legends, myths, and folklore of Europe, Asia, and Africa. Every culture has a story, and it is time to embrace and learn from those elements of the immense and riveting tapestry that makes up humanity and the human experience.

My hope is that anyone picking up the Chronicles of Evermore will relate to one character and know that you as a reader are seen, heard, and beloved. Balanced be and wade ever in the light and night. To this beginning and from my people to you and yours: I bid ye fair.

Tryfan Heights
Blvmenthal Blvffs
Valsworthy
Fournemout
Onryx Loch
Dyfed Landin
Rheged
Larnw
Valley
Cvhlwch Circle
Gu
Scotsborovgh
Camelaan Lake
Cornwall Shores
Brickelwhyte
Tintagel
North
Myrefeld
Abe Bay
(Llyr Lighthouse)
West Evermore
Isles Seas

Murphy's Hold
Orrinshire Pass
Wyllt Way
Lockinge River
Kirekwall
Glastonbury
Pellinore Falls
yesgarth
DuLac Pines
Dragon's Spine
Dunmore
Dynnah Loch
Spitsbergen
Gorre Retreat
Kyner Craggs
en's arth
Sagramore Halls
Porthcrawl
Zeffari
Esau Islet
Kindah

Cadogan Corrie
Glyder Mount
Kuhlkrait
Vulgate's Vault
Dragon's Spine
Penryth
Ri W
Caerdydd Loch
Siege Perilous
Barmwich
Grendel Grove
Odese Whar

East Evermore
Jotnar's Tomb
Grasmere
Wrentlow
Foel's Loch
Bach Haus
Sherhurst Forest
Suthseaxe
Lemstead
rune or
Dursvater
Isles Seas

Once Upon a Wishing Stone

Seven days of the world enshrouded in darkness because a Fomoiri got his knickers in a twist was a sodding way to end life. Being THE Fomoiri Prince of the Hells, Lugh Bheara was somewhat of an authority figure on the subject. Oh, aye! His grandsire was blowing from the Hells, and Lugh would be arsed if he didn't drive a spade into the old smoky bastard's bony chest and send King Balor back where he belonged.

As it were, Lugh shivered in his homespun tunic and trousers, a far cry from the royal he had been. With hands roughened from farming, he picked at the wood splintering from the shaft of the cobbled-together spade his boy had made for him. He didn't dare touch the metal of the spade, wary of the Fae, Nymphs', and Wild Ones' blessings imbued upon it. If he could deal his grandsire a good blow, then he would send his kin hurtling past the Gates of the Hells and forever block the free access Fomoiri had since the dawn of time. The blood and rituals staining the warped metal sent a blue-black sheen over it and Yggdrasil engraved into the iron base glinted between violet and silver.

"Stare any harder, and it'll combust, Fire Man," a twenty-seasonal man drawled from next to Lugh. "Then, there goes the greatest Dragon blessing of all."

Lugh squinted at the reformed highwayman slouching against the barn. "You're the most pathetic Dragon I've ever seen, Cymry. Dragons hoard gold and jewels and vast treasures. You hoard—Wait. What do you hoard again?"

Cymry rooted through his pocket and retrieved a palm-sized river stone with white streaks of unbroken lines crossing the black rock. "Wishes."

Lugh's eyebrow twitched. "I should've eaten you when I had the chance," he muttered, his irritation rising when Cymry handed Lugh the rock. "How is this a wish?"

Cymry guided Lugh to trace each line with his finger while chanting:

"Upon the stone cleaved in half and again aligned,
Make aloud your wish and trace each hoping line.
Come what may, our Fates forevermore unique.
The ring upon our stones shall ever be complete.
Dream upon a hoping line and call upon a wishing stone.
Two parts bound as one, we nevermore be alone."

The ruffian furrowed his fair eyebrows over his steely blue eyes and closed Lugh's hands over the stone. "Now make a wish aloud," Cymry said.

Asked Lugh, "Why aloud? What have you wished for?"

Cymry scratched his head. "Saying it aloud casts it in stone. I wished to be the greatest King to ever walk the pending roads, fair to all and their targe for evermore."

"Of course you did—" Lugh huffed but said to the rock, "I wish for protection of those I love and hold dearest for all eternity." When nothing happened, he focused on Cymry staring down the stone. "Uh, was that it?" he asked, fidgeting when the highwayman collected the rock.

Cymry buried the stone, and with all the gravity of a village priest, met Lugh's stare. "It is done. Your wish is made and may it be granted."

Lugh looked at the mound of dirt, back at Cymry, and out to his fields. He half-squeaked and shouted, "How many times have you buried your wishes on my land, you barmy slitherin' snake? Is that why my crops on the eastside won't grow?"

Shaking his hands from side-to-side, Cymry protested, "Nay, I buried them—" pointing to the right— "over there. See? You're just a shite farmer."

Lugh roared, "That is east! I don't know how you've lasted as long as you have! I should've eaten you, but you're such a shite Dragon, you'd give me indigestion!"

"As you say, Your Majesty. Sure you don't want me to hang abouts, Lulu?" Cymry sang, running his thumb over the old scar upon the upper part of Lugh's wing that was courtesy of himself. "If your Bampi is anything like you, it won't just be the Hells that I send him back to."

Lugh flicked out his black raven-feathered wings. "Cheap shot, you bell-end."

Cymry barked, "Oh, ho! Lugh the Fomoiri Prince of the Hells outdone by a mere mortal with a butter knife! Actually, I take that back. Pembroke had you hanging from a tree like a great big bat with her Earth spells. Don't even get me started on Windsor using his Air to pants your pale arse to outmoon the moon!"

Lugh groused, "If you and yours hadn't protected my girl, I would've killed you."

"Yer girl was the one who stared you down and insisted on us being her trinkets," Cymry said, sniggering at Lugh's miffed snort. "Never would have guessed something so small would square off against a Fomoiri. Between her and I, are you sure you don't want us being your seconds against Old Smoky Pants Balor?"

Lugh's wings flagged limp upon the dusty earth. "There'll be no mercy from my grandsire. It's best you be far from here. If I make it, I'll catch up to you and the others."

Cymry nodded gravely. "You have my blood oath that I'll keep ours safe."

The withered grass surrounding Lugh's farmstead crunched under the boots of the three other people he loved. Turning, Lugh braced himself when spindly arms wrapped around him and the fourteen-seasonal girl squeezed hard enough to strangle a lesser man. He set the spade against the rickety fence and encased his charge in an embrace.

Tangling his fingers in her wild mop of pink hair, he rocked the girl he had taken in since she was nine. "My beastie girl," he crooned.

Llewelyn keened, "Come with us. Please don't stay here. Everyone leaves me."

An older woman in her fifties sniffled and the twenty-two seasoned man next to her passed her a rag to blow her nose. "We'll never leave you alone," the woman said, gesturing to the last highwayman of Cymry's trio. "You have mine and Windsor's word."

Windsor gave a parting thump across Lugh's shoulder. "Pembroke is right, Llewelyn. No harm will ever come to you or any other future Fae ruler."

Furiously, Llewelyn shook her head. "Please, Thad," she implored the endearment for father to Lugh. "Nobody wanted me until you. Don't leave me."

Lugh retrieved from about his neck an amulet fashioned from gray and violet sea glass that had been melded with snowflake obsidian and hosted an engraving of a wolf and raven. He looped the old hemp necklace over Llewelyn's head. "The greatest of wonders arise from blending and melding what is meant to be," he said, pressing his palm over the pendant. "My wife gave me that as our oath to be Bonds of our own choosing. Use mine to find the one that belongs to my wife and son. When they are brought full-circle here, we'll all reunite once more."

Sniffling, Llewelyn tucked the necklace under her tunic. "Promise?"

He hugged her. "Aye, and this means I'm ever with you. It's not goodbye. It's fare thee well until we unite again. Wade ever in the light: be it the sun, moon, or both."

"Fair thee well," she croaked.

"I have your final mission. Find my boy and wife and tell them they were right." He murmured, directing her attention to the others. "Love ever grows in light and night."

She nodded against him. "Wager's on."

Lugh guided her into Cymry's hold. "Take her lest all shall be lost forevermore."

It scorched his soul hearing her cry for him and not going to her as Cymry set her on one of their plow horses and swung up behind her. Pembroke and Windsor mounted their horses. Lugh stepped into his barn to wait for them to gallop off before returning outside. His sole consolation was the spade his son, Finneas Bheara, had given him. Fate had a delightfully sick sense of humor with Finneas delivering to Lugh the weapon he would wield against their shared kin, the demonic Fomorian King Balor.

The irony was not lost on Lugh. He was one of many Fomoiri his grandsire sent to find the future Fae rulers of the Seelie and Unseelie. It was punishment for helping the Fomoiri High King of the Seas, Tethra, for siding with those like the High King of the Tuath Dé Danann, Nuada, and the Tuath Dé Danann God, Dagda. Tethra had become the shame of the Fomoiri, as he chose his love for the slave, Ogma, over his kind. Lugh's involvement had earned him the order to prove that he was not so weak to follow in less worthy family member's and allies' footsteps.

The consumption of the future Fae's souls would ensure Balor gained dominion over the Hells, Life, and Twilight, and herald in a new reign of Hells' Fire. Others were servants, but Lugh was his grandsire's natural-born Soul Bond. Lugh had followed the echoes of Twilight to hunt the veiled Unseelie ruler and the Twilight Phoenix. Sometimes, Lugh found the impression of the Sionnach Fox, a Wild God who worked alongside of the Unseelie ruler to lead the dead home.

One night, the Dark Fae ruler stopped in a boundary ring of yew trees and shrugged off a midnight cloak to reveal a woman with gold and silver gilded wings flaring from her back. Spellbound, Lugh approached until her fingers graced his cheek, startling him as she explored his black curled horns tipped with gold amid his hair.

She lilted, "Hello, Prince Lugh. Come to be your King's champion or mine?"

That night, Lugh abandoned his oath and sealed his duplicity in the rise of the future Fae King through fathering his son. Queen Mabily Bheara became his first true love, only matched when he held Finneas and realized adversaries could become more if they but willed it.

Alas, peace refused to last. After Fomoiri reaped a neighboring Witch's coven to find the upcoming Fae rulers, a youngling Witch named Elden joined the Bhearas. Lugh waited until his son and Elden became teen seasonals before rejoining the search for the other Fae ruler. After years of fruitless hunting, he found an abandoned Aessidhe Fae with vibrant pink hair in a mixed Light Fae and Nymph community in the Larnwelch Valley. Not even her village knew Llewelyn for what she was, not having contact with any Aessidhe Fae for generations. The darkness in her nature repelled most, the sole exception being Druir, a young Wood Nymph lass.

Lugh hid his Fomoiri nature even from Llewelyn, but after having it revealed to his new charge by Cymry and his crew, settled into life as a farmer. There had been no sign or way to reunite with Mabily, Finneas, or Elden.

Three years later, the first animals fell over dead. Then, entire herds. The weather turned frigid and sweltering as if indecisive over what season it was. Lakes and rivers churned as tumultuous as the seas while fish and frogs boiled alive or froze to death.

On the first day of the full solar eclipse, Lugh went before the gathered village of Fae and Nymphs to reveal himself as a Fomoiri and Llewelyn the future Unseelie Queen. Prostrating himself at their mercy, he offered his son's spade and said, "Bless it to win against Balor. I'll stay behind and stall him. All I ask is protect your Queen."

Silence met him until Druir dripped her blood on the spade. "My name is Druir of the Wild Woods and you have my blessing," she said, presenting the long shaft of the spade for anyone else to take.

Cymry nicked his thumb and vowed, "My name is Cymry of the Pending Roads." He smeared his blood over the engraving of Yggdrasil on the spade. "I'm not Fae, but to protect the future Unseelie Queen, I'll take the name of Pendraig to hide her."

Windsor spilled his blood and hesitated in front of Llewelyn. "I won't take a family name, but anyone else within my family will use my given as their surname. It will best hide you amid the weeds, Princess."

Next, Pembroke performed a ritual with her Earth Witchery, christening the spade with the Moon, and avowed, "So mote it be."

On the second day of the solar eclipse, the village summoned the Wild Ones. Cernunnos the Horned God, Artio the Bear Goddess, and many other Wild Gods came on the sixth day. All of them blessed the spade with their blood and a vow to walk with those they favoured whenever a Fomoiri rose high enough to rule Life, Twilight, the Shadows, and the Hells. The only one strangely absent was Sionnach the Fox.

Now, the village had scattered and the Bond between Lugh and Balor itched incessantly. Lugh knew Balor smelled his presence around the Unseelie heir. The tides were still in Lugh's favour as it was unlikely Balor knew if the heir was male or female. It bought them time in case Lugh failed to land a blow to send Balor back to the Hells.

Lugh muttered the mantra Elden had delivered the last he had seen of the lass:

"All shielded by the scions of sight, wind, water, fire, ice, metal, wood, and stone.
The Light of the moon harkens a Dragon rending Twilight and its black heart and bones.
Foiled by the scaly snake,
The lamb gifts its life in bloody Fate."

As a Fire Witch, Elden had Sight and knew something would arise from the battle between Lugh and Balor. *Aye, Cymry Pendraig was likely the intended Dragon, but then who is the lamb? Maybe me? But I'm no lamb,* Lugh mused, considering the spade.

Twigs cracked and Lugh spun around to find Druir of the Wild Woods. She raked her fingers through her sunset red hair and flicked strands to drift upon the dry earth.

He hissed at her, "Druir, you shouldn't be here. Balor will arrive soon."

"I'm counting on it." Druir rubbed her fingers and the tall grasses that had died shot upward with life crackling through them. The green Elemental light of Wood released in the air and the grasses flattened downward in a wave.

"You're a Witch," Lugh said, watching the grass lean back toward her.

"Unlike Fae, Nymphs can be Witches and are friendly with Light Fae," Druir said, finishing a ritual that allowed Balor to enter and contain him while Lugh still breathed.

Lugh tapped the shaft of the spade against his shoulder. "Your kind are not friendly with Dark Fae," he said, narrowing his eyes at her soft huff and the smile hugging the corners of her mouth. "Why so with Llewelyn?"

Druir gave a light lift of her shoulders. "Why not? I made a choice as did you. Still do."

The upturned crinkle of her eyes had Lugh take a harder look at her. She met his stare and the hair about his nape prickled. "What are you?" he whispered.

Another shrug and a splinter of moonlight slid over the ground to paint her in its grace. Nine silvery fox tails materialized behind her before the red at their tips took over to form one. Her hair and features darkened, lightened, and he lost count of the men, women, and children she embodied until she returned to her current form.

Said Druir, "I go by many names in many lands, Lugh. Sometimes Sionnach, other times Inari, Aguara, Húshén, Ogo, Fylgja… I'm of many faces and names."

Lugh shook his head. "I wondered why Sionnach didn't come to bless the spade."

"Ah, but I was the first to prick my finger on it." She reopened the scratch and dribbled her blood on the spade's center. "I blessed it as a Wood Nymph. Now, I bless it as a Wild One. I name you and Cymry the first true Aegis of our people. You are The Targe… The Shield… The Aegis of All."

Closing the blessing, Lugh cut his finger with his dagger and added his blood to the metal until it pooled in the center. The spade hissed and spat, glowing black and humming the trill of the Twilight Phoenix. Lugh bowed and said to Druir, "Thank you."

Across the way and hovering over the trees, a massive black cloud crept forward, harkening Balor's approach. Giving her fingers a final squeeze, Lugh slipped from her touch as she shifted into a red fox.

"Druir, keep my family safe and do me a favour—" at her chirp, he smiled tearfully— "Tell Cymry he's a wanker, but he's going to make a bloody fantastic King."

CENTURIES LATER

The Hells bore down on King Leinnet of the Earth Dragons with each lunge backward in a Larnwelch field as he scrambled from his towering former best mate and brother-in-law, Rallorc. With his pulse banging in his ears, Leinnet begged, "Rallorc, fight it. You must! No Fomoiri should ever hold sway over anyone!"

Blue flashed across Rallorc's Fomoiri-possessed red eyes, and the Jabberwock King hissed, "If you want to live, do as you must, Dragon King! I command you!"

Leinnet cringed, his sob broken and jagged in his throat. How could they know the prophecy declaring Rallorc's beloved wife and unborn child perishing would be by the Jabberwock King's own hand? Blinded by grief, Rallorc performed the dark rituals and became entrapped by the Fomoiri that possessed him through the rites.

Leinnet returned to find scorched earth and bones, the land guttering smoke and Twilight from Rallorc's madness and wrath. The Fomoiri that held dominion over Rallorc was an insidious beast older than King Balor and proclaimed himself as Bres the Blighter.

With scrub grass and rocks slicing open his hands, Leinnet shoved himself farther back. He let his Dragon begin to take hold, his nails growing into thick black talons—

Clink!

The shrill scream that echoed in Leinnet's ears had him glance down at the long, splintered shaft of a rusty discarded spade. Rallorc's jaw gaped and a ball of fire grew into the size of a fist within. Leinnet grabbed the spade, spun it around, and ducked under Rallorc's lower jaw, thrusting it into the toughened hide of the Jabberwock King's chest.

Blood spurted over Leinnet and he said, "I'm sorry, my brother." The spade slipped through his twitching fingers.

"Thank you," Rallorc wheezed, the Fomoiri receding to the Hells from its dying host and eyes as blue as the summer seas returning. "Thank you for freeing me, Brother."

The wind ruffled the blue-kissed white mane of the Jabberwock and his eyes slid closed as he relaxed into Twilight. His body darkened into ash, leaving behind his metal bones, talons, and fangs. The next gust of wind took the rest. Leinnet cradled the metal skull against his chest and whispered, "May you be at peace forevermore."

"Of that, shall he ever be," a dulcet voice said from behind Leinnet, whipping him around to a fox standing with her forepaws splayed over the spade. The fox shifted into a woman with hair glowing a burnished red in the growing dawn. She collected the spade and offered it to Leinnet as he scrambled to his feet.

"Who are you?" he asked.

Not even a rustle of grass broke the spell her presence cast. "The people of Evermore remember me as Druir the Nymph and first Wood Marshal of Evermore, but you know me as Sionnach of the Wild Woods," she answered, setting the spade into his hand, "And you are the third Aegis of Evermore and this—" patting the spade until it thumped against his chest— "chooses the next Aegis to shield our people. You will build anew the promise of greatest sacrifice to Evermore, Young Dragon King."

Leinnet collected the metal bones, teeth, and claws. In Jabberwock custom, the metal from their bodies was fashioned into weapons and jewelry for them to live on in their families. There was no one else in Rallorc's clan, not after Bres forced him to kill his kin. To this end, Rallorc would embody a blade meant to be a Targe for All.

The spade hummed and Leinnet swore someone murmured a prayer of, *"Mabily."*

Leinnet turned to Druir. "You called me the third Aegis. Who were the first two?"

Purring, Druir sidled closer. "The first was Lugh Bheara of the Fomoiri—" at his throaty growl, she tutted and flounced her fingers through Leinnet's ashen hair— "Aye, a Fomoiri Prince who shall remain a secret for now. Swear it on your blood, Dragon King."

Leinnet swallowed, his curiosity warring with his good sense. "My word is my bind. Who is the second?"

Druir traced her finger over the tree emblem engraved into the spade. "I knew him as Pendraig, but you call him the First King of Evermore, Cymry Pendragon."

About the empty field, Leinnet recognized stakes that had been a fence and mound that was a homestead from bygone days. The names of Cymry Pendragon and the first eight Marshals for the Seven Elemental Houses of Evermore were a centuries-old legend and cloaked in as much mystery as the myths connecting them with Evermore's first Queen, Elden Pendragon, and the first Ebony Knight, Finneas Bheara.

The haunting cry of the Twilight Phoenix trilled in the winds of the past as though for a loved one beyond her reach. "A great sacrifice was made here," Leinnet said, spying a crystalline tear flash down Druir's cheek.

Said Druir, "Aye. The Gates of the Hells were ever open to the Fomoiri until Lugh closed and locked them against his kind."

"Yet, they walk amid us," Leinnet spat bitterly.

She snarled. "Only when fools invite Fomoiri to share their bodies for power. Lugh didn't sacrifice himself for that. Sacrifices will continue until we come full circle."

Leinnet averted his gaze to the spade. "We were fools."

She wiped aside her grief. "Name the weapon of your sacrifice, Lord King of Evermore."

Leinnet wondered what she meant when a Pendragon King already sat the throne of Evermore. The spade throbbed and silver flashed over the metal. Leinnet chuckled and said, "Your name shall be *Vorpal*, the name my sister and Rallorc chose for their son. May you be what marks the beginning of the end of all sacrifices. Balanced be, *Vorpal*."

SPRING AND SUMMER ROYAL PROGRESS LOG
EBRILL TO JUNI

Dydd Sul, Ebrill 2

I, King Arthwyr Pendragon, mark this as the first day of what I decree as Royal Progress. We represent The Seven Elements of Earth, Water, Air, Fire, Metal, Wood, and Ice, and at my lovely Queen Guinevere's suggestion, we have embarked upon this great mission of assessing our wonderful realm of Evermore. Since there is no better way to know the needs of my people than to directly mingle with them, I'm riding with my Knights of the Eclipse, and we will be traveling as one movement of progress and hope.

My only contention is the Aegis of Evermore refuses to present Vorpal as would show to the people of Evermore that the current Kingship of Evermore is right and true following the Red and White Duels of Draigs against my father, Uther. Truly, if we shed the secrecy surrounding the Aegis of Evermore's identity, there would be far more acceptance and accountability in that post as well as the Royal Pair of Evermore. Alas, Vorpal remains in the safe keeping of another at Elden's Hearth. Whoever knew two with such opposing natures could wield Vorpal at once? Never in Evermore's history have there been two. Wonders never cease, but I still wish all could know our secret Aegis.

Dydd Llun, Ebrill 3
Bedwyr Wallach

What the Hells is this rubbish in this travel log?

I'm going to kill my cousin. Only Ewain would sign me up for the Progress roster. Mightier-than-thou Healer freak!

To make matters worse, we're stopping at Sagramore Halls and picking up a load of fluff-brained harpies for their debut in the Summer Court. Oh, happy day. Let me vomit now.

This bloody Progress is a trip through the Hells. Arthwyr is only going to see what everyone else wants him to see as King, never the reality. If he wanted to see the realm beyond his nobles blowing hot air up his arse, he should moonlight as a peasant for a few weeks.

Dydd Mawrth, Ebrill 4
Galahad DuLac

Ha! Ewain didn't sign you up for Progress. I did.

We've arrived at Sagramore Halls. These girls are driving Bedwyr up a wall. I'm glad my father insisted I join him on this Progress. Life couldn't be better.

Dydd Mercher, Ebrill 5
Bedwyr Wallach

Sod off, you contentious berk! You're going to rue this.

Since I've been commanded to update the log because of fighting with Galahad, here it is:

We're one day from Zeffari.

Dydd Iau, Ebrill 6
Lance DuLac

Zeffari is a nice village. The people and their crops are flourishing. When I retire my lordship to Galahad, I might stay here. It's much warmer than DuLac Pines. They have these yellow prickly fruits that are divine. So sweet. They candy them, put them in bowls, fry them. So good with rice. Even better in drinks.

Arthwyr put my son and Bedwyr in his Get-A-Long tunic. We almost lost them to Twilight, but it ended up fine. Afterwards, the mayor of Zeffari gave me a coqui-piney-apple drink. They're called piña coladas, and they are great. They make everything about Progress better.

Dydd Gwener, Ebrill 7
Arthwyr Pendragon

We're four days from Porthcrawl and Kindah.

Oh, what am I going to do with my sons? Maryck started picking on Ulrich again. Of course, Ulrich accepted it as he always does. There's too much Cameliard in my youngest.

Bedwyr and Galahad are fighting again too. Thank Evermore we have five wagons to keep them apart. They'd kill each other otherwise.

Dydd Sadwern, Ebrill 8
Constantine

It would be Saturday in my country of Viteliu. We have been on Progress for a week.

The weather has been fair. Thus far, the realm is on its way to recovery from Arthwyr's and Uther's Duels of the Draigs. Assessing the pulse of Evermore and her people has been insightful.

My charge, Palamedes Sasania of Saraceni, has spent much of Progress hung over the side of a wagon and sick. Travel on horse or wagon does not agree with him.

The members of Progress have been fractious. Infighting drags and makes the days longer.

We're nearing Porthcrawl and Kindah. May God bless us and this journey.

Dydd Llun, Ebrill 10
Bedwyr Wallach

Delayed two days because that flaming tart, Lady Jocelyn Sagramore, made supper to express her undying love and appreciation to our village dunce of a King and his merry arseholes. Poisoned the lot of them, except for me, the Saracen puke pustule, and that pious prick priest, all because of some bollocks called Lent and giving up pork in concession to those carpet kissers he loves. Fun times.

Constantine

It's Lent, Bedwyr. Lent! And Islam is a well-respected religion in the East, with a bounty of beautiful and diverse cultures and people. Expand your perceptions more. Also, you could stand to exercise some restraint and sacrifice. Forty days would be good for your soul.

Bedwyr Wallach

I'm exercising a lot of restraint by not killing you all on this barmy trip through the Hells. To reconcile my suffering, this travel log just turned into my version of One Thousand and One Nights: So, not a creature stirred in the abandoned Throne Room. Except that was not quite true of the dark and gloom. Atop old goat Uther's Throne and accursed space, two people made merry as they anointed that place.

Dydd Mawrth, Ebrill 11
Myrddin Emrys

Bedwyr, future generations are going to think King Arthwyr and his Knights are a joke. For the love of Odin, **DO NOT** *add another bloody thing in the travel log about anointing anything else, you ruddy degenerate!*

We continue to Porthcrawl and make excellent time. The temperature from last year's winter keeps the weather fair. With good fortune, the trip will continue to have favourable conditions.

Dydd Mercher, Ebrill 12
Arthwyr Pendragon

Porthcrawl has a lot of resources, and more coming in. The economy is booming. Evermore seems back on track for success. We have entered a golden age.

I got lost in an alley searching for a gift for Guinevere. For the life of me, I can't remember much about the young woman I followed into a shop. It was the strangest thing. When I entered, the only person inside was the old proprietor, Auntie Viv. She told me that what I sought was in the back.

An old cedar box drew me to it. There is something about the cloak I found within. When I touched it, I could hear waves lapping on the beach like a lullaby. That cloak is perfect for the woman who has given me the greatest treasure anyone could bestow on me. I haven't thought of anything else since I left that shop nor was I able to find the place again as where I thought the shop had been was nothing but charred boards and ash after I returned to it. I still taste the ash.

Dydd Llun, Ebrill 17
Constantine

We are on a ferry from Cornwall Shores.

The weather is fair. Palamedes is not. Traveling by boat is as debilitating for him as being on a horse or wagon. Ewain Gorre and Lamorac Pellinore are weary from soothing his seasickness. They've enlisted Bedwyr to help fluctuate Palamedes' body fluids. It seems to be helping.

Dydd Iau, Ebrill 20
Lance DuLac

We are staying on the outskirts of Scotsborough. The town is skeletal. Ruins, really. Like Camelaan Lake, it is a burnt-out husk. The ground is cracked into plates. Scrub grass crinkles from the occasional gust of wind. With little hope for agriculture, the few people left are worn down and rendered hopeless. Destitution clings and serves as a reminder that not all of Evermore is recovered from the Red and White Draigs' Duels. Even after these past few better years, there is still much wrong that hinders our advancement. Some of the locals will not change and see no reason to better our realm. Not if it calls into question timeworn traditions and deep-seated favouritism within Evermore's old guard.

Arthwyr has not been eager to write in the log since Porthcrawl. Something drags our King down and seeing Evermore's people suffering in Scotsborough does not help.

Two weeks later: Dydd Llun, Mai 4
Bedwyr Wallach

We've picked up a loudmouth from Blumenthal Bluffs: Brynn Blumenthal.

My arm's acting up again. Bloody Uther and my father.

That Saracen rat, Palamedes, puked all over Lance. That was nice.

Arthwyr's moping like one of his sons died. Can't figure out what the Hells is going on there. Every time Arthwyr is around Maryck or Ulrich, he gets all quiet. At night, he strolls by himself.

One week later: Dydd Mercher, Mai 13
Gaheris Foxbury

Allo. First entry from me. Just joined the King's Progress from Murphy's Hold with my nephew, Harlan. We stopped at Fournemouth. They had mud wrestling. The reigning Mud Champion of Fournemouth threw Myrddin Emrys into a mud pit. Oh, the look on Myrddin's face.

Bedwyr Wallach

I got Galahad to eat a mud-worm pie. Have some num-nums, cousin. I know you're reading this.

Galahad DuLac

Arthwyr made me write one hundred times: I will not drown my cousin in a mud puddle or suffocate him in his sleep with my dirty socks. *Choke on that, you pillocky prat. Totally worth the sore hand I got.*

Myrddin Emrys

Unfortunately, the adults writing in this log act more like children. Sad state of affairs for our future when people model themselves after any one of them.

Dydd Mercher, Mai 20
Arthwyr Pendragon

I love my people! The village of Kirekwall have great taste. They gifted me a cloak. I'm wearing it everywhere. Unfortunately, Ulrich burned the other cloak the people of Kirekwall gifted to his Queen Mother under the mistaken belief it was tinder because it was made out of sticks.

Our next stop is Iyesgarth. I wonder what wonders we'll find there. So many things to discover in Evermore. So many. Like what I discovered in Porthcrawl. I'm not sure how to address it. Perhaps my advisor, Myrddin Emrys, will make my path clearer. Balanced be, I hope Myrddin's Oracle instincts provide clarity. His wife, Oracle Nimue Abe, confirmed Balance was nigh when she performed my Scrying Ball Divination.

Sometimes I can't escape feeling that I have failed my family, my friends, and the realm. I'm tired of trying to right the wrongs that many generations of my family have visited upon Evermore and our people. Perhaps, our current Aegis of Evermore is right to uphold their secrecy. The less who know, the better. Vorpal will move on to a new Aegis of Evermore if I fail in securing Balance or become the reason it slips past Evermore once more.

CHAPTER 1

DYDD SADWERN, MAI 23
STRAIGHT OFF THE CARROT CART

For every untoward action there was bound to be irreconcilable consequence. Earlier squabbles had now reached a boiling point, fueled by King Arthwyr's decision to go on Royal Progress. This action was likely to spark the inevitable, and as Myrddin observed his confederates, he knew that he had little reason to think otherwise.

Across Iyesgarth's dusty octagon-shaped town square, Myrddin watched Ewain and Bedwyr bickering more vociferously than usual. With his hand on his katana's hilt, Bedwyr circled Ewain like a wolf sizing up its prey. The longer stray strands, on the otherwise short dark hair around his neck, stood out straight. Ewain spun around, green light crackling and his turquoise cloak snapping behind him as he swiped at Bedwyr with his foot. Even from a distance, Myrddin could see Bedwyr's gaze darkening from cinnamon brown to blood red.

Peasants kept their distance, hastening over cracked, noisy cobblestones. The closest merchant set his pottery and dishes below the counter. His neighbor clapped her hands and created an array of brown light that enabled her Wood Element to form a barrier between her fabrics and the two bellicose Knights.

Snarled barks drew Myrddin's attention to Galahad whose wild shouts were directed at Trystan. Perched on Trystan's shoulder, a merlin held an apple in her claws. Fluffing out her feathers, the bird bobbed her head as if in time with Galahad's frenzied screams. As the Knight shook his fist, his robes got tangled on his arm.

Flicking tribal beads over his shoulder, Trystan droned on unintelligibly in his Lietuvan tongue. Silver pockmarked scars and a burned-off brand of a skull with crossbones shaped into scythes from indentured servitude to a pirate lined his bare upper arms, perspiration changing the top of his vest from light olive to deep forest green. Whipping into an impressive about-face, Galahad stomped toward the fountain in the middle of the square and hollered, "That fruit was my breakfast. One of these days, I'm going to stuff that damned bird of yours, you gypsy!"

Muffled snorts from Harlan, the young Foxbury Heir, had Myrddin turning his way. The lad straightened and fixed a more respectable mien to his features but gave himself away as his mischievous bright blue eyes crinkled about the corners as though he was above the whole mess. He compounded his indifference by asking, "Why must Galahad, Ewain, and Bedwyr fight so?"

Myrddin replied with equal nonchalance, "Should be Fire Elementals instead of Water, eh? They're related to the Esau and that family was built to be as tumultuous as the Isles Seas."

Waggling his eyebrows, Harlan said, "Since Galahad stormed off, five ingots Ewain's going to deck Bedwyr."

"Wagering against your allies is unseemly, Harlan."

"Is that a nay?"

Myrddin eyed the Knights. "Five ingots and you brush down my horse."

"Wager's on, Milo—"

Myrddin tensed when Ewain jabbed his finger against Bedwyr. Bedwyr braced as if to throw himself at Ewain, stilled, and jerked his piercing stare to Myrddin and Harlan. Withering his lip, he stalked off, leaving Ewain to curse the air.

"Shite!" Harlan barked.

As the youth dug through his purse, Myrddin wiggled his fingers until the coins were shoved into his hand. "Language, boyo," Myrddin drawled. "I'll leave Lailo's kit out for you."

Summer gourds thumped upon a nearby table as two farmers set their produce on display. Myrddin eyed a clear sky, yet he heard thunder. If it wasn't for the mugginess left from the previous night's storm, he would have shrugged it off. But thinking about it further, he said to the King of Evermore, who was now at his side, "A storm might be on the way."

Arthwyr emitted a disinterested grunt and strode toward Iyesgarth's mayor, Lincoln Limawit, who was pontificating on a makeshift platform. After a brief conversation, Arthwyr spun away from the mayor and yelled, "Behind you, Myrddin!"

Earth quaking under Myrddin's boots sent chills racing through his legs and up his spine. Like hailstones hitting against glass, pebbles rattled noisily on the uneven cobblestone surface. A fast-approaching billowing plume of dust heralded the rattle and slam of a horse-drawn cart racing over the ruts in the bumpy street. With his heart bounding, Myrddin shoved Harlan aside. As the wagon drew closer, the small figure of a girl perched on the front seat came into view. She snapped the reins as a cream-colored steed and its rider sped after her.

The pursuer hollered, "Stop, you hooligans! Unhand my produce, you little berks!"

The girl in the cart howled a laugh that sounded like crows cawing. Wood skidded over the stonework of the town square, and a change in terrain kicked up even more dust. The cart lilted to one side, and the wheels screeched on the cobbles. Myrddin glimpsed a teen-seasoned boy in the bed of the cart, the lad's features fixed in vivid green.

The wagon veered again, yanking the shire horse to and fro as if the animal and the cart were toys. Rearing up, the poor beast lashed its forelimbs. The girl dropped the reins and vaulted from the driver's seat, landing on the bed of the cart. Wild hair whipped around her freckled features as she snapped her fingers, and Fire singed the straps and hemp holding the harness together before rocketing to the Pendragon Royal Banner.

With a screech, the mayor yelled, "Not the banners!" to which the fire leapt to the neighboring flags for the Seven Elements and Oracles.

The horse gave a mighty lunge and its harness broke. He darted across the square, his hooves sending sparks in all directions. In his flight, the terrified animal surged toward Galahad, who stood stock still and gaping in the midst of the chaos.

Rushing to Galahad, Myrddin reached for the Water Elemental's cloak. The fabric barely brushed his fingers as Galahad was wrenched backward and tumbled into Trystan. Pure muscle galloped past, and the horse's flank shoved Myrddin into both men. Blue light wreathed Galahad and Trystan as their lips met, the sharpness of their Soul Bond activation filling the air like fire-scorched charcoal. Myrddin caught the flash of Trystan's hazel eyes as Galahad covered the three of them with a large Water array.

Trystan pushed Galahad into a stall, as the cart's long hitch zipped by Myrddin, who threw himself backwards to avoid becoming impaled. The wagon crashed, and cabbages and carrots exploded midair; the vegetable missiles whacked Myrddin in the chest with the force of a trebuchet launch. He gagged and flailed his arms, gripping a clump of greens, as he fell onto the cobblestones.

As a rapidly spinning wheel flew off the cart, the fleeing townsfolk scrambled in a mass of humanity. The wagon fell hard on its side and more vegetables went airborne. Clinging to the cart's tenuous frame, the boy in the back vomited over the side. Lance DuLac became the victim, his doublet a disgusting mess. Arthwyr evaded the spray of puke, but a shoe struck his forehead and flew upward, its shoelaces tangling in a line holding the King's welcome banner. A whoosh of air upset his equilibrium and Arthwyr fell backwards onto his arse.

Barreling toward the fountain, the wagon sent birds screeching into flight, an abundance of feathers drifting in the air like leaves in an autumn breeze. Blind, deaf, and oblivious to the mayhem, the village's old Healer, Dottsie, flicked crumbs onto the ground for the birds.

Motion became a wave of turquoise and purple, guiding Myrddin's attention to Ewain as he vaulted into the square's fountain. A blue array appeared in front of Ewain, and his hair whipped about his face. The exterior edges of the array turned green with an incandescent pulsing glow. Water rose into two shimmering walls, and the center of the array expanded until both columns swept forward.

Myrddin climbed and swayed on his feet until the water blasted him back into Lance. Lance smacked his palms against the ground and a green light shot up from beneath the soil, the earth rippling forward like water toward the old Healer. The ground erupted into a protective barricade and the wagon splintered into a thousand pieces. Shot from the cart, the youngsters flew forward. The boy bowled over Ewain as the girl overshot the fountain and flattened Arthwyr for a second time. A twang snapped through the air as the lone fluttering banner for the Fire symbol drifted in a final fanfare of tepid greatness over the King.

CHAPTER 2

PHOENIX RISING

Carrots and cabbages drooped about in orange and purple piles as they dotted the cobblestones and hung limply on the sagging lines overhead. The shire horse nosed a ripe head of cabbage in passive interest. Their faces set in shock and awe, the villagers tracked the tumbling vegetables as sections of the wooden cart lay scattered throughout, with Viera Tillwith and her brother, Garrett, in the center of the calamity.

The crack of canvas drew Viera's attention upward. The one remaining line, with the King's welcome banner, whipped in the wind, together with a shoe—her left.

Their farming neighbor, Cletus, stomped his foot and pulled at his hair. He grabbed some of his ruined vegetables. "My feckin' produce, you little barmy Tillwiths!"

He brandished a fistful of carrots at her and her brother, but Viera ignored Cletus and turned her gaze to the beet-red faces of both her father and Mayor Limawit.

A vein bulged on Mayor Limawit's temples as he screamed, "Sully Tillwith, your damned kids again!"

Viera's father stood next to the pumpkin stall he rented each year. He lowered his bushy eyebrows and his gaze all but disappeared.

The King of Evermore, his bent crown hanging precariously from his head, staggered to his feet, small sticks jutting at odd angles from his robe. Toadstooled porcupines high on fairy dust rotated in fewer circles. He arched his neck back to the burning banners, stretched out the one for Fire, and blinked at it.

Viera's stomach lurched when she connected what had happened. She had knocked over the ruddy King of Evermore! Edging away from Arthwyr, she stilled upon meeting her mother, Rhoshlyn's, emerald glare. Garrett flopped into a pile of wet robes and belched water onto the pavers like a beached fish.

Viera called out to him, "I told you we'd be famous."

It wasn't until their father crossed in front of him that Garrett scrambled upright as a long booming laugh rumbled through the air.

"If only more villages entertained me like this," the King bellowed, still laughing as he walked toward the children and their father, who were now standing together.

"Yes, my Lord King!" Mayor Limawit sputtered as he tried to keep up with Arthwyr's pace. As soon as they reached the Tillwiths, he added, "Two of our youngest citizens are a true comedy duo. We call them Tillwith-Dee and Tillwith-Dum. Guess which one's which?"

Viera craned her neck. "Who are you calling a comedy duo, you stodgy old codger?"

The mayor cupped her jaw with his hand, covering her mouth completely. "Such sweet young children."

She ground her teeth into his palm until the mayor yanked it away from her. As he walked off rubbing his hand, she sent him a breezy smile.

A man approached, wearing the black-and-gray-colored robes of the Ebony Knight. "Sire, it would be fortuitous for the boy to learn another trade."

The King stroked his beard. "What have you, Lance? What would you recommend for the lad?"

"I'm sure we can find a suitable use for him." And to Garrett, Lance asked, "How old are you, son?"

Garrett gulped and shoved his sodden black hair behind his ears. "Sixteen springs, Milord."

Lance hummed and turned to Viera, who ogled at the sight of the targe emblem on his shoulders showcasing each phase of the lunar cycle and more than confirming his office as the Righthand of the Kingdom. "And you?" he asked.

Shying from him and standing closer to Garrett, Viera squeezed her lips into a thin line. She glanced at the splotches along the fountain, a handprint on the stone a grim reminder of how a noble could flip from tolerant to lethal as fast as the wind changes direction.

Lance's head moved as if following her stare and a stillness settled in his frame, the corners of his mouth twitching down. He faced her again, and she relaxed at the light dip of his chin as if he understood her fears. He turned to Garrett. "How old is your sister?"

Garrett stuttered, "Fourteen, soon to be fif-fifteen summers, Milord."

The Ebony Knight said to Arthwyr, "My King, perchance Battle School and defending The Pass for the boy. He's of a good size, and with proper training can be a solid asset."

Garrett's face turned from green to stark white. His father stepped forward and addressed the King: "Milord, we are but humble farmers. Our growing season continues, and I will need my son for the harvest. It is but him, my wife, Rhoshlyn, my daughter, Viera, and me. My wife can no longer bear children. Sire, I beg you for your mercy and good will."

King Arthwyr eyed Sully. "The peasantry can serve Evermore best by defending its land. You may have your son for harvest, but he'll train at the base camp near Orrinshire Pass during winter. Now, your children provided quite a bit of fun for us, but that good man has lost his produce. I'm not going to make you pay for our enjoyment, so from my coffers the farmer will be compensated. So mote it be."

Cletus sank to his knees. "Thank you, Your Majesty. Thank you."

A noble in red and black Fire robes stepped forward. "Aye, Myrddin, is there anything you wish to add?" Arthwyr asked as he adjusted his crown.

Myrddin pointed to both the Fire banner and to Viera. "My Lord King, what of the girl?"

"She did set quite a few banners on fire," the King said. "Mine included. That demands some consequence."

"A shame to waste her potential here in Iyesgarth when she could be a great boon for Evermore." Myrddin chuckled. "We might even save this poor man from losing a cabbage or two in the future."

"Fine," Arthwyr said. "Induct her into the Fire Temple at Elden's Hearth. For now, we add her to our Progress."

Horror filled Viera. She squawked, "Don't I get a say in any of this?"

The King rubbed his forehead and said to Myrddin, "You may give her a choice if you want. I daresay, the two of you will make quite the pair as Apprentice and Master."

Myrddin offered a slight bow to the lass. He settled his stare on the scowling girl and asked, "Why wouldn't you wish to join the Fire Temple, child?"

"What good would it do me?" She folded her arms in front of her. "And my name's not Child, sir. It's Viera."

"Ah, a fine name," said Myrddin. "It means truth. You can harness your talents under the tutelage of a Fire Master. A great many things can come from this."

"So, I go to the capital and learn how to tend a hearth elsewhere?" She scuffed her remaining booted toe against the packed ground. "I already figured that out for myself—here."

Myrddin shuffled closer. "You deserve to become an asset to Fire and to Evermore. Your Fate will be more than you can ever attain here."

From beneath the bangs of her long hair, her green eyes flecked with brownish-gold met his gaze. "Fine. Show me what you can teach me."

Myrddin presented an orange-yellow array with runes sliding into place that throbbed above his fingers. He nurtured the array until embers hovered over his skin, the borders illuminating as light and heat melded into a sphere that weaved over his palms.

Viera sighed and said, "Anybody can do that. Hells, if a cabbage had half a brain and half an Element—" Her father cuffing the back of her head drew her up short. "What, Da? It's true. Even I can do better than that."

Myrddin raised an eyebrow. "Fair enough, lass. Let's see your better."

Viera lifted her hands and plumes of smoke erupted from the heavily packed soil. Glittering black sigils snaked over the ground as two runes writhed together as one. The other Knights tensed, a few fidgeting more than others, their hands straying closer to their weapons. Myrddin spied Bedwyr in the shadows, gripping the hilt of his blade as he pinned

Palamedes with his free hand to a stall to keep the Saracen youth from scuttling closer.

Myrddin blinked and pivoted toward the girl. A screech shattered the quiet as Fire burst forth from the sigil. He jumped when a bird ascended, the phoenix's wings flaring like flames in a hearth, but not the slightest finger of fire touched him or any of the spectators. Gilded wings caught sunlight and undulating orange and red plumage slid into individual arrays he'd never seen before.

With hot embers sputtering and falling down to earth, any thatched roofs might catch fire and the buildings would burn to the ground. But the lass flicked her fingers, the embers burning out and black soot wafting harmlessly in the wind. The fiery little imp bounced on the balls of her feet.

The dark sigil on the ground still glimmered. Myrddin stared at the image shining on the soil—the clear depiction of a firebird in flight, its head thrown back, as proud as the lass who had created it.

A wooden robe rustled next to Myrddin. Arthwyr's voice carried a hushed quality as he asked, "What do you think?"

Myrddin glanced toward Viera. "She will do, Milord. She will do just fine."

CHAPTER 3

IYESGARTH'S REALITY

How this day had changed. Myrddin remembered the morning all too well. He was not sure when resignation became his default reaction. Perhaps it began earlier with the unappealing sprawl of the Larnwelch Valley, sway of its parched high grass and stilted grains, and stench of soured mulch stinging his nose and eyes. The Maids' constant harping along the way hardly helped. And the visit to Iyesgarth had just begun.

As the King's retinue meandered through the village, Myrddin's attention centered on the drab, mottled, gray buildings. Even the mud people from Fournemouth had added flair and color to their town. Conversely, Iyesgarth, where locals brought their harvest for the Lord of the Fief, appeared as tired and dejected as an old man. Myrddin counted no more than ten buildings. Only one was a two-story structure, and likely the home of the mayor.

Nay, he was wrong.

Down an alley, there was a three-story structure, an inn of sorts with a stable bordering the far side. Closer to the central market area, worn banners hung limp and tattered on hemp lines. They stretched between buildings, in a crisscross pattern like a child's game of cat's cradle.

However, several tangles balled the lines, and flocks of birds perched on the longer portions and forced the hemp lower.

The fountain in the center of the town square had been scoured. So, some effort *did* go into sprucing up the place. Myrddin dreaded to think what the fountain had looked like prior to their arrival, as discolored splotches still populated the bottom of the stone basin. The scrubbed outline of a hand drew a shudder from him.

Myrddin squinted at the Elemental banners: Air, Earth, Fire, Ice, Water, and Wood. An orange, blue, and white flag represented Air. The Earth symbol was composed of three triangles depicting a cream-topped mountain range. Similar to Air's banner, Fire was red, yellow, and black for Fire as gray, white, and blue made-up Ice. The Water symbol was an S-shaped purple line separating bright blue from forest green. Wood was so simple a child might have drawn the series of tree growth rings. A dingy gray banner with hands all over it stood for the Oracle's symbol. Oddly, no banner displayed Metal's colors and design.

A pointy object jabbed Myrddin's side. When it poked him a few more times, he bit the inside of his cheek and struck his fist at a dead, deep-fried rat bound to a stick.

Lance DuLac bounced back on his heels as Myrddin missed him with a sizzle of his Fire. Sweat had darkened Lance's rich brown hair along his neck, and the heavier gray and black robes of his office had damp patches around his shoulders and chest. Swishing the souvenir in a salute, he held the rat's snout near his brow.

"How old are you again, Lance?" Myrddin asked.

"Thirty-eight winters," Lance replied, dipping his souvenir like a wand from a fantasy tome, "not that you care one whit."

"Where in Evermore did you get that?"

"From a stall. Couldn't *not* buy it. They had a special. Buy one, get one. Isn't it great?"

"Only you would find such a thing an idle amusement."

Lance sniggered. "Hardly the only one. Looks like Bedwyr already has plans for his."

Across the way, the Knight of twenty-one winters held up a taxidermized squirrel as a gaggle of noble girls passed him. He tucked the stick into his belt and grinned as one lass fluttered her fan in his direction. The afternoon sun caught the silver flecks in her plaited hair and the glitter in her aqua Water robes.

"When is Lady Sagramore ever going to learn?" Myrddin groaned. "She's mooning up the worst tree she could find."

Lance mumbled distractedly, "She definitely needs to be careful with her attentions."

"With how Bedwyr rebuffs her, and the bad blood between him and her father, that should have settled things long ago."

Lance tapped the rat against his side, flipped it over, and scratched its belly. "Cuchulain expects his daughters to wed well and bear fruit. Bedwyr outranks even us. Can you blame her for going after him?"

"That might be the case if it were anyone save him. Cuchulain still wants an execution, and he shan't settle for anything less."

Darkness settled on Lance's features as a coarseness entered his voice; one reserved for the few descents into irritation that he so rarely displayed after his late father-in-law trained him in courtlier demeanor and carriage. "He shan't have one with Bedwyr. He had his pick of leftovers from Uther's and Jormund's depleted forces. Bedwyr is off limits, and the sooner Cuchulain gets over it, the better."

The fine hairs rose along Myrddin's arms, and he murmured, "He's right behind us, isn't he?"

Lance gave the slightest dip of his chin. "Play along. He's been messing with that thing all morning."

A hand latched onto Myrddin's, and the snout of a fried lizard poked his nose. "Sneak-sneak, lizard-assassin attack!"

Myrddin stared past the dead creature, not to Bedwyr but to a boy of fifteen springs prancing around in front of him. "Oh, the horror. Felled by... whatever the Hells that thing is."

Palamedes Sasania twirled his dead toy from one hand to the other. "I've graduated into stealth mode." The Saracen boy pointed at his hazel eyes and directed his fingers at the square. "If I got you two, then it's time for me to up my game to Master of Sneakering."

"Wait!" Myrddin hollered as the boy moved away, missing him by inches. "Oh, bloody Hells!"

The boy slunk toward Bedwyr, who had his back to him as he faced a stall of deep-fried creatures. Palamedes no sooner lifted his lizard when Bedwyr snatched his dead squirrel from his belt. He smacked several places on the youth and dropped him like a load of potatoes. Whistling and twirling the squirrel in a lazy circle, Bedwyr stepped over Palamedes and strolled to the next stall.

Sitting, Palamedes shouted, "Ninja-goo is the greatest!" He jumped to his feet and chased after Bedwyr. "Teach me more ninja-goo, Master."

Bedwyr flailed his squirrel at the boy. "Dammit, no, you Saracen plague! Get away from me!"

Myrddin pinched the bridge of his nose. "This keeps getting worse and worse. Can we go home yet?"

He was interrupted by brown and green paint just missing them. "They must have finished the Wood symbol this morning," Lance said as he quickly moved away from any drips hitting him.

As more paint splashed on the ground, Myrddin grunted and said, "Remind me not to stand under any of the banners."

As they drew closer to the center of town, the last two banners took up the most prominent positions in the square. Bless Iyesgarth for having a Metal symbol after all. Its standard, two silver swords with gold hilts superimposed on a black circlet, was bright and well cared for. The only better-kempt banner was one with a silver Dragon gripping a gold chalice and a sword in its front claws. After King Uther decimated villages for failing to display the Pendragon standard, every village now kept one. Iyesgarth's leadership was lackluster but not stupid.

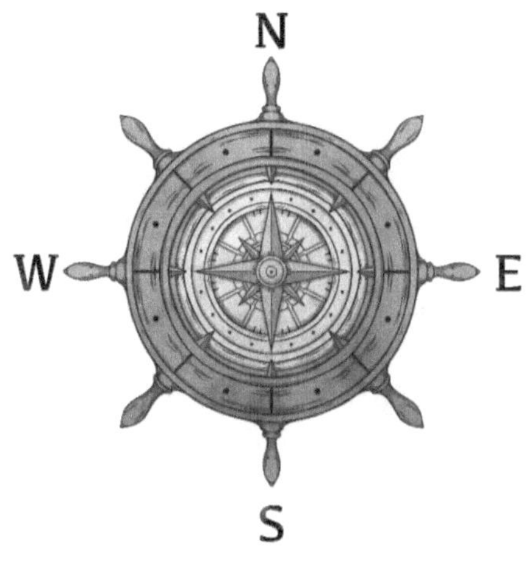

CHAPTER 4

ISLES SEAS AND SEA GLASS

Spittle pinged against the metal vessel next to the trapper. Crevices lined the man's features as he squinted from his rickety chair. A brindled dog, with half its lower jaw and canines framing its scabby nose, grunted next to its master.

A breeze rattled the dead creatures hanging above the wooden table, their vacant eyes fixed on Myrddin. His teen-seasonal daughter, Maerna, suffered from a headache back at camp, and he felt he owed her a souvenir.

Upon accepting a bird statue from a villager in a coastal town, she had cupped the dung-molded bird and trilled with a high-pitched squeal, "Oh, how charming!"

Days later, Myrddin found the same souvenir glued to a support beam in one of their wagons after the noble boys had repurposed it from a firepit. Maerna had not been thrilled with its revival, but was too polite to air her disdain; instead, she punched wide holes into linens and sewed her discontent with elaborate embroidery.

Refocusing on the matter at hand, Myrddin considered the dead animals and their protruding tongues and small faces now affixed forever in wide-eyed horror. If he brought her one of the dead animals, he imagined her pert nose crinkling up as she pulled her thin lips over her teeth—then she'd light his arse on fire. Or she would *accidentally* embroider a flower on the seat of his trousers or along the crotch. Definitely no dead anything for his daughter.

Arthwyr broke the 'spell' as he pushed his shoulder against Myrddin, who rose to his full height to stand over him. Arthwyr flinched and stepped back as the Mage of Evermore flicked his fingers over the King's nose and said, "No matter how much you stretch, I'll always be taller."

"Not fair." Arthwyr scratched his neck, rattling the entwined sticks that formed the cloak Kirekwall had gifted him. "I wonder what else my realm will provide for its royal guests."

Myrddin tapped his chin. "Roll out a straw representation of you, light it on fire, and dance naked under the flames."

Arthwyr laughed. "Sounds like my kind of entertainment—if it wasn't me doing the dancing."

Myrddin gestured toward the fountain. "Wait 'til you meet the Healer."

They faced a full-figured old woman throwing feed to a colorful array of birds. The woman shifted to the side, and a thunderous fart trumpeted loud enough to scatter the birds.

Arthwyr quickly put his back to the fountain, shadows crossing his countenance and his head bending forward with the slump of his shoulders.

Worry surged through Myrddin, and he readjusted the sticks to lie flat on Arthwyr's cloak, saying, "What's wrong? You've been melancholic since Porthcrawl."

The lines around Arthwyr's mouth deepened. "Your wife said Balance for the realm was nigh."

"Did she, now?" Myrddin said, taken aback that Nimue had not told him of this Divination.

"Around my kingdom there are signs of Balance everywhere in our people."

Myrddin stood silently and fixed his gaze on Arthwyr. "What exactly is bothering you?"

Arthwyr closed his hands over Myrddin's wrists, his fingers clenched so tightly his knuckles went white. "How can I be at peace knowing I have a bastard out there?"

Myrddin sucked in a harsh breath and dragged Arthwyr into the shadows next to an empty stall. "Was it the lass your father bought for your First Night Ritual?"

Arthwyr sighed. "Aye, mess of a situation that was. You know that Uther postponed my First Night until I was twenty-five autumns. Some tripe about that age holding great promise."

"Great promise, indeed. The lass conceived."

"Her name is Ursula, and I gave her a purse outside of the one my father promised her for teaching me my body. He would've killed her afterward, so I told her to disappear and... surprise... twenty-three springs later, I ran into her in Porthcrawl. My son was at their stall, a real Pendragon. No denying the steel in his blue eyes even if he was across the way from us."

"What does the mother want? Your bastard recognized?"

"No. She didn't want anything."

Myrddin thumped Arthwyr on the head with the flat of his hand. "What possessed you to not take a draught? My brother forced me to take one for my First Night. No bastards for the Emrys."

"My father told me it was handled."

"Of course, your father did. Wanted something to hold over you." Myrddin caught the way Arthwyr thumbed a whorl on the stall table next to them. "How is Guinevere handling it?"

"She doesn't know," Arthwyr replied, scraping his fingernails over the darker lines in the tabletop's swirl.

"Oh, bloody Hells!"

Arthwyr clapped his hand over Myrddin's mouth and brought their noses scant inches apart. "Would you tell Nimue if you found out your First Night delivered you a bastard, draught or not?"

"Fair enough. How do you want to handle this?"

"I don't know. I gave Ursula another purse to pay for my failure as a father. When we return home, I'll fully consider my options."

"You should tell Lance. Maybe Bedwyr."

"And send my Ebony Knight and Bedwyr to an early grave?"

"Nothing surprises Lance. As for Bedwyr, he'll laugh in your face. Later, when he realizes you've spawned another Pendragon, he'll drown himself in Moon Mead. It'll take the entire Elven Shrines of Ribeena to air him out."

Arthwyr grumbled, "I should have come to you sooner. Forty-seven winters and much more capable, eh, my cantankerous Soul Bond?"

"Go or I'll light your arse on fire."

Arthwyr strode across the square as Myrddin visited the stalls. Various merchants and farmers displayed their wares and produce on tables. If he were a betting man, he would wager some of what he saw was not local but from far away.

He spied baubles of glass jewelry and paused to study the pieces closer. Laid out by color, glass glittered atop a burlap sack. *Strange how talk of Porthcrawl and the Isles Seas came full circle to a display of sea glass.*

Myrddin selected a trinket from the rough material, draping the black leather of a necklace over his hand. As he brushed his fingers over the sea glass, warmth sparked through him. *Curious.* He traced a violet tinge atop the frosted, grayish-white surface. A wolf and raven engraved in snowflake obsidian was melded to the sea glass. Both were fashioned into the shape of a fang. He imagined any boy of status liking it.

Robes shuffled as the haggard old man running the stall bowed over his goods, uttering a fawning, "Milord."

Myrddin returned the bow and held it for a few seconds. "Good sir. Balanced be."

"Balanced be."

Myrddin weighed the burgeoning collection his daughter already had in her possession. He examined other jewelry, some items fetching for a young lady. One with the illusion of raindrops dripping from silver wire held his stare. He reached for it.

"Choose carefully, Milord," a low voice hissed, not at all sounding like the old man.

Myrddin tensed and turned to the ancient vendor hunched over his wares. A flicker of orange slid over the man's muddy brown eyes. For a split second, Myrddin swore a younger man stood there, flames licking through a wild mane of chestnut-brown hair.

Myrddin addressed what he assumed to be an apparition: "Who are you?"

"Noeman, Milord," came a quick reply as a grin flashed across the man's features, and when Myrddin blinked the old merchant was back, saying, "My friends call me Noeman."

A sparrow hopped onto the counter. Myrddin shooed the bird to the wooden rafter over the stall. "So many damned sparrows," he muttered when the bird fluffed out its bright feathers and one drifted onto the table. "They must be quite the nuisance."

The merchant chuckled. "Invite a host of sparrows to your home, and you will find the beginning of the end."

Myrddin grimaced at the superstition. He studied the necklace and scraped a fingernail over a strange rune carved on the back. "I'm not familiar with this engraving. What does it mean?"

Noeman's eyes flickered in the afternoon sun as he leaned forward. "My apologies, Milord, but the strangest things arise from blending and binding what is meant to be. Only two pieces have such marks." He emitted a soft, deprecating laugh. "It's not my best piece. Flawed in many ways. Little wonder no one has bought it yet. I have much better goods, if you wish to see them."

Myrddin shook his head. "How much for this one?"

The merchant chewed on his bottom lip. "Five shinnies, but are you sure?"

"It will do." Myrddin picked through his purse for some ingots. "I have a daughter who favours the most awkward things, just like her grandmother. She'll adore this piece more than the others."

His crow's feet wrinkling into gullies, Noeman extended a liver-spotted hand to Myrddin. When he saw the amount that he was being offered, his voice shook: "Milord, this is too much!"

"Use it to find a nice inn and a hot meal on the way back to the Isles. I believe you've come from quite a way to wish our King good luck and balanced fortune. Would I be right?"

Noeman nodded and enclosed the necklace in a packet of wax paper, his neat folds forming a three-dimensional envelope.

A hot breath at Myrddin's elbow tensed the muscles in his arm. He slanted one eye downward to the youth next to him. Ginger locks gave away Harlan Foxbury's family as sure as the coat of arms with a snarling fox on a yellow shield sewn upon the sleeves of the lad's cream-colored tunic.

Myrddin raised an eyebrow. "Aye, Harlan."

The boy of fifteen autumns poked at a piece of red sea glass with veins of white and yellow flames attached to a braided red-and-white leather cord. "How do you know that all of these items come from the Isles?"

Myrddin studied the piece for a moment, flipping it and smoothing his fingers over the rune on the back. Petrified redwood and forest-green jade were emblazoned and sealed against the glass, a fox and a phoenix carved within the dark pendant. As he handed it to Harlan, the merchant hummed a tune Myrddin recalled, which was an old saw his mother had taught him: *"From oceans blue, smooth edges true. Edges sharp and jagged, known origins become ragged."*

Harlan gently rubbed the sides of the shard. He nodded to the merchant and handed the necklace back to him. The old man placed the piece of jewelry on a fresh sheet of wax paper and with little effort folded it into a swan.

"Take it in good tidings, young Lord," the merchant said as the boy reached for his coin purse. "This Lord has already paid for it. So, your charge is to bequeath it to someone dear. Aye, the one meant to be your counter in Balance."

Both bowed to the merchant, and Myrddin nudged Harlan toward a nearby empty stall. "Have a little miss you're gifting that to?" asked the Mage, more than a little curious about the answer.

"Nay," Harlan was quick to reply, but Myrddin wasn't so sure as he watched the boy gently caress the wings of the paper swan and secure his prize within the leather sporran clipped to his belt.

"You'll figure it out one day," Myrddin said, smiling and mussing Harlan's hair. "When you realize who that belongs to, no one else will ever make you feel as whole."

CHAPTER 5

TILLWITH SECRETS

After Dottsie the Healer and Noeman entered, Rhoshlyn Tillwith closed the door of her home, which was inside two huge oak trees that had grown together. Rhoshlyn heaved a great sigh and tightened her grip on her children's Royal Contracts. It had been a long day, and a longer walk home, stretched to extremes because during the entire trip Dottsie and Noeman had carried on like fresh Soul Bonds.

Rhoshlyn unrolled the parchment for Garrett's Royal Contract. The King's flowing script and Lance DuLac's blockier print lined the bottom. Off to the side, Lord Gorre was listed as a witness. Garrett's shaky scrawl of acceptance was made worse by his smudged thumbprint.

Rhoshlyn secured the parchment and set it on the table. She loosened the tie on Viera's Contract and opened it. King Arthwyr Pendragon's signature appeared first, with Lord Myrddin Emrys signed below it. Just as Viera was about to sign her Contract, a Knight of the Eclipse had rushed in. He yanked the document from the table, and so he could sit and read it in good light, he shoved Lord Gorre from his chair.

This Knight ripped up the original Royal Contract and beckoned for Mayor Limawit, who as a matter of policy always attended the formal conscription signings. As the mayor bent closer, the Knight pounded his fist on the table and yelled into his ear, "What arsehole has two children sign a binding agreement without an expiry of terms? Take this shite back or I'll drown you in that pissing-tank fountain outside!"

If not for the intercession by this Knight, whom Rhoshlyn had learned was Bedwyr Wallach, her children would have entered into a lifetime of servitude instead of seven years. Chirping broke up Rhoshlyn's thoughts concerning her youngsters' futures.

Dottsie pointed at the sounds coming from a sparrow sitting on a limb that was touching an open window in the kitchen. "Time comes full circle," the old Healer said. "My little Lord and Lady have chosen, and a fine choice it will be."

Rhoshlyn sent a prayer, to whatever ancestor was willing to listen, to keep her children safe. It was especially hard letting go of her little spark, but it was necessary. There was nothing for Viera in Iyesgarth. Rhoshlyn had known this from the moment her fiery daughter had released her first shrill cries as she entered this world, the newborn bellowing her arrival before Dottsie even had time to announce the child's gender.

Rhoshlyn's eldest sat at their wooden dining table, his lanky frame perched on a wooden chair, his toes curled to the side of it. Garrett's bushy black eyebrows furrowed into a solid line, his slackened jaw clearly defining his weary acceptance of his plight.

But Viera would be different, her mother was certain. Her daughter would fight her Contract. Myrddin Emrys would rue the day she was conscripted, as it would be a long time before he would gain anything of benefit in exchange for her service.

Rhoshlyn immersed herself in the sensation of loam against her bare feet. The cool earth of the natural ground in her home calmed her, steadying her as she reached into the soil to touch a root. Wood Elementals felt the tendrils of existence that made an oak a tree. As an Earth Elemental, she sensed influences surrounding the oak like the sigh of life from the roots into the ground.

Her husband's family name was Tillwith. Yet, to the villagers, the name was the butt of many a joke, as the Tillwiths would till anything because they were farmers and people of the earth. Not much countered this thinking, and Mayor Limawit and his lackeys lifted their collective noses at them. If they only knew the truth.

Tillwith originally was Tylwyth, the latter the handle of a people long eschewed and ridiculed. Hence, it was not a "safe" name, and this fostered the need to change it. Indeed, Dwarves, Elves, and Dragons held more prominence, as Tylwyths were classified as the "Seelie" and fantasized with catching Fae lights at night or smoking fairy dust.

However, the Seelie and their darker cousins, the Unseelie, were real beings. The Seelie embodied the light; Unseelie the dark: Life and Twilight—and believed never to join as one.

When Rhoshlyn, an Unseelie, was a young woman and looked across the fires she routinely danced around, it was then that she celebrated both Life and Twilight—witnessed by the stunned gaze of one with Seelie blood. They were natural enemies, with uncountable wars fought betwixt them, yet as night slipped into dawn, the Unseelie blood of her Ancient Aessidhe heritage recognized this opposite as her Soul Bond.

As for Viera, the phoenix she had summoned required a special skill and a power not seen for many generations. Thankfully, an Ancient had not been present. An Elf or Dwarf would have known what Viera had done and what she was.

Viera's Seelie/Unseelie heritage had always been evident to Rhoshlyn in another way, because despite the constant head-butting between her husband and her daughter, an esoteric language coexisted between them. However, Sully and Viera were not the sole benefactors of veiled communication. Rhoshlyn padded over to her son and knelt next to him. She smoothed back his hair, looked into his dark brown eyes, and whispered, "I have a secret for you."

Sully sauntered into the kitchen, not concerning himself with what his wife might be saying to their son. Steady as the earth he tilled and the Element that predominated him and his wife, flights of fancy and dreams of a different life had always been beyond him.

Sully had only wanted three things from life: his crops to grow well, his family to benefit from the bounty of his efforts, and for his home to remain standing. Yet now those goals had changed, along with his desires. For so long, he denied this was occurring, but what was once whimsical—and his little girl's pastime—had exploded in epic proportions. His daughter had rent the fabric of their small town and rattled the fiercest of Evermore's nobility.

With Viera's groans and the squishing of dough filling his ears, Sully circled around to her side. Viera pounded the dough, her grunts increasing as if to somehow drown out his presence. Misery was etched on her face, and this pained Sully, whose thick mustache twitched involuntarily.

She grumbled at the chore, but his voice stopped her: "Daunting tasks are like untilled tough soil that require the crust of the earth to be ploughed through diligence and patience, Little Sparrow."

Viera bristled. "Yuck, another farming story, and *Little Sparrow* is a baby name."

Dipping his fingers into the bowl of water next to Viera, Sully sprinkled the dough to soften it. "Ever will you be my little sparrow."

He patted ground pumpkin flakes into the dough, adding the sweetness he only included in his family's bread. Covering her hands with his, he kneaded the flour into the best loaf they would ever eat. "I learned this secret from my father, who learned from his, and so on."

All the currency in Evermore could not move him to sell the bread they baked this day. Memories are made from things like this. And, someday, Viera would understand the reason behind her father's support of her conscription.

CHAPTER 6

LITTLE GREEN MEN AND SPARROWS

Punishment, in the form of another travel log entry, had descended upon Bedwyr for threatening to drown that idiot mayor in the fountain. As Bedwyr climbed into the wagon, he spied Palamedes adding to the log and he gritted his teeth.

The quill, as if operating on a mind of its own, scribbled over the travel log and ink splotches dribbled on the parchment as candlelight flickered and cast shadows in the dimness of the wagon. Palamedes' stifled snorts and giggles broke the silence.

Bedwyr peered over the boy's shoulder. "What are you doing?"

A sharp gasp interrupted the chuckles as the Saracen youth whipped around so fast that the joints in his neck popped.

Palamedes answered in a parrot's voice: "Arthwyr said we should all make an account of our observations for historical and educational purposes."

"Arthwyr said 'the adults,' not snot-nosed little brats like you." Bedwyr snatched the log and read Palamedes' additions. "Seriously? Little green men and orange sky ships." He snapped the book shut and cuffed the boy over the head with it.

"Aww! That hurt!" Palamedes' lower lip trembled. "The log is boring. It says I puke everywhere. That shouldn't be in there. It should be an accurate account."

"It is, you little puke pustule."

Wood creaked and the wagon swayed as Father Constantine clambered over the tailboard. "Am I interrupting something?"

Bedwyr flipped open the book and jabbed his finger repeatedly at Palamedes' scribblings until the priest took the log and read it. Constantine grabbed Palamedes by his tunic and hustled him to the rear of the wagon.

Constantine raised his voice, which was rare for him. "Palamedes Rasim Sasania! Little green men and orange gliders? 'Tis bad enough certain adults write like that!"

"Then I could do no worse," Palamedes said as he dropped to the ground. "Father, I made the travel log interesting. Give me five minutes and that log will undergo a revolution."

"It's a travel log, Palamedes, not a rag to use in the latrine. With the way you've written that, it's like something from the Heavens visited us."

Constantine tossed the log to Bedwyr. "Finish your account of what happened in Iyesgarth. Afterward, I'll include my observations. Heaven forbid anyone sees this who's toadstooled on fairy dust. I can only imagine someone like Gaheris Foxbury, who seems to live on fairy dust, embellishing the part about little green men."

It was night, the flames from the candles weaving in the faint wind. Bedwyr slouched onto a wooden bench pulled from one of the wagons. Beyond the camp, the night sky seemed to envelope the world. He picked up the quill and inkpot, balancing the travel log in his lap. Opening the book, he returned to where Palamedes had left off. As he pinched the corners of the page to rip out the Saracen's lunacy, he couldn't help himself. Leave it! Little green men it was!

A chirp drew his gaze to the darkness overhead, and it took everything in him not to throw the log in the direction of the noise. He made out shiny little Hells pits for eyes in the boughs of a tree, but he chose to ignore his interloper and instead touched the tip of the quill to the parchment. As ink drowned the fibers in darkness, a milky stare framed with riotous hair surfaced in his mind. Fate was a twisted slag in crossing his path with the old Healer in Iyesgarth. The cold phantom kiss of the Healer's fingers had encircled his wrist, driving shivers deep into his body.

"I've been watching over that girl, Viera Tillwith," the blind Healer said to him as she tightened her grip, nails dulled but with the pressure forming half-crescents on his skin. "Help her, Milord. If you don't, Evermore is forfeit. All life is forfeit. All of us."

Two sparrows darted around Bedwyr, and the female landed on his shoulder. He'd know that sparrow anywhere. *To see her again was*—Bedwyr interrupted his own thoughts, saying aloud, "I promise not to let the girl be abused. This I pledge on The Seven Houses."

He ran his thumb along the pages of the log, the whiffle of air and subtle noise soothing him. If he wrote what he'd experienced, too many people would see what lay within the pages, yet he had to provide at least a narrow outline of the future. Balance at present was nigh, but to what conclusion would Evermore reach if he didn't contribute the truth as he knew it? Yet if Balance for Evermore is to be attained through Viera Tillwith, is she the end or the beginning?

Chirp, chirp.

The haunting trills of a song filtered across Bedwyr's awareness, snaring his attention to the female sparrow twittering away. He could not write what the girl meant to Evermore in blatant terms, but there was nothing against couching his observations in the flowery bollocks of symbolism that the bulk of the nobility devoured voraciously.

He refreshed the ink on the quill and beneath Palamedes' contribution began his entry:

I, Bedwyr Wallach, witnessed the rise of a phoenix.

Chapter 7

The King's Progress, or Lack Thereof

As gray diluted the morning sky into the first hints of a brilliant summer tableau, Viera viewed the path leading away from her home in a different light. Her senses attuned to each nuance. The farther away she traveled, the more crushing the reality of her circumstances, and this weight bent her forward.

While Myrddin's horse plodded down the trail, her fingers dug into his arm secured about her waist. When Myrddin grunted, she forced her fingers to relax as the smooth hickory-hued reins remained coiled around a fist splotched with ink.

The ride was uneventful until the horse slipped on a rocky patch and stopped fast, almost throwing Viera, who began to tremble.

"Easy." Myrddin tightened his arm over her waist. "You're all right."

She quivered in the saddle, her squeaks clawing past her throat, making it clear that she wasn't sure about her well-being.

Myrddin patted her on the shoulder. "Really, you're fine. Lailo here is a gentle mare with good sense." He clicked his tongue and the horse settled into a comfortable gait. "My daughter was not good at riding at first."

"You have a daughter?"

"Aye. Her name is Maerna. You'll see her soon. She's fifteen winters."

Viera tightened her grip on his arm, tense over what she viewed as awkward news yet not knowing why. "Is she like you?" she asked.

Myrddin was silent for a few seconds. "Yes and no. She is of Fire, so we share many similarities. But she's quiet for her age. I fear she might be too scholarly. Takes after her mother, Nimue Abe, who is The High Oracle of The Oracle's Guild."

Myrddin was full of surprises. Only a King had more influence than a High Oracle. Viera swallowed the lump that had formed in her throat. "Is that common knowledge?"

He chuckled. "It's common if anyone knows my wife."

Her gaze went to the twin black and silver Dragon ear cuffs coiled around and fanning the top part of his unpierced ears. "Are you really a Lord or a pirate?" she asked quietly.

His eyes rounded and he blinked down at her. "What makes you ask that?"

She pointed at the ear cuffs. "I heard Mayor Limawit say only pirates and not so nice people wear ear cuffs and earrings."

Myrddin snorted. "He's a fool then. Some in the nobility wear them, but these are the Emrys Ear Cuffs. They designate me and my spouse as the Heads of Emrys House. Each Noble House has a certain effect and wears them only when acting in the stead of their fief or for certain ceremonial purposes."

"What do you mean by ceremonial purposes?"

"Festivals or when an heir is coronated into their Lordship or Ladyship. There's also a ceremony for when an heir takes a spouse or Bond and that person is coronated too."

Viera grinned. "Like a King or Queen."

Myrddin laughed. "Similar. For some Noble Houses, they are recognized with a crown if that is the effect worn by their Heads. The Noble Houses used to be their own kingdoms and those effects were the way to distinguish their Royal Pairs. However, that is long past and the Pendragons are our rulers."

Lailo picked up her gait, and soon Viera relaxed in the saddle and settled into the mare's smooth pace over the mostly level fields they now passed through. It was definitely different being high up and not sitting in a bumpy wagon.

Viera playfully poked her fingers at the saddle's hard pommel and said to Myrddin, "I've not been on a horse like Lailo. We have them harnessed and pulling a wagon. Never riding one."

"As my Apprentice, you'll travel with some regularity. Riding a warhorse is something you will get used to over time."

"Aren't warhorses supposed to be stallions?"

"Depends. It gets down to what the Knight or guard is most comfortable with. There are those who prefer the faster mares who do not tire as quickly, but when going into battle, many would rather ride atop the largest male steeds. I have a big stallion named Ken, but Lailo is just as capable in a fight." Lailo snorted and tossed up her head, as if proud of what her Master had said.

Wings beat a few yards away, a rush of white birds rising above the knee-high grasses of the valley they had recently entered. The abrupt flight of the birds startled a herd of deer, which ran from the taller grasses and dashed toward the trees.

Myrddin leaned close to Viera, so near that his breath warmed her hair. "I've been wanting to ask you something for a long time."

"What?" Viera barked, fearing the question.

"Why steal the cart?"

Much easier than what I expected. She hunched over, her fingers tracing the lines of wear along the pommel. "We weren't stealing. It was a jest. Supposed to be the biggest one ever. We were going to hide the cart in the woods, but we got caught by Cletus."

"Caught in more ways than one," Myrddin said, motioning in the direction of the deer dotting the outskirts of a tree line. "What if the wildlife got to it?"

The heat rose from her neck to her cheeks. "Never thought about that." She screwed her face toward the sky. "Thinking is overrated."

"I see," Myrddin said in a voice steeped with sarcasm and mumbled something that sounded suspiciously like, "Hells, what have I done?"

They crested a hill overlooking three wagons, along with a collection of horses hobbled and grazing near a stream. A figure stepped from behind the closest wagon, and the sun glinted off his sword and crown. As King Arthwyr approached, another man rounded the wagon and followed him. Viera recognized the second man as Lord DuLac, the Knight who had laid claim to her brother's future.

"Introductions are in order," said Myrddin as he cinched Lailo to a tree next to the grazing horses. "You haven't had a chance to meet a lot of people on Progress. Frankly, a few were missing and some others indisposed after you and your brother's welcoming ceremony."

They walked over and the King immediately began staring at Viera. She returned his stare and marveled at the faint silvering in his tawny hair and beard. When his brow crinkled, she realized that in meeting his gaze she might have offended him, so she ducked her head.

A huff and his laugh drew her eyes back to his. "You'll make a wonderful addition to the Court in time, lass. I see great things coming from you."

Her teeth began clicking as she said, "I'm a peasant, Sire. I wouldn't dare dream of the Court."

"You should sit with Lance and Trystan. Not all my Lords are of the finest breeding. Some mercenaries even fill my ranks. I don't pick those I trust most because of their family trees or the size of their purses."

The King thumped Myrddin's arm. "When we return to Elden's Hearth, there are some reoccurring issues we must—"

The King halted his oratory as loud screeches filled the air. A tall canvas-covered wagon swayed, and a boy flew from its cloth opening in the rear.

Viera stared at the puffy pants and vest the boy wore. Powder dusted his light brown features. He yelled back at the wagon, "I don't want to be anywhere near you tarts, either."

A man in a long black cassock ran from another wagon, grabbed the boy by his collar, and whipped him around, shouting, "Palamedes Rasim Sasania, what is wrong with you?"

Palamedes crossed his arms; his features set in mulish defiance. "They blew girly powder on me. You can't make me go back in there, Constantine. I'd rather walk."

Constantine planted his hands on Palamedes' shoulders. "You're not walking all the way back to Elden's Hearth."

Palamedes stomped his feet like a baby in a tantrum. "Then I want to ride with Bedwyr!"

"What would possess you to want to ride with him? He hates you."

"I don't get motion sickness with him." Palamedes pointed his finger at four girls jumping down in unison from the wagon. "He's way better than them. Anything—even highwaymen—would be better than that!"

Leading a horse toward the stream, Bedwyr broke into a run once he spied Palamedes, who latched onto his arm. "I can ride with you, right, Bedwyr?"

Bedwyr shoved the boy onto the ground and stepped over his small form, kicking dust in his face in the process.

Undaunted, the youth whipped around and latched onto Bedwyr's legs.

Windmilling his arms, Bedwyr lost his balance and fell over. Startled, his horse whinnied and high-stepped around him. The animal tossed its mane and lashed its tail, settling down and poking its nose at both of them as if they were some sort of novelty.

As Bedwyr rolled onto his back, he lifted one booted foot but couldn't manage a clean kick with it. He hollered at his young nemesis, "Get off me or I'll make sure they never find your body!"

Palamedes squirmed forward on his stomach and howled long and loud enough to rival a wolf pack. "Don't leave me with them! I'll give you my good kidney!"

Bedwyr managed to stand on one foot and drag the youth after him. "I don't want bollocks from you! Now, get off me!"

Palamedes, unfazed, said, "I'll be great for you, you'll see."

"Let me go, you little bugger!"

Myrddin said to the King, "We have this going on, and we're supposed to be setting examples for our countrymen?"

The King stared at Bedwyr and Palamedes as they continued to wriggle around and scream at each other. "Between our Water Elementals and the girls, I can't decide which is worse."

Viera scoffed, "And here you thought I was bad."

Myrddin knelt in front of her. "You're going to love riding with the Maids."

CHAPTER 8

EARTH, AIR, AND FIRE

When faint tremors teased beneath Myrddin's fingers, he squeezed Viera's shoulder. The girl shifted closer to him. He could practically smell her feverish thoughts as she stared at the blood staining the cloth. Seeing a prince bleed—let alone the Crown Prince clipping his brother across the leg in a mock spar—must be disconcerting for Viera.

Appraising the superficial wound, Myrddin nodded at the Healer next to them. "This is Lord Lamorac Pellinore, Viera." He pointed at the blue triple spiral symbol with evenly spaced arms curved to the right on Lamorac's upper sleeves. "Anyone wearing a triskele is a Healer."

Thumping their boots, Maryck and Harlan perched on a wagon tailboard. Pink kissed Viera's cheeks as Maryck grinned rakishly and winked.

As Ewain twined a poultice over Ulrich's leg, two silver lions with their paws locked over a serpent adorning his sleeves rolled as if fighting over their prize.

"You three should know better than to spar without an adult present," Ewain grumbled. "You, especially, Ulrich. It's not like you to act so foolish."

"Well, he's fifteen summers." Lamorac draped his arm over Ewain's shoulder and teased his fingers along the other's back until Ewain brushed him off. "Young yet and still open to the start of many an adventure."

Ewain secured the bandage. "A few tragedies too."

Chuckling, Maryck led Harlan in dropping from their perches and bowed to Viera. "Milady, would you like to see a trick or two," he added, blustering at Ewain's growl, "with an adult present, of course."

Far too much went into that offer and Myrddin bristled. "Don't let me catch you playing Court games with her."

Maryck backpedaled as if he had stepped onto a field of caltrops. "We meant no offense," he said, leading Harlan and Ulrich into a fast retreat around the wagon. "Welcome to Royal Progress, Milady."

Viera scuffed her boots on the gravel and squinted at the triskele on Lamorac's robes. "What's your Element?"

"I align with Water," Lamorac said, collecting a claymore from the wagon.

"You have a sword?"

He let her touch the hilt and secured it to his belt. "Aye. I'm a Healer and a warrior."

Constantine emerged from behind the wagon, holding at arm's length a cauldron containing the burnt congealed remnants of breakfast and wafting an acridness that singed Myrddin's nose. Gagging, Ewain and Lamorac fanned bundles of herbs in front of their faces and made themselves scarce.

"Another meal attempt by Lady Sagramore?" Myrddin asked.

Sheepishly, Constantine nodded. "Gaheris took the fall with a new Wood array he was practicing when he knocked this over."

"Good on him."

"Quite."

"Have you seen my daughter? I want her and Viera to have a chance to get to know each other before tossing my new ward into the fire with the other Maids." Myrddin mentally ticked through the other girls he hadn't seen as well. "And what about Brynn and Delilah?"

"Maerna is at the stream with Brynn. Delilah might be with them or Trystan."

As Constantine fell into step with them, Myrddin introduced Viera and the Catholic priest to one another, adding, "Father Constantine is from Viteliu, a realm south of Evermore."

Viera didn't respond, but Constantine smiled, as if he knew something was bothering her.

As they ambled down a path, Myrddin and Constantine chatted idly when screams broke up their mutual pleasantries. Myrddin squinted in the direction of the stream, the clear source of the yelling. "What now?" he murmured.

Others heard the commotion as well, and Trystan jumped from a wagon and raced around Constantine who dropped the cauldron. Hot behind Trystan, Delilah tripped into Viera, the Maid's massive, white-streaked brown braid slapping against Myrddin's arm with such force that he had to hold her up to keep her from toppling over.

Another screech set all of them charging toward the stream, which had a broken stone wall bordering the sharp drop of the embankment next to it. Myrddin planted one hand on the stone wall and vaulted over it.

Trystan remained where he was, gripping Delilah's shoulder, his hawkish gaze on the group at the rivulet. He was laughing as more screams drew Myrddin's gaze to Brynn, who stood over Jocelyn. With the amount of mud covering her, Lady Sagramore might as well have been born of the swamp. Three other girls had their fine clothes and their fancy hair plastered with dripping mud as they, too, fretted and squawked, but Jocelyn fumed the loudest, her cobalt eyes steeled on Brynn as she raged at her.

Releasing a ball of sludge from an Earth array, Brynn covered them again, cutting short their protests. "You all wanted my secret for soft, beautiful skin. Now you have it."

Jocelyn daubed her face with a silk handkerchief as a glob of goo dropped from her forehead and splattered all over the delicate cloth. "You gave us nothing but sludge, you natter-brained chit! You're worse than that desert rat!"

"No, Joci, I gave you a facial," Brynn replied and stuck out her tongue. "It's hardly my fault a sow's ear can't be turned into a silk purse."

Picking his way around what appeared to be either mud pies or compressed horse manure, Myrddin spotted his daughter standing next to a crate of dishes. "Observing or participating, Maerna?"

Brynn stepped over to them and answered for Maerna, "She's washing the dishes. I asked for her help and she agreed."

Myrddin bit back a groan. Brynn Blumenthal was his second Master's youngest daughter, and what she lacked in size she made up for in spirit. Her father, Lord Dinadan Blumenthal, did not raise wilting flowers, and Brynn's mouth got away from her as a matter of course.

Myrddin let out a huge sigh and directed Viera in front of him. "Introductions are in order."

Even in her decrepit state, Jocelyn perked up. "Oh, thank Evermore. This Progress has needed a scullery maid." She stripped off her filthy shawl and tossed it at Viera. "Go on, girl, I expect to see not a speck of muck on it."

Myrddin caught the shawl in midair and tossed it back to Jocelyn, "Begging your pardon, Lady Sagramore, she's not a scullery maid! She's my Apprentice—and will be treated as such!"

Brynn's shrill laughter earned a flinch from those nearest her, and she said, "Hah, you fluff-brained harpy! You got told well, didn't you?"

Red overtook Jocelyn's pale cheeks. She shook like a pot bubbling over a hearth.

The situation quieted down as the Maids of Evermore cleaned themselves off as best they could. Myrddin directed Viera in front of Maerna. "Viera, this is my daughter, Maerna." They smiled at each other, and Myrddin nodded to the girl hovering next to Trystan. "And this is Lady Delilah Cuhlwch. I believe you've met Trystan."

Viera nodded and turned to Jocelyn and the other nobles' daughters.

Myrddin gestured and said, "Jocelyn Sagramore is, ah, to the far left." He pointed at three other girls. "This is Felicia Cornwall, and this is her younger sister, Constance Cornwall. The last one in Wood robes is Tavrina Cuhlwch.

Brynn bounced over to Viera and flicked her forehead with a single, well-aimed finger. "I'm Brynn Blumenthal. But I don't need an introduction. Harlan and Palamedes haven't stopped yakking about you." She encompassed Viera with a wave of her hand and stuck her nose up in the air. "Can't imagine why they're smitten with you. You don't look like much. If you'd like, I can fix that for you by giving you a facial."

CHAPTER 9

WOE TO THE COMMONER

Bloody Hells!

A few hours into setting out that day, Viera, now relegated to traveling with the Maids, drummed her fingers on the raised tailboard. Digging her nails into the wood, she stared out the back of the wagon, a noble girl's nasal voice grating on her ears with her latest inanity: "Pink is far out of fashion."

Disgusted with her predicament, Viera looked toward Maerna, who punched large holes into the handkerchief she was embroidering. Delilah Cuhlwch, even though herself a Maid, didn't seem to be tolerating the silly banter any better, because beneath her dark eyelashes her violet eyes held just a sliver of their usual glimmer.

Brynn clambered over Felicia Cornwall, kneeing the girl in her side. "Move it, you cow," Brynn said, without the slightest hint she was joking, and plopped herself onto the driver's seat.

Lamorac was holding the reins, and he braced himself to keep from being shoved off his perch.

Opening a large tome that took over her lap, Brynn jabbed her finger at a page and asked him, "What would happen if I tripled the anise in this?"

He scanned the text and made a face. "You better pray you're next to a latrine."

"Really?"

Viera pretended not to see the impish grin streaking across Brynn's face, but there was no mistaking what the look presaged.

The wagon moved along without any conversations from within until a moan disturbed the temporary quiet. "The odor in here," Felicia said, waving her fan frantically, "is making me faint."

Not to be outdone as the center of attention, Jocelyn fanned herself with greater ceremony. "Oh, how blue the sky is. We couldn't ask for a better day."

Myrddin had ridden Lailo up to the rear of the wagon, and he'd likely heard both girls' drivel firsthand. He leaned as close as he could without falling off his horse and whispered to his new ward, "How are you holding up?"

Viera straightened. "I cannot fathom how fortunate I am to be in such inspiring company." *I heard that from Brynn and already found a time to use it.*

"Duly noted," he said and cast her a wry grin. "In another hour, we'll let you out to ride."

"An hour that will seem like a year," Viera said as her Master yanked on Lailo's reins and the horse galloped off.

Lifting herself up from her position in the back of the wagon, Viera peeked past Lamorac. The fields were the same as hers at home. Tears stung her eyes and she sniffled.

Never one to miss a chance to nettle, in a grating voice, Jocelyn asked, "Are you crying?"

Cheeks warming, Viera focused on the other girls to find even Delilah eyeing her for an answer. Viera said nothing but could see Maerna wince when her embroidery needle pricked her finger as she furiously worked on her rosettes.

Jocelyn folded her hands over her skirt and jutted her shoulders forward. With a shimmy of her upper body, she lowered her voice into a husky tone that reeked of insincerity and said, "Sometimes young children need a good cry."

Viera buried her hands in the folds of her homespun dress and gritted her teeth. "I'm not a bawling whelp. I don't need a gaggle of geese yeah-saying me."

Fury warped across Jocelyn's features as she lifted her dainty nose and sat upright. "You're little more than a guttersnipe—a parasite feeding off the blood of your betters. I don't see why Lord Emrys would bring you under his tutelage." She sniffed indignantly. "He'll soon see that you're doomed to fail. As for me, I can see you selling yourself within a month of our return in the Red Lantern District of the Hearth."

Viera could do nothing except grit her teeth—for now.

A short time later, as Myrddin promised, the girls were allowed to ride outside the wagon. Though, for what it was worth, it was a paltry concession. The others got to ride. Viera was resigned to riding in front of Galahad as Myrddin had overrode her protests with, "No one rides a horse without some training. You were about to expire a few hours ago from Lailo!"

Not that there was anything wrong with Galahad. He was perfectly well natured and even let her hold onto his mare's reins. Camie, an Arabian with a high bluish shine, ambled at a sedate clip belied only by the whipcord muscles rolling beneath her hide.

At first, it wasn't so bad. Then, Jocelyn rode past and sniggered. "Perhaps you should've started out with a stick horse."

Now, Jocelyn made a production of flipping a delicate fan as the Princes and Harlan rode alongside the white mare she'd propped herself upon as if she were Queen Guinevere herself.

Constance Cornwall, for her part in the charade, twirled a fan in front of her face and parroted her older sister's earlier nonsense, proclaiming, "Oh, I'm a little faint."

Harlan, ever the gentleman—and an easy touch for any of the Maids—slipped Constance's reins over the pommel of his saddle and allowed her to lean against him.

Jocelyn couldn't help but respond to the attention Constance was receiving, so she said to Ulrich Pendragon, who was riding beside her, "This jaunt through the Valley has tried our delicate sensibilities and constitutions." She turned to Viera and Galahad. "We are not used to manure."

Jocelyn's arrogant sarcasm triggered something in Viera's mind. Manure had a definite place in farming, as it served as a fertilizer to nurture the soil and ultimately make crops grow better. But manure had other uses as well. When there was little in the way of dry wood, especially during the first cool nights of autumn, it could be used to light a bonfire. All it took was enough heat to create a flicker of a flame—and poof.

CHAPTER 10

FLAMING ARSEHOLES

"Lee-lee-lee-yahoo!"

What the ever feckin' Hells have I done to deserve this?

The youth behind Bedwyr cupped his mouth, amplifying his Saraceni shout and repeating, "Lee-lee-lee-yahoo!"

A shrill wail from afar assaulted Bedwyr's ears. He tightened his grip on the reins and chewed on his inner cheek. "Sit still, you little bastard! And shut up!"

Another yodel from Palamedes earned a hiss from the eagle hawk perched on Bedwyr's shoulder. The messenger bird fanned its wedge-shaped tail, surprising the boy and causing him to bounce sideways in the saddle.

Bedwyr elbowed Palamedes, hoping he'd fall off and break something, perhaps his neck. The Maids had made clear how much they despised Palamedes, and Bedwyr loathed the boy with equal disdain. However, Bedwyr didn't like much of anybody. People were not his forte, and he was happy that way. He was also a man of few words, becoming talkative only when vilifying people, the Sagramores ranking at the top of his list of those he relished disparaging.

It was with little wonder that Bedwyr sat idly on his horse as that idiotic blond fluffball, Jocelyn Sagramore, held on to her mare's mane for dear life and caterwauled across an open field. Amused, he tracked the flight of the mare and the cone of fire coming from the horse's arse. *Who knew Fire could do that?*

Myrddin urged Lailo to chase after the runaway horse and the terrified girl. Not far behind him raced Viera and Galahad on his mare, Camie. Fate was keen on entertaining Arthwyr, Lance, Ewain, Trystan, and the noble boys as well, since they all thundered along on their steeds in hot pursuit.

Lailo barreled toward a reservoir and came to a halt. Jocelyn's horse was not so alert. Myrddin could only watch in horror as Jocelyn's mount jerked to an abrupt stop in front of the pond and Lady Sagramore flew over the horse's head and into the water, her screeches becoming gurgles as she nosedived into the silt-filled pool and disappeared below the waterline.

Bubbles churned in the sludgy water and arms thrashed up. Soon, mud and water exploded around the girl from her reflexive use of her Water Element. But she was not safe yet, as the heavy brocade skirt she wore repeatedly dragged her under, her face the only part of her that remained in view.

As Jocelyn floundered the others arrived, slid from their mounts, and ran toward her. They all stood at the edge of the pool, as if in a trance. Myrddin swung off Lailo and called out. "For the love of Evermore, somebody pull her out before she drowns!"

Kneeling next to the pool, Ewain dipped his hands into the pond just as blue lines appeared. Water churned around the girl, rushed upward in a column, and Jocelyn was shot, wailing, into the air. She soared high until gravity took over, and luckily for her a haystack cushioned her landing. Tumbling on the straw with her mud-filled skirt draped over her head, sludge gushed from her as she grabbed at anything to try to stop her movement.

Maryck Pendragon beamed. "I just knew Progress would get more interesting."

"Yep," Viera crowed. "And now who's got better tricks?"

Myrddin stalked toward her, saying, "Of course you had a hand in this. We need to have a long—"

Muffled yelps interrupted him when Jocelyn slipped on the wet hay and tumbled down the sodden pile. A long guffaw coming from Maryck overwhelmed Jocelyn's cries, because when she was able to stand a rich layer of manure formed a thick beard on her slender face.

Viera laughed herself hoarse, continuing well after Maryck had quieted down.

Jocelyn lunged forward, staggering under the weight of her waterlogged dress. She released a guttural snarl and screamed, "You—"

Cow manure slid into Jocelyn's mouth. She gagged and threw up. Every single person, except for Viera, slinked backwards. Galahad pinched his nose and breathed through his mouth.

Viera darted around at her puckish best and railed at Jocelyn: "Didn't your mother ever tell you to fertilize with manure, not eat it? Clearly being highborn has its limitations."

Jocelyn howled, "I'm going to drown you like the worthless rat you are."

She took a step toward Viera, who bristled at her. Myrddin wedged himself between the potential combatants. "Girls, calm down!" he yelled as he grabbed Viera.

With heat hissing over her like the sound of meat sizzling in a fry pan, Viera backed off. Myrddin took her by the shoulders and bent her forward, one arm secured around her middle. She stiffened, likely well familiar with her father slippering her on the occasion for some misdeed. Before Myrddin had a chance to make true on it, she was hauled forward into an ebony gambeson and lighter gray hauberk, and swept off her feet into Lance's arms. Lance deposited her next to the King but kept his hands over her shoulders as he turned to Myrddin.

Seething, Myrddin glowered at the Ebony Knight. "Lance."

"Remember that time when my son and Bedwyr were youths and stole a boat and crashed it into the pier?" Lance asked, blocking Viera from view.

Myrddin hissed, "Aye."

"Remember how my wife had you and Arthwyr collect them from 10-4's local garrison?"

"Aye. Elaine was certain if you retrieved them, you would slipper them into next season."

"She wasn't wrong. Think of this as me returning the favour. We're even."

Galahad rubbed his hand over his haunches. "You slippered us anyway."

"But the difference was that I wasn't angry when I did and you live to the current age of twenty-one springs. Imagine that," Lance said, bending at Viera's eyelevel. "You have two choices, Milady. Either you ride with me or you ride with Arthwyr. What say you?"

She stuttered, "Ya-you, I guess."

"Good. And, Viera, I recommend you don't light anyone else's horse's or their arse on fire, or I'll personally hand Myrddin my slipper."

He straightened and clicked his tongue until his mount, Troyes, trotted over to him.

Arthwyr waved the others toward their horses. "We'd best be on our way. There's a river a mile or two up. We'll break for the noonday meal." He nodded as Jocelyn made her way to him. "And, you, ah... can clean up there, Milady."

"Thank Evermore for you," Jocelyn said and sniffled. "At least someone around here knows how to treat a young lady."

Viera let loose a shrill cackle. "The *lady* in you died with the shite you crawled from."

Myrddin dug his fingers into her upper arm. "That's enough, Ward. I don't know what possessed me to take on... oh, forget it."

As they walked off, she informed him, "I'm not a wart! Why do you call me that? You even call Lord Lance a wart. There aren't any boils on either of us."

He buried his fingers in his hair and said through gritted teeth, "A *wart* is a boil or pustule, you little fool. A *ward* is a dependent, child, or Apprentice."

She leaned forward and delivered a new level of Hells upon him. "Ward, Wart. If you say it fast enough it sounds like the toads croaking back home."

Releasing a deep sigh, Myrddin waved her toward Lance before he changed his mind and slippered her with his boot. "*Wart*, just get on the bloody horse."

Chapter 11
Civics Lesson

Everything, from the quiet lap of the stream to the subtle pop of wood from the campfire, annoyed Viera. The rougher section of the log she'd perched herself on didn't help, either, as it dug into her legs. Everyone else was bustling about the camp as she opened the book, still trying to figure out what the drawings meant.

When glowering at the dots, circles, and characters didn't force some semblance of sense into what she was reading, she created jagged ruts in the dirt with the heels of her boots. She saw nothing she understood; so, gritting her teeth, she smacked the leather-covered parchment across her knees. "'Study the book,' he says. 'It'll tell you everything,' he says."

Across from her, Gaheris Foxbury, the Lord of Murphy's Hold and also the Balancer of Evermore, quit stoking the fire. "Having trouble over there, lass?"

She whipped the book around and shoved it under his nose until his eyes crossed. "Myrddin wants me to study this bollocks!"

Gravel crunched nearby as Myrddin arrived just in time to hear Viera complaining. Behind her Master, Bedwyr trailed with his eagle hawk on his shoulder and a messenger tube in his hand.

Myrddin took the book from Viera. "Wart, how is this bollocks?"

With a rock, she drew a picture of a fork on the ground and jabbed her foot at it. "The only thing that makes any sense in that ruddy book is this fork meant for eating."

When red bloomed over Myrddin's cheeks, he clenched his fists against his sides and shook from head to toe. "That's *Algiz*, you little idiot!"

"Who names a fork *Algiz*? It's a fork! A fork, a fork, a fork, a fork!"

Bedwyr stopped midway through unfolding a missive and snarked at her, "Are peasants really this stupid? Wait. Don't answer that. The closest your kind ever comes to the Metal rune is when chasing someone from your shite town with pitchforks."

Myrddin smacked Bedwyr with the book and said to Viera, "*Algiz* is symbolic of protection. We protect with weapons, which is why *Algiz* is the rune for Metal."

Bedwyr snorted and perused the letter his feathered messenger had delivered. He crinkled his nose as he cursed, "Dammit! Lost another manservant according to my equerry."

"After Dante, you couldn't keep a manservant to save your own life," Gaheris said, craning his neck to peer at the letter and cackling as he winked at Viera. "His equerry wrote, 'Stop being such a bollocksy little shite and scaring off everyone I train or do your own damned ledgers.' Ah, he even drew himself frowning at the end"—to Bedwyr, he whistled long and loud. "That man has you whipped better than those Wallachian horses your family prides itself in."

Scowling, Bedwyr passed the information on to Myrddin. "Oh, and Uther's leftovers are conspiring again."

Myrddin appeared stunned as he flipped over the single page to see if anything was written on the back. When satisfied he'd read everything, his tone was dour. "Glastonbury? I didn't think that any of Uther's allies still lived in Evermore. At least not now."

Myrddin handed the letter back to Bedwyr. "You'd better show this to Arthwyr and Lance. In the meantime, I'll try to educate my wart."

Viera hissed at Gaheris, "You can't leave me with him! He's going to kill me."

Waving his hand, Gaheris said, "Too many witnesses."

With a smirk, Bedwyr chimed in, "That and you're already in the travel and supply logs. I added you last night between a sack of potatoes and wheel axle."

"Seriously, you little gremlin!" Myrddin barked at him.

Bedwyr waggled the message over Viera. "Have fun teaching phonics to Goobstump the Troll there. Remember, start simple like frog eat fly."

Myrddin snapped his fingers, sending a spark of fire at Bedwyr, who dodged it and with Gaheris cackled. "For the love of Evermore, she's not a Troll," Myrddin called after them.

After the Knights left, Myrddin turned to the book and pointed to the first page. "You read the words, right?"

"How many peasants can read?" Viera snapped.

A strangled wheeze escaped him. "How did you sign your name on the Contract?"

"Everyone, including the village dunce, learns how to sign his or her name."

Myrddin grumbled but sat closer to her. "Let me start from the beginning. We use traditional realm words, along with figures, for each of the seven elements." He opened the book to a page with several diagrams of katas. "Air is *Awyr*. *Pren* is for Wood. *Metel* for Metal. *Gweryd* for Earth. *Ia* for Ice. Fire uses *Tan*. Last is *Dwr* for Water. It may take time to learn all this, but it will come to you."

Viera threw her hands up in the air. "This isn't helping. There are words and squiggles like people on some pages and circles on others." She jabbed at one picture and laughed. "That looks like a snake eating its arse!"

"Actually, you're not far from being correct. It's a snake consuming its tail. *Ouroboros* to be exact." He tapped a symbol that looked like a mouth without teeth, which was drawn at an angle on the right side of the page. "See this? That's *Kaunaz*. It's in the center of every Fire array. Sometimes it covers another image, but it's always dead center."

Since she was a Fire Element, this interested Viera and she sat up, saying, "Really?"

"*Kaunaz* is a rune." He directed her attention to the blocks bordering the array's outer edge. "These are sigils, with runes in them."

"I see two runes in each of them."

Myrddin's eyes lit up. "Maybe there's some hope for you yet." He drew two of the runes in the soil, their larger size making each more defined. "Runes are like an alphabet of words. When combined, they read as sigils that direct what is to be released into the realm. The Oracles also have the rune *Ansuz* in their symbol of two hands holding a gray scribing ball."

Viera gave a hint of a nod. "I think I understand."

"You'll understand more in time." He pointed at two other runes in the book. "*Isa* is for Ice and *Laguz* is for Water."

With her finger, she traced the straight-lined rune for *Isa*, as well as *Laguz's* similar rune with a crook going to the left. Perplexed, she asked, "Why aren't they the same? Ice is made of water."

"What melts ice?"

She pursed her lips. "Heat?"

"That's the primary difference."

"So?"

Myrddin went into a lengthy discourse on Elements bonding with one another, with Water Elements absorbing heat and therefore not becoming solid, whereas temperature influences Ice to become solid. It sounded so obvious that it was simple, but he got into a deeper explanation that made no sense to her at all.

"Ugh!" she groaned. "All I heard was water, heat, and ice! The rest, forget it!"

"Surely your villagers and parents taught you something about The Seven Elements."

Viera stuck out her tongue but just as quickly drew it back into her mouth when Myrddin growled at her. She said, "I know that the days of the week are based on specific Elements." Collecting a stick, she scratched the four Elemental symbols of Metal, Earth, Water, and Wood into the soil in front of her.

Exasperated, Myrddin said, "You didn't even draw your own Fire Element. I hope you know more than just its existence in you. And what about Ice and Air? Or did you not pay attention in your schooling?"

"What schooling?" Viera scraped her boot over her drawings, blurring them. "The only lessons were for Metal, Earth, Water, and the occasional Wood Elemental."

If she were to judge from his grimace, the way Myrddin pressed his fingers into his temples looked painful. "You mean no one came from a Fire Temple to evaluate you?"

"Why in Evermore would someone come to Iyesgarth? I don't even understand why you came."

He shook his head in dismay. "Village leaders or Lords must alert Temples of outlier Elementals. A representative of the Element assesses the situation and brings back the Initiate for training, which should have occurred with you."

"Obviously, that didn't happen!"

Myrddin paused in deep thought and asked, "When did your Fire first present itself?"

She wrinkled her nose. "When I was born, I made the fire flare in my home's hearth. At least, that's what my mum and da said."

Myrddin tapped his chin. "After seeing what you did in the town square, I can't say I'm surprised, but I expected an interlude with you."

Viera blinked. "What does that mean?"

"When a child is born, there's generally a settling period before Elemental presentation. Not always but usually within six seasons of the Elemental's birth. Though it's not uncommon for a presentation to happen later if we have an oddity like Bedwyr or Lamorac."

"How were they an oddity?"

"Bedwyr was nine winters when he presented as a Water Elemental. Lamorac didn't present until he was fifteen." Myrddin snorted. "He's been late with everything throughout his entire life. Couldn't even decide if he wanted to be born in summer or autumn." Her Master rolled back his shoulders, the joints cracking as though in empathetic protest. "Your village did you a great disservice. They should have reached out to the Lord of Iyesgarth."

Curling her fingers, Viera pressed them tight against her palms. "Mayor Limawit is a gigantic wanker."

He arched his eyebrows. "Language, young lady!"

She pounded her fist. "He's always had it in for my family. Two autumns ago, my mum should've won the potluck contest for pies and cakes. He cast the deciding vote for brine-soured kippers. Have you ever had that? It's a disgusting little fish sifted out of the mud and shite that's pickled. Hells, he barely let me win last summer's Ugliest Pig Contest! Should have substituted mine for the mayor himself."

Slapping both hands over his face, Myrddin dragged his fingers down his jaws. "You still must watch your mouth."

"Not for anything concerning Limawit. He's a ruddy coward. Mayor Keyne Senan was far better." She laughed, recalling the only time the man had been any less than his usual jovial self while approaching the nobleman who had led an army through the town square. "At least he didn't piss himself when he met Lord Wallach."

Viera had been feeding the birds with her best friend, Peg, and Dottsie on the fountain when Jormund Wallach stopped, sniffed as though he had smelt filth, and stalked toward them. Senan had intercepted the noble, with orange Elemental light dancing about his fingertips and his Air—a rare Element in their village—swirling about the square. There was no saving Senan after he stepped between Lord Wallach and the fountain. Dottsie had enfolded Viera and Peg in her embrace, spouting gibberish that had Jormund snarling and retreating as if what ailed the Healer was contagious, calling her a mad she-bitch to boot. Crimson and black blood splashed as he rounded on Limawit, who had found himself promoted as his predecessor's body cooled scant feet away.

Myrddin straightened. "What do you mean?"

"Jormund Wallach led a force through the Valley seven summers ago." Viera worried her lip, her mind returning to the man with blue warpaint staining the skin about his eyes into a mask, across the bridge of his nose, and blue vertical lines streaking from his temples to his cheeks. "He gutted Mayor Senan in front of the entire village. Senan's blood is still on the fountain. Limawit was next in line to be mayor. Standing in front of all Iyesgarth, he pissed himself and blubbered for mercy. It was embarrassing."

Myrddin got up. "Wetting his pants was the smartest thing your mayor ever did. Your village would have been totally destroyed otherwise." A moment passed. "What lordship oversees Iyesgarth?"

"My father said we're in Dyfed's domain even though we're close to the outskirts of the Ynyr duchy of Gwent. I was told, before they clasped hands some centuries ago, the two regions used to fight over us."

"If you were under Gwent dominion, you would be dead. Limawit, losing control of his bladder, saved you all. Your other mayor likely displayed too much confidence, and Jormund found that threatening."

"How close was Jormund Wallach to Bedwyr?" asked Viera.

"Father and son."

"Scary."

"Aye," Myrddin said, sounding ominous. "Even Bedwyr feared his father until the very end."

Myrddin's tone bothered her as she asked, "What changed?"

His bunched jaw foretold the severity of what was to come: "Bedwyr murdered his own father and was complicit in the death of Arthwyr's father, Uther Pendragon."

Chapter 12

Fire Lessons

Lladdwyr perthynas meant betraying your own blood, the term translating into old tongue "kin killer." In Iyesgarth, performing *lladdwyr perthynas*—especially on one's own parent—was a crime that demanded the offender's death. The last time such a heinous crime occurred it rent the community in half. The accused, a young son, had a legitimate excuse, as he was protecting his mother from his drunkard father, but it mattered little and the youth drank the poison the village leadership handed him. It was the only leniency granted the boy, yet much better than being drawn and quartered or subjected to a Blood Eagle in the town square.

Myrddin's revelation made Viera's skin prickle, and she asked him, "How is it that Bedwyr is still alive without paying for his guilt?"

Myrddin tensed. "What do you mean?"

"Since the realm follows the law of *lladdwyr perthynas,* how come Bedwyr wasn't executed?"

Myrddin's wrinkles became more defined and aged him. "The entire nobility deserves that sentence more than Bedwyr. He was the canary we ignored in a gas-filled mine."

She wondered what skeletons hid within the murky confines of Myrddin's remark. "Ah, do you mind explaining this in a way I can understand? Remember, I wasn't around."

"Sorry. It's a difficult story to relate, and I got ahead of myself. Bedwyr was about this tall—" Myrddin held his hand across from his waist— "when he begged us to hear him out. Jormund Wallach told us that Bedwyr was a disturbed child, crying wolf. We realized all too late that Bedwyr had warned us correctly about the monsters among us. If we'd listened, the Red and White Duels of the Draigs might have been avoided and countless lives saved on both sides."

"How old was Bedwyr?"

"Nine winters." The corners of Myrddin's eyes sagged. "I promise to listen if ever you come to me. I'll not make the same mistake I made with him."

She studied his sad countenance and said, "I guess."

Myrddin's voice started breaking. "Your slipping through the cracks explains a lot. Your mayor should've reached out to Elden's Hearth. Too much goes awry when an Elemental does not learn from those of the same Element. Even though you demonstrated amazing control with your Element, you have deficiencies. We will fix these, but for now tell me about Fire."

"Well, it's hot and it burns."

He glared at her. "Aye. Anything other than that?"

"Uh, it lights a hearth. No other Fire Elementals are anywhere about the village, so there was nothing."

Myrddin clenched his jaw. "Great. With your limited knowledge of Fire, how were you able to produce something as advanced as that phoenix?"

"I didn't know it was *that* advanced?"

"It's not in any book I know of. How were you able to come up with that firebird?"

She chewed on her lower lip. "I don't know. It just felt right."

"Well, you could be Reactive."

"Huh?"

"You've no formal training, and you work on instinct. Your Fire channels itself through whatever stimulates you. As for me, I have to plan every move with Fire, such as right now." He created delicate flames that produced intricate wisps of gray smoke that whirled into a tight spiral. "With no mentor, you stumble along until you have it the way you want it. You've learned your present skills through necessity yet without proper conditioning."

Confusion rippled through Viera. *Isn't necessity how everyone learns anything?* She drew her hands together. "Does that mean you can train me to do better with Fire?"

"I will certainly try. So, you are aware, some of the most powerful Elementals in history have first learned their elements by necessity. The first King of Evermore, Cymry Pendragon, is one of the most notable Metal Reactives."

"Are there any others?"

"Daegyn Dyfed, the future Lord of Dyfed Landing, is one. He's fourteen summers and an Earth Elemental. He has his own story to tell."

Viera swallowed. "Who are the others? And can I talk to them?"

"You're not going to want to hear the answer."

"Why not?"

"Bedwyr is another one. But keep your distance. As I'm sure you know, he doesn't suffer people well. He's never entertained an Apprenticeship. Arthwyr even tried to get him to take on Maryck, but the Knight refused."

Viera had learned a lot about Maryck from the Maids and said, "If Bedwyr wouldn't take on the Crown Prince of Evermore, I guess there's no chance he'll give me the light of day."

"My best advice is to stay away from Bedwyr. If you get on his bad side… well… you won't like the result."

"Why do you fear him so? Aren't you one of the most powerful Lords in Evermore? I hear you're also the Mage."

"I am indeed the latter. As to the former, power only holds true meaning when based on what a specific situation requires. Be wary of trifling with any Knight in the Eclipse. Each deserves his title." Viera felt a chill run down her back. "And whatever you do, don't attempt to cozy up to Bedwyr. Only ill could come of it." He turned back to the book. "Fire has ten main katas. There are more advanced ones, but the first ten are our base and—"

"We learned a little about katas but none of it made sense," Viera said, happy to interrupt what she found very boring.

Unfazed, Myrddin continued, "A kata is a sequence of moves. In Temples, you learn your katas as a means of control and mastery."

Myrddin placed his hands palms down and tilted toward her. After a brief period of concentration, he lifted his hands and began tracing an elaborate circle in the air, and in a few seconds yellow light rippled into a throbbing array. "This is *En,* the first kata, which is a defensive maneuver. You use this kata to deflect something or someone from coming at you."

The array shimmered and she gulped, noting it was beautiful but also unnerving.

Myrddin lowered his hands and canceled the array. "The next one to learn is *To*, which is another defensive maneuver, except it's more for close-range contact." A sharp move brought his elbows against his sides, his fingers splayed as he brought his arms into a peak in front of his chest. He closed the kata by shoving his hands outward.

Too soon they moved on to the third kata, *Tre*, but by now the entire process was a blur to Viera.

Over the next hour, Myrddin repeated the moves for *En*, *To* and *Tre*. Viera tried to emulate him as best she could, but her unrefined moves were awkward and uncertain, and she created little more than a flicker of a flame here and there. When she returned to the Maid's wagon, she was sweaty, exhausted, and frustrated.

I'm never going to get this, and, ugh, there are seven more katas. But I've got something up my sleeve that I'm positive is better than all the katas put together, and nobody knows about it.

Yet!

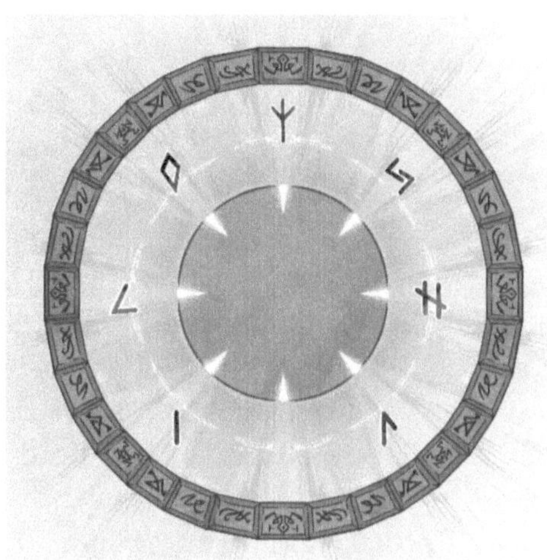

CHAPTER 13

LIGHT OF THE MOON

Thin soup softened the bread Viera dunked into a wooden bowl. She scraped her spoon over a dent near the top of it. A quiver skirted across her shoulders. She was certain she was being watched, which proved true, because as she glanced up from her meal, she met Jocelyn's narrow-eyed glare.

"Peasants sleep with pigs in the winter," Jocelyn blurted, elbowing both Cornwall sisters but speaking directly to Viera. "Papa says it's because they are not far from them."

Viera was about to pounce on Jocelyn when Bedwyr stopped in front of her and called to Arthwyr, "All's well, Arthwyr. Should be a quiet night."

Arthwyr waved toward the bubbling cauldron. "Care to break bread with us and then ride to Glastonbury?"

Next to Viera, Galahad stilled with his spoon midair before it clattered into his pewter bowl. "Why are you going there?"

"What's it to you?" Bedwyr asked, sneering down his nose.

"Strange how you're slinking off close to the last known sighting of Avalon."

"You sound like a scorned bitch. Want me to bring you back a favour? What does the little Princess of the DuLacs want? Ribbons?

Girdle?" Bedwyr toed the ground and sent a pebble skittering toward Galahad. "Oh, I'm sorry. They're fresh out of mud worm pies for you."

Galahad lunged to his feet, spilling broth on his trousers. "You bast—" he said as Constantine strolled past and shoved a bread roll into his mouth.

Rapping Bedwyr over the head with a long loaf of bread, Constantine nudged him toward the cauldron. "Find a seat and eat," Constantine said, ladling soup into a bowl, "or I'll fry you."

Disregarding Myrddin's warning concerning Bedwyr's antisocial nature, Viera motioned to the space next to her. "Lord Wallach, would you like to dine with us?"

Bedwyr recoiled as if a snake had struck at him. "I eat pig, I don't dine with it."

Jocelyn and her pack couldn't laugh loud enough, but that ended in a hurry when Bedwyr said, "That amuses you harpies? I don't recall saying I'd break bread with any of you, either." Bedwyr sniffed in the girls' direction, and his features morphed into disgust. "One of you reeks worse than a pig." He held a stare on Jocelyn, who stilled as if a statue, even holding her breath until he turned away.

Snatching the bowl from Constantine, Bedwyr sat by himself at the farthest end of the long bench everyone was seated on. "Rather eat with my horse than with any of you," he said in a voice loud enough for everyone to hear.

Rumored to have Bedwyr's interest, Felicia Cornwall sat nearest him, and after a few minutes sidled closer. She smiled coyly and cooed, "Milord, I want you to know that —"

"Be gone, Felicia!" came his quick rebuke, cutting her sycophantic drivel off midsentence. To add further insult, he pointed her away as one would a two-year-old.

After she ate, Viera took a short walk. A bird's tweeting drew her to a crate left next to the river, and a sparrow, female by its smallish size, and with odd shading about its otherwise dullish-brown wings and head, perched atop the lid. A large, colorful male sparrow soon flitted onto the crate. Three white specks lined its black beak, and a dark-gray bib marked its breast. Its bright orange feet completed the bird's picturesque appearance. It took Viera but a few seconds to realize she had fed both birds when she was with Dottsie the Healer in the square. Despite being blind, Dottsie had described these birds, and she had a name for each.

"Suzume," Dottsie said was the name of the female, but when Viera tore off a big crumb and called out to the bird, she wouldn't take the morsel. No matter how many times or in how many different ways she pronounced Suzume, the sparrow didn't come to her.

Dottsie told Viera not to fret, the bird was an old friend who had at last found its way home, and she was likely tired and not ready to meet anyone new. The sparrow had many names, as well as her mate who shadowed her. How a blind person could tell color was only one piece of the puzzle, because Viera didn't understand the Suzume reference either. But Dottsie said many strange things, like when she called Viera by the name "Viviane" for over a month. When Mayor Limawit overheard the blind Healer repeatedly addressing Viera in this manner, he claimed that Dottsie was daffier than a looned-up duck on Moon Mead. Still, Dottsie sometimes made sense.

When certain she'd butchered the sparrow's name again, Viera gave up and murmured, "Golly." To her amazement, the male instead hopped over and took the crumb from her finger.

Viera broke off some more crumbs, and the bird voraciously tore into them. The female bounded closer, crowding Golly and pecking at whatever he hadn't yet eaten.

"Tilly is what I'm going to call you," Viera said to the female and pushed some morsels her way. Black edged Tilly's wings, and rich violet rippled over the bird's head. The phoenixes that Viera summoned looked much the same, although when their feathers opened, they shifted between red, yellow, and white.

She extended her finger toward Tilly, a new friend forever. The bird jumped onto it but did not prick the skin with its sharp talons.

A call out from Myrddin halted Viera's trip down memory lane, and she bid farewell to her feathered friends and made her way back to where her Master was standing. He patted her on the back and said, "You're done for the day," and he guided her toward her wagon. But she wasn't tired and remained outside, in time to hear a discussion between Myrddin and Bedwyr.

Myrddin held out an athame with a hilt braided in gray and burgundy leather.

Bedwyr shoved it aside, saying, "I can handle Uther's leftovers without that blasted thing. All your brother's blade ever brings anyone is misery."

Myrddin pressed it into Bedwyr's hand. "Yet, Hamyll insisted you have it. Take it, and if you don't like it, return it when you come back from Glastonbury."

Bedwyr closed his fingers over the hilt. Below its base, an ebony stone winked in the firelight, and as he slid the sword from its sheath, gleaming steel emerged. Bedwyr resheathed the blade and hung it next to his saddlebags, but he turned to Myrddin and said, "You're the one who should have it. There have been reports of highwaymen about. You need to be careful, Lord Emrys."

"I will be diligent, as always." Myrddin waved Bedwyr off, adding, "Balanced be and fair winds to you." The younger Knight mounted his horse; the mare did not even sway from her rider's movements, displaying how horse and rider were enviably attuned to one another. His horse cantered away in the direction of the late-setting sun.

From the corner of her eye, Viera glimpsed a large oak on an embankment not far from the river's edge. She set her mind to enjoy a night secured in the cradle of the tree's roots and beneath the blanket of a starlit sky.

The pulse of the girl's life thudded in the man's ears. She was curled up against the roots of the oak, her thin peasant dress providing little warmth. The chill in the air should have chased her closer to the fire.

The moon, fat and round, loomed above. Cast in the shadows of the tree's branches, several figures lurked. As tall grasses rustled, an owl hooted. Sinews and tendons popped as shadows became elongated. The odor of urine, dried sweat, and long-stale food overpowered the cool night air.

The highwayman who had discovered Viera returned to the eight who had skulked farther back, waiting for his signal to close in on the camp. But when they learned of the girl, their heads swiveled toward the tree where Viera slept, their slavering jowls twisting into grotesque leers. Moments later, cackles barked as all four highwaymen materialized.

Unbeknown to any of these marauders, a man hid himself on a tall branch in the tree. But he was not just a man, he was Twilight. The others of his Order called him the Marshal. Fools, the lot of them. He was The Eclipse.

As he rose and jumped, wind covered his grunt, and not even a whisper of noise marked his descent from the bough of the tree. His cloak brushed Viera, and she twitched in her sleep but that was all.

Beneath the moon's glow, the highwaymen spread out, slinking along as they flanked the oak, not knowing that the Marshal lurked nearby. They had ever been his prey! He wanted to lunge and kill them all, but he had to know the extent of their capabilities, and if there were more of them. His best option was to use the girl as bait, so he chose to let these highwaymen believe they could do what they may to her.

CHAPTER 14

THE MARSHAL AND THE HIGHWAYMEN

As a man's squeals pierced the fog of slumber, Viera startled awake. A branch crackled and clothes rasped against stiff grass. Sweat, grime, and urine invaded her nostrils. A figure emerged like the ghostly visage that commonly materialized when early dawn rolled onto the fields. Viera, however, was certain this was not a shade. Much worse, this was a flesh-and-blood highwayman, a societal fringe feeder who came during the night. Good people never encountered them. Or so it was said.

High-pitched laughter rattled her bones, and a voice said, "Good eve, pretty."

Viera lifted her hand, ready to blast the man with a Fire array just as he slammed something metallic around her wrist. She heard a clink, and her Fire was sealed tight as a cold emptiness pulsated from what was a bracelet of some sort. She yanked at the metal until her wrist bled from its rough edges. She screamed, "What is this?"

"It's an Elemental breaker, pretty. Don't you like it? It means no Element for you." The man's foul breath heated the nape of her neck. "Want to play, little one?"

A yell rocketed past her throat, and she kneed the man in the groin and bolted from the nest of roots. Thick blades of grass dragged over her legs as the river's waters called her to safety. She threw herself from a knoll and rolled head over heels until she landed on her feet. Like wildfire, pain spread through her legs and she crashed to the ground. She pushed up and took a step, but roots twisted upward like knobby knees and sent her skidding and yelping over the rocky bank. Agony washed through her right leg and she collapsed.

At the sound of twigs snapping, she could hear her heart beating. She spun around and the highwayman let out a guttural cry and reached for her, twisting his fingers in her hair. He thumped her skull against the ground, and her vision swam as blood coated her tongue. As the highwayman's putrid saliva spattered her cheeks, his scabby lips twisted into a gnarled leer. Gripping her throat, he pressed so hard that her neck bones cracked from the pressure.

Her vision clouded and all she saw were dark splotches. Behind the man, crimson coalesced into two celestial pinpricks of light. Death beckoned and lassitude slid through her limbs as she floated toward Twilight.

The highwayman's nails scraped her neck and tore her skin, his full weight on her and his breath directly in her face. Choking, she sucked in what air she could. Her lungs were ready to explode, but she wasn't ready for Twilight yet. She found the strength for one final attempt to save herself and managed to flop onto her side, but her assailant pushed himself to his feet and flashed a steel blade in the silvery moonlight.

Certain she was done for, she closed her eyes. But instead of dying, snarls and the clash of swords clanging against each other rang in her ears. Through blurred vision she watched two darkened forms fall backwards as a gurgled scream pierced the night.

Viera covered her ears and sang, *"Little sparrow, sing me away, past the darkness and into day. I give you honey and milk, you give me fortune and silk."*

Popping noises filled the silence, and a spray of warmth splattered her side. The stench of stomach contents filled her nose, and her own insides churned at the squelch and smell of excrement being released. The victor whistled the tune Viera had sung, and this terrified her more than the fight itself.

The winner's boots came toward her, making sucking sounds as the man slogged through patches of deep wet soil on the embankment. A jolt shot through her as each step drew closer. She pulled her knees over her belly, desperate to protect what she valued most. Once again, she closed her eyes.

A strange sweetness settled on her tongue. Warm gloved fingers plucked the edges of the iron band on her wrist. Metal clicked and the breaker stayed in place but the clasp sprang open.

She felt her Fire begin to trickle back to her, but there was no time to revel because ragged panting assailed her eardrums. Her eyes flew open, but it took a few seconds to connect the panting to the shadowy crimson-eyed beast that stared at her—and from its maw a wide tongue that licked its black-lined lips.

As a gloved hand settled over her face, the beast faded in wisps of smoke. Warm liquid dripped over her quivering skin and dribbled a path down her neck, the fluid's heady slickness indicating it was blood. A gravelly voice rasped into the shell of her ear, "Don't move if you know what's good for you."

Her Fire smoldered but lay too deep beneath the surface for her Elemental core to be of use to her. Indeed, the breaker on her wrist was loose enough for her Fire to continue its path through her, but not release from its cinch over her wrist. When Viera thought it couldn't get any worse, a whine came from something clamoring for release from within her core. *What is this thing? Is it inside me or from the breaker?*

"Pathetic," the voice said, low and cold. "You're not even worth the blood in your body. Hardly worthy of The Eclipse. But I can show you what you can be good for."

The rush of fabric whipped in the air and a belt buckle jangled. Viera shook like the leaves on a branch in a gale wind. Fearing the worst, she sobbed, "Please, don't."

She waited for the cold kiss of his skin on hers. *That's what happens, right? There's no other way. This is how it's going to be for me.*

She waited. All motions stilled. A hand pressed hard over her mouth.

"Just sleep," the man said, and what seemed like the swell of a wave crashed over her, dragging her into the dark. "Just sleep," the voice repeated.

Whoever he was, he made her blood boil and twinges of pain lance her body. Viera flailed her limbs in defiance of what she assumed was the man's demand that she succumbs to his carnal wishes—and ultimately Twilight.

Her tears slid past her tired eyelids until she could cry no more. It was then that the pressure eased from her, and the breaker dropped from her wrist and into her hand.

"Sleep," she heard him once more, and she drifted into darkness.

Metal dug into Viera's hand and her eyelids snapped open. To her utter shock, there was no pain radiating from between her legs or blood caking her thighs. The dark night sky felt as stifling as what had cut away her Fire. She didn't know how long she'd slept, but she was elated that the rest was adequate enough for her and Fire to be one again. And just in time, as tall grass rustled and a dark figure appeared along the ridge of the embankment.

Viera staggered to her feet, and to her utter shock, there was no pain radiating from between her legs or blood caking her thighs. A twig snapping had her flying into a shaky facsimile of the third Fire kata, *Tre*. Fire flared from her palms and the breaker fell to the ground. Instinct and the kata lessons sharpened her attack, and the drills Myrddin had shown her took on a new life.

The intruder scrambled for safety to avoid the release of yellow Fire bathing the embankment. Her second attack produced an explosion of orange that lit up the hillside. The next assault waxed deep red until black rippled from its center.

Viera heard a harried shout coming from behind a tree: "Wart, it's me!"

Viera stared, hands outstretched and quaking, as Myrddin ran toward her. She cried, "I had no idea it was you. I— "

"Don't talk. You're safe. I'm here." Myrddin slid his arms under her knees and lifted her to him.

Viera looped her arms over his shoulders. Great shuddering gulps of air dragged his familiar scent into her lungs. Bit by bit, her stiff muscles relaxed as the heat from Myrddin's body warmed her.

Arthwyr's voice called out, and Myrddin hailed him to join them. "What happened?" the King asked Myrddin.

"Highwaymen," Myrddin said. "Bedwyr warned me about them. They must have been following us. I found one… what's left of him."

The cool night air seeped past the thin material of Viera's dress. She twisted away from Myrddin as soon as she saw Ewain and Lance arrive. Lance prodded his boot at a glistening heap, and the nudge turned the head of a dead man toward Viera. Her gorge rose in her throat as she stared into the eyes of the highwayman who undoubtedly was her assailant, his mouth contorted into a rictus of horror. The macabre scene was made worse by the sharp bones of his ribcage pulled outward. Viera gagged and Lance shifted between her and the mutilated corpse, but not before he bumped it again and a round metal object dropped from the dead man's coat pocket.

Lance asked Viera to relate what had happened. When she finished, Ewain, who was washing the blood off her face, said, "At first glance, I thought a wolf had mauled her, but there are no scratches underneath the blood."

"Thank Evermore that the Marshal is on the hunt," Lance said as he bent down and picked up an unclasped breaker, the metal object that had been dislodged from the highwayman's coat. "The Marshal carries a master rune key to pop the locks."

"That dead highwayman put that thing on me," Viera said and cringed. "I couldn't use my Element. It was gone."

Ewain said, "You wouldn't be able to. It's an Elemental breaker. Makes it impossible to conjure up an element." He checked the marks on her wrist and legs and massaged her ankle. To her relief, he reported, "You shouldn't have any permanent scars, and nothing is broken. You'll be all right. Just very sore."

Snatching the breaker from Lance, Arthwyr asked, "How in Evermore did a highwayman get a hold of one of these things?"

Lance groaned, "We need to find out. And fast."

Myrddin said, "Viera said she thought there were many more highwaymen other than this one. Shouldn't we send our Knights to search for the rest of them? They can't get too far away?"

Arthwyr tucked the breaker into his robes. "Not tonight. They have too much of an advantage in the dark, and we don't know how many are out there."

"But what about the highwaymen who *are* escaping? We can't just let them go."

"If the Marshal is after them, he'll hunt them down until they're all gone. They made their bed; they get to lie in it." Arthwyr said to Viera, "I'm sorry this happened to you, but thank Evermore that the Marshal was able to protect you."

Everyone settled in at the camp, the Knights patrolling the perimeter as Lamorac guarded the wagon with the seven girls and four boys huddled within it.

Galahad approached Myrddin from the fire pit. "As soon as we heard the commotion, we secured the camp. When the screams stopped, we feared the worst. What happened?"

"Highwaymen. One attacked Viera. The Marshal saved her."

"Did the highwayman get to her?"

"Not according to Viera," Myrddin said, as he set Viera down next to the firepit. "The Marshal found him first. At least, that's what I think happened."

Galahad poured a goblet of water and passed it to her. "Did you see him?"

With a tremor in her voice, she rasped, "Him?"

"The Marshal."

"No," she replied sharply. "He covered my eyes when I tried to look at him."

Galahad frowned. "You didn't see him at all?"

"It was too dark."

"What did he say to you?"

"When it was over—" her voice breaking— "He told me to sleep."

"He doesn't want her to know him," Constantine said, from where he observed on the other side of the firepit. "He must have his reasons."

Myrddin said, "I agree with Constantine. And let's quit for the night. Viera's been through enough. We'll have plenty of time to discuss the Marshal tomorrow, and in the days that follow." He turned to Viera. "Unless there's more you want to add right now."

Her skin got cold. Never could she reveal the full extent of her experience with the Marshal. Not when there was no telling what lingered beneath the surface of his cryptic comments.

"No, I'm fine," she muttered. "No canary in the mine this time."

CHAPTER 15

DOG FIGHTS

It had been three sleepless nights since the highwaymen's assault, the ghost of them lingering on everyone. Trying to eat her morning meal, Viera poked the thick gruel in her bowl as if stabbing it. Something as simple as an air pocket popping in the mush made her jump. Ewain had watched her struggling with her food and said, "You should concentrate on eating. If nothing else, you need to regain your strength." He gave her shoulder a pat.

"I can't stop thinking about what happened. I should have done more." She wiped her eyes.

Ewain knelt next to her. "Doing anything else would have been a deadly mistake."

"How is that?"

"Have you ever had to fight for your life?"

"Nay," she murmured.

"The three basic instincts of survival are fight, flight, and freeze, and not necessarily in that order. You did all three. That's pretty impressive."

"I was pathetic at all three."

"You're here, aren't you?"

"I wouldn't be if not for the Marshal. I had little to do with my survival."

"You're wrong. You fought with everything you had in you." Ewain combed his fingers through her hair and untangled a knot. "Flight means you live to fight another day, and you managed to run. Freezing means you blend in and hide so your enemy can't find you. You hid long enough for the Marshal to come to your rescue. The instincts of survival get down to a matter of degrees, and you succeeded with all three at one level or another."

"Yeah, well, I'm not sure about any of it."

"Think on it, Viera." Ewain rose and dusted off his robe. "When fighting to survive, not everything we do will be right. What's most important, we learn what to do differently if it ever happens again. As for your inability to act right away, this is normal for anyone who experiences a breaker for the first time."

Lamorac came over to tell Ewain that he'd found some herbs to restock their supplies. The two walked off, and jealousy stirred in Viera as Ewain's lighthearted laughter drifted back. He was twice her age, but she found him appealing, not much in a physical way but because there was an inherent sense of compassion and understanding encompassing him. Like water should always be a source of calm and he well embodied it, almost in spite of the other Water Elementals in the group.

Air moved, but not by the wind, as a black form in robes and a cloak dropped down on the other side of the fire from Viera. The race of her pulse did not slow when she recognized Bedwyr, who swayed to one side and righted himself with a violent jolt.

His black hair stuck out on the sides, and blue circles shadowed his eyes like bruises. A wet smear of white went from the corner of his mouth to his neck. "Bloody Lamorac and Gaheris and their damned fairy dust. I'm going to kill those bastards," he muttered, a slur thickening his words as he held his hands toward the fire.

Viera edged farther down the bench on which she sat. Flight it was.

Sending Bedwyr a crooked glance, and seeing he was preoccupied, she took the opportunity to shimmy along at a deliberate pace. She was making decent progress until a twig snapped under her foot, which drew Bedwyr's attention.

The abrupt stillness in the man preceded a motion so swift that one second she stared at him, and the next the sunlight blazing over a metal edge blinded her. Blinking against the sting, she flinched at the steel hovering in front of her nose. She went cross-eyed until her vision settled enough to discern a metal lined wooden fan. Past the fan, Bedwyr's gaze had lost its weariness in the face of wariness.

An ache in her chest reminded Viera that she needed to breathe and her next few quaked past her throat. His gaze lowered and the burn of his regard seemed to linger upon the bruises marring her neck. Like the slow withdrawal of a fox retreating into the brush, Bedwyr clicked shut his fan, returned it to his belt, and settled across the fire again, yanking his collar tighter against his neck as she did the same.

He sniped at her, "I see no one heeded my warning about the highwaymen."

She was too terrified to reply, but Galahad came up, eliminating the need as he leaned between her and Bedwyr and said, "Rough few days, eh, lass? And aren't you a little bedraggled, Bedy? There's this thing called a mirror. Want to borrow mine?"

She managed a feeble nod, her gaze zipping between Bedwyr and Galahad.

Bedwyr glared at Galahad as though he wanted to dissect the other Water Elemental piece by piece. "Say, didn't I hear you mewling for your mummy last night?"

"At least I didn't kill mine. You're an even greater monster than your mother ever imagined." Galahad spat and nudged Viera back. "What with you being like your father."

Their restraint snapped in unison. The pair lunged, and Galahad pushed Viera away, sparing her from being shoved into the fire pit, as both men rolled over the crates and other makeshift benches where Viera last sat.

Bedwyr leveled a kick at Galahad's underbelly. Galahad doubled over as he recovered and knocked Bedwyr flat on his back. Viera heard the sound of boots rushing toward the campfire as Myrddin dropped in next to her and moved her farther out of harm's way.

Bedwyr, his hair touching smoldering embers on the campfire, arched his back and pushed off the ground. He charged Galahad and sank his teeth into his shoulder, forcing a stentorian-level yell from the other Water Elemental. More screams marked the moment, some rather garbled, until Galahad grabbed Bedwyr by the hair and pushed him away. Bedwyr made the mistake of charging him again—and Galahad knocked him on his arse again.

"I've got Galahad!" Lance shouted as he ran up to his son. "Somebody, get Bedwyr!"

Bedwyr rose as Arthwyr darted in front of the pair, but a fist coming from Galahad clipped the King's jaw. Arthwyr flew backwards from the blow and flattened a wicker basket.

Myrddin vaulted over a log and tackled Bedwyr, twisting the front of the younger man's robes and slamming him against the ground.

Bedwyr squirmed until a smack from Myrddin knocked his head against a log and a cry erupted from the wounded Knight. His daze lasted just a few seconds and he screamed, "Feck you to the Fomoiri!"

Arthwyr scrambled over and pressed his arms hard against Bedwyr's chest, but he had to jerk back to avoid the incisors that would have bitten off his earlobe. "Dammit, I never should have taught you that trick," he said to Bedwyr.

As light flickered at Viera's feet, a faint purplish glow snaked across the ground. It melded into solid shapes and the rune for the Water symbol appeared as shades of violet throbbed and darkened.

"Feck! Run!" yelled the King, and everyone, including the combatants, tried to flee. All attempts were to no avail as an enormous wave splashed the entire area and steam billowed from the fire. Soaked to the bone, the group turned toward Lamorac standing with a seething Ewain next to a wagon that was safely away from the deluge.

Lamorac milled about, toeing aside a few chunks of burnt wood. "Heh, took long enough for the showers to arrive."

His job done, he sauntered toward a nearby tree, his low whistle drifting back as a reminder of his power.

Ewain, less than a year older than Lamorac's thirty seasons, stalked toward his soaked confederates. "I don't know who's worse. The children or the man-children who are supposed to be the models for the children."

Marching into the middle of the sodden gathering, Constantine brushed Ewain aside and said to him, "You're too close to take them to task, Lord Gorre. You shan't take a position grounded on righteousness when you are part of the problem yourself."

With pink dusting his pale cheeks, Ewain sputtered.

Constantine asked Galahad, "What brought this on between you two?"

Galahad clutched his shoulder. "He's an arse."

"You started it," Bedwyr said, squirming between Myrddin and Arthwyr, "and I'm going to finish it."

"You think you're the big bad wolf, but I've been kicking your arse for years!"

"Bullocks, I let you think you won!"

Myrddin jammed his fingers in Bedwyr's neck, cutting off any further comments, and rounded on Arthwyr, "How many times did we fight like this?"

Arthwyr rolled his eyes. "How many times did I win?"

"Only because I let you."

"Wonderful examples of maturity, all of you," Constantine said as he shook his finger at the males standing nearest him. "One or both of you exchanged insults. Both of you probably lunged at the same time."

Scoffing, Bedwyr grumbled, "You know so much, you should become an Oracle."

Myrddin motioned Bedwyr to the stones lining the far perimeter of the fire pit. The Mage went over to Viera and pulled her off to the side. "You're very lucky the Marshal was around. Do not stray from the wagons again without telling someone first."

Icy tendrils crawled across her skin, and as she rubbed her arms, she managed a weak, "Aye, Master."

He pushed her wet bangs from her eyes, his gaze sliding over her as concern softened his countenance. "I don't think anything Maerna or even Brynn has will fit you, but you can't stay in those clothes."

Constantine dusted off his cassock and stroked his chin as he appraised her. "Palamedes might have something she can change into. If you don't mind, it'll be baggy but a better fit."

A muscle twitched along Myrddin's jaw and he sighed. "Better than looking like a drowned rat. Lady Sagramore would delight in that far too much after you made her slum it through that pond, Wart."

CHAPTER 16

PEACE BY ANY OTHER NAME

An hour later, Viera descended from the Maid's wagon and walked the short distance to the wagon containing their healing supplies. Scarves and fans decorated every square inch of the Maid's interior wagon and never mind the dueling perfumes that threatened to strangle the air. Viera winced at the aqua gauzy netted material hugging her arms. The white pants were looser than even her worn homespun dress, but material called elastic tightened the waist and bottom of the pantlegs. When she pulled, the elastic stretched and conformed to her body and movements.

Rounding the wagon, she slowed at finding Gaheris had joined Constantine and was tending a new fire with a cauldron of barley cawl. She worried her inner cheek with her teeth as she took in the Foxbury Lord adding root vegetables into the barley soup while sipping on a horn of ale. It was odd witnessing noblemen as comfortable cooking and attending to the daily grind of camp when that was usually the labor of peasants. Even odder that someone as highborn as Gaheris was so intimately familiar with root vegetables, as he was ever digging them from the soil and adding them to the meals he made.

Awkwardly, she cleared her throat. Gaheris glanced over the battered rim of his drink and choked on it as his gaze settled upon her.

Perched on a nearby log, Constantine snapped his fingers next to Gaheris' ear when the Foxbury Lord ogled her. With heat burning across her cheeks, she headed toward the other fire pit.

Gaheris hailed her and said, "Don't go near that campfire, Milady." Rubbing his hands together from the chilly day, he added, "Bedwyr brought several back."

"Several what?"

"Highwaymen."

She perked up. "Are they going to be our prisoners while we're on Progress?"

"Only if the decapitated can walk," Gaheris replied and snorted.

The image of ragged strips of flesh dripping from a bloody neck came into Viera's mind. Shuddering, she looked in the direction of the campfire, glad a wagon blocked her view. "He decapitates the men he kills?"

"Generally. Or he displays them."

"What do you mean?"

"Bedwyr stages the bodies in gruesome ways." Gaheris picked up a twig and idly drew the Wood rune of *Ingwaz* on the soil. "Criminals tend to steer clear when they see mutilated corpses, especially with the heads missing."

Robes rustled and Lance appeared, carrying two burlap sacks. When he spied Viera, he stumbled to a halt and swung the bags behind him. Too late. Viera caught a glimpse of the stiff black stains covering the fabric.

Knowing he'd been found out, Lance brought the bags in front of him and said to Viera, "You don't want to go near the campfire, eh?" He whistled and trotted off with the heads in the sacks as if carrying melons to market.

Viera wasn't satisfied with Gaheris's response prior to Lance's interlude. "Why bring back the heads?"

Gaheris cleared his throat for so long that Constantine answered for him: "Bedwyr collects bounties on criminals and fugitives. He… well, to put it mildly, has a high prey drive."

Gaheris chuckled and tapped the twig against his palm. "Bedwyr might not be so effective after what one highwayman did to him. His left arm was acting up as he went to Glastonbury. During his search for Uther loyalists, he got into a skirmish and some bastard put a breaker on him."

"Is he all right?" Viera asked, ambivalent about Bedwyr but legitimately concerned because of his value to Progress.

"It comes and goes. Last night the pain was intense, and he had a pretty high fever." A tight expression settled on Gaheris's features. "Lamorac and I gave him an elderberry-and-fairy-dust draught. Bedwyr became so out of it he swore he *smelled* rainbows and threw up on Lance."

Viera plucked at her sleeve, sliding it up and down over her arm. "Did the guy who put the breaker on him escape?"

"Oh, Hells no. That poor sod is food for the wildlife."

She cringed, caressing the lingering, deep bruise where the breaker had abraded her wrist. "Didn't the breaker take away his Element?"

"That's never stopped Bedwyr. He doesn't need his Element to fight effectively or to kill an adversary."

Constantine inched his fingers toward the crucifix peeking from the fuchsia cincture banding his waist, and he said to Viera, "He was trained to fight wearing a breaker."

Viera propped her chin on her knees. "He must be really powerful. I couldn't dream of touching that level."

Constantine tucked the crucifix within the cincture. "Bedwyr is far from invincible. Gaheris has knocked Bedwyr's block off. And Galahad occasionally tops him. There are a few others who give him as good as they receive, as well."

Gaheris added, "Palamedes' brother, Segwarides, laid Bedwyr up in the Infirmary for several days." He snickered. "I didn't even know it was possible to do what Segwarides did with a stick, and he's a Fire Elemental."

She wrinkled her nose. "A Fire Elemental beat Bedwyr with a stick?"

"Ask Constantine."

The priest nodded. "Saraceni fighting styles are different from what is taught in our realm. Segwarides is a Master in *Tahtib*, *Nguni*, and *Razmafzar*."

Gaheris snatched up a new twig. "Bedwyr got cocky. He never anticipated Segwarides would know Evermorean fighting styles along with Saraceni techniques." He chuckled. "Bedwyr won't fight Myrddin either. No one in his right mind would want to pick a fight with the Mage."

Said Viera, "It's hard for me to assume that my Master could ever beat Bedwyr."

"Myrddin's style is unpredictable. He knows the katas of each Element, and he's adapted them to release as Fire."

Constantine bent toward her. "Be wary of assumptions. They have been many a powerful man's—and woman's—downfall."

Her mind circled back to the highwayman that attacked her and her breathing grew short and sharp. Pressing her knees to her chest, she squeezed her eyes shut and tried to breathe through her nose and out of her mouth as Ewain had instructed her. A subtle sweetness plumed over her before thick material dropped over her. With her breath hitching in her chest, she jolted and almost lurched into Bedwyr kneeling across from her. He flinched, exposing the mottled bruising encircling his throat.

As if of its own volition, her gaze could not tear from the handprints and he must have noticed as he flicked his fingers to indicate his neck. "Want to know what I did to the man who put his hands on me? How to get rid of the fear growing roots inside of you right now?"

That drew her stare from the marks to lock eyes with his, a darkness purling through her to hear whatever secret he could reveal to combat her night terrors. "Aye," she whispered, a tremor entering her voice that had his forehead knitting.

"I leaned into him—" Bedwyr's voice lowered, urging her to shift closer to him— "sank my teeth into his neck, and ripped out his throat. Fight like a bitch, don't snivel like one." The sodden man staggered to his feet and made shooing motions at them. "Make yourselves scarce. I'm not riding soaked."

With wet fabric squelching, he disappeared into the back of the wagon. The suck of his boots preluded the drop of both over the side, narrowly missing Gaheris, who set the cauldron so it would stay warm over the fire but not boil over.

Gaheris shoved Constantine past the wagon and gestured for Viera to follow. "Come, lass," he shouted into the wagon— "Some things you can't unsee once you've seen 'em!"

From the shadows, Bedwyr barked out, "Feck you, ya ginger blighted bastard!"

Viera hurried after Gaheris, who led her and Constantine to another wagon. Once they reached the other side, she settled on a barrel and tucked her arms in the sleeves of the cloak, marveling over whatever trick Bedwyr had used to dry the fabric so fast and well. Lavender enclosed her as if in an embrace and she closed her eyes when her muscles relaxed.

Giggling interrupted Viera's thoughts and Jocelyn flounced past with her pack. Viera's nemesis stopped and huffed, "Already reaching far beyond your station, I see."

Tavrina and the Cornwall lasses turned their noses up at Viera, fluttered their fans, and crossed over to their wagon. Maerna and Delilah loitered farther behind, their expressions blank and gazes averted. Appearing around the side, Lance handed them into the back.

"Bloody Hells!" Brynn's voice shot out from the wagon's interior. She hauled herself onto the driver's seat, flung open a book, and buried her nose in it, adding loudly, "Fluff-brained hussies, all of you."

Viera turned to her present company. "What's really going on with Jocelyn?"

Wincing, Gaheris flopped onto the ground. "That would be the green-eyed monster."

"Yeah, and then some. But there has to be more. The two of us have been through enough that she should be backing off. She has to know she can't beat me because of my Fire."

Gaheris jerked his eyes in the direction of the girls' wagon. "On the first night into Progress, Felicia tried to cozy up to Bedwyr. She failed. So, Jocelyn tried to do better."

Viera quizzed, "Better?"

From where he sat on the tailboard next to her, Constantine gestured toward the wagon Bedwyr had commandeered. "A formal Bond with Bedwyr is desirable for many reasons. He chewed out Jocelyn royally for trying him. She needed it. Sharp tongue, that one."

"What does that have to do with me?"

"He extended what little chivalry is in him to preserve your dignity. This," Gaheris said, rising and tucking Bedwyr's cloak about her shoulders, "is a loan. In the Game of Bonds, he presented this to you as a token. At least, that's how Felicia, and more important, Jocelyn, views it. He scorned them, and they see you as achieving what they couldn't."

"But I don't know anything about this cloak."

"You don't have to. All that mattered is what the Maids think it represents."

"I'm more confused than ever. Bedwyr has done nothing but ridicule me. He loathes the air I breathe."

Gaheris gave a toss of his head and his red hair seemed to flame in the morning sun. "Again, it doesn't matter. He's the last Lord of The Seven Houses. He gives his House symbol only to his Bond, his heir, or to recognize a new King or Queen of Evermore. As to the latter, he continues to refuse to recognize the current rulers."

Viera was shocked at that revelation. "He hasn't recognized King Arthwyr or Queen Guinevere? Doesn't the nobility have a ceremony to acknowledge its rulers?"

Constantine shifted and exchanged a look with Gaheris, once again answering what the man didn't want to discuss: "There was a coronation, but Bedwyr refused to attend. In relation to the Kingship, the way The Seven Houses are set up, it's not required. Nor do the Houses have to support either ruler. Bedwyr invoked that right. He won't formally ally with this King or Queen."

Gaheris checked the back of the cloak. "As for you, he hasn't presented any House symbol, although the Maids don't know this. So, you're safe from his bid—but not the speculation surrounding this cloak."

A shudder worked through her body. "I don't want to go back in the Maid's wagon wearing this thing."

Nudging her shoulder, Constantine said, "You can ride in the wagon I'm driving."

"I heard you were assigned to the Maid's wagon."

"Because of issues between the Maids and Palamedes, Lance decided otherwise. He's having enough of a time keeping our Water Elementals from burning and razing the valley."

"More like flooding it." Gaheris snorted and indicated Lamorac leaning against a tree with his back to them several yards away. "Though, Lamorac is calm."

Constantine rolled his gaze upward. "He smokes enough fairy dust that he's just five toadstools from joining a Kumbayaist circle."

Gaheris scratched his jaw. "Just five?"

Viera whipped around toward Constantine. "What's a Kumbayaist?"

"I'll answer that," Gaheris said, pawing through his robes until he unearthed a small purse. "A Kumbayaist is anyone who takes an oath of peace. They sit in a circle of toadstools, singing and discussing eternal, blissful harmony."

The pungency of fairy dust coiled in the air from the pouch as Gaheris rolled to his feet and sauntered toward Lamorac, who straightened and in greeting lifted a fag with smoke swirling from the glowing end. As the pair passed back and forth the stick, Viera muttered, "We call them tree-huggers."

Constantine guided her to the second wagon. "Let's get you settled in before Palamedes returns from his breakfast."

As they walked away, she glanced back to Gaheris and Lamorac to see if they were still upright. "Could Gaheris really beat Bedwyr?" she asked.

Chuckling, Constantine said, "He has a few times."

"How?"

"Gaheris does not have to wait for a Soul Bond to mature, boost, or smooth out his Element like most people. He was born completely Balanced and powerful. You remember when Gaheris said that Myrddin is unpredictable in a fight?"

"Aye."

Sweeping his gaze around them, he inched closer and murmured, "How do you think Gaheris knows this? It's no different from how he knew about Bedwyr and the cloak you're wearing. He can be bested, and he's also not invincible. But never underestimate him or any from Foxbury, or this will surely be your downfall."

CHAPTER 17
NEW ALLIANCES

Viera sat, her back a straight line, as the Saracen boy lay draped over the long bench inside the wagon, his legs braced against the canvas. Palamedes shuffled a deck of cards, his gaze fixated on his hands. With the sway of the wagon, his hair rippled and giggles bubbled from his throat.

Pressing her body to conform to the wooden boning of the wagon, Viera eyed him curiously. *Crazy perhaps?* Was she stuck in the wagon with a crazy person?

The Saracen boy continued to giggle like a loon.

Are all Air Elementals like this? Is this malady contagious? Feck, what if I catch it? A habit, long believed dead by her, reemerged. Nail biting was a horrible thing to do, but desperate times called for equal measures. With each snapped-off nail, the sound seemed to crack louder in her ears.

Palamedes' giggling was unrelenting, and she became even more unnerved when he slinked his way over to her.

He pressed his finger to his lips and whispered in a voice so soft Viera could barely hear him, "I'll tell you a secret."

Anything had to be better than his incessant laughter, so she nodded.

"After I learned Bedwyr was sick, I smoked fairy dust with Gaheris and Lamorac. I haven't felt so good, ever." He peeked at the priest sitting on the driver's seat. "Don't tell Constantine. He'll kill me and tell my brothers. Then they'll kill me dead again."

Her jaw dropped.

"Girls are stupid, but I like you," Palamedes said, opening his eyes wide. "Tell me, how did you light that tart's horse on fire?"

"I did not light her horse on fire. I sparked the mare's gas with my Element. There's a difference!"

He brayed like a donkey.

Constantine twisted around. "Any problems I should be aware of?"

"Of course not," Palamedes said, composing himself quickly. "Please don't make me sit with the girls in the other wagon."

"If you cause trouble, you'll be back there, young man, I assure you."

"We were just playing."

Constantine waved dismissively as he turned around.

Facing Constantine, Palamedes said through the side of his mouth, "You have no idea how boring this entire trip was until you blew up the welcome ceremony in Iyesgarth."

Viera leaned closer to him. "I had no idea."

An excited gleam appeared in his eyes. "It was the talk of the town—and Progress. That phoenix was amazing. Gaheris and Lamorac were jealous they missed it."

She gestured at Constantine. "What about *him*?"

"Father Constantine is an old man and a stick in the mud."

Palamedes flinched as the priest turned around in his seat and pointed at him, barking, "I heard that."

"I wasn't hiding it."

"Hooligan."

Palamedes said to Viera, as if nothing had happened, "You have pretty eyes. It's why those girls are jealous."

"They have nothing to be jealous of."

Palamedes rested his elbows on his knees. "You are way prettier than those tarts. They flutter their eyelashes enough to take flight, if they were lucky to be Air Elementals. That and titter away."

"What got you calling them tarts?"

Any joviality left him. "My older brothers and I come from Saraceni. It's an eastern realm with a lot of sand and little water. Evermore calls it a desert." Palamedes tugged at the hem on his vest. "Our father is Lord Aglovale Pellinore. My brothers grew up with him, but he's like a grandfather to me because I was a last blessing he had with my mother. The Draigs' Duels called him back from being an Emissary. My uncle was more like a father to me until..." he trailed off, gripping his arm and shivering as he blinked as though trying to clear his eyes of tears, "He's the reason we had to flee and my oldest brother, Safir, lost his birthright as the next ruler of Saraceni."

Circles. He talks in circles. "What does that have to do with the girls?"

"None of us will inherit Pellinore House because other members of the family are the heirs. Jocelyn somehow knows this, and she calls me and my brothers sand monkeys."

Heat sizzled on Viera's neck. "She called me a guttersnipe and a pig." A new determination set her mind in motion and cemented her resolve. She thrust out her hand to the Saracen boy. "We both need to avenge our honor. She's shamed us and sullied our names. This means war. The enemy of my enemy is my ally."

Palamedes didn't hesitate interlocking his fingers within hers and clasping her hand in his. The steady thump of his pulse against her palm startled her, but her own heart beat just as strong as they closed their personal oath with a unified promise: "Evermore!"

After the stop, Constantine did not make Viera and Palamedes change wagons, to the great joy of both youths. As they moved along the trail, Palamedes told stories that fascinated Viera, especially when he used his Air Element to create weaves that imitated the roll of sand dunes. Viera now hung on every word Palamedes spoke. A desert was something from fantasy. The only thing that rolled in Iyesgarth were hills and pastures.

Enthralled with tales of Saraceni nights and sands glowing under the hot desert sun, she could now listen to Palamedes for as long as he had the wind in his lungs. All was fine until the wagon slowed to a stop next to a stream and the loud bang of the tailgate dropping jolted her. She hit her head on a wooden support and cursed just as a book sailed through the air and smacked against a barrel with grain in it, spilling some. The book fell onto the wagon's deck, flying open to a page displaying a detailed sketch of a man's penis.

The noise had caused Constantine to turn around, and the whiff of parchment drew his attention to the open book. Dark red quickly stained his olive features as he grabbed the book and closed it.

Before he could say anything, honey-blond hair framed Brynn's face as she dragged herself over the tailboard. Sweat dripping down her forehead, she held out her hand to Delilah, who was coming up behind her.

"For Valhalla's sake," Delilah said, shoving aside Brynn and slumping onto the wagon bed, "save that damned book but forget the rest of us!"

Brynn and Delilah both ducked as a bag flew past them, the contents spilling all over the floor. Two hands latched onto the tailboard, fingernails digging into the wood. Viera bit back a squeal when a mass of inky hair, like that of an imaginary loch monster emerging from the depths of a lake, slowly lifted into sight.

Blowing long tresses from her face, Maerna demanded of someone, "Help me up!"

Grabbing the back of Maerna's robe, Brynn hauled her inside until she flopped onto the floorboards in a most undignified manner.

"Bloody Hells, man!" Delilah said as she scooted along the baseboards. "What are you trying to do, beat the ruddy King back to the Hearth? The three of us have been trying to catch up to you ever since the last stop."

Constantine asked sharply. "Why do you three not want to be with the other lasses?"

Brynn planted her hands on her hips. "There's not enough ducats in the realm to put up with their bollocks."

Delilah plopped next to Viera. "You can ill afford no allies. Jocelyn aims to turn the entire Court against you as soon as she steps her dainty feet in the Hearth. We can help you thwart that."

Rising, Palamedes slouched onto the seating across from Viera.

Guilt bubbled in her. "What about Palamedes?"

Brynn shouldered past her and joined him. "Clever girl. When we offered, it was not exclusive to you."

Palamedes' jaw quivered. "Truly?"

She gave him a toothy grin. "There wasn't much chance to get to know you. Hi, my name is Brynn. I like books and long walks along the… blaw!" She mimicked someone vomiting. "Aye, you get the idea, right?"

Maerna dragged herself upright. "We're all going to have to get along. It would be in our best interests to try."

Biting her lip, Viera allowed her gaze to travel over the trio. They had not participated in tormenting her, what with Maerna keeping vigil over Viera when Myrddin went about his morning duties. And Brynn flaunted rules, challenging Knights with a bullheaded determination and Fomoiri-may-care attitude. Viera studied Delilah and Maerna. *Judgment's still out on them.*

Viera offered her hand to Maerna. The girl blinked and stared at it, her eyes going dead, as if she was in a trance—or worse.

What Viera didn't know was that Maerna had stilled because her parents' Oracle blood stirred deep within her. Part of her feared the reach across the divide, because when Viera's emerald eyes met her gaze, her preconscious shifted into horrifying focus. Her respiration grated against her ears as two shrouded figures in front of a fireplace clouded her vision. Fire encompassed the room and all burned. Shapes mutated into cinders and eventually dust, the remaining particles fading into nothingness. The drag of years slid past in seconds, quick in the rush of realization, slow in the execution of what was inching ever nearer.

As Maerna had stared into the darkened hearth, she thought all had been lost. She was lost. A breath found purchase in the quiet. When soft ghostly wailing keened in her ears, the pulse of new life echoed. Over the icy hearthstone, sparks ignited once more. She blinked against the ethereal cobwebs clinging to her mind.

Chills had snaked down Maerna's back when she'd first glimpsed Viera Tillwith. Now she had her confirmation. Brynn and Delilah twitched, and their outlines quivered, fresh with what she had glimpsed long ago. She could not divine their Fate—not when theirs were closely entwined with hers. It was the one inexorable rule that anyone with Sight was warned against challenging. Those who gleaned the knowledge of their Fate always regretted looking far ahead instead of what was immediately in front of them. Many an Oracle fell into such a trap, and the outcome never boded well.

Maerna had looked into Viera's soul. Fear of Fire was not a weakness for one with Dragoness blood, especially not for an Emrys. As she reached across the divide, she closed her fingers over Viera's forearm. Fate was not to be cheated. Nor was Twilight.

Chapter 18

Reactive Insecurities

Axles squeaked in unrelenting rhythm as the wagon's wheels ground their way down the bumpy road. Myrddin shifted his attention from the draft horses' languid pace to the back of the wagon.

His mouth agape, Palamedes lay on a bench and snored. Next to him, Brynn was sprawled out and snoring louder. A book lay half open on the floor as her fingers brushed the pages in tune with the wagon's motions.

Maerna and Delilah, their blankets cushioning them, slept on the other bench. The Emrys daughter's embroidery basket was mercifully closed. Myrddin had lost count of how many times he'd sat on one of her misplaced needles.

Dice were scattered on the wagon floor, along with random cards wedged between the uneven seams of the planks, all the offshoot of teaching Viera the time-honored game of Four Suits. The game was tied not only to the currency of the realm but to the nature of the Royal Bonding as well. It was important for the Maids to learn this card game proficiently, as lacking expertise could prove a disastrous shortcoming.

Distressed murmurs brought Myrddin's stare to Viera, her back pressed against the bench behind him. Sleeping as fretfully as she had since her narrow escape from the highwaymen, she clung tightly to the cloak Bedwyr had lent her, burrowed within its folds like a small owl safely ensconced under its mother's wings. When they had stopped for their midmorning meal, more than a few eyebrows raised when Viera stepped outside wearing the garment.

A grunt from Palamedes had Myrddin switching his thoughts to the lad. Nothing concerning any of the children in the wagon was easy. Safir Sasania, one of the Saracen boy's older twin brothers, had voiced concern over Palamedes witnessing their mother's murder. His Element had become increasingly unstable, and the mere mention of his uncle, Shahzaman Sasania, charged the air around Palamedes, the crackle sharp enough to sting whoever was nearby. Worry grew that the boy was becoming Reactive like Bedwyr.

Safir had sought Myrddin's judgment of his younger brother, believing the best way to make an accurate assessment was to see Palamedes in a different environment and away from him or his twin, Segwarides. Lord Emrys now wished he'd never accepted the task.

A grievous error had also been made in collecting Lady Jocelyn from Sagramore Halls. When her father, Lord Cuchulain Sagramore, saw Bedwyr, their brief time together settled into insults over Bedwyr's late mother, Karen Wallach, with Jocelyn smirking throughout. By happenstance Palamedes was present, and if anything ever nettled the boy, it was those who belittled their mothers, as he had no respect for those people. When Myrddin considered this later, it explained a lot of why Palamedes held Jocelyn in such low regard when he first met her. Of course, she quickly exacerbated his disdain by her own doing.

As the horses pressed onward, his gaze settled on a tree in the distance. It was under another such tree that he'd sat with Lance, Constantine, Gaheris, their Healers, and Arthwyr to discuss helping Viera. Bedwyr had unwittingly given the answer to their concerns by gifting Viera his cloak, even if it was to be temporary.

Whimpers dropped Myrddin's attention to his shaking hands as he rolled up his sleeves. The Seven-Elemental array Lamorac had drawn with ink and blood darkened Myrddin's wrists. Myrddin activated the sigils and kneaded his wrists until his scent strengthened. When the array shimmered in mother-of-pearl light, he lowered his arm close to Viera's nose and her breath stirred across his wrist. Her squirms increased and tapered off.

Imprinting. A ritual of questionable means if there ever was one. Families naturally did it with their children. It fostered a sense of security and home for younger members. What Myrddin did was not natural in the sense of familial bonding. Used on a child with the wrong intent, it could wreak mental havoc through enhancing dependency.

Myrddin waited for Viera to slip into a deeper sleep and removed his hand, sick to his stomach over engaging in the ritual with one not of his blood.

Constantine and Myrddin had taken turns driving, and the priest pulled up the horses for watering, a quick graze, and rest. The sadly familiar snout of a dead rat on a stick poked Lord Emrys in the side.

"How long are you going to keep that damned thing?" he snipped at Lance.

After giving Myrddin an exaggerated salute with the stiff rat corpse, Lance tucked away his atrocious trophy in a thick leather bag that hung on his belt. "Until the novelty wears off, I've still got a few more jabs left with my friend." He patted the pouch.

"It's appalling what amuses you." Myrddin pointed at a discolored patch on Lance's gray tunic. "Is that where Bedwyr and Palamedes puked on you?"

"Neither. The Tillwith boy got me. I'm running out of unsullied tunics. Bedwyr hasn't helped my wardrobe either. The front of my other trousers looks like a First Night jaunt through a brothel. Bedwyr might have been smelling rainbows from that draught we gave him to ease his discomfort, but it came out white."

Myrddin could not help but laugh. "I take it you held vigil over Bedwyr last night?" At his remark, he noticed a slight frown cross Lance's features. "How are both of you holding up?"

"It's nothing either of us can't handle."

"You're not Bedwyr's father, Lance. He's not your responsibility."

Distance seeped into Lance's expression. "Someone should've been," he said, his voice soft but with a brittle edge to it. "Anything else you wish to add regarding that topic, Lord Emrys?" When Myrddin opened his mouth, Lance added, "It wasn't an invitation." Myrddin gave a clipped nod, his attention drifting to Constantine prodding the ragtag youths from the wagon for bush breaks, food, and drink.

Following the swivel of Myrddin's head in the direction of the group, Lance gave Myrddin a pensive stare. "The real question is, 'How are *you* holding up?' You've been twitchy of late. What troubles you so?"

Myrddin lowered his chin and slumped his shoulders. "I have erred most grievously. I took Viera from her home, deluded into believing I'd be the one to train her. I've failed her miserably. Every time I look at her of late, it's like nails clawing at my sides, it pains me so."

"What happened was beyond your control. The only people to blame are the highwaymen—and I guess the Marshal in a way." Lance patted Myrddin on the shoulder. "You did nothing wrong."

"I vowed to her family that I would protect her."

"The Marshal came to her defense." Lance paused in thought. "When are we going to tell Viera about him?"

Sweat dampened Myrddin's neck, and he tugged on his collar to wipe away the moisture. "Arthwyr and I decided it would be wise to keep that to ourselves. The Marshal also doesn't want her knowing anything more."

"She might see the whole thing differently. Especially concerning him."

Myrddin grimaced. "Evermore only knows what that revelation would bring out of her. Several nights ago, she growled and bared her teeth at me."

Lance chuckled. "You make her sound like a wild animal."

Myrddin grabbed Lance's hand. "You weren't there. She has no formal Fire training, other than what little I've taught her, and absolutely no grasp on how to make a true array, yet she released an imperfect one."

Lance's nose crinkled as he slowly said, "You said she almost fried you with a damned powerful array when you came up to her at the river. Either she can make one or she can't. Which is it?"

"You know how your Second has that blasted memory of his and can recall everything?"

"You're not telling me that we've got another Gavyn Foxbury on our hands, are you? Cause if so, you're fecked."

"Well, she creates half-formed arrays and releases them, thereby bending the laws of Elemental arrays. That shan't be possible for anyone."

Lance stroked his chin. "We've seen it with Daegyn Dyfed, who is the same age as Viera. I thought Carydoc was joking when he first told me about it, until I saw it myself. And Palamedes uses his Air without creating an array."

"Viera's arrays are even more volatile."

Lance's eyes widened. "How so?"

"They're going black. Any insight into that, Lord Ebony Knight?"

The stark pall gracing Lance's skin was answer enough. He sent Myrddin a beseeching glance riddled with equal parts determination and encouragement for more information.

"Black is possible only for the final deadliest offensive arrays of an Element," Myrddin added. "Mind you, those are arrays I have yet to teach Viera."

Doubt crept onto Lance's features. "You're saying she's producing those without having learned them?"

"No. She's taking arrays meant for defense and molding them into offensive arrays. She changed the third Fire kata into an offensive array. A black *Tre*. I didn't think it possible, and I'm considered the expert in Fire katas."

Lance shook his head, glanced at Viera's wagon, and gave his head another shake. "Damn. That is a bit of a problem. What's the chance her brother is the same?"

"I couldn't get a reading on him," Myrddin said and sighed. "There's something about the Tillwiths. The oaks growing inside their house had *Yggdrasil* carved into them."

"You think it's anything to worry about?"

"Aye. Something dark; something light. Keep your eye on the boy."

"It will be interesting how his training unfolds." It was Lance's turn to sigh. "What of your lass? Surely you aren't giving up on her so soon."

"I truly believe it would be wise."

"I truly believe it would be most foolish of you. You know who you must seek counsel from. I'll have to do the same for the boy as well."

"Carydoc will be most insightful."

Lance grumbled, "Adding a few steps to that dance? Nay, Dagonet specializes in hard cases. After all, he is the Spymaster of Evermore."

Myrddin grimaced. "He also uses his Metal Element to dawdle in alchemy and play the Fool at Court."

"All true, but his pranks serve Evermore well. Our enemies think he really is a Fool, and by entertaining them, he often learns vital information that keeps the realm safe."

Myrddin was asked to drive another wagon, this one holding stores, with Lance riding beside it on his horse. They hadn't even made it to the next ridge when the ruddy Court Fool's new Elemental array on the wagon's wheels activated—an array that repeated Dagonet's sharp cackling laughter, several less-than-ideal ditties, and his howling the accursed *Are We There Yet* song over and over. *Bloody feckin' Alchemist!* Didn't help that the center of the array included a caricature of Dagonet wearing a beret with his orange hair sticking out from it.

Myrddin wanted to return to Elden's Hearth just for the satisfaction of killing Dagonet in front of everyone. He growled, "He's a Fool who feeds off theatrics and chaos."

"Ironic, innit?"

"Meaning?"

"Reactive Elementals are Dagonet's forte."

As the song grated on his ears, Myrddin yanked the horses to a halt and scrambled down to singe the arrays. To his utter horror, the song changed and belted out even louder, "Rolling, rolling, rolling along the bog! Singing, singing, better than a frog!"

Throwing up his arms into the air, he said, "I'm thinking that we should ignore this lunatic jester and seek out Carydoc. Daegyn and Viera came from loving families—"

"That is where the similarities end." The muscles in Lance's jaw bunched. "You delay the inevitable by ignoring the obvious."

"I'd rather seek the right kind of help so I'm not chasing my tail all over Evermore."

"What has you quailing over keeping her? And be honest."

Myrddin voiced what he feared most: "All right, I'll tell you exactly why I feel the way I do. I've not seen such power in an Elemental since Bedwyr. I was terrified of so much raw energy that I refused to Apprentice him. As was everyone else. Now I see the same in her."

"It took a special type of person to finish Bedwyr's training." Lance steeled his eyes on Myrddin. "Three to be exact. Dagonet will be most excited that we've brought him the type of student he prizes most."

Myrddin grumbled, "That's what I'm afraid of—more than anything."

CHAPTER 19

LIGHT, TWILIGHT, AND SHADOWS

Late that night, Viera deftly picked her way over the uneven ground, dodging high grass and avoiding boulders. No one stirred in her wagon when she quietly slipped away, and there were no untoward sounds coming from the darkness surrounding her. Still, she hugged the cloak tightly against herself until lavender and another sweeter scent teased her nose and she relaxed.

Wood crackling in the campfire drew her to the warmth and safety it provided, no different from her flannel blanket offering a sense of home and security. Controlled flames also meant that someone was maintaining the fire; someone alert to movements outside the camp; someone who provided protection.

Viera squinted at a figure who was blurred by the smoke from the fire. As she walked closer, shock flared through her as Bedwyr came into view, glaring in her direction. She glanced over her shoulder, praying that his focus was on someone or something other than her.

He propped an elbow on a crate and planted his chin in his hand. "No one is behind you."

"How do you know?"

"Just know that I know. There's nothing but shadows, the same as the ones you're standing in." Bedwyr swatted at a bat that flew too close to him. "Do you plan on scuttling off to your Master, or are you just going to stand there like the scared country bumpkin you are—and do nothing?"

Viera found courage by pulling the cloak tighter about herself. With her stare locked on him, she stepped from the shadows and strode toward him. "I'll make my own choices, not you."

The burning cedar released a calming sweetness, but when a knot in the wood popped, she flinched, making it impossible for her to conceal her true fear.

"I left you an out," he said and snickered. "Now what will you do against the big bad wolf, little piggy?"

She sat on a log bench across from him. "Not go squee, squee, squee all the way to Myrddin, that you can be certain of, big bad wolf."

Bedwyr looked past the perimeter to the stillness of the tall grass. His lapse in judgment did not justify the girl being subjected to a highwayman and a breaker. Especially since a breaker, albeit a highly modified version, had dug into his wrist and cut all the way to the bone. It had been some time since he'd practiced with a breaker, but the bastard who had dared to put one on him rued that miscalculation, because he had used his innards as chum to catch breakfast.

From across the fire, he heard, "How is your arm?"

Bedwyr glared at the girl, clinging tightly to the cloak he'd lent her. She slinked back a little, and he held his stare on her until he believed she wasn't going to ask him any more questions. But something else happened he could never have prepared for.

A pale limb slid free of his lent cloak, and yellow light flickered over a small upturned palm. The array writhed and spun like an out-of-control needle on a compass, runes dancing and shimmering and twisting to her Element. Black throbbed from the center of the array, and Bedwyr read the first Fire kata. But it wasn't *En*. Instead, it was a bastardized blend of the first and the sixth, *Seks*.

Viera's face showed a blend of fear, uncertainty, and disappointment. The array shifted into the second array of *To*. It was Bedwyr's turn to flinch, as arrays were not supposed to be turned into a different array. They were made, released, or dismantled, not created in one form to be switched to another. Elemental laws, as they were known, didn't allow this.

Bedwyr studied her concoction, noting this one had *Seks* and the fifth Fire kata, *Fem*, smattered into it. "Your array is wrong."

"How is it wrong? I released the other one into it." With yellow and black expanding from the center, the array rippled outward.

Bedwyr had to say something. "You're missing runes, and others are jumbled. Got a little *Fem* in your *Seks*."

Her cheeks seemed to take in the red of the fire and rush to her hairline. "You were listening when Myrddin taught me the fourth, fifth, and sixth kata!"

"If I remember correctly, there was a little pig squealing sex is *Seks* to her Master, who is now missing a quarter of his beard from that lesson."

She buried her face into her knees. "Doubt you would be any better a Master than him, even though he's awful. The bar's set low."

"If Myrddin had half a clue, he'd run you ragged and then try and teach you. At least, train you in meditation scenarios." Bedwyr flicked a pebble at her array and quivered when it hissed and spat. "You shouldn't be able to do what you're doing if you were a normal Elemental."

"Whoa, big bad wolf, I *am* a normal Elemental." She lifted her face, squinting at him. "What else could I be?"

"If thinking like that helps you sleep at night, so be it."

She raised her arms and released her *To* array into the sky. It flared outward, the colors brilliant, and Bedwyr's eyes stung as it flew by.

Haughtiness etched itself into the girl's face, and she beamed, "It must have been perfect for it to release. Myrddin told me it had to be perfect or it would fizzle out."

"For normal Elementals, it disperses, but for one who is Reactive, perfection seldom matters." Bedwyr mirrored her mien to equal her arrogance. "You define what is normal to suit your needs and purpose. Normal means nothing to you because Elemental laws don't bind you."

"Did your father or your Master teach you that?"

Snarling, he pointed to her wagon. "Get back to Myrddin or I'll drag you to him."

Viera shrugged and trotted off. Groaning wood announced her ascent into the wagon, and Bedwyr immediately designed a Water array, focusing on the third Water kata, *Mittsu*, which against the firelight gleamed black as dried blood.

Bedwyr's fingers formed a complex design, shimmering ebony lines and a hint of violet edging the center. As his Element pulsed through him, he released the array. Crimson fluid swelled up and rushed past the campfire, the flames quickly sputtering out.

The curse still thrived. Blood and Twilight remained his trade.

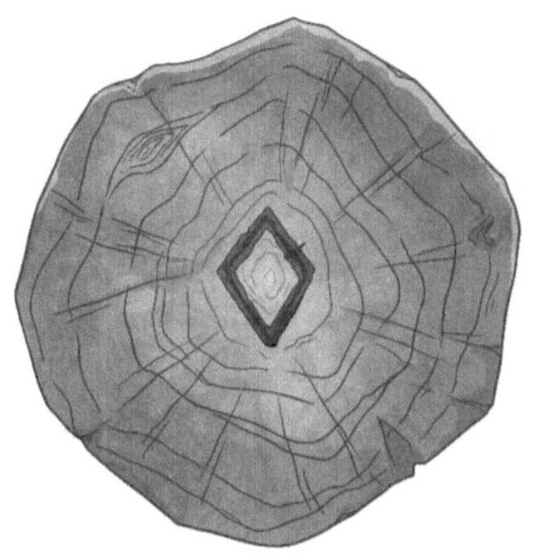

CHAPTER 20

SWAYING WITH THE BREEZE

As the sun peeked through fluffy clouds the next midmorning, Lamorac Pellinore, atop his big steed, Gales, approached Viera. An earlier drizzle, providing a much-needed reprieve from the summer mugginess typically plaguing the valley this time of year, promised a good day for riding. When Viera extended her hand to Gales, the horse tossed aside his black-and-white streaked mane and pushed his nose against her palm.

"Time for you to learn how to ride a real horse," Lamorac said as he dismounted.

The offer surprised Viera, and within the hour, she was perched on Gales as Lamorac walked alongside the horse with her sitting high in the saddle, her thighs squeezed tightly over what little of the stirrup fender her short legs could cover. It would be a long time until Viera reached the stirrups, but she was grateful to Lamorac for giving her the opportunity to experience what it was like to sit on a magnificent stallion.

Lamorac was content to walk beside Viera and his horse for the rest of the morning, but as afternoon rolled around, he had to get off his feet. However, he didn't send Viera back to her wagon, sitting her on the saddle with him instead.

Viera could not have been happier. She liked Lamorac, finding him fun to talk with and enjoying his stories. She especially appreciated that he treated her like an adult.

His conversation turned to the Foxburys, and they interested her greatly as they were rumored to have stronger loyalties at times to Dumnonia, the Dwarven realm north of Evermore, than the Pendragon banner. Lamorac seemed particularly keen on Gaheris' older brother, Gavyn, whom he referred to as the Tactician of Evermore, and she asked why he was called this.

"Gavyn is Lance's Second, and he's a brilliant battle planner. He definitely earned his title after helping Arthwyr burn and loot Tintagel, a fortress believed to be impenetrable. The buildings had thatched roofs to make it easier for the ocean breezes to cool them. But if the roofs ever caught fire, it would be the same as dry tinder igniting."

"So, he's a Fire Elemental?" she asked.

Lamorac chuckled. "No, far from it. He's Wood." He peered at Viera as if sizing her up. "I think you're mature enough to hear this, so here goes. After several days of whoring his way through the town of Tintagel's many brothels, Gavyn figured out the local birds nested in the roofs but scavenged their food past the fortress walls."

It was Viera's time to chuckle. "So, he's a bird watcher who likes, well, you know. But what's that got to do with anything?"

"Gavyn had our soldiers net the entire flock outside the fort, tie wood chips to their legs, and light the kindling. Birds had to land somewhere, and the closest place for many of them was on the thatched roofs."

"Bloody Hells," she cried out.

"More like flaming Hells, but you get the idea."

"What about the birds?"

"With all that roasted pigeon around we didn't have to worry about dinner, if that's what you're asking. As for Gavyn, he sunned himself on the beach—in his bare arse with the whores from the brothels—as Tintagel burned to the Hells and back."

An image of a much older Gaheris frolicking on a beach and waving a roasted pigeon on a stick smoldered in her mind. She muttered, "He sounds as mad as Dottsie."

"Gavyn has his own form of madness. He's—"

Lamorac abruptly pulled Gales to a halt. Viera squinted into the late afternoon sun to make out two wagons and a horse next to a tree.

Hooves thundered from behind as Arthwyr and Lance raced past on their horses. Myrddin rode up a moment later and shouted in an irate tone, "He's got a bounty."

Lamorac shouted back, "Dammit!" and Myrddin rode off.

"Who's got a bounty—and on what—that it's got everybody upset?" Viera asked as she swung her leg around so she was now riding sidesaddle.

Lamorac jumped down, helped Viera from the stallion, and knelt in front of her. "The Knights of the Eclipse aren't all fun and games, even though it might seem like it. There are certain duties demanded of us." The lines on his face darkened, and he reached up and fussed with his reins. "There are reports of increased activity of highwaymen."

Shaking, she leaned in close to Lamorac. "Do you think they'll strike again?"

"There's no way of knowing," he said, fixing his eyes on the scene ahead. "The Marshal's activities should have convinced them not to go after Progress, but…." Lamorac's voice trailed off.

They mounted Gales and rode toward the wagons and the tree. As Viera looked up at the branches, a cold pit formed in her stomach. Two figures hung from a thick limb, spinning around as though the wind was playfully twirling streamers. This far out in the valley, farmers placed bwbachs in the fields to scare birds away from their crops, a prize given each year at Novamber's Samhain Harvest Feast for the hay-stuffed mannequin that performed its duty the best.

Viera hoped it was two bwbachs dangling from the limb, but as Gales brought her closer, two men hung from the thickest bough of an old oak tree, one man still jerking. The other man was obviously dead, his neck stretched so far and at such an angle that it was clearly broken. To make his death scene even more gross, his tongue hung out like that of a lolling dog, and his eyes appeared ready to burst from their sockets.

Galahad attempted to scrabble up the tree but the slick bark hindered him. Lance tried to boost him up by the waist, but Constantine pushed him aside and told him to help grab the feet of the man who was still alive. This relieved the pressure on the man's neck, and when Galahad made it up the tree and was able to release the noose from around the man's throat, the fellow dropped onto Constantine and both men tumbled to the ground.

Viera observed Bedwyr nonchalantly leaning against his horse, a spool of hemp hanging from his saddle's pommel. Two separate lines of the tough fiber ran up the tree and over the bough.

Arthwyr marched forward and shoved Bedwyr. The King pointed at the highwayman now gulping for air like a fish out of water. "That's not how we administer justice."

"Last I checked, we're in Dyfed territory," Bedwyr monotoned, "and over here highwaymen are subject to martial law."

Bedwyr and Arthwyr argued until a raspy voice grated on Viera's ears. His hands tied behind his back, the highwayman who'd received the reprieve was on his knees, groveling between gags, "Thank you, my…my Liege. Thank you for…for sparing me. I promise to always… always do right by Evermore. Always."

Bedwyr walked over and stood behind the man, his fingers hooked onto the hasp of his dagger. Viera inched nearer the man, and the stench of urine, sweat, and rotted food brought back the awful memory of the highwayman who had undoubtedly intended to rape and kill her.

Bedwyr took out his dagger and pointed it at the man. "Is this the man who attacked you under that tree by our camp?"

She took a hard look at this highwayman. A ball of tension curled up in her chest and a bitter taste, like curdled milk, settled over her tongue. It wasn't him. Never could she forget that one's face spraying spit against her cheeks. Even amid the wreckage of a corpse, the glazed eyes of her attacker and his mouth wrenched open in a horrified rictus had pierced her deeper than his nails biting into her flesh. "No," she whispered, wishing she had it in her to lie just this once.

Bedwyr directed his next question to the cringing highwayman. "What do you have to say to the lass one of yours attacked?"

"I'm sorry. I'll, I'll never do it again." Tears streamed down the highwayman's craggy features. "I swear it. I'm sorry, Milord. My King."

Bedwyr entwined his fingers in the man's oily hair and yanked his head back until his grimy throat was exposed. "I'm not your King, but I'll accept your apology in flesh."

Steel parted flesh as smooth as a ripple across a gentle stream, and blood bubbled and gushed from the cleaved throat. Bedwyr slashed open the gasping man's gut, intestines and yellowish fat spilling out. The highwayman uttered a final scream as pink grayish coils slithered down his legs. Brown oozed from the highwayman's trousers, adding to the grisly mess.

Viera turned away, sobbing. *I admit I wanted him dead, but not like that.* She covered her mouth to keep from throwing up. Bedwyr and Arthwyr began arguing again, this time quite loudly, and it took her mind off the horrific death of the highwayman.

"Pay up, Arthwyr," Bedwyr sneered in Arthwyr's face.

The King turned to the mutilated corpse and yelled back at Bedwyr, "The Marshal—"

"Is a notion you Pendragons conjured up to scare fools into goodwill and honor." Bedwyr flicked blood from the blade of his dagger. "What honor do these scum have for those they plunder, rape, and murder? I did you a great service." He pointed to the dead men. "That's two. Pay your due. You owe me a bounty for both capture and execution."

"You deserve nothing."

"You will pay me or I'll alert the noble families that you aren't good to your word for dealing with highwaymen."

Arthwyr pulled out a small but elaborately stitched purse. "Compassion wouldn't kill you."

"Yara. Yara. It doesn't feed me either."

He opened the purse and counted out some coins and gave them to Bedwyr, who summarily dropped the money into his own pouch.

"Come, over here, lass—" Bedwyr motioned to Viera— "it's your turn."

Every muscle in her body tensed as she made her way to him. He told her to hold out her hand, and he placed several coins in her palm.

"For each highwayman you catch," Bedwyr said casually as if discussing the weather, "the bounty goes from one shinnie to two shillings, to three ingots, four drams, five shekels, and six krones per head. Never expect silver or gold for a first catch unless you're a bounty hunter or mercenary. That's your due, lass, for two caught—one at the river, even if the Marshal killed him—the other here, who told me he was at the river."

Viera glanced between the eviscerated corpse and the coins in her palm, which were a fortune to her. "But I didn't catch anyone or do anything."

Bedwyr wiped the excess blood from his fingers into her hair. "'Tis fine. Even bait has its use at the table."

CHAPTER 21

HAIL TO THE HIGHWAYMEN

Despite the rolling hills and pastures, there was no hiding the nearby sulphur mines of Dunmore. The air held an undercurrent somewhere between perspiration-soaked clothes and rotten eggs. Viera's eyes burned, begetting a watery stream. Myrddin had decided it best that she stay in Bedwyr's wagon, and away from everyone else. Burying her face in Bedwyr's cloak provided her only reprieve. As for Lord Wallach, the pungent stench from the mines was not helping him recover from his arm injury, which was plaguing him as much as ever.

To her amusement, Bedwyr secured a scarf about his features until occasionally his forehead would appear and his gaze would peek over the gray cloth, making the Knight the image of a Hood of Locksey—a villain that children loved to play-act to—who kidnapped and ransomed the innocent. Most often, however, when Bedwyr wasn't asleep, he idled away the time cursing the smell, Jocelyn and her harpies, and certain Knights of the Eclipse on Progress.

Arthwyr brought the procession to a halt on a hill that allowed an unencumbered view of Dunmore, and to everyone's relief a strong breeze was blowing in the opposite direction. While strolling about a meadow, but careful to keep within eyeshot of Lamorac as he stood outside Bedwyr's wagon, Viera marveled at how much she had learned about the Knights—except her current wagon mate, who every day became more mysterious.

Late the previous evening, Palamedes had slipped into Bedwyr's wagon. Viera was certain that the boy didn't know she was enshrouded in blankets in one corner, because she heard him murmur, his voice tight and aching: "I miss her so much. Why couldn't my uncle just let my mother leave?"

Bedwyr's voice slipped above the wind buffeting the canvas covering the wagon: "Men in such positions only care to fuel their ambitions and desires. Women and children mean nothing unless they serve a boon. Your mother knew this. Mine learned it. We are their legacies. It's on us to carry on in their behalf."

Because it was so outside his normal character, it took a few seconds for Viera to realize that Bedwyr was the one consoling her friend.

"Remember your mother, Palamedes," he continued, his voice low and full of understanding, "for what she was to you—and you to her. Women nurture their children into becoming their legacies. You'll always be more to her than to anyone else, no matter where your future takes you."

The wind picked up, rocking the wagon, and the ensuing constant clamor which made it impossible for Viera to pick up any more of the conversation, and the fog of sleep soon overtook her.

When Viera awoke the next morning, she had become sandwiched between Bedwyr and Palamedes, a mass of blankets entangled everywhere. After they extricated themselves from all the flannel, no one said a single word to the other as they left the wagon.

After an unchaperoned but necessary trip to a nearby stream, Viera collected wild strawberries she had spotted along the way. She dropped an unripe strawberry into her mouth, the fruit souring her tongue and puckering her lips. But the acidity held its own attraction, and she ate another.

A small copse stood clustered on the side of a nearby hill, and bright yellow fruit weighed down the branches of one tree. Strawberries might not have been a roaring success, but gooseberries might be better, their flavour also acidic but with a sweeter aftertaste.

Standing on the balls of her feet, she plucked bundles of the lower-hanging fruit and placed her prizes in the folds of her skirt. But the higher she reached, the farther her top rode up and exposed her back. As she extended her arms to their absolute zenith, she heard a garbled grunt and a strange warmth ran the entire length of her bare back.

Then a loud exhale blasted heat all over her. She spun around to find sagging skin framing black eyes atop a massive nose and mouth, all of this right in her face. It was the scariest creature—all yellowish brown, lanky, and lumpy—she had ever seen. Just when she didn't think it could be any more frightening, the beast, which had a mass of drool coming from its mouth and nostrils, spit out an enormous, well-aimed wad of stinking saliva that hit her directly in the forehead. To add the ultimate insult, the beast stuck an absurdly long tongue into the pouch she'd formed in her skirt and licked up some of the fruit she'd carefully tucked away.

Screeching and wiping off the mess, she stared past the creature's long muzzle to a man sitting astride the animal. A faint tinge of red from the sun darkened his skin and reminded her of light almonds and, of all things, Palamedes. The rider's brown and black leathers creaked as he arched back toward another man—huge and with skin as dark as charcoal—sitting atop a shaggier version of the first animal.

Viera lowered her arms and peeked past him to four other riders.

A man with red hair, much farther back from the others, was riding a horse instead of one of the monsters. "Heya, Fair Lass," he hollered to Viera. "Mind stopping and talking for a spell?"

She blinked at how familiar he sounded.

Another man drew closer. She gasped at the mass of tattoos plastered across his bald head. She didn't have time to conjure Fire, so she did what any intelligent person would do. She dropped her berries and ran screaming down the embankment: "Highwaymen! They're riding monsters! Highwaymen! Hells, they're feckin' bloody everywhere! Highwaymen!"

CHAPTER 22

SPEAK OF THE FOMOIRI

Water skimmers darted across the placid stream, their bodies gliding against the gentle current. Silver flashed, jaws snapped, and a fin breached the surface. A single splash signaled the end of one water skimmer, parts of the insect bobbing until another trout swallowed the leftovers.

Bedwyr liked to observe the play of fish hunting their meals. As an insect wing drifted into his hands, its thin, weblike structure stuck to his wrist. He flicked off the remnant. His pain had subsided, the fever he'd experienced was done with, and the itch from fairy dust and elderberry wine was no longer an issue for him. The presence of the girl had softened the bite of his infirmity, although he'd never admit it to anyone.

Sloshing drew Bedwyr's attention to Palamedes as he kicked his legs in the most awkward version of a back-crawl he had ever seen. Floundering, the boy dipped below the water. The sputtering and wild flailing, however, did not answer the Knight's hope of Palamedes not resurfacing; because, miraculously, the boy splashed his way from one side of the widest part of the rivulet to the other, where he stood on the bank and shook off water like a dog would do it. To signal his achievement of not drowning, he waved his arms at Bedwyr before scurrying up the embankment and out of sight.

The dryness of fairy dust still lingered in Bedwyr's throat, and to him it was as if he had swallowed sand. Concentrating on his Elemental core, he purified the water in front of him. Eddies of gray swirled in the liquid he cupped in his hands and drank, its coolness providing soothing relief.

He was as relaxed as he had been in some time, when the air cracked around him. He blinked as frost formed beneath his knees, covering his pants in white patches as icy fingers raked across his back like chalk on a blackboard. His heart bounded against his chest, aware of only one other who possessed the knack to sneak up on him so effortlessly.

Bedwyr stood and faced a man with long brown hair and a healthy glow warming his pallid features.

"Nice of Uther's pet Marshal to emerge from the shadows," Bedwyr said, adding a derisive smirk for good measure. "Happy hunting, Lord Fire Marshal?"

The man's bright blue gaze twinkled. "Lord Fire Marshal, now? I rather liked when it was just Hamyll Emrys." Gray scudded across his irises like clouds rushing from the horizon into a heavy storm. "I saw the girl several nights ago."

The remark prickled Bedwyr's skin, and he flexed his fingers over his katana's hilt. "What made you take notice?"

"Hard not to. She's powerful. And marked!" Hamyll leaned closer, his height casting a shadow over Bedwyr. "I look forward to my time with her."

"Another has a bid," Bedwyr said, scrambling to get his thoughts together. "He'll train her."

Hamyll clasped his hands at his waist. "For now, perhaps. But don't pretend you're unaware of what your House charter demands of you."

Bedwyr narrowed his eyes on Hamyll. "I know my oath."

"Good." The Fire Marshal squeezed Bedwyr's shoulder. "Just know that the girl will one day be mine."

Bedwyr sneered, "Not for quite some time."

"Then make sure her Master trains her right." Hamyll returned Bedwyr's sneer. "In truth, it's of no real concern, for she will most assuredly be mine."

"What heartless creature did you become when you went to Glastonbury?"

The corners of his mouth dipped hideously, and he yanked Bedwyr so close that the Knight's forehead smacked into the skull of the ebony creature Hamyll had become. The acridness of funerary fires choked Bedwyr, and he shuddered in the creature's hold as yellow pooled over the spirit's body and morphed into bleached bones.

"You know what lurks beyond the veil, dear one," Hamyll said, the ragged rasp of another familiar voice slithering past his full lips. "You know what approached me—what came to take me—gullible little lamb that I was." He released Bedwyr and retreated a few steps in the waltz of give-and-take that had defined them since the Draigs' Duels. "It never suspected that the bait was the hunter. But now it's me and I am it. Wish I may, wish I might; wish I'd risen again that night."

Bedwyr stepped toward the apparition. "I know your other name. Imagine if it was I who summoned you." He stretched up as tall as his 5-foot 8-inch frame would allow. "You're welcome to try me, if you can own up to it. But know I can try you too."

"I'd love to see you try, dear one." Hamyll shifted back from Fomoiri to his human form. "My Mistress added a little flare to my arsenal." Fluorescent swirls and designs made him glow as if beneath moonlight. "If there's anything I miss most, it's you. If I could, I'd take you home with me."

"You can't though."

The ethereal glow faded from Hamyll, and the air became heavy. "No, I can't. I'm not the one meant to bring you home. My Mistress made it clear you're not mine to take."

"Have you spoken to your brother?" Bedwyr asked, taking pleasure in the tension appearing along Hamyll's jowls. "And what of your lovely niece?"

"You know how this works for me now. Myrddin and Maerna are no longer my family. It's the price for becoming what I am."

"Why did you do it?" Bedwyr asked, his tone calming down. "The Duels of the Draigs were over. We won."

"Aye, but I didn't win. There was no happily ever after for me." Hamyll fussed with his sleeve, sliding it back-and-forth over a thin bracelet strung with green, pink, and blue clay beads that were faded and chipped. The beads jangled against silver-and-gold charms engraved with the kanji for Water and Fire. He rolled his thumb over each one. "After your father took her, there was no coming back for me. I couldn't live without her. Not anymore."

Swallowing hard, Bedwyr said, "Stay away from this one."

"I can't make that promise."

"You need to try. She's not ready for you. Hells, no one is ever ready for you."

Hamyll knitted his brow. "Of course, that's true. But she'll seek me out on her own, you'll see. The two sparrows she calls Golly and Tilly have chosen well."

Bedwyr scowled. "Those damned things are as subtle as a landslide."

"Only to those who know what they are." Hamyll chortled. "Everyone else sees them as annoying little buggers begging for a meal. Although, Golau is more of a pig than—"

Loud screams drowned out his words. Bedwyr spun toward the shrieks, recognizing the raucous howls of the very person they were discussing.

"Speaking of the Fomoiri," Hamyll said, "she screams for you instead. Make sure my idiot brother trains her well."

Crashes came from the opposite side of the stream, and Bedwyr ran toward the ruckus. A crack split the air, and a blinding light burned across his peripheral vision, smoke rising from scorched earth and freshly charred ground.

Palamedes threw himself over the slope and skidded to the bottom, yelling, "Viera's screaming and running down the bank!"

Another screech followed fast on the heels of his announcement.

"Evermore, she's a ruddy headache!" Bedwyr grumbled to himself. "What's the standard return policy on Apprentices? Myrddin definitely might want to give her back. Hells, even Hamyll might give her back if he ever has her."

Hooves pounded in the direction of her screams. *Damn! How many times was she going to find highwaymen? If this keeps up, I won't have a shred of amusement left to idle away my time!*

CHAPTER 23

FINDING SID

Viera slipped over loose rocks and sank in the wet pockets lining the sandy embankment. She rounded the bend of the river and skidded to a halt. Whipping around and thrusting out her hands, she dug deep into her Fire. The scattered form of *Seks* melded and came into sharp focus, with not a hint of anything other than black in the array. Sweat dotted her neck as she split her attention to summon both *Tre* and *Fem* as well. The arrays crackled to life and writhed as they moved into a flanking position and encircled *Seks*.

Wending around the bend, the man in brown and black leathers skidded to a halt on a gravelly patch of embankment. "Oh, Hells!" he barked just as a man with short black-and-gray-peppered hair jumped from his horse and ran into him. Both men tumbled to the ground, and the man in leathers did a great imitation of a goldfish out of water.

"Indeed, Segwarides!" came the reply.

Viera had seen enough and released *Tre* on them. The man called Segwarides, lying belly-down on the ground, shouted, "Ya Allah! What is she, Cary?"

A youth darted into view as a wash of deep green rippled through his chocolate hair. He slowed and called out, "Cary!" in a high-pitched tone that revealed his youth—and his fear.

"Get back, Dae," Cary called over his shoulder. "She's like you."

"Feckin' Odin-damned, flea-bitten, Taffy-thief!" She threw her hands outward and released two arrays that expanded in consort with the flare of her temper. "Eat this, bastard!" she added with equal fervor.

The red-haired man tackled the boy at the same instant *Seks* brushed his robe. With his throaty curses filling the air, he rolled away from the lad and ground out the fire. When he was able to stand, his brown-and-green Wood robe stirred Viera's insides.

He quickly crouched, locked his gaze on her, and unsheathed his broadsword. "Heya, Fair Lass. You've faced a stripling whelp. How about someone a little more mature?"

The confidence in Gaheris' voice caused her throat to tighten. He edged closer, and Viera reached deep within her Elemental core. She formed her hands into the last kata Myrddin had taught her, and a shrill howl was followed by crackles and pops that became deafening. The image of a terrifying wolf appeared, flames flaring high above its snout, its black lips slathering fiery spittle over gleaming canines as its crimson gaze took in everything at once.

A throaty rumble vibrated in Viera's ears as her creation called out into her mind, "What's my name, Mistress?"

"Sid," came her reply. "My precious Sid."

Gaheris leapt up from his crouch. He crossed his broadsword over his chest and let out a bellow that punched her guts.

Viera flattened her hand so it appeared like a blade and lashed it toward the man, ordering, "Sic 'em, Sid."

The flaming wolf shot forward from her array—black, red, and flickers of white heat sweeping past her.

Scrambling backwards, the man who had brazenly challenged the young girl spun around on his heels. He linked his arm into Dae's; his sword rattled from his grip and clattered onto the gravel. He used his spin and momentum, shoving himself and Dae into the water with a loud sploosh. Bubbles appeared on the surface until the pair had to come up for air, this occurring at the same instant.

The two men still on the ground rolled behind some large boulders to avoid the wolf as it sped past. Sid appeared not to know where they had gone, but he snapped up the discarded sword by its basketed wrist-guard, dragging it behind him. He had, however, flicked his tail near enough to Segwarides to singe the man's boot.

The man and the boy thrashed around in the water, their heavy robes encumbering their movements.

Viera patted her knee. With a wave of its tail and his gleaming red orbs fixed on her, Sid returned, with Viera telling him, "Good Siddy. That's a good boy. Good Siddy." She caressed his ears.

Whimpering playfully, he wiggled his backside and dropped the sword at her feet. She collected it and staggered under its weight. "Hells, it's heavy," she said under her breath, but she managed to swing it above her head so all of them could see it. She announced: "Hands up, arseholes! I've got fire and the pointy end and I'm not afraid to use either!"

Boots crunched on the hard ground behind her, and a bark of laughter had her peeking over her shoulder. For the first time in her life, she was happy to see Bedwyr, who approached with Palamedes not far behind.

"Look, Lord Wallach," Viera squealed with glee. "I got these highwaymen all by myself—" glancing at Sid— "well, mostly by myself. And I didn't have to stab anybody."

CHAPTER 24

HOGTIED

Whistling, Bedwyr cinched hemp around the less than thrilled Saracen's wrists. In his years of hunting criminals, he never dreamt his fellow Knights would be among them. For ranked Knights, they surely got caught with their britches down, and by a no-account serf no less. Oh, how gloriously they had slipped in their own mess.

Palamedes held out the rope he had collected from Adur, his brother's camel. The boy gave a little bow to Segwarides, who with his twin, Safir, were almost twice his age.

"For the hundredth time, you fool," Segwarides growled through clenched teeth at his little brother, "we aren't highwaymen. The Queen sent us to help you root out highwaymen, you ruddy-minded infidel."

Bedwyr shooed Palamedes from his brother and tightened the bindings around the man's wrists. "All I know is that some heathen assaulted a poor lass in the fields. Wait until the King sees—" lowering his voice and winking at Segwarides— "how his Knights treat ragamuffin serfs. Try beating that with a stick."

Palamedes snickered and parroted, "Yeah, try beating that with a stick."

With his arms well-secured behind his solid frame, Segwarides huffed until smoke puffed from his nostrils. "Enjoy this, Betti. When I get free of these—"

"Silence, heathen." Bedwyr lightly rapped Segwarides in the head, smirking when the Saracen's long silky dark-brown hair flipped around wildly and covered his eyes. "Prisoners talk only when spoken to."

Muffled grumbles brought Bedwyr's attention to the man who had saved Daegyn from a good sunburn, none other than Gavyn Foxbury, known as the Tactician of Evermore—a title he relished—and the only person who was gagged. Considering how the Foxbury triplets prided themselves in the practical joke arena, there was no way Bedwyr was letting the prank of a lifetime slip past his grasp; so, he had stuffed a scarf in Gavyn's mouth so he couldn't tell Viera his name. Bedwyr had agreed that her captive was Gaheris Foxbury, making the ruse all the merrier since his cloak's colors and sigils didn't differentiate one Foxbury from the other.

Bedwyr pinched Gavyn's cheeks. "Where's that damned Gringo of yours, huh?"

Fury blazed in Gavyn's blue eyes as smothered ravings rose behind the gag.

"No bother," Bedwyr said, shrugging but keeping an eye out in case Gringolet snuck up to attack and defend his Foxbury rider, "Don't worry. Your pig of a horse will return to Harlan. Consider yourself lucky I'm not turning you over to Harlan myself."

He knocked Gavyn's legs from under him, forcing the Knight to his knees. Bedwyr said in a loud enough voice that Viera was sure to hear, "*Gaheris*, you've shown your true colors. Scaring poor Viera half to death. Arthwyr will be beside himself."

Shuffling past Gavyn, who was writhing to try to free himself from the hemp binding his wrists, the gloating Knight chortled as he went over to the other *captives*.

Viera stood next to Daegyn Dyfed, with Bedwyr's hunting knife trained on the youth. Whenever he twitched, she prodded him with the handle. Not that he could twitch much with the way Bedwyr had him tied up like a Yule goose and slung over the rump of the boy's own horse.

Daegyn shouted at Bedwyr, "I kill you, you bloody, looned-up slag of a wanker!"

With the guard of his fan, Bedwyr rapped Daegyn on the head. He rechecked the binding as his attention shifted to the last member of the

"Highwaymen"—and much everyone's senior—the Lord of Gwent and the Steward of Evermore, Carydoc Ynyr.

Bedwyr carefully checked out Carydoc. Though a healthy man of fifty-three autumns, it would not do for this highly revered Knight to become injured during this escapade, and a little concern for his well-being would go a long way.

Asked Bedwyr, "Comfy? Don't want you carking it before you die from shame."

"Thank Odin my pride died long ago," Carydoc said as he slumped in his saddle, to which Bedwyr had tied him rather loosely.

Gathering the reins, Bedwyr waved Viera and Palamedes toward the other two *prisoners*. The girl whistled for her wolf, and the animal trotted up to her.

Bedwyr came over and crouched in front of Viera's conjured entity. A mirrored, blood-red gaze met his stare as the wolf wagged its tail. "All right, lassie. Tell your Hellhound to sit, roll over, and play dead."

Said Viera, "His name is Sid, not Hellhound."

"Same difference." Bedwyr waved his hand impatiently. "We need to get a move on. You've got a bounty to collect from Arthwyr."

Segwarides groaned, "You can't be serious."

"As the plague," Bedwyr drawled. "I'm ransoming you bastards. It's the least you owe society for bollocksing up so gloriously."

Viera exclaimed, "Wow, really? I'm liking this bounty stuff."

"Aye. These three are on the Most Wanted Registry—" pointing at Gavyn, Daegyn, and Carydoc— "and since they're the leaders of their gangs, you've hit the jackpot, sweetheart. Three gold lakhs, one for each."

Palamedes jabbed his brother's side with a twig. "How much for this lunkhead?"

"Not quite a lakh, but a silver lira for him." And to Viera, "Not a bad haul."

"There were two others!" she blurted, suddenly remembering them. "A big bald guy with tattoos all over his head, and a guy who was all black!"

"I wouldn't be too worried," Bedwyr said and patted her shoulder. "They'll show up. Anyway, you get to bring Gav… ah, Gaheris back."

As Adur mouthed Palamedes' hair, he shrieked and caressed the camel's long neck.

"You've got the heathen scourge," Bedwyr said to the boy as he clicked his tongue and led the horses. "Don't worry. That slobber sack you call a camel is part pig. He'll follow."

CHAPTER 25

ADVICE IN MASTERING AND REACTIVITY

Tapping his boots over the edge of a tailboard, Myrddin watched Viera stroking a camel's elongated jaw as Segwarides held its halter. She giggled when Adur pressed his nostrils against her neck for a treat.

"Lord Numidia," she asked, turning to the Knight who was holding the reins of the second camel. "You come from a land farther south than Constantine?"

"Aye, little bird. Alkebula to be exact," he said, his voice deep. "And you may call me Bors." He handed her a strip of apple jerky. "Ibil is a Bactrian camel."

Viera placed the treat in front of Ibil, and the camel picked it up in her fat lips and quickly gobbled it down. She giggled again, earning a smile from Bors Numidia, a man of eighteen winters who was a Metal Elemental and the Mercenary Prince. Muttering under his breath, Myrddin rolled his gaze upward at the relish the younger nobleman delivered to Viera over his compatriots' capture. He told her that he and Ector Kyner, the latter the bald man with tattoos all over his head, had watched the entire scene unfold as they sat on their animals and hid within some trees dotting the embankment.

"He's our tattooed menace," Bors said, sniggering as Segwarides shushed him.

"What's his Element? How old is he?" Viera asked, digging her boot into the earth.

Segwarides wiped some drool from Adur's rolling jaw and flicked it on the grass. "Earth and sixty-two summers—" he grunted when another string of drool dripped onto his boot. "Lord of Kyner Craggs and the house of the—"

"Griffs," she said, clasping her hands and bouncing on her feet. "House Kyner used to be the Griffin House with catbirds of all shapes and sizes at their beck and call."

Chuckling, Segwarides said, "Aye. Hermes, the last known Griffin in Evermore, turned to stone and to this day guards their main feast hall."

"Lord Kyner's much older than I thought he would be."

"He started balding in his thirties," Bors said, grinning as her eyes rounded, "and gave up on combating it in favour of tatting. If you look closely, you'll find each Kyner child and grandchild, as well as Arthwyr, Guinevere, and both Princes, in his tattoos."

Ibil lowed for another treat until Bors passed Viera more treats. Bors pointed between his camel and Adur. "As you can see, Ibil is a darker orange and fluffier," he said rather lovingly. "Her type has two humps. Adur is a dromedary and has one hump."

Viera laughed. "But they both like sweets the same."

"Aye. But Adur is a bit more temperamental."

Segwarides passed Adur's halter to Palamedes. "Long as his rider is about, he's fine. Would you like to sit on him?"

"Of course," she said, touching the stirrups that were too high for even Segwarides to lift his foot to. "You're going to have to show me how to get up on him."

"There's a trick to it. You cannot ever mount or dismount from a camel like a horse. Not without hurting or killing yourself." Segwarides clicked his tongue and Adur lowered to the ground, his knees folding in such a way that had Viera gaping.

He helped her mount the beast, adjusted the girl's legs, and snapped his fingers and barked, "Hup, hup."

Huffing mildly, Adur rose and Segwarides patted the camel's rump. A strip of apple jerky quieted Adur as he extended his long neck and snatched the treat from his rider. Viera worked her fingers along the camel's hump, marveling over his coarse and wiry hide.

After a few minutes of a plodding and bumpy walk in a circle, Segwarides helped her down. She stroked Ibil and waved for the trio to follow her a few feet from the camels. When she brought up her hands, the last array Myrddin taught her materialized and a Firewolf burst from the center.

As flames danced over its body, Myrddin stifled a gasp and shuddered. Carydoc was right. The girl had bound a Cú Sídhe to herself. Myrddin had not wanted to believe what others had said about Viera's manipulation of Fire, but there was no denying what was crying for affection and wagging its tail.

Long before Dragons and wilder Ancients fled to the northern realms, Cú Sídhe had faded from Evermorean lore. Myrddin's mother spoke of the legend with bated breath, telling her son that an Emrys ancestress bound one. According to the myths, Cú Sídhe came as wolves, jackals, and foxes, and took on their forms based on the ability and strength of their Masters.

Carydoc's earlier conversation replayed in Myrddin's mind. Viera's power was evolving. The howl that spilled from her that night made much more sense. A Cú Sídhe had paced inside Viera like a caged animal, to be released only when she was under great stress. The blood the Marshal had painted on Viera created a fracture in the barrier holding back the Cú Sídhe, and now it could be conjured up at the slightest whim.

A chirrup broke his concentration. Landing next to him, a male sparrow fluffed out its proud body. Myrddin squinted at the white specks on its beak.

"I can't believe you followed us from Iyesgarth. Your Mistress is over there teaching her new pet to fetch."

The bird hopped closer and perched on a crate. It cheeped and settled on the wood, its delicate claws poking out from beneath its belly.

A female, much smaller and dullish brown in color, settled next to the male. The rapt attention each paid to the other had Myrddin believing they were communicating. He had no idea why he felt this way, but he thought they were discussing something sinister.

He mused out loud, "What else is following us from that Hellshole of a village?"

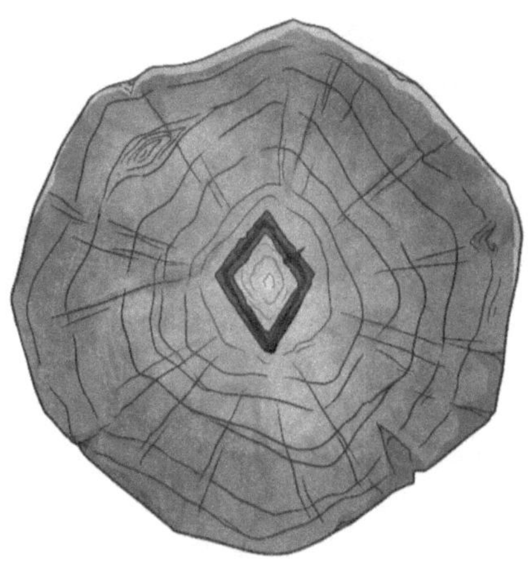

CHAPTER 26

GAVYN FOXBURY

Snorts and thumping hooves broke up the din of field crickets whining. Viera watched the large destrier frolicking like a colt, the horse's dark tail and mane snapping in the breeze. He thundered up to his Master, stopping a breath away from Gavyn Foxbury.

The Knight patted the animal's sooty palomino hide, grabbed a stick, and held it in front of the horse. He then tossed the piece of wood far into an adjoining field. The horse shot off, covering ground at breakneck speed, and snatched up Gavyn's missile. Viera gaped as the stallion returned with the stick hanging loosely from its mouth and deposited it in Gavyn's hand. *All dogs should do as well.*

She had been observing Gavyn working his stallion, Gringolet, as she was taking a break from the broadsword lessons that she was receiving from Carydoc, who was also instructing Daegyn. She'd heard a lot about Lord Daegyn Dyfed in recent days, courtesy of Myrddin educating her to Dyfed Landing's overall culture, of which Iyesgarth had been traded into the fiefdom.

She had imagined someone much senior to the youth, who stood across from her, as the Lord of Dyfed Landing, a formal title the young noble would receive when in under two years he would reach sixteen summers. Albeit it was rather young to become the Lord of his House;

the age of young Lords coming into their title ranged from eighteen to twenty-one and depended on the House and the circumstances that led a new Lord to claim the reins of his duchy. As for now, despite his noble pedigree, she could see him fitting right in with the boys from her village.

His cheeks reddened whenever his gaze met hers, the green flecks in his brown eyes taking on a deeper emerald. The warmth of him brushing against her borrowed Saracen garb prickled her skin as Carydoc instructed on deadlocking between blades. It was not unheard of for the Dyfeds to Bond with those of common stock, as the last Lady of Dyfed Landing, Daegyn's mother, Melinda, had been a horse trainer and stable hand.

On the final deadlock, Carydoc settled his hand over her straining arm doing more in countering Daegyn. "Lower yourself here. I know you don't like it because it feels like ceding to him but—" he guided her to drop by centimeters and Daegyn's stick buckled forward— "you've now broken his form and it grants you the ground to slide under and into him."

Now, it was her turn to feel heat bathing her cheeks as her practice stick pressed firm along Daegyn's stomach. "Oh, thank you, Milord."

Chuckling, Carydoc deftly plucked the sticks from both. "That's enough for now, Milady. If you ever want more lessons, you know who to approach."

Carydoc trotted off, slinging his arm over Lance and trading jabs with the sticks. Daegyn scratched along his neck, his gaze returning to her and opening his mouth when jeers erupted from the noble boys and Gaheris standing nearby. Daegyn mumbled an apology to her and joined them, darting glances toward Viera as his peers ribbed him.

A moment later, Gavyn stormed by Viera. He put Gaheris in a playful headlock while walking into the middle of the noble boys, who teased Daegyn for being beat by a girl. She fretted that Gavyn loathed her, and she feared making him any more of an enemy. So, she had avoided him since his "capture."

When Viera learned that Bedwyr had substituted Gavyn for Gaheris, she wondered about the reason, as the Foxbury Noble meant nothing to her except that she was incensed that someone she had gotten to know a little and liked—had become a highwayman. Oh, how stupid Bedwyr had made her feel, yet maybe this was the idea all along.

She spied Harlan, who acknowledged her with a wave but quickly turned his back to her when Daegyn said something to him. Harlan had been nice to her and had even complimented the Saracen clothes as Jocelyn called them trollop threads.

That seemed about to end. Harlan wouldn't choose her over his father. People—at least in her village—never picked outsiders over family.

Constantine walked into the gaggle of boys, grabbed Gavyn's arm, spun him around, and wagged his finger in the Knight's face. "Where's Budgie, you carrot-topped menace?"

Gavyn huffed, "Heckling some vixens."

"In Elden's Hearth," Constantine asked, his voice rising, "or here?"

Gavyn held a closed fist in the air, whistled, and a moment later a loud cackling sound pierced the air. Perched on a tree limb, a large gray bird with red tail feathers bounced on its legs and made "wolf whistles" at the Maids sitting on the tailgate of their wagon. This was followed by a shrill voice calling out, "Puta! Puta! Puta! Budgie found puta! Lots of puta!"

Palamedes and Segwarides had also just come on the scene, and the bird's repertoire gave the young Saracen all the ammunition he needed. He hooted and jabbed his finger at the girls, hollering, "A bird called y'all tarts, you tarts!"

Segwarides cuffed Palamedes, but the boy had already done his damage.

Viera edged past Ewain, who leaned against a barrel and glowered at the vulgar parrot. Off-white halos framed the bird's white eyes as he bobbed his head and continued to whistle. Viera laughed as Budgie arrogantly spread his tail feathers.

Sandalwood blanketed her like the flannels back home. Despite the similarity to her father's scent, she flinched at Gavyn's proximity. Hooves thudded and Gringolet shoved a branch against Gavyn.

The man glanced at the horse's offering and said, "That's not the right stick, and you know it. Go find the right one, you lazy cow."

The horse dropped the branch, snorted, and cantered off.

"Heya, Lass," Gavyn said, the first words he'd spoken to her since the *incident*. "I hear my son and brother are taken with you."

She tensed when Gavyn knelt next to her, held out his arm, and whistled.

Budgie fanned out his wings, swooped low, and landed on Gavyn's outstretched, leather-sheathed wrist. The bird opened its charcoal beak to take some sunflower seeds from Gavyn, the parrot's dark tongue darting out and black specks lining the bottom of the animal's cheeks.

Viera bit her lip and murmured, "I'm sorry for trying to kill you, Milord."

Gavyn chuckled and smoothed his fingers over the feathers on Budgie's back. "You're hardly the first, and you won't be the last lass to make the attempt, of that I'm certain."

CHAPTER 27

OF ALL THINGS GRAY

Constantine held out a large bundle for Viera and said, "Myrddin requested I bring these clothes for you. No more lent garments. These are yours to keep."

Viera didn't know what to think but she went inside her wagon and began trying on the outfits, quickly becoming embarrassed at the various swaths of her skin that became exposed as she tried on the clothing. She covered herself with a shift and undertunic and poked through the mass of outfits the priest had given her.

She pushed her arms through the sleeves of one robe and tugged the collar around her neck. The folds of the fabric, which exposed an inner robe, curtained her thin body but opened uncomfortably to expose her undertunic. The inner robe was blue, the outer robe a smoky gray with black sigils of ivy and sparrows along the hem.

Finished with her first attempt at donning new garb, she managed to hop down from the wagon, but she tripped and fortunately Lance was there to catch her. She gasped at seeing him bare-chested, but her gaze locked onto the burns encircling his upper arms and the number *314* tattooed in black blocky letters as Constantine passed Lance a gray peasant tunic.

The Ebony Knight tugged on the tunic, and as if reading her mind said, "During Uther's time, Wards of the Keep received ward brands. It designates you as a type of property of the House."

"Will I be branded?" she asked softly, clutching her robes about her and shivering.

"Nay. It's an archaic practice most Houses don't do." He gave a slow spin. "What say you, Constantine? Still earthing the peasant look."

Constantine pinched his nose. "Does it fit, you lummox?"

"Gloriously and no stains."

"Ten ingots it shan't remain that way. Daegyn's going to get you next."

"Oh. Becoming a wagering man, eh?"

"Get out of here." Constantine shoved another bundle into Lance's arms and sent him on his way. "I'll show you how to tie off the robes, Viera. They can be a little confusing."

He situated the robes around her, and the patterns on the hems showed up better in the sunlight, prompting Viera to ask, "How did you come upon this robe with the little birds on it?"

"Lamorac mentioned that you have an affinity for sparrows."

She smothered a string of curses. *He must have been sneaking around and heard me talking out loud to the birds!* She muttered, "That was kind of him," not meaning a word of it.

She made her way back inside the wagon and emerged tugging at a sash. Her fingers slipped when she twisted the cummerbund too tight, and she squealed.

The priest acknowledged her latest struggle, saying, "Trystan and I come from different places, and we find your robes mystifying as well. The first time I wore Evermorean robes, I went to a feast in your people's underwear. Gavyn said it was the traditional attire that a noble bride wore on her Bonding Night."

"You're joking?"

"Nay, I'm not. Good thing it was in Murphy's Hold. It would've been a deadly error to make in the capital."

"Seems innocent enough. How is that?"

"Aye, seems innocent enough, but Uther and Jormund would've been alerted." He lifted his gaze to meet hers. "During the Draigs' Duels, I was a spy and masqueraded as Myrddin's cousin."

She raised an eyebrow. "You have an accent much different from ours. Would it not give you away?"

"N-n-not wh-wh-when I st-st-stutter." Constantine stopped the act. "Some nobles are closed-minded toward those they view as flawed. It proves their greatest failing."

He was full of surprises, as he called to Budgie and the parrot landed on the wagon's aft hitching post and eyed Viera.

She cautiously approached the bird, but when it didn't fly off, she inched closer. "Is he yours or Gavyn's?" she asked the priest, assuming that Budgie wouldn't have responded to Constantine if they didn't have some sort of relationship.

"The best answer would be neither," Constantine said as he sauntered over and scratched the back of the bird's head. "Budgie picks who he wants to consort with—" hesitating, he lowered his chin. "Budgie has a certain capacity toward vindictiveness—a natural level of hatred. From what I gathered, he was bonded to an Alkebulan Wilds Master before his partner was enslaved and murdered by a famous pirate known as Gafforio the Grimm. Budgie chose Trystan after deciding Gafforio wasn't worthy of him. Gafforio is likely where Budgie picked up his *colorful* vocabulary."

Viera found the story funny and asked, "How did you get close to Budgie?"

"When the Duels of the Draigs was at its peak, Trystan and I entered Evermore through Orrinshire Pass. Trystan left with Arthwyr but he gave me Budgie to take to Elden's Hearth."

"How did Trystan get Isolde?"

"I gifted her to Trystan. She's a yearling chicked from Maerna's mated pair."

"Why did you and Trystan split up?"

"Trystan's appearance and speech made it impossible for him to hide he was a foreigner, and if he'd continued with me, Jormund's men would have found him out. Arthwyr needed Trystan as a Wilds Master, so it was an easy decision. Me, I'm more used to blending in."

Viera shivered, no longer finding any of this humorous. "Weren't you just as afraid of being discovered?"

"Aye. Many risks went toward securing the realm." He gave his head a fitful shake. "I walked straight into the lion's den. There was no way out for me if I failed and the Emrys would have been even more compromised. After an—" pausing with his brow furrowed— "incident with Myrddin's youngest brother, Maerna was kept in the capital to ensure Myrddin and Nimue remained docile. Uther demanded one of his allies, Dub Foel, to become Maerna's bodyguard."

Viera went still, her gaze widening at the mention of a man tied to a House as infamous and dark as that of the Foel Witches. "Did he hurt her?" she rasped.

Constantine smiled ruefully. "He never acquired the chance. The current Head of the Abe, Haruki, is as disagreeable a man and Lord as his father, Naboru. Uther errored and tried to fine Naboru for Bonding the last pureblooded Heiress of the Llyr on an archaic law that forbade noble Heirs and Heiresses from compromising bloodlines by sullying themselves with peasant stock."

Grimacing, Viera said, "Aye. Our taxes got raised when our Lord Darren Dyfed Bonded his wife, Melinda. But I don't see how the Abe-Llyr was a mistake for Uther."

"Uther forgot one important factor surrounding that law," Constantine said, a wicked smirk stretching across his features. "You see, if another noble family questions the nobility or capabilities of an older noble family, the second family can demand a fine, a duel, or both."

"So? What's that got to do with anything?"

Snorting, Constantine said, "The Abe predate Pendragon House by a thousand years."

Viera blinked and her lips parted. "What?" she croaked.

"House Pendragon had to pay a hefty fine to Abe for questioning Naboru, who emptied out a few Royal Accounts to be made whole. Uther learned to keep his fingers out of Abe-Llyr affairs. Myrddin married the oldest Abe-Llyr daughter of Naboru. It would not do to anger or insult the Abe-Llyr over an Emrys Heiress tied to their House through her mother."

"Then, why wasn't Maerna moved to their House?"

"Haruki is disagreeable but not stupid. He could ill-afford all of the Houses going against him as a new Lord. Moving Maerna under his purview would do just that." Constantine tapped his temples. "However, Haruki used the law his father had used to spite Uther again."

Uncertain of where this was going, Viera asked, "Why would Uther question Lord Haruki's claim when he already did that with Lord Naboru? That doesn't make sense."

"Uther didn't."

"All right. Then how did Lord Haruki use the same law?"

Said Constantine, "Uther demanded Dub Foel to be Maerna's bodyguard under the premise that Dub was the best choice, which would have worked if those under Abe employ weren't the best bodyguards in Evermore. For that matter, when Maerna was born, the Abe gifted her the services of her youngest uncle, Abe Daisuki. He was already her bodyguard and replacing him was an insult not to be tolerated by the Abe. The only satisfactory recourse was for Uther to either pay a fine or have his man duel Daisuki."

"What happened?"

"Daisuki dueled and used flowers to beat Dub."

Viera glanced at a nearby patch of yellow-horned poppy, having a hard time seeing the danger of flowers short of using them for a poison. "Flowers in a duel? Surely you jest."

Constantine laughed. "Serious as the thorns from a rose. Some Nihon Wood Masters weaponize flowers, plants, and trees. Daisuki is Evermore's Master of Sakura-Nihon cherry blossoms, Fuji-Nihon wisteria, Momiji-Nihon maple, and Sugi-Nihon cedar, which is a rarity even by Nihon standards as he is a Wood Master of All Seasons. In Nihon, trees such as Sakura stand for spring, Fuji for summer, Momiji for autumn, and Sugi for winter." The priest sobered. "Daisuki remained Maerna's bodyguard, and as affable as he is, he made sure I knew that I would be more fortunate to die at Uther's hands than his for any failure. I had to be careful."

"Why take such a risk for a place that's not your home?"

"My birthplace stopped being mine when I was seven autumns. Home is not a piece of land; it's the people who live in it that make it what it is. Besides, homes grow with the people who join them."

"Speaking of joining a family. Why is Myrddin not bothered with you dressing me? Shouldn't he insist on one of the other girls? This sounds like the perfect bonding experience for them."

"He's aware of the friction between some of you and figured it would be good to give you breathing room. Do you want me to call for Jocelyn?"

"Nay." She crossed her arms. "Jocelyn keeps salting the wounds—not me—and could you imagine what she'd do?"

"I'm not in agreement with how it's being handled, but you're going to have to stand more on your own, and I'm afraid that a Lady's garb is not going to make the Maids in Court automatically welcome you. The old guard, so to speak, will have a bit to say whenever they can make life hard for you."

"Can't the King do something? He lets them get away with whatever they want."

Constantine's fingers played over his crucifix. "Arthwyr toes a precarious line. Families like the Sagramores, Cornwalls, and Cuhlwchs could throw us into another war. To prevent this, Arthwyr avoids certain court issues and traditions. Sniping between the Maids of the Court is one area he won't touch unless it's for the most serious of offenses."

Viera lowered her head. "I should have stayed home."

"That's letting them win. You asked about Arthwyr but not the Queen. Guinevere will set everything straight with the Maids whenever they go too far. She will not tolerate a mockery of her Court. Even Lord Sagramore bows to her."

"The Queen sounds ferocious."

"Uther intended to prearrange Arthwyr's marriage to a weak wife with a weak Ice Element." He leaned back on his heels, and his voice became pensive. "Instead, he met his match with Guinevere."

"Because a serf-smoothy is so scary."

"Ice makes a phenomenal weapon under the right conditions." Constantine finished adjusting her cummerbund. "Myrddin thought you would be more comfortable with me than him."

Viera thought a moment. "But you're a man."

"My vows insist I remain celibate. The easiest way to explain it is that I made a vow to Bond with the God of my religion. I made that oath prior to meeting my Soul Bond."

She eyed him, piecing out each word deliberately to better understand. "You've met your Bond but will not Bond with them."

"Not in the sense of a marriage, no. There are other ways to satisfy a Bond. I made my commitment to God a long time ago. My Bond Mate made their commitment. We're on good terms, and that is all our type of Bond requires."

As she considered Constantine's personal history, Viera thought about Segwarides' brown and black leathers. "Why don't you and Segwarides wear a symbol of your Element or a family coat-of-arms?"

"Segwarides and his brothers fled their home after their uncle overthrew their mother. Since they aren't Evermorean, they're uncomfortable wearing the Fire or Air sigil."

"What about you?"

"My family forsook me." He rubbed at his wrist before stilling and shoving his sleeve down to hide a suspicious scar along the bones of his wrist and the darker curve of a line across his skin. "It's unwise for me to wear anything that hints at them. Such a symbol could draw unwanted attention."

A clatter drew her gaze to Trystan, who walked up and wiggled his fingers and held out a shiny metal hair ornament that he handed to Viera.

Viera accepted the pretty bauble just as Constantine yelled out, "Trystan!"

Trystan shrugged. "Isolde like. Isolde took." He bowed to Viera. "Yours now."

The priest grimaced. "What he means is, Isolde filched it from some poor merchant." He sighed and shook his head. "There's no returning it now."

Clutching the piece, Viera returned Trystan's bow. "Thank you for the gift."

"Thank Isolde. She likes you."

Trystan raised his voice to the scowling priest and garbled something in his rough tongue that ended with Constantine massaging his temples.

"Fine. I'll get Ewain." Constantine said. "He can help you with it."

She wrinkled her nose. "Why Ewain?"

"He's a Water Dancer for the main temple in Elden's Hearth." Constantine squeezed her shoulder. "Decorative pieces are something he knows. Evermore only knows where it would end up on you, if left up to Gavyn."

Bedwyr argued with Arthwyr as Carydoc and Segwarides stood next to the King. "I expect you to pay the full ransom to the girl on our return to the Hearth," Bedwyr said.

The King crossed his arms. "Why am I paying you for my own people?"

Said Carydoc, "I'd argue the same, but she gave us the drop. She deserves the reward."

"Pay her, Arthwyr," Segwarides urged. "And give Palamedes a share as well. I don't want to hear him forever whining that he was cheated his due for securing me."

"Fine." Arthwyr handed Bedwyr a pouch. "Bleed me dry, eh, both of you? And don't even start with that doesn't feed me tripe you like, my bratty little light."

Bedwyr palmed the pouch, turning to meet with Lamorac for the next round of balms and bandages for his arm, and drew up short when Arthwyr grabbed his uninjured arm. Quirking his eyebrow at the dour expression Arthwyr gave him, Bedwyr swallowed. "Aye, Arthwyr?"

"There's something we must discuss in private—" Arthwyr waved Carydoc and Segwarides off— "Something happened in Porthcrawl."

Bedwyr shrugged off Arthwyr's hand. "What? Got drunk on pissgut in some tavern and made a bedding mistake with some trollop. Tansy will fix that."

"Tansy isn't effective twenty-three springs later, you little gremlin."

Bedwyr laughed until he realized Arthwyr hadn't joined in. His sniggering tapered off as Arthwyr lowered his chin and his shoulders drooped. Bedwyr wasn't laughing when he grabbed a tankard and dipped it into a barrel of mead. *Bloody feckin' Hells.*

CHAPTER 28

THE CURSE OF THE SEVEN HOUSES

Viera rounded a wagon and stilled as she spotted Lamorac fussing with a bowl of liquid goo and standing with Brynn next to a crate on which Bedwyr sat, bare-chested.

Bedwyr saw Viera and turned to Lamorac "Told you we should have done this in the ruddy wagon, you addle-brained wanker."

Lamorac ignored his abuse, saying only, "Sorry."

Brynn swung her legs around as she sat on the tailboard. "I'm not," she said, while folding a linen. "How else am I going to learn?"

Bedwyr twisted toward her. "You just don't want another tirade on how you should behave from that blond shrew and her pack."

Brynn batted her eyelashes. "Bedy, you need to be nice to me because I helped you leave that gift in your paramour's bedroll. Otherwise, that dead-squirrel backscratcher can return to *your* bedroll. What's the saying in Dyfed about friendship gifts—You scratch my back and I'll scratch yours?"

From the corner of her eye, Viera watched black-and-blue ink spiral into intricate arrays atop Bedwyr's pale skin. As she moved closer, she became aware of Gavyn perched on a barrel drinking a tankard of mead. She asked, "What are these?"

"Long forbidden and forgotten arrays of the original Seven Houses of Evermore," Gavyn said as he set down his drink. "Each family represented an Element: Red for Llewelyn and Fire, green for Druir and Wood, blue for Esau and Water, orange for Windsor and Air, brown for Pembroke and Earth, white for Cadogan and Ice, and gray for Wallach and Metal."

"Myrddin told me the other Houses died out."

"For the most part," Bedwyr said, groaning as if in considerable pain. "The Esau were the last to die out. The only one left is my family, the House of Metal, Gray, and Wallach"

"Weren't those born to the Heads of those families always of the same Element of the House they represented? Aren't you of Water?"

Lamorac released a dark, mirthless laugh. "Aye, and now you see the conundrum Jormund faced in the birth of his son and rightful heir."

Dropping to the ground, Gavyn kicked up trail dust. "Jormund despised Bedwyr for failing to be born of Metal, so he violated the laws of nature no different from what the rest of The Seven Houses did for many generations." He stood over Bedwyr and poked the lividest of the marks on the Knight's torso. "The Seven Houses weren't honest in their sacrifices."

Viera stepped back. "What do you mean?"

"The Seven Houses performed rituals assuring that their heirs were the correct Element." Lamorac shooed Gavyn away and drew his finger over the marks obscuring ropy raised scars and carvings. "If an infant was presented as different from what was expected, then these were painted on them to change their element."

Brynn gently elbowed Viera. "Future Heads who presented late had a choice. Usually, they moved their Twilight to conform. I mean, who doesn't want to be Lord of his own House?"

"There was no choice or explanation given to me," Bedwyr said to Brynn as he presented his carved-up shoulder to her for more work. "My father took the *Books of Metal* and gave them to Uther and his allies."

Viera was liking this less and less. "What happened?"

There was a dullness to Bedwyr's features as he answered: "Galahad was their intended victim. When he and some others escaped Evermore, my father offered me as their experiment."

"Uther and his cronies failed to understand, for a successful shift in an Element to be possible, the person had to be willing." Lamorac smoothed a balm—Brynn and Ewain had meticulously prepared—over the worst marks. "Their plans went wrong because Bedwyr was unwilling and fought the process. With infants, they know no better."

"Their determination knew no bounds," Bedwyr hissed as his shoulder started to bleed. "When I resisted, they carved and tattooed it into my skin with woad."

"It was gruesome. If you didn't realize it, woad is used to dye fabric blue. It was never meant to be applied to humans as its horribly caustic and leaves burns on the skin," Lamorac said as he wiped the remainder of the healing solution from the rim of a bowl. "Certainly nothing a child should endure from people who are supposed to love and nurture him."

Viera twisted her fingers in her sleeves and asked Bedwyr, "How old were you?"

"Fourteen winters, but they didn't complete carving me up until I was sixteen winters." Bedwyr flexed his bad shoulder and inhaled sharply through his nose. "It did nothing in the end. I'm still of Water."

As if what was happening could affect her, Viera clutched her own shoulder. "You said there were books. What happened to them?"

"From the Hearth's Library, I collected *The Books of the Seven Houses*. I couldn't find *The Books of Metal*." Cold settled upon his features. "I took the others to a courtyard and burned them all and—"

"Arthwyr secured *The Books of Metal* before Bedwyr got to it," Gavyn interrupted, sniggering into his mead. "The Scribes were in an uproar."

"Did the King ever tell you what he did with them?" Viera asked Bedwyr.

Bedwyr gave her a cynical look. "Arthwyr knows what I would do with them if ever given the chance."

Brynn collected the linens and Lamorac wrapped a poultice around Bedwyr's arm, and like a fresh rain over a field of lavender and peppermint, the mixture of herbs in the bandage filled the air with invigorating scents. "The curse of The Seven Houses lives on despite good sense saying it should have ended," Lamorac said as everyone took in the fragrances.

Brynn weaved bandages over Bedwyr's abdomen, and after tucking in the last strip, she turned to Lamorac. "So, you'll consider me for an Apprenticeship?"

"I'll discuss it with your father and Ewain," Lamorac said, and to Bedwyr, "The irritation and swelling will go down, but you'll need to take it easy. I'll have Talia look in on you and change your bandages every day."

Viera noted the faint line of tension running along Bedwyr's jaw and the knitting of his forehead, so she quietly asked, "Who's Talia?"

"A little fairy who waves a magic wand, and—magically—clean stuff happens." Gavyn's broad grin was a glaring indication that this was all bollocks.

Viera braved asking Bedwyr about Talia, and he said, "Talia is my servant."

She imagined a dour manservant with no sense of humor; aye, a twitching messy wreck of a human being. "He must be very brave."

"*She*," Bedwyr replied, scowling at her. "*She* must be very brave."

Lamorac snagged the tankard of mead over Gavyn's protest and said, "Talia has made it her life mission to corral in Bedwyr, Foxburys, Dagonet, and Lance on a regular basis."

Brynn chortled into her sleeve. "Then, there's the Wallach equerry that helps run Tryfan Heights. Now, two of the biggest scandals of the Court and both surrounding Wallach servants."

"Hush," Lamorac chided, though amusement lent a mischievous sparkle to his eyes.

Viera wrinkled her nose. "How could an equerry cause a scandal? Don't they just train and break horses."

"Aye," Gavyn said, ignoring Lamorac and winking at Brynn. "They do but Bedwyr's equerry is a former Viteliuian slave and member of the Catholic church."

Viera cast a bemused glance at Bedwyr as she recalled how dismissive he was of Constantine and his priesthood under the same faith. "I find it hard to believe such a man is one of your servants."

Bedwyr smirked. "Dante was indebted to the Catholics through his peasant family. There is little of him that is truly Catholic. When Dante no longer functioned the way that they wanted him to, they sold him to a family called Sforza who in turn gave him to Foel House."

Cold shook through Viera at the mention of the Foels. "Is his connection to the Foels the reason behind the scandal?"

Lamorac elbowed Bedwyr and Gavyn, sending them warning looks before turning to Viera and Brynn. "Dante is of very few words. His slavery made him taciturn and the practice of Foel House removing their servants' tongues had many believe him mute and slow of faculties. The man is far from it and fully has his tongue and wits about him."

"Oh," Viera said, furrowing her brow and looking at the wicked delight all but igniting from Gavyn and Bedwyr. "What does that have to do with anything?"

After Lamorac glanced at Bedwyr, who sobered and gave a guarded nod, the Healer said, "After negotiations amid Wallach and Foel House, Lord Tegid Foel gifted Dante's slave contract to Wallach House. At sixteen, Bedwyr was deemed too young to command a man like Dante. In effect, Dante became Jormund Wallach's manservant."

Viera whipped her head between Bedwyr and Lamorac. "Oh," she breathed, her gaze settling on Bedwyr, who swiped the tankard of mead and gulped it down. "Yet, he still works in Wallach House?"

Bedwyr tossed the empty tankard to Gavyn. "Aye. Dante served my father, but he is only loyal to those he respects. Rumor has it, Dante was far more loyal to Tegid and those Tegid cherished most. The negotiations that I was central to secured Dante's unwavering loyalty. After Dante's actions following the Duels, I have no reason to doubt my equerry's fidelity."

Curiosity burned through Viera. "What did he do?"

"Slaves and servants were spared arrest after the Duels, except for those who inspired suspicion. Dante fell under the latter. He was imprisoned and regularly brought to the Throne Room for questioning. Since he never spoke a word, Arthwyr and the others couldn't free him as they didn't know where his loyalties lay nor kill him without a trial proving he was an enemy."

"How did they—you realize the truth?"

Bedwyr chuckled. "Constantine and Uriah started a conversation in Viteliuian about how to ensure a man tainted by my father was removed from my service without compromising me, and Dante kept side-eying them enough for them to realize he was Viteliuian. Later, Constantine went to Dante's cell to deliver ink and paper under the presumption that the reason Dante did not speak was because of the removal of his tongue and not understanding Evermorean."

Gavyn refilled his drink, took a swig, and smacked his lips. "Dante wrote that he would tell all if Constantine and Uriah served as his translators for the Court. Imagine our surprise when in front of the Court Dante told us in Evermorean that he knew we had to try him. He vowed every secret he heard would be reported into the trial registries if we dared to harm a hair on Bedwyr's or Talia's heads. To prove it, he divulged several secrets from both the East and West that had the Court in an uproar that persists to this day."

Viera blinked, blinked again, and then burst out laughing. "He said he'd tell all and he did. I'm surprised he was allowed to live."

Lamorac helped Brynn roll extra gauze and return it to a case. "Dante is only a liability when people go after those who hold his allegiance." He lifted his finger and waved it at Viera and Brynn. "Dante is an expert poisoner, an Earth Elemental, and one of the best equerries this side of Evermore. Though, you will not likely see much of him as Dante only ventures from Tryfan Heights at Bedwyr's summons."

Bedwyr scoffed. "You have the Sagramores to thank for that. Those blonde menaces and their pet servants stirred up a bunch of rot that cost me the best manservant I could have had. I doubt there is a person alive that could match Dante. All the other ones have been wastes of air."

Lamorac pitched a ball of gauze at Bedwyr that bounced off of his head. "You keep hiring timid mice to set you and your affairs to rights. Dante had the bollocks to put you in your place. Though be honest, he loathes balancing your accounts when he is on them."

Snorting a laugh, Gavyn said, "Funny you say someone with less bollocks than all of us happens to have more." With a wink at Viera, he added, "Though, that's a tale for another day."

Viera had to think about that remark twice and she still couldn't sense of it as she rummaged through a pile of clean garments sitting outside the wagon. She gestured toward the House symbol on Bedwyr's doublet. "Why don't others wear their coat-of-arms on their chests?" she asked anyone listening.

Lamorac answered her: "Only the Heads of The Seven Houses and the Royal Pair retain the right. Not even Royal siblings, such as Ulrich or Maryck, can wear a coat-of-arms on their chests. Only a King, Queen, or Head of The Seven Houses is allowed this privilege. The only brief exception would be if there was to be formal adoption between Houses."

Viera spied Lance leaning against a wagon. "What of the Ebony Knight?"

"Again, only Arthwyr, Guinevere, and Bedwyr carry that right," Lamorac said rather emphatically, surprising Viera by his tone. "And since Bedwyr is the last head of The Seven Houses, you will see no other wearing his coat-of-arms."

Carydoc had come over to sample the mead, and listening in, said, "Aye, there is one other who bears the right."

Viera darted a glance his way. "Who?"

"A Wallach Bond or heir," Carydoc said, handing Bedwyr a tunic from the stack of clean clothing. "Ah, but 'tis a daring lass who takes such a gambit for the first part of that prospect."

He winked at Bedwyr, who turned away and grumbled about meddling old codgers.

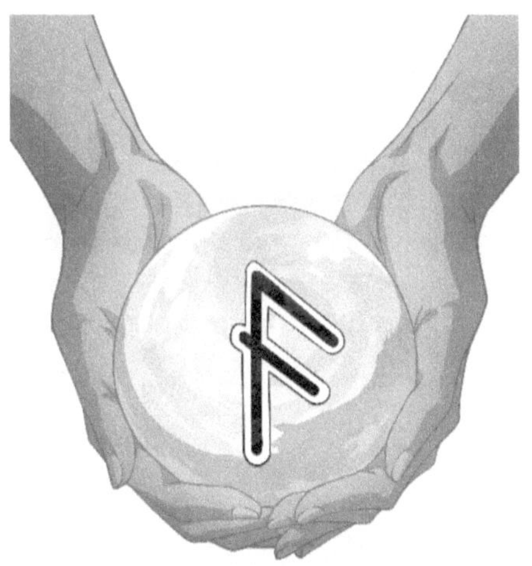

CHAPTER 29

DIVINING BALANCE

Eyes as black as night and outlined with crimson kohl peered from the spire of The Oracles Guild. A river of the woman's dark hair rippled from the wind, obscuring the faint red lines curled into an intricate pattern over her forehead. Its brilliance faded, only brightening when the time grew closer to roam the shadows of night.

Along the lime-green sleeves and bottom hem of the Nihongo robe Shiori Murasaki wore, white foxes jumped from lily pad to lily pad beneath a crescent moon. She considered the figures along the edge, the gleam of their armor blazing across the entire expanse.

Tap. Tap. Shuffle. Tap. Her concentration was broken.

Gray Oracle robes swayed, and Lubaba Cuhlwch stopped next to the woman, a slight stoop to her frame as she tottered closer, a highly polished wooden cane keeping her upright.

Skin crinkled around Lubaba's hazel eyes as she straightened and her brown, white-streaked hair twisted in the light breeze coming through the window. She said, "Ah, I see, Lady Murasaki."

She could only wonder if Lubaba really saw the same thing. Shiori Murasaki, retainer to Karen Wallach and Water Elemental Master to Bedwyr Wallach, looked to where her former Apprentice lingered on The Ridge. The depth of the relationship she shared with Bedwyr was as undeniable as it was immutable; aye, no tighter than if they were actual Bonds.

At the sight of Bedwyr, her whole body warmed so much it tingled, and her normally morose nature lightened. His time had come. Prior to her next journey, was it necessary that she get more than just a glimpse of her prize student? He was assuredly ready. Of course he was. She did not train the meek or weak. Shiori made the decision to let Fate take its course. She morphed and leapt from the observation window, her rouged lips pulling up and the peaks of her sharp canines gleaming in the sun.

From her vantage point in the North Tower of the castle, Nimue Abe observed Progress as it gathered along The Ridge. Under her breath, she called out the katas for Fire, then switched to Nihongo and repeated the sequence. Abe Naboru, her father, had never put much stock in Evermore's Oracles and the traditions the people clung to, not even when Nimue rose in the ranks and eventually assumed the post of High Oracle. To his way of thinking, her achievement meant little when Divination was much older and therefore more rooted in Nihon than Evermore could ever comprehend.

A harrumph drew Nimue's attention to Guinevere standing in the entranceway, the Queen's sophisticated facial features as rigid as granite. If there was ever a Court favourite that Abe Naboru had, it was the unflappable little snow princess who grew into the Ice Queen of Evermore.

Guinevere turned to an open window and nodded toward the people, horses, and wagons amassed atop The Ridge. "Look who returned sooner than I had hoped."

Both women smiled at one another as a whisper of cloth betrayed the presence of another in the large, heavily draped room. Nimue said, "Come out, Eerie. I know you're hiding in an alcove again."

Eerie Chia, Nimue's honorary niece of eighteen winters, shuffled from behind a wide column. She curtseyed to both ladies and walked toward an elegantly carved table with the scrying ball on it.

"Even with your Sight, no one except the Oracle administering the divination and the one the divination is intended for are supposed to be present for Scrying Ball Divinations," Nimue said rather sternly. "You know this, and it's been a rule ever since Uther made his divinations public and brought war upon Evermore."

Nimue was concerned with what Guinevere might be thinking about Eerie's blatant abuse of protocol, but the Queen was preoccupied with what was going on outside her window with Progress. For her part, Eerie acted unfazed by the rebuke. With a flick of her fingers, she sent her silvery-white hair over her shoulders. Her Element caught the strands, and a gauzy orange array flashed to mark her use of Air. Stopping in front of the low table, she toed the smaller pillows into a defensive line against a heart-shaped one. She plopped onto the pillow, her skirt billowing from the graceless drop. A letter peeked from the top of her corset.

Nimue tsked. "Filched someone's mail again?"

"Come now, Auntie." Eerie shoved the letter deeper into her corset and readjusted her ample bosom. "We know as far as my Soul Bond's concerned, what's mine is mine, and what's his is mine."

Nimue folded her hands within the sleeves of her robe. "As I said, young lady, Scrying Ball Divinations are meant to be between the individual and one Oracle, and no one else. You are going to have to leave, and I don't want you in here again when a Divination is taking place. Do you understand me?"

"How could I resist, Auntie Nimmy?" Eerie twisted a few strands of her hair around her finger. "I only wanted to confirm what's best for the realm."

Nimue pulled back the sleeves of her robe. "What do you mean?"

"I want to hear also," came Guinevere's voice, loud and clear.

Eerie lowered her gaze to the scrying ball. "The pieces are gathering."

Each woman stood on one side of Eerie as she bowed over the globe. Clouds roiled within the crystal, followed by flashes of lightning lancing through the dark, sparking and lashing against the glass constraining the mayhem. A bolt of bright light signaled the end of the storm.

Guinevere, normally unmoved by most anything, flinched but remained standing next to the table and the ball, the latter now cloaked in darkness. Eerie moaned and yellow flared from the orb's center as seemingly hurricane-strength wind whipped around inside the crystal. As quickly as this latest turmoil began it ended, and a vision emerged. Somewhere, far beyond Evermore, the sun hung high over shifting sand dunes. A bazaar bustled with people covered in as many different clothes as colors in the world, and all the buildings were heavily sand-pitted. Wide, luminous orange eyes peered out and vanished within a sandstorm.

Eerie weaved her fingers at the ball and said, "The last Architect will lead her blood to what, one day, we will need most—and another shall rise."

Eerie moved closer to the scrying ball. Two shades, one apelike, the other a nondescript outline, skittered across gray stone. They stopped and the creature launched itself at the shadow cast in flowing robes. Another blurred figure joined them, and the creature settled on the pairs' shoulders, everything fading into a wall.

Sand pinged against the glass and slid away. A black wing skirted the sides of the scrying ball as four hands, two black and two white, clasped. Eerie pulled back from the globe. "Two from afar and two from near will strike a deal," she said. "People from many lands will join once more."

Fire swelled and metal gleamed until darkness once again consumed the sphere. Nimue said to the Queen, "My apologies, Your Majesty. I had hoped that the answer to Balance would emerge from within."

Eerie placed her hands over the ball, and when she removed them, the orb was clear. "Balance is complex," she said as she ran her fingers over the smooth crystal. "Destruction is as much a form of Balance as growth."

"Which means?" the Queen asked in a not-too-pleasant tone.

Eerie reached across the table and set her hand over the Queen's stomach. "Sometimes we must burn the land for new growth to occur. You and yours have ensured one will rise from the legacy you have already born and determine Evermore's Fate."

A fresh shaft of light shot through the window and sent a prism of colors dancing on the wood floor. The Queen asked Eerie, "Do you know the signs that will mark the event for Evermore?"

Eerie sat back. "It has already begun," she replied smugly.

Knocking had them looking toward the wooden door leading to a staircase.

"Enter," Nimue said, swathing the scarves over her scrying ball, "if you dare."

Hinges squealed as a youth of eighteen autumns entered. The future Lord of Rheged knelt, his pitch-black hair framing his cheeks in a wild tousle as if he had run from the parlor to the top of the tower. He held the position until Guinevere signaled for him to rise.

"Lord Eryck," the Queen said and held out her hand, "what brings you here? I thought you were in my parlor guarding the Ladies?"

He kissed the Queen's hand and bowed at the waist to Nimue and Eerie. "My apologies for interrupting. Grandmother sent me and Uncle Elyan to escort Queen Guinevere to the Throne Room for the King's arrival. She already sent my grandfather and Lord Pellinore to greet Royal Progress on The Ridge."

"No need," Nimue said, "Is your uncle downstairs?"

Eerie clattered to the window. "Knowing Elyan, he's on the other side of the hall—" she pitched her voice higher— "trying to be all menacing while cowering from the webs of Fate like a scared girl."

Thumps on the stone steps preceded Elyan Rheged appearing in the doorway. "Who's scared now?"

As he tucked Guinevere's arm under his, Eryck waggled his eyebrows. "When I came in, there was a shovel in Lady Abe's scrying ball. Guess it was predicting you, Uncle."

"Obnoxious chick."

"Caw," Eryck imitated the grating call of his house's raven totem, "Caw."

The Queen sighed and gestured toward the door. As they proceeded toward the door, Guinevere looked back at Nimue. "Would you mind escorting my husband when I'm ready to receive him and the others, Lady Abe?"

Nimue curtseyed. "Aye, Your Majesty."

As soon as they were alone, Nimue joined Eerie at the window.

The young woman tossed her head back and swept her hair into a wild cone of silver, her magenta gaze gleaming in the morning light pouring through the window. "The sun ascends, and," Eerie said, "like the rise of a phoenix, our beginning will be as glorious as our end."

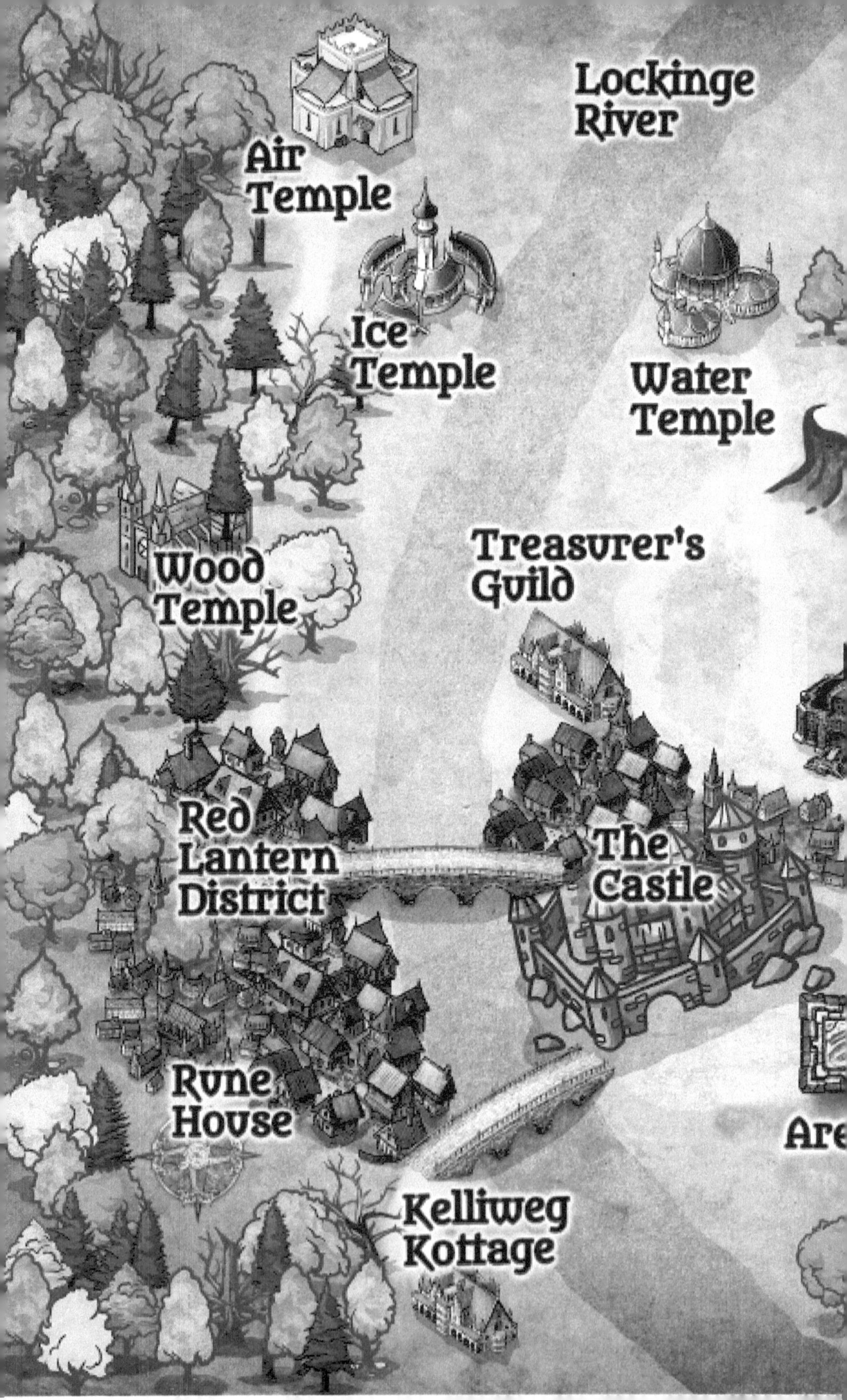

Air Temple
Ice Temple
Lockinge River
Water Temple
Wood Temple
Treasurer's Guild
Red Lantern District
The Castle
Rune House
Kelliweg Kottage
Are

Elden's Hearth
The Ridge
le
Oracles Guild
Earth Temple
Metal Temple

CHAPTER 30

ELDEN'S HEARTH

"Whoa!" Viera cried out, not knowing what to think as she stared at the capital of Evermore for the very first time. "So, this is Elden's Hearth?"

Maerna, who was riding next to her, said, "Aye," appearing clearly amused at Viera's reaction as they sat on their horses high atop what was known as The Ridge.

Ewain had lent Viera a tan and white skewbald mare from Gorre Retreat's stable after a brief stay in the holdings. His home buttressed Dynnah Loch, its squat reddish brick buildings casting a welcoming glow over the lake. From the towers, she had ogled the yellow and evergreen topped buildings of DuLac Pines across the way. It had been surprising to see evergreen trees dotting Lance's holdings as they grew from the roofs like her home.

The mare turned her neck and snorted against Viera's leg. She slipped a sugar cube from her pocket and held it out for the horse.

"Please tell me what I'm looking at?" she asked Maerna.

Getting Progress ready to make its formal approach to the capital was no easy chore. For the Maids, however, there was a lot of time to kill. So, for the better part of the morning, Maerna pointed out locations all over the Hearth and its surrounding lands, giving Viera an extensive history and geography lesson:

"The Sagramores own the southern fief of Dynnah Loch. The Queen and her brother, Balin Cameliard, have their natal home of Spitsbergen on the eastern edge of the lake. Prince Ulrich might inherit that duchy and become the next Lord of Spitsbergen, unless he rises to the Throne."

Viera stole a glance to Ulrich chatting with Lance and Trystan, Isolde preening her feathers on the younger prince's shoulder from where the trio observed the capital on their mounts. "You say *might?*"

Red dusted Maerna's cheeks when Ulrich turned toward them and she ducked her chin. "Balin has two stepchildren he's considering calling his heirs. One is a boy older than Ulrich's fifteen summers, so he *might* be the successor to Cameliard. What has the nobles in an uproar is that both stepchildren are born to a peasant wife, but Balin is of the mind that his stepson and stepdaughter are better suited than even the son he shares with his wife. For now, however, he has staff training them on how to be the Heads of Spitsbergen."

Viera laughed. "Sometimes it seems a whole lot better to be a peasant. You haven't mentioned the Emrys duchy. Can we see it from here?"

"Our duchy is called Wyllt Way, and it's in the northeastern mountains of Evermore, so you can't see it even from up here. Farther south from Wyllt Way, and closer to Spitsbergen, is Pellinore Falls. The last eastern mountain duchy is Kyner Craggs. There are ceded duchies from Uther's surviving allies that are no longer part of Evermore."

Viera's attention turned to the enormous castle next to the Lockinge River. "That thing is bigger than any building I could ever imagine."

The fortification, constructed from huge slabs of gray and white stone, was the personification of strength and power. With its turrets and parapets piercing the sky, its architecture served as mute testament to mankind's defiance against all odds and its continued challenge to nature. Four towers were erected, one on each corner of the imposing wall surrounding the castle, creating the effect that these structures were the cardinal directions on a compass. Perhaps a trick via the angle of the morning sun's rays, the westernmost tower appeared dark and hollowed out.

Viera settled her gaze on the gardens, in full bloom and providing a rich tapestry of colors exploding across the castle's grounds. She also couldn't help but stare at the pools of water designed in shapes she recognized, via Myrddin's training, as serenity symbols.

"Are those pools to swim in?" she asked Maerna, her mind already carrying her into the cool recesses of the water.

Maerna furiously braided her reins. "Not if you're polite and understand that they're called *purity* pools."

Gruff burring laughter drew Viera's attention to Gavyn joining them astride Gringolet. "If you ever name something pure or chaste," Gavyn said, "there's a guarantee it won't remain that way for long, lass. How are you finding the fair view so far?"

"It's beautiful. Do I sleep in the castle," Viera asked and handed her mare another sugar cube, "or do I stay in the slaves' quarters?" She meant that to be taken as a joke, but Maerna gasped and cringed into her saddle.

Air whistled past Gavyn's parted lips as he checked to see how far away Arthwyr was from them. "Slavery is outlawed here!" he hiss-barked at her. "Don't ever breathe a word of that in front of Arthwyr. He'll lose his mind!"

"I didn't know that was a sore spot. Seriously, I'm sorry."

Gavyn sighed and slouched in his saddle. "Slavery is indeed a sore spot. It was one of the first things Arthwyr outlawed when he gained control of the Throne. So, there are *no* slaves here. As for your question, it depends on the House and how many children are in it. The Emrys are protective of their children and keep them in their quarters with them until they Bond, go into a trade or Mastery, or reach their House majority at eighteen."

They relaxed into following Gavyn, and Viera turned the conversation to the quaint village of Elden's Hearth. It had the vibrancy of a thriving community, its buildings with eaves and gleaming paint catching the sunlight. Even from afar, the flowers appeared fresh and full of pleasant scents. The variegated greenery of the tree-lined streets added another outpouring of color and life to the capital.

"Noble families have houses, some even full manors, about the capital. When you turn eighteen seasons, the Emrys will set you up in an apartment there or maybe in the castle," Maerna said and pointed at a residence in the center of the sprawling capital. "Our residence is closer to the town square."

Gavyn gathered Viera's reins and led her mare around a large twisted oak. Patting the tree, Gavyn said, "It's called the Watchman. Legend has it the first Wood Marshal, Druir of the Wild Woods and a Wood Nymph, planted it from a seed that came from her native village. There are all sorts of myths surrounding her. Some say she ever favoured foxy things as foxes were her constant companions. Others say she was thick as thieves with Llewelyn the First Fire Marshal, Windsor the First Air Marshal, Pembroke the First Earth Marshal, and King Cymry Pendragon himself." He lifted a branch of the tree to reveal engravings that were varnished and sealed to last as long as the tree. "They used to ride up here and remember the one who sacrificed everything for them and the entire future of Evermore."

Viera stretched in her saddle and dragged her thumb over the symbols of the Marshals, the Pendragon emblem, and the lunar sigil of the Ebony Knight. Strangely, with the way the sunlight filtered through the trees, the last symbol almost mirrored phases of the sun as well as the moon. "How do you know this?" Viera asked, paying particular mind to the carving of an oak tree encompassing them all.

"Druir's descendants Bonded into the Murphys and then bound them into the Foxburys." Gavyn led her past the tree to where its limbs reached out as if toward a large estate bordering the river to the south of the capital. "That manor is called Kelliweg Kottage. The Kelliwegs lodge there, but most prefer the House of their main trading company in Porthcrawl. The only Kelliweg Knight is Lord Baudwyn, and though he retains a full-time residence in the castle, as he is the Treasurer of Evermore, he lends it to his niece and her husband, Garyth."

Viera chuckled. "Where does Lord Kelliweg stay if not the castle?"

"He keeps a flat between the Wood Temple and Treasurer's Guild. Likes the quiet better."

Viera slithered her reins from him. "Seems odd, given he can live in a castle."

"Try telling him that and you'll be treated to one of his special looks he reserves for Foxburys and village dunces." Gavyn wagged his finger in front of her face. "And he swears both are interchangeable."

"It's complex to explain to someone who's not… sorry. Let me give you some examples." Maerna straightened herself in her saddle. "Daegyn inherited his parents' chamber assigned for Dyfed Landing, but he's adopted by Carydoc Ynyr, so he lives in the Ynyr residence in the castle until he's sixteen seasons."

Said Viera, "Don't get mad at me for asking, but if I wasn't staying with you, where *would* I be living?"

Maerna gave Viera a somewhat annoyed look, but she replied calmly, "Young Maids of the Court either stay with their parents or with chaperones appointed by their families. Many take rooms provided for the Ladies-in-Waiting. Before you ask the obvious, it's unacceptable for Unbonded men to enter those rooms under most circumstances. And to assure this doesn't happen, older Ladies of the Court rotate chaperoning duties."

"What about the Royals?"

Maerna raised an eyebrow. "They stay in the upper levels of the castle. The Emrys' Chamber is on a lower level but we do have a balcony."

Just outside the main entrance rose an imposing tower standing equal in height to the castle's tallest structure. Unlike the gray and off-white stone used for the castle, this building gleamed with polished white rock and dark wood fitted around the doors, windows, and in between the various sections. Viera pointed to the tower.

"It's The Oracles Guild," Maerna said. "We call it The Guild for short."

"Does the highest part have a name?"

"The topmost feature is the Spire. It's where my mother, Nimue, who is the High Oracle, performs Divinations." Fondness filled Maerna's features. "She splits her time between the castle and The Guild, but she doesn't hold quarters there unless my father is away."

Viera's eyes shifted to some smaller but still impressive structures outside the castle. "What are these… wait, I've got this, they're for the Elements." She glanced from building to building, and it was her turn to rise up in the saddle. "Whoa! Some addle-brained wanker plastered a hearth onto the banner for Fire!"

Maerna snorted into her sleeve. "I'm sure you'll see that's fixed to your liking in no time. While we're on these buildings, let me explain which is which." Viera nodded, but she wasn't happy with what had been done—for all to see—to the banner degrading her Element.

Maerna waited a moment for Viera to collect herself and said, "There are Temples for each Element, obviously seven Temples altogether. The one that's directly south of the castle and abutting the Lockinge River is appropriately the Water Temple."

Viera flicked her reins toward two buildings that were decidedly smaller than the others. "What are those?"

"The one in gold and wood is the Treasurer's Guild. The circular one is for the Runemasters and called Rune House. Law enforcement is mostly tied to Rune House. It's also where breakers are made. From here, it kind of looks like one too."

"I definitely don't need to be told about them." Viera boosted herself a little higher in the saddle. "Where's the Healers Guild? I don't see anything with a Healer's sigil."

Gavyn broke off a twig and squeezed it until sap stuck to his fingers, showing it to her. "You wouldn't. Each Temple has its own Infirmary, and the castle has one as well. Healers circulate between all the Temples, regardless of Element. Sometimes an injury requires the coolness and ease of Water or the balm and Wood of a plant. Other times, Fire cauterizes wounds. We don't limit ourselves to what's in one Temple."

Viera spotted the Earth Temple. "Look at the flowering hedges lining the way."

"Aye, flowering plants adorn the path, but what gives us sustenance is in the large pots in the front. Across from Earth is the Wood Temple. A lane of trees marks the way to it."

Out of the corner of her eye, Viera could make out the Air Temple's blue and white airstreams, crossing over an orange circle, displayed on a large sign at the structure's entrance. Even from their distance on The Ridge, chimes could be heard tinkling in the wind.

Across from that building, the Ice Temple's reflecting glass shimmered in the morning light; shades of gray, blue, and white banners were on proud display, its symbols glittering on the flags like fresh snowflakes in the sun. Maerna said that she found the entire image beautiful, and Viera agreed.

By contrast, to the east of the Water Temple, a dark gothic structure, built with straight-line architecture, displayed spires instead of banners that marked the way leading into the building. Engraved upon the front of the edifice was the Metal symbol.

When finished with the Temples of The Seven Elements, Viera thanked them for making something simple that could have been quite complicated.

Soon, the Knights brought their horses into formation, and the signal was given to move out. "Come," Gavyn said, guiding them back around through the trees and brush. "The Hearth awaits."

"Ready to meet your new home?" Maerna said, extending her hand to Viera.

Viera squeezed Maerna's outstretched hand. "Aye."

The wagons followed the Knights, and halfway down The Ridge the road split in two directions. Arthwyr motioned and the procession followed him on the wider of the roads. Within minutes, two Knights approached from Elden's Hearth and greeted their King. Percyval Rheged led the way, with a black inverted chevron and three ravens sewn into the fabric of a gray banner flapping behind him. Aglovale Pellinore followed, displaying a purple standard bearing a yellow lion.

Arthwyr and Myrddin rode side-by-side, and the King said to his main advisor, "For as long as the flames light the hearth of Fire, Evermore will stand."

If Viera could have heard this, she might have had a different opinion of the Fire banner she'd found so demeaning.

CHAPTER 31

HOME SWEET HOME

Progress officially ended as the King and his retinue arrived on the arrival landing of the castle grounds, because what followed was a frothing mass of humanity moving around without any sense of direction whatsoever. Nine small siblings running helter-skelter was indicative of the disorganization of the entire ceremony. Viera learned that the harried mother trying to corral her brood was Tippy Foxbury alongside her equally agitated Bond, Kae Kyner, the Seneschal of Evermore and Majordomo at the castle. For Tippy's part, she was a Wood Elemental and classified as a Wood Sister, which was a prestigious title. At some point, the middle Foxbury triplet, Garyth, emerged from the crowd and assisted in separating a blond seven-year-old Kyner boy from intimidating his sister with earsplitting calls as the older girl screamed, "Mum! Rory thinks he's a Griffin again!"

Viera took in everything Maerna was telling her until a small gray cat skittered to her side. Patches of fur stuck out from it, scars lined its face, and its bushy tail kinked in two places.

Viera called to the cat and put out her hand to pet it, but it arched its back. Not put off by this, she clicked her tongue and this time presented her hand, palm up. The feline caressed her fingers with its pink nose, and Viera was able to scratch behind its ears, without incident.

"Aren't you a pretty puss?" Viera said, wanting the animal to like her even though her remark was far from what she really thought of the cat's appearance.

A condescending sniff announced Jocelyn, her cronies at her side. Blue swirled into a pattern near Jocelyn's fingertips, and a globe full of water formed over the cat. With a snap of her fingers, Jocelyn released the water. The cat squealed as if run over by a cart, and it raced across the landing in front of the castle.

Viera rolled up her sleeves. "What did it ever do to you?"

"Nothing, but you liked it." Jocelyn sniffed. "That's enough reason for me."

Before Viera could grab Jocelyn by the hair, Palamedes shouted, "Oi! I found Moggy!"

High-pitched yowls marked the cat's bouncing in the air, its kinked tail thrashing like the blades of a fan just starting up. Palamedes ran behind the cat and created a swirling orange array that writhed into intricate spirals and curlicues.

Galahad rushed over to Palamedes, screaming, "Hells, Palamedes, put Moggy down!"

"He doesn't like heights?" Palamedes said, his tone indicating he knew well the answer.

"No, he doesn't enjoy heights!"

Palamedes lowered Moggy and Galahad grabbed his cat. Still terrified from Jocelyn's cruelty, the animal latched onto the Knight's robe and yowled the same piteous howl as earlier. Fortunately for Galahad and the cat, Trystan sauntered up and disentangled Moggy's claws from Galahad's many layers of garments.

His good deed done, Trystan walked off. Galahad was about to give Palamedes a piece of his mind, and maybe his boot, when the Saracen lad let out a sharp yelp as a tall man with darker skin, but lighter than the boy's, began alternating rubbing his knuckles across the young troublemaker's head and smacking his rump with a slipper.

Viera looked between this man and Palamedes. His hair was much shorter than the boy's shaggy locks, but the raven color and texture were a perfect match. He wore crimson-and-ebony brocaded fabric displaying gold-embroidered geometric shapes and flowers.

The man twirled Palamedes around to face him and tucked the slipper into his pocket. With a lightly accented tenor, he asked, "What did a little idiot learn about cats today that he should've learned in Saraceni a long time ago?"

Palamedes grumbled, "They don't like water… or air, I guess. I—"

Before the boy could finish his latest round of inanity, Segwarides ran over and captured the tall man in a bear hug. When the pair pulled apart, they gripped each other's shoulders. There was pure silk on the tongue each man used to communicate with the other, the flow of conversation smooth like water but with a depth that warmed like fire. They could be cursing each other to the Hells and back, for all Viera knew, but it still sounded poetic.

They stopped talking, and the strength of the taller man's affect seemed to consume all light. There was little denying the quiet power he exuded, as it was clear he could lead a realm with a mere flick of his fingers or subdue an army with a carefully crafted lift of an eyebrow. From travelers going through her village, Viera had heard stories of large black cats that commanded a preternatural sense of majesty in lands far east of Evermore. She envisioned this man commanding the same level of respect as the sveltest of leopards.

Stepping around Segwarides, the man loomed over Viera and asked, "Who is this lass?"

Myrddin had arrived in time to hear the question, and he stood beside her and placed his arm around her shoulder. He said in a proud tone, "Safir, this is my new Apprentice, Viera Tillwith. Viera, this is the true Shahanshah of Saraceni, Safir Sasania."

"Shah what?" she asked, glancing between the three Sasanias.

"King would be the nearest translation in our language," Myrddin said.

"King?" Her gaze darted to Arthwyr standing on the other side of the landing amid the Kyner children, with Maryck grimacing, as the children darted close and clattered off with high-pitched squeals when the King caught and tickled them. "More than one lives in Evermore?"

"Aye," Myrddin said and nodded, "There are others you will also meet who are welcome guests and allies of Evermore." He gestured toward Segwarides. "Safir is Segwarides' twin, and of course that makes him Palamedes' brother, as well."

Viera's gaze slid over to Tippy Kyner, who was chasing after her children. One little boy yanked on Gales' tail and used it to drape over his curls like a wig. Another boy licked the muzzle of Ector's horse, and the animal rewarded him with a huge slobber.

Safir shuddered. "Our mother was smart. She stopped after that little idiot." He winked at Palamedes. "One lunatic is enough to have in the family."

Palamedes brayed until a shadow swooped low over him. With its wings flapping loudly, a large raven flew past Viera. The bird landed on Percyval Rheged's shoulder and stuck out its leg. As the Chancellor of Evermore took the letter from a case on the bird's thigh, the raven squawked and poked its beak against the Lord's neck.

"All right, Fenius, I see my grandson has spoiled you." Percyval handed the bird a strip of jerky he kept in a pocket in his robe, and in a booming voice so everyone could hear, he announced: "Our Queen sends her blessings and welcomes you back, and now she is prepared to receive you formally. Tippy, you're summoned to return for your Seven Sister duties. Lady Gorre awaits you outside the Throne Room."

Jocelyn, who was standing right next to Percyval, stiffened. "My apologies, Milord, but we've just arrived. Should we not present ourselves without the dust of travel still upon us?"

His green gaze crinkling, Percyval said, "You can, Milady, if you wish to offend Her Majesty."

Percyval organized the group who was to meet with the Queen first. Panic surged through Viera when she discovered she was not going to be with the Sasanias, Healers, Galahad, or Constantine. However, she let out a huge sigh of relief when she spotted Myrddin, Maerna, and Lance in the same line with her.

At the crunch of boots against hard ground, Viera glanced at Bedwyr leaving Carydoc and walking over to Percyval. "Safe to assume I'm invited to be in this group," he said to the venerable Lord Rheged. "It wouldn't be a party otherwise."

Percyval grunted. "In your case, it's not an invitation but an order. Though, we all know how you abide by those." He gave Bedwyr an uncompromising look and joined the others dispersing from Progress. "Wait here until someone is sent to accompany you to the Throne Room, and if you're smart you won't leave."

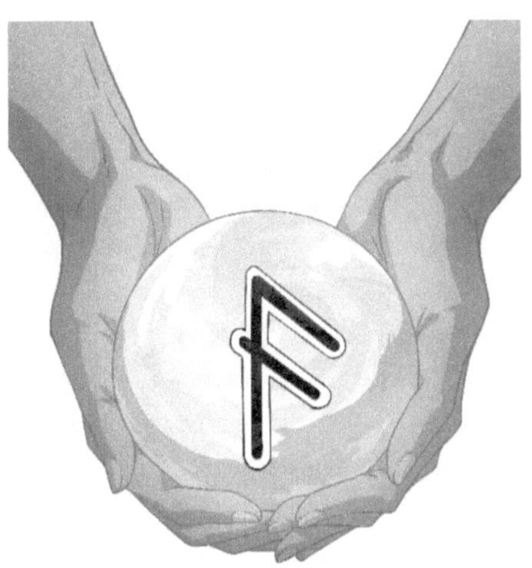

CHAPTER 32

WOMEN OF SIGHT

Standing outside the massive doors that led inside the castle, Viera bounced on the balls of her feet until Myrddin seized her by the shoulders. When she squirmed, he tightened his hold and she settled down. As she jutted out her lower lip, he tweaked her ears and she bolted from his grasp.

"I'm bored." She sent her one-hundredth glance to the doors. "How long must we wait?"

"Until the Oracles grace us with their presence and tell us to come forward," Myrddin said and patted her shoulder. "Be patient, Wart. It's called tradition."

Grumbling, Viera trailed her gaze over the stairs to the landing. A large statue of a man overlooked the steps, the sun glinting off of the metal band encircling the crown covering his long hair. The Elemental and Oracle runes were engraved in the crown.

She tugged on Myrddin's sleeve and pointed at the statue. "Who's that supposed to be?" She arched her eyebrows as she had seen Myrddin do many times. "He looks a little like King Arthwyr."

"That's because he's Cymry Pendragon, the first King of Evermore."

"I don't see a statue of his Queen."

"Elden was the first High Oracle of Evermore. Hence, Elden's Hearth. Her statue is in front of the Oracles Guild."

"Are there statues at all the Temples?"

"Aye. Each of the first Heads of The Seven Houses has a statue. When we visit the Fire Temple, you'll see Llewelyn behind the landing altar."

Heavy wooden doors boomed open and a female clad in gray robes exited the castle. Wind pulled her almost all-black tresses into a long cascade down her back. In similar attire, another woman appeared behind the first. Her medium-blond hair with its silver streaks gleamed beneath the sun.

The first woman came toward the returning nobles, the other woman trailing behind, her ornate cane rapping on the stone. A flicker of white preceded a much younger woman arriving at the top of the stairs. Silvery white hair formed a halo over her head, her white cloak a blur with the sweep of her mane. Purple and magenta flowers teased the edges of her skirt.

The corset she wore was another thing. The pale swell of the woman's ample bosom was pushed up, her cleavage on full display for any who dared to look.

Leather creaked, fabric rustled, and metal jingled in a ripple effect as everyone bowed, knelt, or curtseyed to these women, whom someone in the crowd murmured were the Oracles.

Viera bowed at the waist to the approaching trio until an elbow jabbed her in the side. She heard a hiss to find it coming from Maerna, who had just sidled up next to her. Maerna bent one knee, swept one foot behind her, and held her long skirts outward. Scrambling to change the greeting to a curtsey, Viera spied the first woman pursing her lips.

Dipping her chin, Maerna whispered, "Nimue Abe, my mother and the High Oracle of The Guild."

If that was not surprising enough, the younger woman drifted past the High Oracle, advancing toward Viera as though they were old friends, her deep pink eyes unnerving in their intensity and confidence.

When she drew even with Viera, she slowed and huskily purred, "About time, little phoenix. We've been waiting for you."

She swiveled away just as quickly as she had arrived, leaving Viera to whisper to Maerna, "Who is she?"

"Lady Eerie Chia," Maerna replied just as softly. "Her mother, Aisling Chia, is the woman behind my mother. Eerie is Carydoc Ynyr's daughter and—"

"Hello, Beloved, miss me?" Eerie said, her voice more than loud enough to drown out Maerna's quiet delivery.

Eerie stepped over to Bedwyr, hooked her arms over his black-leather-clad shoulders and dragged the Knight down to her for a kiss. Equally shocking to Viera, and by the stunned looks on their faces, to Jocelyn and the rest of the Maids as well, he pulled Eerie flush against his doublet and let the kiss linger.

CHAPTER 33

MINE

Footsteps echoed and metal rang against the gray stone of the corridors. Along the walls, torches and sconces lined the corridor as strange stones glowed in some places. Viera prodded one such stone and jolted backward; nothing happened.

Nimue's velvety voice jarred Viera's attention from the stone. "They're lumistones. Only Metal or Earth Elementals can light them."

Enthralled with the cast of violet, Viera poked it again. She covered the lumistone, marveling at the coolness until her hand warmed the surface. Red glowed beneath her skin.

When she turned toward Nimue, the woman lengthened her stride and met Aisling's pace. During Myrddin's introduction of Viera as his ward, Nimue had been less than welcoming.

Stopping in front of a suit of armor, Viera considered steel that was polished to such a high shine it blinded when the lumistones reflected over it. They all looked the same, but Eerie had said to look for the differences amid the many. Strange, and apparently Eerie was one touched with an Oracle's Sight like her mother, Lady Aisling.

After rattling the debuting Summer Court, Eerie had flounced toward the stables and purred in her wake. "Don't be late, lover. I want my souvenir, but first there's a wittle baby brother I must find."

Bedwyr had reached into his pocket and said, "I'll give it to you now."

Eerie licked her lips. "Sexy times on the landing?"

He clasped a string of gray pearls about her throat. "We'll exchange the second one in private, hmm?"

She peeked past Bedwyr's shoulder to the noble girls, the burn of her gaze having a few shrinking from her. "Welcome to Court, Ladies. Be mindful of where and on who you put your fingers." She licked a long strip along his neck and nipped his ear. "Don't keep me waiting too long, Beloved. I'll start without you."

The sudden groan of metal had Viera stilling and focusing on another suit of armor. In its gloved grip was a broom, and the helmet was a butter churn with a feather duster seemingly sprouting from its top like a potted plant. She snorted at the face of a fox drawn on the helmet.

As she stared at the weird mishmash, air whispered over her neck, fingers ghosted along her skin, and a breath blew against the shell of her ear. Whipping around, she found no one was there, but she observed the drift of fabric at the far end of the long corridor. Her pulse hammered in her ears, only to be overpowered by the click of boots in the distance. *How is it possible something could have gotten that far away so soon?*

As she turned to hurry after the others and the corridors twisted about into a labyrinth, a thick nasally voice murmured, *"Come, little Usagi. Come find the night."*

This was followed by other voices too low to make sense of what they were saying, even when she stepped out into a large atrium with marble stairs leading up to a magnificent landing that had seen better days. On the second level, two massive dark doors loomed like the ones rumored to lead into the depths of the Hells.

With each step Viera took, greater chills crept through her. Even in the dim lighting, a spider web full of dust could be seen waving in the air that whistled through a broken window. Dirty gray curtains hung loose and ragged as glass lay scattered on the window ledge and floor.

Then she heard, *"Ni-San. Ni-San,"* the words bouncing over the cold stone walls. Viera trembled as the single voice shifted from one to two different speakers, each repeating, *"Ni-San. Ni-San,"* in unison—and becoming so loud it hurt her ears.

At the clamor of heavy footsteps and chainmail clinking, the hair rose on the back of her neck. Leather rasped over cloth and crackled in her ears as she was consumed by the smell of soaked fabric and sodden animal hide. A shrill wind swirled, and cold settled over her like ice on bare ankles.

Garbled and charged with despair, a deep baritone reverberated through her bones: *"Eyes on the floor. Don't look up. Don't meet his gaze. Don't."*

Viera whimpered as this voice changed into a child's lilting sob: *"Ni-San, I'm afraid. Ni-San, will the Marshal rise again? Please, Ni-San."*

A darker rumbling tone drowned out the light whimsy of this latest voice, saying: *"Close your eyes. Tip your head back. Lean. Wade into the light."*

The voices rose together, a husky growl overtaking the jumbled cacophony with one word: *"Mine."*

Wood groaned and Viera squinted at a dark patch on the dusty steps. *How had I not seen that?* As she stared, the patch grew outward—black and slick—and spilled down the stairs.

Another voice husked, not like any of the others but a seeming combination of all of them: *"Mine. You're mine. Evermore, mine."*

With panic laying siege to her body, Viera stumbled in circles around the atrium. The room morphed between decrepit and bright and polished—and back again. Near the stairs, two figures slowly came into focus. A crowned man ascended and another followed. Both men stilled as if they had heard something and turned toward Viera.

Ah, Bedwyr and Arthwyr.

Except they weren't. The dark ochre of the second man's hair was shorter than Bedwyr kept his, but the unnerving crimson of his gaze could be none other than Jormund's—the man who led his forces through the Valley. And the madness in the crowned man's eyes was not anything Viera had ever seen in Arthwyr's gaze. The hair on Viera's arms stood straight as she recognized Uther Pendragon.

Jormund prowled closer, dark promise settling upon his features. Delight glinted in Uther Pendragon's gaze as he unsheathed the engraved reptilian hilt of his infamous blade, *Vorpal,* and brandished it at Viera.

Chainmail rattled in the shadows nearest her, and four figures strode forward. As she glanced around the atrium, more shock rippled through her as the dingy staircase returned to the gleaming glory of its early years. A shadowy figure—a younger Lance—drifted past Viera, the robes of his office mirrored in a woman walking beside him.

Viera blinked. *Are you Lance's wife, Lady Elaine DuLac?*

Two more men followed the pair; one, a much younger Myrddin.

The third man stopped next to Viera, his chestnut-brown hair framing his blue eyes. *Who?* She could not shake that she knew him from somewhere. He smiled at her as Myrddin approached, and he turned to him.

An arm grabbed her from behind, and she released a screech that echoed throughout the atrium. Thrusting her hand against this person's chest, Fire warmed her fingertips before she recognized who it was, fell into Lance's arms, and fainted.

When she came to, Viera looked past Lance to a man with a blend of yellow highlights laced through his sandy hair and beard. His icy blue gaze swept over her. She didn't know who he was, but when the frigidness of his stare softened, his similarity to Ulrich Pendragon became undeniable. The relaxed slope of his shoulders revealed a white unicorn bowing its head to a cross on a heart-shaped emblem embroidered upon the sleeves of his outer robe.

He asked, "May I touch you, lass? Just want to make sure that you're not hurt."

She glanced at Lance, who nodded, and she did as well. "This is Lord Balin Cameliard," Lance said, rubbing her shoulders, "The Chamberlain of Evermore and Queen's brother."

Balin ran his fingers over her, keeping his moves slow and careful while lingering on her face, throat, and arms—and nowhere else. He rolled on his feet and rooted through his trouser pockets. "She's chilled. Likely from shock. Keep an eye on her." He opened a tin, broke off a thin brown square, and passed it to her. "Thin mint. Should calm you down some."

Viera eyed it from deep below her eyelashes and turned away.

Balin let out a long sigh. "Lance, for the love of Evermore, please tell me she knows what chocolate is." He groaned. "She looks like I just offered her manure to eat."

"Probably thinks you did. She's a peasant from the Valley." Lance took the square and broke it in half, popped a piece in his mouth, and made a show of eating it. "See, Viera. Perfectly safe." He handed her the remaining part.

Reluctant, and waiting for him to spit it out, Viera took a small nibble on the edge. As soon as the sweetness teased her tongue, she devoured the rest.

Balin offered her a few more squares. "So, Viera, is it?"

She hummed confirmation as she licked at the roof of her mouth.

"Want to tell us what happened? Take your time."

From behind him, Bedwyr moved stiffly into the room. He glared at the two doors shrouded in darkness that harkened across the antechamber like sentries indeed guarding the gates to The Hells.

Swallowing around the thick coating of chocolate and mint on her tongue, Viera swept her gaze over the steps. Once more, dust lay thick and dreary like a blanket of gray snow. Beneath the heavy layer of ruin and forgotten time, the black spill was no longer visible. The four who had been in the atrium were gone, as well. She had expected to glimpse at least the shadows of the Mad King and his most loyal minions. But nothing except the wind giving off the haunting sounds of a sobbing child filled the dank air.

Lance's voice broke through her musings: "Can you tell us what you saw?"

"Aye," she managed to say after considerable time passed. "A child kept crying. Terrified. I still hear it. Afraid the Marshal would come." She turned her head away.

Striding past her, Bedwyr stalked the stairs with his cloak billowing behind him like a wraith rising from the ashes of a funeral pyre. He stopped and scraped his boot over the spot where Jormund had stood. "Stop blubbering," he said to Viera. "It's in the past, and the past can't hurt anyone anymore."

Her words poured from her mouth like boiling water: "Aye, but the Marshal… I think it was him… he insisted, 'Mine!' over and over."

CHAPTER 34

THE QUEEN OF FOOLS

Sunlight streamed through large bay windows, the Elemental and Oracle symbols gleaming from floor plates on the white marble floor. Silver room appointments lightened the Throne Room further, lumistones opal and mother-of-pearl detailing adding their own special luminescence. Along the walls, flowers in ornate boxes provided a striking array of reds, blues, pinks, and yellows. Green vines were draped from wooden trellises placed along the bottoms of the windows, and long strands of blue and violet morning glories created a perfect contrast to the ivory paneling.

Maerna was savouring the airiness of the spring blooms when a growl drew her attention to Viera scuttling backward from stepping on Bedwyr's boot.

Bedwyr swiveled on his heel. "Stop gawping at the crown molding."

"Crown molding my arse, you ruddy Troll." Viera kicked the back of his boot, causing him to stumble. "Oops. Did I do that? My apologies, Milord."

"If you two don't behave," Arthwyr said, setting a hand on their shoulders, "I'm going to treat you to my favourite punishment."

Maerna swallowed and looked at the seam of her boot.

"I'll hang you off a parapet, if you put us in that ruddy Get-A-Long tunic." Bedwyr gripped Arthwyr's sleeve and dropped the limb from him. "You'll never find her—Alive."

A throat cleared and all attention went to the Seven Sisters. Two of the Seven Sisters drew back their shoulders and exchanged looks as an older one of "theirs" stalked forward like an uncaged cat on the prowl. The Gorre family symbol from Ewain's robes adorned her sleeves. Her gray hair, pulled back into a tight bun, gave off an equally pinched expression, her thin lips further accentuating the severity in the metallic-blue stare that seemed etched into her eyes.

"You had best fix your approach or you'll be out these doors," the woman said in the same cultured accent that Ewain had, poise dripping from her address and manner.

Not a person in the welcoming party didn't stiffen and pull themselves from a slouch. Even Arthwyr bowed to the woman, saying, "Good morn, Lady Saris. A pleasure for you to greet me—"

The woman narrowed her eyes. "Your mother would be beside herself with that posture and address. Stop slouching."

Arthwyr straightened, his features coloring under her remonstration. "Aye, Lady Gorre."

"Much better." She glared over her shoulder at a woman in Earth robes chortling. "Anything to add, Lady Rheged?"

"No, darling," Lady Rheged drawled, "You've once more shriveled the most stalwart of men with a tongue sharp as an asp and frown as stern as a gargoyle."

Maerna said to Viera, "The one in blue and purple robes is Lady Saris Gorre. She's over sixty seasons, the Water Sister of the Seven Sisters, and a retired Healer. She married a guard of the Court and had nine children. Many of them are highly prized Healers in the Elven and Dwarven Courts north of us. The one in Earth robes is Lady Blanche Rheged and one of the Heads of Rheged House."

Viera tugged at Maerna's sleeve. "What's with this Seven Sisters thing?"

"The Queen has an entourage of Seven Sisters, each representing a different Element. Seven Knights also serve as her envoys. You've already met three of them."

"I have?"

"Aye. Your new self-appointed Bampi—the one my father introduced as his primary Master when he escorted us into the Hearth—

Lord Aglovale Pellinore is the first. Lord Garyth from the landing, and the Queen's brother, Balin Cameliard."

"Are The Seven Sisters related to the Queen in some way?"

"Nay. They come from different families. Their main credential is their Element and the Queen's approval. Though, some are from Queen Igraine's reign like Ladies Saris and Blanche."

The Seven Sisters formed a line that extended from a staircase leading to not one but four thrones on a raised section at the rear of the massive room. A horn blared once, and The Seven Sisters waved everyone onward and toward the thrones arranged for the Royal Pair and their immediate heirs. The thrones were intricately carved from a combination of ash, oak, holly, and yew to symbolize the perpetuation of Evermore via the trees that ever remained green even in the middle of winter.

Maerna slowed and bent to murmur when Arthwyr sputtered, "Feckin' Hells!"

On the raised dais, a lone figure lounged with legs swaying over the King of Evermore's throne and his head lazing in the Queen's lap, a platter of cheese and grapes within his arm's reach, on a small table. He sipped from a golden goblet encrusted in jewels.

Viera, eyes bulging, twisted from Maerna's grasp. "Who is he, and why haven't the guards lashed him to a pole so he can be drawn and quartered?"

Meeting Viera's wide-eyed stare, Maerna kept her tone even but with more than a hint of sarcasm. "*That* is a Knight of the Eclipse, Lord Dagonet Vagary, the man who might well have been King instead of Arthwyr."

Before Viera could ask any of the hundred questions likely running around in her head, a jester's bells rang from Dagonet's curved footwear.

He said to Arthwyr, who was stepping up to his throne, "Ah, the prodigal King has returned to his castle at last." He tossed a grape and caught it in his mouth. "Alas, a usurper has arisen to claim the royal perch. Balanced be, what will ye do, oh, great Lord King of Evermore?"

Arthwyr scoffed. "Dagonet, I see you've made yourself at home."

"When have I never been at home, dear King?"

"Indeed."

Dagonet scratched the black star-shaped mane about his neck. Beneath the bay windows, his patchwork doublet of silver, black, and gold diamonds gleamed from the sunlight entering the room. Waggling his eyebrows, he sipped from the goblet.

"Who let the Court Fool usurp good reason and replace me so soon," Arthwyr said, fixing a wounded look at Vagary and Guinevere. "Dear wife, you have betrayed me and laid quite the hurt upon my heart."

The Queen looked up from the man in her lap. "There was a usurper?" She released a mirthless laugh. "Who knew there was a change in the Court Fool I sit next to?"

Arthwyr blinked and said nothing. Dagonet clattered down the stairs, burgundy half-skirt flouncing around his hips, and barreled into Bedwyr. The diamond-shaped Vagary emblem of common theater and marionette masks rippled. The gold one's teeth bore a feral grin as the silver mask's mouth dipped and three tear droplets dotted its cheek. Dagonet kissed Bedwyr's cheeks and rumpled his hair into thorough debauchery, flouncing to the doors and hooking his arm through Lance's to spirit them into the hallway.

Guinevere rose, a glimmer of sage green sliding over her blue and gray robes. She descended the steps leading to and from the thrones, her glittering train trailing behind her. The clink of eleven ice gems shone in her hair and sent prisms of color over the stairs. Striding forward, Balin held out his hand for his sister and tucked her arm under his.

As they moved forward and approached Myrddin, she pulled her hand away and said to him, "Introduce our future Ladies of the Court, Lord Emrys."

As Myrddin posed one girl at a time in front of Guinevere, each girl curtseyed and held the position until the Queen waved her off. When it got to Viera, Myrddin hesitated a moment and said, "Viera, ah, Viera Tillwith, Your Majesty."

Guinevere leveled him with a cold stare. "Anything else with that, Lord Emrys, or am I to guess?"

A bright flush overwhelmed his features. "She's my new ward."

"Of course." She stared at Viera and returned to Myrddin. "I've heard of this girl, and I wish you well with her. From what I'm told, you'll need my good wishes."

The Queen waved for Blanche Rheged, the Bond to Percyval Rheged. The Earth Sister curtseyed to the Queen, who said, "Please call in your Rheged boys, Lady Rheged. House Rheged and Tippy will escort the new Ladies of the Court to their quarters."

Lady Rheged turned her attention to ticking over each girl with the calculation of a huntress in her vibrant green stare. With a toss of her dyed black hair, she pinched Brynn's cheek and strolled by her. "Yes, Your Majesty," she said, her accent a derogative drawl, "Quite the darlings. Hardly can wait to see which little strumpets become… oh, yes… such belles of the ball at Summer Court."

After the Earth Sister slipped outside, Guinevere had the entire group of Maids stand in a single row. She said, "You will be our newest Summer Court, and I hope you will be a credit to each of your Houses." She walked along the line so each girl could curtsey to her. "I do not tolerate certain behaviours in my Court. You are all potentials for my sons—" pausing pointedly in front of Jocelyn and Viera— "regardless of your station. Please take this to heart. Don't give me cause to be disappointed."

In unison, they said, "Aye, Your Majesty."

Guinevere allowed Balin to take her hand again, and they made their way to Arthwyr, who was leaning against a pillar and appearing amused at his wife's address to the Ladies of the Court.

Guinevere said, "I'm glad you find me so entertaining. If you wish, Arthwyr, you may take your Throne back. Dagonet has left, so one fool for another is not much of a loss."

CHAPTER 35

THE KING'S REVEAL

Maerna flinched at the stanchions clapping over the marble floor. A peek toward the doors revealed Blanche entering with two men in Rheged Wood livery flanking her in rigid unison. The men stopped; the shared green of their gazes locked forward with only the lightest shading in the younger man's. As if aware of her attention, the younger slanted his gaze toward her and winked.

Tippy departed from the line of Seven Sisters and approached them. "Time to sort you into your new rooms, young misses. This is Lord Eryck Rheged, heir apparent of Rheged," she said, signaling for the youth to join her and indicating the older man, "and his uncle, Lord Elyan Rheged. They will help get everyone situated, so you can ask us any questions you may have."

Pity reared in Maerna when Eryck escorted the girls from the Throne Room. Despite the Queen's warning, this bunch was primed for flirting—and then some. Maerna watched Jocelyn and Felicia catch up to Eryck before they had even left the room, fluttering their fans more in his face than theirs, as Brynn trailed behind them.

Guinevere waited for them to exit and groused, "It begins." She drifted toward Bedwyr, hesitancy slowing her pace until she was in front of him. "Constantine sent word you were injured in Glastonbury. Anything I need to know, my little light?"

"Nay," he said, rigidly and squinted. "Just a few discontented curs that I gelded."

Toying with her sleeves, the Queen sighed. "Take care of yourself. You know that I see you as my own."

"Really? Then you should see to your own stepson, Your Majesty."

The King shot up from his slouch. "Dammit, Bedwyr!"

Her Ice cracked in Guinevere's voice. "Husband."

Arthwyr swallowed. "It appears my father has defamed me again, Beloved." His expression faltered at the twinkle of ice crystals and a drop in the room's temperature caused by Guinevere's ire. "We should outlaw First Night. It's rife with problems."

"Indeed," the Queen said as a crack pealed in the air and a thin coating of ice settled upon everyone.

Harsh, rapid breathing drew Arthwyr's stare to Balin, who stood with his arms pinned to his sides. "How could this come to be?" Balin grieved. "Didn't you take a draught to ensure no bastards?"

Arthwyr took a few steps from his brother-in-law. "My father assured me the lass had taken it."

"Of course." Guinevere slipped her arm into the crook of her brother's. "What is your bastard's name, and where is he now?"

"Mordred. He lives in Porthcrawl with his mother, Ursula."

"What do they want? A title? Formal recognition? The throne?"

"Nothing. I only spoke to his mother." Arthwyr lowered his voice. "The boy doesn't know anything about me."

Guinevere rubbed her temples. "I must think on this."

"How do you wish to handle delivering the news to my uncle and cousin?"

The Queen dropped her hands as if her head had caught fire. "For the love of Evermore, no! This stays in this room. I don't want a breath of it outside these doors."

"Kae and Ector should know."

Air stirred Air Sister Yuliya Blumenthal's, orange, blue, and white Air robes. "Not with how Ector is. The news will reach Porthcrawl by lunch."

Arthwyr glowered at the Seven Sisters, who returned his regard with unimpressed glares.

"It's in our best interest to keep it hushed." Myrddin thumped Arthwyr's arm. "Remember how Ector reacted when the princes were born?"

"He had Maryck on the highest turret," Guinevere said, huffing, "telling him nonsense about light, shadows, and the sun touching every bloody thing. Then, repeated it with Ulrich."

"Then not a peep shall occur outside of here," Arthwyr said, shaking his finger at Bedwyr. "Truly, you little brat. Not a word."

Bedwyr smirked. "The lark has landed."

"I'll give you the lark has landed, you ar—"

Guinevere stepped on Arthwyr's foot, saying, "And don't even pretend you planned to inform me. You and I will have a private meal tonight, Husband. We have much to discuss."

CHAPTER 36
THE ANCIENTS

Maerna and Viera had to wait for some of the other Maids to get settled in before they could go to the Emrys Chamber. Maerna took Viera for a short tour of their section of the castle, arms linked together as if the girls were old friends. She spotted some royal guests, as she referred to them, and a giggle caught in her throat as she squealed, "Cousin, my Cousin!" to the younger royal lad.

The boy released an eager laugh, slipping past his Elemental Master and dropping all formality as he scooted toward Maerna.

She curtseyed to him and fawned, "Your Highness!"

He gave her a gentle frown. "None of that stuffy stuff when I'm free of my duties. You know it's Wil or Wilhelm." Her fifteen-winter cousin yanked her upright.

Maerna said to Viera, "This is my distant but Royal cousin, Prince Wilhelm Auraboralis. He'll rule the human realm of Auraboralis in the north after his father, King Anders." She dropped her voice to a low murmur. "He's my favourite cousin, though you're in for a time of it with my mother's side." She signaled to Viera, by shifting her eyes, that she'd explain the meaning of that remark later.

Viera curtseyed. "Milord."

Myrddin had told Maerna that Wil was in Ice training with King Bercylac Bredbeddle, the Elven King of Ribeena. Maerna had found many things fascinating about the Elven King when she first met him years ago: light-green skin, multicolored hair, and that he was now 382 winters old; but, strangest of all to her, he was an Elf who stood 5-feet 10-inches tall. It was after encountering his family and even guards that she realized Elves were far taller than the legends let on and came in as many colors as what existed in the world.

She asked Wil, "How is the Ice training with Bercylac going?"

"Fine, I've just learned—"

"He means the Ice Pop taught him how to sneeze out a blizzard!" a gruff voice barked as a tiny well-muscled man thumped toward them, the Elven King at his side.

Maerna caught a glimpse of the green triangular symbol of a war hammer crossed with a shepherd's hook sewn on the shoulder of his tunic. At 4-feet 5-inches, Lord Gereant Dumnonia was the Dwarven King of Dumnonia and taller than most in his realm. He was one of the oldest Dwarves at 547 autumns.

Gereant wrapped his muscular arms around Maerna and pulled her down to him, his thick red beard scratching her cheek. "Hey, littlest Dragonling, ya bury any Fox Lords while you were out there with Progress?"

All the while Gereant greeted Maerna, she could see Bercylac bending toward Wilhelm. The warmth faded from his aristocratic features, his pupils expanding and drowning out the pink surrounding his irises. Wrenching Wil behind him, Bercylac released a crackling Ice array.

As Bercylac moved to the opposite side of Viera, Gereant whipped around and closed his meaty hand on the battle axe strapped to his belt. Dwarves and Elves were known throughout history for their competitiveness between them. For the pair to take up flanking positions, something must have set them off.

Maerna whirled to learn who had garnered their attention. She groaned. Of course, it was Viera.

Catlike. It was the only word capable of describing the Elven King slinking toward Viera. There were wildcats in the woods near her home, hunting at night when humans were not around. Sometimes they prowled on the rock outcroppings in the valley. When she harvested truffles, Viera glimpsed their shadows and markings as they blended into the trees and brush. As the Elven King's slit pupils dilated, she took a shaky step backwards, imagining herself hiding in the underbrush as he hunted her.

When the short Dwarven King made his move, the heavy clunks of his metal-tipped boots were a far cry from the graceful glide of the Elven King, and the clatter of his armor created even more racket with each step he took. If nothing else she could easily outrun him. It was the tall winsome Elf who gave Viera pause. The famed Ancients were rumored to be shorter than the Dwarves, but the Elven King was taller than Bedwyr, though around the same height as Nimue, who was tall for a woman.

The Dwarven King was the first to draw his weapon, brandishing his battle axe at Viera and hollering, "Who are ya? And what brings ya here?"

Viera blinked against the sting of tears. She looked to Maerna, who said, "Milords, perhaps you might be so kind as to explain what has you so upset."

"Her kind shouldn't exist." Bercylac flanked Viera. "The Council of Ancients must be informed."

With her heart bounding against her ribs, Viera became lightheaded just as someone shoved her, forcing a yelp from her. The sharp crack of wooden fans snapping open obscured her view and silver gleamed from its edges.

With both fans on full display, Bedwyr stood beside Viera. Using the fans as a guard, he guided Viera away from the Ancients and to safety behind Maerna. Bedwyr checked Viera over. Satisfied she hadn't been harmed, he said to the Kings, "I'm not supposed to exist either. What makes you think the same of her?"

The morning was looking to be a success until Gereant stood opposite the shock of a lifetime—and at 547 autumns and counting there was not much under the moon and sun that could surprise him anymore. At first, the girl, Viera, didn't inspire much awe. Snarls twisted about in patches of her hair, although the top had been smoothed from the recent introduction to a hairbrush. And even though she wore a Maid's dress, she was of the peasant variant, obvious by the way she walked and carried herself, her awkward curtsey to Wilhelm a definite giveaway.

All of that, in and of itself, wasn't vexing. What had Gereant upset was his not picking up right away on the real oddity the lass presented before Bercylac hit on it. No matter. He stood across from the girl, his battle axe ready and his body bristling for a fight. It surprised him that this was Odin's design for the day.

Wood cracking and steel sending shafts of light across the room drew Gereant up short. He blinked at the Wallach whelp, whose crimson irises had his hair prickling. Gereant marked the fan's smooth steel that lined its wooden panels. They called these deadlier versions Tessen. The wood was very sleek, from the sakura tree in Nihon. Legend had it, bodies were buried under the trees and blood soaked into the roots, staining its flowers pink. There was a point in his expansive lifetime when Gereant had ridiculed the utility of a fan. That day had ended when he saw firsthand what Bedwyr and Shiori Murasaki could do with Tessen. Never again would he underestimate a lady's frivolity repurposed toward creating Twilight for a foe.

As his fingers twitched over the leather adorning his axe's handle, he could count on one hand how many people Bedwyr had opened those fans to defend.

Bercylac stepped forward and said to Bedwyr, "You don't know, do you?"

"I know that you hunt a girl who understands nothing of other Ancients," Bedwyr replied, shifting his weight from one foot to the other and weaving like an alpha wolf seeking to protect his "own" from a challenger. "You have a duty to ease younglings into the way of the Ancients. Scaring this one serves no purpose."

With a sharp inhale, Bercylac said, "You are full of surprises."

Gripping Bedwyr's sleeve, Viera asked, "What is it you don't know?"

Gereant huffed, "He doesn't know what ya are."

Bercylac rapped his fist over Gereant's helmet. "It's fair enough. They haven't been part of The Council of Ancients for several generations." Turning to Viera. "Lass, you have Fae in your blood."

A certain blankness entered her gaze as she asked, "Isn't being Fae good? The Fae are all happy and Fae lights with catching lightning bugs in jars."

Gereant muffled a curse as he secured his battle axe to his belt. This one was painfully ignorant, and he fumed over how she was oblivious to what she was. "Lass, that would be the Seelie. The Light Fae as humans call the fair folk."

"So then, I'm part Seelie?"

Now it was Bercylac's turn to fret, and bitterness swept across his features as he grumbled, "You are part of an Ancient line we have not seen since the early days of The Council. Your kind died out a long time ago."

The girl released Bedwyr's sleeve. "How am I Fae, if I'm not Fae?"

Shoving his hand into his pocket, Gereant closed his fingers over a small sachet. When the tiny metal disc encased in the cloth hummed, chills ran along his spine. Could she be the one they had been waiting for a few centuries for?

As Gereant caught Bercylac's eyes now steeled on Viera, he was certain that the other Ancient felt the same as he did with the other half of the disk he carried, and he said, "There is another type of Fae: the Unseelie. The last known Unseelie was the Unseelie Queen."

Viera asked, "What's the difference between the Seelie and the Unseelie?"

"The Unseelie are the Dark Fae."

Viera's voice shook. "What's that supposed to mean?"

Gereant brought out the pouch and removed the metal disc from it. The hum became more pronounced, and Viera's scent thickened throughout the room, its sharpness coating the Dwarven King's tongue for the first time in hundreds of years. Bercylac tensed next to him and slowly nodded.

"Your blood, lass," Gereant said, stepping away from Viera, "rings of Twilight."

CHAPTER 37

THE HANDS OF THE KEEP

Bells plinked into a rasp in the stone corridor. Mews alerted Lance as he rounded the bend and spied Galahad kneeling on the uneven pavers with a sea of fuzzy little bodies twining around him. Lounging across a burlap sack draped over a wooden crate, Moggy observed the other keep cats as Galahad fed the mousers from a sack of feed flavoured with jerky. Behind Galahad, Trystan held a stack of small bowls that he passed to Galahad. Flicking his fingers to acknowledge the pair, Lance fell into step behind Dagonet, and the Court Fool led the way to the kitchens. With a wiggle of his shoulders, Dagonet skipped toward the doorway as the headiness of roasted beef and baked bread filled the hallway.

Thumping the doorframe, the Fool shouted, "Hark, the return of the prodigal child."

From a long wooden table, a woman slapped at the dough she was kneading and snarled a curse. A yellow headscarf—with vibrant black and red tribal designs—gave away Talia Ward's birthright, a heritage she clung to with fierce determination even when Uther relegated the uniform for castle staff to brown burlap.

After the Duels, Bedwyr had delivered his House's servant robes to Talia in front of the nobility, in line with the time-honored tradition for accepting an applicant into employment. As the newly minted Lord Wallach, the first servant Bedwyr chose—and in the Throne Room no less—was quite the honor. No sooner had Talia shaken out the robes and stared at their nondescript nature, she folded them up and fixed Bedwyr with a crinkled smile that had Lance gulping and shrinking from the looming fallout, which was immediate:

"Child, you need some color in your life," she said, patting Bedwyr's cheek and shooing him off. "Let's just turn these into the rags they're meant to be, and I'll help you find the way."

An hour later, Bedwyr gawked at her in the kitchens until she chanted a childhood song that once scared him and Galahad. *"Tethra skulked from the Lockinge. He reaped me village, but he didn't reap me. The Picts arrived; then, took all who died. Me hid away in the murk and dark; the harbor seals call 'hark' as they bark. Tethra skulked from the Lockinge; he reaped all the survivors but didn't—Sklerp! Crunch! Squelch!"*

Bedwyr never once objected to anything Talia wore, and the running joke around Court was that she could murder another member of the castle's staff and Bedwyr would turn a blind eye.

Shuffling from behind the table, she set her hands on her lean hips. "Oh, now you grace us with your presence, great Ebony Knight!"

Grimacing, Lance bowed to his childhood friend and honorary sister.

"Come now, you behemoth. Where's my hug?" Talia bustled over to him, the slap of her sandals against the wooden floorboards drawing attention to the Ghanaian colors and intricate beading woven into the strap. "You nary see your sister-in-law in weeks, and you stand gawping like yesterday's dead fish."

As Lance held her close, the collar of her robe dipped low and displayed her former slave symbol and her number, *315*. Dark raised skin around her neck matched similar marks about her wrists and ankles. Less than creative subjugators developed a simple enough method for branding their human chattel. Their captors heated chains in the forges and wound the metal around their screaming, thrashing victims.

At the tender age of ten summers, Talia received her brands upon arriving in Porthcrawl. Soon afterwards, in Elden's Hearth, she had been selected to become a Siren for the Red Lantern District. To her good fortune, Kef, the old Kitchen Master of the castle, had bought her contract from the auction house, ensuring that she found service in the kitchens in the castle instead of working for the brothels.

A soft giggle and sharp cackle drew Lance's attention to Micah Vagary and Primula Fiori. The two women sat at the table reserved for kitchen breaks, and they pored over an old tome.

As Lance regarded the book, he noted that it was the registry Kef had kept of all those who worked in the castle. Lance's own name and ward number, *314,* graced the page beneath his fellow wardmate, Jarvis. Lance tapped the edge of the book. "What are you reading about?"

"The three of us were reminiscing," Talia said as she returned to her food preparation table. "A shame Kef didn't see the end."

"He lived long enough to free us."

She daubed a towel under her eyes. "I still can't believe he used all his money and everything else he had to free us so we could serve Lords, Guilds, and Temples instead of whoremongers and pimps."

Lance glanced at the old stool where Kef used to smoke his tobacci, a tin of the crushed leaves left on it each year for him on his birthday. "Kef would've been proud."

Dagonet rounded Lance and played with Micah's hand. He waggled his eyebrows and applied teasing kisses along his Soul Bond's arm. Pulling a breadstick from a basket, she batted him over the head. Encircling her waist, he settled on a wooden bench with her next to him. If Dagonet had been King, today Micah would be the Queen—a far cry from baker. She had accepted her station gladly, however, knowing she had performed a vital role in protecting her husband's true identity during the Draigs' Duels. To some in the Royal Pair's most Inner Circle, she was as responsible as anyone for Arthwyr's ascension to the Throne.

As Talia placed warm rolls and honey on the table, Lance settled in next to Primula. Scooping a few tablespoons of sugar into some dark tea, he said, "Nice to have the Hands of the Keep back."

"Not quite everyone," Dagonet said as he swiped the heel of a roll and popped it into his mouth. "Lord Sagramore has been sniffing around, and some of the servants have had to stay away. Old Cuchulain is as devious and dangerous as ever."

"How so?"

"His consternation grows with his curiosity."

Worry grew into a stone in Lance's stomach. It wouldn't do for certain nobles to know who contributed to the Duels, least of all the participation of anyone in this room. If it got out, there was no telling the effects it would have on commoners, even this long after the Duels was over.

Lance stirred his tea with more vigor than required and sloshed it over the sides of his cup. "Did he find out about any of the Hands?"

Dagonet deferred to Primula, who said, "Nay—" smacking her lips resolutely— "he's chasing ghosts."

Micah looked to Lance. "But can we be sure that Bedwyr maintains his silence?"

"He was one of only a few people who knew that the Hands were involved," Lance replied swiftly. "He could have revealed your secrets many times over. There's certainly no reason for him to do it now."

Micah flicked sugar from her hands as her fingers trembled. "That's not reassuring," she said, peering low beneath her bangs at Lance. "Witch hunts come in many guises, more to peasants than to the nobility. If you might remember, it wasn't that long ago when a Foel Lady pointed a finger and someone burned."

The remark cut Lance to the bone. He was all too aware of House Foel marking his wife a Witch—and the result. His voice rose. "Bedwyr was adamant that the peasantry wasn't involved." Scanning the kitchens for his adopted brother, he couldn't change the subject quick enough. "Where's Jarvis?"

"Your brother isn't the one who brings you here," Dagonet said and scoffed. "A little bird said I'd receive a visit from you and an Emrys' Dragon."

"Who told you that?"

"Trystan."

Lance stilled, his small knife at mid-swipe on buttering a roll. "It's surprising Trystan would take such initiative. Constantine must be more worried than I thought for Trystan to act."

"Aye, right to the point, are we? You're quick to look for insight into Reactives, yet you ignore the quieter student of such learning who's right in front of you. No one gives our church mouse quite as much attention as he is due. I'll give you credit, though, you thought of me." Dagonet ran his finger over the rim of a goblet. "How long will it take for Safir to figure out who he needs to seek for Palamedes?"

Talia picked at the dough stuck to the webbing between her fingers and said to Dagonet, "Look how long it took us, and with what was right under our noses."

"Mistakes were made," Dagonet agreed. "But this time, the boy has people who love and care for him."

Lance pondered where the conversation was going, and admitted, "I might have acquired a Reactive myself. I'll have a better idea when the boy begins formal training at the Battle School this winter."

Micah twirled a strand of her brown hair. "You haven't tested him?"

"I've had limited contact with the boy, whose name is Garrett. I'll know more when he's formally sorted. My concern lies in the similarity he may have to his sister."

The playfulness sapped from Dagonet. "I'm assuming the one you refer to is Myrddin's ward."

"Her name's Viera Tillwith," Lance said, observing the waver of Dagonet's gaze and knowing that the Court Fool dissected everything twenty-fold as he assumed a lazy slouch of his shoulders, which at this moment were stiff and upright.

"How Reactive is she?"

"Bedwyr comes to mind."

"Then there is far more than similarity," Dagonet asserted.

"What do you mean?"

Dagonet traced his fingers over Micah's wrist. "I briefly saw the lass once when she was with Bedwyr. His gaze never strayed too far from her in the Throne Room." He shifted his eyes to his Bond's. "Bedwyr is aware of something. Exactly what, that's the question."

Like any mother worth half her salt, Talia eyed Lance with the fervor of a lioness looking after her cub. The light caught her eyes, and the briefest pattern of a spider web crisscrossed her hazel gaze. "How much do you suppose Bedwyr is seeing of *Her* in this little miss?" she asked.

Lance thumbed a knot in the wood on the tabletop. "Too much, it seems."

CHAPTER 38

GRAMMAR AND COURTLY EXPECTATIONS

Chimes clinking loudly in the rafters drew Viera's attention from the ebb and flow of the voices that were making her very nervous. Perched on a couch in her Master's chamber, she twisted her fingers in her robes. As Myrddin and Nimue argued on the balcony, the High Oracle's voice rose, harsh and caustic enough to strip paint. "Have you lost your mind? Why in Evermore did you bring her here?"

Myrddin shouted back at her, "I couldn't just leave her there."

"So you drop her into a viper's nest, right here in the capital?"

Viera watched a flash of gray robes dart across the slim partition of the door separating the balcony from the living space. Nimue must have caught sight of Viera, because the door clicked shut with such finality that the glass panes shook.

Viera strained to hear more, but between the closed door and the now lowered voices, there was little hope of making out anything they were saying, so she settled back against the cushion she had propped up on the couch.

Fire crackled in the hearth and abated the natural chill of the room. Compared to the rest of the castle, this section was steeped in shadows and dark walls. Fortunately, rugs staved off the chill always present in the stone floor. She wondered why her Master kept quarters nowhere near the station in life he deserved.

Viera considered the smaller individual room banked in an alcove that she and Maerna shared. The Emrys Chamber contained more space than the quarters provided for the other Maids of the Court that she'd been allowed to visit. Books, with strange symbols adorning their spines, filled the other alcoves. In the main living room, scrolls were sprawled over a large desk, and some chairs were scattered around an oblong table.

A four-poster bed was pressed against a wall; furs and quilts tucked into drawers fitted neatly below. Beyond the bed, an entryway led to the balcony where Nimue and Myrddin had their argument. The balcony overlooked a forest of evergreens.

Maerna cleared her throat as she entered from their room. She was swinging a book on grammar from side to side. Viera moaned as if stabbed with a rapier.

"None of that," Maerna said, shoving the book across the table. "Every Lady of the Court can read, and you'll be no exception. Now sit up here with me."

With lessons from Myrddin, Maerna, Constantine, Brynn, Viera had grasped letters quickly enough to learn words and even simple sentence structure.

Maerna opened the book and began her instruction. Viera grumbled but read the small words making up the sentences her roommate pointed out for her. Though reading along at a pace she believed was good, she felt a spark of utter brilliance. Dragging her thumb over the pages, she harrumphed and imitated Jocelyn's haughty preening: "You do realize most of the servants can't read," she drawled, smug in her delivery.

Not giving her the slightest glance, Maerna slinked over to the couch. "Whatever gave you that impression? The Scribes give free lessons to any who wish to learn."

"You're kidding, right?"

"Nay, I'm not. The Queen even gives lessons to the servants, when she has time. She also teaches Viteliuian, Gallian, and Allemanian to the Court Ladies."

"She knows Constantine's language?"

"She's Catholic, as is Balin. Constantine is their priest, and he delivers sermons to them in Viteliuian." Maerna reached over and picked up her latest embroidery project.

Viera flipped a random page in her grammar primer. "I can't believe that the Queen teaches servants and Ladies alike."

"The Queen's kind and patient toward those who want to learn," Maerna said, lifting her gaze briefly from her embroidery and pointing her needle at Viera. "She was the chief advocate for the Temples, Guilds, and Libraries to open their doors to any and all, and she's also the reason why it's not illegal for peasants to learn how to read. You, as much as anyone, have her to thank for that."

For all the good that promised to be, Viera could not shake the dread and hopelessness she'd felt when the Queen settled her gaze upon her in the Throne Room. "She seemed so cold to me. Like she could not stand to be in anyone's presence for long." Viera sat on the couch with Maerna. "There's something wrong about the Queen. Not that I know what I'm saying, but her Element felt colder than it should be."

Maerna set her embroidery aside and drew her legs up onto the couch. "It makes sense that she's colder. She is an Ice Elemental, you know?"

"I understand. But if everything is right about her, why are Bercylac and Wilhelm not near as cold?"

"I see that nothing gets past you." Maerna stretched out her legs and bracketed Viera against the couch. "Not a word of this outside this room. Vow on your Element."

"Swear on my family trees."

Maerna wrinkled her nose.

"Those trees mean the world to my family." Viera rested her back against the armrest. "My family would kill me if they found out I swore on the trees and because of this something happened to them."

"Fine. Swear on the *trees*. Just don't you dare breathe a word of this to anyone, not even to my parents." Maerna glanced around and shifted forward. "You know how we Soul Bond with someone who Balances us out?

"Aye."

"The Queen lost her Bond during the Red and White Duels of the Draigs."

"But the King is her Soul Bond, right?"

"The Royal Pair aren't true Soul Bonds. They're both Bonded to other people."

Viera gulped. "Who is the King Bonded to?"

"My father."

Twisting around on the couch, Viera stared through the glass window panels at her Master's back. As if sensing her stare, he looked over his shoulder and met her gaze. His eyebrows furrowed and he shrugged as he faced his wife again.

An uncomfortable warmth spread up Viera's neck and covered her cheeks. "You have to, ah, kiss your Soul Bond to become Balanced, don't you?"

Maerna shook her head. "No, you don't. All that's required is to share body fluids."

Viera made a disgusted face, causing Maerna to swat at her. "Not like that, either! My father and Arthwyr shared their blood in Fire Wine."

Viera pressed her nose into a cushion. "Then that's not as freaky," she mumbled weakly and peeked at Maerna. "Why isn't your father on the Throne with the King? Royal Bonds are meant to rule together."

"Are you bloody stupid?" Maerna screeched. She looked over the couch and waited a few seconds to see if her parents had overheard her outburst. Neither looked her way, so she lowered her voice. "It's unheard of in Evermore."

"Why?"

Maerna twisted her braids, tightening and snapping them. "Because it's deemed unnatural, Viera." She dropped her hair and set her hands on her lap. "There must be children to secure the Royal Lineage. You can't have that with a Royal Pair who shares the same gender."

Sticking out her lower lip, Viera muttered, "That's not fair."

"Life isn't fair. My father and Arthwyr made the best of their circumstances."

"Can you say they're truly happy, though?"

"They love their wives and children. To put to rest what you're thinking, I've never known either to be close like *that*."

"It's still not right for a true Royal Pair to be denied their rule." Viera picked up the cushion and tossed it. "Maybe that will change someday?"

As a pensive glaze bordering on black settled upon Maerna's eyes, she pursed her lips and tilted her face in the direction of the fireplace. "Perhaps, but it will have to be a Pendragon to make that change, and I doubt we'll ever see that in our lifetimes. And likely nor will our children or grandchildren. There is too much wrong with the thinking of the nobles in the realm."

Viera got up and went back to the desk and the grammar book. "You said the Queen's Bond died. Who was it?"

"Her name was Karen Gorre. Aye, Viera, the Queen's Bond was female." Maerna wrapped her arms around herself. "And she was Bedwyr's mother."

"Nay! For real?"

"Aye, she was indeed Bedwyr's mother." Maerna sucked her lip into her mouth, and when it slipped back out, it was swollen and red. "Karen was a victim of the Duels, and our side failed her. Whatever you do, don't talk about her to anyone, especially the Queen or Bedwyr."

Door hinges squeaking signaled Myrddin and Nimue's approach and silenced any further discussion. Viera craned her neck, her eyes roving over the pair. The discord between them had subsided, as their expressions indicated amicable neutrality.

In a gesture reminiscent of when Bedwyr tucked his hands into his long-sleeved cloak, Nimue slipped her hands into her flowing sleeves. She faced Viera. "You're officially welcomed into Emrys House. The tailor, Florian, will come tomorrow and measure you for Fire initiate robes and formal clothing. At some point, I'll take you into the village for other clothes."

"Aye, ma'am."

Nimue collected her gray cloak, pulled it over her, and fluffed her hair down the back of the shiny fabric. She kissed Maerna on the top of her head, patted Viera on the shoulder, and kissed Myrddin on the cheek. "I have a senior Apprentice completing her final Mastery as an Oracle." She paused at the door and pierced them with a glare. "Husband, you'll tread carefully as I assist Zabrina in shedding her Element. Don't make me regret conceding to this."

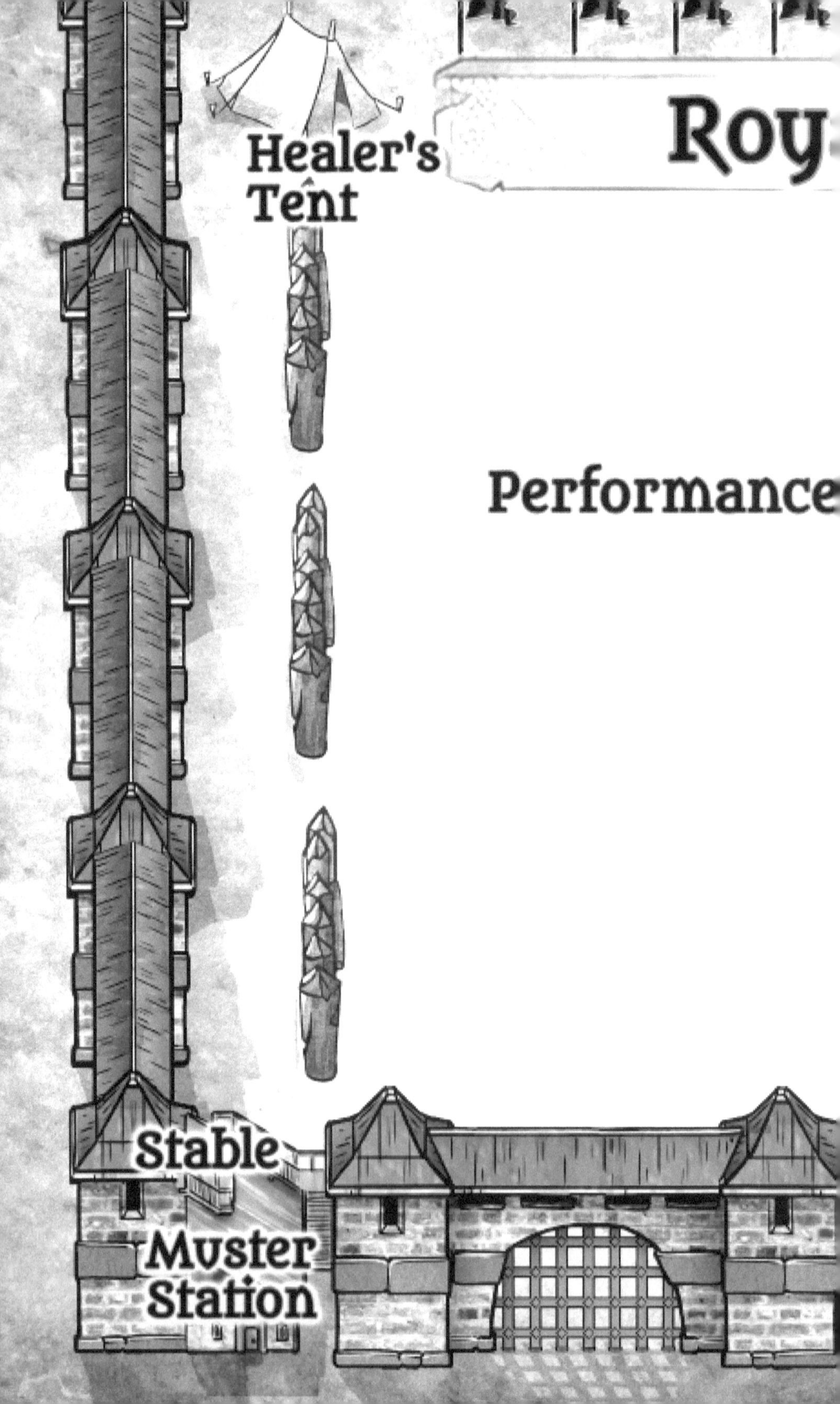

Healer's Tent
Roy
Performance
Stable
Muster Station

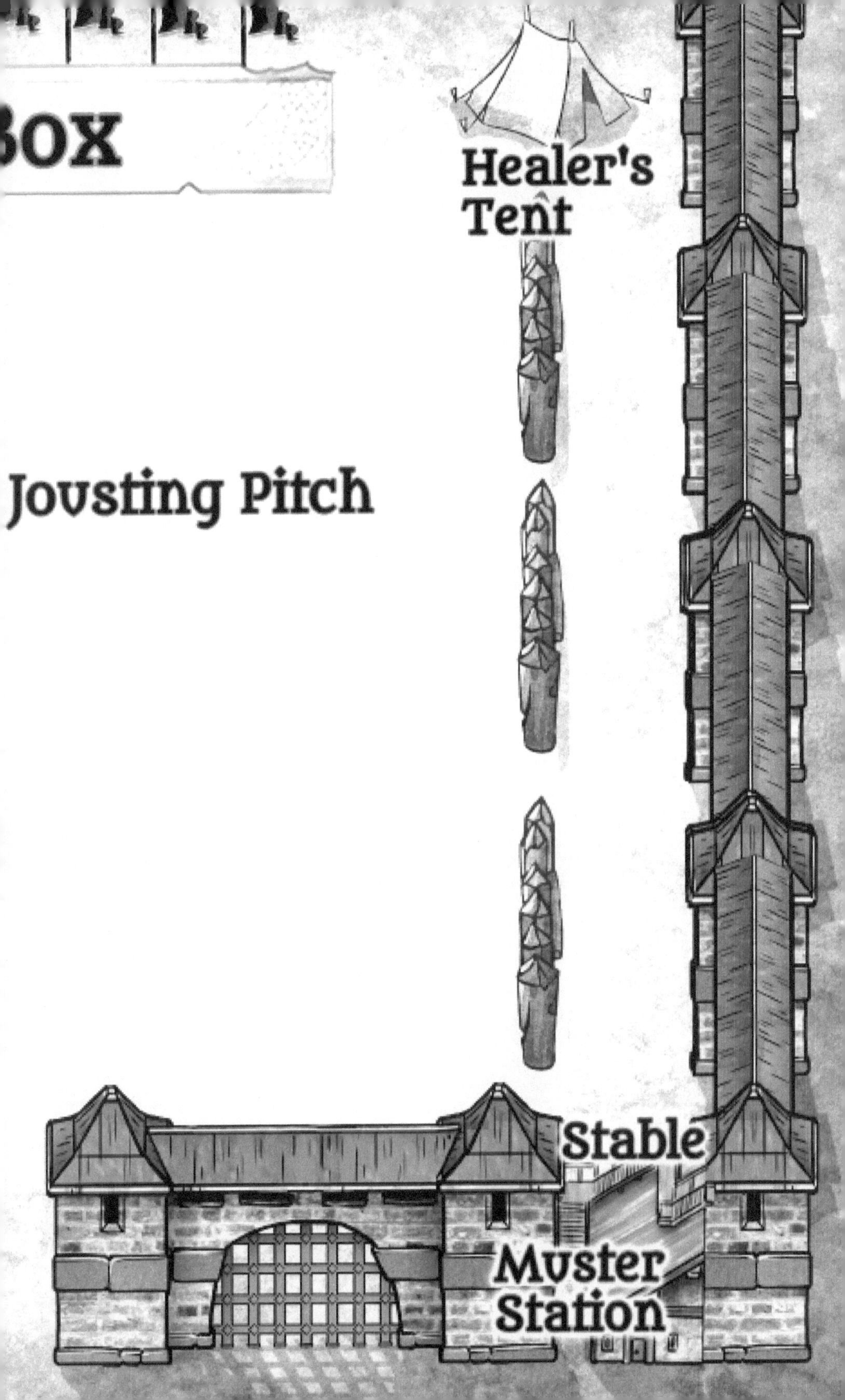
Box
Healer's Tent
Jousting Pitch
Stable
Muster Station

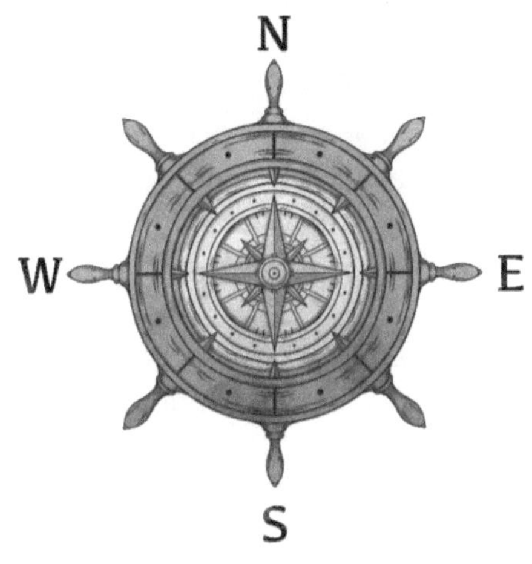

CHAPTER 39

A JOUST BY ANY OTHER NAME

If the chaos of arriving at Elden's Hearth overwhelmed Viera, it held no comparison to the preparation required at the castle for the Jousting Tournament commencing the Alban Hefin Festival. Myrddin's primary Master, Aglovale Pellinore—who insisted Viera call him Bampi because youngsters, Maerna in particular, viewed him as a grandfather of sorts—visited the Emrys Chamber. Myrddin had asked for this meeting to discuss Viera's Royal Contract with him and to elicit his support to have it approved by the Treasurer of Evermore, Lord Baudwyn Kelliweg.

As Myrddin and Maerna led Viera around the Arena, she didn't know what to make of the pitch. The long field was sectioned off, in the middle of it a long track of packed earth set apart for jousting and chariot races, rows of wooden bleachers lining the sides of each venue. Bells clanging and banners cracking in the wind drew Viera's attention to the flagpoles lining the perimeter of the Arena. At the far end, the Pendragon banner waved high over the Royal Box, the Cameliard unicorn a little lower but still prominent.

Bors Numidia's laughter drew Viera's attention to the future Mercenary King parading toward them. She gasped at the black-skinned man, wearing a gold crown adorned with rubies and sapphires, walking next to Bors. Viera looked from this man to Myrddin and back again, trying to decide who was taller. When he got closer, he had Myrddin beat by a few inches, making him a bona fide giant at 6-feet 8-inches in height.

The man narrowed his beetle-black eyes on Viera, and she curtseyed to him, albeit warily. Her courtesy didn't soften his mien, as his nostrils flared and a wide scratch deepened across the bridge of his nose.

After exchanging greetings with Myrddin, Bors said to Viera, "This is King Morien Ziyad, from Marrakesh. He's also a Knight of the Eclipse, and His Majesty is from Alkebula, same as me. We arrived together, with the Sasanias."

Bors had smiled at Morien Ziyad as he introduced him, but this had no effect on the King's deportment. Morien scowled at Myrddin, and in a deep bass voice he drawled, "This the peasant you bought from the turnip cart?"

"Carrot cart," Viera shot back as she stood on her tiptoes. "Just how tall are you?"

Jerking his chin downward, Morien Ziyad eyed her with an unblinking stare. "It speaks," he said in a tone that one would use on the village dunce.

"*It* is a teen-seasoned Evermorean girl," Myrddin said. "The trick is getting her not to speak." He scoffed, "At least she doesn't click her tongue to communicate like people in your country."

"Careful. Remember, it's by the grace of my charity that I didn't conquer your land as you were on your knees after the War."

As their discussion became more heated, Bors slipped between them and guided the arrogant King toward the muster stations. The young Knight called back to Viera, "All's well. We're friends now. Good to see you again. May your Alban Hefin be light."

Waiting for him to be out of earshot, she asked Myrddin, "Is that arse for real?"

Myrddin bent down to her eye level. "Morien Ziyad is from a family of conquerors. After the Duels of the Draigs, he came to assess a takeover but decided it was far better to cultivate an alliance."

"We seriously could've been taken over?"

"Aye. You have Safir and Bors to thank for his decision. Corruption was rife and a lot of underground black-market dealings were going on in the south. Morien brought honest commerce to the ports and eradicated the seedier elements. He now oversees the southern ports of Evermore."

Trumpeting had Myrddin hurrying Viera and Maerna to an open section in the bleachers, which was in the first row. Two helmeted riders trotted their horses down the Arena, the telltale markings of Gales giving away Lamorac as one of them.

Myrddin pointed at the large gray horse opposite Gales. "Balin and Lamorac are breaking the field. They're opening the bids for favours. After that, the registry for jousters begins."

Myrddin and Viera had just taken a seat when Gaheris stopped by and offered his usual greeting: "Allo."

Viera poked the fox-faced helmet he carried. "Are you jousting?"

"Aye, as is Gavyn," Percyval sniped from behind Gaheris until he stepped aside. The old man added, "You better get signed up lest I lose good money on you, boyo."

Gaheris arched an eyebrow. "You're not wagering on a Rheged or Gavyn?"

"Blanche has wagered on them already, but I gotta keep the ungrateful bastards on their toes even with my money on you."

As Gaheris shook his head and went to register, Percyval sat next to Myrddin and glanced at Viera. "When's this one going to joust?" Percyval asked.

Myrddin whipped his head toward Viera, who shrunk under his regard. "Are you crazy? The Court was in an uproar for months after Shiori Murasaki did it. The Sagramores and Cuhlwchs had her barred and disqualified for being an Ancient."

A drum roll announced the opening Joust. Both combatants lowered their lances to their squires, who removed a large circular token from each and placed the discs on a row of dowels. The tokens registered the jousting order, and each dowel held a metal version of the Knight's House symbol, along with a number to designate birth ascendency if more than one member from the same family was participating.

Maerna handed her father a metal circlet with many distinctly colored ribbons attached to it, some with ornate embroidery on them. "Which one?" Myrddin asked.

She blushed and indicated Lamorac.

Myrddin said to his daughter, "You may go after Gaheris and register your favour for Lamorac to approach and collect it after he and Balin are done."

As Maerna left and caught up to Gaheris, Viera ran her hand over one of the ribbons. "What does all this mean?" she asked Myrddin.

"It determines the favour an eligible young lady can give to her jouster of choice. If it's done wrong, a lass might proposition a jouster for a marriage Bond instead of asking for a simple token of appreciation."

"Can I do one?"

"Wart, after you reach your fifteenth season, you'll have ample opportunity."

"And I get to pick who I want?"

"No," Myrddin snapped, the terseness of his answer startling her. A moment later he added, "Until you are eighteen seasons, you will seek my approval of your choice. If I say no, you pick someone else. That's it, and there will be no discussion."

"Why so strict?"

Myrddin growled, "There are men here with far less honor than the ones you have met thus far. They believe that noble blood outweighs that of others. They will lay claim to you with no intention of making you their Bond." Fidgeting, Myrddin shared a look with Percyval. "For the first time you participate, favour Gaheris, Lamorac, or Segwarides. They won't dishonor you or force a claim."

Viera surveyed the dowels hosting the jousters' coats-of-arms. The foremost central dowel displaying the House of Metal stood amid the others. Three dowels on either side of it lacked particular distinction, but the dusty sun-bleached sigils for the other extinct members of The Seven Houses flanked the last surviving House. The empty dowels bordering the orange House of Air and white House of Ice were spaced as if the nobility feared that getting too close would spell their demise.

"What about Lord Wallach?" she asked. "Would I be allowed to favour him?"

Myrddin snorted. "No one favours Bedwyr in a joust. Too many scandals surround him. Arthwyr has even suspended him from competing."

"Isn't it expected for all nobles to joust, as well as all Knights?"

Percyval grunted, "Most do—" side-eyeing Myrddin with delight glowing in his gaze— "though some are stuffy old stooges without a lick of spirit for it. Your Master learned it from his Masters, your new Bampi Aglovale and that old goat, Dinadan Blumenthal."

"Saith the man who dared Dinadan to compete and got wiped across the pitch with of all things a mop," Myrddin said and stroked his beard. "Quite the sight witnessing a reigning Jousting King get deck-swabbed by the Lord of a House full of reformed pirates."

Percyval kicked pitch dust in a cloud over Myrddin's boots. "Lass, you'd best understand that when Bedwyr's blood gets kicked up, he goes for the kill. Not many can get him to back down when he gets like that either. Though, I'd pay a small fortune to see him go against our favourite Treasurer."

Viera asked dubiously, "A Treasurer against Lord Wallach?"

"You have any familiarity with old Foel House?"

Her skin pickled. "I've learned that they're a House of the foremost duelers." She gulped. "There are rumors of their ladies being Witches."

Myrddin said, "This isn't appropriate at—"

"Boyo, I swear I'll box your ears off!" Percyval shouted, cutting him off. "Shielding your wee lass from certain truths that creep about the Hearth shan't do her a lick of good. Hiding it allowed it to go unfettered until it became the shame of us all."

Myrddin sagged in his seat and wrung his hands in his lap. "Aye. I understand."

When Percyval turned back to Viera, she shivered at the broiling fury in his worn green eyes. "Right on both accounts. Carian Foel was an accomplished dueler and a Court darling during Uther's reign. He saw himself and his lackeys above the law. I spent a decade as a Runemaster trying to catch him."

"Why?" asked Viera, barely above a whisper.

Dragging his teeth over his cracked lips, Percyval said, "He and his pack had a penchant for little lassies. Kept it to slaves and peasant girls in the beginning. Carian was clever and there was no bringing him or the others to justice. As with that type, they never stop, only get worse."

"That's horrible," Viera said, reeling at the strain lining Myrddin's features. "What happened?"

Myrddin turned away but said, "Carian raped the wrong girl and ran afoul of the wrong man. Lord Kelliweg challenged him to a duel. He ripped out Carian's heart and ate it with his Second and Third—both Kelliwegs—as it still beat, in front of the entire Court."

Said Percyval glumly, "Twelve years dedicated to nailing that bastard Carian and some mousy Treasurer managed it in under a half-hour. I near retired that day out of shame." He let some time pass before adding, "Word of advice, lass. Don't ever cross Baudwyn Kelliweg."

A jangle of heavy metal came from Bedwyr as he and Eerie sauntered toward the Royal Box. As Bedwyr came closer, his fans clicked against a slimmer sword with a diamond pattern crisscrossed on its hilt, but what drew Viera's attention to the Knight's belt were the three gleaming ebony batons made of wood and the silver chain linking them together.

Eerie had her arm looped through his, and she wore a silver headdress covered in amethysts that sparkled radiantly over the spill of her white locks.

Eager to get off the current conversation, Viera asked Myrddin, "Why the tiara?"

"Eerie is the current Queen of the Dance of the Elements. The winners of the Joust and Queen of the Dance share Thrones during Mala."

"Wonder what Bedwyr thinks about this since he isn't allowed to compete?"

Myrddin didn't answer, favouring her instead with a tight smile as Gaheris and Maerna rejoined them.

Viera pointed to a ribbon with fancier embroidery on it than any of the others. "It's pretty," she said as she stroked the runes and family sigils. "Does the jouster get to keep it?"

Myrddin chuckled. "Nay, the ribbons all get burned in a ceremony afterwards."

"Why?"

"It's a ritual meant to wish the jouster a safe, good, long life."

She opened her mouth to protest the concept of destroying the ribbons when a horn sounded and the first set of jousters lowered their lances and charged toward one another. Her pulse raced with the horses, and she pressed against Gaheris when a loud crack from the lances impacting the shields rang across the pitch. Miraculous to her way of thinking, both riders remained in their saddles. The horses galloped back into position, turned around, and charged at each other again. Once more a loud crash was heard but the riders were still seated.

Not even pausing, the jousters angled their lances and their chargers ran at each other at full speed a third time. Viera gripped Gaheris' arm, and she flinched hard from the third impact, which was louder than either of the first two passes.

"You all right, lass?" he asked.

"That was amazing! Who… who won?"

"Those were practice runs. That's why both Knights are still mounted. When it's a real joust, one or both will hit the pitch."

From behind her, a bark of laughter caused Viera to spin around. Viera exhaled a sharp breath at seeing Eryck Rheged's striking green and brown leathers. His rakish black hair shone under the sunlight as he stepped down from the bleachers and passed a group of busily chatting Maids, who fell silent as they tracked him. He was joined by Harlan, who spun around and gave Viera a wink that had her ears burning.

Rolling his gaze upward, Myrddin asked Percyval, "Have you seen your brother? I need Aglovale's help with Lord Kelliweg. He said he'd meet me here."

Percyval straightened, his features taut. "A few mousers got into the communal prayer room. My nephews' prayer rugs were burned. The ones from their mother. Aglovale and the twins went into town to try to find new ones."

Myrddin sighed in utter dismay and said, "Where is Palamedes?"

Percyval pointed at the boy, hunkered on a bench next to Constantine. Palamedes nodded to him as the priest rubbed the youth's shoulder.

Maerna tugged on Myrddin's sleeve. "Why don't we keep Palamedes and Father Constantine company?"

Myrddin grumbled, "All right, you get settled down with them." He turned to Viera and said rather meekly, "Wart, we'll just have to go at Baudwyn on our own."

"Give Baudwyn the Hells," Percyval said as the two of them stood to leave. "Then send him my way," he added as if he meant it. Judging by the sour expression on Myrddin's face, Viera thought it safe to assume no one wanted a piece of Lord Kelliweg—under any circumstances.

CHAPTER 40

THE TREASURERS

If there were two things Viera had learned since signing her Royal Contract, it was that she would never be able to assume that anything about her life in Elden's Hearth would be permanent, and that nothing she was involved with would ever occur without turmoil. Viera had never felt more scared as she walked with Myrddin toward a Healer's tent erected on the side of the Royal Box. As the two of them approached the tent, the stiff canvas whipping in the wind created an unsettling noise. Myrddin squeezed Viera's hand, but the kind gesture didn't allay her fear in the slightest. If anything, it made her pulse race faster.

They entered the tent, and she spied a Foxbury scion leaning against a table, a woman standing next to him. In the middle of her curtsey to him, the Lord said, "Howie, lass."

Viera nodded and replied, "Lord Garyth."

He winked at the woman muffling a laugh into her sleeve as he said to Viera, "How do you know which brother I am?"

"Gavyn always says, 'Heya,' Gaheris uses, 'Allo,' and when you and I first met, you said, 'Howie.' It's the only way I can tell you three apart."

"She's figured you out," the woman said, smiling wide as her long blond hair slid along her face like curls of honey splashing across sweet cream. And to Viera, "Harlan has told me a lot about you."

Viera blushed but didn't want to ask if the reports were good or bad.

Garyth set his hands on the woman's arms and said to Viera, "This is my wife, Reese." He sidestepped her and gestured to the other occupant in the tent. "This is her uncle, Baudwyn Kelliweg."

Viera stared at the man sitting behind a small table in the darkest corner of the canvas enclosure. His goatee and pencil-thin mustache were impeccably maintained, and not a gray hair on his head was out of place. Gone was the presumption of some battle-scarred brawler more animal than human, and for the life of her, she couldn't imagine his unmarked hands encrusted with another's blood. Or the gore—of someone he'd just killed and eaten a part of—dripping from his mouth and down his chin. One of Baudwyn Kelliweg's trimmed eyebrows arched as he tapped the calamus of a raven-feathered quill over a cloth to remove any clotting.

"Just who we're looking for," Myrddin said, bowing to Lord Kelliweg. "We've just come from your chambers at the castle. Not finding you there, we rushed right over here."

Baudwyn snapped the book shut and placed his quill in an inkwell. "How interesting, Lord Emrys."

Myrddin dug inside his robes and pulled out a neatly rolled-up scroll with a ribbon around it. "My apologies for not presenting this to you under less chaotic circumstances. Please understand, I'm certain everything is in order, and that's why I didn't rush."

"And you decided to wait until Alban Hefin was underway to get this to me?"

Myrddin said nothing but held out Viera's Royal Contract for the Treasurer of Evermore. Baudwyn made no move to take the proffered document. As the moment of silence stretched on, Myrddin teetered as Baudwyn continued to stare at him until he lowered the scroll to his side.

When Viera also twitched at what was taking place, Baudwyn turned his stare to her and offered his hand. At first touch, a surge sizzled through her and she fell back into Garyth. With the hair frizzing along her neck, lingering tingles darted through her arm. And she was Fire!

With clipped movements, Baudwyn removed a white monogrammed handkerchief displaying *BQK* along the edge, and he wiped his hands. "Well, aren't you sensitive," he said, folding and tucking away the linen. "I won't be touching you again."

Viera murmured, "Why is my arm numb?"

Baudwyn's features held the calculus of a predator toying with its prey. "I don't give away my secrets." He held a flat stare on Myrddin.

Myrddin untied the ribbon cinching the scroll and unfurled the document. "Is something wrong, Lord Kelliweg?"

"Clearly there is—" Baudwyn waved a finger at Myrddin— "for you to present a Royal Contract like this."

"As I said earlier, we couldn't find you in the castle."

Sitting up straight, Baudwyn braced his arms on the table. "You knew whenever I was at the Treasurer's Guild, and you've had more than enough time to find me." He growled as Myrddin started to open his mouth. "Don't even think of saying whatever verbal incontinence you're about to spew. I'm thirty-five winters, Lord Emrys, and hardly an idiot. Yet, I'm starting to wonder about you."

Myrddin stepped forward. "I don't like what you're implying."

"I don't like anyone trying to make a fool out of me, either." Baudwyn snatched the scroll and set it next to his elbow. "You planned all along on passing me this Contract to sanction while I'm in the throes of the mayhem going on with Alban Hefin."

"I assure you, it was unintend—"

"Don't finish that, because no matter what you say it would be utter bollocks." Baudwyn directed a pointed look at his niece. "You know my opinion of powerful men taking advantage of females, especially young ones."

Reese stilled, a stark look consuming her smooth features and giving her the appearance of being made of marble.

The tension in the tent was broken when a couple slipped inside and stilled at the sight of them. In similar brown and gold robes to Baudwyn, the new man tucked his dark hair beneath a small circular scrap of white cloth pinned with simple silver hairpins to his curls. "Linny," he said, helping the woman into the second chair, "you may have my seat."

Baudwyn said to the pair, "My apologies, Lord and Lady Rava. Myrddin has brought the business of his House here."

"I must ask, Milord—" Lord Rava turned to Viera— "would the matter at hand concern Miss Tillwith?"

Viera attempted a bow, stumbled, and righted herself. "Aye, Milord. But how did you know? I haven't seen you in Court."

He motioned toward the symbol on his upper robe sleeves of the four suits of diamond, club, spade, and heart in gold positioned respectively on a black-and-white two-by-two checkerboard pattern. "I'm a Treasurer, same as Baudwyn, and have been in the Treasurer's Guild this past week. To answer your question, we have some mutual acquaintances."

Viera tossed back her head and snapped, "Who might that be?"

"Constantine and Palamedes, as well as Bedwyr."

Myrddin tugged Viera closer and whispered, "I'm liking this less and less."

His voice was not low enough, as Lionel said, "And well you should not like what I'm about to say." He pointed at Myrddin. "I like you, Myrd—"

"I don't like him at all," Baudwyn barked, cutting off Lionel. He opened the scroll and began reading it.

Lionel cleared his throat and stepped behind the table. "I've always respected you, Myrddin, but what Bedwyr had to say doesn't sit well with me."

Myrddin huffed, "I'm surprised Bedwyr brought Viera up at all, considering his attitude toward people in general."

Their banter continued until Baudwyn handed the Contract to Lionel, who scanned it and said, "Bedwyr doesn't meddle in other people's affairs unless—" He stopped reading as if it was his own death notice. "Wait! He signed as the witness?"

"He also intervened in the signing of her original Contract," Myrddin said. "Bedwyr insisted on an expiry of terms before letting us proceed."

"Ah, he had an issue with the language from the beginning," Baudwyn said, placing his chin in his hands and tapping his fingers along his cheeks. He turned to Viera, "Mind answering a few questions, lass?"

Viera observed the tight set of his jaw, and she gave her head a weak shake.

Baudwyn leaned forward. "You aren't an Emrys by blood, and I'm in a position to set aside your Contract if I'm not happy with it."

She blinked repeatedly. "But the King signed it, and his word is law, isn't it?"

"Normally, yes." Baudwyn accepted the scroll back from Lionel. "But Arthwyr treads carefully around a Kelliweg—and especially one his Queen has Knighted."

She sputtered, "I thought only the King could Knight someone."

As though approaching a flighty animal, Lionel gingerly stepped around the table and said to Viera, "Guinevere made a point of Knighting me, Baudwyn, and five others. We are loyal to the King, but our responsibility is also to the Queen."

"I hold no such loyalty to either," Baudwyn said as he motioned for Garyth and Reese to leave.

As soon as they departed, the canvas flaps stirred again and Constantine entered the tent. "All is well?" he asked in a jovial tone.

"I was about to question Miss Tillwith about her Royal Contract," Baudwyn said while drumming his fingers on the table. "Anything you know about it?"

Fussing with the cat's eye rosary beads dangling from his cincture band, the priest avoided even a fleeting glance at Lionel. "I had hoped not to be brought into this."

Said Lionel, "Rather late for that, given the concerns you expressed to me right after the Contract was signed." He bent at the waist to Viera, and a star pendant slid from the folds of his robe and dangled on a silver chain. He said to her, "Answer honestly. If we decide to remove you from Myrddin's care, is there someone you trust among us?"

She could not have been more unprepared to answer a question of such importance to her. Viera didn't know why, but she found his star ornament strange, hypnotic even, and she wondered if Lionel Rava was a Witch. Her voice was rife with uncertainty as she answered, "I'd rather not go with anyone else. But if I must—" glancing at the priest— "I guess Constantine… or Lamorac … maybe Ewain."

"Good choices." Lionel turned toward Constantine. "What say you?"

Constantine tucked away his crucifix. "I'll put her up, if it comes to that, though it might send a few tongues wagging. As Healers, Ewain and Lamorac can better quell the rumor mill. Of course, there's always Bedwyr."

Said Baudwyn quickly, "He skirts a thin line of acceptability, and even if he agreed, it would destroy both him and her in the eyes of the Court. We all know who would raise the most protest."

Viera stared at her Royal Contract, now rolled up and sitting on the desk. "Why would that hurt his image? Isn't he Bonded to Eerie?"

Myrddin groaned, "Not formally. There's little doubt given how Bedwyr and Eerie are, but they haven't hand-fasted in a Bonding Ceremony yet."

As Viera's mind stumbled over his remark, she said, "They're not married?"

"Oh, they're merry all right," Lionel said, laughing until Linny smacked him with her sandal.

"Let's not get ahead of ourselves," Myrddin said and steered Viera toward Baudwyn. "Your questions, Milord, if you will."

Baudwyn steepled his fingers and addressed Viera gently: "How old are you?"

Viera flexed her arms and planted her hands against her sides. "Fourteen summers. I'll be fifteen summers during what you call Mala."

"Are your parents aware of everything in this Contract?"

She spared a glance to Myrddin for guidance. Receiving none, she offered meekly, "They were present when it was signed."

"But do they understand what is says?"

"Uh—" lowering her chin— "maybe."

"What does *maybe* mean?" Baudwyn asked, briskly unrolling the contract and taking another look at it. His brow furrowed; he pressed his lips into a thin line. "They can't read, can they?"

She swallowed. "No, Sir. They can't."

"Can you?"

She cringed at her embarrassment, but Myrddin placed his hand on her shoulder and she looked up at him as he comforted her by saying, "No one will judge you for whatever you say."

She turned to Baudwyn. "I can't read well, Milord, but the Emrys and others are helping me do better every day."

Baudwyn tapped the parchment. "I'm of a mind to void this right now."

Shivers coursed through her as she pleaded, "Milord, please don't. The Emrys are wonderful to me, and I promise to work even harder at reading. Please don't—"

He held up his hand, staving off her protests. "I'm not notarizing this." He took the contract and slipped it into a leather case. "Myrddin, I expect you, Arthwyr, Bedwyr, and Miss Tillwith in my office three days from now. We'll discuss the contract in full so all parties understand where they stand."

Viera gripped Myrddin's arm. "Am I being removed?"

Enfolding her against him, Myrddin crooned low in his throat. She clutched at him until ink, parchment, and steel soothed her nerves. The more she inhaled the scent, the more she relaxed until she peeked past her Master at Baudwyn.

The tent flap blew aside and Gavyn loped toward the table. "Heya—"

The crackling charge Viera had experienced when touching Baudwyn grew into a steady din in her ears. Through bared teeth, Baudwyn growled, "Get Bedwyr, Arthwyr, and a Healer in here now. Myrddin Emrys, I can't believe you imprinted yourself on her!"

CHAPTER 41

IMPRINTING WOES

After Gavyn hustled Viera, the Ravas, and Constantine from the tent, Viera observed the summoned Knights and King embroiled in their debate. Linny had left to ready the Queen for her arrival and alert the ruler to the need for her attention. Viera thumped her boots against the stairs wrapping around the outside of the muster station to the towers overlooking the Arena and whispered, "I messed up, didn't I?"

Gavyn stared into the blue remains of his serf-smoothy and handed it to her. "Not really."

She sipped the melted blue ice. Like a dog awaiting a signal from its master, Gavyn angled himself toward the Healers' Tent. It remained to be seen who held his lead, but her ingots were on Baudwyn holding far more power over Foxbury. Many a Pendragon and even the Marshals failed to shake Foxbury fidelity from the family's dyed in wool allegiance to the Dumnonian Dwarves.

At a sharp glance from Baudwyn, Gavyn had spirited them from the tent chattering all the way, "You've got to try a serf-smoothy, lass. Just haven't lived until you've turned your tongue purple!"

In near tears, Viera protested, "But I don't have any money!"

"Don't worry! It's on me," he all but barked in his haste.

Grimacing, she stuck out her tongue and it definitely was purple from her original red serf-smoothy. The only time in her experience a tongue was any other color was if someone was sick or dead.

She caught Baudwyn jabbing his finger at the other Knights and the Contract as he howled, "You unbelievable berks!"

Gavyn draped his arms over the guardrail and muttered, "Baudwyn doesn't have children. He doesn't understand how beneficial imprinting can be."

Like Viera, Lionel sat on and tapped his heels against the stairs. "One could argue it's abusive and immoral when it's done on those not blood related."

"The same can sometimes be argued of family. Little close to home, eh, priest?"

Constantine climbed the stairs and settled behind Viera. "My family used it to foster blind fanatic loyalty to my bloodline."

He rolled up his sleeve and presented his arm to Viera. The faded black ink of an eagle and large snake with a babe in between them stained the olive skin of his wrist.

"Families, who use such a ritual, tattoo it on members of their families' wrists. It's a natural reservoir for imprinting because our scents release from this area." Constantine smoothed his fingers over the tattoo and the sweetness of herbs tickled her nose. "In my old family, when a child turned five, they received the brand as a present."

Lionel groused, "Don't hold back. Tell her what they did to you, lest she not be wary of what Myrddin has done."

"I made a mistake when I was young." Constantine tilted his wrist and the sunlight caught thin lines about the edges of the brand. "My family sent me away and completely cut me off from them. The way they used imprinting forced dependency upon them and was addictive. I su— suffer—suffered until my Masters supplemented it with a healthier form of imprinting."

She shuffled backward and relaxed against him. "What is imprinting?"

"There are two types. Natural familial imprinting occurs from exposure to the same people in a family," Gavyn said, snatching Constantine's wrist and rolling his thumb over the thin scars. "Children and parents in a family have a natural inclination toward it. Ever enter your home and relax from the smell, lass?"

She nodded.

He released Constantine. "That's typical and natural imprinting."

"What's the other type?"

"It's a blood ritual that heightens the scent of an individual and encourages a sense of security." Gavyn showed her a small brand of a fox's profile above the pulse point of his wrist. "I imprinted myself on Eryck Rheged after his parents died and he became my Apprentice. It kept him calm and supplanted the loss of his parental bonds."

Lionel pulled the silver star pendant from under his brown robes and fussed with it until it was centered on its chain. "Those are different circumstances. What Myrddin has done borders on overstepping propriety."

Collecting the empty paper cup of Viera's first treat, Gavyn crushed it into a little wadded ball. "I would've done the same," he said, setting the ball over his palm and flicking it at Constantine with his fingers. "Masters use the technique to help students during the initial phases of training. Especially young ones prone to homesickness."

"There are benefits to it, Lionel." Constantine grabbed the ball and lit it before Gavyn could try it on another victim. "It's how Galahad survived the flight over the Isles. Lucan had to do it to keep him alive."

Viera narrowed her eyes. "Who's Lucan?"

The men fell silent.

Affecting a smile that teased as much as encouraged her curiosity, Gavyn said, "That went arse over ankles."

Lionel groaned. "Don't even pretend she wasn't going to find out about it."

"So, who is he, or who was he?" Viera pressed.

"Lucan Cornwall and Tor Cuhlwch were Galahad's and Bedwyr's initial Masters. But it's best not to bring up these names to either Knight. They respect Tor, but Lucan is a bitter point for Bedwyr."

Gavyn sat on the stair below hers. "Do you know of the scandal surrounding our Queen and Lance?"

She stiffened. "Aye."

"Uther started and spread the rumor." Constantine's low voice startled her into looking at him. "Arthwyr was in Orrinshire Pass and Lance close to Camelaan Lake when Uther had his loyalists begin telling tales about the Queen and her new lover. Uther despised peasants and foreigners, and he tried to execute Galahad and Guinevere's father, Uriah Cameliard, as well as Lance's wife, Elaine. Balin and the Princes were in Spitsbergen and escaped to the Pass."

Lionel jiggled his foot. "Uther imprisoned Uriah and the others. I was serving them when they were arrested. My wife and I were servants in the castle. Tor was charged with executing them. Instead, he helped them escape."

"What about Lucan?" Viera asked, rapt by the story. "You've only mentioned Tor."

"Lucan sent messages to Arthwyr and Lance. Then he freed those he valued most."

"What do you mean?"

Lionel massaged his thumbs. "Don't ever breathe a word of this to Bedwyr."

"I won't, I swear."

"Lucan left Bedwyr and his family in the dungeon to rot and die. He was thirteen."

As she imagined a boy of thirteen winters with his family locked in the dark underbelly of a castle, she rocked herself at the chill seeping into her bones. "How awful!"

"If Lucan had freed them, Bedwyr's family might be alive today."

Gavyn winced. "Only Bedwyr and Shiori Murasaki survived. Bedwyr never forgave Lucan."

Viera gulped down the rest of the blue serf-smoothy. "What happened to the others?"

Lionel stretched and set his hands behind him on the stairs. "Elaine and Tor sacrificed themselves, taking a few men with them into Twilight. Guinevere and the others escaped over the Isles Seas. Uriah was released after the Battle of the Hearth."

"And Lucan?"

Dropping his chin to his chest, Lionel gave a faint twitch of his shoulders. "He kept Galahad alive through imprinting himself on Galahad. Galahad was thirteen springs. It was the only way. Lucan finished Galahad's training and passed into Twilight when Uther ambushed Guinevere. He defended her and died for it."

Viera murmured, "Then, Arthwyr killed his father and became King."

Twitching, Constantine muttered, "Something like that."

As a man with the Cornwall shield of downward pointing gold bezants forming a triangle led a small group of men toward them, Constantine and Lionel scrambled to tuck their crucifix and star pendants under their robes. The Cuhlwch boar emblems decorated a few sleeves, and the Sagramore men sported a family emblem of stars.

A man with the Cuhlwch symbol snorted at them as the others scowled.

Gavyn barked, "Halt. Is that any way to greet your betters?" Gavyn motioned toward one with the DuLac emblem, "Come now, Greshit. Lance expects better from his nephew."

Greshit bristled, but lowered himself to a full kneel on the floor and bowed forward over his hands clasped upon his knee. "Lord Second, I hope Fate smiles upon your jousting."

"Much better. The rest of you, on your knees and beg Lord Constantine's and Lord Lionel's forgiveness."

The Cornwall noble opened his mouth. "But—"

"Don't be an even bigger embarrassment than you already are, Tremayne. Kael won't be pleased to hear a nephew of his and mine is ignorant of hierarchy."

When they knelt, Gavyn clapped his hands. "Now roll over—"

"Are you shitting—"

"Roll over and show your bellies like the bitches you are to your alpha."

They did as commanded, and the fine sand dusted Tremayne's black and white streaked hair in splotches.

After a minute, Gavyn impatiently gestured for them to rise. "Disrespect and attempt to intimidate these two again, and you'll have an audience with myself, Lance, your Heads of House, and the Royal Pair. I'll put in a special request that you spend a season at the Battle School and become my personal project. I love my hobbies."

Shuddering, the group nodded and slunk past.

"What was that about?" Viera asked.

Gavyn winked. "When you curtsey or bow all the way down, you do so to the Pendragons, Queen, High Oracle, and Bedwyr. In more formal situations, you do the same for the Ebony Knight and his Second. Though, Lance and I rarely enforce it."

"Then, what was that?"

"They're arseholes."

Viera parted her lips and stared at him. "Will you make me do that?"

"Nay. My family has taken a liking to you." Grimness settled on his features as he nudged Constantine. "Smudging the truth won't prepare her for the dark nature in this Court. Dagonet is affable but vicious. He sent innocent and guilty to the gallows when it pleased him and furthered his goals."

Despite the summer heat, chills dragged like nails over Viera's back. "I heard Dagonet was almost King."

"Aye." Constantine turned in the direction of Dagonet. "He stepped aside in favour of Arthwyr."

Viera watched the excitable man in jester attire strutting and blowing into the wrong end of a horn, much to his spectators' roaring delight.

Gavyn squeezed her arm. "Shadows lurk within Bedwyr. Be wary of what glooms possess him. Everyone here is capable of insurmountable darkness."

Gavyn baring his teeth like a rabid fox resurfaced in her mind. "Like how we met on Progress," she said.

"I like you, but if you had been any less, I would've put you down. Killing takes a level of inhumanity."

Constantine growled. "Don't scare her."

"There are Noble Houses who will eat her alive. Lass, don't ever let yourself be alone around men from Sagramore, Cornwall, or Cuhlwch. You're no better than an animal to them."

Viera snapped at him. "Really? And, they're Knights?"

The hard edge faded around Gavyn's jaw. "No. They're not." He pointed toward the Healers' Tent. "They won't sit at the Table of the Eclipse with Bedwyr there. Though, Kael, the current Lord of Cornwall, refuses his House their rightful seats for other reasons. Mostly Cornwall is a broken House. Kael is an exception to the first rule."

Grumbling, Constantine gritted out, "Fine. She should know about the Battle of the Hearth."

Lionel steepled his fingers over his lap. "Arthwyr didn't end Uther's life. Legend has it, they crossed swords in an epic battle." He peered at her from beneath hooded brows. "Be wary of what forms legends. The story given is often not the one most true."

"There was a prophecy. Uther's Twilight would come from the commonest denominator. The one who led and paved the way to Uther's conclusion was," Constantine said, as the horns bleated the Queen's arrival, "Shiori Murasaki."

CHAPTER 42

DRAWING CONCLUSIONS

Constantine had joined Myrddin and the others, leaving Viera in Gavyn's and Lionel's company. She sighed and rubbed her eyes, which stung from staring too long without blinking at the Healers' Tent. She tapped her foot in consort to the Queen's tossing of her head like a proud mare annoyed by flies. It remained to be seen if Guinevere's irritation was being caused by insects or curious passersby, the Seven Sisters forming a human barrier around her and Arthwyr, and quickly redirecting any wayward souls.

Beneath the Royal Box, Percyval Rheged and Ector Kyner had taken over the chore of checking in last minute jousters. Even from afar, Viera could tell Ector was far more jovial and welcoming with the entrants he handled. Those subjected to Percyval all but fled across the pitch after he accepted their coin and slapped a numbered array on them, snarking, "Hells' bells, all of Kelliweg would eat yer hearts out. Is that a butter knife or a sword on that one's belt, Ector?"

As a charcoal pencil's soft scritching stopped, Viera peeked at the book on Gavyn's lap. Gasping, she snatched it and stared at her likeness on the cream-colored vellum. "You drew me?"

Gavyn tapped the drawing. "I'm always capturing what inspires me."

She took in the burst of her freckles. "This sketch is amazing."

"As is the subject."

Viera flipped several pages back, pausing at a naked woman with a half-lidded sultry stare. Dots lined the woman's breasts, and a dusting of hair trailed below her. Viera snapped the book shut and scrubbed her face with her hands.

Throwing back his head, Gavyn laughed. "Careful what you peruse."

She sputtered through her hands, "I can't unsee it! Why was she naked?"

Lionel shook his head and turned away from both of them.

Gavyn flipped through the sketches and settled on a page. When he presented the book to her, she shied away until she saw Sid, who was drawn so accurately it was as though he could come to life on the parchment.

"You only saw Sid for a short while," Viera said as she gently touched the corner of the page, "yet you captured him perfectly."

A shadow spilled over the book as Lionel said, "Gavyn has a remarkable memory. Once he sees something, he can put it on paper. It's a talent he uses to woo women."

"Aye," Gavyn said as he wiggled his elbow against her side until she giggled. "Pick something for me to draw."

She glanced around the Arena. Chirps drew her attention to Golly, perched on a nearby barrel. She pointed at the sparrow. "Draw him."

"As you wish, Milady." Presenting his back to Golly and flipping to a fresh page, he added, "Prepare to be astounded."

In just a short while, Gavyn smiled and handed Viera the book that now contained a sketch of the sparrow. The drawing was just as realistic as the picture he'd made of Sid. "This is incredible," Viera remarked.

Lionel said, "Few know of what I'm going to tell you now, so you'll have to promise to keep it to yourself. Can you do that?"

"You should know the answer to that or you wouldn't ask."

Lionel nodded sheepishly. "Gavyn's skill at artistry is how we got intelligence into the castle during the war. As a Wood Elemental, he knows what sap makes ink invisible. He drew pictures like that woman and other provocative things over the information we wanted to hide from our enemies."

Viera flipped back to the naked woman. "If he drew over the ink, how did you see it?"

"There are special ways to raise the lettering underneath."

"There has to be more. What about getting this and whatever else you learned to our soldiers?"

"You are indeed a clever one. My wife and I are from Russka, and Dagonet knew we were fluent in Russkan, Yiddish, and Hebrew. He told us what he overheard that would benefit our army, and Linny sewed the information into a code in those languages, as if they were messages of hope for the poor and orphans. However, I delivered and translated the enemy's secrets to our leaders in the field."

"Why did you leave Russka?" Viera asked, causing Lionel to quickly raise an eyebrow.

"We weren't welcome in our homeland because of what's called our ethnicity, which means who we were descended from, and the Russkan nobility chased us out." A shudder visibly spasmed within his shoulders. "However, Guinevere's father, Uriah Cameliard, accepted us. He provided our Servant Contracts as a bridal gift because he wanted his daughter to have people true to her. Our King entrusted those contracts to Percyval Rheged and he kept us in the castle. When Arthwyr emerged victorious in the Red and White Duels, he revoked our Contracts and raised us to Lower Nobility as reward for our war efforts."

Gavyn returned to the page with Golly on it. "Look at the other side."

Viera turned the page and stared at the drawing. She was holding a broadsword, with Sid next to her. The Fire arrays she had summoned were stark and jarring in the wash of a shadowy backdrop.

She tightened her fingers on the edge of the paper. Half afraid of an underlying reason that would deny her request, Viera asked, "Can I keep it?"

To her pleasant surprise, he tore it out and handed it to her. "Why not?"

Viera carefully folded the drawing and tucked it away as she watched Myrddin follow the King and Queen to the Royal Box. Constantine stood in front of Baudwyn and another man in Wood Elemental robes.

Gavyn hugged her gently and said, "You'll be fine."

The scent of sandalwood rising from his robes soothed her as she relished this reminder of her father, but she asked rather tartly, "How do you know I'll be fine?"

"Imprinting done right is reciprocal."

Pulling away, she looked him in the eyes. "What does that mean?"

"Imprinting brings out the instinct to protect." Massaging her wrists, he smeared traces of charcoal over them.

She sniffled. "I should have lied."

Lionel patted her shoulder. "That would have made it worse."

"I hate Lord Kelliweg."

"You shouldn't."

Viera ripped herself away from them. "Why not? He's making everyone hate me."

"Oh, bubeleh, he's not," Lionel said as he stepped forward and thumbed away her tears. "He's making sure no one takes advantage of you. He wouldn't be fighting so hard for you if he didn't care about you and your future."

With that remark, Lionel walked across the pitch and joined Baudwyn. As Constantine crossed the pitch with the Wood Elemental, Baudwyn could be observed watching them intently. However, after a brief conversation, Baudwyn and Lionel left.

Gavyn urged Viera upright, and they thumped down the steps to the pitch. She half-hid herself behind him the whole way. When they reached the bottom, she scanned Constantine for any hint of her future, but the priest maintained a blank mien as the new man stopped in front of Gavyn.

Gavyn said to the other man, "Lord Alistair Kelliweg, to what do we owe the honor of the presence of the foremost Runebreaker and Runemaster of Rune House?"

Hooking a thumb into his belt, Alistair drummed his fingers over a badge clipped to it. "Baudwyn wants me to address Miss Tillwith and to observe her reactions."

"You mean how far under Myrddin's sway she is from the imprinting?"

"Aye."

Gavyn nudged Viera to stand beside him and said, "You can trust this man. He's just making sure of the extent of the imprinting."

Viera stared at the two emblems decorating Alistair Kelliweg's brown leather sleeves. "Are those Rune House emblems, Milord?"

Lord Kelliweg nodded and pointed at the bottom emblem with the Seven Runes for the Elements pointing outward from a gray circle. "For Runemasters," he said, then indicating the top emblem of a gray and black band enclosing the Elemental Runes, "this one is for Runebreakers because it's symbolic of a breaker nullifying an Element."

She shuddered and blurted, "Those are horrid looking," before realizing what she'd said.

He chuckled. "That they are."

His unexpected reaction relaxed her greatly, and as she gazed at him this gave her the confidence to say, "You have strange eyes. I didn't know people could have splotchy eyes that are half-gray and half-brown."

Alistair shared a look with Gavyn and remarked, "She's too alert for anyone subdued from imprinting."

"That she is," Gavyn quipped and rolled his clear blue eyes upward.

"I still need a sample from her," Alistair said while removing a dagger from its sheath on his belt. He came over to Viera. "This is a special dagger Runemasters use to collect body fluids. I require a few drops of your blood to assess it for imprinting markers."

At Gavyn's flashing his thumbs upward, Viera held out her hand to Alistair, who pricked her index finger with the tip of the knife. The silvery blade seemed to attract her blood, darkening it as the Runemaster's emblem glowed on the knife's hilt. Alistair sheathed the dagger and swiped salve over the small wound, immediately staunching the flow of blood.

Examining her finger, she asked distractedly, "Now what?"

Alistair replied, "Baudwyn will see you, Myrddin, Bedwyr, and the King in his office three days from now." He nodded toward Constantine. "The good Father will be taking you back to your friends, as Myrddin is currently having a much-needed conversation with the Royal Pair."

"Is Constantine my guardian now?" Viera asked, her eyes welling up.

Alistair smiled compassionately at her. "Nay. You are still with the Emrys, at least for now. Try not to worry too much and enjoy the events on the pitch. All will be made right in three days."

CHAPTER 43

VIERA'S HONOR

"**C**ongratulations to our two finalists," Arthwyr said from where he stood on an amplification array. "I refrain from saying who I wagered on. I've a wife and Ebony Knight who might have words with me afterward."

The crowd laughed.

"For now, may the best man win." Arthwyr waved his hand. "So mote it be, whatever it may be."

Balin smacked down his visor and moved into position; Galahad guided Camie closer to his starting line.

Dagonet lifted the horn to his mouth. He yelled, "Ready, steady," the trumpet's blare taking the place of "go." Galahad spurred Camie forward, the Knight's lance at the ready and his body primed for the impact of a hit—should Balin get lucky, according to Myrddin.

The first three passes were uneventful. When they hit the pitch and their horses wheeled back to the muster stations, each combatant supplemented their weapons sparring with a kata from his Element. Water and Metal nullified each other until Galahad's final Water kata overwhelmed Balin like the swell of a flood's inescapable vortex, and the twenty-one springs Herald of Evermore was the champion. Viera would never again doubt the power Water had against Metal.

During the course of the day, Viera had moved up the bleachers until she achieved her goal of making it all the way to the top, which, considering her short stature, was where she could get the best view of the action.

In late afternoon, Galahad's and Balin's final joust and spar was completed, and Viera hopped from bleacher to bleacher, carefully avoiding people as she navigated her way to the bottom.

She was making great progress until her foot caught on a loose board, and she spilled onto a man below her. Instinctively, she threw her arms outward and grabbed onto his back.

He whipped around, a snarl twisting across his features, and stepped aside. Viera crashed onto the bleacher and yipped from the pain flaring from her back and neck. The man bent down and hauled her close, his cobalt eyes inches from her face. She clutched at his shoulders, her fingers sliding over his fine clothing.

He shoved Viera away and pushed her down the remaining bleachers until she landed on the ground. He walked after her and sneered, "What little street rat dares sit on this side?"

Loud snickers drew Viera's attention to Jocelyn, who was making her way toward them.

Viera's greatest pain was now in her shoulder, and it was becoming more intense when a sharp crack against her jaw snapped her backwards. She saw stars as darkness threatened to pull her under. Whispers grew into a rush of noise. A shake snapped her back—in time to see the same man lifting his closed fist to her.

Squeezing her eyes shut, she braced for the second blow.

A strangled yelp and a thunderous crash jolted her, and she opened her eyes. Metal clanged and voices rose above the din as Eerie led her away from a gaping cluster of bystanders. As a flurry of sand bit at Viera's aching body—her pain seemingly coming from everywhere—all she could do was weep.

With weapons drawn, Lance and Galahad rushed over from the Royal Box. At the same time, Morien, his meter-long takouba blade already unsheathed, charged from a muster station.

On the field, Bedwyr had his blade drawn and the steel planed across his body at a diagonal fighting angle. His eyes were the color of fresh-spilled blood, their depths taking on a predatory glow. For the briefest of seconds, Viera swore his teeth flashed under his lips.

He teased, "Harris, time for you to become a eunuch and replace the manservant you cost me." He spat at him but missed.

"Keep baying, you cur. Everyone knows Sagramore House did you a favour with that one," Harris Sagramore said as he delivered short jabs with his broadsword at Bedwyr's unprotected legs. "I've been hoping to have a go at you since the day you were whelped."

Harris twisted around to stab Bedwyr in the neck, but his blade only swiped the air. Morien reached the pair and fitted his massive body between the two, sand swirling like a dust cloud as the three men dragged their boots over the pitch.

Bedwyr scaled the Marrakeshan Knight and pushed off Morien's broad shoulder with his boots. He curled and sailed over the Sagramore Lord. Closing a gloved hand over Harris' chin, Bedwyr wrenched back his opponent's head and Harris crashed to the ground.

Bedwyr pulled the wooden rods from his belt and sent them into a sweeping arc. They banged against Harris's legs and elicited a painful howl from him as the silver chain spun around his limbs, cinched tight, and hobbled him into crashing face-first onto the ground.

Bedwyr buried his fingers in the man's hair and hauled him upright. He reached onto his belt for a fan, the gleam of metal reflecting the late sun from its polished edge.

He was about to run the fan across Harris's throat when Arthwyr's scream rang out, "Bedwyr, no!"

Savagery blazed in Bedwyr's gaze and bore into Viera like a living creature. Fire pulsed through her belly and a dark hiss filled her ears. *Yes! Do it!*

Bedwyr dragged the edge of the fan over Harris's throat. As blood splashed the sand, it clumped the granules. He shoved Harris facedown into his own gore.

Drawing in ragged gasps, Harris held his fingers over the seeping wound.

Morien grabbed Bedwyr from behind and squeezed the wind out of the Knight, temporarily incapacitating him.

Myrddin reached Viera and pulled her close. With his warmth blanketing her, she held onto his robes. The worry in his gaze faded into raw fury.

With her mind swimming, she whimpered, "I'm sorry. I didn't mean to—"

"Silence," he hissed and reversed on his heels so sharply that his cloak snapped against her ankles.

As he strode toward Harris, the old but venerable Lord of Sagramore Halls, Cuchulain, moved at an identical pace toward Myrddin, who acted first by flashing his hand in a sharp cutting motion. At the sight of a Water kata bursting into rolling waves of flames, Viera blinked against her stinging eyes. The other man performed the same movement, and his Water crested and crashed against the other. Myrddin rapidly created another Fire kata. The ground shook and the wood splinters from previous jousts and spars sparked to life in flaming chips that danced in the air.

A black array shimmied into existence, the edges crackling with heat and the pungency of charred wood. Myrddin swept his foot outward into an Earth kata. When a molten shaft burst from the ground, people started running to the other side of the Arena. Jocelyn's father jerked out of the way so he wouldn't get hit by any of the debris.

Both men moved backwards, arms raising in preparation for another bout, when Baudwyn stepped forward and shouted, "Stand down!"

Myrddin sneered. "Back off, Baudwyn. I'm protecting what's mine."

Looking between Viera and Myrddin, Baudwyn said, "So, it *is* reciprocal." When neither man moved, he warned, "I'm serious. Not even Bercylac will be able to ease the pain I'll give both of you. It shan't take much for me to shatter your Elemental cores. Just consider how long it takes a core to heal. You'll wish I'd ripped your hearts out."

Whatever that threat meant had Myrddin retreating but growling at Cuchulain, "What's the meaning of your son striking my Apprentice?"

"This guttersnipe is your Apprentice?" Cuchulain scowled, the wrinkles in his face like deep ravines. "One would never know with how she's dressed. She reeks of peasant."

"The girl is in Fire Initiate robes, and anybody knows this, let alone a noble. You nor your kin have leave to strike any ward of the Fire Temple."

"Then teach her better manners. She draped herself on Harris. I saw this. He's entitled to uphold his honor."

Boots thumped over wood as Daegyn stepped down from the bleachers. Evergreen twined through his hair akin to ribbons braided into a spool of hemp. "I saw what happened too. What kind of bastard blames a girl for tripping?"

With blood smeared all over his neck and clothing, Harris staggered but managed to stand upright. Ewain glowered but came over to attend to him. He was rebuked and sent away as soon as he confirmed the injury superficial.

As hysterical burbles spilled from Viera, she squeezed her hands into fists to still the tremors and keep from setting Harris on fire and charring the life out of him forever.

"Laugh away, guttersnipe," Harris said to her, smiling darkly. "Word has spread about how you handled yourself on Progress. You piss yourself over the Marshal."

Bedwyr flicked the blood on his fans at Harris. "Careful, Harris. I still have some reaping left in me."

Cuchulain straightened and his smirk revealed a slight overbite in his jaw. "You're like your father, Bedwyr. You always had a soft spot for useless runts who deserved to be drowned. My, my. This one looks a spitting painting of your little sister."

Bedwyr snarled. "You keep *her* out of this."

CHAPTER 44

VIERA'S FAVOUR

Viera's gaze lingered on Harris and his shuddering shoulders. She would have found this funny if not in so much pain herself. A soft hand stroked her face and she was enveloped in lavender.

"Observe, little phoenix," Eerie chimed. "Learn how a woman reigns in a world where men think they rule."

Viera watched in anticipation as Eerie went over to Harris.

"You would protect me, Lord Harris?" Eerie asked.

Harris displayed the mien of a hound picking up a fresh scent. "You don't have to stay with a Wallachian dog. You can find a better mate in Sagramore than a traitor who ruins your good breeding and reputation."

Dimples formed on both of Eerie's cheeks. The edge along Harris' jaw softened until gurgles rattled from him and he clawed at his neck. With his face darkening into puce, his knees struck the ground and billowed a cloud of sand. An orange array with *Hagalaz* at its center sizzled into black over his head.

"Oh, Harris, any woman worth half her salt wants a man worthy of her." Eerie circled him, her well-defined muscles rippling beneath her velvet skin. "Why on earth would I want a lamed bitch when I already have the most powerful mate on my arm—and in my bed?"

She bent down and imbedded her nails into the side of his neck. As he gagged, Eerie snapped her fingers toward the cowering noble girls. "Never settle for second best, Ladies. There's nothing worse than holding the lead of a man unworthy of you."

Shaking with fury, Cuchulain bunched his jaws until pops emitted from the joints. "Fine talk when you chose a violent, blood-lusting beast over proper breeding. How long before he turns you into the rabid dog he is?"

With her eyes locked on Cuchulain, Eerie flicked her wrist and Harris began gasping for air. "Don't worry, Lord Sagramore, I have the ability to take Bedwyr's breath away whenever I want." She made the same wrist movement and Harris choked again, holding his throat this time and turning beet red. "The only difference between us is he's quick about it. I like playing with my toys."

"For the love of Evermore, stop this," Arthwyr ordered.

Eerie took a peek at Viera and said to Arthwyr, "Aye, my King, I will do as you command." With a click of her tongue, Eerie released her Air Element around Harris, and he collapsed to the ground, his hacking coughs drawing more than a few gasps from the spectators.

Eerie snapped her fingers at Bedwyr. "Come, love. You promised me an afternoon of utter sin. I find your lack of worship unsatisfying."

Bedwyr crouched and whipped his fan in front of Harris's face as a bead of blood dripped down his chin. "Touch that girl or Eerie, and I'll fold you like origami and leave you for Galahad's ruddy cat to bat around the gardens."

Rising, Bedwyr shot Viera a look she couldn't interpret. It was as though he was disappointed that he had to come to her aid. She had little time to think about this, as Ice splintered from a snowflake array and formed a shield of white that covered the ground. Footsteps crunched on the hardened surface. The entire crowd started to bow. Viera, however, couldn't move from the waist down because frozen tendrils slid around her legs.

Viera lifted her gaze in time to see Guinevere stepping next to Arthwyr, who said, "Cuchulain, do you know why I give my Queen free reign?" Arthwyr offered his hand palm-up to Guinevere until she set hers in his. "Despite our differences, my wife stands equally alongside me and I equally beside her. I wouldn't have it any other way."

"That's foolish," Cuchulain groused. "You're King, Arthwyr."

"Aye, I am King." Arthwyr let several beats pass. "But whom do you fear more?"

Cuchulain swallowed as Arthwyr continued, "I grant compassion and understanding as she provides reason and reality. My wife could kill you just as soon as look at you, and even my father and Jormund feared her in the end."

Guinevere's eyes were laden with ice as she said, "Give me due cause, and there shan't be much left of you or yours when I'm through, Lord Sagramore. Don't disappoint me again."

The Seven Sisters arrived and curtseyed to their Queen. "Come, Sisters," Guinevere said, "My husband will determine their sentence."

As Viera observed their departure, the tendrils unwrapped themselves and vanished into the ground. Viera's scalp prickled when Saris and Blanche peered over their shoulders. Lady Gorre wore the face of a cat considering what it wanted to do with a cornered mouse. Lady Rheged, however, tossed several men a flirtatious smile. Viera relaxed as they cast the last of their disparate looks—Saris's to Cuchulain; Blanche's to Harris.

Viera tensed as Bercylac crouched in front of her, his wild teal, rose, orange, and green hair blocking her vision and making her dizzy. As an Ice Elemental, the Elvin King provided her much-needed relief as he touched her sore jaw, and soothing coolness spread from the brush of his fingers. He followed this by running his hands over her back and neck and shoulders as Viera told him where she hurt the most.

When Bercylac was done, Arthwyr asked, "Will she be all right?"

"She'll be fine. The swelling and pain will be something else, though. I'll make a balm for her in the Infirmary. She should stay there for the night."

Arthwyr nodded and strode over to Harris, shoving him onto a bleacher. He loomed over Harris, his expression promising steel slicing through flesh, and blood weeping over the blade. Viera shifted her weight from one foot to the other, witnessing the same madness Uther's gaze had displayed in the atrium of the West Wing. Somewhere inside Arthwyr the presence of his wicked father lurked; of this she was certain.

But just when Viera believed that Harris had breathed his last, Arthwyr stepped back and said, "I try to do well by the people in my kingdom, peasants and nobles alike." He poked his finger on Harris's forehead. "Don't ever raise your hand against that child again. As for your punishment, you'll pay the Emrys for the damage done." The King turned to Myrddin, asking, "How much would be fair and reasonable?"

Myrddin thought a moment and said, "Nothing, Sire."

"Excuse me?"

"He struck her, not me, so he'll pay me nothing. Instead, he's in her debt. She can call a favour from him whenever she desires. That is his fine."

"Clever, Myrddin." Arthwyr gave Harris a smug look. "I could not have come up with anything more fitting, especially given the Sagramore males' views on girls and women." The King gently laid his hand on Viera's arm. "Within reason, though. You shan't ask for him to kill or maim." And to the dishonored noble: "You're indebted to Viera Tillwith for one favour, Harris Sagramore. You. No one else in your family but you and you alone. So mote it be."

CHAPTER 45

MOTHERLESS

Peeking from beneath his brown cowl, a man observed Arthwyr prowl across the pitch to the commoners' side of the Arena. The Ebony Knight flanked the ruler alongside Balin. When they stopped near the bleachers where the man perched a few rows above, they turned as Myrddin Emrys escorted the girl who had been struck from the field.

The King's head moved as though tracking those from Sagramore, Cornwall, and Cuhlwch. "Harris wouldn't have an arm if she were my daughter," the King said.

The observer noted Lance gesturing toward two men in Treasurers' robes. "I'm putting an addendum on her brother," Lance said, "The Sagramores aren't allowed contact with him."

The man in the bleachers waited for everyone to pass, brushing his hood from his greased black hair and slipping a weathered journal into his satchel—lest anyone spy the silver moon adorning the cover.

On the pitch below him, several peasant and noble children played hopscotch. One lad tripped, scraped his knee, and howled as he clutched his leg.

A matron stopped chatting with some women and rushed over. Her robes hinted she was upper nobility, the Griffin crest confirming her Kyner relationship to the King.

She knelt and cooed to the child, "Hush now, little lark. You're all right. Someone will get your mum."

The peasant boy rubbed his stained sleeve over his face, and she hugged and rocked him until his fussing settled. When the boy's mother appeared, she smothered her son in her lap. Noble and peasant crouched together, their laughter floating as aimlessly as the air around them.

Disgust burned in the man. A few months earlier his mother had been like that woman and her son. Now, his mother had disappeared from his world, only the faintest wisp of her scent remaining in their humble shack on the shimmering white sands of Porthcrawl's coast. Nearby protruding rocks held their carved initials in their secret shared language; in a tradition as mother and son, she insisted on adding a new set after each Alban Hefin.

All he ever had was his mother and an old family torque his mother wore from her childhood that related her family history in a gibberish code no one else he had met ever understood. It was some song-of-the-sea from the waves crashing against the berm and the seals beckoning to play that he had been nursed in. He still used the code of his mother to sign his name as much to confuse as to defuse attention. Most barely glanced at a peasant's signature. Those that did rolled their eyes but accepted that fair few commoners could read and it was a boon for one capable of signing their name.

Now, the man did not even have the torque to succor him as it went the way of his mother, both fading into the sea as if the old sea Fomoiri Tethra himself swept her into its inky abyss. He scratched his palms until they bled, the bite of pain the whisper of a memory when he came home from the schoolhouse on the edge of the city, his lips swollen and his hair askew from another childhood scrap. Other children had both their mums and thads. Other children had answers to why one parent or the other could not be there for them.

Children were mindless and cruel. They had no filter to temper the hurt their words inflicted. He wanted to crush them all, rend them limb from limb and revel in their small bodies split open and discarded like rotten fruit beneath the unforgiving sun. His mother had always assuaged that bottomless chasm of violence, tempered it like water cooling metal from the forges of Hells' Fires. And now she was gone.

There was only one reason she had left when she had promised she would not go.

She had not known that her son had observed her conversation with the King of Evermore. Market day's bustle had drowned out their discussion, no matter how hard he strained to learn what had made his mother's face shift into a cold mask and the King's countenance go pale. He watched his mother pull her threadbare robe closer to her lean form and slide her long black hair inside the fabric in an attempt to warm her.

Arthwyr untied a package and held out a white cloak with silver trim, and he handed it to the man's mother. Her features thawed, her expression morphing into wide-eyed shock. It was a beautiful robe, and his mother changed with the exchange, her life forever altered into something no longer recognizable—the additional gift of coin guaranteeing the permanency of the transition.

His mother was going to prepare dried fish for their evening meal. But the man had other plans as he checked the oyster beds at the beach, plucking a few who dared to expose themselves. Peering into the tide pools, his hard blue stare reflected from the ripples across the water. Within the small glimpse into the sea, urchins and mussels brightened the bottom. They were ill-fated when the surf had pulled out—and further doomed as he collected them. The crab traps were next, the fishing nets afterward.

"Arrr. Arrr. Arrr," the harbor seals barked when he passed them on his return to the wind-worn shack he knew as home. As the amiable creatures bobbed their heads and hobbled closer, he tossed them some fish. "Arrr. Arrr. Arrr," he heard them express their appreciation.

He entered their humble abode, dropped the family livelihood on the wooden table next to the door, and emptied what they would keep into baskets. As he crated his catch, he called over his shoulder, "Good haul today, Mum. Even enough for the seals."

Silence drove a private message deep into his soul, no different from the last words wrung out for the send-off of a loved one long cold and deep in the embrace of Twilight. He turned, stilling as his mother stood next to the kitchen table, her grayish-brown gaze on the beautiful robe with silver starfish embroidered on the trim. In the lantern light, an ethereal luminescence slid over the fabric.

Tears mapped the freckles covering his mother's face, pouring all the way down to the black moles on her pale throat. Birthmarks she called them. When he was little, she had shown him the ones she had on her chest and stomach. The coarse bark of her laughter filled the room as she said they were a map that always showed her the way home.

He had a smattering of pale white dots along his stomach, half-formed and not as striking as hers, and he always wondered if they would someday turn black. He had stared at those marks often. Why were hers so dark?

She had told him a funny story when he first asked why there was no father for her little "sea urchin," as she called him.

This time, her tale was not as funny. Nay, it was heartbreaking and his vision misted as she pressed the purse into his shaking hand and kissed him on his forehead.

As his remembrance of the past swam around in his head, his mother pushed open the door of what had been his home for twenty-three springs. A brisk salt-sea breeze smacked into him like a blow from a powerful fist.

She slid the robe over her frame, and the sunlight framed her in a way he'd never seen. The wind blew the door shut and wood cracked against the jamb. He ran and wrenched open the door, screaming for his mother, wind battering him like nettles on coastal briars. Not even a race around the shack revealed where she was or where she had gone. She had disappeared, leaving the low bark of the harbor seals as her final lullaby.

The overwhelming wash of onions shattered the man's reverie. He blinked at the gnarled face of a man with rheumy eyes. Licking his lips, the other said, "Ingot for a thought?"

"Sluagh, we talked about this. Scouting means separating."

"Ah, so it does. Me and the boys are done." Sluagh removed a purse from his grimy tunic. "A few purses short, but none a noble will miss."

The man rose and followed Sluagh down the steps. A few rail-thin boys paused near the muster stations and sent hungry stares at them as several scraggly men hung about the exits. The man rolled his wrist, flashing a V sign with his fingers. At the signal, the other highwaymen and Sluagh merged into the crowd.

A snapping banner drew the man's steely stare to the Pendragon coat-of-arms. Rage built inside of him and grew like an inferno.

His mother was Ursula.

Ursula left because of his father.

His father was Arthwyr Pendragon.

Arthwyr had stolen his mother from him.

His name was Mordred, and he was going to burn Evermore to the ground.

CHAPTER 46

THE TREASURER'S DECISION

To Viera's chagrin, the time had come to learn of Lord Baudwyn Kelliweg's decision regarding her relationship with Myrddin. Myrddin came for Viera, and the two of them met Arthwyr and Bedwyr outside the Throne Room. Everyone rode in the King's coach to the Treasurer's Guild.

Her vision blurred as the King's horses pulled the plush carriage along at what she thought was a ridiculously slow pace. She started to cry, realizing that she would likely have a new Master—a new everything.

Viera had tucked the page that Gavyn had drawn of her into a pouch, which she now rubbed for luck, her fingers shaking and misery settling deep into her bones. Myrddin watched her twitching and asked that the coach be stopped.

Myrddin gently stroked her wrist, and the gesture soothed her racing mind somewhat. But when the coachman clicked his tongue for the horses to start trotting again, her stomach became so tight with each turn of the coach's wheels, she believed that she might meet Twilight before they reached the Treasurer's Guild.

Once they had reached and were inside the Treasurer's Guild building, Garyth greeted everyone and led them to an anteroom, where they sat around a circular table that held light food and drink.

Garyth sat next to Viera and said, "There's nothing for you to fear."

Shivering, she focused on him and blinked at the Foxbury coat-of-arms superimposed on an oak tree embroidered on his sleeves. "Why the different coat-of-arms?"

"Being married to a Kelliweg affords me the right to wear a blended House symbol."

She ran her fingers across the Dragons on her robes and whimpered, "I don't want a new House symbol."

Before Garyth could say anything, a bell sounded and Alistair Kelliweg stepped into the anteroom. He walked over to them, the bracers on his arms and wrists glowing a soft gold. "Baudwyn is ready for you now."

The room they entered was stately, with not a thing out of place. Baudwyn Kelliweg was his usual impeccable self, wearing an ornate cloak with sigils that Viera had learned represented his House, the rich garb also displaying other symbols which identified him as head of the Treasurer's Guild. He sat behind a massive desk, a half-dozen heavy wooden chairs laid out in front of it, all in one neat row. Alistair approached him and bent to whisper in his ear. Baudwyn narrowed his eyes at Viera, and her pulse thudded in her throat as she realized for the first time that his irises were pure white with a thin gray border.

He thanked and dismissed Alistair, who left and closed the door behind him.

Viera's Royal Contract was lying open in front of Baudwyn. He asked everyone to take a seat, and he addressed her: "This is scary for you, and I understand you're upset. Frankly, you have every right to be." He kept his gaze on her, but the previous coldness and fury were absent as he continued, "It's imperative you're trained to harness and understand Fire. Given what I've heard about you, it would not be remiss for you to have two Masters, rare as that is for females. Either way, to not be able to fully control your Element would be a disaster and—"

Myrddin jerked around in his chair, causing its wooden legs to squeak against the stone floor, which halted Baudwyn's delivery. The Treasurer exchanged a look with Myrddin. "Lord Emrys will no longer be—"

"You can't!" Viera yelled, jumping up from her chair. "I should get some say in this, right?"

Baudwyn sighed long and loud, and the faintest grin crossed his face. "Nay, Miss Tillwith, you don't get any say. I'm not removing you from Myrddin."

Gulping, she managed, "But you just said that Myrddin will no longer be—"

"Performing the imprinting ritual on you. As it relates to you, he's permanently banned from it." Baudwyn gave Myrddin and the King a stare that would kill if it had arrows. "As soon as all of you are back at the castle, the Queen insists on a few words with your Master, here, and *His Royal Majesty,* to express her displeasure with the way your entire situation was handled."

Viera was so overwhelmed by the reprieve she'd been given, she smiled at Bedwyr, who continued to remain strangely stoic throughout everything. She thought about Garrett. "Your Lordship, will my brother's Contract be looked at too?"

"His is different from yours. But don't worry—" favouring her with a full smile this time— "I'll be reviewing it in detail shortly. Unlike some in this room, Lance reached out to me the day he returned to the Hearth. If it's not fair, there will be Hells to pay and he knows it." Baudwyn shot a hard look at Arthwyr. "If I must, I'll cancel it in its entirety. But let's hope it doesn't come to that."

Viera nodded her appreciation for Lord Kelliweg's concern.

Reaching into his desk drawer, he removed what appeared to be a coin and held it out until she took it. "This is a Kelliweg Pence. It's not real currency—but a token meant to bring you sanctuary if you ever need it. Show it to any Kelliweg and that person will house you. You can use it again and again, if need be."

It looked nothing like the money of the realm; it was a pure black coin that warmed as soon as her fingers touched it. She smoothed her thumb over the edges. "How do I know who is a Kelliweg?"

"My House symbol is on the other side." Baudwyn tapped the Kelliweg emblem on both his sleeves. "Anyone in my family has the right to wear it, regardless of birth order. The same for all who marry into Kelliweg House." He nodded toward Garyth and said in a tone that could be taken many ways, "As you can see, Garyth also wears it when he's stepping into the Kelliweg side of either business or pleasure."

She flipped the coin over and stared at a gold inlay with tiny diamonds bordering an oak tree, electrum making the leaves appear green. "I thought you hated me—" lowering her head— "and I have to be honest. I didn't like you much."

He held out his hand to her. "It's not my job for you or anyone else to like me. It's my responsibility to assure that no one cheats our realm legally, morally, or financially."

"But, Milord, I'm just a peasant with no standing whatsoever."

"There is no realm without having people from all walks of life in it. Rulers have no throne without the support of those who put them on it—or keep them on it." Baudwyn paused as if at a loss for words but quickly recovered. "You are everything to our realm, and don't ever let anyone convince you otherwise."

Viera took his hand and closed her fingers over it; the earlier shock that had numbed her arm now nothing more than a slight tingle. As she tightened her grip, something felt right about the Treasurer of Evermore and the token he'd given her. She didn't understand what Baudwyn Kelliweg meant about her importance to the realm, but he had assured her of a better life, and now it would be up to her to see it through.

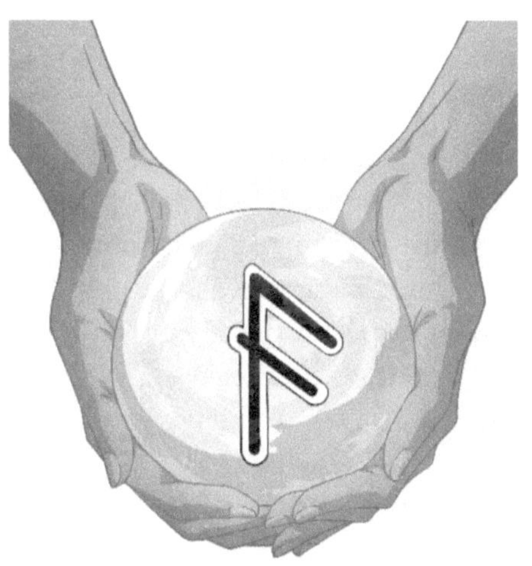

CHAPTER 47

FATE AND MATES

The silent specters of the stars glinted through the velvety blanket of the cloudless night. Bedwyr leaned against his balcony guardrail, Alban Hefin now a memory. Lantern light illuminated the Lockinge River and snaked along the shadowy landscape. It was tribute to the light of day and the benefits reaped from its generosity.

He relaxed into the slow return to normal thrumming through his veins. Royal Progress had taken its toll on his mind and body. His already thin patience was sapped and chafed from being under such intense scrutiny and rigid constraints. As for his physical condition, the raw ache of his left arm flared up often, a nightmare this time of year when memories reemerged from the arrays carved into him six Alban Hefins ago.

Rage unfurled like a rousing Dragon and he clenched his teeth. On this spot, his father once lifted him for the parade of lanterns and murmured tales against his ear. Bedwyr stalked from his father's favourite spot and leaned against the opposite banister. "Sweet memory," he snarled, folding his arms over the railing, "built upon lies."

Lavender teased him and satin whispered against his bare back. Eerie kissed along the solid stripe of his spine. As her nimble fingers slid from his waist to his sleep-trouser's hem, her body heat cut through the chills the night air had driven into him.

Her husky voice bathed his ear. "What troubles Milord from important matters of state?"

He tugged her against him, his hands stilling over the arch of her back. She peeked up at him from beneath her wild glistening bangs, an impish gleam lighting her alabaster features.

She shuddered in his hold, the heave of her chest against his bare skin inciting a thrill far lower. "Glad to have you back," she cooed as she pressed into him.

Bedwyr stroked her hips and pulled her even tighter against him. He brushed aside her satin negligee, smirked at the uptick in her breath, and softly traced her smooth-as-cream waist. He slid his fingers lower, and her skin flinched and his heart thudded in counterpoint. He settled his hand over the small of her back and lifted his gaze to her wet eyes.

Bedwyr drank in the way her shivers coursed through her. "What are you willing to gift me for my return?"

Eerie rolled her hips into his. She pulled away but he followed her. Undulating against him again, she giggled at the sharp intake of his breath. Her voice lowered into a croon:

Pinnacle of light, pinnacle bright,
The first one I glimpse this night;
Desire I may, desire I might,
For you, Milord, are the desire I most desire tonight.

Eerie sashayed into his chamber and crooked her finger for him. He looked back at the meandering trail of lights coursing with the river, and a brilliant light streaked through the sky.

She continued with her lilt: *"My Lord, my wish is waning with my pinnacle of light."*

"Wish I may, wish I might," Bedwyr said, thanking the shooting star, "I've got my desire in my bed tonight."

Joining her inside, Bedwyr gripped her wrist and luxuriated in her pulse beneath his palm. "Why will you not let me Bind with you? Don't you want the world to know I'm yours?"

"Ah, that is what's been bothering you. Cuchulain rattled you, did he?" She kissed his neck. "That girl doesn't help—but she is our Fate."

He gently shoved her onto the bed and straddled her. Gooseflesh prickled his skin when she traced his carvings and tattoos. "I'll push her away," he said, his breathing ragged. "I shan't have her between me and my promises."

"She is your promise, darling. She and what comes after. It'll be your duty to see her and the others through. It's your blooded oath to Evermore."

He rested his forehead against hers and observed the quiver of her eyes. "You're sure it's them? There are no other possibilities?"

"The girl is your promise." Eerie bucked her forehead against his. "The boy is mine."

"He's really annoying, you know that, don't you?"

"They are our responsibilities." Eerie slid her hand below his waist, coaxing a moan from him. "Besides, we hardly need the red strings of Fate to be one. I'll always be yours." Her eyes narrowed. "And may Evermore help the fool who covets mine."

Bedwyr ran his fingers below the smooth roll of her stomach, and it was her turn to moan. Breathing heavily, she said, "Now make good on your wish. I have an appointment tomorrow for an awkward noonday meal across from the Sagramores. There's an old dog and his lamed bitch I must show some mating marks to."

CHAPTER 48

LANCE DULAC'S STORY

It didn't take long after Alban Hefin for the staff to fall back into their standard routines throughout the castle. It was Lance's tradition to attend to the servant quarters as they had been his home in the early days of his Wardship. Lance pressed his fingers against the wall, and the granite seemed to shiver as the cracks smoothed into solid stone. He followed the path to the next turn in a lower section of the castle, the area of the original servant quarters.

Abandoned alongside another infant at the Earth Temple, Lance was an unwanted bastard. Not that anyone could confirm he was a bastard; the person who'd left him that winter evening didn't provide the slightest hint as to his origins. The Earth Masters believed he and the other child, later known as Jarvis Ward, were from two separate families, the primary difference being that Jarvis was found in a burlap sack, while Lance was abandoned without any care for his comfort or survival.

Lance was naked and blue when Carydoc Ynyr stumbled upon them. His cries had started to fade into Twilight; his only saving grace being the volume of noise from Jarvis and Lance's placement next to the other babe.

Whoosh! Whoosh!

Lance heard it and then felt the rush of icy air on his face and hands. He ran his fingers over the walls in the cold, dark hall, seeking where the frigid blast was coming from. But no cracks or bulges appeared, so he checked out the ceiling, which was low enough that he could touch it. Nothing.

Sheew. Sheew.

The air sounded like a whisper. He scanned the walls, his gaze dropping to the stone floor. The whisper faded. With slow movements, he continued down the corridor, old ghost tales creeping into the edges of his memory.

Sniffle. Sniffle.

The sound was different from the others, definitely human this time. He edged his way toward an open doorway. As the sniffling repeated, a sharp pang throbbed in his chest. He hesitated at the threshold and peeked into the room. Curled up and with her bony arms tight about her knobby knees, Viera had her face buried against her legs. At the sight of the lass in the abandoned hearth, Lance was hit with another kind of pain.

He stepped over the threshold, his robes dragging over the stone. She jerked her red-rimmed gaze up to him and scrubbed soot into streaks across her skin. "I'm not crying, dammit!"

Lance blinked. "So, what are you doing?"

She dropped her chin onto her knees. "I got lost. Jocelyn's a stupid bint."

"Thanks. That was enlightening." He walked over to the fireplace and sat on the hearth bench. "Distance makes the heart grow fonder. Proximity makes distance most desired. Royal Progress is a great way to figure out who not to spend extended periods of time around."

Viera snorted. "Jocelyn called me a pig again. I want to go home. I miss my mum and da, and my best friend, Peg."

"I know it's not easy being here," Lance said, rubbing her back, "but you must learn to harness your Fire. Yet, sometimes I wonder what would truly be for the best."

She leaned into him and hummed a tune that stilled his hands. He furrowed his brow, trying to place it. When he did, he looked down at Viera. Shiori Murasaki and Karen Wallach had sung about sparrows in both Nihongo and Evermorean to Galahad and Bedwyr. And Nimue had sung the same song in Nihongo when Maerna was an infant.

Lance crooned the off canter tune an elderly maid once sang while wiping away the younger wards' tears. *Too ra loo* had been their staple until Constantine brought a fresher melody from Viteliu. "The tune your humming is from Nihon," he said, "Would you like to hear one that Constantine brought over? Little secret. He sang it to Bedwyr a long time ago."

She sat up, her eyes brimming with curiosity. "All right."

"Keep humming your sparrow song," he said and started to sing in the same lilting tune:

Fare thee well, little light of mine.
I want to let you shine.
Through the bend of path amid the trees,
The airs of change take you past the valleys.
Far beyond the crests of surf and beach,
Past the rise and peek of the moon's reach.
Fare thee well, my little love,
As the sun's keep brightens above.
Distance breaks and draws us apart,
The pieces gather whole again, my heart.
I may not be near for your sorrows.
The wind and my love hold you forever morrows.
Fare thee well, little light of mine.
You will always shine.

When he concluded the song, Viera said, "Without you and Myrddin, I wouldn't have a chance over here. I just wish some things could be different."

"Unfortunately, *she's* not going away."

"I should have set Jocelyn's arse on fire and not her horse's tail."

Lance started to chuckle, when a shadow filled the doorway. His gaze darted to a thick, tall male leaning against the doorframe, tufts of blond-and-gray-patched hair flaring out, the spiciness of sausages and cured meat rising from his clothing.

He walked forward, winking a blue eye. "What have we here?" he asked amiably.

"This is Viera Tillwith," Lance said, patting her shoulder. He looked to the man and said to Viera. "And this fellow is Jarvis Ward. When we were babes, we were found together, abandoned at the Earth Temple, so we consider ourselves brothers. Jarvis is our Master Brewer and Butcher. If ever you find yourself in need, you can trust him and his wife, Talia."

Jarvis' whiskers twitched upward. "So, you're the Apprentice Myrddin took on." Viera nodded, and Jarvis held out his hand to help Lance stand. "You know, there's better places than here to overcome matters of the heart, eh?"

Lance accepted his assistance and did the same for Viera. "Aye." He clapped the ash from his robes. "If anyone asks, you found a hearth to clean. Cinders get everywhere."

With a snort, Jarvis sauntered toward the door and brushed his thick fingers over where two sets of initials, *JW* and *LW*, had been carved into the jamb. "Even boys sometimes need a spell of hearth-cleaning to overcome the doldrums. As Lance will tell you, there's this lovely garden right this way." He pointed ahead. "It's the Queen's favourite."

Viera twisted her fingers within the folds of her Fire robe. "It's pretty, I take it?"

Before Jarvis could answer, Lance said, "It's… it's beautiful… beautiful all year long. I go there for contemplation." Regret welled in Lance at what else was in the garden.

After Alban Hefin, his visits increased. His wife, Elaine, and daughter shared the same date of Twilight as Karen Gorre but different years. He was far from the only one to spend late nights in the gardens where their ashes were interred. Bedwyr visited the markers around Alban Hefin, Homage to the Ancestors, and birthdates. It would not surprise Lance if they crossed paths soon under shared mourning.

As they stepped outside, Lance blinked until his vision readjusted under the afternoon sun. Willows and oaks grew in separate sectors. Flowering plants were plotted out into an array of colors. The grass was springy and soft, as if begging for bare feet to run through it. Against the castle walls, trestles helped the crawl of roses and ivy form a tapestry over the stone.

Viera said, "This is truly beautiful. I want to look around."

"There are fountains in the back." Jarvis said. "I'll give you an ingot if you catch me a frog."

She crinkled her nose. "Why do you want a frog?"

"If I kiss it, I might get a princess, eh?"

"What would Mrs. Ward think about that?" she asked as she walked off.

Jarvis laughed and hollered after her, "You got me there."

When silver flashed in the corner of Lance's vision, he veered toward the lone apple tree his son and Bedwyr had climbed as children.

A silver apple hung by itself from the lowest branch. Snapping the stem, he rubbed the fruit.

"Isn't this a trick?" Lance poked the apple. "Someone painted it to look like an apple from Avalon. What's that old legend?"

"If you find a silver apple," Jarvis said, eyeing the fruit suspiciously, "someone has either found Avalon or returned from there. This has Palamedes written all over it."

Unsheathing a dagger from his belt, Lance cut into the fruit and the juice dribbled onto his fingers. "My ingots are on Daegyn." He handed Jarvis half as he licked the juice from his other hand. "Here. We'll take it to Arthwyr and act as if it's real."

"Before or after I kiss that frog?" Jarvis lifted his piece and his lips parted on a wheeze.

Lance followed Jarvis's stare to the interior of the apple. His breath caught in his throat—the inside of the fruit was gleaming silver.

CHAPTER 49

MEMORIAL HALL AND
THE CHAMBER OF THE ECLIPSE

Since there was no chance that she would be getting home anytime soon, Viera took advantage of her free time by learning as much as she could about the castle, and in doing so continued to educate herself to Evermore's long and complex history. It helped that Myrddin and many others were willing to freely share so much with her. She often wondered why she was seldom if ever refused an answer to a question, but she wasn't going to challenge this.

She and Palamedes had become good friends, and they liked to explore the castle together, albeit often with Myrddin and the Saracens as chaperones, as this provided an opportunity for an adult to keep an eye on them.

On this day, Myrddin and the Saracens were formally showing them The Memorial Hall and The Chamber of the Eclipse.

Beneath the torchlights, metal alloy gleamed from two columns of statues lining the corridors. Viera giggled when Palamedes held his mouth agape and waggled his tongue at the statues. Myrddin slowed his pace and looked over his shoulder at them and Maerna.

Viera fluttered her eyelashes and earned a snort from Myrddin, who dragged her by the arm to keep pace alongside him. He stopped and said, "This is Memorial Hall, which is dedicated to past and current Knights of the Eclipse. The Chamber of the Eclipse is down there."

She pointed at the end of the Hall. "Is that where the Knights congregate?"

Segwarides fell into step next to her. "Aye, and just your luck that today you get to see inside."

Up ahead, Tippy Foxbury and two of her daughters were pouring wine into a bronze bowl in front of a large metal statue. The matron bowed, the girls emulating her as the three of them finished their task and scurried off.

Viera marched up to the statue. "He looks like a Foxbury."

Safir rested his hand on her shoulder. "He was. It's Renard Foxbury—Tippy's father—as well as the triplets: Garyth, Gavyn, and Gaheris."

"I can see why people come here to remember those they lost to Twilight," Viera said. "I hear most cremate their loved ones. In my village, we're not so lucky and bury them in the earth. It costs money to have a big funeral pyre."

"It's not a Saraceni practice—we inter ours in a family tomb. I wouldn't mind going the way of my Evermorean forebears to embrace Fire in its fullest sense, but Islam doesn't abide it."

Viera stared at the teasing smile forever immortalized on Renard's face, and she especially liked the staff slung over his shoulder. Despite being cast in a medium as rigid as metal, his image was the essence of ease.

"Renard passed into Twilight last summer," Myrddin said as he removed a cloth from his pocket and wiped the rim of the bowl Tippy and her daughters had just filled. "His efforts in the Draigs' Duels earned him his place in this corridor."

The solemnity in his tone had her soften her voice. "Master, what did he do?"

"He helped commoners, Ancients, and fugitives alike. That crafty old fox paid lip service to Uther and his ilk while sneaking people out. Uther and Jormund never suspected him."

She glanced at the other statues. "Why are none of you there?"

"We will be." Segwarides bowed toward Aglovale's statue. "The commissions are taking time. The deceased Knights are first."

"If you cark it, you get a fast pass?"

"That's one way of looking at it. I'm in no hurry." He sobered and gestured toward a statue pedestal. "For those retiring and ready for the next great quest, their memorials also receive priority."

Viera lowered her gaze to the placard for Lord Dinadan Blumenthal, which was attached to a marble base. He was Myrddin's secondary Master, and Myrddin had pointed out the frail old man in passing when he gave her a tour of the Library.

"Arthwyr wants Dinadan's statue in place before my Master passes into Twilight." Myrddin's voice broke, and he shepherded Viera and Palamedes toward the chamber. "This way now."

Matching sentries were stationed on either side of two large wooden doors. When the group of them approached, Myrddin nodded and the guards opened the doors, which they closed as soon as they stepped inside the room. Darkness filled the chamber, and the low creak of wood startled Viera as they walked forward.

Safir nudged her aside and padded farther into the room. "Let's get some light in here."

The scent of fresh campfire wood filling Viera's nose. The flicker of an array formed a low ball of flames over his hand, and Fire leapt into the braziers and sconces.

In the center of the room stood a large circular table with finely upholstered chairs situated around it. When Viera drew closer, she spied a map of Evermore embedded under the smooth resin of the table's top. Over the coastline, blue and white glints created the impression of waves.

"Did The Knights of the Eclipse make this?" she asked.

"Nay," Myrddin replied. "The table was a gift to the first rulers of Evermore, Cymry and Elden Pendragon. Legend has it a maid appeared in the mist rising over Avalon, and once she gave this table and another like it called the Monarch's Mirror to Evermore, she faded in the mist and Avalon faded with her. Unfortunately, the Monarch's Mirror has been lost since the other Pendragon castle, Siege Perilous, fell in the East hundreds of years ago."

"That's quite a story," Viera said. "What was her name?"

"No one is sure. Though, some legends say Gyda Annwyn or Mab. Others she was an Elf or a Nymph. Others go so far as to imply she was a Bean-síghe."

"A what?" Palamedes asked, adding his usual giggle.

"You wouldn't find it so funny if one of them ever visited you," Myrddin said and gave the boy the evil eye. "The name means 'washer woman,' but it's a female who haunts streams and rivers and washes the clothing of a person who is about to meet Twilight."

"Yuck, makes my skin crawl," Palamedes said, scratching himself for effect.

Viera thumbed the runes carved into the tabletop. "Where are The Seven Houses on here?"

Myrddin pointed to the Lockinge River bordering the edges of the castle grounds. "The Seven Houses started in Elden's Hearth. The Temples today were each family's original homes."

"So, Bedwyr lives in, and owns, the Metal Temple?" Palamedes asked, appearing serious for the first time.

Safir shook his head. "Nay. The Wallachs, Cadogans, and Esau left the Hearth and formed separate duchies to maintain neutrality. They were the only three who did, but the Druir, who are Wood Elementals, became partial to visiting Foxbury, which is also Wood, and there is a longstanding rumor that some Druir cousins bred into that family. A few Pembrokes of Earth Bonded into Rheged."

Myrddin indicated the Temples for Druir and Pembroke on the map. "The main Houses still maintained their residency in the capital." He settled his finger on the Air Temple. "The last Windsor Lords were nomadic and looking for a new place to settle. Nothing came of it after the last Lord of Air, Archibald, embraced Twilight and his ashes were interred in the Air Temple."

"That must've been sad for the Pendragons. I heard a bard sing Cymry and Windsor were close—friends even—before Evermore was formed," Viera said. "Unless something bad happened between the Pendragons and Windsors, I can't imagine them parting ways."

"By Air Marshal Archibald's and King Dernion Pendragon's time, the closeness between House Windsor and Pendragon had disintegrated to bare civility. They were no longer as close as Cymry and Windsor had first been."

"What was the first Windsor's name?" Palamedes asked.

"Windsor," Myrddin said, smirking at the faces Viera and Palamedes made. "Windsor and the other Marshals did not have family names. Their names became their family names. Cymry himself did not have a family name. Pendraig was something he came up with after hearing his first Ebony Knight, Finneas Bheara, had a full name. It intrigued him and later Pendraig became Pendragon."

Viera asked, "So, Windsor and Pendragon never recovered their friendship?"

"The curse leveled on Archibald from entering Cadogan House, the Ice Lord's domain—is what ended their distance, as he lost his entire House. It was only through Fate that Archibald Windsor and Dernion Pendragon ever found common ground again."

"What was the curse about?" Viera asked.

Myrddin waved toward the snow-covered mountains on the map, which were past Orrinshire Pass. "The Cadogans settled in the Forbidden Grounds between Evermore, Ribeena, and Auraboralis. Prior to joining Evermore, the Jotnars attacked the Cadogans, slaughtered them all, and laid a curse on the first person who entered. As Archibald was that person, the House of Air perished." He dragged his finger to another area of the table. "In answer to Palamedes' question about the House of Metal, the Wallachs forced the Dwarves and Trolls to move from this old Dumnonian duchy. Tryfan Heights has been the home of the Wallachs ever since."

"I don't see the Esau," Viera said.

"You see Esau Islet, don't you?" Segwarides tapped his finger over the largest island off the coast that was shaped like the head of a Dragon. "It still stands as a retreat of sorts. At least, the parts that have not fallen into the Isles Seas."

"Where's Wyllt Way?"

Chuckling, Myrddin led her to the other side of the table. "This is home." He pointed at a castle in the northeastern mountains. "Mining towns line the mountains to the Isles, but they all aren't in our duchy."

Viera followed his finger to Pellinore Falls and Kyner Craggs. Confusion stirred when she picked out a few more castles farther east of the three holdings. "What about these?" She traced seven more castles. "Shouldn't the table end at the boundary here?"

"Five noble families stood behind Uther when we struck Elden's Hearth. But after word reached them of Jormund's and Uther's Twilights, they pulled back."

"There's seven, though."

Myrddin pointed to two of the castles on the far eastern boundaries. "Arthwyr had two younger twin sisters, Morgaine and Anya. Uther gave them into Bonding to strengthen alliances with Kings Holger Danuske and Talisen Bach."

Viera thought for a moment but quit trying to figure out where this was going. "What does that all mean?"

"As Uther's daughters, Morgaine and Anya had claims to Evermore's Kingship. The five other duchies tried to rally behind them as Pendragon contenders."

"Then we could have a real blooded Queen Pendragon on the Throne?"

"Could have, but the Pendragon sisters loathed their father," Myrddin said, bitterness in his voice. "When we won the Duels, they came to Elden's Hearth with their husbands and heirs. They bent the knee on the condition it was the last time they would for a King of Evermore."

"Isn't that ceding?"

"The Danuskes' and Bachs' loyalty was never cast in stone. Bonding two Pendragon daughters secured little more than two generations of fidelity and trade."

Chewing her lip, Viera stared at the castles. "Knowing how Arthwyr is around his family, I don't see him giving up on his sisters."

"The five other duchies didn't take kindly to Anya's and Morgaine's refusal to retake Evermore. They attacked the Danuskes and Bachs on their return." Myrddin walked away from that side of the table. "After repeated attempts to reach Morgaine and Anya failed, we gave up two summers ago. There is too much land between us and them to send an envoy."

Viera bent over and examined the holdings bordering the north. "Master, if the table is from so long ago, how does it have newer Houses?"

"After the final eve of a festival, the interior displays the current state of the realm." He traced the edges of the table where strange carvings flickered with ebony and silver trim.

Viera made a pass around the table but gave up trying to figure out where each Knight sat. A scent she couldn't place drew her to a chair. She pulled it out and looked at Myrddin.

He circled to the opposite side of the table and said, "You may sit."

Viera settled into the seat and jumped at the lingering warmth from the cushion. *Who sat here just before we came in?* She laid her hands on the table and worked her fingers over the wood. "Where does the King sit? And which side is the head of the table?"

Safir sat across from her. "That's the beauty of the table of the Eclipse. There is no head of it. We're equal when we sit here, and no one opinion has more weight than any other."

Myrddin took the seat closest to the fireplace. "Arthwyr usually sits on the side I'm on, but he takes other places around the table, as well. He likes to keep us on our toes."

Viera looked down at the chair she was in. "You mean I'm sitting where the King might have sat?"

Myrddin steepled his fingers. "Nay, the only place Arthwyr does not sit is where you are now—and the chair next to you. That seat beside you was designated solely for the House of Water. Today, however, Bedwyr sits in it as both the Lord of Metal and of Water."

Viera rested her fingers over the leather on the armrest. This chair was the only one made of ebony wood and with upholstery the shade of congealed blood.

She poked the armrest and it emitted a metallic tang. She gulped, "Who sits here?"

"The Marshal—and only when his position is needed to set Evermore to rights."

CHAPTER 50

THE FIRE TEMPLE

Myrddin split his attention between Viera skipping steps and Maerna strolling up the stairs of the Fire Temple. Smoke billowed from the landing altar; the large brazier's fire snuffed out. With a mulish expression, Palamedes squared his shoulders as Safir chastened him, "There's a slipper with your name on it. I need to break in the soles and the best option would be your arse."

Myrddin bent toward Viera and asked her, "What do you most wish to see now, Wart?"

She pranced up the steps of the Fire Temple. "Fire dances and fighting katas. Not those weak katas you showed me earlier, Master."

"Maerna can go with Safir and give Palamedes a tour of the Temple." Myrddin arched his eyebrow at Segwarides. "I'll show you the more aggressive techniques in *Tan* with Segwarides. He can give you hints on speeding up your attacks in minor ways."

Rooting through the satchel he'd braced against his robes with a wide belt, Segwarides removed a thick journal held together with a leather strap. He unwound the binding and flicked open the latches that kept the book intact, careful to hold in place the additional pages he'd recently added to it.

"You have much to learn before I'm of half the mind to tutor you," Segwarides said, opening to a page with figures performing katas; numbers and equations were scribbled on the margins. "Including more of the maths from Lionel and Baudwyn; for that is how you learn to speed up many of your moves."

Viera stared at the journal, likely not understanding how numbers had anything to do with lighting something with her Fire. To her, snap her fingers and there's Fire—BOOM.

Flames arched with the sailing motion of Viera's hand. Safir tracked the firebirds and gauged the adjustments she'd made to her stance. The phoenixes soared in a lazy circle around the training room and stirred a quickening of his pulse. Not even the most powerful Saracen Masters produced anything so effortlessly. Other Fire Masters observed Viera from the upper observation level, and the wonder in their expressions made it clear that they were equally impressed with what they were witnessing.

Glancing at the training room's entrance, Safir stepped closer to Segwarides. Heat swept near his shoulder as a phoenix sped past, its long tail fanning out behind it.

Viera spun around, her arms extended from her body and palms outward, and the birds raced by her, swooping upwards into a series of complex aerial maneuvers. Without warning, one of the phoenixes dived toward her, and flames erupted and engulfed her in a curtain of black.

Safir stiffened and spied his younger twin, ashen-faced and wide-eyed, as he edged backwards from the wall of Fire that enveloped Viera as numerous fresh arrays sparked to life and twisted into glowing embers. A phoenix blurred into a wash of blue and black as the other remained bright with Fire from its initial release. The birds flew in tandem inside the Temple chamber, their arrays shuddering and expanding, lightning crackling from their centers.

Other Fire Masters shouted and dragged their students into the halls. Safir caught twenty-six summers Xavier Cuhlwch's withering sneer as he grabbed the collar of an Initiate's robes and hauled him to safety. Safir saw something in Xavier's eyes that hinted of a Witchery accusation being leveled upon Viera. Even as he realized with chilling certainty the girl had noosed her neck, Safir knew too many powerful people who would quash any action taken against her.

However, dread took root, weighing heavily on him as waves of electricity coursed through his body and straightened his hair in places. His uncle's Fire arrays had begotten a lightning array that created a bolt of energy which found its way to Safir's mother, and there was no purging her charred flesh from the Saracen Knight's memory.

Whirling, he pushed Segwarides toward a door and shouted, "Run! It's like what Uncle did when he killed Mâmân!" Safir raced over to Myrddin. "Myrddin, get back!"

Blazing heat swept over the stone floor, molten rock bubbling and oozing from the cracks and coming up just short of Myrddin's boots. Safir latched onto Myrddin's arm and dragged him behind the safety of the door, which Segwarides was already using as a barrier.

When the shrills of the phoenixes quieted, Safir shoved the pair into an alcove and shielded them with his body.

Multiple elemental releases burned in the air. The door flew shut, flame-retardant runes preventing its immediate destruction.

Soon, silence reigned until the door lazed open and the calming twitter of birdsong filled the hallway. As the three men peeked past the alcove, Viera strolled into the corridor like nothing had happened. Two sparrows flitted around the room, landed on her shoulder, and warbled. The more colorful one of the two sneezed; its feathers puffed out and white ash drifted in the air.

Viera stroked its head as the other sparrow gently glided onto her outstretched hand, its color flickering between black and purple and turning a dull-brown. After setting the bird back on her shoulder, Viera giggled as it bounced over and inched closer to her neck.

CHAPTER 51

SLEEPLESS NIGHT

Startling awake, Bedwyr blinked shadows from his vision. Bone and wood clinking together drew his attention to the lone shell mobile hanging from the rafters above his bed chamber. His mum and Galahad's mum, Elaine, had made the decorations that sounded like waves cresting on a beach, especially on a night like this when the castle was particularly drafty.

Bedwyr spared a glimpse at Eerie's moon-kissed hair as he slipped from his bed and dressed with the barest of movement. There were some things he needed to keep from her, and it would not do to wake her when he had to find solace in a way that no one could provide, not even his lover.

As he crept toward his door, an age-old rhyme played back in his mind, its lyrics coming from a long-lost and much-missed voice: *Ni-san. Ni-san. I heard a birdy say. Ni-san. Ni-san. Why won't you come and play?*

The moon lit the way, making the gypsum shine in the white gravel path leading through the Queen's favourite gardens. Bedwyr had stopped outside Gavyn's chamber, banging on the door as if a siege was imminent, yet a still-as-a-crypt response greeted him. Truth be told, he should've expected that Gavyn was drowning himself in drink, nowhere near recovered from the anniversary of Renard Foxbury's Twilight—the father who had been so vital to his son after his boy's Soul Bond had met Twilight so swiftly. It had been shocking to see Gavyn on Progress, clean shaven and having shed the black mourning robes he'd worn every day since the preceding summer. Still, it rankled Bedwyr that Gavyn could not muster the strength to go with him on a night like this. The past haunting both of them so harshly, he didn't see how Gavyn refused. But he had, so Bedwyr carried on alone. Though, they would've both been drinking anyway.

As he scanned the path he walked in the moonlight, a glint of blue flashed on the otherwise dark surface. He estimated the distance he'd come thus far, kicked at the stones near his boots, and dropped a pebble on the trail as the low pulse of light from fireflies drew his attention. Fae lights are what dreamers and fools called them, and he could see why.

He swept past the memorial stone for Elaine DuLac to a grave site in the back and against a wall overgrown with a wild outcropping of golden saxifrage. Often, people whispered how he'd failed his mother by not maintaining Karen Wallach's memorial better, but he knew her too well. She would not have wanted an altar without nature cradling her memory. Not when she'd entwined ivy around the stones that she laid out to commemorate her rabbits and ducks that passed beyond their mortal coils.

Bedwyr forced his fingers to remain loose, lest he crush the delicate blooms in his hand. A pebble clicked in his pocket as he stopped in front of Karen Wallach's memorial stone. He recited: "Once upon a time, there was a family: two parents, a son, Handel, and a daughter, Grissa. As for the father and mother, there was something different about each of them. The father feigned affection while the mother was trapped and beaten down with only the love for her children sustaining her."

Bedwyr pulled out a stone, kissed it, and set it on her memorial. "As the father went to his trade, the mother collected little white stones from the river. She enchanted them with the water and laid most of them along a path leading from their home. Dividing what remained between each child, she taught them how to make Water stones and how to follow them, always in the hope that someday they would escape."

Bedwyr touched his mother's name on the memorial stone, his voice softening with reverence once more: "One day, their father accused their mother of being a Witch. In front of the entire village, he drowned her in the river. The children were certain that the sin of their mother would find them as well."

He knelt and pushed aside the carpet of foliage covering the grave. A braided diamond and obsidian circlet was engraved at the stone's bottom. The black volcanic rock hid an interior circle of a sapphire Witch's Knot.

"That night, the children fled. They followed the stones, the villagers and their father chasing them, until they found the river." Bedwyr traced the Witch's Knot with his finger. "When they slipped down the embankment, their mother stepped from the water, her final enchantment whispered upon her last breath to the river in which she had met Twilight. Her children understood, grasped her hands, and the river rose and swept them away."

He lifted his gaze from the symbol that true Witches embraced. "I promise that great-great-grandmother Grissa's story won't die with me. One day, I will teach your heir our truth."

Leaving her memorial, he slipped through the hedgerow. Deep in the recess of the wall was an oft overlooked space between the bushes and stone. He crouched and searched until his fingers brushed a hard surface. As he pushed aside the plants, a flat marker with the name *Wysteria* in Nihongo appeared, the gravestone gleaming under the moonlight from the flecks of mica in the rock.

Wysteria Wallach had been six springs. Bedwyr removed a sprig of lavender from his robe and placed it on his fourth sister's memorial. He recalled her laughter rippling like a bubbling brook as her brown eyes crossed when she was happy. Tragically, when her Element presented as Water, she succumbed to plague a week later. Fluid filled her lungs and nothing could be done. At least that's what his father claimed to anyone curious enough to ask. Bedwyr knew different. Water—Hells, his father had a hand in the loss of all of his seven siblings. At last, he understood what his father was, but nine winters was a hard age to learn such a fact. Water touched Bedwyr but would not take him. His father loathed Water, but a male heir meant more until a suitable one arose.

He worked from Wysteria's gravemarker to find his older sister, Seren, who met Twilight at just one season. She was Water as well, but fever supposedly took her. Bedwyr did not remember Seren, but his mother and Shiori told him that she was a joyful child.

His second sister, Iona, liked Water fine and the Element embraced her as she turned two winters. *Pat-Pat Cake* was her favourite game, her inky gaze lighting up as she pumped her fists in the air, and Water rose from any cup, glass, mug or pot nearby.

To avoid getting wet, Bedwyr was teaching her *Little Pig Goes to Market*. What would he not give for her to drench him again? At five winters, he had to say goodbye to Iona; because, one day she was there and the next she was gone. He was too young for the details, but he became suspicious of Water.

His fifth sister, Rowena, came when he was seven winters. At six months, Twilight claimed her. When Bedwyr last saw Rowena, her face was puce, small, and scrunched up.

When Daphne was born, he swore Twilight would not have her, but she was taken at the cusp of her reaching one autumn. Bedwyr was eleven winters at the time, and he found it impossible to forgive himself when her head fell at an odd angle on the funeral pyre. All evidence went up in a blaze of fire and smoke. He knew better than to leave her unattended. He had tried. Evermore, he had tried!

Fear had gripped him when his mother bore a healthy baby boy. Bedwyr was fifteen winters and knew enough. Wine had frothed in the goblet when he brought it closer to his mother, indicating his father would kill that son.

Constantine—that stupid well-meaning bastard—stopped him from smuggling the infant into the village, afraid Bedwyr intended ill for the innocent babe. Aye, the priest handed Bedwyr and the child right back to Jormund. Despite his best attempts, Fate stole his brother and Bedwyr paid for it, marks burned deeper on his chest than any others his father had visited upon him.

Jormund had named the second Wallach boy Halwyn and erected a raised marker for him. Sons were worth more than daughters—no elevated monument to mark useless daughters.

Bedwyr set a sprig of lavender on the grave and murmured, "I'm sorry, Raito. I couldn't save you from him, but I would never allow that bastard to call you worthless. Mum called you another one of her lights. I know she approves that I changed your name to it."

He found the last marker, and his vision swam at his worst pain and loss. His third sister was Olwen, and she would have turned fourteen summers when he became the only remaining Wallach child, at sixteen winters. He missed her singing: *Ni-san. Ni-san. I heard a birdy say. Ni-san. Ni-san. Why won't you come and play?*

Tracing her name with another stem of lavender he had with him, he placed the flowering plant on her grave, along with a sprig full of cherry blossom petals that he'd broken off Cuchulain's favourite tree.

When she was small, Olwen climbed that tree and Cuchulain would send Bedwyr to bring her down from it. She'd wail to no end, so to appease his little sister he carved her nickname into the trunk.

He had etched her nickname into her grave marker as well.

It meant "Sparrow."

Suzume.

CHAPTER 52

DUNGEON CRAWL

As rustling broke the silence in the hall, Viera edged closer to the shadows, darkness providing safety from where the light of the sconces did not reach. She paused at the bend of the corridor and listened for anyone—or anything. When she peeked around the corner, she was met with blessed nothingness. Running into Tremayne Cornwall on patrol had sent her sprinting down several corridors and hiding behind a suit of armor; Gavyn's throaty growl juddered her nerves as she recalled his warning never to be alone with a male from House Cornwall.

Slipping down what she hoped was indeed a vacant hall, Viera struggled to remember which way led to the kitchens. She entered a grand atrium Lance had taken her into when she first came to the castle, and she faced a gilded staircase with opulent appointments.

Two open doorways, each trimmed with handsome wood and shiny metal inlay, loomed ahead. Lance had urged her to steer clear of one. *Damn, which one?* She clenched her teeth and strode to the far side of the atrium.

Flames wavering in the sconces cast flickering shadows over the floor. She heard the rustle of fabric coming from down one hallway, and in the limited lighting she could see skirts weaving farther down the corridor. Viera's curiosity forced her to take a glance down the other hallway. A chill ran up her spine. How quiet that passageway seemed, like Twilight had descended on the corridor and time stood still.

A hiccough coming from down the hall hinted that someone was nearby, and the sconces seemed to glow brighter, as if inviting her. She pulled her wrap around her shoulders and followed the lights.

She had not travelled far when the wood she walked on started to pop with each step she took. She glanced at the floor but couldn't see it clearly, and when she looked up her mouth went dry. The flames in the sconces were dying out.

A chuckle was followed by, "Come, little Usagi. Come into the dark."

Viera swallowed when heavy footsteps filled the passage and a wet thump echoed behind her. She whipped around, bracing herself to find Tremayne—except there was no one. Steel glimmered in what little light came from the open doorway, and metal grated against the stone floor. A sticky substance lapped at her boots.

Her cry for help bounced off the walls. Stumbling backwards, she spun on her heels and fled down the hall as fast as her legs would carry her. Air raced, rough and cold, through her burning lungs, her feet clinging to the stone and propelling her around a bend and into the next corridor. The sound of her pursuer's footsteps not abating, she burst into a large room. On the far side of it, she was faced with another doorway to consider entering.

Brisk wind blasted through the room, and a shadowy figure appeared near a stairway, the only other potential exit she could access, as there was no way she could go back in the direction from which she came. With a screech, Viera drew up short, and the toes of her boots caught on a small rug. She fell and slid across the stone floor, scraping her knees.

Viera rolled and brought her hands up to protect herself, but thickly woven silk caressed her outstretched legs, and a stare as dark as the deepest night met her anxious gaze. Red and yellow markings stood out on a woman's otherwise pale forehead, and she wore an outer robe with maple leaves appearing to drift along the hem and its sides.

The woman looked over her shoulder to another woman, this one wearing a violet-and-yellow outer robe. The second woman turned to Viera, her green tear-filled eyes narrowing on her. A loud hum came from this woman, which grew into a buzzing din no different from cicadas drowning out the lullaby of birdsong.

Shadows began to stir as if alive, and the ghost of Jormund Wallach slithered down the stairway toward the second woman.

This woman shoved the first woman at Viera and shrieked, "Run, Shiori. Don't let the Marshal have my children."

A shadow eclipsed Shiori's entire as she touched Viera's shoulder. The second woman was thrown to the floor. Jormund's wraith wrapped his arm around the woman's waist, but she drove her elbow into his abdomen, screaming, "Run, Suzume!"

A man with greasy, patchy hair and yellow teeth emerged from the shadows behind Shiori. He fixed a wild-eyed stare upon Viera and whispered in a gravelly voice, "Come, little Usagi. Come sweetly."

Viera darted past his outstretched arm, voices of those who should be dead echoing in her head as she fled the madness snapping at her heels. Diving into another hallway on the opposite side of the room, she scraped her knees again on rough stone, the sound of jingling chainmail forcing her through the pain to stand upright.

Darkness had her feeling her way along the walls, their dampness making them like sodden tapestry. Half-blind, she raced around a corner and stumbled down some long steps. Exhausted, several times she slipped but fear kept her rising to her feet.

The chains kept rattling her way, and her pulse banged at her temples as the noise crescendoed. Tripping down the last few steps, Viera landed on her knees again, which were now a bloody mess as they hit against the damp stone. Hysterical laughter burst from her, and her sides heaved from each expulsion of air. As she ran her fingers over the stone flooring, slick mud squished between the joints. In wet patches over the worn stone, water dribbled as if mimicking the tears streaming down her face. Nearby, a languid drop plopped loudly as it added itself to a puddle on the hard surface.

If hopelessness had a smell, it was the dungeon, which she was certain she had found. A cell door yawned open and banged against its frame, the squeal of hinges sending her scuttling into another cell, where she threw herself into the shadows. Pressing her back flush against the stone wall, she shrank into herself. Cold seeped into her clothing and pierced like knives into her seizing body. *Please let me become one with the dark.*

As she pushed her face against her robes, she inhaled traces of Myrddin's ink and paper scent, which suffused her with the momentary calm she desperately needed.

A whimper startled her into peering out of the darkness and into a cell next to hers. She couldn't make out much, but she flinched when her eyes focused on a youth close to her age. The hitches of his breathing softened her.

"Hello," she said, shifting closer to the iron bars.

When he did not answer, she snapped her fingers next to his face, which was ashen and listless. He stared forward, stoic as the stone around them. A blast of air ruffled his deep brown hair, but he still didn't move.

Tension built when she recognized the gray and maroon on the robe representative of only one other person that she had seen wearing such colors. He was a teen-seasoned version of the Marshal and a younger version of the man from outside the abandoned Throne Room. Viera squeezed her eyelids shut and wrapped her arms around her shoulders.

When a voice filtered through her despair, she opened her eyes to see a younger Myrddin kneeling next to the Marshal, who remained unmoved, as if in a world far away from the dungeon. Myrddin spoke, his words warped and unintelligible despite his proximity. After that received no reaction from the Marshal, her Master rested his back against the bars.

No one should be so unreachable. Slipping her hand past the bars, Viera squeezed the Marshal's shoulder. The same as touching ice, her fingers froze from the intense cold coming from him. Using a trick Safir had taught her, she pressed her Fire into his body. Instead of this producing the desired result, Viera was shot across the cell, hitting the wall hard enough to make her yip. Pulling her Fire Element around her like a blanket, she huddled within it.

The dismal silence that followed was broken by rusted metal screeching and hinges squealing as Myrddin's apparition departed the Marshal's cell, the iron door banging shut and echoing loudly.

The low voice from the abandoned atrium moaned, *"What have I done?"*

CHAPTER 53

WITCHING HOUR

A breeze rattled through the gardens when Bedwyr emerged from the hedgerow. He smacked earth and leaves from his clothing as a patch of mud near his elbow earned a growl from him. He hadn't walked far as he approached the DuLac memorials. He scanned the names until he came to *Cybella*. His mother and Elaine had cooed over the name, thrilled over the addition of a daughter to the DuLac family tree. Removing the last of the lavender from his robe, Bedwyr set it down on her tiny grave in tribute to another lost lamb his father had enabled Twilight to snatch.

Turning away, he climbed the hill to the castle.

In the glow of a lantern's light, Bedwyr made out Talia's statuesque form as she stood in an archway. Her shawl enshrouded her, and a yellow tribal headscarf framed her face. He glanced behind himself, certain she was waiting for someone else, but he saw no one.

"What are you doing out here in the cold, you blithering fool?" She hollered and let out a loud groan. "Bedwyr, you have me sick to Twilight. You're worse than Gavyn, I tell ya. Well, don't just stand there, come on in here!"

He stepped forward and she yanked his earlobe, releasing him just long enough to cuff him over the head. Quick as an adder's strike, Talia secured his ear in her tight grip again and hustled him inside. "I shan't have you catch your Twilight just yet. To the kitchens, you wretched boy."

As he let her drag him through the halls, warmth spread through him at her grumbles of calling him halfwit and dimwit. When they reached an atrium, he spread his fingers over hers. She tensed, her pace slowing as she dug her shoulder into his side.

"My wretch," she said, pulling him toward an archway.

He followed, frowning when she stopped and placed her hand on the wooden door frame. Three spiders appeared on her wrist, a nearby sconce's light illuminating the cross on their abdomens.

Talia blinked, her irises going from hazel to milky white as she droned the tune from her spider tales. Under her spell, the spiders crawled to the arch and launched themselves from edge to edge, shooting forth silken lines that gleamed even in the dim light. When they finished, Bedwyr read aloud the message spun in spider-silk: "*One of these days, you wretch.*"

"Best work yet, Talia. Needs more work on the font. 'You wretch' should be in bold and underlined."

Talia cuffed him. "Years dedicated to becoming an Ananse Mistress," she lamented, stalking through the doorway leading to the kitchens, "and my talents are wasted on web designs for numbskulls."

A glimmer drew Bedwyr up short. He pulled from her grip and stepped in front of the second doorway. Darkness spilled like pitch from the recesses. The light of the torchlight and lumistones flickered in the atrium.

Dark impressions of the past lingered, steeped in tales of the bloodlust rituals in this part of the castle. When he was fresh in his Lordship, he'd haunted the West Wing. He'd listen to the drafts that caused the most eerie sounds to fill the cold embrace of the damp walls.

Uriah Cameliard told Bedwyr that the mind created haunting tricks of fantasy and horror. Shiori said that darkness taints and becomes entrenched in a space. Dagonet laughed, saying that the dark made for a great play on one's imagination; the abyss formed half the basis for inspiration as life's experiences made up the other half.

Bedwyr did not know which was right, believing instead that each position held merit.

Talia gripped his arm. "What is it?"

He did not answer and pressed his hand against the first lumistone. Emerald wavered as the next several lumistones illuminated the hall.

When he scanned the corridor, nothing leapt out at him. He could not fathom what called to him, yet it was too strong for him to ignore, so he turned down the hallway.

His gaze lowered. With his heart pounding fast and hard, he spotted small footprints etched in the dust on the stone floor. Whispers echoed back in his mind, be it imagination, inspiration, or otherwise. But the ghosts that used to linger held no power over him anymore. Memories, however, were another story—and promises even more so.

As he made his way down the corridor, footsteps clattered behind him until long thin fingers gripped his arm, yanking hard and wheeling him around. "I promised to be your servant," Talia said as she lifted her eyes to his, a gossamer haze sliding over her pupils. "Where you go, I go."

Bedwyr sneered, "Then don't come crying to me when an owl hoots in the rafters. I shan't carry you back."

Talia cupped his face with her cool palm and stroked his cheek. "Try not to shite yourself when Tethra and the Picts skulk from the Lockinge." She made exaggerated slurps and bounced on her feet. "They eat all the wretched children who sneak about past their bedtimes."

"Of all the ruddy things," he said, disgust shuddering through him. "You scared the shite out of Galahad and me with that story."

"You two never went wandering the halls past bedtime again, did ya?"

"Bloody hells, you thrice damned Witch!"

She released a cackle worthy of the insult.

They entered a huge room with a high ceiling and a sprawling staircase, and she molded herself to him. No amount of mental cleansing could ever remove the memory of his father slicing his mother's throat on the grand staircase they now faced. His father's voice echoed in his mind, "Kill a Witch during a Blood Moon, reap the benefits thrice-fold."

Little did his father know how right and wrong he was in using a Witch's blood in the ritual, least of all the blood of one who loved her children.

Bedwyr approached another set of doorways, one leading to a garden and the other to the dungeon. He stopped in front of the one he wished none had the nerve to enter, but he stepped directly on the spot where Vertigorn Cornwall had brutally thrown Shiori to the floor for protecting Olwen. Bedwyr eyed the shadows, half-expecting Vertigorn to materialize and lisp, "Come, little Usagi."

Flashing his two fingers in an obscene gesture toward where Vertigorn had stood, Bedwyr muttered, "I got you, you bastard! Uther didn't even have enough of you to scrape together for a funeral send-off, Vertigorn."

Talia said, "Not the only one. Don't even ask what I put in his tea."

Bedwyr took a deep breath. "I'll go first. Whoever is in there could be dangerous or out of their minds with fear. It doesn't help Uther, my father, and Vertigorn removed the lumistones."

As they descended the steps, a pervasive chill leaked from the stone walls, along with a natural musty dampness. Bedwyr gave the moss-coated walls wide berth. The moss had often been the only source of water for those Uther imprisoned. He was one of those people, as well as Shiori. Because their captors fitted prisoners with breakers, he and his family included, not even their shared Element granted them water.

When he stepped into the dungeon, sobs drifted from somewhere down one of the many corridors. Several rows of cells away, an intermittent wind—coming from the boat launch—wailed, occasionally drowning out the crying. Bedwyr blinked away the sting from the salty air as he came to the location in the dungeon he sought, stopping in front of the extremely drafty cell that had been Uriah Cameliard's home for five years. Sadly, Queen Guinevere's father never overcame the rattling chest cough that ultimately spelled his Twilight.

A keening sound called Bedwyr's attention to the cell next to it. In the far corner of what had also been his home, a tiny figure huddled. Memories loomed, clouding his reality with the atrocities of the past. As he approached, he focused on the fine gossamer-thin line between life and Twilight.

He knelt and untied his cloak. When he pulled her forward and tucked the robe over her, Viera peeked up from her knees. A visceral punch of remorse staggered his breathing. She looked devastatingly like Olwen—the desperation in her eyes exactly as he'd remembered from his sister's anguish.

Lips quivering and wet with tears and grime, Viera mouthed, "I want to go home. Can I go home? Please, let me go home. I...."

Swallowing, he looked away. "I'm sorry, but this is your home until your contract ends. You belong to the Emrys."

Nothing prepared him for how severely her slender frame shook. Her small body rocked back and forth even as she muffled her cries within his robe.

Bedwyr pulled her against him, and it was like hugging his sister again. It was the encouragement Viera needed, and her cries became less acute. Her trembling persisted and offered him an aching reminder of what else had happened in this cell.

The Elemental breakers severing prisoners from their elements made it a miracle any of them survived. Bedwyr had wrapped his arms around his last surviving sister to help stave off the frigid chill, while at the same time giving her access to the pittance of hay that they were afforded for bedding so she could at least garner some semblance of warmth. What Witchery he knew helped and he used it as covertly as his mother had taught him what she could. However, his sex blocked him the full powers of a Witch when he lacked a Bond with a female Witch, as no amount of studying his mother's books would ever enable him to overcome his gender deficiency without sharing power. There were a couple of Witchery grimoires squirreled away in his chamber that he had salvaged prior to his father sending the other tomes' ancient pages in smoke and embers.

At one point during the Duels, the Scribes and Healers were 'debriefed' by Foel House for housing questionable and subversive materials that leaned more sympathetically toward Witchery. Bedwyr had ground his teeth while forced to watch Dain Foel paw through Karen's library; the twenty-one springs Earth Elemental charged with eradicating anything smacking of Witchery. The sodding idiot sent an entire section of Karen's romance books to the fires, leaving many actual Witchery articles untouched. Dain was a fool, but a useful one. The irony was not lost on many how a nefarious Witching House led literal Witch hunts, striking regularly at weaker Houses and peasants. After Uther gave Foel House free reign over the investigations, many books 'disappeared' either as a result of the Foels or by Scribes and Healers ferrying as much as they could into hiding.

"Why am I so useless?" Viera asked.

As pressure banded around his abdomen, Bedwyr held Viera tight. Her question was the same lament as Olwen's. Olwen had been too young to become a Witch, and his mother had waited for the opportunity. His sister's first moon cycle opened the door for her to take the Oath of the Moon during her next one. Power could have shifted, the unlocked potential in her blood eclipsing anything Bedwyr might have provided. It had been his responsibility to see her realize that opportunity.

To further their plight, none from Gorre would approach him or Olwen, their mother's House too wary of them and their blood association with their father. Bedwyr had not had confirmation from his mother about Gorre House having an active coven within its waters, but even a fool could put together that Karen Gorre had learned her Witchery from somewhere. One didn't just decide to be a Witch without proper instruction or guidance from some source. The only logical recourse was that Gorre House had a large Witching coven to its name, and it explained why the House was as solidly unified as it was. It wouldn't surprise Bedwyr if there were a few men, who either knew or had suspicions of what their women-folk were.

For that matter, Bedwyr doubted that Gorre and Foel House were the only Witching Houses. Queen Elden, Earth Marshal Pembroke, and Wood Marshal Druir of the initial founding women of Evermore were confirmed Witches, and they had trained Water Marshal Eustace of Esau and to a lesser extent Llewelyn of Fire in Witchery. They reared Witches in their Houses for many generations, their training expanding when a large branch of Druir's descendants moved north to Foxbury and the same occurred with Pembroke's descendants taking up residence in Rheged. Esau had bred into Gorre and DuLac, two Houses that hosted their own full-fledged albeit smaller covens. It was only within the past few centuries and the advent of men, who could not gain the full powers of a Witch without sharing with a female Witch, that such cunning traditions and covens were disbanded by those major Houses.

Bedwyr would not be surprised if 'disbanded' was subjective to those immediately affected by such decrees. His mother was one, and if Bedwyr were to wager, Aunt Saris was likely the one to initiate and train Karen in the ways of Gorre House.

With the screech of metal, Bedwyr squinted at the cell that had imprisoned Hamyll. Viera's choked sobs awoke the remorse lingering in Bedwyr's heart ever since he'd lost Olwen. "It's all right, Suzume. I'm here," he said, "I won't fail you again."

CHAPTER 54

DRINKING BUDDIES

Glub. Glub. Glub.

Careful to not spill any vodka on the wooden table, Lionel lifted the bottle. He caught Dagonet's grimace before the fool schooled his features into neutrality.

"Come now, Lionel." Dagonet said, spreading his long arms over the table. "'Tis a night best served with much firewater. I wish to be numb of memory."

Snorting, Lionel rose and rummaged through the cupboards for the bottles he kept on reserve. A throat cleared when he seemed lost inside one cabinet. He backed away, finding Tippy Foxbury tapping her boot on the wood floor.

Said Tippy, "Hey-hey. Wee in the morn to be finding your cups, dearie." She held out some Moon Mead and Earthshine. "We'll keep it between us if you let a weary mam with too many cubs get some sauce."

Lionel led her to the table. "You've more than a fair deal."

Dagonet took a bottle from Tippy, filled a tumbler, and slid the drink to her.

Knocking back the shot and smacking her hand over her chest, she asked Lionel, "Why are you two up so late, and where's your Bond?"

"Asleep." Lionel settled onto the bench across from her. "I slipped out. Once Linny knew I was awake, neither of us would get a wink."

"Doesn't answer the first part of my question." Tippy licked the rim of her glass, and Dagonet and refilled it.

"That's the pisser, innit?" Lionel said as he savoured the burn spilling down his throat and warming his stomach from his long pull of Earthshine. His glass rattled as he set it on the table, spilt liquor slicking his fingers until he wiped them on his lips. "I dreamt of Alban Hefin, a Blood Moon, the dark, and the Witching Hour of Twilight."

"Aye, now I understand," Tippy said, downing her second drink in quick succession.

Faint tremors urged him to place his palms over the table and still them. "I closed my eyes and my design scraped in the hearths. When I opened my eyes, there were screams and blood was dripping down the stairs."

"You did what you could, Lionel. You survived." Tippy clasped his wrist. "If it wasn't for you, Uther would have held out longer. And none of us would be here."

Bile burned his throat. "I used my darkness to drive a man mad, Tippy. I tainted—" swallowing the sting in his throat— "what should've been pure with what crept between Life and Twilight. I perjured my Fire and led my wife into the abyss."

Strained laughter made both of them jerk around toward Dagonet. "I led the innocent to slaughter," he said, his jagged leer displaying his pronounced canines, "and whispered poison into the ears of a King— and his most loyal."

"No one sin trumps another."

"Aye, dear friend, sinners we all are, from the moment we tear away from our mother's womb 'til our last breath. Your sin drove a mad man madder. My sin led lambs to the slaughter. But lest we forget, our sins ended a reign of terror."

Tippy poured out three measures of Earthshine, one for each of them, and raised her glass. "To the end of corrupt Kings and the Twilight they bring with them."

Lionel tossed back his drink and was about to accept another from Tippy as boots rapidly slapping stone had him pull his glass away. Even Dagonet perked up.

Bursting through the doorway, Talia bolted to the hearth. "We need warm towels! Viera was in the dungeon!"

"Oh, dear!" cried Tippy. "How'd the lass find her way there?"

Talia said, "She got mixed up with the hallways and ended up in the West Wing,"

"I'll make some tea," Tippy said as she scurried to the herb cabinet and packed a combination of chamomile, lavender, and a few other herbs that only a cunning woman would know into a cheesecloth sachet. She held the pouch outside the kettle, waiting for the tea to steep.

Dagonet left and reappeared, towels bundled in his arms. As he passed the linens to Talia, she doused them into a large pot of hot water that was hanging from the hearth.

Lionel stepped around the table as Bedwyr entered with Viera in his arms. A rough protective edge entered Bedwyr's voice as he said, "I have her."

Dagonet tapped the bottom of his stool, creating a rhythmic pattern. His attention shifted to Bedwyr as he snuck glances to the girl pressing against him. There was no refuting the lean of Bedwyr's body over hers.

Tippy sang a Foxbury lullaby about a fawn from Viera's other side. Completing the huddle, Talia had squished between Lionel and Bedwyr. As she snored against Lionel's shoulder, the man lolled from side to side and thumped his forehead onto her headscarf. They had pilfered the cabinets and made merry with a large jug of sahti from Gereant's hidden stash.

As if Fate hadn't enough, a slurring chanty interrupted Tippy:

"Drank meself and me lass with some pints o' sahti.
Got to za bottom, turned, and what did I see?
Instead o' me lass in me bed was me filly.
Sad to say, me horse drinks better than me."

A few crashes followed with a string of curses arising from the corridor. "Any more ya got in there or is that it?" a gruff voice snarked.

A rousing song belted in the hall:

"In the tavern, the boyos cheer me.
Not long 'fore me get more sahti.
Me stumbles right out the door.
Me arse go up and head on the floor.

All the way, me fought the bastards in the alley.
Forgot me sword, but me got a shillelagh.
In the morn, woke in a bonny pig's trough.
Feck ye and yer cow and bugger off."

One of their resident Healers tripped into sight, sucking on the end of a fag and blowing smoke from his nose. "Gav, ya drunken bastard, I was just jesting," Darna Eynon growled.

Lance appeared, and with Darna, lugged Gavyn next to Lionel. Tippy rose and rubbed Gavyn's shoulder until he retreated from her, his gaze inching toward Bedwyr.

"Stood thar, you bastard. Watched you do it," Gavyn slurred. "Waited to the end. Cause—hick—I hated mine as much as you did, but I still needed my Bond so bad."

Bedwyr sneered. "I regret nothing." Gavyn's choked sobs echoed in Dagonet's ears. The only salve was to direct Darna to assess Viera, who checked her over, announcing nothing amiss except the blood caked on her knees.

Darna healed her with his Air, his fag drooping from the corner of his mouth. "Stay out of the dungeons, gil," he said, standing and grunting at Gavyn. "I'll go tell yer brothers and yer priest to come on down."

Gavyn two-finger saluted him. "For a Healer, a Troll's got better bedside manner."

"Bugger off 'fore I make ya eat my shillelagh, ya carrot-topped wanker," Darna said.

Light glinted off a silver tray on the table. Lance squinted and crooned low in his throat as Bedwyr cushioned his cheek on his arm. Wood groaned as Dagonet leant back on his stool. The others had been collected, leaving the four of them in the kitchens until Constantine arrived for Bedwyr.

Viera rested her cheek on Lance's shoulder. "I need to tell you what happened."

"It can wait. You need to rest." Lance rubbed her back. "You're safe, and you're going to be all right. That's all that matters."

She raised up. "There were people in the hall. Scary people."

"What people?" he asked, smoothing her back with his hand. "Who scared you?"

When she clung tighter to him, he looked toward Dagonet. The Fool met his gaze, nothing amusing in his expression, a vicious hunger creeping across his face as he surrendered to his usual haphazard grin. "What scary people?" Dagonet chided. "We can't go snerting through the castle until we know who to look for. Tell Unca Dag and Lance who they were."

Viera pulled away from Lance and said, "Two women came down the stairs. Both with black hair and strange robes. One had green eyes. Jormund came and grabbed her. That one screamed and told Shiori, now I remember—that's the other woman—to take her children and run."

Viera's story got Dagonet to raise an eyebrow. With a slow turn toward the table, he poured a large measure of Earthshine and gulped it down. "What happened next?" he asked.

Viera rubbed her chin. "Shiori almost reached me, but a man with greasy hair and yellow eyes appeared. He threw her against the floor, and I didn't see her again. He called me *Usagi*. The first woman screamed for me to run." She glanced at Lance. "I ran as fast as I could and somehow ended up in the dungeon."

Motion drew Lance's attention to Bedwyr's features blanked into neutrality and his stare locked on her. The younger man laid his cheek onto the table and closed his eyes, but there was little chance he was not listening in.

Dagonet knelt in front of Viera and held out his hand until she placed hers in his. "Shiori Murasaki was the one who went to you. She is fiercely protective. One of the bravest in all Evermore. The other was Karen Gorre, Bedwyr's mother."

Viera shifted closer. "Where are they now?"

"No one has seen Shiori. She's somewhere." Dagonet slowly withdrew his hand from hers. "Karen didn't survive the Duels. She gave her life for her son and daughter."

Viera bit her lip. "What about the man?"

"Vertigorn Cornwall," Lance said, fanning his fingers through her hair. "You needn't worry about him. He cannot hurt anyone anymore."

"He scared the Hells out of me. What makes you say he can't hurt anyone?"

"Bedwyr killed him during the Duels."

"Good." She looked toward the *dosing* man next to her.

Constantine stepped through the doorway. He slowed, quirking an eyebrow at Viera. "Fancy seeing you up at this hour. I'm assuming you're going to be all right?"

She checked her unblemished knees. "Healer Darna healed me. He didn't linger."

"He rarely does. Grendel's Trolls learned his bedside manner." Constantine harrumphed. "Lance, am I taking her or Bedwyr?"

"Bedwyr." Lance prodded Viera into following him. "I've some words for Myrddin."

She slid the cloak from her shoulders. "Thank you," she murmured, holding it out to Bedwyr, "for finding and helping me."

Bedwyr grumbled, "Keep it. It's yours now."

CHAPTER 55

"WE END UP WITH WHO WE END UP WITH"

Trailing behind Lance, Viera shuffled through the corridor, her mind adrift. Lance was the one person she felt she could trust, but she hadn't told him everything that had occurred. Actually, far from it.

With her vision blurred and her voice shaky, she managed, "Does Myrddin really need to know I was down there?"

"He can't help you otherwise, and if anyone can figure out what's pulling at you, it's your Master."

She glanced about the hallway, catching sight of a possible passage to slip down and escape the castle forever. The thought met its end as soon as it surfaced. "I was stupid," she said, hiding her quivering chin with a sweep of her hand. "Myrddin will get mad. I wasn't supposed to be in the West Wing."

Lance stopped in front of a portrait of a unicorn drinking from a pond. "So, you *intentionally* went into the West Wing."

"No! That place scares the Hells out of me!" She started to sniffle.

"If it wasn't intentional, lass, then you've no reason to fear Myrddin or anyone else being mad at you." He tucked her hair behind her ears. "This castle has more than enough twists and turns in its hallways to confuse anybody. When new servants arrive, they struggle to learn the castle's layout, some for many seasons, and they work in it every day."

"Still doesn't make me feel any better."

He led her down and around several corridors and stopped again. "Are you lost yet?"

She fiddled with her sleeves. "Maybe."

He laughed lightly. "Give it time."

"Aye, but the halls all look the same."

"That's the reason for the paintings, like the one right here." Lance pointed to a large gilded picture on the wall in front of them. A dark-skinned man, obviously a Master by his robes and books, was sitting on a carpet with some young Apprentices.

Viera studied the scene. "It looks important."

"Morien Ziyad lent it to us," Lance said. "It emphasizes teaching our future and returning the favour back to those who were patient with us." Lance pointed at a small boy sitting on the edge of the students. "That lad became the King of Marrakesh. He's Morien's great-great-grandfather. The teacher in this painting was little more than a Scribe wanting to do well for his tribe's children. Because of that, his student one day raised him to High Minister—or Grand Vizier as it's referred to in Marrakesh."

Viera inspected a decorative shield on the adjacent wall, and she sighed. "Why couldn't Garrett end up with Myrddin—and me with you?" She flicked her hand toward the painting. "We both would have been better matched as Apprentice and Master." She gave Lance an embarrassed look, realizing how that must have sounded.

"We end up with who we end up with." He brushed dust from the shield. "Besides, I would be a lot stricter with you."

She laughed. "Like you are with Galahad."

"Low blow."

She fell in step alongside him. "Why did you and your wife not have more children? I see you often with the Kyner brood and around lots of other wards, so I know you like kids."

"According to the test from the Healers, we expected a daughter, but it didn't come to be." He tweaked her nose. "She would have been as spoiled and naughty as you."

Viera was embarrassed she had asked him such a personal question and mumbled, "I'm sorry."

"Sometimes we have longer. Other times we must wait. One day, I'll see them again."

"You'll stay awhile yet, won't you?"

"For now, aye. Unless you're trying to get rid of me." Viera giggled and he turned his face to the shield. "I must knock some sense into your Master and keep Arthwyr from coming up with another harebrained scheme. This last Progress nearly undid us all."

"Hey, I came from that Progress!"

"Then it wasn't an utter waste," he replied smugly and chuckled.

A lumistone pulsated on the otherwise drab gray wall. Viera walked over and touched the stone. "Lance, you and Dagonet agree that I saw Karen and Vertigorn, right?"

"You described them well, aye. But what are you really getting at?"

"Myrddin was in the dungeon with a boy in the cell next to mine."

"The dungeon?"

"Well, not exactly like he is now, but it was definitely my Master." She swallowed around her dry throat. "There's something else. The boy with Myrddin was a little older than me, and I saw him outside of the abandoned Throne Room when I first arrived."

"What did he look like?"

"Brown hair, blue eyes." Viera wrinkled her brow and tapped her fingers over her mouth. "Is Myrddin special to him? He's always with him when I see Myrddin in my—" she waved her hand— "dreams, visions, whatever they are."

"Myrddin had three brothers. Hamyll is the only one matching your description." A low burr came from Lance's throat. "Hamyll was Knighted as the new Marshal of Fire when Uther tried to bring all the Marshals' positions back from the grave. Of them all, only Hamyll's post really took."

"What happened to him?"

"Hamyll discovered that Jormund had murdered all of Bedwyr's siblings except one, a sister named Olwen. He did everything he could to hide her, but she was found and executed. For all practical purposes, Hamyll himself died with Olwen. I'm saying this, because when we freed him, he emerged from the dungeon a different person."

"So, if I'm seeing Hamyll, he'll be kind to me?"

"You resemble Olwen in some ways. There's no way of knowing, but he could be trying to protect you."

"Why is that?"

"He was partial to her for good reason—they were Soul Bonds."

Lance waited for the door to close and the girls' voices to fade into the Emrys Chamber. It would not due for any of this to reach their ears, so Lance and Myrddin stayed in the hallway. Lance steadied his respiration, a skill that came as natural as breathing well before Carydoc apprenticed him. His secondary Master, Ector, had often said, Lance was borderline reptilian in his temperament and steady as a rock.

As it were, Lance could count on one hand when as an adult he had allowed his rage to snap beyond his control, but Myrddin had him so exasperated, his voice was quaking: "This isn't working. You need to return Viera to her home if you cannot see to her."

Myrddin bristled. "She has no control over her power and almost killed people at the Fire Temple. All the Fire Masters are too afraid to apprentice her." His voice shook, rising with his panting. "I can't find a Master for her. I'm clearly not worthy of it!"

Lance shoved Myrddin against the door. "You're failing to see her for who she really is, yet you keep trying to fit her in with the same training regimen as other Fire Initiates."

"I continue to look for anything that gives me insight with her. But so far there's nothing in the Library that's helping me."

"That's your first mistake. Stop looking at those damned books. Talk to her and then go to Bercylac. Hells, Gereant might even help you with Viera." Lance retreated. "Go to them. As Ancients, they likely have an answer for a way to train her."

Myrddin gave Lance a single nod and exhaled.

Lance braced his back against the opposite wall and slid down. "People might surprise you. They surprise me all the time."

Myrddin pressed his shoulders against his door and dropped to the floor. "You surprise me enough, Lance." He smeared ink across his cheek. "I'm not sure what to do with her. I have gone wrong in taken up her training."

"Well, that's a start." Lance forced a weak smile, but the gesture was enough to ease the tension. "Initially, you seemed to be under this ridiculous impression that she would be a perfect student of Fire. But she'll never be, of this we can all be positive by now. It would be easier if you listened to Carydoc and let go." This time he smiled for real. "But we all know you won't do that, don't we?"

Myrddin thumped his hand against his forehead. "I'll be a ghost before the year is out if she keeps on with what she's doing, won't I?"

That remark got Lance to change the subject. "I don't know about you becoming a ghost, Lord Emrys, but Viera is now seeing ghosts."

Myrddin sat upright. "What do you mean?"

"She's described Jormund and Uther quite well. Actually, too well."

Myrddin waved his hand as a sign of dismissal. "Jormund was once in Iyesgarth for quite a period of time. He would be hard to forget. And everyone knows Uther, or at least about him. I would be more worried if she *didn't* know who he was."

Lance stared across the hall to the lumpy clay vase Maerna had made with his help when she was just five winters. "That makes perfect sense, but she described Karen, Vertigorn, and Shiori perfectly also. Someone might have told her what Karen looked like, and the Cornwall Maids could have described Vertigorn, but she even described Shiori, who is even more of a living ghost than anything haunting these halls."

Myrddin rubbed his chin. "I grant you, that is a little harder to explain."

"There's more." Lance folded his arms. "Hamyll might be paying her visits. Twice so far. Her description of him is vague, but you know how he was with Olwen, so he could be thinking of Viera in the same way, especially since they're about the same age when Olwen died, and they even look somewhat alike."

Myrddin blanched, "Bloody Hells. What have I got on my hands? Cú Sídhe, phoenixes, ruddy sparrows, and now my brother. What else is Viera going to pull from her robe's sleeves?"

"At least it's Hamyll. It could be Raedwalde and Berwyn." Lance chuckled when Myrddin put his hands over his face and moaned. "Aye, no telling what your older brothers would do in cahoots with her against you. Wouldn't that be a right nightmare?" He paused so Myrddin could compose himself. "My advice to you is to seek out Bercylac and Gereant. Something calls Viera to the darker parts of the castle. But it's the Fae in her that scares her, not the spirits of the dead, and this is where the Ancients can definitely help—if you'll let them."

Myrddin pyramided his fingers. "As for getting scared, I'm surprised that the wild side of her use of Fire hasn't scared you off her brother."

Lance looked back at Maerna's misshapen vase. Traced beneath the handles, a heart surrounded the initials of *ME* and another set that had him blinking and smiling. "You and I are the same. We end up with who we end up with, especially if we do it to ourselves."

CHAPTER 56

LADY OF THE NIGHT

Bedwyr crumpled, his drunken sobs now between Constantine and him as the priest carried him into the bedchamber. He wiped away the dampness from Bedwyr's cheeks and neck, his murmurs for the other Wallach children twisting around in the priest's head; words that fell unbidden and bitter with the salt of sorrow and far too many trials and tribulations, the anguished keens now little more than a broken melody.

When sleep slackened Bedwyr until a crinkle formed on his forehead, Constantine rested the Knight's chin upon the mattress edge and pushed hair from his face. "I should have done more—" pulling the sheets over Bedwyr—" aye, I should have done more."

He collected his desk rubbish bin and placed it next to his bed. "You are a wonder," he said. "May sweetness settle your dreams."

Summoning his Fire, Constantine formed a smoldering array that hovered just above his hand. When he snapped his fingers the array released, and he relished the snap-pop of the dry kindling that flared up in the hearth.

He tugged his collar loose and folded his cassock over his desk chair, swaying between the couch and bed. Swinging his leg to the top of the couch, Constantine pushed up to land on the cushion. When he spied what was on the sofa, he sprang up but tripped on a table leg on his way to snatch a poker from the caddy next to the hearth. He muffled his curses and grabbed the iron bar. Primed for a hint of ill-intent, he prodded the scabbard and hilt now ajar from his flight.

With the poker held tightly in his grasp, he listened to the *monster* in his chamber skitter across the room. Constantine's body itched. He expected the stain of his guilt to show his arms and hands slick with blood, but there was nothing.

Shish. Shish.

At the soft ring of bells, Constantine turned toward his bed. A pale blue Oriental robe, or haori as he knew it to be called, was draped over Bedwyr. Bright orange and red maple leaves were embroidered as if to drift across the garment.

"I know you're here." He brushed his shaking hand over the textured silk and looked about his room. "Come out."

Shish. Shish.

A white blur with a black-tipped tail darted past the couch. Flames dancing in the hearth cast shadows over the wall. Dark and light fused into a vulpine profile, nine long tails swishing behind the fox as they transformed into one. The figure elongated and took on a human form, a wash of fur fading into a snow-white robe with a cherry-red lining. The woman twitched her pointed fox ears, and these as well as her tail faded away. Crimson and gold marks materialized and lay intricately on her forehead.

"Shiori, I had a suspicion it was you." Constantine put up the poker and lifted his hand to shake Bedwyr awake.

"Nay, Priest," she said, her velvety tone staying his hand. "I'm not here for him, so you can continue to take care of my little Usagi for me."

"Your little *Bunny* keeps me on my toes, but I fear that one day it will be me he takes care of, instead of the other way around."

Her burbling laughter warmed him. "I chose right when you put yourself between us." She waved Constantine toward the couch and he sat on it. "You proved me right with that gift."

"Aye, but I'm not ready to face that yet."

"Then don't. Hide it until you are. Wait until you can. There was only so long that I could hide it for you in my little Bunny's chamber. I can do so no longer. Now, it's your turn as it will return to your side regardless of how much you fight it."

A shiver worked down his back at the simple but harsh truth of her remark. "It should only be so easy."

She perched on a cushion, and with her nails, traced the chimera-like features of a metal bat, dragon, and bird engraved upon their curse. "In time and soon you will. Don't fear your how and why. Embrace them. They are what led you to your now."

Constantine nodded at the weapon. "You're leaving us, aren't you? That's why you returned it to me now, isn't it?"

Air wavered around her as the outline of her fox ears appeared and disappeared. "Kitsune are not like your loup-garou. We're messengers and protectors. I can no longer keep my blood promise to the Murasaki or the Uesugi. Inari has waited long enough."

"So, you will go back to your Fox Goddess?"

"I must, at least for now. I cannot please her with dances beneath the moon anymore. And since my Mistress's kit can stand on his own, Inari's time has come and yours and mine is at its close."

Regret and desperation warred in Constantine's mind. "You can come back… and return as you please. Why not continue as you have with Bedwyr… and, aye, us?"

"I can't." Shiori twisted toward the hearth. "I don't have much time left to right my wrongs."

"I don't understand. You look as healthy and beautiful as ever."

"I'm hundreds of years older than you, son of Romus."

She closed her slim fingers over his hand, which was dwarfed in comparison. Delicious heat rippled through him when she slid her fingers up his wrist, and when she brushed his knee with hers, what started out as a soft pang became a raw ache.

Throughout his life, easy landed in front of him on a silver tray. Many priests and nuns denied their culpability, pointing at those caught in carnal acts with members of the cloth as the true sinners. Eyes became blind to mutual complicity. Constantine never denied his sin with Shiori, at least to himself, but he also never consorted with another.

The first time he'd gathered the nerve to kiss her resulted in a blade being placed to his throat. In her culture, kissing was an uncommon display. Only his harried explanation about what it meant in Viteliu had eased her blade from his neck.

Her nails pressed into his palms, and when she laced her fingers through his, her breathing faltered. In Nihon, the gesture was an intimacy only shared between lovers. Shiori moaned loudly and brushed her hand along his jaw, gently touching his cheek.

She murmured, "One journey must end so another may begin. Hold that Bond of yours dear until it's time to return home again." Her breath fanned his chin and she pressed her lips to his.

Silt and other sediment floated along the waterline of the Lockinge River. In the gentle night air, wooden hulls pulled against moorings, occasioning the dock with little more than a lulling whisper. As Dagonet meandered along the wharf, he inhaled deeply, recalling his formative years in this very place. The gritty trade of merchandise and flesh had captivated him no different from the iron chains securing the limbs of the human chattel he observed.

His mother and aunt had arrived amid sweaty bodies packed into a tiny vessel barely seaworthy. Salty barbs, mixed with tales of sorrow and desperation, spewed constantly from faces both sunburned and swollen. Grubby limbs reached for the smallest scrap of compassion, let alone food. The truly fortunate lay beneath those who lived, the misty glaze of Twilight on their corneas a testament to their escape—as certain as the dried blood caked over their orifices.

Dagonet paused and observed the moonlight playing on the dark water, the dart of silver and ivory a shifting allusion to the twisted forms that found their final homes in the quick of the river. The offal in the sediment had not been the only hint of evil to foul Evermore. The Lockinge itself held as much of the memory of Twilight for the people of Evermore as the commemorative stones keeping vigil on the dock.

He bowed toward the solemn statue of a woman with an infant cradled inside a sling hanging over her breast. One of the woman's arms was wrapped around the slim bowed form of an older child. As she stared off into the distance, her other arm was outstretched as far as she could reach in a final attempt to wrest back what Fate had torn from her.

Flowers wreathed the trio, and trinkets were laid at the mother's feet, left from those old enough to remember human misery at its most abject, as many were simply in memory of others lost. Some gifts, however, were nothing more than tokens to convey guilt, the regret of survivors who had lived long enough for the tides of inhumanity to turn from the doldrums into fairer winds.

Hands in his pockets, Dagonet drew closer. He extracted a daisy chain from his robe and placed it over the older child's head. "Sweet tidings, Sofia."

He secured another daisy chain around the infant's small head. No words for this one yet. The babe still lived.

His attention returned to the woman, a mere child when her life was torn asunder. She and her sister were victims of crushing subjugation, their statues more than random people, as they were trafficked into the Red Lantern District of Elden's Hearth. Two fell. One survived. The babe came later but was a symbol of the cruelty that had thrived in Evermore.

From the pouch on his belt, Dagonet removed a string of bells and wrapped his gift around the woman's extended wrist, entwining it over her fingers. Satisfied when the brass balls stayed in place and tinkled in the wind, he knelt in front of the statue. "Good eve, Mother."

A nearby cackle caused him to clasp the hilt of the stiletto dagger sheathed inside his robe. The bells' rhythm, however, stilled his initial impulse to dart from the statues—their soft tones calming him—as they indicated from whom the boisterous laugh had come. "Shalom, fair colleague," he said.

She sat on a piling, her head cocked with a seemingly bottomless stare meeting his. Her lips were pulled into a vulpine smile, or as close to what she could manage in her current form. Starlight and moonbeams glistened off the sweep of her fur, and her tail acted as a billowing silver banner.

Dagonet held out his hand to her. As the fox twitched her ears, she pressed her damp nose against his outstretched fingers. Her breath tickled his palm and her rough pink tongue scraped over his skin. He stroked her ears and pinched the corners, making the tips flop.

"I'll miss you, my dear," he said as he ruffled her neck and the bells sang out to him, louder than before but with virtually no wind to make them jingle. "May the moon ever guide your path in the night." He winked at her. "I'll see you again."

The Kitsune yipped and Dagonet said, "Two reflective surfaces. Water and Metal. I see you; you see me. Now we both see."

She nuzzled his side, her cackle now soft and pitchy. Tail waving behind her, the Kitsune leapt to the nearest wooden pillar projecting from the dock. Her silver form arose from the piling and danced across the celestial weaving of the moon on the inky abyss of the Lockinge.

Dagonet waited until she disappeared and all he saw was the black of night in front of him. "Wade ever equally in the dark and in the light. Fare thee well, Shiori-san."

CHAPTER 57

THE RISE OF A CONTENDER

The smoke, combined with the warm night air, hung like a moldy curtain inside the squalid tavern known as *Kreb's Grogs*. Lumistones sputtered, cracks running through the glowing rocks and telling their own tales of how they had been pried from better buildings throughout the Hearth. Along the walls, wooden signs had been nailed into warped, rotted wood—*Toadstool Way, Big Beaver Road, Cox Avenue*—complete with suggestive images. The musk of unwashed bodies weighed heavily on the room, adding to the already oppressive smell and degrading the place further.

Spindly pedestals swayed to the bumps of drunks staggering by, puddle rings and food spatter staining the tavern's uneven floorboards as permanent evidence of a lack of concern for cleanliness. Any man walking on the floor felt the damp, rotted wood sucking on the soles of his footwear, as if trying to slow him from leaving.

Rats scurried around, snatching crumbs from the floor if not outright scaling the tables and thieving what the tavern help set out for customers.

As one wench plunked down a tray with some crusty laver bread on it, a rat leapt onto the table. Twisting her lips to reveal missing teeth, the woman snatched the fork from the tray and slammed it into the rat's back. The vermin squealed and writhed around the tines pinning it to the table, its blood splattering with each contortion of its body. She ripped the fork away, with the rat still attached, and stormed to the kitchen.

Staring at his meal, Mordred muttered, "There goes tomorrow's breakfast." He used the remaining knife to blend the seaweed paste in with his oatmeal to create something more edible.

After setting aside the knife, he searched the nearest tables for a fork or a spoon. When spotting none available, he contemplated using his fingers until a snort—rivaling hacking up spit—drew his gaze back to the same wench, now standing next to him. She held out the original fork, blood dripping from the utensil and a with a chunk of skin and matted black fur stuck to it.

Mordred accepted the disgusting fork and said, "Thank you, Milady. I look forward to what delight you serve tomorrow with your recent catch."

She smacked her lips. "You get first crack at the sausage in the morn. Be abouts 'fore the sky grays."

He tipped her another ingot, her eyes flashing at the coin a sure sign of what drove her. As she put her back to him and shuffled to the next table, Mordred wiped the fork clean with his sleeve. Spying a tankard of ale on another table, he dipped the utensil into the drink, gave a few quick stirs so the rat's remnants stayed in the drink, and set the fork in his bowl. A moment later, boots thumped loudly behind him and a great mountain of a man settled at the table. Cayne, the locals called the man, lorded over the criminal activity in the district through inherited rite from his father as well as the league of associated villainy who barely remained loyal to his family name.

Mordred was filled with giddy anticipation as Cayne took a huge gulp of his drink and immediately spit it on the floor. A black blob formed a puddle at Cayne's feet as the huge man banged his fist on the table.

"Bitch, why is there rat in my drink?" Cayne bellowed, landing a few blows to the wench's head when she came to look at his tankard. She fell to the floor and he kicked her in the side, hollering, "Ya stupid slag, I should skin ya!"

Amid the woman's desperate pleas and snivels, Mordred palmed his filleting knife and slipped from his chair. Quick as Elemental light flashing from an array, he ducked behind Cayne, jerked his head back, and slit open his throat. As Cayne gurgled and clutched at the wide gap in the skin around his neck, Mordred shoved him against the table. A few chairs scraped but otherwise silence blanketed the tavern. He licked the blood from the knife, careful not to nick his tongue over the harbor seal teeth lined with steel and forming the blade.

"One must ever be happy in a good day's work," he said as Cayne's body jerked uncontrollably, and he fell to the floor, a wet smile gaping from his throat, "What better way to die than to show joy while doing so? The attitude maketh the man. Anyone disagree?"

Several rasping coughs preceded the tankards in the tavern being raised in a toast. Another had fallen to a more spirited usurper, the balance of power shifting once more. Mordred had carefully planned what had happened, intent all along on inheriting Cayne's domain and the spoils that went with it.

Crouching, the new "boss" helped the woman up from the floor. She clutched at his arms, bubbling gratitude. Considering her general appearance before Cayne hit her, she was hardly much the worse for wear, even with blood dripping from her split lips and a good-sized cut on her chin. Despite her wounds, and the glaze in her eyes, she had enough wits about her to watch his every move, as if expecting the man's fists to fall about her ears.

But he surprised her by saying, "Any trouble with this or anything else, you talk to me or my boys. Same with your other wenches here." He used his own sleeve to wipe away her blood and tears. "Anything at all, I'll fix it."

"Course. Best meat we can get goes to you and 'em. Me word's me bind."

It required three men to drag Cayne's corpse to a cart someone had fetched. As if sensing their new leader's regard, they lifted their heads like hounds reeling in the scent of the blood from an arrow-struck boar.

"The Healers will pay a pretty coin for another stiffy," filtered back to Mordred, when someone added, "Unless, you wish otherwise, Milord." One of the scum attending to the disposing of Cayne lingered on the gold bracelets around the dead man's wrists, his fingers twitching as he ran his hand over the jewelry.

With a sniff, Mordred said, "Rune House won't be able to connect me to this or even recognize the type of blade I used. Take him wherever you profit, and I have no need for cheap baubles, so it is yours as well. Just smile as you do it."

The gold bracelets vanished from sight, smiles abounding on the three men hauling off the body. A few people entered the tavern, others departing as if nothing had happened— business as usual.

Another wench brought him a new meal, and he settled in a shadowy alcove across the room, which provided a perfect location to observe anyone coming or going. Scraping his fork over the flaking pewter of his bowl, Mordred ticked through his options. Organizing highwaymen was high on his list but only one of his goals.

As he removed the fork from his mouth, the taste of the metal stayed with him. Perhaps he should seek an audience with his father— assess from the interior as opposed to the exterior? His mother had said the money from the purse came from Arthwyr and Mordred should find him in the Hearth.

Deep into his thoughts, he barely acknowledged two recently arrived, cloaked men passing close enough for their robes to brush against his own garment. One sniffed as if disgusted that his robe had touched Mordred, who weighed whether or not he should stalk these two when they left and relieve them of their purses.

"Bloody drunkard," the haughty voice of one of the men ground out. "You know how to pick the finest of establishments, Lord Jotnar."

Mordred's pulse leapt as if to charge into his throat. *Nobility?* He strained his ears, picking up a sigh from who he assumed was Lord Jotnar. This man said, "Lord Minkrune, any place other than a cesspool will alert Rune House and that wretched Marshal. If it's all the same to you, I'd rather not let him set my bollocks alight."

"Afraid of the brat's fire, Ymir? How unlike the great Lord of the Tomb. Surely you know a trick or two to set him straight, what with all the giants you boast in your bloodline."

"Since you're interested in a reunion with the Marshal of Evermore, how about *you* set it up, Kenneth?"

Mordred peeked through cheap latticework dividing the alcove he was in from the one that the two nobles claimed. Sparks shot above the fair hair of the shorter of the two, and darts of flame outlined his breath on his exhale as he said. "I'll pass, Ymir. Let's just make this quick. Between that Marshal, those two Kelliweg Lords, and Lord Blumenthal's rake, we're already cutting it close to a date with the gallows."

Ymir tensed, his eyes narrowing and his lips thinning into a blanched line. "Did you say Blumenthal's rake?"

Kenneth tutted, a cruel smirk lifting the corners of his mouth. "Saw him abouts the wharf fresh from a Blumenthal knarr. You know what shadows follow him, aye?"

So many possibilities rushed through Mordred's mind as he listened to their conversation. Ymir Jotnar and Kenneth Minkrune were the Heads of two of the Evermorean Houses that ceded after the war. In the major cities of the West, the streets were filled with blood resulting from their Houses' affiliations. Now, two of the famed noble lines—the Lords of the Houses, no less—parlayed in the seediest section of the Hearth.

Wood whined as Lord Kenneth Minkrune shoved his leather-covered arms over his table. "Are you sure coming here was wise? Not even Grendel, any of the Foel Witches, or Agravaine Vulgate himself ever dared come to this dung pit to meet. We could surely have found a suitable place in the East, just as well."

Ymir Jotnar shot out his hand. "If I could have, I would have." He glanced around. "Believe me, I don't want to be here anymore than you."

"Then, again, why are we in this cesspool?"

"Because the Foels' cousin insisted on staking out the Hearth first. Can you blame him for wanting to see the risks we're willing to take for his backing?"

"Still, our allies refused to stick out their—"

"The others are far more obvious than we are, and you know it. Besides, Agravaine's best place is in the Vault. His project keeps him occupied."

Crossing his arms, Minkrune leaned back in his seat. "His *project* should be elsewhere, lest he grow too soft."

"And, pray tell, where would you put that project—Minkrune Manor?"

As if Lord Minkrune had bitten a lemon, a grimace twisted his lips into a trembling line. "All right, his project can stay right where it is. Evermore forbid, I take it on in my duchy."

"We don't have many options. Aside from the money from the mines and from the slaves we're bringing in that we don't use ourselves, there's little to fund another war. We need his financial support if we have any hope of unseating Arthwyr and returning Evermore to the glory it deserves."

"There must be another way," Lord Minkrune said, his voice lowering. "The only option cannot be an invasion. What if this sponsor wants more than we're willing to give? I don't see a Pendragon ruler taking up our charge and then exiling the wolf we invite to dinner."

Mordred cracked his eyelids enough to catch the slow twitch of Ymir Jotnar's head as the older man said, "We have no choice but to trust him. The Houses allied with us aren't powerful enough to go against one tied through blood and marriage to a Foel." With a long sigh, Ymir exposed his pale throat dotted with gray hair from where his jaw met his neck. "It's taken us over half a decade to even court someone to help finance another war. It would take many more years for our ally to muster enough soldiers to stage one himself. So, we both need each other. Us for the science and the people we can bring; him for his money."

Across the room, the door banged as a figure swathed in heavy robes eclipsed the lantern light from outside. Both Lords sat up straighter, exchanged glances, and quickly slid from their rickety benches. The figure at the door kept his features shrouded in the folds of his hood, the candles in the sconces casting enough visibility to display a coat-of-arms on his sleeves in glistening red and gold thread. To Mordred's recollection, there weren't any Evermorean Houses hosting a serpent swallowing a babe, and with an eagle—wings extended— hovering above the snake.

Mordred watched the two nobles cross the room and bow to the latecomer, who made no move to return the courtesy, instead straightening and towering over Lord Minkrune while meeting Lord Jotnar at eye level. With the shift in posture, Mordred made out a chiseled jawline and olive skin but the cowl covered all else of his facial features.

As the three turned toward the door, the late arrival exited just as Sluagh shuffled into the tavern. Lord Minkrune crinkled his nose and withered his lip until Lord Jotnar placed his hand on his comrade's shoulder. The briefest lull in the tavern allowed for Mordred to hear Kenneth spit out, "Latrine creeper."

Sluagh's features twisted as he snorted phlegm. The mucous rattled in the highwaymen's mouth and he hacked a gob at the nobles' boots. "Beastie Easties," he said, weaving his head and shoulders from side to side like a cobra about to strike. "Quick, quick. Ingots to be made in hanging Easties."

Red darkened Kenneth's rounded cheeks as Ymir shoved the other noble outside and kicked the door shut. A lumistone fell and shattered, flares of light shooting out when it hit the floor. Several curses were slurred from those closest, though their remonstrations petered out as the drunkards adjusted to the shadows that they were all too familiar with.

When Sluagh made his way, the highwayman's glazed stare sharpened into the delighted acuity of what it had been many moons ago. Sluagh was one of the few men in Porthcrawl deserving of Mordred's respect and even affinity. Though Sluagh was hard to pin down—flighty and prone to dips in mood and cognizance—a lot more than the man's utility bound him to Mordred. An oath secured him more steadfast than any other he'd had or made thus far. Mordred owed that much to his best mate, Orion.

The clatter of broken rocks upon the table interrupted his ruminations to the lumistones Sluagh had collected. "Ingot for a thought, pretty stone for a krone," Sluagh said, the phrase highlighting his unpredictability.

Mordred opened his mouth and hesitated, lowering his gaze to the shards near his fingertips. Picking up one piece, he ran his thumb carefully over a sharp edge. "What if I told you there was a way to have this realm make up for Orion?"

Sluagh scratched his forehead. "Who's this Orion?"

Sometimes it burned anew in Mordred when Sluagh forgot his own son, the bitter reminder of losing him the final straw that shattered the highwayman and brought him to his current state.

Mordred said nothing, the silence having Sluagh reach across the table for his arm. "Not leave me for this Orion, will you?"

Swallowing the lump in his throat, Mordred gripped the leathery hand of his best mate's father. "Nay, rest assured, he's already gone. One day, however, he hopes to see you once more."

Sluagh twitched his eyes from side to side and loosened his grip. "Orion?" he murmured, a sliver of light flaring across his gaze. "Miss me son. Where is he… sea is cold, Isles is blue. Me son so… blue." He sneered with the vitriol of a wolf snarling at a hunter. "Bloody nobles did not make me son's killers pay. Sodding leeches."

Mordred waited for Sluagh's grumbles to fade. "There's a way to make it all right and—"

"Burn Evermore to ground, aye?" Sluagh asked, straightening from his slouch and licking his lips. "Burn her good and done."

"No," Mordred said, collecting another jagged piece of the lumistone. "I have another idea that will honor your son and my mother better." He released a glow of silver from his Metal and fused the two shards together. Bit by bit, he remolded the stone until it formed a sphere.

Rolling it across the table, he chuckled when Sluagh caught the globe and peered at it as if eager for the trick to reveal itself. As the stone remained blank and unlit, Sluagh held it out to Mordred, who closed his fingers over both the orb and his loyal mate's hand. The pulse of his Element's release made the lumistone glow like he remembered Orion's peridot eyes as he passed into Twilight. That steeled Mordred's resolve as a new oath emerged: "We burn Evermore—" his voice rising— "then we rebuild and rule her anew."

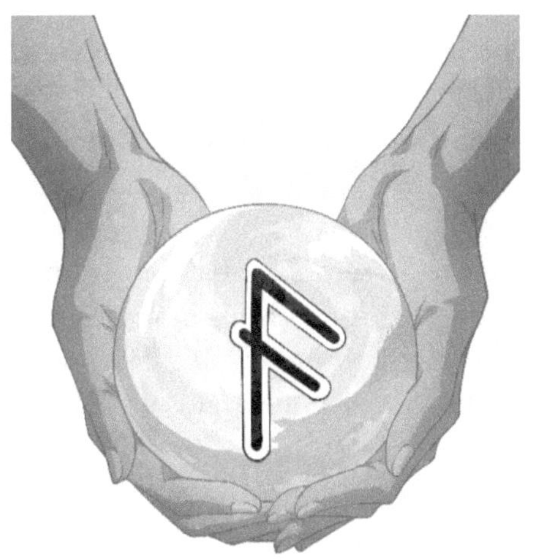

CHAPTER 58

LAID BAIT

Lubaba Cuhlwch's nimble fingers fussed with the locks in Maerna's dark hair as the Maid stared into a mirror and watched Aisling Chia reading a book. As if sensing her regard, Aisling lifted her brown eyes from the text and winked.

Maerna peeked past a curtain to her mother, who sat at a desk of paulownia, a Nihon wood known for its durability yet light weight. Nimue's quill fluttered in the air, as if in tribute to the speed of her writing.

"Any on your list standing out?" Aisling asked, more to interrupt the silence than to elicit an answer.

Papers rustled as Nimue scanned the sheet next to her hand. Her latest Apprentice, Zabrina, had relinquished her Metal and taken her Oath of Neutrality a few days earlier. Nimue flicked her quill back and forth as if it were a miniature sword. "I'm leaning toward Cyrus."

Lubaba stilled her fingers in Maerna's hair. "The Wood Elemental? The little one with big ears and buck teeth?"

"Aye, that one."

"Mm." Lubaba twirled a lock of hair so it framed Maerna's cheek. "Another odd choice. Zabrina worked out well, though."

Nimue shot her a teasing look. "I was not made High Oracle for no good reason."

"No one can ever argue that you were not well chosen," Lubaba replied and chuckled lightly. "You've shaken the tree more than once. All three of us have."

Maerna pulled her hair from Lubaba's worn fingers. A sniffle and a cry brought stares from all three Oracles in the room.

"Oh, dear, did I pull too hard?" Lubaba asked Maerna as she massaged the girl's head. "Or if your braids are too tight, I can do them over."

Maerna didn't respond except to increase the volume of her sobs, which had her mother scramble to her feet and rush over to her and ask, "What's wrong, Daughter?"

Clutching her mother, Maerna said, "I'm… I'm worried about Viera."

"And just what is it that troubles you about her?"

Maerna sniveled. "She sees ghosts in the castle. I'm scared for her." She daubed her eyes to wipe away nonexistent tears.

"She will be fine." Nimue held Maerna in her arms. "I'm sure your father has it figured out."

"How can he figure it out when he's ignoring what she's telling him about the ghosts? She's seen Jormund and Uther." She started to cry again. "She even saw Vertigorn." Maerna paused for effect. "I'm really scared for her."

"Your father is ignoring what Viera is telling him about ghosts?"

"Aye, Mum."

Nimue gritted her teeth. "You needn't worry. Your father simply requires time to adjust to his responsibilities."

"Then why is he trying to dump Viera on a different Master. He doesn't want her anymore."

"Maerna, you really believe that?"

Icy fingers slid through Maerna, but she was committed—no turning back now. "Yes, Mum," she choked out. "He took us to the Fire Temple to find another Master for Viera." In a meeker tone, Maerna added, "He also imprinted on her."

Fire sparked in Nimue's tone. "He imprinted on that child and now he looks to rid himself of her? Are you absolutely certain of this?"

Maerna squirmed in her seat. "Aye. There were letters on his desk. I saw them myself."

Jumping to her feet, Nimue barked, "I just forgot something in the castle!"

The Head of The Oracle Guild yanked on her flaring gray robes and fluffed her hair over them. Tension settled on everyone in the room when Nimue donned the Eye of Sight: two silver chains attached to dual palms cupping a gray circular orb with *Ansuz* engraved in its center. The pendant was what Elden, the first Queen of Evermore—who was also the High Oracle before stepping down—gifted to her daughter. Every High Oracle wore the symbol when deemed appropriate, and it was not brought out on a whim.

In the mirror, Maerna caught her face going pale. An Oracle donning the Eye of Sight was a war declaration if there ever was one. If her father ever realized how much she had manipulated this confrontation, she would be relegated to kitchen duty forever.

She staked her hope on her tactic being necessary to help Viera, but as her mother stormed toward the doorway, Maerna had more than a few reservations concerning what she'd done. If her father somehow managed to abate her mother's fury, Maerna's final three contingency plans were her Aunt Kazue and Uncle Daisuki.

However, her oldest uncle, Lord Haruki Abe, was her ultimate checkmate. He was sweet on his beloved niece. No one wanted Haruki leaving Abe Bay. When he appeared in Court, it was over dire matters or only as a blanket courtesy at certain select points in the year. After the Draigs' Duels, he had received the title of Knight of the Eclipse, but Nimue used it more as his trusted proxy. On rare occasions, the title was proxied by his younger easier-going brother, Daisuki, who frequented the Hearth as a preferred trainer for Houses employing bodyguards.

Setting the hairbrush on the vanity, Lubaba skittered toward the door to follow Nimue. Aisling whipped up her wooden cane from where it rested next to her chair, and this abrupt motion brought a halt to Lubaba's departure.

Aisling waved her cane toward the chair next to Maerna. "Sit back down, Lulu. Fate has decided. This needed to happen."

Lubaba wrung her hands. "I should go with her."

"Nimue hardly needs help with this. Not when Maerna is setting her on the right path." Aisling gave the air another stab with her cane. "So mote it be."

Lubaba placed her arm over Maerna's shoulder. "Then well done, Mae-mae." She returned to fixing the girl's hair as she crooned in her low soothing tones, *"The moon has been arising, the stars in golden guising."*

"You do know exactly what you've done, don't you?" Aisling asked Maerna as she tapped her cane on the floor to the rhythm of Lubaba's song's lyrics.

Patting her cheeks to draw out more color, Maerna inspected her reflection. "Aye. I've made sure Viera becomes an Emrys."

The heavy doors to the room flew open with a loud bang. Gray robes snapped behind Nimue's stiff figure as she stormed into the chamber where Myrddin was conducting a kata lesson with Viera. Viera lowered herself into her seat, but little good it did her as Nimue dragged her chair from the table and pulled her to her feet. "Let's go," Nimue snapped. "We're leaving."

Myrddin hurried up from his desk. "Nimue—"

A low growl hushed him as Nimue stood over Viera, the Oracle's rose perfume easing the girl's anxiety over what was going to happen next. She took Viera's hand. "Why did you not say what troubles you so?"

Viera dropped her eyes to the floor.

"No matter your fears, you must speak up." Nimue bent down so her eyes were level with Viera's. "Any voice is better than none. The softest voice is the loudest when silence surrounds it. Never forget that."

Viera continued to say nothing and stare at the floor. Nimue straightened and rounded on Myrddin, snarling at him, "Our daughter is crying her eyes out. On the way over here, I find out from Lance that your new ward is seeing Jormund Wallach in the bloody keep!"

Myrddin tensed. "Just what would you suggest I do? He's a ghost."

"Finding an Oracle might be a start. Do you think you might know one?" Nimue threw her hands in the air and wrung them in front of him. "Evermore forbid, you and Arthwyr summon an Oracle to purify the dark in the West Wing."

"I'm handling it."

"You're handling it, Myrddin Emrys!" Her voice had pulsated into a roar. She stalked closer to her husband and stopped with her nose able to touch his with the slightest nudge. "Tell me how you're handling it when I hear you planned on abandoning your ward in the Fire Temple? A ward you imprinted yourself on, yet were willing to cast aside knowing the suffering she will endure because of your cowardice."

Viera gasped, her eyes rounding as she looked between them. Myrddin jolted as if slapped, his eyes mirroring hers before he choked out, "Where did you hear that from?"

"It doesn't matter. Husband, it's something you should have been honest about with me from the beginning." Nimue jabbed him in the chest. "Lance also told me everything concerning the little excursion you took her on to the Fire Temple."

"Then you know she set fire to the training arena." He turned away.

She stepped past him. "I thought you were different, but you're like every other Master who treats a ward like a pretty trinket and discards it when its shine fades."

If his pallor was anything to go by, Myrddin took on the gauntness of having a bean-síghe suck the life from him. "I didn't mean for this to turn out like—"

Nimue grabbed Viera's shoulder and herded her out, pausing to deliver coldly to him, "Clearly, your commitment to her goes only so far. I'm relieving her of your presence. If and when you're worthy of her, you can have her back. But only then."

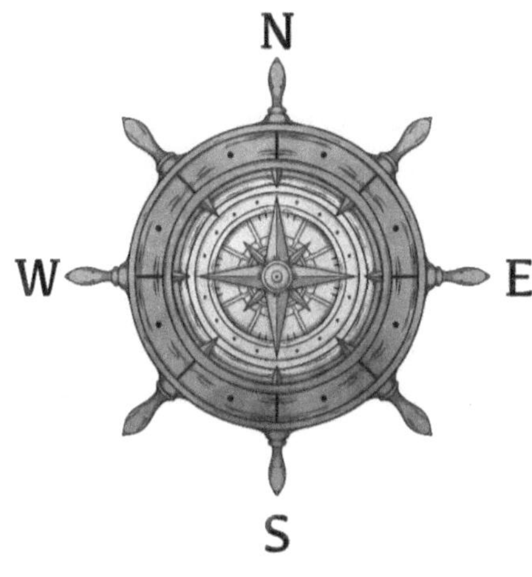

CHAPTER 59

THE DINNER FROM HELLS

Viera's time during the next few days was spread between Nimue and Maerna. She didn't know why Myrddin wasn't around, but since it wasn't unusual for him to have castle business that kept him away for extended periods, she didn't give his being gone that much thought.

Brynn continued to befriend her and help with her reading lessons, and Viera was beginning to settle in at the castle. Maerna had discussed her entering House Emrys on a more formal basis, whatever that meant, but she'd heard nothing further about this.

So, life for her in Elden's Hearth was improving, and no ghosts were plaguing her except in an occasional dream. She was afraid that her somewhat idyllic situation would end, and it did when Nimue told her that her presence would be required for a feast leading into the Mala holiday in the Main Hall, which was a yearly tradition originating from Cymry's reign, but reinstituted far more equally to all ever since Arthwyr claimed the Throne.

Viera tried every trick she could come up with to avoid attending the dinner, and even attempted a few ploys provided by Brynn, but Nimue was too smart for all the ruses. On the fateful evening Viera settled at

Maerna's side as both lasses sat beside Nimue on a bench at an enormous table.

As Jarvis Ward and other servants served the meal, Viera twitched her fingers over the utensils, having no interest in eating and wanting only to leave at the earliest chance. Out of the corner of her eye, gray and maroon robes shimmered. She tensed at the youth now standing directly across from her on the other side of the table. The edges around his face blurred, and she squinted in an attempt to gain a clearer image.

When she recognized the apparition, she whispered, "Hamyll, why are you here?"

The specter staggered a few steps backwards and faded into nothingness. That was the first time a wraith had appeared to her with other "live" people in a room, and this unnerved her as much as being forced to attend the dinner.

The low din of normal dining continued at the table, but with her appetite nonexistent, Viera shoved food around her plate. As she pushed the dish aside, a snicker brought her attention down the table to Jocelyn.

"Food not good enough for you?" Jocelyn simpered. "Don't worry. Shan't be long 'til you're shipped off where you belong. Xavier told us you leveled the training arena in the Fire Temple. Seems you're going to destroy us all if left to your own devices."

Xavier Cuhlwch was sitting across from Jocelyn, and he said, "Indeed, next time you might kill somebody. Or maybe that was your intent all along. The Fire Masters are shocked by your actions. Such power hasn't been seen—" a smile lurking about his mouth as he paused and eyed Bedwyr— "since Bedwyr or a Foel Witch we had to eliminate to assure the realm's purity."

Viera's tongue was gritty and dry as she croaked out a strangled, "I did nothing wrong. My Fire just became too powerful for the enclosed surroundings. It won't happen again."

Of all the Lords whom Viera did not want to see, it was Tremayne Cornwall, but he was sitting next to Xavier.

The Cornwall noble narrowed his acid-green eyes on Viera. "Strange how you deny being a Witch, when I caught you consorting with Lord Wallach not long ago when I was on patrol." He elbowed Xavier. "She was in his arms—as if a damsel—but weaving a spell like a Foel Witch. Then she set her charms upon Lord DuLac. I witnessed him escorting her to Lord Emrys' Chamber, rather familiar like, I might add."

Some of the Maids gasped, but it was at the encouragement of Jocelyn.

Tremayne nodded to those closest to him and angled himself toward the head of the table. "Sire, she might have already corrupted Lord DuLac, and Lord Wallach is supposed to be beyond reproach, yet here we are."

Arthwyr's jaw might as well have turned into a solid block of marble. Bedwyr banged his fist on the table and spoke for his King: "Tremayne, you speak out your arse!"

"Tsk, tsk, you know I don't." Tremayne threw out his hand as if swatting away a fly. "Once upon a time, you dared to fraternize with the Foel Heiress, did you not?"

A cold pall settled on the room as everyone awaited Bedwyr's reply, who averted his gaze. "I did not."

"Bollocks. That little Foel bitch flounced around here all chummy with your sisters. Quite the pack—or I should say coven—considering how they carried on." Tremayne pulled out a long strand of his hair and held it over a candelabra until the flames burnt it to ash. "One wonders if she corrupted both Wysteria and Olwen."

"Those girls weren't Witches and you know it, you lying bastard."

Tremayne grunted. "Tsk, tsk, look how you are into name calling. Let's put this aside and look at the facts. After Lilwy Foel went against Royal decree, the shame she brought to Foel House—"

"Shut your cowardly mouth!" Constantine hollered and stood, the venom in his tone creating a hissing sound as he glowered at Tremayne. "That lass had more honor than you will ever have. She faced down her entire family, including Uther and Jormund. She put her faith in those she believed in over deceitful fealty that would have saved her life. You slander Lilwy Foel's name in what you suggest."

Tremayne folded his arms. "Her father spared her by taking her back to the robin's nest, but nothing could have prevented her execution if she'd returned here." He glanced to his lackeys. "Best to prune a Witch before she turns someone into another Tegid Foel."

Bedwyr turned to the same people from whom Tremayne was attempting to gain purchase. "And I claimed her as my war prize and concession for becoming Arthwyr's Knight. Just think," he said, smirking, "without Tegid's foresight, Lilwy Foel could be flouncing about this room—with a new coven of Maids-in-Waiting—and scheming to turn this entire Court into Witches."

Exchanging his own smirk with Bedwyr's, Xavier chortled and said, "It appears, Lord Wallach, you have been compromised as well as Lord DuLac. Lady Tillwith has enchanted you both more than you could ever know. Fortunately, much too far away is Lady Foel's reach to taint anyone else here." Adopting a pitying expression, he motioned toward Viera. "I will wager that Lady Tillwith is the newest to join this Foel coven. Alas, when you lose a Witch's trinity, it is imperative to usher in new blood, is it not?"

Sending Viera a shrewd glance, Jocelyn turned to Arthwyr. "Oh, my King, the shame of it all! Perhaps a trial *is* in order to assure that we don't befoul justice like when poor Lady Karen was falsely accused. Such a horror to see her body laid out like that. The blood's still there. I go faint whenever I walk by. With any hope, Viera can be cleared and not taste the fire of the stake. What say you, Sire?"

Viera scanned the feast hall for Lance, dread splintering into tremors that promised to undo her when she realized he was not present to defend her honor. One look at Bedwyr, and the devastation in his features left her keenly aware that he was lost in his own memories surrounding that night.

A rattling snort and a heavy guffaw cut through the maelstrom that was out of hand—and becoming worse. "If getting lost on the way to the latrines is reason enough to charge one with Witchery, then I wager that my arse will be burning next," Percyval said, patting Blanche's arm. "Blanche, my love, it's been nice needling you every step of the way."

Blanche offered a low hum. "Gig's up, dear. What do you wish for me to send to carry you aloft to the moon?"

"Any old mop or broom will do."

She inched her stare over him and turned toward Saris. "Thoughts, old friend?"

"Send a wheelbarrow," Saris deadpanned, "nothing short of that will do."

"Milord, you're not a Witch," Xavier said as he snapped his fingers at Tremayne for support, who nodded furiously with panic in his eyes.

Perceval stood. "Neither of you wants to arrest a former 10-4 official from Rune House. Yet, you defile a young girl with no real way to defend herself against you two grown arseholes, let alone against Houses' Cuhlwch, Cornwall, and Sagramore, which led the call for the executions of the survivors in Foel, Jotnar, Minkrune, and Vulgate."

Blanche blew air past her lips. "You lot were so gallant in shaming Isaac Minkrune and Armand Jotnar all the way to the Dragon's Spine, two who broke from their Houses long before the Draig's Duels. We're lucky the third man of the East got rounded up in the village and imprisoned at Rune House. You near plunged us into another war by demanding his execution."

Percyval raised his voice. "You know what you two are? You are a plague on all the good Houses in Evermore!" He pounded his fist so hard on the table that several glasses toppled and spilled their contents.

Appearing unmoved by the censure of someone even as august as the Rhegeds, Tremayne said, "It's best to be wary, Milord. A shinny of caution keeps the realm from bankruptcy and out of another war." His supporters nodded and murmured among themselves.

Percyval wasn't having any of it. "I've heard better drivel from the drunkards in the slums." He turned to the pack of Cuhlwchs, Cornwalls, and Sagramores sitting together in a long row and then back to Tremayne. "Funny how you and Lord Cuhlwch make such remarks about the lass, yet you don't dare make such claims in front of Lord DuLac. Is that because he'd have you two by the throats?"

"That's…." Tremayne's voice trailed off, a tinge of pink dusting his cheeks as both Lance and Galahad entered, took seats at the table, and started passing food between themselves.

Percyval said, "What were you fools saying about Miss Tillwith and Lord Lance?" He winked at Lance. "Something about our Ebony Knight now having a hankering for little girls, right? Lance, they're calling you the next Carian Foel!"

"Really?" Lance said as he dropped a sausage he was about to eat back on his plate. "What brought this on?"

"Tremayne and Xavier are fixing to fry the lass at the stake for her getting lost and spending a night in the dungeon. Apparently, she and I are now part of Lilwy Foel's coven. Hells bells, the lass bewitched you, me, Bedwyr, and who knows who else. I didn't even realize that Tegid's little girl was still alive, let alone able to influence Miss Tillwith. Amazing the power of a child no one can confirm is dead or alive—or even a Witch."

Tremayne and Xavier flinched at the icy stare Lance gave them. He spoke with more vehemence than Constantine and Percyval combined: "Even after knowing such rumors killed my wife and daughter, your impudence in inciting a Witch hunt on an innocent is reprehensible. I believe that a few words to your Heads of Houses are in order, as well a formal complaint to Rune House." He ran his gaze down the row of Cuhlwchs, Cornwalls, and Sagramores, none of whom would look directly at him. "I will not tolerate any of you besmirching my name, hers, or Lord Wallach's."

Percyval strode over to Jocelyn, crinkling his lips into a toothy grin that stretched a few of his battle scars. "Word of advice, lassie. Anyone with any brains knows that it's not wise to insult a Witch, lest you end up puking your guts up like the Foel Witches made others do for far less. Clearly, you are not speaking out of your mouth, hmm?"

Arthwyr had been a silent observer during the entirety of the exchanges. He raised his hand and the large room became quiet as he asked, "Is that all, Lord Rheged?"

"Depends on your verdict."

"You argued your point well, Milord."

Percyval nodded. "Ah, no dungeon time then. Very well." He bent and pecked Blanche's forehead. "Blanche, I live to rue you another day."

Blanche released a peal of laughter. "As do I."

After Percyval swaggered from the room, the diners returned to an uneasy silence. Nimue squeezed Viera's shoulder and murmured in her ear, "Chin up. Show no fear. Maerna and I must deliver some post. Brynn and Delilah are joining you. We'll be back soon."

Viera smiled as Brynn and Delilah sat with her between them and Nimue guided Maerna to the door. The pair halted, bowed, and sidestepped into the corridor as a man entered. At first, Viera turned to her friends until a hiss reached her ears, "Shite, it's him."

Her attention returned to the door and her lips parted at the sight of—*He's a pirate! There's a sodding pirate in the feast hall!* There was no denying that all attention was diverted to the man in a flowing white tunic and leather vest that put his toned and tanned chest on full display. His trousers were tucked into his worn leather boots and a cutlass with several other daggers jangled on the wide belt slung low on his hips. Black hair curled in rakish waves to the nape of his neck and dark stubble lined his jaw.

The man sauntered past the Elves, who had fixed their stares on him; their expressions stoic but harboring an intensity that had Viera cringing at their catlike gazes. With a cocky salute across his brow, the man continued past the gaping courtiers and drew closer to where Viera and her friends were seated. She expected him to keep moving only for her heart to lurch into her throat when he slowed to a halt next to them.

"Milady," his voice had the roughness of the sea with a hint of something courtlier in his accent. For a few seconds, Viera swore he directed his greeting to her until he nodded toward her and Delilah, "Milady's crew."

"Quartermaster Beddoe," Brynn said, dipping her chin. "What brings you here?"

Beddoe flashed a roguish grin, gesturing to the emblem of a ship's helm with a compass in its middle. "Maritime business with your father. I'll be in town for a spell. Little Bonny Lass, I'd say stay out of trouble, but that wouldn't make anything very interesting, now, would it?"

He winked a glowing violet eye at them and made his way to sit next to Lord Blumenthal, who filled a tankard for the pirate. Viera whispered, "Who is he?"

Brynn shrugged. "The third Easterner that Lady Rheged mentioned, and the only one given leave to walk freely this side of Evermore. Beddoe is my father's man and my cousin's Quartermaster. If he's here, then my cousin is sure to be soon, if not already."

She bowed her head in Dinadan's direction, who returned it with a faint bob of his head before focusing back on Beddoe. Unable to tear her gaze from Dinadan, Viera asked, "How old is your father?"

"Eighty-four winters. Stop staring. It's unseemly." Brynn jabbed Viera in the arm with the handle of a butter knife. "My father apprenticed my mother when he was in his thirties and her sixteen. They realized they were Soul Bonds. You can guess the rest."

With heat scalding her cheeks, Viera muttered, "You should go and sit with the other Maids. This spot's reserved for humiliation."

"You should ignore them better. No one's going to go against that performance and call you a Witch."

Viera was so nervous that she had thumbed permanent circles into her cloth napkin. "Who is Lilwy Foel?" she whispered.

"Lilwy Foel was Lord Tegid Foel's daughter," Brynn said and inched closer to Viera. "Bedwyr made a Bonding bid for her that Jormund Wallach and Ceridwyn Foel, Lilwy's Witch of a mother, accepted. The whole thing was quite horrid. Lilwy was eleven and he was sixteen."

Clapping her hands over her mouth, Viera mumbled, "That is gross. She was a child. What in Evermore possessed him?"

Delilah moaned in distress. "They were going to kill Lilwy. Jormund insisted that the Bonding happen when she turned thirteen. Nothing came of it because Bedwyr chose Eerie."

"Where is Lilwy now?"

"None of us know. If she is alive, she's sixteen seasons this autumn." Brynn raised an eyebrow at some noble boys who'd just left the table and walked by. "If you think the Sagramore, Cuhlwch, and Cornwall men are bad, there's no hope for a girl where she's from. As an heiress, it'll be a miracle if she's not married off to some royal prick and utter bastard of a noble. If she's smart, she'll enchant him into a frog."

Delilah said, "The only ones worth anything on that side were Armand and Isaac—maybe Henri Vulgate, and to a lesser degree Dain Foel, Lilwy's cousin, wasn't so bad."

Viera glanced about the table, spying Constantine eying them with narrowed eyes, and lowered her voice. "Isn't anyone from those Houses evil?"

"There's good and bad on both sides." Delilah surreptitiously directed Viera's attention to Master Tailor Florian as Jarvis served him a flagon of homebrew. "Courtiers—mostly Dain's brothers, Dub and Dother, masterminded Isaacky the Icky for Isaac Minkrune's size and because he aspired to be a Master Cook. Lord Kenneth threatened to disinherit Isaac if he didn't rescind an apprenticeship. Isaac fired his House, earned an Apprentice's stipend, and apprenticed under the old Kitchen Master, Kef, and Jarvis. Following him, Armand apprenticed as a Master Tailor to Florian. They were younger sons and didn't give two goats, as they wouldn't likely inherit their Houses. The Court was in an uproar."

Viera bit back a laugh. "That's pretty wicked."

Brynn smirked. "No one ever heard of a noble son firing his House and going peasant. Wasn't long after that Henri did similar, though Dain didn't, and the four of them shared a flat in the Red Lantern District."

Delilah giggled. "Armand and Isaac would've run circles around this Court and gotten us all out of this dinner."

Viera massaged her temples. "You two seem to know everything that goes on around here. Even with you helping, I tried every way I could to get out of this dinner, just knowing something bad was going to happen to me here, but Nimue made me show up. Yet I didn't see Myrddin, and Palamedes and the other Saracens weren't here, either. How come?"

"I don't know about Myrddin," Delilah said, "but the Saracens, Morien, and Bors had this afternoon devoted to prayer. It is Ramadan right now, so they were excused."

"If I'm still around here next year at this time, I'm going to turn Muslim."

Brynn laughed and cracked her knuckles. "There's still some sunlight left. Want to practice spitting like a drunk off the parapets?"

Viera clapped her hands and rubbed them together. "Only if Jocelyn has a stroll through the Queen's favourite gardens planned."

"Why do you think I suggested it?"

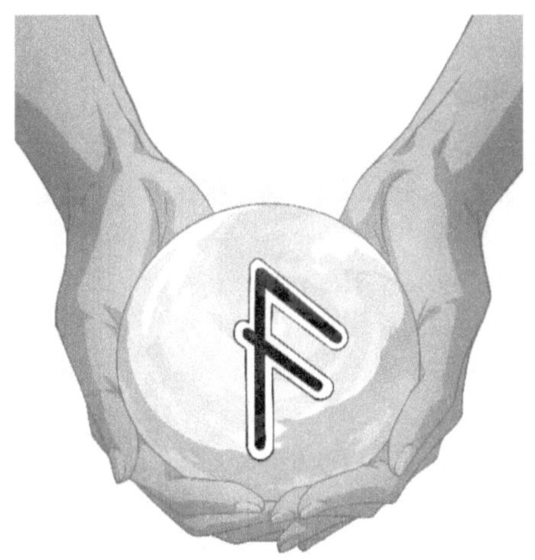

CHAPTER 60

MORE THAN MEETS THE EYE

The High Oracle strode from an archway that separated the castle from the rest of the district. A peasant herded goats down the path, and other denizens hustled through their early afternoon routines. Across the way, a fountain bubbled and two children flicked water at each other as their mothers chatted. An old man, seemingly oblivious to all of them, sat on a bench and tossed crumbs to a smattering of birds. The mutt near his feet dozed, muzzle upon its legs, an occasional huff interrupting its napping.

Viera's attention darted over the continuous flow of activity, and she tightened her grip on her lesson primers and scampered after Nimue. When she caught up with her, Nimue turned and touched her shoulder. Out of instinct, Viera jerked away, her textbooks spilling on the ground. As Nimue knelt to help collect the material, Viera apologized for being so jumpy.

Nimue said, "You've been through a lot lately, but you can start to relax. Your time here will be easier from now on."

"Did you do a Seeing, or whatever you call it?"

Nimue laughed. "No. I just know that life will not be so stressful for you."

How could it get any worse?

Nimue opened one of the books. "I had a hard time learning how to read and write." She traced some words on a page with her finger. "My first few Masters gave up on me."

Viera wondered if that was really the truth, but she asked anyway, "What did you do?"

"There are realms where the written word doesn't flow from left to right but from right to left instead. In Abe House, my siblings and I first learned Nihongo. It's why I had trouble learning Evermore's written word. My seventh Master had to get Shiori to teach me."

"Can I learn Nihongo?"

"When my fool of a husband gets back in my good graces, you can have him work with you on some words, but you need to learn the language of this realm first."

"Can I ask why my Master wasn't at the dinner?"

Nimue waited so long to answer that Viera didn't think she was going to, when she said, "Knowing him, chasing his tail. He means well, but as is the nature of many men, they can be a bit daft. Then there's…." Her face tightened so much that a vein Viera had never seen showed in her forehead. "As I think about it, Bedwyr can show you how to read Nihongo."

"*Bedwyr* speaks Nihongo?"

"Aye, he has Nihongo blood from his mother."

"There's something different about his eyes. He looks like Jormund, or at least the ghost of Jormund that I've seen."

Nimue slowed in front of a stall with wooden chimes clattering out front. "Bedwyr favours his father in many ways, but there is much of his mother in him too. She had blood from the East, and her ancestors were from a powerful line of warriors and clan called the Uesugi. If you must know, my father came from a family of onmyouji heralding to Abe no Seimei. Abe has no meaning here, but his feats are legendary in Nihon."

"What's an onmyouji?"

"They're very similar to this realm's Oracles, but some would argue they meddle in Witchery as they also handle spirits and magic."

"And Uther tolerated your family in this realm?"

Nimue chuckled. "Uther learned that, with my father's Sight, Naboru was a far more cunning warrior and it's not fortuitous to go against an Abe onmyouji. He also didn't want to contend with my mother, the Heiress of Llyr House, and a known House that has a long history of Oracles running in its bloodline."

Oracle or not, odd how she knew I was going to ask her about her parents.

"Does Maerna know Nihongo?"

"She's not as keen on learning my ancestral tongue. Maerna has enough to deal with. Too much, I fear.'"" Nimue stopped in the middle of the street. "Myrddin never should have apprenticed you."

A lump formed in Viera's throat. "I'm sorry."

"You have nothing to be sorry for. Do you understand why I'm opposed to you being my husband's Apprentice?"

"Because I mess up all the time?"

Nimue shrugged. "Hardly. Every student does. You're no different from any other."

Her vision wavering in the sunlight, Viera attempted to focus on a meowing orange kitten in a nearby shop window. "There don't seem to be a lot of people who like me."

Said Nimue, "The kitten is cute, isn't it?"

Startled at the abrupt shift in topic, Viera considered the kitten. "Aye."

Nimue pointed at a less-attractive feline with a patchy gray coat and missing an eye, as it lazed in a nearby planter. "We forget they grow into cats. Life is fraught with events—some good, some bad. Is it fair to make a commitment when times are good, only to abandon what is not so good during times of strife?"

"Nay." Viera held out her hand to the scruffy cat and it butted against her fingers. "Everyone, every animal, deserves the same."

"You're no different."

"I'm a mistake."

"You're definitely not a mistake." Nimue scratched under the cat's chin. "My point is, when someone becomes a Master to another, the person is committed for better or for worse. It's no different from a marriage Bond. We can talk about this more later. For now, I want to show you why I brought you down here."

They came to a shop displaying varnished pots and beautiful flowers. The sign posted outside the door, *Primula's Flowers,* had a long green snake curled around blooms of roses and violets. Viera stared at foliage awash in vibrant color. Iyesgarth grew plants as well, but they were more of the edible variety.

Nimue stopped near a pot overflowing with tulips. "Primula grows the best flowers. They're all steeped in milk and rosewater. It's something Primula learned from her great-great grandaunts, Biancabella and

Samaritana. They convinced her that the mixture makes the blooms grow fuller and brighter."

"Looking at these, who's to argue?" Viera said, and Nimue nodded.

Swinging a water can, a tall slender woman came toward them. "Good noon," she offered.

Nimue stepped aside for the woman. "Afternoon, Primula. How goes the blooming?"

In the wake of her smile, the wrinkles smoothed around Primula's eyes and forehead, shedding years from a countenance and emphasizing a woman who likely turned her fair share of heads in her youth. "Blooms are bountiful as always, dear. Who is this young miss?"

"Myrddin's newest Apprentice, Viera Tillwith. She came with Progress." The High Oracle's quick, sharp peek at Viera made it clear that the current state of affairs with Myrddin was not to be discussed.

Primula smiled at Viera and pruned a few dead ends from some flowers. "Nimue, if you're interested, I have a spot of lavender tea on the hearth. Micah is coming with sandwiches."

As if on demand, the slap of sandals over cobblestone announced a younger woman in paisley robes carrying a basket overflowing with food. "Good noon," she said and waved. Her green stare settled on Viera as Nimue introduced her and explained their relationship.

Micah said, "Nimue and I were Initiates in The Guild. Different years, though." She smiled at Nimue, as if their ages were a realm secret.

"You're an Oracle too?" Viera asked, legitimately excited at getting to know so many of the Seers in The Guild.

With a shrewd glance at Nimue, Micah shrugged. "Nay. It wasn't the lifestyle for me, and my Sight wasn't near reliable enough to—"

"That's not to say Micah is incapable of Seeing," Nimue interrupted. "When she does, her Sight is quite sharp, just not consistent and a scrying ball is not her medium."

Micah patted her basket of food. "I'm much happier baking than staring at a scrying ball or figuring out tea leaves."

Viera glanced at Primula, who was fluffing a flower. "What about you, Milady?"

"As for me, I design floral arrangements for display in the castle. I used to even bring roses for Arthwyr's mother, poor dear."

As Viera looked between the two women, she sensed something well beyond that simple explanation. "So, you two are like the other servants in the castle," Viera said dryly, "except there's something about each of you that's not like any of the other servants. You two ladies remind me more of the Ravas and Wards."

Primula brushed her hand over the tops of her flowers, which leaned toward her fingers as though kissing them. "She has good instincts. They will serve her well."

Nimue placed her hand on Viera's arm. "Aye, but she will best serve all of us to attain our common goal."

Nimue made an intricate design in the air with her hand, and both women made a slight bow to Viera.

Primula said, "Micah and I are part of an intelligence network called The Hands of the Keep. It began during the Draigs' Duels. Dagonet gathered information and relayed it to the Ravas. Linny sewed it in the languages she shares with Lionel."

Micah tugged from her basket a napkin with graceful script hidden in flowers on the cloth in a language Viera had never seen and missed until it was pointed out to her. "Lionel dropped off the clothes for the poor and orphaned to the Temples and other places," Micah said. "He also gave the coded intel to Nimue."

Viera asked, "How did you get the information out?"

"You are a clever one," Primula said, smiling at her. "No one thinks a thing or two about a woman taking a cart of flowers for sale at market or of a man who buys a bloom or two for his Bond or lover."

Micah tucked the cloth back over her basket. "It's amazing how quickly and completely lemon water fades from butcher paper. There's an old Chief near the Pass that would travel miles for a good meal. I fed many men loyal to Arthwyr and sent them on with a little extra love to help them on their way."

Nimue drummed her fingers over Viera's shoulder. "As you can tell, we don't owe our current circumstances to monumental feats. The greatest moments often arise from the smallest of gestures."

Primula pointed at a yellow flower and said, "It's a begonia."

"It's pretty," replied Viera.

"Did you know that flowers have a language?" Primula said as she delicately stroked the petals. "Each one, as well as its color, means something different. A purple iris means wisdom and compliments."

Nimue drew closer to the flowers. "Another way of flattering a bureaucrat stupid enough to believe such things."

Primula harrumphed. "Everyone's a critic."

Viera stroked the yellow flower's waxy surface. "What does this begonia mean?"

Snapping off the fullest blossom, Primula handed it to Viera, who drank in the scent and the bright, sunny coloration of the flower. "It says, may your days bloom with happiness and contentment, and may you find peace with new family and friends."

Nimue closed the blessing with, "So mote it be."

CHAPTER 61

GOLAU AND TYWYLL

Murmurs hummed through the large open space of the Library. At the far end of the room, wood infused with lily oil crackled in a hearth with a huge mantle. Three more hearths were also in use, and farther down on each side of the main fireplace, a grand staircase led to the second level. At the top of the landing, a view of the lower level was afforded a patron. Double doors on the other side of the room led to a large balcony.

The aroma of wood and varnish lingered amid the stronger scent of parchment and ink. Scribes in their yellow robes coasted through bays of cedar wood. Stripes ran down their garments, and decorating their shoulders was an emblem of an open book and the sun rising from its pages. When carrying books, the Scribes gave the appearance of bees with nuggets of pollen moving throughout a hive, the honey of wisdom sweet in their hands.

Myrddin sidestepped a Scribe struggling to carry a mountain of books. He focused on the two Ancients, Bercylac Bredbeddle and Gereant Dumnonia, standing next to a reference table, and he said to them, "I dearly need and request your guidance."

Bercylac wiggled his fingers at Gereant. "Pay up, Doorstop."

"Don't use it all on your hair, Ice Pop." Gereant slapped a silver coin into Bercylac's palm. "Thanks, Dragonling."

Bercylac collected the book that a dour-faced Scribe held out to him. "Much gratitude," the Elf said, lifting his eyebrow when the Scribe sent Gereant a long look. "I promise no ash, booze, or food."

Gereant grinned wryly. "You said nothing about ink."

Bercylac spun the Dwarf toward the balcony's double doors. "No ink either. Come, Myrddin, lest we're banned—Again."

As they went outside, a clear view of The Ridge greeted Myrddin. The blue-green of the trees created a tableau for art students to salivate over. The three men took a seat on a bench that afforded them a view of the tree line. Gereant pulled out his smoking pipe, a work of carved wood combined with finely etched metal, depicting the largest mountain in Dumnonia. From a pouch, he took pinches of herbs and stuffed the bowl with his finger and lit the pipe.

Smoke drifted from the side of Gereant's mouth and his eyelids drooped. "How has yer lass been?" the Dwarven King asked Myrddin.

"I'm no longer sure. Everything I've done with her seems wrong." Myrddin placed his hands listlessly over his lap. "What's worse, I can't find a single thing about the Fae that tells me what I don't already know... or what everybody else already knows."

"It's no fault of yours." Bercylac set the book he had checked out on the table between them; the title reading *How to Water your Dwarf* earned a curse from Gereant. "Humans were not equipped or concerned about Ancients until recently."

Gereant added, "Even the Dragons have more stories writ about them, and there's not been one out and about for centuries." Both Kings laughed.

Bercylac flicked his palm outward and a gray array formed in front of his fingertips. A twinkle of his Ice released a frosted Dragon figurine. The likeness shifted between Dragon and human form and back again.

"It didn't help that the Fae were naturally secretive—the Unseelie more so than the Seelie," Bercylac said as the Dragon shattered into luminescent shades darting everywhere. "When the Unseelie left the Council, no one knew what happened to them."

Myrddin was perplexed. "How could an entire people vanish?"

Gereant pointed when the shattered remnants formed into two figures, a shadow of pitch black and a blaze of light. "Viviane was the last known Unseelie Queen. She tolerated being part of The Council of the Ancients as a way for her people to prosper. But there was bad blood between her and the other Ancients. Eamonn, the Seelie King, didn't make it easy for her. Ya see, the Seelie and Unseelie are natural enemies. Life and Twilight—light and dark."

"Aye, they couldn't put their differences aside," Bercylac said. "When Viviane faded into Twilight and took her people with her, or at least that's what everybody thought happened, at first Eamonn was thrilled. However, he eventually realized that Viviane's seat on The Council provided a form of Balance. But by that time, there was no trace of Viviane or the Unseelie."

"Eamonn even left to try to bring her back," Gereant said and shook pipe ash from his long red beard. "There has been no sign of either him or Viviane for hundreds of years."

Gereant chortled and added, "Who knows, ya girl might draw out Eamonn or his descendants. There's a blood vow to set everything back to Balance within the Fae."

Myrddin slumped on the bench. "What am I to do? I have a student who uses black arrays like a Master and sees specters about the castle. Every time I think I have a way to train her with Fire, something new comes up and I have to start all over again."

Choking on a cloud of smoke, Gereant twisted toward a slack-jawed Bercylac—both Kings absurdly quiet considering their relationship to one another.

Myrddin frowned. "Out with it, you two. What am I dealing with?"

Bercylac asked, "You ever notice a change in her personality or temperament, at times for no apparent reason?"

"She's an adolescent girl. Of course I've noticed that. I see it in my own daughter too." Myrddin caught himself, calmed down, and apologized. "I'm sorry, but I don't understand what you're asking."

"What I'm talking about is different. Most Ancients undergo a difficult time when coming into their own. We call it The Blooding." Bercylac sniffed down his nose at Gereant, which didn't please the Dwarven King, who blew smoke in his face. "It can be rough. Powers awaken and, depending on the Ancient, take time to settle."

Gereant slouched. "My daughter ate my favourite pony during hers."

Bercylac groused, "She ate my prime studding reindeer too, you goatfecker."

"Made her Blooding worth it. I heard he was delicious." Gereant chortled. "And it's not just for little lassies either. Prince Valkyrie undergoing his around the same time Uther attempted negotiations dissuaded your realm from trying a takeover of Ribeena."

Myrddin grumbled, side-eying the irritated expression on Bercylac. "Your son is still one of the most intimidating people I have ever sat next to during negotiations. Uther forced me to switch seats with him because Valkyrie kept eying him up and growling about Blood Duels."

Gereant hummed, blowing smoke circles of hearts at Bercylac. "Makes Fiwa's Blooding sound tame, eh? When that boy of yours finds that Bond of his, it'll settle him faster. Though, you won't see him out of his bedchambers for a while."

Bercylac snatched the book from the table and thumbed through the pages. He held out the guide to Myrddin, who glanced at the section and shoved it back into the Elf's hands.

"No way." Myrddin waved both hands in front of him. "Not even going there."

"Too late, son." Bercylac set the tome in his lap. "Contact with an element, Soul Bond, or drastic life change can incite a Blooding. Viera might be having two of those happening at once."

Myrddin smacked the bench. "What?"

"Her arrival might have prompted her to hunt potential Bonding candidates."

Gereant snorted. "Bedwyr's type did. Don't even pretend that Eerie didn't know what she was doing, Myr. She kissed him twice and dropped her robes for a Moon Hunt."

Myrddin groaned. "It was the middle of winter. No one slept that night."

"You're lucky we stopped you fools from following them into the woods. Though, Eerie always seemed to have everything handled where Bedwyr was concerned."

The memory of carping at Carydoc for letting Eerie accompany Bedwyr back to the Hearth without a chaperone resurfaced in Myrddin's mind. Lord Ynyr had seemed rather unperturbed, even going so far as to say, "I trust my daughter to have this. 'Sides, I'd be more worried over him than her."

Cary had motioned toward Bedwyr, accepting a large bag from Eerie. The younger man had fallen forward, and upon wrenching open the sack, shouted, "Why are there so many rocks in this bag?"

Eerie sang, "Gigantic rocks are a girl's best friend."

Rubbing his forehead until it was sore, Myrddin grumbled, "Viera is fourteen summers, too young to be hunting anyone."

"For a human Elemental, perhaps." Bercylac flicked his long multicolored hair over his shoulders. "A Fae might be quite different."

"Bercylac is just talking." Gereant took a long draw of his pipe, the smoke billowing from his mouth. "Aye, but there were whispers that some Fae walked through time. Whispers mind ya, nothing more."

Myrddin stared at him, then stared some more. "I've not heard of *walking through time.*"

Bercylac grimaced. "Some, like Eamonn and Viviane, could see the past."

"Nimue and Aisling said that Viera doesn't have any Oracle potential."

Gereant shook his head. "The Fae slip beyond the veil of Light and Twilight. They walk in the Shadows of Time."

Myrddin, frustrated with what he was hearing, stood and said, "I still don't understand."

"Your Apprentice might be able to walk back in time," Bercylac said. "It's not ghosts the girl is seeing, but the past." He nodded to Gereant, who nodded back. "We can talk to the girl, if you want. That might ease what she's going through."

Myrddin massaged the burgeoning headache forming around his temples. "I'll take any help I can get from either of you. Just please go gently with her. The last thing any of us need is for her to get upset and unleash a phoenix. She makes them as easy as she breathes."

Bercylac swiveled around on the bench. "She unleashed a phoenix?"

When the two Ancients exchanged a look Myrddin couldn't distinguish between awe and fear, he took his seat and waited for what was to come.

Gereant settled his thick arms over his lap. "What color was it?"

Myrddin threaded his fingers together. "Two."

"Aye, all right, what color were *they?*" Gereant asked.

"Red, with some orange and yellow in them. One changed, though. It became blue and purple and then black. Maybe it had a little white and gray where the blue was." Myrddin paused and let out a loud sigh. "Sorry. They kept shifting, but those were the colors."

Running his hands through the rose section of his hair, Bercylac nervously entwined three strands into a haphazard braid, which he tugged loose and said, "Feck."

"That's all ya can say?" Gereant bellowed as he exhaled smoke through his nose, his outburst and an accompanying snort startling some nearby birds into taking flight.

Myrddin's gaze darted between the Kings. "What's wrong?"

"She is an anomaly," Bercylac said, and cast a deadpan expression at Myrddin. "From the phoenixes you described, she's a definite descendant of the Fae."

"Aye," said Gereant, his tone indicating he was proud of his affirmation. "We smelt the Twilight on her when she first arrived. It's very distinct and why we failed to pick up the rest."

Bercylac added, "She's the descendant of Viviane. But there's more. A lot more."

"What more?" Myrddin asked, dreading the response.

Bercylac replied, "She's not just a descendant of the Unseelie. That lass is a descendant of the Seelie too. Eamonn released Golau, the Light Phoenix. That was the first phoenix you described. Only one worthy of standing as the Seelie King or Queen can summon Golau."

Myrddin swallowed. "What about the other one that changed from blue to purple to black, along with the rest of the colors?"

Gereant drew so long on his pipe that he coughed. "Viviane, the Queen of the Unseelie, commanded Tywyll, the Twilight Phoenix, a bird of the darkest night." Smoke shot from his nostrils. "That's the phoenix that brings us to embrace our own Twilight."

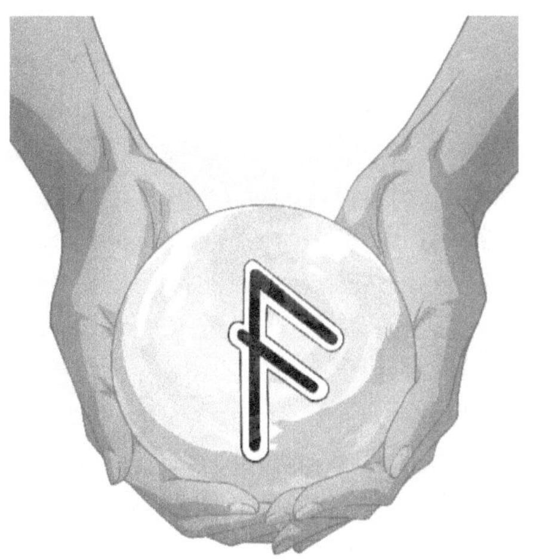

CHAPTER 62
THE SCRYING BALL

Halfway up the flight of stairs, Viera edged closer to the banister overlooking the interior of the Spire. Handsome gray wood blended in with the stone walls to create a trancelike effect, the only variation in color provided by the brass instruments on the lower level that seemed to be aimed toward the rafters.

"Mistress, I hope Myrddin takes his time," Viera said. "I'd like to observe the Oracles mapping the heavens and Divining the future of Evermore."

"Perchance we can do better than that," Nimue said, kneeling in front of a low table with a clear crystal orb sitting atop it.

"How is that?"

Nimue motioned for Viera to sit across from her on a large cushion. "We can Divine *your* future instead."

Viera took her seat and asked, "Why is everything in The Guild the same drab gray? Even the Oracles' clothing?" She spread her fingers over the also gray, albeit velvet, cloth covering the table. "The color makes everything so… so boring."

Nimue smoothed a crease from the tablecloth. "When Oracles take the final Oath, they sacrifice their Element because a prime requirement for our Order is to remain neutral."

Viera raised an eyebrow. "You were all Elementals?"

"Not all, but most. We undergo a long painstaking ordeal that strips us of our Element, requiring the aid of like Elementals and high-level Oracles. I underwent the ceremony before I married. However, there are some who are naturally of Sight but never possessed an Element."

"Do you have to become an Oracle if you have the Sight?"

"Nay. Eerie bound herself to the Air Temple. Young Oracle Initiates hone their skills with the Guild at the same time that an Elemental Master teaches them their Element. Then the choice is up to the person. I see you giving me a strange look. You wonder, why learn an Element only to remove it?" Nimue flicked her fingers toward the rafters. "Did you know that messenger birds are often terribly injured when crossing into battle zones?"

"I never thought about it."

"Most people don't. Many birds are never able to fly again. Some animals seem to know what they stand to lose but perform their duties anyway."

A white raven with a white star emblem on its black collar landed on a windowsill and started gurgling softly. Viera thought it sounded more like a baby crying and wished it would leave. "So why would a bird fly into danger if it can just as easily go somewhere safe?"

Nimue gestured to the bird and it hopped over and jumped onto her wrist. She retrieved a messenger tube from its leg and rewarded it with a treat. "These creatures find meaning and purpose in what they accomplish. Likewise, you must learn your Element to appreciate the gifts it provides. You will learn that your Element is a part of you—but certainly not entirely you."

Viera wrinkled her nose. "I follow some of what you're saying, but a lot of it sounds really weird. I don't think that Fire is entirely—"

"Experience and time will make it understandable. For now, just work on learning about what life brings." The bird flew back to the windowsill.

Viera nodded, happy to be moving on to something else. Gray fog, misting the scrying ball, caught her eye. "That scrying ball was clear earlier, what happened to it?"

"Each scrying ball reacts differently to the person looking into it." Nimue placed her fingers on the orb and traced a wisp of haze swirling within it. "When I was a Fire Elemental, a ball took on the color of my

Element. As I got older, the ball displayed various shades of the color, each one depicting a different aspect of my being."

"That explains why the one the Healer uses in my village always looks the way it does. Dottsie is blind and partially deaf, and her ball is always milky white. She gets a lot of what she says right, though." Viera ran her eyes over the surface, fascinated at the way the colors came alive within it.

"Your Healer's impairments impact her physically but not necessarily her ability to See." Nimue continued to trace the outline of the wisps of fog. "When my final Mistress embraced her Twilight, my scrying ball took on a dark gray. When Maerna was born, my Fire streaked through my natural gray and it became lighter."

Viera inspected it further and asked, "How does it work?"

"Place your hands on the ball," Nimue said and adjusted Viera's fingers over the surface, which was cold to the touch.

The ball pulsed against Viera's hand until it warmed. Wide-eyed, she said, "It's breathing! I feel its heartbeat."

Nimue nodded. "That's because it's you."

Ribbons of red and yellow floated near the edge of the scrying ball, the initial warmth now supplanted by heat so intense that Viera could not have kept her hands on the surface if she wasn't Fire. The ball soon cooled, green oscillating through the ribbons, and a hum rose to match her racing pulse. The scents of her mum's honeyed oats and her Da's bread filled her nostrils.

Nimue said, "A scrying ball reflects the nature and the essence of the one using it." She set her hands on the table. "Your Element has some bearing, as does your current mood and all the experiences that shaped you until now. That's why you see red for Fire and green for Life."

Gold, gray, and black came into focus inside the ball, as did blue. Everything blended together into the outline of a horse, and in the blink of an eye, a wolf appeared. The figure loped against the inside of the glass and panted in front of Viera. She rubbed the surface above the image's head and said, "Hi, Sid."

A moment later swirling colors formed a wingspan, followed by a wash of black and blue sliding apart from the first pair of wings and the flash of a tail flickering in the wake.

Confused, Viera took her hands off the ball. "I don't know what happened, only that I didn't do any of it. Sid wasn't even my idea."

"What you saw is always lurking within you. But there's something else. Please, place your hands back on the ball."

Viera observed Nimue's pupils enlarge and cover her irises as dark as a solar eclipse. So, she did as she was told and once again placed her fingers on the scrying ball.

Fire raged and flames leapt high inside the orb. Viera had expected something to occur with her Element, but she was not prepared for the voices that sobbed until the desperate din of their cries ended only when darkness overtook the sphere. Heat flashed across her back and metal flickered along her periphery. Viera fell backwards and dashed to the window, scanning the grounds and the skies for hints of impending disaster.

Instead, what she observed was summer-warmed grass and well-watered flowers, as paths of tiny white rock threaded through the gardens. Birds glided on the air currents in lazy shifts of motion. Viera glanced behind her to see Nimue extending her hand.

At the realization that the gesture implored her to return to the sphere, Viera spared a glance to the stairs, even though she realized that there was little chance of a successful exit. Fate always had a way of catching up.

As she drew closer to the scrying ball, her body stilled. The orb remained as dark and foreboding as when she'd left it. She sucked in a harsh breath as the High Oracle took her hands and guided them over the perfectly round surface. Crimson, gold, and silver laced through the pitch-black sphere as an emerald sheen slid across it and settled once more into black.

Slumping her shoulders, Viera said, "I'm going to do something bad or cause something awful to happen, right?" She pulled her hands away. "I don't want to do this anymore."

"Twilight and the descending darkness are but fleeting. You're not the cause of the coming night, Daughter of Hearth." Nimue placed her hands on the ball. "You will be what bears us back into light."

Viera didn't know what to think, and the "Daughter of Hearth" phrase made her laugh to herself rather than ask her Mistress what it meant. What bothered her most about her time with the scrying ball had nothing to do with her Divination but with Nimue's hesitation during her last look into the orb. Something was definitely wrong. However, when Viera did ask her about this, she shrugged it off, saying it had nothing to do with her. She found this hard to believe but didn't press Nimue further because her Mistress's eyes remained black as the darkest night.

Micah ushered the shaken woman into her bakery, "Nimue, why are you so pale?"

Nimue said nothing but sank into a chair at the table where Micah rolled dough.

"Don't talk. Let me bring you some tea first." Micah poured the tea and Nimue drained it in one bracing go. When she thought that Nimue had settled down, Micah asked, "What is it? Has something happened at the castle?"

Nimue stared at the bottom of her empty cup. "I've seen Maerna's future. Her path crosses Viera's, and they are both destined for darkness."

Chapter 63

Reflective Surfaces

When he heard the knock on his chamber door, Myrddin hesitated to move from his chair as he continued to mull over his failure with Viera, as well as his difficulties with his daughter.

As Myrddin let him in, Dagonet Vagary sang, "*Oh, piddle dee, would thou look at thee. Cast a stone for thy love up high, thee know not whether thou catch thy love when thee shan't try.*"

Myrddin showed the Court Fool to his couch. "I'm sure you're aware of why I requested your presence."

"Not really. So would you be so kind to enlighten me, oh, great master of the not-so-obvious?"

Myrddin sat next to Dagonet and leaned toward him. "For once, please don't make me play games with you. I've tried to find Shiori to help me with understanding Viera better, but she's disappeared. We both know when she disappears, bodies tend to stack up. Constantine practically threw me from his room when I asked him."

The innocence in Dagonet's tone assured the Court Fool was anything but unaware of all that entailed. "Shiori's gone, is she?"

"Come now, I think you know that." Myrddin came even closer. "I'm going to ask you one more time, and you can agree to my request or leave now." He took a deep breath. "Can we do this without all the theater?"

Dagonet rolled his shoulders and cracked his neck. "All right, we'll do this your way. But it's boring."

"So bore me with the facts."

"Shiori's loyalty has ever been to Inari. Not even her fondness for Bedwyr or Constantine would impinge on her duty to her Fox Goddess. Shiori always places her duty over everything else."

"What about Bedwyr? Does she not have a duty to him?"

"Like I said, Inari is above all else to Shiori. She's her great love— her true Mistress." Dagonet scraped his thumbnail over the fabric on the couch.

"You don't seem very distressed. Since you mentor Bedwyr, shouldn't you be concerned for him?"

A chuckle rippled from Dagonet. "There comes a time when we must say we have done all we can. I have to believe this is how Shiori feels about her relationship with Bedwyr. Let me ask you, Mage, is there not a Master that you're bracing yourself to lose?"

Myrddin tensed. "Dinadan is different."

"How so? Shiori is still alive but beyond your reach. Yours will soon slide beyond his mortal coils. The mirrors aren't so dissimilar, Lord Emrys."

"Perhaps, but could you please focus on Viera?"

Dagonet shook his head and the silver studs on his jester's cap twinkled in the sunlight coming through the balcony window. "Aye, but in discussing the first you have a reflection to peer back on when your obscurity dims your view."

Myrddin's patience was being tested to the point of his wanting to light Dagonet's hair on fire, but he held up and said, "For the love of Evermore, that doesn't make the least bit of sense."

The door to Myrddin's chamber creaked open, and Micah stood in the threshold with a tea service in hand. She squinted at her husband. "Hope you two don't mind my not knocking. Talia was bringing your tea up but I requested to do it."

Said the Fool, "Aye, dear, what timing you possess." And to Myrddin, "We'll clear up our shadowed misunderstandings."

Micah set down the tray at the living room table and came over to her husband. "I think I've a pretty good idea of what you two are talking about."

They settled around the living room table and sipped chamomile tea with honey. Myrddin said to Micah, "Since you already assumed we were discussing Viera, and you would be right, perhaps you can ask your husband to confine his comments to her."

Dagonet partially closed his eyelids and flicked his finger against Myrddin's forehead.

Myrddin jerked backward. "Dammit, Dagonet! Can you ever be serious?"

Dagonet was about to say something when Micah put her hand over his mouth and whispered something in his ear.

Whatever private message Micah had conveyed, Dagonet straightened up in his chair and said, "I have my theories on there being no such thing as Reactives. But I doubt you want to hear them. You're too ingrained in the idiocy of bigger fools than either of us."

Myrddin grumbled, "You've got that right, you ruddy-headed fop."

Micah gave Myrddin a not-so-pleasant stare, which caused him to settle back in his chair.

Dagonet blew her a kiss. "A shame that Reactives are no more dissimilar than conventional learners. Hells, we all react during training. Teaching is its own form of reaction."

"Whoever creates a way to reach past the veil of Twilight and commune with the dead should be a god. I'll give them half my fortune to speak to Uriah." Myrddin dropped his hands to the table. "It'll be less a waste of my time than this."

"I see there's no convincing you of anything in an enjoyable manner. So, what exactly is it that you want to know—in a very boring way?"

Disgust flared in Myrddin as he stared daggers at Dagonet. A weblike pattern formed across the Fool's eyes, and he seemed at a loss for words. Myrddin could not remember Dagonet ever being this wary of discussing anything.

Myrddin lowered his gaze to the rose pattern on his saucer and asked calmly, "Is Viera Reactive? That's all I want to know."

Dagonet smoothed his sleeves and fussed with the ruffles at the ends. "She's as Reactive as one can be. Though, I think you already knew that."

"Confirmation from one with experience such as yours goes a long way." Myrddin toyed with his cup and saucer. "So, what do I do? No one in the Fire Temple will apprentice her."

Flicking his anelace from his sleeve, Dagonet spun the blade about his fingers. "Yours is a similar quandary to what we faced with Bedwyr." He took on a serious mien that made him look even sillier in his jester's hat. "The Metal and Water Temple wouldn't step forward." Dagonet returned his anelace to its sheath. "Jormund made Bedwyr undesirable to the best Masters in Evermore."

"I don't want that for Viera, but rumors are already afloat because some Fire Masters are calling her the next Bedwyr." Myrddin's voice rose in tandem with the panic beating in his chest. "She's being shunned, and I'm unable to stop it."

"Wrong!" Dagonet snapped, slapping his hand hard on the table, the tea set ringing from the vibration as if offering its own protest. "You can stop it. You change her circumstances. You have that authority and the resources."

Myrddin flinched. "Authority and resources didn't help Bedwyr, did they? Not when Cuchulain Sagramore spearheaded the same movement that saw the Foels, Jotnars, Minkrunes, and Vulgates murdered in the streets. We all know the only three spared were Beddoe, Isaac Minkrune, and Armand Jotnar and only by a breath."

Micah growled. "Isaac and Armand were spared because they were good lads. Beddoe had the sponsorship of Dinadan, who vowed a blockade and war if you did not return his man back under his protection."

"There were others. Don't pretend there weren't, Milady."

Micah lowered her gaze and cradled her hands in her lap. "Fine. We favoured Isaac and Armand because they weren't too good to embrace being of the common people. You nobles chose to spare Bedwyr—one of your own. We chose to save Isaac and Armand by securing their freedom."

"Fair enough. It didn't go without those two being harried and humiliated all the way to the Dragon's Spine. The Sagramores didn't get Bedwyr or them, but they certainly ruined them in both the Western and Eastern Courts."

"I did what I could." Dagonet looked to Micah, who offered a smile. "Fortunately, Uriah embraced Bedwyr as his. This made things somewhat easier."

After a long sigh, Myrddin said, "Uriah was a shell of his former self, barely able to stand on his own two feet, yet he was the strongest of us all. He did what so many of us couldn't… nay, wouldn't do."

"You want to know how Metal and Water are similar?"

Startled at the abrupt shift in topic, Myrddin still responded: "They're not. One is solid and the other is a liquid. They couldn't be more dissimilar."

Dagonet poured tea into a sugar bowl, causing Myrddin to wince. "Wrong again," the Fool said. "They're the only two that are reflective. After the Draigs' Duels, I looked at Bedwyr as broken, lost, and filled with fury. Do you know who I saw in him?"

Myrddin didn't even pause, the answer so simple and obvious that only the village dunce would be dumb to the truth. "Jormund."

"Myself."

That revelation jarred Myrddin, so much so that he found himself with his mouth embarrassingly agape.

Dagonet said, "I was never whole and floated through life rudderless and bitter. I wanted to destroy everything in Evermore—and mad enough to do so as I masterminded Uther's end."

Myrddin swallowed hard. "What stopped you?"

"Olwen. She cried for Bedwyr, insistent that no matter what he did he was still her brother. She scolded me that I played with people's lives like they were pawns in a chess game. Olwen reminded me of my own sister, Sofia, and how we had been chips in the games of others as well."

Myrddin's hands fidgeted on the table until fingers settled over them.

But they weren't Micah's, they were Dagonet's, accompanied by his unblinking stare as he said, "Viera's a child. Embrace her as yours. Claim and introduce her in front of the Court as Uriah did for Bedwyr." He released his hands from Myrddin's, and the intensity in his gaze relaxed. "Don't let Uriah's compassion be the only thing that's the same betwixt you and me."

"Aye, but am I the best solution for Viera as a Master?"

"Stop doubting yourself. That's the first step to being the solution." Dagonet lightly jabbed Myrddin's chest with his spoon. "You're a Fire Master, a Knight of the Eclipse, a former Oracle Initiate, Lord of Wyllt Way, the Mage of Evermore, and Arthwyr's Chief Advisor. Your accolades surpass your insecurities."

"I just—"

"You just what? You're the solution for any Reactive who receives lackluster training." Dagonet set his hands on his lap. "Now take the girl and train her properly."

"I didn't realize that the Fate of Reactive students hinged on my training of Viera," Myrddin said dryly.

"For a former Oracle Initiate, it's surprising how thickheaded you are." Dagonet rose and bowed when Nimue appeared at the door. "I return your daft husband to you, Lady Abe."

"Thank you, Dagonet, and good to see you, Micah." Nimue gave Myrddin a look that was not nearly as harsh as those he'd been receiving from her of late. "My desire for coming here from The Guild is so I can have a word with my dense spouse. I'm embarrassed to request a certain place devoid of interruptions and listening ears, if you catch my meaning, Lord Vagary."

Dagonet passed her two wooden placards with the engraving for the *Tit for Tat* and smirked at Myrddin's groan. "You've done so well expanding your horizons that I'm pleased to award your study, Lord Mage. My Bond and I will leave you two to each other, as Micah will go back to the baking of cakes and I to the baking of the idiots in the Hearth."

As Dagonet left, Myrddin grabbed him by the arm and thanked him.

Dagonet said, "Be with the lass what you have always been to others. Bedwyr changed for the better when we challenged where he was and not where he thought he was going. Do the same with Viera."

Chapter 64

Raising a New Daughter

On this short sojourn, long overdue, Myrddin and Nimue were sitting in the beautiful pool of a sauna room at the *Tit for Tat*. Nimue placed a cool wet rag over her hair as a thin white towel hugged her trim form, leaving little to the imagination.

"Clings too much." Myrddin tugged at the towel around his waist. "Nihongo onsen tradition is a wonder in and of itself. Which of your brothers convinced Dagonet and Jubilee to set this up? I can't imagine it being Haruki."

"It was my lovely little sister, Kazue."

"She offered to introduce me to this, drugged me, and set me adrift in Abe Bay. I take it back. This onsen thing might be too much for me."

Nimue clucked her tongue seductively. "Give it a chance."

He released a relaxed sigh. "Why haven't we done this on our own?"

"Because you became tied to the castle." Nimue plucked a goblet of wine from a tray on a floating basket. "I've been enjoying this place with Lulu and Aisling for years."

Myrddin pushed back his dripping hair and squinted when another floating basket bobbed past, this one carrying an assortment of essential oils. "I'm seeing the error of my ways."

"Still shan't get you here for the alternative entertainment Dagonet and Jubilee hosts."

He cringed. "You've seen those?"

Nimue arched an eyebrow.

"With the rest of the Weird Sisters, no doubt." Myrddin picked up his tankard of mulled ale and took in the rocks protruded at various points in the pool and the gentle trickle of water from the decorative wooden pipes. "I'm going to say it again; we should have done this together a while ago."

"We stopped being exciting years ago, dear. War does that. Our spirit was sucked from us." Nimue sipped her wine and wrinkled her nose. "We've no hope of it returning. Maerna will have us both without any hair on our heads as we marry her off."

"What possessed you to Divine her? We agreed not to See her future."

Swirling her wine, Nimue said in a low tone, "I never would have put Viera in front of my scrying ball if I'd had the slightest inkling that it would also Divine our daughter." She met his stare. "Darkness shadows our daughter, love."

"I don't want to start an argument, but did not any of this come into your Sight during an earlier Divination?"

"You know how being an Oracle works. It requires searching for something, and I certainly didn't intend to Divine Maerna. It all happened through Viera."

Myrddin thought a moment. "Is another explanation possible?"

"The edges are smudged, but there is no doubt that Maerna will walk a shaded path." Nimue pressed Myrddin's arm. "Viera will walk in the same shadows, and her future will cross with Maerna's."

"I must ask—" his face taking on horrible strain— "are they our end?"

"I didn't have near enough time to Divine that, but I'm certain that Balance for Evermore is dependent on one or both of them."

"Do you really think they will decide Balance?"

"Theirs and others' Fates are aligning. That's all I can say for certain."

He slid his hand over hers. A tremor raced through him. He took several deep breaths to ease the ache bubbling within him. He loved Maerna, but with all he'd been through with Viera, he found it difficult to even consider letting the peasant lass go. He asked his wife, "What if we separated them?"

"Nothing we do will change what will be." Nimue chewed her lower lip. "Fate will unwind the way it must and should."

Myrddin flipped her hand and traced the creases in her palm, marking the different lines as the lessons from The Guild weaved once more into his consciousness. He recited: *"Those who fight hardest the roll of their dice discover their die was cast and true."* He released her hand, miffed slightly as she gave him an amused scowl, making it clear that palm Divination had never been his strong suit. "How much of this do you think Eerie might be aware of, or has she dared to See?"

Dryly, Nimue said, "She disperses her pearls of wisdom most sparingly."

"Aye, true. What about Bedwyr?"

Dimples formed in her cheeks until Nimue released them with a pop. "Given his vows to Evermore, he either knows far more than he lets on or far less than he finds palatable."

"What makes you say that?"

Nimue stroked his wrist. "His blood oath to Evermore, and his personal honor, demand that he secures the continuation of the realm. My belief is that he's either unaware of the threat Maerna and Viera pose, or he's aware enough to determine them otherwise."

"His lack of action is telling." Myrddin pushed the floating basket and it bobbed over the water. "There are also some new tendencies he's developed that are raising a few eyebrows."

Said Nimue, "Bedwyr's public humiliation of Harris is unacceptable to the obvious Noble Houses, especially since he favoured Viera. That has set more than a few tongues wagging elsewhere, as well."

Myrddin drew his foot against the pool's rock ledge. "I wonder if there is something stirring between them? In two summers, she's marriageable, and Bedwyr has yet to formalize a Bond with Eerie. Is this a concern we should have?"

"Oh, Husband, he's Bonded to Eerie in every way save formality." Nimue arched her back and flicked the water with her toes. "He won't stray from her for anyone else—not even for a dalliance." She plucked a vial from the floating basket. "As Eerie has said publicly, his heart beats for her." The pop of a stopper released peppermint into the air, and she rubbed the oil over her wrists and neck. "Viera might be many things to Bedwyr, but she cannot fulfill *that* role for him. If nothing else, the Fae in her—coupled with what he has become—are not at all, how should I say it… compatible."

He teased, "I don't know what you're talking about."

"Of course you don't," she teased back and pressed herself against him. "It makes this far easier."

"Makes *what* far easier?"

With flint in her eyes and her lips pursed, she announced, "I don't want Viera as a ward in our home anymore."

Myrddin shot straight up in the pool. "What are you saying?"

"Rescind what you must of her Royal Contract. Go to Arthwyr and claim her as a daughter of our House. If you must, put her under the Abe name."

Thrills coursed through him as his wife surprised him, as she had throughout their marriage. "You want her recognized… I… I don't know what to say."

Nimue grabbed a fresh goblet of wine. "The Royal Court doesn't give wards equal treatment, no matter the social standing of the family they are sworn to. I want her viewed in the Court—and with the Noble Houses—as a daughter."

As Myrddin thought about the other Noble Houses' reactions, this tempered his elation. "I don't want to claim her if this will cause our family to be ridiculed."

"In the eyes of some Houses, a ward is little better than a bastard. But there's something else. We raise her as ours, or Harris Sagramore will go after her once her favour is called. Titling her as our daughter eliminates the threat."

"Cuchulain will never forgive and forget what happened to Harris, and the other Sagramore men are spitting images of their father." He bit down on his cheek. "What about the rest of her family?"

"Lance's bid protects her brother, Garrett. Iyesgarth is under Dyfed dominion. Daegyn and Carydoc made it clear where they stand, so her parents won't be in any danger whatsoever from the Sagramores." She gave Myrddin a resolute smack of her lips. "They're cowards, so they'd never do anything on their own."

He scratched his jaw. "You must have known that I wanted to talk to you about titling her with us after everything settled down."

"I didn't See it, if that's what you're asking, but I didn't need to. We're past the point of casting her aside." Her eyes took on an impish glint. "You knew this when you started the imprinting ritual. There was only one outcome. Though, you should know you aren't the only one to have imprinted on her."

Surprise had him popping open his mouth. "How? Who?"

She giggled. "Alistair tested you, Arthwyr, and Bedwyr when you concluded your business with Baudwyn."

"Arthwyr tested positive on it?"

Nimue shook her head. "Bedwyr did, light as it was."

Myrddin ground his teeth until his jaw ached. "The utter gall of him. Time for that whelp to learn what not to touch."

"You'll do no such thing, considering he's ignorant of it and shall remain so in regards to our new daughter."

Myrddin deflated at the steeliness in her eyes. "Aye, Milady." He perked up and kissed her gently. "So, we have another daughter."

Nimue set her goblet aside and grasped the deep cotton of the bath robe he wore. "So mote it be. Our family will gain another daughter."

"You do realize we have some serious fleecing of the Court to do. Our favourite Houses are going to make a mockery of us."

"We can at least count on Kael and Yuliya to distract Cornwall. I suggest coordinating Viera's inclusion into our house as part of her birthday since it is also on Mala. The chaos will throw off Sagramore and Cuhlwch."

"Know what would really work? Doing it in Wyllt Way."

"Nice try, love," Nimue husked against his lips, "but if I have to go through Mala next week, so do you."

"Maerna gets that damned powdered paint everywhere," he griped. "Imagine what Viera's going to do."

She kissed the tip of his nose. "I've already secured Garyth to chaperone for Mala. Reese couldn't volunteer him fast enough. After the ceremony, we'll have the rest of Mala all to ourselves. Would you like a prelude to what we can do?"

As she straddled his lap, he teased his fingers over the towel sliding down her hips and murmured against her bare shoulder, "I'll take the prelude and the encore."

CHAPTER 65

MIDDLE OF SUMMER

As Viera squirmed on the couch, she pulled at the hems of the elegant white robe Nimue had given her. Upon the sleeves and amid a gray background, the white lines of the Abe pentagram were centered amid twin black dragons squared off against each other, red flames spewing from their nostrils. That morning, she had been presented in the Throne Room as a new daughter and Apprentice of the Emrys and Abe without a whisper of protest to mark the occasion. Sagramore, Cornwall, and Cuhlwch had been out for an early morning hunt that Lord Kael Cornwall orchestrated, and by the time they returned, Viera was outfitted into her new station.

To add to it, all the excitement of Alban Hefin paled in comparison to Mala. To Viera, Mala was an extension of Alban Heflin—complete with a Joust—and she didn't quite see why a separate fete was necessary. The only real purpose seemed to be that the extra time between both events enabled ample opportunity for the Jousting King and the Queen of the Dance—currently Galahad DuLac and Eerie Chia—to be readied for formal display.

Giggling dragged her attention toward Maerna next to her in similar robes. Yodeling whipped Viera around as Palamedes darted past

Myrddin. With his white robes fluttering, he vaulted over the couch and landed on Maerna's other side.

Segwarides called from the doorway, "Best behaviour doesn't mean using a couch as a trebuchet launch!"

Peeking over the backrest, Palamedes jeered. "Don't you have a woman of the word in the Library to snog with?"

As Nimue clucked her tongue, she smoothed Segwarides' collar and the front of his robes. "Who is this special lady you have dolled yourself up for?"

"Natalia." Segwarides flattened his hair. "She's a Water Elemental and Scribe in the Library."

"Brother was kissy-kissing in an alcove." Palamedes puckered his lips and blew kisses over the couch. "There was so much giggling going on—from big brother."

Segwarides rolled his gaze upward. "Are you sure Garyth can handle them?"

"It'll be fine." Nimue pulled her long hair into a bun and teased out two strands to frame her features. "Garyth often takes out the boys."

Viera popped up from her seat. "Will we see the crowning of the winners?"

"You will." Nimue tucked Viera's hair behind her ears. "There will be another special ceremony with Arthwyr and Guinevere."

Snickering, Myrddin added, "Strangely, Bedwyr is participating in it."

Viera asked, "What is it?"

"The nobility grants the common class the opportunity to rub elbows."

"Huh?"

"Depending upon the noble, commoners receive the chance to paint us on Mala. Dagonet chooses peasants to ascend the stage and paint blast volunteering nobles."

Segwarides knelt in front of her. "Different festivals suspend the reality of our classes or Element and allow us to be equal. In Eanair, the Homage to the Ancestors is one such celebration. We become equal and balanced for the second month of winter."

Viera sputtered, "No way! Arthwyr will actually let a commoner paint him?"

Segwarides plucked a stray hair from her robe. "Before Arthwyr's ascension, the ritual was only performed amid those within the nobility. He embraces the peasantry and has gained their love and support."

"You said the reality of our Element gets suspended. What does that mean?"

Segwarides chuckled. "The final celebration and paint festival are for everyone. It's why no one uses an Element during it. We become one balanced equation."

"I guess that makes sense. Though, it's not fair to say we're all equal when there's nobody in the Eclipse bereft of an Element."

"Who told you that lie?"

She planted her fists on her hips. "I've seen all the Knights use an Element."

Myrddin lifted his hands, palms face-up, to his shoulders. "Have you, Viera?"

"Which Knight is it? Who?"

"Whoever said there's only one? You'll figure out who one day."

Knocking interrupted them as Garyth and Harlan stepped inside. Garyth handed each youth a satchel loaded with traditional Mala treats.

Viera gasped at the powdered paint and glitter bombs. She threw her arms around Garyth. "You're the best!"

Grabbing a bomb, she scuttled toward the balcony.

Myrddin looped his arm around her waist. "Not in this room."

He snaked the bomb from her grasp but squeezed too hard. The bomb exploded, splattering powder over his beard and eyebrows and showering them in a cloud. A draft blew in through the open doors and blasted them in fuchsia and purple glitter.

Myrddin stared at his recently cleaned couch splotched in powdered paint. He sighed and waved them all toward the door. "It begins."

CHAPTER 66

LIGHT, TWILIGHT, SHADOWS, AND BLOOD

Elemental and Guild symbols decorated the canvas draped over the Mala Court. Viera trembled as she stood next to the Elven and Dwarven Kings, Bercylac and Gereant. Peeking out from the muster station, she took in the packed bleachers. "I'm going to mess up Mala. I don't know what to do."

Bercylac rubbed her back and chuckled. "Lass, you'll do fine. There's really nothing you can do wrong."

She wasn't so sure about that, especially as she glanced at the King and Queen, who spoke to Ewain. The Healer came over to inform Viera that she would be the new Fae representative.

This didn't seem very daunting. She assumed this meant that she'd be introduced and all she'd have to do is stand and wave at the crowd. But Ewain said to her, "The most you do is present Sid or your phoenixes. Nothing too dangerous."

"Who goes first?" she asked, eying the others.

"Zabrina, Nimue's former Apprentice, will for the Oracles." Ewain nodded to the clusters of Elementals. "Gavyn is Wood and paired with Myrddin for Fire. Metal and Ice are the King and Queen. Earth is Morien and you are paired with Trystan as he's the Wilds Master."

Viera peeked at Lamorac and Bedwyr in the shadows. "Why three Water Elementals?"

Ewain favoured her with an unblinking stare and crouched down. Against her ear, he whispered, "Lamorac is without an Element, though it's covered by having him work in tandem with me and a few others. Few except certain Knights know. We put breakers on him during performances to mask it."

"What about Bedwyr?"

"He's too dangerous to pair with anyone else and because of that is last."

"Where's the person for Air?"

"Heya, broads and heifers! I heard ya needed an Air Man," a cheerful voice twanged as a gray-haired man traipsed into the muster station. Upon his upper robe sleeves was the Evermore's Watch version of the Treasurer's symbol, the silver threading of each card suit weathered from regular exposure to the sun and elements than what was typically found on the Watch personnel in the capital.

Arthwyr greeted him, "Chief Dalinger Weiss, I was hoping you'd make it."

Weiss threw him a choppy salute. "Am I with this one?" he asked, clearly sizing Viera up. "What's the limit on your horizons, lassie?"

She gaped at him. "What's that mean?"

"You get me," Morien said, striding over and dwarfing the Air Elemental.

Weiss whistled. "You're going to take some skill getting up in the air."

"What was that?"

"Nothing." Weiss flapped his hand. "It'll be a pleasure working with you."

Morien clipped out each word as though to a village dunce. "Don't make me bury you."

"It's time," the Oracle interrupted, scooping up her scrying ball and slipping outside.

Cheering announced the Oracle juggling the scrying ball and two metal batons. This culminated with shafts of color washing over the Arena as wraithlike images slid over the sand.

As the Ancients strode past, Gereant loosened a looped chain to drag behind him. Bright red Dwarven sigils rippled across the sand and cooled into liquid black. Whorls of aquamarine Elvish skipped over the

Dwarven sigils, twined with them and the black glass forming on the pitch, and illuminated the sand in brilliant mandalas.

The Oracle and Ancients bowed and returned to the muster station. With her light-green robes shimmering, Guinevere passed by Viera and received thunderous applause as she made her way into the Arena. Viera stared in awe as Guinevere performed *Ia* katas, lifting her hands and painting intricate designs in the air. This resulted in sparkling arrays that produced frost which decorated the sand, the ground appearing to freeze under a shield of glass.

The Queen had indeed sequenced an ethereal dance, but it came with what Viera thought was a "twinkling fragility," and she doubted that Ice could stand up against a more volatile Element. This was until Arthwyr, brandishing a metal spear, joined Guinevere. He manipulated the weapon through several complex *Metel* katas, his brusque moves in contrast to Ice's fluidity and appearing to weaken the Element. To counter this, the Queen made Ice whine as she crafted black arrays that clarified for everyone that the ground was frozen solid enough to withstand the onslaught of the force, literally and figuratively, which any Element could produce.

The pair ended their dance with Guinevere taking hold of the spear and Arthwyr's arm draped around his Queen's waist. He bent toward her and their lips brushed, much to the crowd's delight. The throng cheered wildly as the Royal Pair marched in perfect step from the Arena, both as masters of the realm—and as equals.

Myrddin and Gavyn were the next to perform, the latter slinging a wooden staff over his shoulder as he exited the muster station.

Myrddin performed the precise motions of *Tan*, emphasizing pinpoint accuracy and hand-eye coordination. Fire spiraled in aerials, and the audience tensed at how close the flames came to their heads before snapping and moving off.

For Gavyn's role as a Wood Elemental, he spun and twirled, the wooden staff in his hands highlighting both *Pren's* offensive and defensive capabilities. The ground cracked as plant tendrils burst from the soil that had recovered from Ice. Myrddin blasted one adventurous vine that had wrapped around his ankle, and this began a serious competition. Laughter rippled from the audience as the pair swapped Fire and Wood techniques in attempts to outdo one another. They ended their display with a bonfire in the middle of the Arena, further symbolizing unity throughout the realm.

After the pair, Weiss sprinted over Air arrays, his boots no longer on the ground, and dropped into a dance that had his body twirling and tumbling into katas that Palamedes had once told her was a form of Capoeira. Morien stripped off his tunic to raucous applause and slapped his broad bare feet on the ground, earth splintering from the release of Gweryd, as he adopted a wrestler's pose against Weiss. Apparently, Weiss' horizons were levitating his furious partner above the spectators as Morien sent coils of sand wriggling over Weiss.

As Ewain and Lamorac traded with the pair, Viera watched with far more bated breath as Lamorac performed the standard realm katas for Evermore's Watch. It was chilling to know he fought as well as anyone with an Element despite him lacking one. Biting her nails, she wondered who else in the Eclipse had a hidden story amid their accolades.

As the pair finished, Viera cringed, knowing she was to follow.

Myrddin knelt and squeezed Viera's hands. "No matter what you do or what happens, Nimue and I will be proud of you."

Viera was about to say that she couldn't go out there, when Trystan offered his hand to her. "You fine. Isolde watch. I watch. You see." As if in a trance, and with her pulse hammering her ears, she followed Trystan to the center of the Arena.

Isolde took off from Trystan's shoulder, the merlin cruising in wide circles and swooping down to snatch the rings in her claws that her Master tossed high into the air. Catching them with seemingly no effort at all, Isolde dropped each one onto Dagonet's pointy jester hat, not missing it once on the first attempt.

After the applause for Isolde died down, Viera waited as long as she could until it became clear by the untoward noises coming from the crowd that she had to perform in some way. Facing the spectators on one side, she concentrated on summoning Sid or a phoenix. A wing darted across her awareness but fell away too soon for anything to materialize.

She closed her eyes and held out her hand. The wing touched her fingers and tickled the hair on her arms, but nothing happened as she tried to make a Firebird burst forth. She squeezed her eyelids so tightly and clenched her teeth with such pressure that her jaw hurt. With each attempt to peel away the barrier preventing the release of her Element, sparks flashed in front of her. But no matter how much she threw herself into her summoning, her Fire creatures danced out of her reach and their flames died out.

The crowd was now impatient, and what had been mild grumbling was on the verge of becoming downright unfriendly. Viera closed her eyes and tried once more, but again nothing happened. However, when she opened her eyes, Trystan was standing next to her, Isolde on his shoulder. He tossed the merlin into the air and the bird did a few rolls and dives, which quieted the audience.

As Isolde kept the audience occupied, Trystan handed Viera the rings and said to her, "It fine. Wind come and go too. Just wait."

When Isolde did not have another trick left and was back on her Master's shoulder, utter failure and bitterness settled on Viera's tongue: "I can't… I can't control it. I don't know what's happened to me, but I can't even bring up Sid."

Trystan offered a sympathetic hand but she rushed away, only to find Bedwyr blocking her path and holding the blade given to him by Myrddin during Progress. Bedwyr waved the athame at Trystan, and he and his merlin beat a hasty exit.

Viera remained in one place as Bedwyr slashed his bare wrist. Crimson dotted the sand, the bloom of it staining the earlier designs. Lavender and the sweet scent from his robes blanketed her, and her breath caught in her throat. She felt faint, and when Myrddin clasped her shoulder, the touch jarred her from images of blood streaming across ivory granules. She struggled to understand his moving lips but couldn't make out what he was saying.

Viera pulled her gaze from Myrddin, seeing instead the bloody trail Bedwyr had left behind. Someone shouted, the words warped as if coming from a great distance, and she shoved aside Myrddin, the war between fear and concern fighting within her.

A low growl slid past her ears and drew her to Sid, who was licking his jowls as he wagged his tail into a plume of fire.

How did I do this?

Instinct set in before Viera could think about it further, and she commanded her creation: "Sit and stay!"

A moment later, Bedwyr stood in the middle of the pitch, a crimson storm of daggers of reddish-black blood throbbing in a violet light and rotating all around him.

Beautiful but deadly.

Danger flared through Voera and the hair rose on her arms, but she soon relaxed her stiffened muscles as two phoenixes created a loud rush of air as they exhaled Fire and soared toward the blood.

Bedwyr flicked his hands and the blood formed two pairs of fans. He plucked them from the air, and a sharp crack echoed in the Arena when he unfolded the panels. The edges darkened into obsidian, the ebony glass gleaming magnificently. Bedwyr twirled the fans around his body, stopped, and waved Viera forward.

Viera glanced at rows of people seated in the now silent audience. Mouths agape, they appeared torn between the blood, the phoenixes, and each other.

Facing Bedwyr, she lifted her hands into a defensive kata and said to herself, "Ready Set. Begin."

She melded the katas Myrddin had taught her with the Fire dances she was working on. Bedwyr's fighting style was smooth like his Water Element dictated, and early on she found it far more advanced than what either Galahad or Ewain had perfected. For Bedwyr, Metal mixed in with Water, and as hardened blood brushed past her, she had to move deftly to flick aside its potentially lethal caress.

For the better part of ten minutes, blood and fire whipped through the Arena. Viera danced and fought her way past the gore as Bedwyr demonstrated comparable skills at avoiding the scorching heat of her creations.

The crowd went crazy as the combatants stood in front of one another to rest, the two of them posed together like dual eyes in the middle of a hurricane. "I was told to become one with Light, Twilight, and Shadows," Viera said, throwing back her shoulders and lifting her chin. "Someone forgot to mention Blood, eh?"

"Deep down, you had to always know it was there as well." Bedwyr held out his hand to her. "Ready to begin the end?"

She slapped her hand into his and relished the coolness of his Element upon her. "Aye. Balanced be."

White light and black light spilled from their clasped fingers, hot and cold merging and blending into her flesh. She tightened her grip as the white and the black merged into gray, the resulting substance morphing into a huge sphere, his blood array and her phoenixes darting inside. As soon as the last spark died out within the globe, the orb rose and exploded, the deafening blast shaking the Arena.

Viera fell onto the pitch, and when she recovered, she blinked at the gray sand all around her. She lifted her eyes to the crowd, and what began as slow applause became a rush of noise. She didn't know what to think, only that her flushed cheeks told her she had done something that was appreciated.

Bells jingled, the sound of them becoming louder until Dagonet lunged at Bedwyr and wrapped his arms around his prize student. Tossing his jester's hat in the air, he whistled to urge the crowd to revel in his enthusiasm. He pressed a few kisses against the side of Bedwyr's face contorting into revulsion.

Myrddin urged Viera toward the amplification array, and as the crowd quieted his voice carried throughout the Arena as he said to her: "Wonderful talent you exhibited, my Apprentice and new daughter." And to the spectators: "Could not have asked for a better student if I had scoured the entire realm and beyond myself."

Viera stared at him as they stepped off the array. *Did one of those vines smack him and make him lose his mind?* Before she could ask what that was all about, more applause and wild screams deafened her.

Dagonet rushed up and pumped Myrddin's arm. "Lord Emrys, I'll bet you edged us closer to Balance. Just think of all the people who will now view Reactive students in a positive light."

Confused, Viera asked Dagonet, "What are you talking about, Lord Vagary?"

A snort drew her attention to Bedwyr, who had followed Dagonet. "He won't answer that in a way anybody can understand, but I will. As my late Master, Uriah Cameliard, instructed me, 'Lift your hand, wave it, plaster on something that passes for a smile, and pretend you want to be here.'" Bedwyr followed the advice he'd just related, and the revelry increased. He snorted again and added, "Would you look at that? The masses are stupid enough to think they love us."

Raucous howls rose and fell like waves cresting over the shores, the robes of the assembled masses undulating in the bleachers. People were too enthralled with the Fire Girl and the Blood Master, as both were now called, to pay attention to anyone leaving the Arena.

This made it easier for three men to blend in with the shadows around the Healers' tents, the robed figures slipping along the sidelines, their hoods drawn up tight. They were a strange lot, but because oddity during Mala held no special significance in Elden's Hearth, their presence created no unusual interest.

Mordred, hiding behind the back of the Royal Box, waited until one of the three men was even with him. He stepped out in an attempt to halt the man's progress. The other two crowded Mordred to prevent his escape, apparently believing that three against one provided good odds. As Mordred lifted his hood, their sharp gasps revealed their awareness of his unfortunate relations.

Electricity crackled along Lord Kenneth Minkrune's hair, creating sparks as if from a hammer molding golden-hot steel. "He's a Pendragon. Dispatch and scatter."

Whipping his hand forward, Mordred blocked an attempted dagger thrust from one of the other men and twisted the blade from his grasp. "I wouldn't do that if I were you, Lord Jotnar."

"You've the Pendragon eyes and look but not one I've seen before," Lord Ymir Jotnar said as he stared at Mordred, his eyes flashing from side to side. "How is it you know me?"

"I'll answer the first question in due time. As for how I know you, I overheard you in that seedy pisshole of a tavern you and Lord Minkrune were hulking and skulking in."

Stiffening, Lord Minkrune also ran his eyes over Mordred. "Hells, you're the blasted drunkard I thought was spying on us." He swished his hand over his shoulder as if to dust off where he had brushed against Mordred. "We should kill you. You're dressed like a thief. Wouldn't be hard to present you as one."

"Why kill me when we have so much in common, Lord Minkrune." Mordred flipped around the blade that he'd taken for Ymir. "I know you well, Kenneth. You and Lord Jotnar are among the unlucky souls who allied with the wrong Pendragon."

Lord Jotnar's blue eyes widened as he accepted the dagger back from Mordred. "You said we have something in common. Why aren't you in Arthwyr's camp?"

"Let me just say that Kings usually rise or fall through their offspring's actions or inactions. You picked the wrong Pendragon as an ally, but perhaps you can be on the right side of the next one."

The nobles tilted their heads toward the taller man of the group, who'd said nothing thus far and was starting to walk away. Mordred quickly caught up with him and was told, "Join me for a drink? You pick the spot."

"Aye, I'll join you. Hope you like *Kreb's*. It's part of my enterprise now."

"You own it?"

"Recent acquisition with all the surrounding spoils, if you get my meaning."

The man chuckled. "You remind me of my family. They would find you delightful."

Lengthening his stride to match the taller man's, Mordred said, "Wonderful, but I'd like to know who I'm drinking with and sharing confidences."

"Very well." A thick accent took over the man's voice as he brushed back his hood, revealing stiff black hair and gold eyes. "Signore, I am Lorenzo Sforza."

CHAPTER 67

WARS AMID WARS

Oak chairs glistened from polish, and white cloth covered the long tables beneath the dais in the town square, with pots of all shapes and sizes on display. Small mounds of powdered paint formed a rough model of the northern Glyderau Mountains. All social classes sported identical white robes splashed with multiple shades of glitter.

Younger children surrounded the Queen and drew on her. The Royal Pairs' and Princes' white robes had long since lost their purity. However, as the honored Jousting King and Queen of the Dance, Galahad's and Eerie's robes remained pristine.

Festival goers perched on roofs and showered people scampering around below them with cornstarch, flour, and herbs ground into paint and infused with glitter. A rainbow of color billowed down the streets, popping sounds filled the air, and whoops and hollers marked the delight of those who hit their human targets.

Even with all of this, Viera's enthusiasm had waned at being relegated to standing as a silent spectator of the more traditional elements of painting the volunteered nobility. That was until Carydoc Ynyr came up to her and said, "Talia and Eerie have a special request: You get to help me and Daegyn paint my son-in-law."

The thought of being able to humiliate a helpless-to-respond Bedwyr was too much to resist, and Carydoc's summons sparked fresh life within her.

Viera followed Carydoc as Daegyn skipped past both of them to a table covered with pots. Picking up two pots that were half-full, he combined the powdered paint, added glitter, and brought the mixture to Viera.

Pink powder covered Daegyn's cheeks, and his hair rippled a dark green as he held out the custom color for Viera to inspect. "You like green and purple, right?"

She beamed at the blended powder with the glitter mixed in. "It's pretty."

He grabbed a different concoction for himself and marched toward Bedwyr, throwing up a salute to the Knight as he and his "crew" approached. After coming off a death-defying test of wills with Bedwyr, Viera was not sure how aggressively she should proceed, but as soon as she watched Talia and Daegyn—and even Carydoc—splatter Bedwyr, her inhibitions left her and she joined in without the slightest trepidation.

Partway through paint blasting Bedwyr, Viera rolled his sleeves to the middle of his forearms. Instead of splashing paint on his arms, she used her fingers to paint his skin with vines, mandalas, and runes she had learned in her studies. Beneath her fingertips, she felt the steady beat of his heart as it pulsed on his inner wrist, and she noticed that the fan guards on his belt displayed a delicate flower design. She sketched that flower on his wrist and added a tiny bird to symbolize a sparrow.

Viera was eager to see how Bedwyr was going to respond, and she was about to look up at him when an orange cloud mushroomed around her and Palamedes darted away. Yipping, she grabbed a paint bomb from Daegyn's supply and ran after him.

Her attempt to catch him was thwarted as green and yellow bursts of powdery paint blindsided her. She spun around. A blast caught her flush in the abdomen as Harlan, standing behind a barrel, laughed and tossed another paint bomb at her, missing this time.

She had no time to respond because another bloom of color hit her on the arm, but she managed to "escape" and chase after Palamedes as he ran from the square and farther into the village.

Even though he had a decent head start, Viera was able to keep him in view. She raced after him down several alleys and across a bridge spanning the Lockinge, but she could never get close enough to tackle him. She did scream at him, "Just wait until I catch you!" and she knew he'd heard her because he always sped up.

Unfortunately, her performance with Bedwyr in the Arena had sapped a lot of her strength, and she had to quit running after the Saracen pest, her sandals no longer slapping the cobblestones as she brought her pursuit to a halt. To her surprise, she heard the thump of boots coming up fast behind her. She turned in time to see Harlan readying another paint bomb to toss at her. When he saw Viera staring at him, he put his "ordnance" back inside his robe.

Maerna darted by her, splotched robes snapping in the wind, just as Daegyn and Harlan flew past, their boots imprinting the cobblestones with thick powder.

Harlan whooped over his shoulder to Viera, "We'll avenge you and your betrayers."

Viera found the strength to run after him, yelling, "I'll avenge myself just fine."

Harlan hollered back to her, "Not if we beat you to it."

Rounding a bend in the street, she caught Daegyn's green hair glowing whenever the sun's rays hit it, his natural-colored locks blending in with the paint-blasted crowd. Ahead, Palamedes and Maerna clattered down another street as plumes of paint rained down on Viera, her nostrils filling with the powder and burning her nose.

A quarter-hour later, she ran through a weathered arch and caught up with the noble lads and Maerna, who were squatting on the ground near a rotted cross-section of an old wooden beam. Viera broke open a paint-bomb pouch and tossed it over their heads, showering them in fluorescent orange.

Daegyn hollered, "We give up, we're out of ammunition," and the other two raised their hands in mock surrender.

Wary of such a "united front," Viera approached them cautiously, when they all started laughing and pointing to her robes. She knew she was covered in paint, but she wasn't prepared for the splatters of horse manure covering her up to her knees.

"You Taffies betrayed me too." She ran over to a nearby trough and dunked her outer robe in it. "Where are we?" she asked as she wrung out the lower half of her garment.

"I'm not sure, but I know we're not supposed to be here," Harlan said, the tension in his voice making it squeak, "We should go now."

"What is this place?" Palamedes asked, not sounding like his normal confident self.

A low chuckle preceded a gruff voice. "Our humble home."

Palamedes and Maerna scrambled upright, followed by Harlan.

Viera hadn't taken notice of the surroundings, as she was too busy with the mess on her robe, but as she looked around, cold prickled her bare skin. The walls of the buildings, most little more than hovels, were discolored and in shambles. The smell of urine and excrement, mixed with the odor of rotted food tossed everywhere, was enough to gag anyone unlucky enough to pass that way. But not even the rancid odors were enough to deter the man who walked up to them.

"Taffies, eh, lass?" the man said, his rheumy eyes moving slowly between Maerna and the noble boys. "Ye understand the word?"

Maerna said, "We understand all too well. It's us. The Dafydd. We were just leaving, Sir."

A rusty knife dropped from the man's threadbare sleeve, and he caught the dagger by its hilt. "Ye insult me, lass." He waved the blade toward Daegyn. "I can fix that, little Lord. Have her squeal some respect, eh?"

Daegyn shoved Maerna behind him, and Palamedes said, "We were just leaving. Balanced be, and may your Mala be full of summer."

A gray figure emerged from the shadows. The man crooked his foot around the Saracen's legs and swept the boy off his feet. With a yelp, Palamedes struck the cobblestone. The man buried his fingers in the boy's thick hair and jerked the youth's head back until his throat was stretched. The hilt of a tarnished blade smacked the side of his neck and silenced his sharp cry.

"Are we still in the Hearth?" Viera whispered, clutching Daegyn's arm.

"Aye, we're in the Red Lantern District." His face became drawn. "But not a good part."

A tavern door banged open and leathery faces appeared in the windows before disappearing from the stained, dust-encrusted glass. One man left the tavern with his trousers wide open, another with food all over his jacket and his stomach hanging so far over his waistband that there was no way he could ever see his feet. Patches of blackheads and scabbed skin covered his splotched face. He smelled like fetid garlic, so much so that it made Viera gag, and she had to breathe through her mouth to keep from throwing up.

The man restraining Palamedes eyed him luridly and said, "Aye, you'll fetch a good price, laddie."

Daegyn bared his teeth. "Let him go. He's nothing to you."

The blade brushed over Palamedes' throat and blood oozed down the outside of his robe. "He breathes," the man said. "More 'an enough for me."

Harlan said, "He's as noble as us. Do you want that on your hands?"

"He's got nothin' on his robe. No House. No Elemental sigil."

The blade dipped low and sliced through the fabric of Palamedes' upper robes. Small lines of blood ran down his chest from where the tip of the knife had nicked the skin. Palamedes' pupils drowned out his irises as he whimpered and his body shook.

The first man said, "If we gut 'em, let's see if he squeals even more like a little piggy."

A new voice entered the scene, this one with a drawl. "How utterly unimaginative." The man narrowed his muddy-green eyes, stopped a few steps from Palamedes, and added, "Let the kids go, Sluagh." He hooked his fingers onto his belt. "We hardly need an incident."

The first man spat on the ground. "Who asked ye, Easterner? Ye got no business here."

Blinding yellow light throbbed into the rune of *Hagalaz*, forming an Air array. The newcomer flicked his hand, and Sluagh flew straight up.

Squirming in midair, he barked when a flash of metal cut into his shoulder. As blood dripped onto the ground, the man controlling his Air flicked his fingers and released the array, dropping Sluagh into a cistern, his entry causing thick slimy liquid to slosh over the rim of the filthy vessel.

"Sluagh, you're a sad excuse for a thief lord. Start teaching your scabby bastards respect around me, or you'll end up more drowned than wet." The children's saviour turned to the man pinning Palamedes, "My patience is about through, friend. What say we see how much Air I can fill you with before you turn into a balloon or blow up? Now release the boy, or you can be one of my experiments."

The man shoved Palamedes into their saviour's arms. The Air Elemental said, "Pleasure doing business with you, but time to put the kids to bed."

Sluagh emerged from the cistern. He jerked a metal rod from his shoulder and tossed it aside. "Careful, Luxley. No reason ye should sit amongst us and call us friends."

The Air Elemental wiggled his eyebrows at the man covered in slop. "That's Lord Luxley to you, friend. I stopped being a fringe feeder like you some time ago. Now I sit at the table of—" He gave a derisive snort— "great men instead of serving them."

Luxley sauntered down the street and clapped his hands. "Baa, baa, kids."

Viera hurried after him, shooting glances toward the highwaymen behind her. She faced forward and looped her arm through Palamedes' arm. Leaning into her, Palamedes quivered and rubbed his sleeve over his eyes.

Harlan moved toward Viera's side, hesitated, then stepped to the other side of Palamedes. He took out his handkerchief and pressed it against the nicks along Palamedes' neck. "Wait 'til we tell everyone whose arse you kicked," Harlan said.

Palamedes accepted the handkerchief from Harlan. "Really? You won't tell everyone I was scared?"

Harlan bent and whispered into Palamedes' ear, earning a surprised look and expanding grin from him. "I won't tell, if you won't," Palamedes said.

Harlan tapped Palamedes on the shoulder. "Deal, but let's get our stories straight, eh?"

Once they reached a better section of the Red Lantern District, Luxley checked Palamedes' injuries, the man's cloak spilling behind him and revealing green baldrics. His House symbol displayed two white buck goats, horns locked and with fore hooves pressed together, the animals standing upright on their back legs.

Luxley rubbed his sandy-colored beard. "You'll live, kid. But what in Evermore you goaties were doing here begs a few questions. Didn't your nannies and billies ever tell you to keep out of the weeds?"

Maerna sniffled. "We didn't mean to be there, Sir."

Luxley reached into his pocket and passed her a handkerchief. "I've only enough for one." He snapped his fingers at Daegyn. "Didn't your parents raise you better? Offer this little lass there your handkerchief. It's the real reason a gentleman keeps it on him."

Daegyn dug through his pockets and handed his cloth square to Viera. "My apologies."

Twirling his fingers in a circle, Luxley pointed down the street. "Let's go. It's getting late." He led them toward shouts and cheers. "Stay clear of that part of the village."

"Thank you for helping us," Viera said, daubing at her cheeks with the handkerchief, "but why are you doing this for us if you're a friend of those highwaymen?"

Luxley slowed his pace. "We're more like business associates without choice."

Viera frowned, eying the man's much cleaner and expensive attire. "They said you were an Easterner. You don't sound foreign. What realm are you from?"

"Lass, I'm as much Evermorean as anyone in this realm." He gave her a sly grin. "You'll understand this better someday. Actually, someday soon."

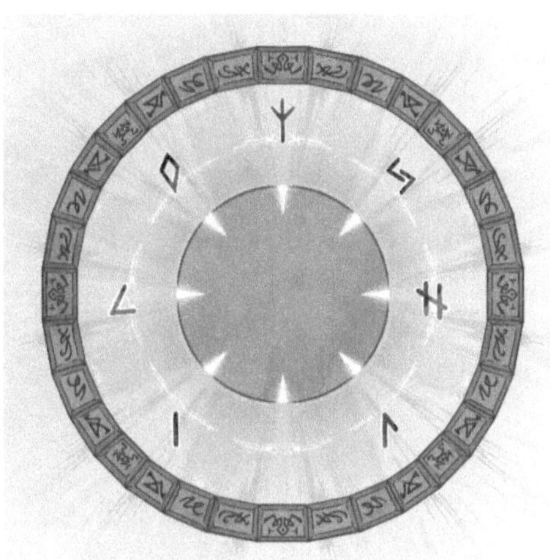

CHAPTER 68

LUXLEY OF THE EAST

When Errol Luxley heard the snuffling in front of *Kreb's Grogs*, he expected to learn of the removal of valuables, a little winding up of the victims, and the unfortunates who were robbed racing past him once they were free to leave. At thirty-five springs, and with him being an old hand at the fine art of flimflam, he knew a mugging when he heard one. But what he came upon was more than a theft. It was the prelude to the selling of children into human slavery, and without his intervention, there was no way the little rapscallions were going to escape from Sluagh and his slavering hellhounds.

Not with how pretty the girls were, and the boys were fringe benefits; the foreign boy likely to fetch more in the seedier exotic markets. The sigils on their shoulders marked these children, and Luxley was not about to burn on the altar of a House bearing the symbol of a fox, a horse, or a Dragon. Best to get them away from this place as fast as possible.

Luxley waited with the children for the pair he sought outside the *Tit for Tat*. The former slave auction house and brothel of old had changed since Uther's reign. It was no longer a den for sex with enslaved whores. Nay, it had been upgraded to respectability, replete with a dining room, quality entertainment, a legitimate inn that rented rooms, and public onsens on the lower level.

However, the backrooms were still open for intimate commerce, where sex was sold and bartered in ways as old as time immemorial. The *Tit for Tat* management was not about to pass up extra income, hence a referral was always available for a well-placed coin. In truth, women and men alike used their bodies for gain and worked the higher-end businesses in Elden's Hearth, since a lot of the "help" doubled as much-desired courtesans.

The pair who left the establishment staggered to a halt at Luxley's salute. Alistair and Reese Kelliweg looked about ready to bolt when Luxley pointed at the children huddled next to him. "Oh, come now, Alistair," Luxley said, "I brought you a gift."

Reese gasped and tripped over to the children, checking them over furiously, "Why are you in the Red Lantern District? Where's Garyth?"

Luxley kept Alistair in his line of sight. "I found them in the middle of a tussle near *Kreb's*. They got turned around a bit from the market."

The Runemaster toyed with the manacles on his belt. "Is that so?" Alistair bent in front of the black-haired lass. "Ingot for a thought, Maerna."

The girl said, "Lord Luxley intervened for us. Thank you, Milord."

Alistair fished out an ingot and gave it to Maerna. "Reese, take them back to Garyth. He's likely worried sick looking for them." He motioned toward Luxley. "I'll see our friend back."

Reese pursed her lips. "Alistair—" she stopped at the sharp jerk of the Runemaster's head. "Very well. Come now."

Luxley waited for them to disappear around a corner. "Good to see you as well," he said, running his eyes up and down Alistair. "Look at you all settled and a hound of the law no less."

Twitching an eyebrow, Alistair shoved Luxley down an alley. "Let's walk before I whistle up one of my watchdogs and put you in the pound."

"Aww, still sore?" Luxley smacked his lips. "Didn't your ma ever tell you to let the bygones go by the river?"

Luxley hit the brick wall of a building face-first, and with such force, that his nose popped and the flesh around it burned. A hand gripping his neck tightened, and fingernails dug into his flesh. When warmth bathed the shell of his ear, he glanced at Alistair. A thin yellow line bisected the lower half of Alistair's gray and brown irises.

"Because of you, I don't have one." Alistair released his hold and smacked Luxley over the head with his fist. "My mother forsook me, as did others in my family. But you're all too aware of this, aren't you?"

Groaning loudly, Luxley popped his nose back in place. "One could argue that you're still alive only because of me." He wiped the blood from his nostrils and spun around. "Your family was foolish to cast you aside, Alistair Foel. Especially when considering what your brother did to your Bond."

Alistair stepped away. "You don't get to talk about that. You gave up that right when you outed me for telling Baudwyn what my arsehole brother and his degenerate friends did to her."

They meandered down the street and detoured into the seedier section of the District. A clear distinction marked the change of scenery, as the buildings were in need of paint and a good scrubbing. Equally unappealing, weeds grew tall through cracks in the cobblestones, and plants sprouted from the walls of the more distressed structures. One corner they passed was where they had found Reese crumpled and tossed aside like garbage, just nine years earlier. Fourteen seasons was an awful age to learn about men in packs, least of all a troupe led by one who was trusted and a darling of the Court.

"You did the right thing," Luxley said quietly. "You must know that. What I did, and your taking Reese's namesake, saved your life. You could just as easily have been alongside your brethren when the executioner's axe kissed their necks."

Alistair Kelliweg nee Foel stopped in the shadows of an overhang. Sunlight pouring through holes in the dreary gray canvas showed dust mites circling his hair. "You don't get forgiveness from me, Errol. Not when there were innocent Foels in the lineup who had no hand in the war efforts."

Luxley winced. "Neutrality in a war is as bad as picking a side. How many thought what happened to Reese was wrong but kept their silence? Omission and lack of action are as devastating as participating directly in war crimes."

"Errol, go back to Sherhurst Forest." Alistair's voice sounded heavy, carrying a weariness with it that seemed to bend his body forward like that of a man much older than his twenty-seven winters. "Not even Baudwyn could pardon you if word got around that you were in West Evermore. You'd be viewed solely as an Easterner, and there would be no reprieve."

Alistair retreated the way they had come. No one would question the most renowned member of the Runemaster's Law Division for paying a visit to the seedier areas of town to seek out criminals.

And very few criminals escaped the Runemaster's Court, but the one older case Alistair Kelliweg had yet to resolve was Errol Luxley's. For now, Luxley remained safe as he hid in the shadows of Evermore, the pendant hanging on a braided chain under his robes as much a symbol to rally behind as it was a yoke every Head of his House had donned since the realm first came together under Cymry Pendragon's banner.

Shoving the past into the locked vault of his mind, Luxley reminded himself of the vow he had made to his bloodline. But no one else could ever know what it was until a new dawn rose from the darkest night.

Fixing his gaze on his former bestmate's back, Luxley tucked his hands in his pockets and closed his fingers over a smooth metal bracelet. "Just because my home is in the ceded territories doesn't make me any less of an Evermorean." He toyed with the clasp as the metal leached some of his Air. "We're still the same people. You should understand that better than anyone, given your bloodline."

Alistair stilled but did not turn around, bitterness in his voice like the thickest of draughts. "It's only because you saved my Soul Bond, I'm pretending I never saw you." He pointed to the east. "Now, go home!"

Alistair turned away and disappeared down another alley as Luxley meandered toward *Kreb's Grogs*. Part of him wanted to run back and tell Alistair what had been bubbling like a pot too long over a fire in the ceded territories. Almost to the tavern door, he reversed his walk, determined to do just that, but he stiffened when he bumped into Ymir Jotnar. A curse perched on Luxley's tongue, but he kept his composure.

Ymir sniped, "Ah, Luxley, you goat. How is our King of Thieves? Keeping busy?"

"Having a smashing good time." Luxley tipped a salute over the corner of his brow. "Anything I can do for you, Jotsi? Get ya a drink, meal, heart to eat?"

Ymir drew his thin lips over his teeth. "One day you'll outlive your usefulness. I look forward to being the one to gut you and your entire den of miscreants."

Removing the brass bracelet from his pocket, Luxley waved it under the taller man's nose. "That day shan't come. Not when I'm the only one making your *new* Elemental breakers."

Snatching the breaker, Ymir examined it. "What makes this different from any other?"

"Ah, that's the beauty of it. Nobody will know the difference until it's on. The normal rune keys won't work to open it. You want to see what I'm talking about?"

Ymir whistled. "Get over here, Sluagh."

The highwayman slinked away from the tavern landing, muttering, "Aye, wretched Lord of the Tomb."

Ymir yanked the highwayman closer and snapped the breaker on Sluagh's wrist. His caterwauling bounced off the building like the screeches of a cat caught in a mousetrap. Sluagh frenetically grabbed at his wrist as he dropped to the ground. Tears streamed down his face and death by axe seemed as though it might be kinder. Soon, whimpers and sniveling replaced the screeches. A dull film covered Sluagh's rheumy eyes, and whatever strength was in his jaw appeared to have left for good. Tremors danced through him, and those closest to him retreated into the shadows.

Luxley knelt and used the special rune key for this breaker to release its hold on Sluagh. He waved for someone to haul the whining highwayman into the tavern. "Give him something strong. The effects last for a while."

He handed the breaker and rune key to Lord Jotnar. "Works the same way every time. Anyone never introduced to a breaker will be passed out for several days. Others will be useless, or close to it. People with experience might regain consciousness faster, but they'll still be on their arses. Look at Sluagh's condition, and he's had to wear a breaker many times."

Tapping the rune key against the clasp, Ymir played with opening and closing it. "It shouldn't be too hard to find where you hide your plans."

"Aye, if there were any plans, but there are none." Luxley pointed to his head. "It's all locked away in here, Jot-Jot."

"Torture unearths so much." Ymir smiled deviously, as if his cynicism needed embellishment.

Luxley arched his tongue to display the underside. "Nay, no matter how much you make me scream, I'll be unable to give you the plans."

"You don't need your tongue."

"But I do need the roof of my mouth." Luxley laughed and spit. "Want a peek?"

Laughter drew Luxley's attention to Lorenzo Sforza, whose tall shadow went all the way to the top of the wall. "For a thief, this odd fellow has his charm," Lorenzo said, his heavy accent seeming to devour and then regurgitate his words, the cold of his stare akin to a Basilisk freezing its prey in the embrace of Twilight. "You need to be careful you don't become too in love with yourself, Errol Luxley. I'll still kill you at the drop of a hat, no matter how much you know. Oh, I agree, it would be hard replacing you—but not impossible, Signore."

Another man stepped from behind Lorenzo. "So, you're the one who can revolutionize breakers and runes? How intriguing."

As Lorenzo introduced Mordred Pendragon, Luxley's mind wandered past Elden's Hearth. It loped over the mountains and across the East to Sherhurst Forest. For his family and those under his care, Luxley allied with those stronger than any of them. What other choice did he have for now?

The conversation with Alistair Kelliweg left a bitter aftertaste as he followed his new cohorts into a hive of deceit. Errol Luxley of Lemstead could not revel in the joys of a stiff drink of Earthshine, decent food, and like company. His tongue coiled as though swallowing a mouthful of ash as he raised his glass and, in a monotone, offered a faux exuberant toast to his confederates: "All hail our future King of Evermore, Mordred Pendragon!"

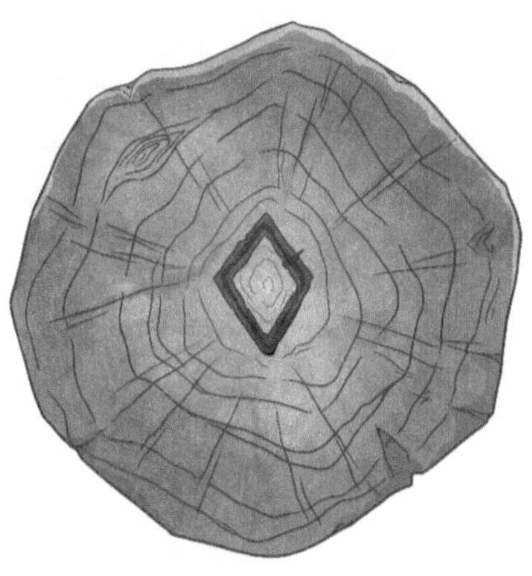

CHAPTER 69

MISSIVES FROM AFAR

Constantine put the finishing touches on his letter. The sigil of a Basilisk devouring a child peered at him; opposite the serpent stood a black imperial eagle, its tongue hanging from its beak and its wings spread at the ready to take flight.

He capped his inkwell after a final flourish of his signature upon the parchment: *Constantine*. Nothing aside from his given name ever closed his missives.

A screech rattled through the air as a gray body hit the side of his face, a charcoal beak clicked in his ear, and wings flapped against his cheek.

Budgie's harsh shrills rang inside his head: "Get some puta! Get some puta!"

Constantine righted himself and gritted his teeth to keep from cursing out loud. The Alkebulan gray whistled, his head tapping against Constantine's shoulder. His talons dug into the priest's cassock. Budgie dropped into the hood of Constantine's cowl, the material pulling so tightly across the priest's throat that he had to readjust it or choke.

The bird gargled, "No Popobawa Putas here."

Sighing, Constantine caught the parrot's dark-gray beak between his fingers as the bird poked its head over his shoulder. "Could you at least try and not call them Devil putas? Tippy and the Queen near turned you into a pin cushion over the Kyner children overhearing that."

Cackling, Budgie snarked, "Shetani puta! Thar goes Shetani puta! Yo-ho-yo! No Popobawa Puta portside!"

With a resolute shake of his own head, the priest said, "You are right. None for you here, you naughty bird."

He released the beak and stroked it. Budgie made a clicking sound and gently pecked the priest's fingers with a playfulness rarely reserved for the man. However, the parrot quickly tired of this, settled into the cowl, and squawked, "Too cold for Popobawa putas."

Leaning back in his chair, Constantine peered at the open package on his desk. Inside, a velvet bag contained beach glass and pottery from Sardinia, a gift his former Master, Father Benedict Medici, had sent for Galahad. There were also beads for Trystan and a silk scarf for Palamedes. The gifts were like those a doting grandfather showered upon his grandchildren for merely existing.

Constantine glanced at a package that had slipped out from under his bed. A few gifts lay within it for Bedwyr. All had been rejected but kept aside for the day when the Knight's anger subsided, and he would forgive the priest and accept the presents. At least that was the hope.

A jarring bang on his chamber door startled Constantine from his musings. "Come in—" raising his voice— "Come in before you break down the door."

The door flew open and Gavyn sauntered over to the priest's desk. "I know. I'm late."

Constantine gave an aggravated nod and raised up in his seat. "Budgie's napping in my cowl, so I couldn't leave my chair." He held up his letter. "I just finished replying to this post."

"Oh?" Gavyn snatched the parchment and went to the hearth to take advantage of the better lighting. "When did this arrive?"

"Two afternoons ago. I've been hesitant to respond."

As he read the letter, Gavyn drummed his fingers over the mantle. "You're afraid?"

"You would not be incorrect in saying that, my friend. I'm uncertain as to what ends some of these people might wish to attain."

"Flowery language shan't send me skittering into the shadows. You might have fooled Uther and Jormund, but you're hardly going to fool me." Gavyn tapped the edge of the letter as he gave the text another read. "You fear your family will darken your doorstep, eh?"

Constantine muttered, "That's always been a real fear of mine."

"Do they know Trystan is here? What about the Sasanias, Galahad, or even Bedwyr?" The mention of the latter's name caused Constantine's head to raise up.

"I don't think they know, but I'm not sure." Constantine shook his head. "I'm just not sure about any of this, and especially if they've learned I'm here."

"How could they possibly know? You're a man long dead to them." Gavyn handed back the letter. "I can't imagine any of them believing you survived this long on your own."

"If they ever came here, they would insist on proof of my being dead, and they would accept nothing less than my corpse. They would do anything to get it—or to learn if I was still alive." Constantine stole a peek toward his bookshelf where he secreted his private correspondence. "To assure everyone's safety, I should leave the realm."

"As long as you remain in Evermore, you stand little chance of anyone from the outside harming you. That applies to Trystan and the others, as well."

Interlacing his fingers over his stomach, Constantine twirled his thumbs in a tic the priests from the rectory failed to cure him from doing. "If only it worked like that. Me aside. Traian—" he bit his lip hard, stuttering to cover the slip of tongue that was Trystan's true identity— "Trys—Tryst—Trystan is partially responsible for sinking the flagship of Gafforio the Grimm's pirate flotilla with Gafforio aboard to save me. He turned on a Master who bought his indentured contract. That has blood consequences. There is much to fear for the both of us."

Gavyn faced him. "I'm not joining you on Sundays. Silent contemplation works only for those with minds too full. And you look like yours overfloweth at the cuppeth."

The priest groaned. "You hang around Dagonet too much. What in the name of Evermore is that supposed to mean?"

"I go to the loveliest establishment for the deepest of musings. You should try it. I can get the owner to give you a free sampling. You shan't ever think too hard again for inspiration."

"Dare I ask what business you speak of?"

Gavyn licked his lips and lowered his voice to a husky drawl. "The *Tit for Tat*. Best brothel in Elden's Hearth—" eyes lowering to the cowl— "Many a fine *puta* there."

Budgie scrabbled from Constantine's cowl and shot onto his shoulder. Bobbing, he squawked, "Budgie want to see puta! Lots of puta! Budgie like lots of puta!"

"That's my good boy," Gavyn said to the parrot and rested his hand on Constantine's shoulder. "Ready for some puta. Lots and lots of puta."

Sighing, Constantine levered himself from his chair. "Lionel's right. You're a pig and in perfect company with that blasted bird."

"I want to take Budgie with me as I make my *visits* tonight."

Constantine shot him a stern look that turned into a grin which he quickly wiped off his face. "You sure you want Budgie with you?"

Wiggling his fingers, Gavyn enticed Budgie to settle on his shoulder and rubbed the bird's cheek. "Aye, I do. I get far better puta with him around. Wenches love a talking animal."

Whistling, Budgie leaned toward Gavyn's ear. "Ready for some puta. Lots of puta."

Constantine went to touch Gavyn's arm, but the Foxbury scion snatched his hand and held it to his own heart. "Don't fear reprisal," Gavyn said, "We take care of our own. Embrace us for what we are, knowing we will always be there for you, no matter what."

"Thank you, and—" Constantine stopped abruptly when he noticed the unnatural ridges around Gavyn's eyes. What he saw in Gavyn's features was a war between desperation, fear, and the questioning of resolve. If Constantine had not been so close, he would've missed the veil lifting enough to glimpse the shadows lurking across the veneer Gavyn deftly painted across himself.

"Gavyn, seriously, how are you?" Constantine asked softly, his friend's façade shifting again from a dour canvas to the cavalier scamp he projected publicly.

"Everything's fine," Gavyn said, tense lines deepening at the corners of his mouth defeating his remark. There was a wooden quality to his features, as if strings manipulated his appearance as an afterthought.

"When someone says he's fine, it usually means he's not. Often, it's even a cry for help."

As Gavyn pulled away from Constantine, the priest lunged at him and held him near. Gavyn turned his head away and said, "That's right for most everybody else… but not for me. I'm fully capable of… handling myself."

"You sure about that?"

"I'm managing, Father Constantine." Gavyn bit out each word, his muscles straining under Constantine's tight hold on him before his voice softened. "I'm handling it. I am. Really."

Constantine focused on Gavyn's sad eyes, remembering Renard Foxbury in an alcove with his eldest son, hyperventilating in his lap, across from where his son's murdered Soul Bond had lain, the blood still warm from where Bedwyr had drained that soul's life. The fracture had been brutal, Gavyn becoming a shell of himself at the decision not to save his other half.

"How long before you stop managing it and start recovering from it?" asked Constantine.

Gavyn averted his gaze. "When it stops hurting." His eyes shifted until they stilled on a wooden cross on the wall.

"Your father made a mistake by imprinting himself on you."

Heat overtook Gavyn's stare, and he withered his lip into a sneer. "Unlike your family, my father had my best intentions at heart, and he saved my life."

"The path to the Hells is paved with good intentions. You need something other than what you've been doing to cope with Renard's death, and someone else imprinting on you or your reckless philandering is far from helping."

"And what, dear Priest, would you suggest? What great counsel do you have for one who's far from being a lost little lamb?"

"I don't know what I can say or do to help you overcome your grief." Constantine smiled weakly, hoping this would ease some of the tension in his friend's countenance. "Just keep in mind that my door is always open to you. Don't forget this."

"Like I said, I'm fine."

"So you say."

An irritated huff preceded Gavyn muttering, "Just remember, that door of yours swings both ways. I checked the hinges."

"Ah, you're back again to menacing us poor mortals. I guess that's a good thing." Chuckling, Constantine clapped Gavyn's shoulder, careful not to upset Budgie.

"Like you had any doubts. Now go pray or whatever it is you do on your knees." Gavyn shuffled toward the door and hesitated in the archway. "Consider my offer. I know this wonderful wench who can Hail Mary the Hells out of any man bent on absolution."

Snatching an apple from his desk, Constantine threw the fruit at Gavyn. He ducked and it hit the wall, Gavyn's laughter exploding just as another voice greeted him: "Avast, me cousin! Just the man I'm asearching for in these troubled waters."

The click of beads and a tangle of feather-strung blond braids framed a woman as outrageous and immoral as Gavyn. Perched upon her shoulder, a large lizard turned baleful eyes on Constantine, who gripped his crucifix and pulled it closer to his throat. The woman dipped the brim of her tricorn hat in his direction. "Good Father," she said, dangling a bottle of mead between her fingers, "Care to join us?"

"Thanks for the offer, Lady Blumenthal, but I'll have to refuse this time." Constantine eyed the lizard closely as it hissed and ate one of the feathers from her hat before hacking it out. "Besides, your First Mate is critical of most men in your company."

"Call me Imogen, dear Priest," the woman said with a false pout while stroking her lizard's sailfinlike tail, "and Smeeg here will make an exception for you."

"Perhaps one day, I will join you. Just not now."

Imogen shrugged and danced her fingers over Gavyn's chest, crooning to him,

Whiskey-oh, yo-ho-ho. Whiskey-oh, yo-ho-ho.
Avast me mateys, up high and down low.
To the top of ze mast we go.
With the wind, the sails ablow.

Yo-ho-yo, the blues abreeze.
The horizon and squalls are for me.
Ho-yo-ho, the wind and seas,
Amid the sun and moon, I be free.

Gavyn's eyes widened before narrowing. He leaned closer to her, growling the rest of the tune with her and earning a light giggle from his cousin:

Whiskey-eh, yay-hay-yay.
To starboard we must sway.
Taste the salt from the ocean spray.
At port side, me cannons bay.

Hay-yay-hay, I be astern.
I man me helm and the seas churn.
Yo-ho-yo, a land lubber's life I spurn.
Yay-hay-yay, a pirate's life do I yearn.

Imogen pressed her hands over his chest. "Lovely as always, Bloodsworn Blumenthal Bosun. I've a little proposition for you, cousin. It involves our favourite people."

Gavyn sniggered. "Oh, and who might they be?"

"That upstart cousin of ours and my former fiancé. Word has it, Tremayne is tendering an early courtship bid on my dear little Brynn, and Xavier is pulling out all the stops to help him. Now, I can't have that, can I?"

"And you want me to help you stifle those two?"

Imogen's radiant green eyes sparkled. "In all of the nastiest ways you can imagine. My dear Quartermaster awaits us in my chamber. Beddoe will support us from the shadows."

Gavyn looped his arm through hers. "My dear, yours is not even a proposition. What you're suggesting has been within our compact ever since I first helped you escape Xavier's dirty little claws."

As the duo cackled over Imogen's past and her leaving Xavier at the Bonding altar, with a baby's bootie no less, Constantine massaged a burgeoning headache and sank into his chair. Between the two of them, he couldn't rightly say which of this duo was worse. Regardless, Evermore help Tremayne and Xavier. Knowing Imogen, the punishment would involve Smeeg's chasing the two of them throughout the castle. The priest thought he might tender a betting pool on whose arse that lizard bit first and how long it would take for that to become infected and need to be removed.

CHAPTER 70

FATHER CONSTANTINE

Boots echoed in the corridor. On the cracked flagstone, pools of water collected in the crevices. Constantine patted his robes for his key, locating it in his left pocket. Seven had been dispensed between himself, the Ravas, the Saracens, the Royal Pair, Balin, and Myrddin.

He slid the key into the latch, listened for a muffled click, and pushed open the door. Air whooshed from the empty communal prayer space. Constantine surveyed the cobbled-together altar. The wooden table hosted a large crucifix he had brought from Viteliu. The bible that Father Benedict Medici had gifted him lay open next to the Ravas' *Torah* and a menorah.

Guinevere had visited recently, as her favourite white candles flickered and danced in the draft, the tease of her perfume lingering in the room to assure her past presence. Constantine blew out the candles and whispered a prayer to acknowledge her attendance. Her faith did not prevent her from joining Arthwyr in Evermore's traditions and rituals. The pair bolstered acceptance of the varied beliefs practiced in the realm, and for this, the priest was most grateful.

Constantine dipped his fingers in the brass vessel next to the door. The water soothed the heat of his thoughts. He crossed himself and entered the room. At the front of the pews, he knelt and crossed himself again.

Observing the altar and a faded design on the white altar cloth, Constantine let his mind drift across the Isles Seas to a continent far away and to a life he no longer claimed as his.

He was seven seasons when his father, a powerful man in Milan, abandoned him in seminary. Constantine came from a family that raised silkworms, owned vineyards, and grew olives on sprawling lands. However, beneath their public facade, the Sforza family dealt in armaments, slavery, and usury. To absolve their sins, they paid blood money to the church, greasing the palms of their religious leaders to solidify the *Familia's* respect.

A shudder slithered down Constantine's back. His largest fault had lain in befriending and often playing house with a servant's daughter. He made the error of telling his family he would marry her. The announcement was met with stony silence and his swift insertion within the walls of the Santa Maria Sopra Minerva of Romus, Milan's Duomo being too close for his father's comfort.

Constantine rubbed his fingers over the patch of waxy skin near the curve of his jaw. His father had backhanded him and the Sforza family signet ring had torn deeply into his cheek. As his blood dripped past his hands and stained the tablecloth, more care was extended to saving the linen than to dressing his wound. To close the gash, his mother had sealed it with her Fire, leaving an immutable memory that seared his brain as severely as the burn had his skin.

A decade later, Constantine refused to give his father a false alibi, and for this reason, he had outlived his utility. It secured his Fate and permanent expulsion from his *Familia*, with execution the only accepted recourse for disowned family members like him.

Father Benedict Medici and Constantine's second Master, Bishop Francis Borja, were his staunchest allies. Unknowingly, Father Medici had booked Constantine passage on a ship under the Sforza fiat. The ship's captain, a pirate captain of a vast enterprise and flotilla known as Gafforio the Grimm, learned that Constantine was a fugitive. Constantine's saving grace was a Lietuvan gypsy named Traian Kurjeris and a foul-mouthed parrot. He owed his life to the pair for helping him escape the ship and reach Bishop Borja's abbey.

It was there that they met Guinevere and the others; there that Traian stumbled upon Galahad in a garden; and there that Traian embraced Trystan as an easier name for Galahad to pronounce.

This past year, and with increasing regularity, Francis and Benedict sent missives to one another, and these letters often reached Constantine. Sforza was on the move again, and as Constantine doubted that his father knew what had become of him, it was unlikely though not impossible that they pursued him.

The Sforza patriarch's nature was to be relentless in seeking and striking down his enemies. He knew no other way. Even though Constantine had offered to leave, deep down he was certain that running was not the right approach. The people he now loved would not let their homeland be easily breached, so he was much safer in the castle than anywhere else.

Memories of the Duels of the Draigs weighed on Constantine's waking moments as much as they consumed his dreams. Some of the sacrifices had come at far too great a price. The Wallach children were an example of the cost of blood for power.

Constantine came back to his current reality and balled up the dark fabric covering his knees. "I need you now, Shiori." He pulled his cassock tighter. "God and Inari be with you. Bedwyr was not the only one you put back together."

Creak. Thump. Thump. Click.

Fabric swished as frankincense and myrrh tickled Constantine's nose, and he craned back toward the man striding down the aisle. "Good noon, Safir."

With a practiced flick of a finger, Safir Dariush Sasania, the former and hoped to be future Emperor of Saraceni, lit a wick with his Fire. He genuflected to the crucifix, in deference to the priest's religion, and sat on the pew across from Constantine. His tone solemn, he said, "I expected I'd find you here."

"I've been mourning the past."

"More like sulking."

"It's hard not to."

Shadows covered Safir's face as he sat up and looked toward the altar. "Life is full of regret. I wish I confronted my uncle, especially since I'm the oldest. I should have protected my mother." He wiped his eyes on his sleeve. "I should have stood by her."

Safir's lament made Constantine think about what he might have done to save the babies Talia Ward lost during the Battle of the Hearth. "I could have done something for Talia as well as the Wallach children," Constantine mumbled.

"You did all you could. If you hadn't, who else would have died?" Safir rapped his knuckles over the pew. "Jormund murdered his family and brutalized his oldest son. It doesn't make it better, but his actions put everything the rest of us did or didn't do in perspective."

"I still agonize over what else I could have done."

Safir leaned over. "Would it soothe you if I said, 'May the hands of Jormund be ruined, and ruined is he?' Like Abu Lahab, the only person cursed in *The Koran*, Jormund deserves that too. Everything he touched crumbled to ash and ruin, and the people along with it. He is worse than a kelb—ah, the word here is dog. What animal allows others to rape and pass around his wife's servant like meat to be taken a bite of and tossed from one slavering hound to the next."

The last comment stung like bile in Constantine's throat, and he pressed his fingers over his jugular vein. Shiori covered up the abuse she suffered with yukatas and fancy kimonos, layering them to shield her as she considered the attacks as tests of both her physical and mental endurance. But they weren't just exercises to prove her mettle, because when she and Constantine began paying attention to each other in a carnal way, for the longest time, the barrier allowing her to free herself of the past seemed insurmountable.

Constantine dropped his hand from his throat, and his fingers twitched on his lap. Safir rubbed his jaw so rigorously that a burgundy circle had risen on his olive skin. "Uther was just as bad," Safir said. "His daughters hated him and Evermore, so much so that they insisted as long as Arthwyr left them alone they would never contest his throne."

"There's more to Morgaine and Anya Pendragon than the hatred they harbored for Uther and Evermore. They received more than what most Kings allow."

"Ah, but they were potential Queens in their own right. And even more so when Uther bargained them as Bonds into their husbands' houses." Safir rolled his eyes. "Arthwyr couldn't prevent their marriages, but the situations took care of themselves." Safir came over and set his hands upon Constantine's knees and pressed down until Constantine met his gaze. "As for all else, guilt is the worst punishment we lay upon ourselves."

"Thanks, Saracen Shiori," Constantine said sarcastically after a long pause. "I don't know what I would do without you."

Darts of light softened Safir's stare and dimples appeared in his cheeks, drawing out the youthful future Shahanshah of Saraceni that he had been before his uncle's coup and the deaths in his family had hardened him forever. "The real Shiori would smack you over the head with her fan." A half-smirk broke across Safir's face. "I still can't believe Viera caught Segwarides. Palamedes has been trying for ages and hasn't come close."

"My opinion of that boy is that he will turn out fine when he gets older." Constantine nudged Safir. "There's a lot to be proud of with him, even though he continues to play the scamp whenever he can get away with it. Which is most of the time."

"You and the Ravas have done wonders to help shape him." Safir sighed and his eyes lost their luster. "Priest, my little brother needs more than what Segwarides or I can give him." Burying his fingers in his rich black hair, Safir pressed his face against his hands. In the candlelight, a few stray strands bordered on silver.

Constantine wrapped his fingers over Safir's wrist. "What's wrong?"

Safir's hand shook. "Palamedes responds to you. He looks to you as more of a father figure than he sees in either me or Segwarides. You've filled that role for him since the moment we arrived." He blew out a large breath. "Now I must be honest with you."

"Have you not been honest with me up until now?"

"Of course I've been honest with you." Safir took a playful swat at the priest. "What I meant by being honest with you is that I sought you out today for a reason, which is to ask if you would be Palamedes' Master."

With his heart fluttering and his chest swelling with gratitude, Constantine set his hands on Safir's shoulders. In measured words, he replied, "I'm too close to you and Palamedes. You need someone unconventional to handle him; someone who will command his respect. I'm definitely not that person because I could never discipline him adequately."

Safir grimaced but settled a resigned look on Constantine. He thought a moment and smacked his lips. "Do you think that Bedwyr might apprentice him if I let him hang Palamedes from a chandelier anytime he gets out of line?"

Constantine let out a loud guffaw that echoed in the tiny room. "You had better get a count of how many chandeliers we have in the castle. Seriously, you might never find your brother if Bedwyr ever got too irritated with Palamedes' antics."

Entwining his fingers in his hair, Safir relaxed on the pew for another idle Sunday afternoon with Constantine that they shared in each other's company since starting the tradition three years ago. "Funny how that moves him to the top of my list," Safir said.

CHAPTER 71
BUILDING BLOCK REVOLUTION

Hammers banged on the long landing stretching into the village of Elden's Hearth. Loud groaning preceded rock being placed to support the bridge's arches. Upon a table stood a balsam wood model of the same arch bridge. The reproduction gleamed a varnished yellow under the summer sun as dust bounced off its protective barrier created by an Air array.

"You ruddy Odin-be-damned fool," the venerable Master Mason, Peter Decole, snarled at a man loitering next to the table. "I swear, Reddrom Pinkerton, you're the sorriest excuse for a Mason's Apprentice I've ever set my eyes upon." The old man's temper had several workers scattering, and they sent pitying glances at the Apprentice, who was wringing his hands.

Reddrom Pinkerton lifted his gaze from the blueprints sprawled across the table. "I'm sorry, Master Decole, but I don't understand. Shouldn't we save materials? Arch bridges have no weak points I can see."

Decole planted his blocky hands over his hips. "You little arse, arch bridges need more support along the sides, but their weakest point is the middle. That's the first thing they teach in masonry school. It's why we add beams at the midpoint to bolster the weight the bridge can handle, you fool."

Reddrom considered the blueprints and the bridge spanning from the castle to the village of Elden's Hearth. "You sure are smart, Master. Maybe one day I'll think like you, eh?"

Decole sucked on his teeth. "If it weren't for how dumb you are—" stalking toward another model on a different table— "I'd wager you wanted these damned bridges to collapse."

Another man ran up and passed the Master Mason two large satchels full of parchment. "Your blueprints for the bridges in Porthcrawl."

Decole accepted the pouches. "Aye. I'll leave tomorrow and be back in a few weeks."

The man nodded and both men headed to the other table, Decole's voice drifting back to Reddrom: "This bridge will withstand all seven Elements hitting it at one time. You don't have to worry about cracking or splintering. As for Ribeena and Auraboralis, the plans for them are in my office. My idiot Apprentice over there can show them to you." He pointed toward Reddrom.

The Apprentice waited until Decole was well out of sight before turning to the book of final plans laid out in front of him. He picked up an eraser and removed bracing from the master plans and inserted supports that had no relevance to what the bridge could tolerate if under attack. Readjusting the drawings took him no time at all. There was a certain skill he had learned in cleanly removing a line and inserting another. Drawing perfect circles was another talent he had developed to a high level of proficiency, both skills assuring his acceptance at twenty-three springs—an age surpassing typical masonry students.

Decole's original student had met with an untimely end. Such a shame when someone so full of promise drank past his limit, only to find Twilight in the Lockinge River. The perfect replacement had been hired by Decole's company, or so it was thought. Within the first few weeks, Decole had found the new man utterly worthless as a mason and barely acceptable at dealing with paperwork. Regardless, the ninny was too hard to replace this far into the project.

Glancing up, the Apprentice observed his highwaymen masquerading as workers. They lingered next to a large scaffold. When he dipped his chin, the highwaymen moved as one solid unit past the construction trolleys. A loud crack preceded the platform tipping over, stone dust pluming the building site like a cloud rising from a volcano. In the wake of the chaos, the highwaymen slinked past the Apprentice.

One of his henchmen placed a hand on his shoulder and leaned in close. "Bring back other plans, eh?"

"Nay, not now. I'll meet you tonight. In the meantime, have some fun with Master Decole, Sluagh."

Sluagh slit his eyes like a snake's and pulled his lips over his cracked teeth. "He's not our Master. You're our Master, my King."

The Apprentice waited for Sluagh and the other highwaymen to leave, his attention turning to the other plans so he could set about altering their designs as well.

Soon, Lord Jotnar would escort the Apprentice to the ceded region to meet with their allies.

Quirking his lips into a sneer, Decole's Apprentice, Mordred Pendragon, quietly sang:

> *Evermore 'tis breaking down.*
> *A new rule rises dark with renown.*
> *Shields resounding, warhorns sounding,*
> *The West shouting in the din.*
> *Arrows singing, chainmail ringing—*
> *Loki promises the East and me a win."*

CHAPTER 72

RAFTER SNEAKER

Three days was too long in Palamedes' opinion to be searching the marketplaces in and around Elden's Hearth and not be able to procure a real prayer rug. Oh, there had been all sorts of fakes foisted on him, pointed out in no uncertain terms by his brothers, as the few merchants who sold Muslim goods had proved altogether unreliable when it came to rugs. Palamedes had assured Safir and Segwarides that he was up to the task, but he didn't need Nimue to look in her scrying ball to tell him that his brothers were losing their patience with him.

Normally, Palamedes wouldn't be concerned one way or the other, but this was different. For the first time in his life, he was given the responsibility to do something worthwhile, and he wanted to make his brothers proud of him. He had convinced himself that this was the day he would find a bona fide prayer rug—and he would be correct.

What he settled on was larger than a traditional prayer rug, as it was more the size of a small carpet, but it met all the other criteria. Both Segwarides and Safir spent the entire afternoon analyzing the fibers, colors, design, and knot-count per inch and deemed the rug satisfactory. After that, his brothers managed to acquire the aid of Lionel, Constantine, Daegyn, and Palamedes' cohort of girls to help haul it back to the castle with quite a few curses to go around. Upon seeing what they were up to, Gavyn offered his services in the form of delegating the retinue into walking into walls and suits-of-armor. Gavyn had escaped having to sit for hours as a master painter made Arthwyr's upcoming birthday present of the Knights of the Eclipse, the day allotted for the Foxburys' and Baudwyn's sketches. Between laughing his arse off at Gavyn's antics, Palamedes learned the Foxes already had designs on adding their additions to the renditions of the painting.

Palamedes had sloshed through in a puddle outside the castle grounds, and his gray sirwal was covered with brown splotches of mud as he skittered across the corridor to the communal prayer room. After surveying the area to make certain he was alone, he scurried inside.

Islamic, Catholic, and Judaic artifacts shared the table in front of the altar. Palamedes ran his fingers over a silver candelabra. Above the altar, a man in a loin cloth and a crown of thorns was nailed to a wooden cross. Gold-and-silver braided coils made up the frame for the crucifix, making this the most ornate part of the room. The man bound to wood was unnerving. No amount of effort answered for Palamedes the attraction by a mass of people to a person becoming one with a cross.

He found priests to be an especially strange lot. Their lifetime of avowed chastity confused him most. His backside still bore the marks from when he had questioned Safir about perhaps having a "fuller" relationship with Constantine, since they spent so much time together.

When voices echoed in the corridor, Palamedes lifted his foot onto an orange array and launched himself up to the rafters. *Creak. Squeak.* He settled onto a robe he'd left for rafter-sneaking, as he liked to refer to his gross invasion of privacy.

Lionel entered, carrying a salver full of clay. Fire runes and a combination of Russkan, Yiddish, and Hebrew symbols bordered the silver platter, and small flames flickered from the edges of the plate. He set down the large serving tray and, using his control of Fire, adjusted the intensity of the flames.

Linny soon followed, locked the door, and joined her husband. They gathered some ash from the nearby hearth and drew a circle around the platter at the spot where it sat on the altar.

Lionel took a dagger from its sheath beneath his robe and pricked his thumb. He passed the knife to Linny, and she did the same.

They extended their hands over the platter and spoke a blend of the Fire, Earth, Air, and Water katas as they each allowed four drops of blood to fall onto the clay. The contents shimmered, and wispy fingers of smoke whorled from the center and rose high in the air. White ash on the clay smoldered into gray before turning dark and starting to take on a shape. After passing their hands around the clay four times, it solidified into the black form of a one-foot-tall figure with feline characteristics, its ears becoming pointed and a tail whipping around its back.

Palamedes bit down hard on his lip to keep from squirming on the rafter and making noise as Lionel, in Hebrew, addressed the transmutation he and Linny had created. The figure's head lurched upright and its bright red eyes gleamed in its shadowed face. Reciting passages from memory, Lionel rounded the creature, making a complete circle. He repeated this in the opposite direction, Linny at his side throughout.

After the fourth rotation, they stopped in front of the altar and the strange incarnation crawled close to them. A squeak scraped from its throat as it shook itself free of residual ash, and smoke drifted from its nose.

Linny extended her hand, and the creature bucked against her palm and wrapped itself around her wrist. A purr rumbled from its throat.

"Good morn, golem," she said. "You had a pleasant sleep for a spell?"

Maerna rubbed her arms as if they were cold, which was not the case. As she trailed closely behind Palamedes, Maerna combed her hair with her fingers, her tight braid staying the nervous habit. She grumbled, "I'm not so sure this is a good idea."

"Golems are so neat. The one Lionel and Linny summoned a few days ago even did tricks." Palamedes stopped and turned to her. "If a golem can do tricks, think of the other possibilities."

Poking Maerna's upper arm, Viera skipped ahead of them. "Yeah, like no more chores!"

"If our parents aren't using these *things* to perform the jobs the servants do," Maerna said, glaring at both of them, "there might be a good reason for it."

Viera drew her finger across a table in the hallway, creating a line through the dust. "Who wouldn't want dancing feather dusters or brooms that sweep on their own? Even with the servants, we're still left with a lot of chores the golems could do for us, right?"

Maerna remained silent to that.

Said Palamedes, "There's something else we can't forget about. Brynn got slippered for entering Constantine's room under false pretenses in a Muse's getup. We owe her for getting us the key."

"Brynn did that to get what she wanted," Maerna muttered. "I can't believe she wants to take part in First Night. Her father's scouting candidates for her."

Viera ran ahead to the door leading to the prayer room, leaving Palamedes and Maerna by themselves.

Waiting for Viera to get farther away, Palamedes bent close to Maerna. "Brynn is really going to do the, ah, with somebody who's not her Bond?"

"Aye. Some tripe about, 'If boys get to do it whenever they want, why shouldn't girls have the same opportunity.'"

Palamedes lowered his eyes. "My brothers won't let me. They believe that everyone should wait until marriage. Though I think that Segwarides and Natalia, that's his Bond, might be getting more *involved* with each other. Still, I give Brynn credit for saying what she believes." He raised his eyes to Maerna's. "We're not telling Viera about First Night, are we?"

Once again, Maerna remained silent. However, this time she gave a brief nod.

They caught up with Viera at the door to the prayer room, and Palamedes began rummaging through his pockets. After a harried search produced a negative result, red-faced, he admitted, "I think I, um… lost the key."

"That you did." Viera dangled the key on her index finger. "You need to be more careful where you put things." She fumbled with the locking mechanism. "Trystan and Dagonet are attentive teachers."

"Figures you learned it from them." Palamedes manipulated her fingers over the metal, showing her how to use the key. "They're not the only ones to learn from."

"I see." Viera batted her eyelashes. "Maybe I could teach you a trick or two."

Maerna gently elbowed past them. The prayer rug was rolled up, bound with leather straps, and set upright in a corner.

"We keep it like this so it won't get stepped on." Palamedes stuck out his chest. "When we stand it on end like this, we preserve it so it isn't sullied with dirt."

"Or infidels like Gavyn," Viera said, adding a smirk.

"Never thought about that. But I guess you're right."

Palamedes rolled up his sleeves. As if in a trance, he lifted his hands. The Air around his fingers became wavy. A white plume solidified into an Elemental array. Saraceni lettering appeared around the edges, the design writhing as if in a sensual dance as Palamedes released it.

An easy exhale slid past his lips, and the bindings on the prayer rug came loose. Palamedes flicked his fingers and the carpet came away from the wall and levitated. Jealousy flashed through Maerna at how Air reacted to the smallest gestures he made. In the past, she had watched in awe when he had controlled Air without even utilizing an array.

The rug unfurled, and it settled on the floor. Palamedes guffawed like a loon as he plopped himself onto a pew and pointed at the rug, his hand weaving back and forth like a snake searching for prey. Maerna followed the direction of his finger, and her jaw dropped.

In neat gold thread, Talia had embroidered an arrow and *This End Up* along the length of one long edge. According to Palamedes, this assured that the prayer rug would always be facing Mecca.

Viera plainly wasn't having any part of it, going so far as saying "If that's an arrow, you could fool me. It looks more like a boy's dangly bits."

Maerna glared at Viera and groaned. "We should leave. Linny and Talia will be coming here after they finish tea in the Queen's parlor, which could be any time now."

"We don't want to go yet." Palamedes bent to trace Air symbols over the edges of the rug. "All of us must gather ash from the fireplace to make a circle around the carpet."

Maerna reluctantly complied, and the three of them, with ash from the fireplace, coated the stone floor around the perimeter of where the rug rested.

Palamedes stepped away from their collective efforts and surveyed the result. He raised his hands to create the sign he had seen Constantine use for approval.

Maerna shuddered. "I hope this doesn't cause anything bad to happen."

Producing a small paring knife from his pocket, Palamedes pierced his thumb and passed the knife to Viera. "For better or worse, we spill our blood together," Viera said as her thumb started to bleed.

She handed the bloody blade to Maerna, who tightened her fingers into a white-knuckled grip on the small handle. Maerna fixed her eyes on the carpet until nervous snuffling drew her gaze to the intent stares of her friends. She uttered, "I'm not a wallflower—" clenching her jaw— "I'm a Dragoness."

Slashing open her thumb, she cradled her hand in her robe.

Palamedes said, "Recite the Air kata along with me, and we must have seven drops of blood for each Element. No more. No less. And we have to circle the rug together, exactly seven times." Palamedes used his hand to make circles in the air. "Maerna, you'll recite the Metal and Water katas. Viera, you do the Earth and Wood katas. I'll take Ice too. We'll go in the sequence of Air, Metal, Earth, Ice, Water, and Wood until we close with all of us doing Fire together."

After they nodded, he began the Air kata: "*Ek, Dui, Tin.*"

As he spoke, they held out their hands: "*Char, Panch, Cha.*"

They circled the prayer rug: "*Sat, At, Nau, Das.*" He nodded to Maerna.

"*Eins, Zwei, Drei.*" Maerna guided them in dripping seven droplets over the rug: "*Vier, Funf, Sechs, Sieben, Acht, Neun, Zehn.*"

Viera took up the Earth kata, confident from practicing with Brynn: "*Moja, Mbili, Tatu, Nne, Tano, Sita, Saba, Nane, Tisa, Kumi.*"

Palamedes sang the more musical notes of Ice: "*Sami, Ohta, Kyehti, Kulma, Nelji, Vitta, Kutta, Ciccam, Kaavci, Oovce.*" He offered a playful leer with the last kata and added: "*Love.*"

Maerna recited the Water sequence with ease: "*Hitotsu, Futatsu, Mittsu, Yottsu, Itsutsu.*" She even mimicked the flowing movements Ewain performed at the Dance of the Elements, finishing with: "*Muttsu, Nanatsu, Yattsu, Kokonostu, To.*"

Viera had no trouble with Wood, as her sharp voice called out the katas: "*Nane, Jees, Tree, Kiore, Queig, Shey, Shiaght, Hoght, Nuy, Jeih.*"

Palamedes grabbed three of the small sticks used to light the candles. He passed one stick to each of them and waved his over the rug until Viera and Maerna copied his movements. He had Viera light their sticks with her Fire, and they in turn lit the candles on the altar. Bubbling laughter filled the room as smoke wafted over the carpet and they chanted, "*En, To, Tre, Fire, Fem, Seks, Sju, Atte, Ni, Ti.*"

However, not so much as a whisper of air circulated, the rug remaining limp on the floor. Palamedes nudged the edge of the carpet with his boot.

Viera gave the other side of it a little poke with her toe, asking, "What did we do wrong?"

Deep in thought for a long moment, Palamedes shot up and slapped his hands together. "I know what to do next! We have to do seven circles the opposite way, reciting the katas backwards! We must bring everything back to where it began!"

Viera rolled her eyes, but Maerna's facial features tacitly said that they had come too far to turn back now. So, as soon as Palamedes finished with Air, Maerna bit the inside of her cheek and began: "*Zehn…Neun…Ach….*"

CHAPTER 73

BADGIR

An hour went by, with Palamedes trying everything he could think to bring the prayer rug to life, but even his use of Air didn't help. The Saracen boy sat listlessly in the middle of the carpet, resigned to the reality that he had failed miserably.

Viera, sitting by a corner of the rug, agreed with what no one had said but what everyone was thinking: *This was a waste.*

"Look on the bright side." Maerna pointed at the bloodstains splattering the rug like dried fruit in bara brith bread. "We spilled our blood in the spirit of camaraderie."

"That's right," Palamedes said, bitterness seeping into his tone. "We spilled our blood, and I'm going to lose a lot more of mine when my brothers get hold of me." He shook his skinny arms. "I probably won't have much left when they get done with me."

"We could always lie," Viera suggested, "and say that Constantine spilled some holy wine on it." She caught herself. "All right, a lot of holy wine."

Palamedes shook his head. "He wouldn't dream of going anywhere near our prayer rug with holy wine or anything else. If Constantine even found it unrolled, he wouldn't touch it. He'd get us to move it."

"Any other brilliant plans?" Maerna asked as she repositioned herself on a pew.

A swirling globe of Air appeared below Palamedes' hand, the rich threading of the fabric attracting his attention as the flickering candles created a shimmer across the darker shades of the rug. He reached toward a corner of the rug and stopped halfway, as the edge rose on its own and brushed his hand. Viera and Maerna sat speechless.

The material writhed like a beast rudely awakened, and Palamedes shot to his feet and jumped from the rug. The rug began to shudder; the pulse of life being infused into its fibers. The carpet shook itself, levitated a few feet, and the edges became illuminated.

Palamedes screeched, "What do we do now?"

"How are we supposed to know!" Maerna hollered back at him. "You're the one who made this thing!"

Viera stepped past both of them and rubbed her fingers over an edge of the rug, her Fire seeming to sooth the carpet's anxiety. Her high voice cut through the shrieks still coming from Palamedes and Maerna: "I'm Viera. What do you want us to call you?"

She didn't get an answer, but fifteen minutes later, all three of them had a seat on the rug. Their initial fears had faded as it rolled playfully through the room like a puppy investigating every nook and cranny in a new place. As they floated above the pews, they pushed away from the walls when they drifted too close. The only problem any of them experienced was when standing on the rug, as this resulted in the carpet buckling and the person tumbling into the center.

Palamedes, being his old self again, said, "Viera's right. We need to have a name for our friend here."

"Why not just Carpet or Rug," Viera said as she clapped her hands and snuffed out a flickering candle. "Make it simple: Hey, Carpet! Hey, Rug!"

Palamedes threw up his chin. "I'm not calling her Carpet or Rug."

Maerna ran her fingers over the dense material. "What makes you say the rug is a her?"

Palamedes smiled. "She told me when I called her a good boy."

Maerna jerked up. "She talks to you?"

"Aye. Doesn't she talk to either of you?"

Both girls scrunched their noses and said as one, "Nay."

The rug purred, wiggled when touched, and butted their hands like a feline but shook itself like a dog.

Viera asked Palamedes, "What about your native language for rug?"

Palamedes groaned. "I'm not calling her Sijada."

Maerna tapped her chin. "What about a description that has nothing to do with a rug?"

"Like?" asked Palamedes, seeming genuinely interested in her answer.

Maerna fidgeted with her sea glass pendant of a wolf and a raven. "Uh, well, it's got a lotus flower on it too," she offered.

Viera jabbed a finger at Talia's additions. "That's not all she's got on her."

Palamedes grumbled, "I'm not naming her that."

"Oh, come on. It would be great."

He jutted out his lip. "Safir would kill me."

Maerna asked, "What is a lotus flower called in your language?"

"Zahrat alluwts."

"Viera's right. Rug might be best."

Palamedes gritted his teeth and focused on the altar candles. Idiots with no imagination called something for what it was.

"It's all right, you old wind catcher." Viera scratched the rug and giggled when the material arched toward her nails. "We'll come up with something."

Wind catcher. Palamedes had not heard that name in a long time. Not since Her and the home he left behind. In Saraceni, windcatchers ventilated their palace and the towers that reached high into the sky.

His mother took Palamedes to the highest spires and they read the air currents, images of grandeur taking shape on the wind. She created illusions in the sandy boundaries beyond their palace, and she wove tales around this. With each smooth flick of her henna-stained fingers, mirages danced. The same that saved her from the blade her first husband ordered for each new bride gracing his Throne. His mother had scrabbled her way to the very top—until she ruled from the perch meant to be her last seat.

"Badgir." Palamedes petted the rug. "Your name will be Badgir."

Viera squirmed a bit at the name. "What does it mean?"

"It was my mother's nickname. It means Wind Catcher."

The fabric levitated higher, its surface quivering gently in the air.

Maerna gripped the carpet. "I'm scared. What's it doing?"

Palamedes lifted one hand to direct the rug closer to the floor. As he set his palm on Badgir, emotions roiled through the boy's mind. One scattered thought sharpened into a crystallized declaration of intent.

With only a few seconds to form a counter thought, Palamedes didn't react in time and Badgir lunged.

CHAPTER 74

DISTURBANCES IN EVERMORE

Myrddin glanced at the Knights who were present in The Chamber of the Eclipse before locking his eyes on Arthwyr and saying, "I feel a disturbance nearby."

Arthwyr gave him a bemused look. "Care to explain?"

"I hear laughing. Lots of laughing. Some people are having far too much fun, and at our expense. I sense destruction. Lots of destruction."

Arthwyr sat upright on his chair. "Good Evermore, invaders?"

"Much worse. Our children are running amok."

Gavyn smirked and peered over the rim of his goblet. "Ah, the many joys of those we bring into the world." He tipped his mead in a salute to no one in particular. "In truth, good thing it's not a horde of invaders amassing across the river."

"Could be yours causing the grief," Balin said as he kicked the leg of Gavyn's chair. "Thank Evermore you only produced one issue."

Gavyn scrambled to right himself and said to Baudwyn, "Hold my mead."

"Sit," Baudwyn enunciated, "or Jarvis will need to roll you out in a wheelbarrow."

Arthwyr asked Nimue, "Milady, can you See anything yourself?"

Massaging her temples, Nimue murmured, "All I can tell is that it's worse than the Princes, Daegyn, and Harlan combined."

"How is that possible?" the King asked, his tone indicating genuine concern.

"I'm sorry, Arthwyr. I can't See exactly what is happening. All I know is that something occurred that will make us all very uncomfortable. And it will get worse before it gets better."

Morien growled, "I'm not here for this. Figure your children and Apprentices out on your own time."

"He's right." Arthwyr picked up a silver apple and examined it. "For now, let's focus on these Avalonian apples that keep cropping up in the gardens. How are you after eating this, Gav?"

"I had the best night at the *Tit for Tat.*" Gavyn blew them a kiss. "Might be an aphrodisiac. Can I eat the rest? Just to test and make sure. Quality control."

Lionel dragged the bowl of apples closer to himself. "You're so full of shite your eyes are brown."

Gavyn smacked his lips and lifted his finger.

Bedwyr cut him off. "Please don't eat any more of those accursed apples. It's bad enough you can't fix stupid. There's no reason to compound it."

"Oh, look who woke up from his cat nap." Gavyn banged his hands over the table. "Have a nice nap-nap, Bedy?"

Rose perfume enveloped Myrddin, and he bumped his shoulder against Nimue as she said, "We'll get them later. All will be unveiled."

"Argh!" Maerna screeched.

Viera was too afraid to unwrap her arms from Palamedes' waist to buffer her ears from Maerna's high-pitched whining.

Not that she was any better, hollering at the Saracen, "Make it stop! Make the damn thing stop lest it kills us and everybody in the castle too!"

"I'm trying." Palamedes pulled up on the rug and commanded, "Stop, Badgir!"

The demand ignored, the rug blasted down a corridor and sent an ornamental shield flying off the wall. Wherever the rug took the trio, loose items were dislodged and destroyed. A large mirror shattered, shards sent everywhere, causing servants to fall to the floor and duck into alcoves. The lucky ones carried something that could serve as a form of protection. However, there was no safeguard for a maid lugging a full chamber pot, its contents drenching the poor woman unfortunate enough to be on the way to empty the vessel.

The next sharp turn Badgir negotiated on her own took the freshly conjured golem into the main dining hall, which was being readied for the evening meal. Meals were tossed in the air as much of the staff dived under tables and others ran for their lives, joining in Maerna's howls.

Musicians were practicing, and not knowing what was really happening, they burst into the requisite musical fanfare for the Royal Pair, assuming this was a comedy show that was also in rehearsal. Some members of the Royal Orchestra figured out this was not comedic theater, and they added to the chaos in their attempt to escape with their instruments in tow. A few others, oblivious to what was going on around them, continued playing. As orange slices lodged in its strings, a violin released a grating squeal that was so obnoxious it caused the musician to finally stop to consider what was taking place around him.

Screaming, one limber servant vaulted onto the table and raced down the length of it. It was all Badgir needed to become enthused enough to play with the man, and she gave chase. The fellow stepped into an enormous platter of bread pudding, and he slipped and skidded forward and off the end of the table. He careened into the orchestra pit and landed in the middle of a large bass drum. The musician, who was trying to get the drum out the door and to safety, could only throw up his hands and scream as he started to beat the servant with his drumsticks.

Badgir entered an open corridor leading to the kitchens, and the rug dived into a man carrying live chickens tethered together by a string. The birds screeched, flapping and writhing until they escaped his grip. One bird became wedged in a fold in the rug, right in front of Viera, and she found herself spitting out feathers.

Ahead of them, Jarvis dropped a tray and food flew everywhere. Jarvis threw himself onto his belly, barely missing getting bowled over by Badgir. Wind whistled and ruffled Viera's robe. Clutching Palamedes, Viera looked toward an open doorway, from where the breeze was coming. Badgir darted outside and careened toward the sky.

Extending her hand toward some low dense clouds, Viera called into Palamedes' ear, "Could you get Badgir to take us through those clouds?"

He tightened his grip on the rug. "Clouds, Badgir? Can you take us to the clouds?"

The material rocked gently back and forth.

Her voice thin and ragged, Maerna said, "Slowly, please."

Palamedes slid his fingers over Badgir. "Aye, very slowly."

The chicken in front of Viera screeched, "Puckah! Puckah!"

Viera passed the bird to Maerna and said to it, "You should consider yourself lucky. After all this, there's no way they're cooking you tonight."

Maerna stroked the head of the terrified chicken. "That's not helping."

Viera shrugged as Badgir drifted toward the cloud.

Before long Viera was staring at the twining blue thread of the Lockinge River, the distance from the ground making her question if hiding behind a cloud was a good idea. She elbowed Palamedes. "This isn't as much fun as I'd hoped."

"What do you mean?" Palamedes asked.

I've got to say something? All right. "Clouds are boring."

"I know how to make it better." Palamedes patted the rug. "Who wants to see how fast Badgir can go?"

Oh, shite, what have I done now!

CHAPTER 75

LESSONS IN PROPER COMPORTMENT

The pianoforte's gentle plinking accented the calm provided by the wooden chimes that clinked together in the breeze coming through the open window. Flowers blossomed in vases set on handsome wooden and marble tables, and ornately designed chairs faced a raised dais that Jocelyn stood behind.

She had just finished the opening segment of her dissertation. During a respite, she focused her attention on the Princes and other young male nobles, since only the most deserving belonged in the company of the Maids of the Court. Indeed, the noble boys present in the Queen's Court were deserving of her consideration, except for Harlan Foxbury, who demonstrated his immaturity by slouching with his legs spread apart, his head tilted back, and his mouth moving as he appeared to be ignoring Jocelyn and counting ceiling tiles to himself.

Jocelyn deemed most of the other Princes and the older male nobles perfect for her. She found Eryck Rheged especially fetching. At eighteen seasons, he was two seasons older than her.

She glanced toward Daegyn Dyfed and suppressed a wince. Since Carydoc left him in the parlor, the young Lord, who had turned fifteen seasons shortly after Alban Hefin, had buried his nose in a book on horses. Good Evermore, could he spend a moment not obsessing over his family's damned herd? He bored Jocelyn to tears with his plans to rebuild Dyfed Landing. She crossed him off her list, as well. Hence, there were two she found unworthy of her.

As she deliberated with herself further, Wilhelm Auraboralis would be perfect if not for the blight of being a foreign Prince. Alas, perhaps he was the third she'd have to remove from her inventory of viable prospects.

Jocelyn made a mental note that he could have Viera or Brynn. Aye, wouldn't either of them be a match made in the Hells for him?

"Lady Jocelyn," the Queen said, sipping Elven lily wine from a crystal flute, "please recite the next lines."

Jocelyn wiped her mind clean of her ruminations, her mother's lessons coming to her with the ease of water flowing off a duck's back: "Your Majesty, a proper young lady embodies the essence of propriety, serving a shining example of how a house is run, an estate managed, and a kingdom ruled. She has the hand of the industrious, the mind of the sage, and the heart of the fair."

Jocelyn gave a smooth flick of her new fan to acknowledge the applause coming from those appreciating her flawless delivery. Executing an exaggerated curtsey to Her Majesty, she had to catch herself from falling over.

"Well recited, dear." The Queen nodded in the direction of The Seven Sisters. "Her diction was clear as a bell, as well."

The only dark-skinned servant who attended the Queen whispered something into Guinevere's ear, irritating Jocelyn. That maid exercised far too much familiarity. Rumor had it, the woman had publicly bid to be Bedwyr's servant. A crying shame the Lord of Metal accepted her into his service.

Jocelyn's vitriol ran to another less than worthy peasant, as the brown-haired Jewess serving pastries wasn't any better. If either worked in Sagramore House, those women would be lashed until their pride lay in tatters like the skin flayed from their backs.

Guinevere clapped her hands. "Jocelyn, dear, would you kindly recite thy mother's *Advice for General Conduct?*" The Queen sent a cautionary glance at Maryck Pendragon, who at sixteen seasons was next in line to the Throne. "I fear young Ladies of the Court aren't the sole benefactors of such counsel."

A smirk disappeared from Maryck's face, and he sat up in his chair.

Jocelyn curtseyed again, with more care this time, and she tapped the edge of her fan over her lips. She mentally mused to herself: "Tap once on the edge to draw their stares to you. Twice to let them know your lips are supple. Thrice to show you are a woman." She fluttered her eyelashes. "When thou goest on thy way," she said aloud, flicking open her fan and rolling it in lazy designs, "go thou not too fast."

Her sycophants quietly voiced their approval among themselves, acceding that these were the same pearls of wisdom their mothers had taught them. They all understood the proper ways to conduct themselves in public, with Jocelyn their undisputed bellwether.

Brimming with confidence, Jocelyn spoke with more authority: "Brandish not with thy head—" noticing Brynn setting down a book— "nor with thy shoulders cast."

Lord and Knight Dinadan Blumenthal did his daughter no favour in allowing her to engage in far deeper reading than the other Maids. Even worse, he accepted candidates for Brynn's First Night, thumbing his weathered nose at the advice from great men such as Jocelyn's father. Whoever allowed a girl such loose freedom? If she raised her robes once, she'd have no problem rolling her hips to accept another; no different from the most common of strumpets traipsing about the docks. A girl should be chaste and pure to receive her husband.

Jocelyn hoped that her cousin, Tremayne Cornwall, would be successful in wooing Brynn. During the next week, he would present the first of many tokens of his affection, all to avert the brewing scandal. How honorable and self-sacrificing of him—and starting with a dozen red roses no less—all for that foolish bint's sake. No honorable man would ever want anything less than a chaste woman between his sheets during Bonding Night.

She spared a glance at the book in Brynn's lap. It was not befitting for a Lady to dirty her hands in learning the healing arts. Ah, Tremayne would break Brynn of that soon enough.

Jocelyn approached her favourite part of her recitation by saying, "Your Majesty, I find these next words the most important of all." Yet, as she recited from a prepared litany, the guttersnipe resurfaced in her mind, and irritation washed through her, dulling her delivery. A dark cloud that appeared in the sky outside a large bay window heightened her disgust.

Faint clucking startled Jocelyn into looking for the noise, and she lost her place in her speech. She hoped that Her Majesty would scold the simpleton once the culprit was discovered.

She started again just as a large shadow darkened the window. *For the love of Evermore, when was that cloud going to pass?*

Loud shrilling wind rattled the pane in the window, and Jocelyn marveled at how a gale could develop on an otherwise beautiful day. Just when she thought the wind had died down, a blast shattered the glass and tiny shards rained down everywhere.

A carpet flew into the room; the guttersnipe, the sand monkey, and Lady Maerna astride it. A squawking chicken shot off the rug, coming straight at Lady Jocelyn, who uttered the only epithet she could think of to express her dismay: "What the FECK!"

Brynn plucked the fan from her lap and covered her face to conceal her amusement. Jocelyn was on the floor in a sprawl of petticoats and robes; a chicken perched on her head and its beak pecking through her once perfectly coiffed plaits of silky blond hair.

Her facial features set in her Ice, Queen Guinevere sat motionless in her chair above the dais. Brynn couldn't help herself from what she did next. She curtseyed to the Queen and to The Seven Sisters and finished Jocelyn's speech: "…from swearing keep aloof. For all such manners come to an evil proof."

Considering Jocelyn's loss of control and blurting out the ultimate curse word when the rug came through the window, had the carpet arrived after she'd finished her speech, Jocelyn's hypocrisy would have been epic. Still, Brynn had made her point, and she snickered at the raw fury reddening Jocelyn's features.

With Jocelyn shrieking and unable to free herself of her garments, and her toadies only making her predicament worse, the Queen continued to sit motionless in her chair, her entire being as stationary as a slab of granite. Everything in the enormous room seemed to be suspended in time, but it did not take long for the Hells to descend on the Queen's Court.

Smacking a wooden ladle over her palm, Linny Rava marched through the room. Fire sparked through her gaze as her short legs ate up the distance to the dais. Closing in on the other side, Talia Ward covered the expanse like a svelte cat in pursuit of a meal.

The rug drifted past Brynn, sunlight catching the gold-and-silver thread in the fabric. The sting from Tippy's slippering was worth sneaking the key from the priest's chamber. Anything to see this magical carpet in action.

The Queen moved slightly, and a sheet of her sparkling Ice shattered on the floor. It was beautiful and impressive—but above all else scary. Guinevere's face remained as stoic as ever, not hinting at all what she was thinking.

The rug rose and snapped its edges at everyone who was seated at the long table.

Brynn shuffled closer until a hand on her shoulder tore her from her awe. Eryck Rheged hesitated and pressed his handkerchief against her face. It was then she realized her cheek stung from a sliver of glass that had glanced off of her. He waved at her to stand behind him. She wrinkled her nose but acceded to his request.

"For the love of Evermore," Linny screamed at Palamedes, "did you create a golem?"

Palamedes scratched his jaw and turned away, mumbling, "Ah, maybe."

More of her Ice shimmered in the air before smashing onto the floor. Guinevere raised her hand and turned to Talia. "Please put everything back to rights." Talia bowed to the Queen. "Good. I need to work out a few things with my husband and his merry band of fools."

"You three, come with me," the Queen said, pointing her finger at Palamedes, Viera, and Maerna. "And bring that infernal rug too. Linny, you better come along as well. We don't take the creation of golems in this realm lightly."

Guinevere stopped at the door before facing Jocelyn and the chicken. The white hen appeared content to be perched on Lady Sagramore's head, the Maid's hair sticking out at all angles. Jocelyn's acolytes had managed to get the petticoats under her main garments, but her robes looked as disheveled as her hair.

"For the love of Evermore, fix your robes and get that chicken off your head, Lady Jocelyn!" Guinevere shot around toward Eryck, as he couldn't muffle his laughter any longer. "Lord Rheged, since you find this so humorous, please mark that bird as one of my personal animals. One whose health and safety you shall be responsible for, as I won't have it gracing your plate anytime soon. Now get it off her and take it to the pen with my lambs."

"Aye, Your Majesty," Eryck said as the Queen departed with her victims in tow.

He glanced at Brynn and switched the handkerchiefs out, summoning a Wood array and gently attending to the scrape as he said, "But a surface wound."

"Thank you, Milord," Brynn said, as he returned the sullied handkerchief to his pocket and kept the second against her cheek. "When would you like this one back?"

He untangled the chicken, tucked the irate animal under his arm, and clicked his tongue when it started to cluck. "You can keep that one. It's on Rheged House." Winking as he passed Brynn, he sauntered toward the door. "Who'd ya wager on in this joust, Milady?"

Brynn removed the entwined piece of oak and bamboo he had given her as his indulgence in return for the favour that she had given him during Alban Hefin's jousts. Using her penknife, she diligently added another notch to the bamboo half and whispered, with no small amount of heat suffusing her cheeks, "You, Milord."

CHAPTER 76

SHADOWS OF GOLEM

If there was ever a march toward an execution, it was the one the Queen led the trio on as they made their way to The Chamber of the Eclipse. Guinevere moved at a brisk enough pace, but the journey seemed unending. Maerna shivered at the thin press of the Queen's mouth and her steady stare forward. The slightest things grated on Maerna, and even Linny's gently shuffling steps played hard on her frazzled nerves.

Jarvis appeared and wrung his hands. He started to open his mouth, but the Queen fixed him with a look that had him snapping his jaws closed.

Sweat dampened Maerna's robes, perspiration sliding down her chest and below her stomach. A lump formed in her throat and she found it difficult to steady her breathing, the erratic thump of her pulse bounding between a fast trot and an all-out gallop. Metal statues loomed in front of her, the cold bronze of their gazes piercing Maerna to the quick. They, too, judged her, it seemed.

Much sooner than Maerna liked, her party reached the doors to the Chamber. The pair of guards at the massive entryway stood in awe as the rug floated behind the group, both men too stunned to even blow their horns to signal the Queen's arrival.

Guinevere pointed at the entrance and demanded, "Just open the door."

The doors slowly swung open, yawning with the heavy creak of ancient wood and timeworn hinges.

Almost every Knight sat at the round table in the Chamber of The Knights of the Eclipse. Mild amusement filled Arthwyr's warm tones as he took in the trio of children who had just entered.

The King remarked, "What have we here?"

The Queen snipped, "I'm not sure, Husband. Tell me, my King, am I no longer to fathom my reality? Have we lost ourselves down a rabbit hole?"

Pointing at the fabric flapping behind the children, Gavyn asked, "What is that?"

The rug began to undulate, as if to wave at the assembly. A few of the older Lords paled, some gave blank stares, and others held looks of wonder. Garyth and Gaheris tilted their chairs back and appeared to be appraising the carpet's value as it hovered above the main hearth in the front of the room.

Maerna massaged her temples as she walked toward her parents, Nimue's stare burning with an intensity that the girl had rarely seen in her mother. Nimue said to Myrddin, "Oh, look, Husband. Our disturbance came right to us."

Myrddin groaned. "I hate it when you're right."

Everything was wrong. Viera believed that the positive relationships she had developed with the Knights and Lords was now a thing of the past. Gone was the ease these people displayed around her. In place of their comfortable countenances, stricken faces twisted into jagged images indicating anything but pleasure at their being in her presence. She sent beseeching glances to the adults who she felt might still stand by her side.

Head bent low, Ewain Gorre ignored her and shot looks at Bedwyr.

Lionel Rava sat upright in his chair, his gaze aquiver and his features a sickening shade of gray.

Viera scanned the other nobles in hope of finding someone to provide her with the slightest hint of reassurance. Of course, that would be Myrddin. Or at least he should have been able to mitigate the fear building in her. But Lord Emrys would be no help, as he stood behind Arthwyr as the King paced at the front of the Chamber.

Walking back and forth, Arthwyr resembled a lion on the prowl. Each time his gaze settled upon Lionel, his azure eyes glowed a fierier hue, as if being touched by an increasingly intense flame.

Crack. Everyone sitting round Viera jumped, including her, at Arthwyr slapping the table. Even the normally unshakable Gavyn released a distressed whine in sympathy for Lionel.

Arthwyr splayed his hands on the table and bent over it, throwing his shadow over Lionel. "You taught that lad this!"

Cringing as though he wished to hide within his chair, Lionel sputtered, "Of... of course not."

"Silence!" Arthwyr grabbed the front of Lionel's robes and shook the man. "Why would you show the boy something so dangerous? How could you be so foolish?"

"Let go of him right now," Bedwyr yelled, lunging from his seat and twisting his fingers into the shoulders of Arthwyr's robes, "or Evermore help me, I'll take your head off!"

Arthwyr released Lionel. "You of all people know the danger he's created for us."

"All the same," Bedwyr said as he returned to his seat and Lionel slumped into his chair, "touch him again and you'll need the Glitterball to fix your hand."

"Would you like to repeat that?" the King said, storming toward Bedwyr.

Bedwyr braced his hands on the table and rose from his chair. "Touch him again—"

Metal squealed and a silver tray caved inward. Drinks frothed and spilled over, slicking the resin table. Lumistones ruptured and faded into hunks of cold stone.

Both men took a step forward, and right as either was about to take a swing, Palamedes shouted, "Stop it, please!"

"Keep your silence, son," Aglovale Pellinore said as he steepled his fingers into a triangle over the table. "You're in enough trouble."

"Lionel and Linny did nothing wrong!" Palamedes shouted, his face flushed and his eyes shaking. "They didn't know."

Safir's voice rumbled from across the table. "What was that, little brother?"

Palamedes flinched and blurted, "I hid in the rafters of the prayer room to see the ritual."

Arthwyr, who was standing inches from Bedwyr, stepped back and collapsed into a chair. He peered at Bedwyr and sighed. The Knight went back to his seat.

His expression bitter, Safir shook his fist at Palamedes.

As for Segwarides, the candles nearest him flickered wildly as the fire in the hearth roared. Touching his Fire, a small array created a heated wash of bright light that strengthened the flames even more. Face flushed, he grabbed onto the leather armrests of his chair as if trying to squeeze the life out of it, and he looked away.

Lionel made a slashing motion with his hand, and the flames settled into a low crackle. He said to Palamedes, "I'm so angry and disappointed in you." His voice strained. "What you did is a violation of trust in every way possible."

"I'm sorry," Palamedes cried out. "I didn't mean to do any harm or upset anyone." He went on to explain how he got Viera and Maerna involved.

Lionel pointed his finger at the boy. "What you did is not only dangerous to others, bubeleh. You and your friends could have been injured or killed as well."

Linny went over to Palamedes. "Golems are not toys." She wrung her hands. "As you learned, blood is spilt to produce them. The slightest mistake and the creator can lose control. You had to know that. There's also the—"

Arthwyr abruptly stood and announced, "I've heard enough, and I believe penalties are in order." He steeled his eyes on the trio. "And I don't mean minor ones."

Myrddin paled and scrambled to his feet. "No, Arthwyr."

The King, clearly still in no mood for anyone telling him what to do, pointed Myrddin to his chair. "Sit down."

"But he is a child," Constantine said, lunging from his seat and pulling Palamedes into a hug. "He made a mistake. Can we not just leave it at that? I'm certain he will never do it again."

"The boy learned something dark. Very dark. Then he showed what he found out to others." The King came up to Constantine as Palamedes cowered behind the priest. "What should be done so he doesn't get it in his head to try this again?"

The priest shielded Palamedes from the King's view and didn't respond.

"Lionel released the Hells on my father and the residents in the castle," Arthwyr said as he stepped back, crossed his arms, and stared at Viera. "This gives me no pleasure, but all of you must learn." He turned to Lionel. "Show them the creatures you conjured in this castle that drove a King mad."

Lionel bowed low, his gaze downcast and a tremor quivering across his shoulders. "As you wish, Sire," he said hoarsely.

Collecting a pot of water, Lionel doused the flames in the hearth. The wood snarled as if alive and smoke began to fill the room, causing people to cough.

Dagonet's chair shifting backwards jarred Viera, and his teal eyes seemed to be full of fear as he pulled her close to him and guided Maerna to her parents.

Many Knights moved around in their seats, as if experiencing the onslaught of ants running up and down their legs.

"Don't expect me to support you with this," Constantine said to Arthwyr as he placed his arm around Palamedes' shoulders. "I've followed you in many things, but I won't in this. I respect your judgment, but don't ask me to step aside from one I view as my own."

"Then all will witness a corrupted golem, up close." Arthwyr nodded to Lionel to continue.

Viera swallowed when Lionel returned to the hearth. He performed a series of hand maneuvers and followed this with bloodletting and chants and incantations. Lionel raised his hands to the top of the hearth, and shadows grew longer in the room. Fingers drumming over the table brought Viera's attention to Bedwyr, who was staring at her. He scowled and pulled back his upper lip to reveal his teeth. Viera found that eerily reminiscent of the Marshal when she was attacked by the highwaymen, but she quickly erased the thought.

The faintest twitch of Guinevere's jaw betrayed her underlying apprehension, as it appeared that no one in the room, save Bedwyr, was immune to the severity of what Lionel was doing.

Air stilled into an uneasy calm reserved for a funeral. The temperature dropped with the slow rise of Lionel's hands over the charred wood and ash in the bottom of the hearth. A dull whine came from the fireplace, and shadows flickered without the aid of anything obvious to cause this. Clawed fingers lashed from the hearth, clutching burnt wood in their grip. A collective flinch had robes rustling, and gasps sounded in consort with the crack of flames that flared brightly.

Beads of light blinked until a sea of crimson and yellow filled the open space in the hearth. Viera grabbed onto Dagonet's arm. The whine became a piercing squeal, and she clapped her hands over her ears. The shrilling noise was so loud that it seemed to vibrate in her head. She shrank back and Dagonet held her tight, quivers sliding through her frame as a black creature came into focus.

Ash swirled as several more of Lionel's creations materialized. Black shiny bodies emphasized the hideous contorting motions of each golem as it became more fluent in its movements. The hearth was filled with the sound of brittle bones cracking, as if a hundred chickens' necks were being snapped in rapid succession. This extended into a series of muscles popping and bones grinding, the din stopping only long enough for another wail to add to the chilling cacophony.

The golems pulled their glistening ebony lips over their jagged black teeth to display equally black gums, their mouths filled with putrid-smelling carrion. As the stench of decay spread throughout the room, Viera gagged and turned her head to keep from puking on Dagonet.

From Bors Numidia to Balin Cameliard to old Aglovale Pellinore, no one seemed unaffected by the stench. Everyone that is, except for Bedwyr, who rested his chin in his hands, limbs upright, and elbows on the table. His eyelids drooped as if ready to doze off at what spilled from the hearth. He went so far as to let out a loud yawn.

The rest of the people in the Chamber were not so cavalier, as the fear in the room was palpable. A golem shook itself, and its body shuddered as its bones cracked with each jarring, unnatural movement. It cocked its slick charcoal head. Steady clicking rose into a squeal. With an earsplitting howl, the golem lunged forward and Hells' Fire glowed in its blooded eyes.

As it smashed into an unseen barrier, its beet-red gaze locked onto Viera while it flashed its teeth and caterwauled even louder. "Lionel, please make it stop!" she shrieked as she grabbed onto Dagonet with all her might. "Please!"

Lionel looked to Arthwyr, who nodded.

Lionel raised his arms, moved them around in complex patterns, and said a few incantations in a tongue foreign to Viera. Agonized wails knifed through her head, and this scared her so much that she thought she might pass out from fright. However, the golems writhed, withered, and soon only stinking meat filled the bottom of the hearth—and the noise stopped in her head.

Constantine held Palamedes in a chair as the boy shook and sobbed throughout the entire ordeal. Kneeling in front of the youngster, Lionel cupped the Saracen's cheeks and smeared them with ash from the hearth. "Don't ever summon another golem. Do you understand?"

Palamedes cried so vociferously that Constantine had to comfort him as one would a small child. But Lionel pressed his charge until the lad said he would never even think of conjuring another golem.

Viera had regained her composure and looked at the Knights sitting at the table.

To a man, darkness lay heavy on the faces of all of them.

CHAPTER 77

SHADOWS OF THE PAST

For reasons all her own, and which didn't make sense to her when she thought about it later, Viera assumed that Palamedes' humiliation in front of the Knights and Lords was the end of the punishment for everyone. This, however, was quickly dispelled when the King waved the three of them to take a seat. He talked privately with Dagonet and Myrddin as they retired to a table at the far end of the room, well out of earshot.

Time stretched as uncomfortably as a clothesline pulled taut enough to snap at any moment. Viera shivered, uncertain if another half-hour of her worrying would fray her anxiety to the point of breaking her in two. The Knights and Lords weren't doing much better. Chain mail clanged and wood protested at the constant shifting of restless bodies.

The three men finally stood and went to their original seats. The King joined the Queen in front of a freshly kindled fire that was starting to heat up the room.

The fire was the only thing warming the area, because when Arthwyr placed his hand on his wife's shoulder, Guinevere drew her chin down and stared menacingly until he pulled it away. They did, however, speak to each other in low voices for several minutes.

Viera tensed when the Queen looked toward her and her friends. The icy chill of Guinevere's voice stood equal to the resolve in Arthwyr's eyes as she announced to everyone: "In what is to come, I stand with my King," she said, leading Arthwyr back to the table and the pair sat across from Viera and her friends. "So mote it be."

Arthwyr gestured toward Viera, Maerna, and Palamedes. "We were remiss in allowing you three such freedom as you currently enjoy. There are consequences for your folly." He looked at Safir and Segwarides. "I trust you can handle your brother."

The men stood and bowed, saying as one, "Aye, Your Highness."

In clipped tones, Arthwyr directed his next order to Myrddin and Nimue. "I don't need to impress upon you to properly chastise Viera and Maerna. They are just as guilty in the making of that… thing."

Twisting his fingers into his trousers, Palamedes corrected the King. "Badgir."

Arthwyr released a low hiss, his mild temperament being tested once more. "Excuse me."

"Her name is Badgir, Sire." With a swallow, Palamedes bowed at the waist. "I named her for our mother."

Safir snarled. "Little fool."

Palamedes straightened and planted his hands on his hips. "At least one of us shan't forget her."

With his eyes flaring, Safir made a move at his little brother, only to be brought up short as Segwarides slipped between them and shoved Safir into a vacant chair.

"I can handle this," Safir said, biting out each word through clenched teeth.

"Not right now you can't." Segwarides pinned down Safir's shoulders. "Don't forget yourself and do something you would regret, something like our uncle did."

Safir's features softened and he appeared as though he might cry. Segwarides hugged him before kneeling in front of Palamedes. "We're not trying to forget her. However, creating this golem could've ended in tears and heartache for all of us. We miss Mâmân, but her time is complete. She died for us—not for you to sacrifice yourself to try to bring her back." He took Palamedes in his arms. "We know that was your ultimate goal."

Brushing back his tears on Segwarides' robe, Palamedes said, "It would be better if she was back."

"For who?" Segwarides shook him. "We do not want the dead with us. We want the living. You are that. Not her. Not now. You will have her forever later."

Segwarides pulled his younger sibling against him. "We'll figure out something to ease your pain as you continue to remember and love Mâmân. For now, you are to be with either me or Safir, or a chaperone of our choice, at all times. No going anywhere on your own—at all. Do I make myself clear?"

Palamedes nodded and Safir added, "We'll figure out the rest of your punishment later."

Palamedes looked confused. "You mean there's more?"

Said Safir, "There is much more to come. What you did had potentially dire consequences, and you will not get off lightly."

Arthwyr cleared his throat. "That said, you three will start cleaning the stables. Less idle hands might eliminate thoughts of similar acts of foolishness. This will continue until I say otherwise. Oh, and this means every day of the week."

Myrddin said to Arthwyr, "I believe you have something to say to Lionel."

"Aye, I do." Arthwyr motioned for Lionel to stand in front of him. The guilt he felt was obvious in his voice. "I deeply apologize, Lionel. I should have explored everything further before taking you to task."

Lionel offered an appreciative smile. "Sire, I might have reacted the same if I were in your position. You had nothing to guide you."

"I should have asked questions instead of jumping to conclusions. You'll also determine a punishment."

Lionel drew Linny close and the pair conversed in Russkan. Coming to a decision, Linny moved in front of Lionel, who set his hands over her shoulders in support, and she said, "You three are going to school. Temple school, where you are kept busy."

Arthwyr clapped his hands. "Excellent. I'll take applications for volunteers later."

"Now for the hard part," Constantine said from his seat at the table. "What about the rug?"

The King said to Lionel, "Since you destroyed the others in the hearth, surely you can do the same with this one."

Palamedes squirmed free of Segwarides' hold. "No! Please, no! Please, don't kill Badgir!"

A loud boom reverberated throughout the room, and a black array formed in front of Bedwyr.

Arthwyr folded his arms over his chest. "Bedwyr, is there a problem?"

"Paws off the toe rag." Bedwyr released the array and another sharp bang elicited a collective shudder from those at the table. "It wouldn't do for you to dismiss what took so long to come to us."

"Excuse me."

"Don't you dare touch that golem. The boy keeps it. You may not be willing to pay me what I'm owed, but in this, I'll collect part of my due."

The King jumped up from his chair. "You cannot be serious."

"Why have an issue now, Arthwyr? You preserve *The Books of Metal*, yet it's hypocritical how you bend for one but not for the other."

Arthwyr's lower lip quivered. "You know why the books must be preserved."

"No, I don't know why. What we *do* know is the devastation they can cause when they're in the wrong hands." Bedwyr pressed his hand over the House symbol on his robe. "As the last of The Seven Houses, it's my right to have them destroyed."

"I can't destroy the last legacy of—"

Bedwyr hissed at Arthwyr, "I'm going to repeat, you're a hypocrite." Sweeping up a jug from the table, he tipped a salute to the rest of them and strode toward the exit. "Don't punish them too harshly without punishing yourself first."

Bedwyr stormed out the door, which slammed behind him. Viera clenched and unclenched her fingers as she turned her attention to Arthwyr. As if the weight of his crown were too much for him to wear, he appeared small sitting next to the Queen.

"Remember our vows, Arthwyr," Guinevere said, twisting a silken handkerchief. "We promised to be Bedwyr's guiding lights. He and Karen were never the mistake Jormund was." She dotted the cloth under her eyes. "Are those books really worth safeguarding when they cost us so much?"

Arthwyr heaved a sigh. "We can't let them—"

"Let them what? Exactly what do we value anymore?" Guinevere turned to the trio who had caused the day's upheaval. "Each of you in my parlor after you have your midday meal. I won't tolerate my realm falling into ruin because of you three." She glared at the Knights at the table. "And even less so from those who won't take their heads from their posteriors long enough to breathe anything beside their inflated egos."

For all the strength Arthwyr had shown earlier, he was clearly not the same person. Guinevere added to his distressed state by saying, "If you choose to punish Bedwyr for speaking the obvious truth, your bed will be in the stables, Arthwyr." She picked up her gown so its edges wouldn't touch the floor and departed from the room.

Wooden chair legs screeched against stone as Dagonet pushed up from the table. "You weren't there, Arthwyr. Neither were most of the people in this room. For this reason, above all else, anyone not there has no right to judge."

Arthwyr started to speak but sighed.

"You can't answer because you weren't there. So let me tell you what happened. There were bodies everywhere. Lionel thought his golems had escaped his control." Dagonet turned to the others at the table. "Thank Evermore that Shiori and Constantine found Lionel before Bedwyr came upon him, or he would have been gutted."

Ewain said, "Even though we weren't there, we're here now, and—"

"Hold on before you go any further." Dagonet leaned over and braced his arm on the back of Ewain's chair. "Many of you had your chance to make amends. But now, you're well past the point where you can pass judgment." Pulling back the chair, Dagonet bent forward until he was nose to nose with the Healer. "You were Bedwyr's blood. You were Olwen's too. That little girl screamed for you. Where were you, Ewain?"

Looking mortally wounded by Dagonet's words, Ewain lowered his chin and his tears dripped onto the table. "You're right. I was not where I should have been… certainly not when it mattered."

Dagonet strolled alongside the table of The Knights of the Eclipse and ran his eyes down each man occupying a chair. "How many of you sat in the very seats you're in and raised your hand when Bedwyr was selected for execution, ignoring that he was the same boy—and he indeed was just a boy at the time—who handed you the keys to the realm? Do the honorable thing and raise your hand now if you raised it then."

As half the Knights lifted their hands, Viera murmured denial when her gaze fell on one man—Myrddin—who had his chin tucked against his chest and his hand in the air.

Dagonet came to Viera. "Do you want to know where Bedwyr was as the people in this room voted on his Twilight?"

She bit her lip and managed a very weak, "Aye."

"In the Infirmary, nearly dead after Uther had tried to kill him." Dagonet waved at those sitting at the table. "These bastards didn't even have the guts to wait for him to recover before judging him."

"That's not fair, Dagonet," Aglovale said as he slapped the table hard and grimaced. "It was a war. Mistakes were made. People suffered. Many men and women lost themselves in the necessity to survive."

"People suffered and lost themselves to necessity, eh? Shiori suffered but was stronger than everyone here, me included, and I risked my life every day so we had a chance." Dagonet walked over to Viera and Maerna. "Fire tests women, and they emerge from the forge far stronger than many men. You have to rebuild most men. Yet a woman does it to herself, by herself. You lasses remember what I just said."

Dagonet waited for a response but nobody said a word. "Shiori's statue isn't outside these doors." He paused, letting his words sink in, heavy and uncomfortable if the twitches were of any meaning. "None of the women who gave their lives to win the war are memorialized in or around this castle."

Arthwyr frowned. "There isn't much I can do about that now."

"Oh, is that right?" Dagonet grabbed a pitcher of mead and flung it into the fire. Flames erupted, sharpening the air with the drink's heady mixture. "Try another excuse, Arthwyr. Make it as entertaining as I do."

Sweat dotted Arthwyr's forehead as he stammered, "It would…it would take time to make such changes."

Dagonet bared his teeth in a macabre grin, his incisors sharp and pronounced. "Do not let our father be the excuse for your shortsightedness. I didn't step away from my rightful role as King for you to be a coward, brother. Nor did our sisters."

Viera gasped. Looking around the table, she found a few wide-eyed stares.

Stepping past her, Arthwyr came over to his brother. "It's too late for me to repay and make things right for Morgaine and Anya." He hesitated and caught his breath. "I promised you that I would do everything I could to repair our father's wrongs, and I've held true to my vows. But I must have time, and I believe you understand that as well."

"Memorials to our women are a reminder to everyone in the realm to have the courage to seek change for the better." Dagonet came over and slipped his hand in Viera's. "Don't deny women the respect they've earned in shaping our destiny."

Arthwyr folded his arms. "I cannot yet make the changes you or I desire. Not when there are Noble Houses who will throw us into another war over it."

"Then," Dagonet said, walking toward the doorway, "you have no further need of my counsel."

Arthwyr called after him, "Tell Bedwyr that I'm sorry."

Dagonet scoffed. "We both know what he'll say to that."

"Perhaps, one day, I'll give him what he wants. Then maybe he'll forgive me for being the biggest fool of all."

Arthwyr slowly faced everyone seated at the table of The Knights of the Eclipse, and Viera saw something in his manner she had never seen. It appeared that he didn't care what anyone thought about what he'd revealed. It was as though a huge burden had been lifted from his shoulders.

CHAPTER 78

FIRST NIGHT, FIRST BITE

At first glance, the trio's time cleaning up after the horses was more symbolic than anything else, since the Knights' rides were well-attended by stable hands and grooms who had long histories with the animals. This didn't mean that the stalls wouldn't need cleaning, but the task didn't take more than a couple of hours each morning, at most, as the regular workers took care of replacing the hay, which also meant that the manure was removed.

Oddly coincidental to her punishment, Viera enjoyed her chores in the stable because it brought back pleasant memories of her home. It made her feel good to be around the horses and other farm animals. However, she never let on that she enjoyed her "penalty," for fear of Arthwyr giving her something she really did despise. Maerna and Palamedes also seemed to have settled into the routine, and the friends spent much of their time talking.

One day, after the three miscreants finished their chores, Gavyn came by the stables to exercise his stallion, Gringolet, just as everyone was leaving. Viera struck up a conversation with him and sent her friends on, wanting to enjoy more time in the stables and perhaps have the opportunity to talk with him further when he returned his horse.

A while later, she was in the middle of feeding the summer lambs in a makeshift pen when she turned to find not Gavyn but Lord Eryck Rheged sitting at a small square table the stable hands regularly used when playing cards. Laid out in front of him, he toyed with a favour adorned with Blumenthal sigils that Viera recognized as Brynn's.

She frowned at the favour and said to him, "I was told those were burned when the jousting ended."

So absorbed in the favour, Eryck jolted with his gaze flashing toward her before he palmed a stained handkerchief back into his sleeve. He stopped fiddling with the ribbons and rewarded her with a not-too-subtle leer. "That's usually true, unless of course the recipient decides to treat one as an indulgence. A jouster gets one *special favour* during his tournament career, and I chose your friend's favour as mine."

Viera scoffed. "When you could have any lass, why Brynn?"

Eryck flashed a wide smile that displayed his teeth. "Why indeed?" Disgust must have shown on Viera's face because his bravado quickly faded and he secured the favour in his hip pouch and added, "You needn't concern yourself. Regardless of the whispers that shadow your friend, and with ever-increasing regularity, I might add, Dinadan would never tolerate any man treating a daughter of his as a Muse."

Viera finished feeding the lambs and put away the buckets. She dusted off her hands and went over to him. "Why are you here?"

Eryck snorted. "Likely for much the same reason you're lingering about."

"What is that supposed to mean?"

Gavyn returned with the horse and turned it over to his groom to have it walked and sponged down. He raised an eyebrow and smiled at Viera. "I know you aren't hanging around here because you can't get enough of my company, so what do you have on your mind?"

She leaned against a stall, saying, "I don't think you'll soften your words to protect what someone referred to as my *delicate sensibilities*."

"Ah, but what about his?" Gavyn asked, hooking his thumb at Eryck.

Eryck retorted, "You apprenticed me. I've got none."

Eryck and Viera exchanged smirks before she narrowed her eyes on Gavyn and said, "The Maids have been atwitter about Brynn and her asking to take part in First Night, First Bite. Then, I heard from one of the Pendragon boys, Maryck to be exact, that Arthwyr wanted to ban it."

Said Gavyn, "'Tis true, but I can assure you that the tradition Arthwyr wishes to eradicate remains alive and well—and will continue to stay so."

"Oh, please," a voice said, startling Viera as Gaheris Foxbury came up behind them. "You two going to discuss this like adults or children?"

"You've been listening?" asked Viera, crossing her arms in defiance.

"I was all the way at the far end of this building with my mare, Morgan, but sound carries in here." Both brothers nodded to each other, communicating without words, and Gaheris continued: "Viera, if you want to hear how First Night really works, you and Eryck best sit together because I'll wager he's here for the same lesson about—"

Laughter cut him off midsentence as Garyth walked over, took one look at the three of them, shrugged, and dragged a chair up to the table. He kicked up his feet onto the fence of an empty paddock and chucked a packet of cherryroot fags to Gaheris. "Baudwyn should be down soon, and you suddenly picked up my habit, dearest brother. We're meeting Alistair over that old goat that slipped our best corralling."

Gavyn grunted. "You know what they say about goats. If water can pass through a fence, aye so can a goat."

Before Viera could ask what they were on about, Garyth said, "So, still interested in First Night, First Bite?"

"Just how did you know what we were talking about?" she barked, miffed that it seemed everybody was aware of her curiosity concerning the ritual.

"I was standing right behind Gaheris. If you want privacy, you need to be careful with what you say in this stable."

"It seems so, doesn't it?" A deep breath followed her smug comment. "But I would like to know the facts about First Night, First Bite. The Maids are talking about Brynn like she's no better than a strumpet in the Red Lantern District. I don't understand why she'd put herself up for that kind of ridicule."

"Come now," Eryck said and sat up in his chair. "Nothing wrong with a girl who has a little fire in her belly. I wouldn't mind my bride teaching me a trick or two during our Bonding Night." He gave Viera a look that caused her to shake her head.

She snickered and said, "It's also being discussed by the Maids that Ulrich Pendragon will be going through his in two weeks."

Gaheris said, "That's what my brother meant about the tradition being alive and well. Though, Harlan says that Ulrich is trying to not participate and have the practice shutdown. However, it's too late because his brother, who *is* the Crown Prince, has already indulged in his. At best, Ulrich won't have to do it. At worst, he can just sit there and stare at the girl until he runs down the hourglass."

"Harlan follows this autumn," Gavyn said to Viera.

"Is there anything that's truly private around here?" Viera asked, wondering why Gavyn thought she needed to be aware of anything concerning Harlan. "And, aye, Brynn doesn't care… just doesn't care. But I still can't believe her father is agreeing to this, also knowing how it's going to sully the Blumenthal name."

Garyth shot out, "Lass, that House's name has been tainted long before this. As for the rumor mill, it's always enjoyed a steady presence around here. Just so you know, Palamedes, Wilhelm, and Daegyn will be up soon after Harlan's First Night."

"How do you think it will go for those three?" Eryck asked, sporting a smug grin.

Garyth replied, "As for Palamedes, it's not a Saraceni practice. Their people believe in marriage first. And Wilhelm won't do it. Bercylac would never forgive him. As for Daegyn, he's just turned fifteen seasons, so it might be a spell longer before he's considered ready."

Gavyn tapped his fingers against the table. "There's something else that's seldom talked about, and this applies solely to Wilhelm. Women are far more equal in Elven, Auraboralis, and Dwarven tradition." He surprised Viera by what he said next: "Perhaps when more men stop looking at women as if they owe us their bodies, equality won't be such a problem."

Eryck glanced at Viera before turning to Gavyn. "Unfortunately, that's not the type of society we live in, and you know it. Pray for the day we stop waving the bloody equality banner we cling to so fiercely—when we act just the opposite. At what point do you start affecting the change you so hope for instead of waiting for another generation to do it for you?"

Whatever Viera had thought of Eryck's immaturity, he had turned that around completely. But when Gavyn stared at his former Apprentice, the younger man shrank from his scrutiny. "You are very young yet, Eryck," Gavyn said. "It's hard to bend old ways to make for new, and yet change comes as much from within as from outside. It is best to observe what naturally unfolds."

Garyth had grown quiet, his stare blistering in its intensity as he glared at Gavyn, his voice shaking as he said, "What naturally unfolds are often real monsters walking in skins that cloak their true intentions. If you should remember, some seemed to be our dearest. Surely you haven't granted a pass to Carian Foel and his pack of scum, who preyed upon my wife when she was fourteen? Few in the old guard stood against the Court darlings; aye, the dirty bastards who said she asked for it. I'll never forgive them, regardless of their reasoning, and I hope you haven't either."

Gavyn dropped his gaze to the table and his shoulders crumpled inward. "Point taken," he managed, his words sticking in his throat. "My apologies, brother."

One issue kept nettling Viera. "I'm sorry to keep bringing up the Maids, but they tell me that First Bite is when a woman introduces her body to a man. And, specifically, a whore is used for this. What I don't understand is how this applies the other way around. When a man introduces his body to a woman, as will be the case with Brynn, what is the man called?"

Garyth let out a long guffaw. "They call Gavyn a whoreson dog." Gavyn even laughed at that, and when they quieted Garyth added, "The participants really don't have names per se. The Maids are being sanctimonious. Think of Eerie and Bedwyr. She is hardly a whore or he a whoremonger. The idea of branding people with a vile name is stupid, something the Maids do out of indignant self-righteousness."

Color infused Eryck's cheeks as he fixed his gaze on Viera. "Since we're on this subject, what do youths who are of age in your village do when they're *interested* in one another?"

Her face heated, hopefully not nearly as bad as his, and she bit at a fingernail that had long since met its match with her incisors. "They sneak off, a lot of times during festivals. We call it hay-rolling. Sixteen seasonals Bond fast in small villages. We find someone we like—and that's it. Our choices are limited."

"Is it proper Bonding?" Eryck asked in a deep voice that had Viera raise an eyebrow.

"Is it ever?" she blurted, surprising herself at how eager she was to respond to Eryck's question. She took a breath and added, "An old blind Healer named Dottsie has a scrying ball that works well enough for most." She stilled her fingers, which she had been tapping on the table and mumbled, "Anything else?"

Bracing his arms over the table, Gavyn said, "You mentioned the word 'whore.' Or I should say that the Maids have made this brilliant distinction despite knowing these people are called Muses. And to be clear, it's not just women who are Muses. Men and Ancients are also in the mix. In truth, Red Lantern Districts have always provided a place for unconventional art and nonconformist culture to flourish. The most highly regarded actors and actresses in our current society work as Muses. They are fountains of artistic expression."

Eryck smoothed his fingers over his sleeve. "I learned much from mine, and I'm eternally grateful to the woman who taught me to put my future wife above myself."

"If that's so, why does Arthwyr want to do away with First Night?" Viera asked.

Said Eryck, "It's not actually what he's against. It's the Red Lantern District because it was home of the Slave Quarters under Uther. The King believes that it's still being used for human trafficking, so it's not just the disgrace from the past he's trying to get rid of. It's what might still be happening there in the seedier parts."

Gavyn dug out a scrap of parchment from deep within a pouch he carried on his belt. A sketch of an upside-down heart was drawn over another heart, with the letter N inside it. "We still see former slaves bearing their brands. The N is an old sign for those trafficked into the brothels during Uther's rule."

Eryck pointed at the sketch. "The Muse who taught me had that brand, but it had an S instead. I never considered it before, but what is that supposed to mean?"

"Aye. Foreign slaves were called Sirens, hence the S. Those who were native to our realm were called Nymphs, thus the N. It's actually very insulting to those who are true Nymphs or have a Nymph bloodline." A cold fury burned in Gavyn's eyes that was equally shared in his brothers' eyes. "Especially given Druir, the First Wood Marshal of Evermore, was in fact a Wood Nymph and Foxbury House shares lineage with her."

Shying from that potential bundle of lit kindling the Foxburys held over that slight, Viera asked: "Why didn't Arthwyr just outlaw the brothels a long time ago?"

"Dagonet convinced him otherwise."

"He supported it?"

Gaheris nodded. "Dagonet grew up in one. To outlaw the trade, too many people would be left homeless and starving on the streets because they had no skills beyond brothel activity. Arthwyr wanted to act, but he had no way of providing for the workers."

Viera groaned. "Has anyone in the nobility at any level *not* gone through with this stupid ritual of First Night?"

Garyth sniggered. "Found my Soul Bond before it and skipped the festivities—" he elbowed Gaheris, who had gone pale— "someone else threw up all over his."

Gaheris raised his voice over Garyth. "Bedwyr refused when Jormund bought him a girl the same age as his sister, Olwen." The intense compassion in his tone caused his voice to falter. "Instead of participating in his First Night, Bedwyr helped her escape."

"Got the Hells beat out of him for doing it too," Garyth said sharply. "In front of the entire King's Court, Vertigorn implied that Bedwyr was *bent* a certain way." Viera gave him a puzzled look, and he explained: "Jormund laid the shame of homosexuality, and its punishment, on his son."

Viera pressed her fingers to her lips. *Bedwyr—bent? How in Evermore could any of those dumb bastards get that impression?* Just yesterday, she spotted Bedwyr exiting a storage room, his clothes rumpled and hair mussed. Eerie had slipped from behind him, unabashedly displaying dark love marks on her neck like the gray pearls he had gifted her from Progress.

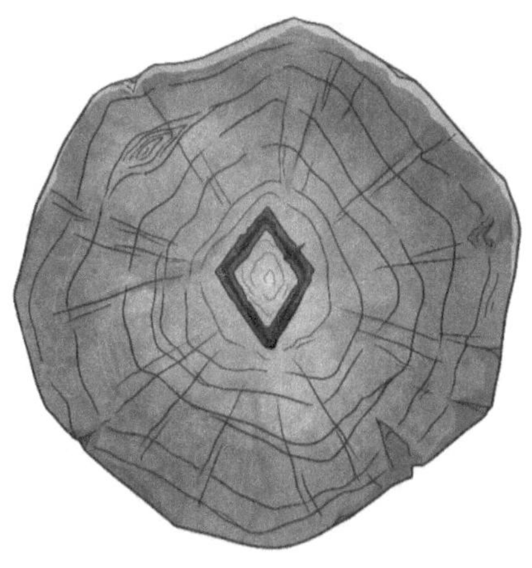

CHAPTER 79

VERY PERSONAL RELATIONSHIPS

Viera was not done with the Foxbury brothers or Eryck. She tugged on Gaheris's sleeve, jerking back when he faced her quicker than she expected. "We're taught in Iyesgarth that Soul Bonds are between a man and woman. But since coming here, I've heard about same-gendered Soul Bonds. They are considered outcasts. Why isn't this accepted if it's a natural possibility?"

Said Gavyn, "You're not wrong about that, but it's not widely accepted because—"

"Because it's purist nonsense," Gaheris interrupted, running his fingers through Viera's hair. "There is a lot of stock placed on a family line continuing, and through only blooded Bonds producing children."

Her eyes darted back and forth between them and settled on Gaheris. "You obviously don't believe it."

"If I believed it, I would not believe in myself, Viera." Gaheris pinched her cheek. "I was born fully Balanced. There is no other person out there for me."

She contemplated what she was going to say next, not wanting to offend Gavyn. "Tippy has ten children. You only have Harlan. Why is that?"

With a low snigger, Gavyn reached into his doublet and removed a vial of bright pink fluid. "I take regular draughts and visit Healers to assure I have no more children. Not even my hay tosses, as you call them, will result in a bastard."

Viera worried her lower lip about what she would ask next: "Don't you want more children with your wife?"

Gavyn uncorked the vial and held it under her nose until the sickening saccharine scent burned her nasal passages. "We find each other repugnant and our marriage a convenience." He drank from the vial and set it on the table with a sharp clink. "We drew up our conditions. Collette received a title, and she has the run of the manor whenever my brothers and I are away. It's not written out, but it's understood that I perform my duties to Foxbury House and shield her from the wrath of the Sagramores and the Cornwalls."

Viera's thoughts screeched to a horrified halt as her mind flashed to Jocelyn and Harris. "Your wife is a Sagramore?"

"Aye, Collette is a Sagramore. Wyndel and Corla, both in Twilight now, were her parents, not that you should care." Gavyn eyed her with a flat stare. "Once Harlan was born, we parted ways in the bedroom. Our arrangement is the best we could hope for."

Viera felt comfortable enough to ask Gavyn, "Why would you settle for something like this? Isn't it the reason for Seeing Ceremonies?" He gave her a puzzled look, so she added, "What I mean to say is, what about your actual Bond? There must be one."

As if to wash down the subject, Gavyn took another pull from the vial and licked the sheen from his lips. "Jormund Wallach was mine."

Viera's arms puckered like the skin on a freshly plucked goose. Her throat tightened. "You said 'mine.' Mine what?"

"Jormund Wallach was my Soul Bond. The one I was fated to achieve the most Balance with." Gavyn nodded at Garyth. "Unlike some Fate smiled upon at birth with a little more enthusiasm."

Eryck said, "If your Soul Bond shares your gender, there's nothing shameful in it. It's the handiwork of Balance at work, right?"

"It's not that simple. There are certain factions who are no more understanding now than they were then."

Eryck slammed his fist on the small table, causing it to buckle. "Why should those Soul Bonds be counted as less than any other? It's not right."

Garyth snapped at Eryck, "Don't speak as if you know anything of it. Not when people have been lashed, castrated, and burned to death in public for even alleged homosexuality."

Eryck dropped his hands onto his lap. "Milord, I didn't mean to—"

"It's not for anyone outside those Bonds to decide."

Eryck tucked his chin against his chest as Garyth stood and shoved his chair under the table. Movement drew their attention to Baudwyn leaning against the nearest archway.

Garyth said, "I'm rather done with this conversation."

Eryck murmured to Garyth: "I didn't mean to upset you. I'm truly sorry."

"Me too," said Viera, who attempted a smile that fell as soon as she mustered it.

Garyth looked back at them. "We live in a much gentler time now. Arthwyr would never allow a ridiculous scene like Uther concocted for Bedwyr."

"Or an equally absurd punishment," Baudwyn added quickly, flashing them a predatory smile, "if he valued his Metal and life."

With that, the pair departed and the tension dissipated.

Tapping her fingers together, Viera shared a look with Eryck. "So, Jormund Wallach, eh?"

"What is there to say? One look in a scrying ball, and I got the bastard!" Gavyn chortled a laugh edged in brittleness. "I kept shaking the damned ball. Don't like the answer, eh? Jostle the ball until the right one floats to the top." A rough sob rasped from his throat. "Except, no amount of shaking or dashing the ball into a thousand tiny specks erased my Fated One."

Viera didn't remember ever feeling more tormented at hearing another person's lament. "That is so sad."

She hugged him, tensing as he said, "Bonds are meant for Balance above all else. They can be between family, friends, and Masters with their Apprentices. Jormund wanted nothing to do with me. He wouldn't even entertain becoming my Master."

"That's beyond awful," Viera said, her eyes welling up.

"Bonds aren't everything. Compatibility, just like Balance, does not mean you have to accept what Fate gives you." A flicker of light seemed to fracture Gavyn's features. "I knew Bedwyr intended to kill his father. I caught up to them and could have prevented it, but I chose instead to lose my Bond."

"And it broke you," Gaheris said in a conciliatory tone.

"Aye, but I regret nothing—" Gavyn's face held a pain akin to being punched in the gut— "not even when Jormund's eyes went gray and the sonofabitch smiled at both me and Bedwyr. Last thing Jormund bloody Wallach said to me was, 'Sorry.' Then he said, 'Thank you,' to Bedwyr. Whatever the feck any of that was supposed to mean."

Accepting what it must have taken for Gavyn to pour out his soul, Viera gave him a moment to compose himself before she whispered, "Can I ask you about Dagonet?"

He glanced at his brother, who shrugged. "Uther frequented the brothels. He broke in new girls for First Bite. Dagonet's mother was one. She died young."

Shuddering, she asked, "Did Uther know about Dagonet?"

"It's why he brought Dagonet into his Court as a Fool. Uther wanted him to always be aware that he was a King's son—and a bastard to boot."

Gaheris said, "Few knew about what Dagonet contributed to the war effort until the very night Uther died. Poetic justice, I guess it's called. In one fell swoop, Dagonet's mother was avenged, Uther's reign of intimidation and terror was brought down, and the nobility was shaken to its core."

The street lanterns glowed about the neatly arranged square as Garyth observed from his station at the living room window. As his mind buzzed, he pressed his forehead against the pane of glass. The earlier discussion in the stable warred with his unease of Luxley in the Hearth.

"What are you doing, foolish Husband Mine?" a groggy voice asked from behind him. "Come back to bed, Garyth."

"Can't. I'm thinking," Garyth said, grimacing, "I can't fathom how you can sleep at a moment like this. Luxley knows about all of us."

His Soul Bond's warmth seeped into the back of his bed robes as an arm coiled around his waist and a hand palmed his stomach to turn him from the window. Following the directive, Garyth faced Baudwyn as his Soul Bond drew them flush together.

Baudwyn said, "Alistair confirmed that Luxley left with a few herding dogs and some new members to join his enclave of thieves."

"Baudwyn, he knows and can—"

"Garyth, I made a decision for you, Reese, and Alistair that hurt all of you."

Garyth shook his head. "You made a decision and sacrifice that kept us all alive through the Duels and beyond."

Baudwyn grabbed Garyth's wrist and led him to the couch. After shoving him onto the leather cushion, Baudwyn settled next to him. "I nearly destroyed us and our sanity. Or do you forget when we couldn't handle being parted for any longer because of our Bond? Nay, Garyth. Listen," he said, pausing to gather a breath and continue, "I masterminded a paper marriage between you and Reese, as well as hid Alistair from the Foels by making him a Kelliweg. Part of my design was to inflict anguish on Alistair by denying him Reese. Look where my revenge and hubris got us all."

"And it saved us all."

"It doomed us to a lie that's overtaken our lives. We can't be our true selves in public without our entire house of cards collapsing about us. Eryck means well, and that might one day be what frees us all."

Garyth buried his face against his hands and groaned. "I want to strangle Eryck for his naïve idealism on all Bonds going public, but Harlan insists on he and Balin seeing him finish his Wood Mastery. Gavyn and I are at odds on the pair for obvious reasons; for me, Eryck's being too optimistic, and for Gavyn, his natural rivalry with Balin. Gaheris thinks we're both being blockheads."

Baudwyn coughed a laugh into his hand. "And he's not wrong." At the cross look Garyth gave him, he shrugged. "They're what Harlan needs. Someone with the agility of a sapling to grow and the solidness of an older tree to better moor him."

"Now look who's being naively optimistic," Garyth snarked, twitching and starting to rise from the couch. "Hells, I need to go do—" flailing his hand— "something!"

Baudwyn tugged him back down, and the wild splintering about Garyth's Elemental core subsided as his Soul Bond used his ability to void the excess Wood. Similar to Lamorac Pellinore, Baudwyn lacked an Elemental ability and could bolster and recharge an Element, but unlike Lamorac, his true prowess came in depleting an Element similar to an Elemental breaker.

"Do you know what I love about trees?" Baudwyn asked, waiting for Garyth to nod before continuing, "They can live through the worse conditions so long as they have light, water, soil, and air."

"Are you saying I need to be watered?"

Baudwyn laughed. "Want to know what else I love about trees?"

Garyth asked, "What?"

"They evolve with the times. Don't be angry with Eryck for wanting a better future. You did the same during the Duels." Baudwyn shucked his outer robe, and in a rare departure from his usual fastidious habits, dropped it carelessly over an armrest. "Each ring inside a tree marks its life and experiences. It changes and surpasses many of the initial constraints against it."

Garyth worked off his undertunic and dragged Baudwyn to straddle him as he fell against the cushion. "I am left with no choice but to acquiesce to Eryck's being Harlan's Master." He grinned. "How much did Gavyn pay you?"

"Not enough for me to not wear him down on accepting Balin, my Fox."

Garyth laughed. "Seriously, how much did Harlan pay you to have his way, my Hunter?"

Baudwyn stoked Garyth's Wood core until it unfurled, but he pulled away and said, "Harlan didn't pay me enough to not kiss and tell."

CHAPTER 80

YOURS

Pinpricks of light dotted the night sky. Viera's bare shoulders weren't tolerating the chill very well as she sat upon a pilfered cushion on the balcony outside her bedchamber. The rest of the Emrys were at a dinner with Arthwyr and Guinevere that Viera had managed to beg out of after coming down with a small cold. Grabbing the cushion, Viera went inside to the room she shared with Maerna, and even with a fire blazing, she had to rub her arms to get warm.

She was tired but sleep had refused to come. Not since she was awakened by what had materialized in front of the hearth when she'd started to doze off—something that was too strange and frightening for her to enjoy the wood crackling in the fire.

The ragged lurch of the golem Lionel had conjured resonated in the dark corners of her mind. "Damn my curiosity," she muttered. "How long will I have to pay for my stupid decision to follow Palamedes?"

A glance around the room no more convinced her to try to sleep than when she lay awake with her eyes wide open as a cold, steady draft bit through her bedcovers and her sleep robe. Soft burbling and a light touch on Viera's slipper drew her attention to Golly. He puffed out his feathers.

"Come, silly bird," Viera said, relocating to the Emrys' common room. "I'll keep you warm."

Viera got comfortable in an armchair as Golly hopped onto her palm. She stroked his breast as he pressed his tiny body against her fingers. "Where is Tilly? You didn't leave her scrounging for a meal alone, did you?" At his chirrup, she giggled. "Ah, so the lady of your night left you for another, eh?"

Viera stretched her legs, her joints and muscles feeling good as she did this. Sliding her hands from the folds of the cloak Bedwyr had given her, Viera positioned the cushion on her lap, disturbing Golly, who decided to perch on the candelabra on the mantel over the fireplace.

Annoyed that she'd caused the bird to leave, she tossed the cushion aside and pulled the cloak closer around her body, getting herself caught in the fabric. "Shite, am I this clumsy?" she uttered. "Yeah, seems I am," she added as she struggled to free her arms from the garment.

Viera thought she heard a chuckle, but the sound was so faint that she assumed it came from afar, perhaps from someone on the ground several levels below her window.

Considerable time passed, and she began to fall asleep in the chair. She decided to go back to her cot, but as she started to get up, she stiffened. The hair on her arms stood on end as her heart raced. The apparition of Myrddin's younger brother, Hamyll Emrys, stood an arm's length from her.

He chuckled, mimicking unmistakably the first laugh she'd heard. Breath hitching, she lifted her eyes to Hamyll's sapphire stare, and everything around her seemed to float. Firewood snapped, jarring her attention to the specter, which was now sitting on the couch. How much time had passed, she didn't know.

Viera blinked at the strangeness of the room. Much of the furniture was the same, but it was the removal of her sleeping cot from the alcove, and its replacement with a bird's perch that convinced Viera she was somewhere else. She rose and began circling the room, looking for other differences—of which there were several subtle variations. She stopped in the space between the couch and the armchair.

Movement startled Viera into whipping around, and she yelped. A new ghost sat in the chair she had just vacated. Riotous red hair slid over his emerald gaze, and he reminded her of Renard Foxbury's statue in the hall that memorialized those who had met Twilight to save the realm.

Viera retreated from him and frantically lashed her arms at the air. A gray-and-burgundy clad sleeve encircled her waist and dragged her onto the couch. She started to scream, but when Hamyll made no further attempt to subdue her, she quieted down.

She couldn't take her eyes off the face that was right in front of her. *Warm. So unlike when you were in the dungeon.*

A glance about the room flooded her with concerns. *Where was Myrddin?* There was no sign of the younger version of her Master, who in the past had followed Hamyll into this in-between world where she found herself.

Across from them, the redheaded man dusted off his robes. Saluting, he sauntered from the area and exited into the hallway.

The Fire Marshal phantasm suddenly raised his hand as if to hit her. Viera folded up and whimpered, "Please, don't!"

The strike never came. The ghost closed his fingers around her hand, and she gasped at the rush of warm energy pouring from him. The heat licking against her palm was like the touch of soft ash from her hearth at home. And when the apparition squeezed his hand over hers, Viera smiled at him. He lifted his hand and placed it on her shoulder. She tensed but relaxed when he made no further advance.

Viera, now at ease, tilted her head. The ghost mimicked her movement, which she found mildly amusing. But she still asked in a more serious tone: "Hamyll, are you here because of Olwen, or are you here because of me?"

Hamyll's wraith dropped his stare to their hands. Tears poisoned the air, overwhelming Viera with their weighty sense of sadness. She tightened her fingers over his, the instinct to comfort too hard for her to set aside.

The specter lifted its head back to her.

Viera blinked when Hamyll as the Fire Marshal climbed to his feet, and it stunned her when the couch squeaked from the release of the ghost's weight. *Was this sort of reality truly necessary?* She found everything happening in front of her impossible to fathom, and this added to the mystique.

The room went out of focus for a moment and shifted back to her room, fire crackling in the hearth, and the alcove holding her and Maerna's cots exactly as she'd known it. Boots thumping nearby drew her attention to a much older image of Hamyll. Dark chocolate hair framed him, except that silver teased through it and laugh lines crinkled his skin. The wraith took her fingers, patting its hand over hers.

Tears clung to her eyelashes when the specter walked toward the door. As it reached the doorway, Viera clenched her sleep robe and asked, "Do you see me when you look at me, or do you see Olwen?" She gave her head an irritated shake. "If you want her, why come to me? What are you even to me?"

Hamyll's image shifted between its older and younger self until it settled on the teen-seasoned one. It nodded at Myrddin, who had just appeared. Viera decided this was also a ghost, which was confirmed when it glided to the doorway. Hamyll's apparition turned to Viera as it slipped into the hallway with Myrddin's specter, and it uttered:

"Yours."

CHAPTER 81
THE BOOKS OF WATER

Still reeling in his drunken stupor, Bedwyr slumped on the table in his chamber. Alcohol stung his nose and eyes, a precursor to the Hells unleashed from the floodgates of too much Moon Mead.

One bottle near his outstretched hand was larger than the others. Bitterness threatened to overwhelm him and he growled at the bottle, the amber sheen of the glass akin to his father's frigid stare as Bedwyr went to his knees in front of the entire Court and begged for the life of his last living sister's best friend, Lilwy Foel. She was ten autumns—two mere weeks shy of eleven—as she pulled her fingers into her wrinkled sleeves and her mother prowled in front of her.

Bedwyr would never forget the sound of the snap as Ceridwyn Foel halted in front of her mousy daughter and slapped Lilwy so hard that the girl flew backwards onto the marble floor. Lilwy's yelp was met with laughter, and as she lifted her gaze—one eye gray and the other mottled with brown—there was little denying that her agony should have engendered pity. But there was not a smidgeon to be had. Not even her enchanted father, Tegid, had managed to claw his way past the ignominy Ceridwyn and her twin, Carmryn, had saddled him with for hiding Lilwy in the Foel apartments bordering the castle.

With those braying for more blood in the exact spot Olwen had died a few months earlier, Bedwyr knew Lilwy's time had reached its end. As Jormund slunk down the stairs from the throne to stand behind the girl, Bedwyr saw his two remaining sisters and Lilwy whispering secrets in the Library. With their heads bent low, the three holy graces schemed against their evil older brother and their even more nefarious cousins.

Lilwy had been one with the trinity of innocence and summer daisy chains wound into wild girl hair before culture coiffed rebellious locks into the custom of Ladies-in-Waiting. Bedwyr intended to let the good die young, the same as the rest of his siblings. Indeed, it was the plan, until she turned her anguished gaze his way. In that moment, it would not be her last day, of this he would make certain or meet his own date with Twilight.

His father was inspecting his claymore, not even the mercy of an axe granted to cleave Lilwy's head from her body, when Bedwyr strode past the whimpering lass. Her haunting pleas for mercy, not for herself, but with the insistence that she didn't want another to die because of her, played on his mind. Bedwyr, not yet a man, prostrated himself in front of his father, the marble floor cold as ice against his forehead.

Not knowing how he gained the confidence to defy Jormund, he pleaded, "Father, I request mercy for the one I wish to bind to our House. Lady Lilwy Foel would be a credit to the House of Wallach."

After a long pause that made Bedwyr's skin itch, Jormund asked Ceridwyn Foel, "Has your daughter bled yet, Milady?"

Licking her rouged lips, Ceridwyn fixed Lilwy with a burgundy stare. "Nay, Milord, she has not, but I could arrange it immediately if it is your will."

"When do your girls typically bleed? It wouldn't do to take one too young."

"Thirteen seasonals for most. The longest, fifteen."

Jormund huffed and motioned for Bedwyr to rise. "Since you're so eager to have a wife, you will Bond and bed her then."

Ceridwyn bent and hauled Lilwy upright, her nails digging half crescents into the girl's tiny wrists. "If you should wish for me to induce her moon cycle early, it is but a simple draught, Milord. No trouble at all, and she'll bleed within the day."

The cold Bedwyr continued to feel burrowed into his gut, but through the grace of Odin, he maintained a blank façade. "If you will it, Father, I'll bind her presently."

Even under the thundering beats of his heart, Bedwyr maintained a tone of legitimate interest in Lilwy. Anything short of this and she would once again be under the claymore. His other fear was that her horrid bitch of a mother would persuade Jormund to have Bedwyr perform the deed that very night.

Consummating a Bond was a private affair between the couple, the pristine white First Night consummation sheet bled upon to prove the virginity of the receiving partner, with the cloth whisked from the bedchamber afterwards for immediate inspection. If he must, Bedwyr would bleed out a rat or bird over both and coerce Ewain, Lamorac, or Aunt Saris to confirm Lilwy's maidenhead as torn. At worst, he could order Shiori to illusion herself as Lilwy. No matter what he did, it would further damage his already tattered reputation, but better this than a dead girl on his conscience.

For once, Bedwyr had good luck shining upon him, as Jormund set his arm around his son's shoulders and husked in a disconcerting gravelly tone, "Sometimes, patience is the best seasoning. Let your future Bond savour the anticipation of her Bonding Night. Two years is enough time to build her—expectations." His father's gaze slid past him to the Foels. "No more than that. If she's not bleeding by then, she'll do so on her thirteenth autumn."

Bedwyr read between each word, aware it was a form of torture meant to hang about Lilwy's neck like the stiff and unforgiving hemp of a fresh noose. He had bought her time but delivered her to a new Hells of his own design. She would suffer for his compassion, and everyone else would love every excruciating second of her misery.

Jormund cupped Lilwy's chin and kissed her forehead as tears streaked her quivering cheeks. The Lord of House Wallach straightened, met her terrified eyes, and said, "It's early yet, but I'm sure you'll forgive my eagerness to bestow upon you my preemptive blessing. Welcome to my House, child. You'll do great things for our illustrious future. May many springs bless your womb."

Bedwyr hid his loathing for his father as Lilwy was made to curtsey through her tears and express gratitude to the man who orchestrated her future rape—and to a youth forcibly commissioned to make it happen. So much for evading the minutiae of Bedwyr's earlier First Night when he assisted his victim's flight to freedom instead of her bloody violation. He should have known his father would make up for that. And he had.

When Lilwy's father emerged from his enchantment two days later, Bedwyr insisted that his future wife must rest at her home under Tegid's care and personal protection. Over the shock at what he thought was going to happen to Lilwy, her father wailed like a child as he stood on the landing of the castle, effusively expressing his gratitude to Bedwyr for having his daughter spared. Of course, Ceridwyn was nowhere to be seen.

Bedwyr saw Lilwy a few times during the two years before her coming-of-age. At the date of her twelfth seasonal, he had been charged with presenting a gift from his father and House Wallach, and to personally observe his little autumn maiden opening it. Hatred surged anew in his stomach when it turned out to be an hourglass to countdown the exact time until Lilwy's reprieve from formal Bonding expired. It was cruel seeing the life drain from her face as she forced a grateful smile and made a speech, oft-practiced with gritted teeth in private, to appease her sadistic mother.

The summer before she turned thirteen, that hourglass served as a silent sentry over her mantel. Bedwyr had coaxed her to close her eyes and think of her happiest memory. After a prick of his dagger against her thumb, he dribbled her blood onto the sand in the hourglass and carved an ancient Witchery rune at the top of the frame. When the sand spilled to the bottom, a memory of Lilwy and his sisters, catching frogs in the gardens of Elden's Hearth, flickered in the glass.

Lilwy caressed the hourglass with reverent fingers and asked how he did that, to which Bedwyr replied, "The blessing of the moon has a long reach." He closed his hands over hers and pulled her into an embrace that had her shaking in his hold. "When next I see you, it will be in Tryfan Heights, the night before our Bonding. I convinced my father, your family, and the King, it is only right for us to consummate our Bond there."

Not loving Bedwyr but knowing she had no choice except to abide by his wishes, her tears burned as she pressed against his tunic. "I vow to bring spring to House Wallach."

"Lilwy, it's not what you think. Follow the waterstones in my sisters' garden. I secured you safe passage and sanctuary to Auraboralis. King Anders will meet you at the end of the trail. Don't ever look back. Not even when you're safe in Auraboralis." He let go of her and added, "Fare thee well, and wade ever in the light, Lilwy."

Two months later, the outcome of the Draigs' Duels was decided, and he prayed that Lilwy had either peacefully embraced Twilight—or she had stabbed her mother in the throat with a darning needle and freed herself of that monster forever.

"You've bled your last enemy, Father," Bedwyr said to the larger bottle as his fumbling fingers squeaked over the glass. "Ha, I'll see you again in Hells, and we can discuss this further."

Boom! Boom! Boom!

The three jolts shot through Bedwyr and were fatal to his musings. He groused at the large wooden peg that, in his maddening condition, he had not placed correctly to allow the door to his chamber to serve as a legitimate barricade, and which now made him vulnerable to visitors from any quarter. When the knocking increased, Bedwyr fell forward onto his face. He mulled feigning death if it meant he could get some sleep.

He would not be so lucky either way, as Ewain shouted, "Dammit, Bedwyr! I can smell the Moon Mead all the way out here in the hall, you drunken bastard!

Bedwyr staggered upright, the desire to wreak havoc on his cousin bolstering him. But his uncoordinated stumbling made getting the peg free of the iron latches no easy chore, and a section of the wooden pin broke off. When Bedwyr was able to throw open his door, the peg banged against his chamber's stone wall, satisfying him because he wished to repeat the process on the side of Ewain's skull. Or at least to use the heavy door to wedge his cousin against the rockwork—and leave him there.

Bedwyr kicked the chipped–off part of the dowel into the hallway. "What brings you to my inner sanctum, another attempt to air me out?" Bedwyr slammed the door closed just as Ewain cleared the threshold, delighting at the line of tension forming along his cousin's brow. "Try going at me again, and I'll hang you off the highest parapet in the castle!"

Ewain gave the empty mead bottles in the room a long look. His expression became dour and he ran his fingers through his hair.

Bedwyr stilled. *Oh, feck this!* With pointed jabs against the other's shoulders, he shepherded Ewain to a chair at his desk. "You don't get to beat on my door and enter my chamber like we're going to have a heart to heart. If that's your goal for coming here, you can get the feck out!"

"Bedwyr, we must—"

"Evermore, this *is* what you came here for. Get out now, Ewain!" Bedwyr clenched his fists so tight that the veins in his wrists were livid against his skin. "Out! Out! Out!" he yelled at the top of his lungs.

Ewain extended his hand in a calming gesture that would have worked when Bedwyr hero-worshiped his cousin. But no longer. The brush of his fingers over Bedwyr's robe snapped whatever restraint was holding him in check. He lashed out, sending Ewain into a bookshelf.

The impact sent a few books to the floor. Bedwyr grabbed the collar of Ewain's outer robe, and not releasing his grip, he rammed his body against the wood again, adding two more books to the pile.

"You're still my family," Ewain said, the cool brush of his Water Element numbing the pain from Bedwyr's death-tight grasp. "Surely our mutual blood still counts for something."

Bedwyr snarled into Ewain's face, "Oh, that's supposed to mean something? Where was that relationship back then?" He gave a mirthless laugh. "Aye, somewhere alongside my father's, right?"

Ewain's features darkened. "You'll never know the depths of my sorrow and guilt."

"Then go drown in both. I hope your pain festers and rots your soul." Bedwyr held Ewain even tighter against the bookcase. "When you close your eyes, I pray you see the two of us. In this way, you will see my failure as your failure as well."

Ewain angled his body, and Bedwyr had no choice but to release some of the pressure. The pain in Bedwyr's voice, however, didn't abate: "You could have saved us. You had a duty to your blood. But you failed all of us." A sob escaped his throat. "You could have taken Wysteria and Olwen into Gorre Retreat. If you had, they would still be alive today."

"I should have." Ewain freed himself from Bedwyr. "I'm so sorry."

Bedwyr spat at him. "No, you're not! You raised your hand in support of my execution. While I was in the Infirmary, you let those Sagramore, Cornwall, and Cuhlwch swine drag me into the bloody courtyard!"

"I tried to stop them."

"You could have tried harder! A lot harder! I was nearly in Twilight's cradle, yet you let the vultures in to have an even bigger slice of me publicly!"

His memory, the fragments once blurred and disjointed, were now vivid and ordered. His captors had barged into the Infirmary, hauling his limp body to the courtyard as Harris dragged the still dripping executioner's axe over the carpets and flagstone behind them. Tremayne and Xavier held Bedwyr over the wooden block. He languished for so long, with his head pressed against the slab, that dried blood from a previous execution had flaked and formed a dark line on his throat.

As Harris brandished the axe to send Bedwyr to Twilight, no one present knew what *domine benedic et protégé familiam meam* meant, or how Constantine, without an array, had produced an exploding sun in the courtyard.

The blast sent those thirsting for blood scrambling over themselves as someone shoved aside the Cornwall and Cuhlwch scum pinning down Bedwyr's shoulders. A wolf's-pelt cloak slid over his bare back, and though his vision was quite foggy, Bedwyr could make out tawny hair and brown eyes as Anya Pendragon gave succor to his weak grip on life. She had believed in him, and she had saved him. No one else would. Bedwyr was part of her bargain not to contest the throne.

His guilt weighed on him every time he thought of Anya. He had a choice and could have followed her. She had promised he would always be welcome in Bach Haus. The last time he saw Anya Pendragon, she waved at him from her horse. The sun glinted from her Bach diadem and sent flashes of lupine images on the ground. But when her older twin, Morgaine, turned her dark head toward Bedwyr, her icy stare might as well have been shooting arrows at him.

Morgaine's cold regard had been the same when she stood aloof in the courtyard as his execution almost came to fruition. It was only after Anya threw herself over Bedwyr that Morgaine demanded his pardon or the immediate ascension to the throne. Morgaine didn't care one way or the other, especially about Bedwyr, but Anya made her care. Anya made everyone care.

When the Pendragon sisters rode off with their husbands and children, no one could predict it was the last time they would ever be seen in Evermore. Who knew that the ceded duchies would attack the Pendragon sisters and their families? Bedwyr tracked the sisters until the Jotnar, Vulgate, Minkrune, Foel, and Grendel Houses made it impossible to travel on their lands, even for a single person under the cloak of darkness. There was just too much area to cover, and because of the fear of reprisals, virtually no one was willing to help Bedwyr with information. So, he went back to Evermore, defeated in his quest.

Bedwyr's jaws quivered. "Why did it need to be Anya to sway you to support me?" He groaned and grabbed for the large bottle, but it was empty and it shattered when he threw it into the hearth. "How many times did a ruler have to come to my defense before you would stand beside me?"

Ewain came over to Bedwyr and cupped his face in his hands. "Who do you think sent for Anya?" He stroked his thumbs along Bedwyr's tense jawline. "I knew I couldn't stop them. But I also knew she could."

Bedwyr weakly wheeled away from Ewain. "You sent a woman to do your work?"

"Cousin, that's not quite correct. I sent a Queen who they could ill afford dishonoring. If they hurt Anya or imprisoned her, they wouldn't survive the reckoning."

Bedwyr staggered to his table and tossed another bottle into the fireplace. The crash and splintering of glass on stone didn't help the headache fast settling on him. He groaned at the spread of Moon Mead on the base of the hearth, when a heavy thump hitting the floor drew his attention to where his cousin was kneeling.

"I tried, Bedwyr. I gave you *The Books of Water*. How was I to know…."

"You saw the carvings. You knew the lengths Uther and my father would go to ensure their goals." Bedwyr stared at his cousin's bowed head. "How could you not, Ewain? How could you not see what they conspired to do?"

Ewain clasped his knees and sucked in a harsh breath. "Who would remotely assume that they were capable of such an act?"

"You read the books." Bedwyr tapped his boot over the stone. "To complete the ritual, the blood of those who performed it was required. You were aware I would have to consume their blood to staunch the instinct to close it myself."

Ewain shuddered and disgust twisted across his features. "I never thought Uther would go to such lengths to ensure he wielded power over you. There was no reason to believe he would slip you his blood and carve his control into you as he did."

"You did no great service in hiding such knowledge." Bedwyr toed the broken glass into a pile and braced himself against the bookshelves. "I'm the monster you wished to avoid creating. Thank you, Cousin, for making me into what I am."

Bedwyr banged his hand over the wood. A large tome spilled onto the floor, its cover facing up in silent recrimination of its contents. Ewain glanced at the title, and he shuddered as he swallowed and carefully leafed through some of the pages.

The Healer jerked away from the tome, as if it might bite him. "Good Evermore! You've had *The Books of Water* all along! You told me you destroyed them."

Bedwyr scooped up the book and threw it across the room. It struck the fourposter's frame and the bed shook. "Get out! You're not welcome here! Haven't been for a long time!"

Ewain opened his mouth but closed it. His turquoise cloak rippled from his movements as he stopped in the doorway. "I truly am sorry."

Click. The sound of the door's latch was soft but no less final.

A breeze made the curtains flutter around Bedwyr's balcony door. He collected the book and dropped it on the edge of his bed. Bedwyr caressed the worn leather. Cracks edged the Water symbol, flakes threatening to chip off at the slightest brush of a finger over the fragile surface. Bedwyr opened the last *Book of Water.*

His mother's kanji graced the back cover. It read: *Ai, Yurushimasu, and Raibu. Love, forgive, and live.* She was able to do all three. Bedwyr closed the book and set it on his lap. No matter how many times he stood over his hearth, he could not let *The Books of Water* become enveloped in flames. Not when his mother lived on between the yellowed pages.

CHAPTER 82

PROMISE OF THE ESAU

Ewain observed from where he stood over the Infirmary bed as a sleepy murmur earned a chuckle from Gaheris, who said, "Fine. One story, Staunis. Then you sleep."

A hand lashed out from the covers, the child's gaze swimming like the racing sun in the sky after a spring rain. "You won't leave, right?" eight-seasons Staunis Cornwall whispered, his voice quaking as if threatening to break if the answer was nay.

Gaheris gave a nod, likely to appease the child and as a signal to Ewain and Lamorac that they would discuss the boy later. "Aye, Ewain, Lamorac or I will be in here at all times. We promise."

Staunis made himself into a tight ball, his thin arms folded around his tiny torso. He whimpered loudly when he brushed one of the many bruises covering his body, injuries administered by the family who was supposed to love him. Despite his resemblance to his father, Staunis Cornwall lacked the cruel features necessary to be a copy of Vertigorn, which did him no favours in House Cornwall because his mild appearance was perceived as weakness and made him a favoured target for abuse.

Ewain wondered if the Cornwalls who mistreated the child ever thought in doing so that they might be setting the pattern for another Vertigorn, who would ultimately turn on them.

Lord Kael Cornwall and his wife, Lady Yuliya Blumenthal, had spent much of the day in the Infirmary after Gaheris found several Cornwall youths assaulting their much younger and smaller cousin. It was just a matter of time before Staunis perished or hardened into a monster like his father. Either way, the choice was being made for him, as he was being forced to absorb ridiculous levels of cruelty—and it was escalating.

Slats creaked as Gaheris settled on the bed. The boy's face lit up when the Knight started, "Once upon a time, there was a wee fawn. He pranced in the meadows as sweet clovers swayed in the wind. The call of his mother sang for him to come home and...."

Gaheris slid down the bed frame, his long unruly hair preventing Ewain or Lamorac from seeing his face. After the boy drifted off to sleep, Gaheris quietly left the Infirmary.

As Ewain watched over the bed in which Staunis ever so gently snored and twitched in his sleep, metal clinked and herbs tickled his nose. "Let's get some tea in you," Lamorac said, urging Ewain toward the small kitchen and rest area set aside for the Infirmary staff.

"Aye," was all Ewain could say, still obsessing over what would likely be the boy's Fate.

Lamorac adjusted the lanterns and stopped next to another bed. Delilah had tripped on some ragged flagstone. Her mother, Nalinda Cuhlwch, had delivered the lass to the Infirmary that morning. Bruises and a split lip from the fall marred her pretty face. She would likely recover unscarred, but Ewain questioned the girl's purported clumsiness. Jormund gave similar reports for Bedwyr's injuries, which occurred with uncanny frequency but was hushed away as the boy's need for attention.

Lamorac rummaged through a cabinet for an extra quilt, which he tucked around Delilah.

On the way to the kitchen, Ewain glanced back at the two children and said to Lamorac, "Do you ever resent the family I cheated you out of?"

"Fate can't be cheated." Lamorac guided Ewain onto the lone couch, and he shuffled over to the hearth to stoke the fire. "Our futures were decided long before either of us could cheat the other out of anything."

Ewain scooted along the old sofa, mindful of the frayed threading in one armrest. He placed his hand on the table that served as the dining and draught prep area for the Infirmary. Stains splotched the wood. He picked at a purplish one he had personally been responsible for when starting his Healing Mastery.

"If you still feel so guilty, you can make it up for me," Lamorac said. "I'd like for you to agree to help me apprentice Brynn."

Ewain stopped scraping his nail over the stain. "Are you sure she's the student for you? You've never expressed interest in an Apprentice because you shy from letting many know of your absence of an Element."

"She has a lot of natural talent for Healing and would make the perfect Apprentice for me." Lamorac sighed and pulled the kettle from the hearth. "The only point of contention is that I can't teach her Elemental Healing. I'm hoping you can help with that, but only if you're willing to take on her training too."

"If it's what you desire most, then I'm in agreement," Ewain said, his voice strong. "Brynn has promise and it would be a waste to not engage her in the Healing arts."

Steam, rising in oblong swirls, rose from the misshapen clay mugs into which Lamorac poured the tea. He sipped the vanilla and lavender brew, saying, "Thank you. Otherwise, I would've had to ask Darna if he had any interest in assisting me with her." He snickered and added, "Fate would need to have a sick sense of humor to allow that to happen, don't you think?"

Ewain peered over the rim of the mug Lamorac handed him. "She's a twisted slag, isn't she?" He flexed his fingers over his mug. "I went to see Bedwyr."

Lamorac let out a faint groan. "I should have known you would after that epic departure he made. Was he still charged with acrimony?"

"Aye, Bedwyr is full of rage and bitterness. There is so much of Jormund in him now—and virtually nothing of what he was like before the Red and White Duels."

"You can't get back what you lost. And certainly not with Bedwyr."

Ewain bowed his head. "What hurts so much is that I squandered every decent opportunity I had with him. He begged me to take Olwen into my care."

Lamorac set his mug of tea on the end table on his side of the sofa and closed his fingers over the pale hands next to his. "You didn't have much say in the matter, did you?" After Ewain shook his head, Lamorac said, "Olwen was not your own. Jormund had full control of her."

"I should have offered to take the girls. We knew how little Jormund valued daughters. There was a chance I could have saved them both." Ewain's vision misted. "As I look at it now, there was a damned good chance."

"You were young, and the freshly titled Head of House Gore. You did what was best for your family." Lamorac squeezed Ewain's hands, the calluses from his sword training pulling against the other man's smoother skin. "Karen didn't reach out to you. You only had what Bedwyr said to guide you, and I can't imagine that being much help."

Ewain pulled away. "Karen was a shadow of herself. I let her convince me that her frail appearance was the result of the strain from her pregnancies. I should have paid closer attention to her, but I was too afraid of what I might find."

Rising from his seat, Lamorac said, "We all should have."

Ewain picked up a small book on the end table, which detailed the use of emollients for cuts and burns. Tracing a page's margins, he could not erase the shock of what had found its way to him on the floor in Bedwyr's chamber. There was no shaking off what The Seven Houses embraced to maintain their reputations. A deeper pain burned where an ancient Water symbol pendant rested over Ewain's sternum, the twin of another pendant that had been given to another Gorre by the last Water Marshal, Tobias Esau. Tobias had predicted a new Marshal would make Water burn anew with a dance of fire and ice unheard of across the Elements. It was not time for that one yet. Only one other in the East shared the same oath to see Water crest again.

"*The Books of Water* still exist," Ewain said, the taste of his words souring his tongue like a bitter draught. "The last one is in Bedwyr's library."

Mouth agape, Lamorac stilled. "Are you sure it was the last one?"

"Aye and I saw it my with my own eyes."

Lamorac groused, "Why is Bedwyr keeping the very information used to place those runes and Elemental arrays on him? It makes no sense why he hasn't tossed those books in a flaming hearth and turned the pages with a poker until the very last line was white ash."

Ewain motioned for Lamorac to sit, which he did. "I think I know the reason, and it's because Karen drew pictures on the pages and wrote on them too. My father was furious with her. Bunnies and ducklings everywhere, along with cute song lyrics and funny little messages in the margins. When my father tried to upbraid her, her doe eyes melted him and he couldn't punish her. He believed she shined light in a sea of darkness."

Lamorac snorted. "Did she know that the last book was a recipe for how to strip an Elemental—and an explanation of how to force an Element to change?"

"Certainly not when she was a child playing in the books. But in the end, she did." Ewain lowered his eyes. "In her last letter to me, Karen said that Jormund would kill her and use her blood to force Bedwyr's Element to change to Metal."

"When did you receive the letter?"

"After Bedwyr and Shiori staggered into our camp. We assumed they were war prisoners who'd escaped." Ewain tapped the tabletop as if counting the time. "Who would have guessed that Shiori had taught Bedwyr how to hunt and kill people like a savage? Thirteen of Jormund's and Uther's best men, dead and mutilated beyond recognition."

"Bedwyr freed them and told them they had nothing to fear from us. Of course we assumed he had betrayed us." Lamorac laughed cynically. "Ewain, it was a massacre—the likes of nothing I'd ever imagined."

No matter how hard he tried, Ewain could not forget every detail of what was left of the lined-up bodies upon his return. Bedwyr and Shiori had ripped out some of their victims' throats and boiled the others while they were still alive. Those unfortunate souls had popped and split open like overripe fruit beneath a swollen sun, their bodily fluids providing the only liquid for them to simmer in and ultimately explode. Thank Evermore that Bercylac and Gereant were there. They prevented anyone foolish enough to try to get between Shiori and Bedwyr, lest that person become a victim as well.

Lamorac recalled: "After we tended to Bedwyr's injuries, you journeyed to Gorre Retreat because of the arrays burned and carved onto him. You returned with the books to a reaping. We finally knew who had been culling Uther's and Jormund's men in droves."

"There's another part of this that tears at me to this day."

"And Bedwyr has opened that wound."

"Aye, he's opened it very wide." Ewain gripped Lamorac's hand. "Karen's letter arrived at Gorre Retreat the same day I returned. She begged me to help Olwen." He sobbed. "When I went to retrieve Olwen, Jormund had already killed her and Hamyll was imprisoned."

"You could not have done a thing to save them or keep Hamyll out of the dungeon."

"You're so wrong." Tremors raced along Ewain's shoulders, and his voice was weak as he rested his head against Lamorac's chest and sobbed some more. "I failed them all. Great-grandfather was on his deathbed when he demanded that someone from the Gorre family take the initiative to right the wrongs of The Seven Houses, and I vowed to fulfill that oath. Hells, what a joke that turned out to be. I can't even get Bedwyr to talk to me."

Lamorac kissed the side of Ewain's head. "What makes you so certain you haven't righted a lot already?"

Ewain pulled away. "I have righted nothing."

"You delivered *The Books of Water* to the one person who was supposed to have them." Lamorac lightly bucked his forehead against Ewain's. "It might not be you who rights the wrongs you have pledged to rectify, but it could be you who gives another the chance."

CHAPTER 83

A Kulning Lullaby

Lupine silhouettes slid across the floor as if they were loping over an icy tundra. Lumistones flickered, sending red-and-orange light knifing through the dancing figures. From the fireplace, Sitka spruce popped. As the bouquet of its fragrant dry sap seeped into the chamber, it mixed with the acrid tang of sulphur and char.

Boots echoed in the hall outside her room as the imaginary wolves continued to dart over the flagstone.

Bang! Bang!

A rough voice violated the heavy wood doors as aggressively as the knocks preceding it: "Lord Vulgate requests an audience, Milady."

The woman contemplated the stone relief of Vulgate's Vault that hung on the wall, the masterfully carved panel inlaid with obsidian, agate, and gypsum from the largest volcano in the duchy. She'd often said that if this artwork was located anywhere else but her prison, she would find it beautiful.

She adjusted her crown, tucking loose hairs under the braids common to the Bachs and Danuskes. Smoothing her countenance into the blank expression she had learned in her father's Court, Queen Anya Pendragon locked her gaze on the doorway and commanded: "Enter."

The door creaked open and two men in heavy boots marched toward her with a rickety brindle greyhound following behind the Lord of Vulgate's Vault. The younger of the duo kept his attention on Lord Agravaine Vulgate and not her. Appraising his arrogance and poor Court manner in the presence of Royalty, even if she was deposed, Anya noted the unmistakable Pendragon jawline.

She turned to the smirk filling Lord Vulgate's face, immediately drawn to the long three-line cuts breaking the right side of his black hair. No amount of tinctures could heal where Anya had ripped into him in the beginning of her imprisonment. A closer look at Agravaine's eyes revealed a weariness, even as he set his hand on the greatest source of his shame to the Vulgate name. The old dog arched his head into his master's touch, cloudy brown eyes as devoted and trusting as when Agravaine stoutly refused to put a crossbow bolt between his beloved pet's eyes to claim his manhood as a Vulgate man.

Giving a slow turn of her head from one man to the other, Anya said to the Lord of Vulgate's Vault, "Well, Agravaine, don't hold me in suspense any longer."

He bowed, his fire-bright orange gaze piercing in their intensity. "Wouldn't dream of keeping you in suspense, Milady."

"Then why are you and your newest monkey here? Stand up straight now, little monkeys. Fly for your Queen."

Both men clenched their jaws and Agravaine laughed derisively, "Ah, Milady, we're hardly here to entertain you." He turned to the other man. "I'm honored to introduce you to your nephew, Mordred Pendragon."

"Nephew, you say? He appears rather wanting, just like his grandfather."

"Don't speak ill of your father." Agravaine lifted his hand, offering it to her. "You'll show King Uther and his name some respect."

"I'll do no such thing." Anya presented her cheek for him, all too aware of the violence that his father and his Twilight-kissed elder brothers enjoyed doling out indiscriminately, and especially to women. But she knew how to nick him where it hurt the most. "Why don't you hit me, Milord? Your Jotnar maid comes tomorrow morn—and she will see the bruise on me."

Horror flared across his face.

"I shan't lie when she asks." Anya made a show of licking her lips. "Your little band of traitors might have cleverly removed me from my House, but if she knows what is really going on, imagine the opportunities that will open up for my return." She licked her lips again. "And what I shall do upon that happening."

The fear and hurt in his eyes secured her victory in this little bout of repartee, but her success would be pyrrhic. He would nurse himself to temporary oblivion via a few bottles of fire wine as the portrait of his father loomed over his desk and glowered at him. Third born, and the shame of Vulgate's Vault for not having the same insatiable appetite for blood and women as the men in his family, Agravaine was the Lord of his House by default. A few cousins even came before him in his father's pecking order, but their reaching an early Twilight in Uther's and Arthwyr's War required Agravaine to be handed the title.

"If I'm going to lose my favourite prisoner, it will be because I had a far happier end with her," he said, intimating affection that had since grown stale from her. He surprised her by pointing to the old marks. "As you can see, Mordred, your aunt has been a real prize. And a feisty one, at that."

Mordred made a grotesque smile and remarked, "*'Has been?'* My apologies, Auntie Anya, but you've outlived your usefulness, it seems." Mordred straightened. "When shall we schedule her execution, Lord Vulgate? No use continuing to feed her if she's not going to offer anything of value in return."

Agravaine blinked and looked past the younger man to Anya. He would shield her, and even free her, if need be, long before anyone seriously entertained that possibility. However, Mordred's sinister attitude gave Agravaine considerable pause, so he said, "Although your enthusiasm is inspiring, my future King, we can ill afford the Bachs and Danuskes becoming unruly. They will not strike when we have their Queen."

"But they don't aid us, either. Would threatening her not force them under our yoke?"

"They won't bend to intimidation, even if we execute her." Agravaine rubbed the scars where Anya had scratched him. "They made that clear when we killed her daughter and sent the corpse back to them."

"How was that, Lord Vulgate?"

"They carved up the little girl, used her ribs and lungs to make wings on her back, and returned her with a message taped to her skinned skull: *We transformed something worthless into something honorable. Just try and do the same to our Queen.*" Agravaine grimaced and pointed at Anya. "This twisted slag laughed and praised it as art—worthy of royalty."

Anya chuckled ruefully, refusing to show the slightest tinge of sorrow, which ran so deep that she wanted to personally cut out the Foel Lord's heart who murdered her little girl. One of those blasted triplets—Dub or Dother—had murdered her daughter and Dain, the youngest of that thrice-cursed pack, ferried her body back and forth. The veiled message—her husband, Talisen Bach, had notched in their girl's ribs—was gut-wrenchingly clear to Anya: *I'm sorry. So sorry. Please forgive me.*

Committed to perpetuating the ruse until the time would come when she could savour her revenge, Anya said, "It was the truest form of art. My darling daughter found a higher purpose."

Mordred scoffed, "How utterly inspiring. I'll make certain your head drops right after my father's hits the basket so you both can serve a higher purpose together."

No other Pendragon had ever reminded her so much of Uther. It made her loath Mordred all the more, and it brought her joy in rattling him. "Saving the best for last?"

"It's so nice to be understood." Mordred bowed and kissed her hand. "I look forward to having a beautiful relationship with you until the very end, Auntie Anya."

"Aren't you a darling?" she said in her best Rheged drawl.

Mordred's blank stare revealed he was too far removed from the nobility to have met Blanche, the current Rheged matron who spoke in an identical manner.

"We'll be the best of friends till the end." Anya pinched his cheek. "I can't wait to dote on my new favourite nephew."

Agravaine grabbed Mordred by the arm and hauled him toward the door, saying on the way, "Mind your clever words, Milord. She's a wolf in sheep's wool. As soon as you turn your head, she'll go for your throat. Smeeg, come!"

The greyhound licked her hand—foolish as it was to trust her. Yet, as cold as she was, she could not bring herself to strike him. Wagging his tail lethargically, the dog slipped past Agravaine and Mordred to the hallway outside of her chamber.

Mordred tipped her a salute and added the double wink that was pure Pendragon.

"Toodles, dearest nephew," she hollered. "Don't let the Fomoiri bite you—especially if the wolves are there first."

The door to her chamber slammed, and she listened for their footfalls to fade and counted, "*Eins, Zwei, Drei, Vier, Funf…*"

When Anya was certain they wouldn't disturb her again, she dipped her hand under the neck of her robe. Glass clinked as she pulled out the necklace her husband, Talisen, had given her for their Bonding Ceremony. Anya ran her fingers over lupine-shaped pieces of sea glass and lingered on the ones meant to symbolize the two of them, which were blue like the sea yet worn on the edges to be emblematic of wearing away but never yielding to the endless roll of the tides.

The breakers on her wrists might have defeated her Metal, but nothing could take her crown other than the cold grip of Twilight. The Bach Crown was hers, and none dared touch it except a Bach Royal. Not when dire consequences followed any fool brazen enough to lay hands on the surface. One of her enemies learned his lesson of doom as he fell foaming at the mouth and vomiting his life onto the floor.

"You're mine, poison and all," Anya said to her diadem as she massaged the lupine carvings configured within its design. "Never will anyone know you were boiled in wolfsbane and the blood of the Bachs. And because my blood is included, I'm now as much yours as you are mine."

She went outside on her balcony, the lava flow in the distance lighting up Vulgate's Vault, the sight accentuated by the occasional flames shooting high into the sky from the mouth of the volcano, as if the maw was birthing living beings.

Coughing while taking in the heavy air that was coming her way as the wind shifted, Anya turned her back to the volcano and ran her hand over her forehead. On a far ridge, the sitka forest waited like a clandestine lover for a Bond who had been away too long. At night, she pretended that the branches were not skeletal fingers reaching for the sky but the gentle fingers of her Bond instead. She found it easy to make believe in the dark, as some things remain shrouded even from the moon.

Anya stepped to the railing, the distance to the ground much too high to consider escaping this way, and she placed her hands to her mouth. This high up, her voice traveled like a herald's from atop a church spire. The lilt she sang was what Talisen's mother had taught her.

"Close your eyes and listen," her mother-in-law had whispered, holding out a handful of grain for a cow. "Hear the wolves, dear?"

"That's not a wolf, Freya," Anya said, observing a girl calling in the cows. "It's Ylva, kulning."

"Ah, but who began kulning?"

"Farmers and herders."

"Oh, you sweet fool." Freya crinkled the tanned skin around her gray eyes. "Anya-pup, it was the wolf. It is Fenris's gift to his chosen children. We call our herds home, but we first learned to call each other. Kulning to us is like wolves worshipping the moon. It's how we thank our God, but it's also how we communicate in private."

Anya stepped in front of a lantern hanging on the wall behind her. The light penetrated the sea glass in her crown and cast wolves into the night sky. *See me. I'm here.*

As if it were the aurora borealis, a ribbon of light blazed above the sitka forest. Anya intermittently paced back and forth in front of the lantern, sending an ethereal message: *Hello, Talisen, my dear husband.* The light on the other side spook back: *Hello, my Queen.*

CHAPTER 84
THE ARCHITECTS

Three sweaty, teen-seasoned, tired children ambled into The Chamber of the Eclipse. As Bedwyr skulked past the slow-moving trio, Viera smothered the urge to stick out her foot. Consequences be damned! As if sensing their relief working in the stables, Arthwyr had upgraded them to working the abandoned stable on the eastern end of the castle, citing the main stable as a warm-up. Included was Bedwyr chaperoning them, and aside from helping an injured rabbit and her kits from an accident in the accursed stable, he was a merciless slave driver.

Bedwyr slumped into his seat next to Dagonet, dumping an armload of papers with magic squares and *Luo Shu* diagrams he had been working his way through as he minded Viera and her friends onto the empty chair beside him, which was designated for the Marshal, who, as always, wasn't in attendance. Laying his arms on the round table, Bedwyr dropped his chin over his forearms and closed his eyelids, his breathing slowing into the deceptive calm of sleep.

Shuffling over to him, Viera muttered in his ear, "Sleeping Beauty, you are not."

Bedwyr grunted, peeked up, and made a vulgar hand signal. Viera coyly turned so that no one but the grumpy Knight could see her, and she returned the gesture.

Viera focused on the others sitting around the table. Something good must have come about for the Saracens, as both Safir and Segwarides sported large grins.

Safir loomed over his younger sibling. "Congratulations. We have found you a Master."

Jumping up from his chair, Palamedes cried out, "I'm already set to take my Air test! I'm able to pass it just as I am!"

Segwarides shook his head. "Oh, no, littlest brother, you are not. That test determines knowledge. For someone in Evermore, if they pass it, they are not required to redo their lessons or become a Master."

Added Safir, "There are different requirement when you are assigned a Master. Everything is more intense." He cracked a grin that made him appear years younger than his twenty-eight seasons. "You'll see."

Arthwyr plucked a scroll from the table and showed it to the lad. "Only the head of your household can determine whether or not you're apprenticed. Safir just had to make the decision. I would have gotten to you sooner, but we've, ah… been kind of busy lately." At that remark, several Knights squirmed around in their chairs.

Safir accepted the offered scroll and unrolled it. "Congratulations, baby brother," he said, rolling it back up and tapping it over Palamedes' head. "It's royal decree. I've whored you out and made sure it was legal. No running from this. You'll accept the Master you are given."

Behind them, the door opened and fancy slippers padded over the stone floor.

Voice husky, Eerie purred, "My King, I'm here for my new Apprentice."

"Perfect timing, as ever, my dear." Arthwyr gave her a big hug.

Eerie paced behind Palamedes like a sleek cat scoping out an injured bird. She stopped at Safir's chair. "I accept Palamedes Sasania under my tutelage, Lord Sasania."

Palamedes straightened his shoulders, and he set his jaw in a stiff line that diminished the curve of his face. "What if I say no?"

Eerie spun toward the boy. Air whistled through the chamber and lifted her flowing skirts. Her voice shifted from a husky throb to a harsh growl, and her purplish-red eyes turned black. "You have no choice in Fate."

The sigils bordering the table glowed blue. A dish of lumistones cast a bright light that streaked straight up, and red apples in a wooden bowl turned silver.

The table vibrated and the top started to spin violently, sending Bedwyr flying into the Marshal's chair, which skidded backwards until its legs caught on the stone and flipped on its side, tossing Bedwyr on his head.

Viera stumbled into Gavyn, who said, "Who knew the ruddy tabletop could move?"

Aglovale wheezed, "Never has in all my years sitting here."

Staggering up from the floor, Bedwyr snarled, "And it won't do it again in all your remaining years."

Bedwyr slid his katana from its sheath. Hopping onto the table, he settled upon the middle. Sparks launched upward from the wood, and Bedwyr's hair puffed out around him.

Bors, who had fallen on his arse, began laughing and pointing at Bedwyr. "Didn't know you people got like that!"

"Shut up, Bors!" Bedwyr shouted as the tabletop spun some more. "You were white like the rest of us when Lionel conjured up those feckin' golems!"

The silver apples scattered around the table like marbles. One rolled under Bedwyr's boot, and he crashed belly down onto the table. His katana flew across the room and lodged into a spare chair that was placed against the wall.

Trying to dig his dagger into the tabletop but having no success, Bedwyr yelled, "I hate this bloody thing!"

As if in objection, the round table of The Knights of the Eclipse belched a gray cloud of smoke that covered Bedwyr, and it quit spinning. A flash of light shot out from the gloom, and the map of the Evermore that was always on the table went black before returning to its normal colors. When the dust settled, the back of Bedwyr's robe was coated with something akin to tar.

Bedwyr spat out dust as electricity snapped and crackled from the black puff that would someday be his hair again. "First bloody feckin' rugs and now the bloody feckin' table. I should not have gotten up this morning." Smacking the tabletop, he glared at it. His rant ended as he ran his fingers over the map, and in a subdued tone he muttered, "Avalon."

Viera went to the table and leaned in next to Bedwyr. The word *Avalon* appeared where Elden's Hearth had been written, the letters shimmering in a silvery blue light. Air stirred Viera's hair as Arthwyr reached past her and flicked aside a silver apple. Myrddin and Lance stood over the new name on the map as the other Knights crowded around as well, each man eager to sate his curiosity.

Arthwyr brushed his fingers over the lettering. He jolted backwards when the name shimmied and melded into the map. He looked to Eerie. "What does it mean?"

"All I know is, Balance is nigh." She placed her hand on Palamedes' shoulder.

"What's that got to do with me?" Palamedes asked.

"You were Divined to be my Apprentice when you took your first breath, little Prince." Eerie straightened, her eyes now clear and bright. "The pieces are gathering, Palamedes, and you will be an Architect like your mother."

Palamedes stared at her. "How do you know?"

"Your part in the grand design of our realm was decided when you were born."

Looking dumfounded, Palamedes asked, "What's an Architect?"

"In Saraceni, Architects make or break empires. Our mother broke her first husband's rule and made the Sasania Empire hers." Safir pulled Palamedes into a hug. "That's the greatness of Architects. Their names become part of time immemorial. To be known as one is our highest honor."

Arthwyr clapped Palamedes' back. "You shall become something great, Son."

Segwarides challenged the King's remark: "He won't *become* anything, Arthwyr."

The King gave the Saracen a rather uncomfortable look. "I don't understand."

"One does not become an Architect." Huffing a laugh, Segwarides tousled Palamedes' hair. "One can only be born that way."

Fate reared deep across Alkebula and into the middle month of Agosti. In the Sasania Caravan, Alibaba Sasania's day was like many that preceded it. At nineteen seasons, it was his responsibility to run the monkeys and birds through their tricks, brush their mounts, and feed and water the animals.

After carrying water for his mother, she directed him to mash chickpeas and returned to reading a letter.

"Is that from my cousins, Mâmân?" he asked.

She nodded, her expression softening. "Your cousin, Palamedes, is an Architect. Safir performed the rituals and Palamedes passed every test. There hasn't been one since your Auntie Cehrazad, may Allah ever smile upon her. How wonderful one arises so soon in our family."

"May Allah ever smile upon our family." He snuck several nuts into his mouth until his round cheeks bulged.

"You'll always be special to your—" Mâmân continued, as she caught him, "Ali, you little monkey!"

Ali ducked the snap of her towel and just avoided running into Marjanah as she rounded the wagon. Beneath the silvery veil covering her olive skin, a glow filled her violet eyes.

He hooked his arm into hers and spun her from Mâmân's scolding. Tugging Marjanah's diaphanous indigo sleeve, he asked, "Want to come with me into town for supplies?"

Marjanah giggled. "As long as I get a treat."

Sharp whistles pierced the air as Janus joined them, juggling three bags. Pale splotches dotted his dark skin from his palms to the middle of his forearms. His grin revealed gold crowns tipping his incisors and stretched the mirrored lighter patches of skin around his eyes and cheeks. "Here ya go, Ali," he said, tossing a bag of rupees into Ali's hands. "Try not to waste it all on sweets or Sinbad will have you dancing from his fire whip."

After placing the final order for supplies a few hours later, Ali slid the money pouch into his pocket. His gaze lifted to the sun and he calculated it was early afternoon. He rejoined Marjanah leaning over an empty fountain in the town square. A nearby stall hosted streamers as he guided her to it and said, "Yours could use a new addition."

"I'll need some for the bangles and necklace my mother gave me." Marjanah jiggled the gold bracelets on her wrists. "My bride price for that husband I'm soon getting."

"You're fifteen springs, Marjanah," Ali said slowly. "One more year and you can marry."

"My mother says to choose wisely the man I give them to."

As he was about to ask her what she valued in a Bond, Ali shuffled around the side of the stall and gaped at his aunt, Cehrazad Sasania. His dead aunt.

When his aunt slipped around the stall's corner, he gave chase to the specter, ignoring Marjanah's frantic bemused cries. At last, he drew up short in an empty alley and next to a stall with a wooden counter.

Marjanah arrived and asked, "Ali, what are you doing?"

The smell hit Ali as a small hand caught his shoulder. He stared at flashing teeth and into wide glowing eyes. Loud squalls announced a cage crammed with at least thirty of the creatures.

The stall merchant slapped a hand on the counter. "Silence, you stinking lemurs!"

Ali locked gazes with the one holding him. "How much for one?" he asked.

"Three rupees a piece."

Ali handed over the money. "This one."

The man ripped out the creature, and threw it over the counter. As he drew a bloodstained knife, Ali swept the animal into his arms and hollered, "What are you doing?"

The merchant blinked. "Don't you want to eat it?"

Marjanah screeched to rival the animals. "Ali, do something!"

Another animal stuck its hand through the wire and grasped for the one in Ali's arms. The other flailed its hand toward the cage. With a shiver sliding up his spine, Ali realized they were Soul Bonded. He passed the one he bought to Marjanah and counted through the money over and over with the same result. Not enough for them all. At least until Marjanah thrust her golden bangles and necklace into his hands.

Ali tried to return them. "I can't ask you for your bride price, Marjanah."

She stamped her foot. "It's not for you. It's for them. I'll never speak to you again if you don't come back with all of them, Alibaba Sasania!"

That night, Ali sat still as stone as his older brother, Sinbad, stomped up to him and crossed his thick black arms over his broad chest.

"What possessed you, Ali?" Sinbad hissed, his Fire pluming in a cloud from his nostrils.

Gulping, Ali said, "These creatures can be as good as the monkeys and birds, Sindhi."

Sinbad roared, "Dreamers don't keep us fed, Ali! Get your head out of the sky."

"So, I can be like our father?" Orange shimmered around Ali as his Air crackled from his temper. "The same man who murdered Auntie Cehrazad and you're hellbent on becoming!"

Sinbad's features fell. "Someone has to grow up, Ali. We can't all be like you, her, and Palamedes." He strode from the fire. "They go back, Ali. I'll talk to the merchant."

Jingling brought Ali's gaze to the solemn figure across from him. "I'm sorry, Marjanah," he said. "I lost your bride price for nothing."

Marjanah smoothed her nails over the cooing animal in her arms. "You kept your promise." She bent and her kiss warmed Ali's forehead. "Thank you, my Husband-to-be."

Gob smacked, he sputtered, "Nay, Marjanah. I lost your bride price."

Marjanah said, "My Baba's going to kill you, but he knows I am always right about this. You already are the husband I deserve and want to call mine."

She skipped over to several girls decked in saris and kaftans as they hovered next to a nearby wagon. Her friends shrieked and clapped, Janus joining them as he shouted, "Milady, let me look at the bejangle he put on your wedding gift! Oh, look at that tail!"

The troupe disappeared in a flutter of dupattas and silks around the wagon.

An hour later, Sinbad returned and set down a second cage full of the animals. He wagged his finger at Ali and said, "You better be up at the arse crack of dawn before it cracks to train them, Ali." He flopped next to the cage and added, "There's a merchant missing his eyebrows. Strange when they combust like that. We move on tomorrow."

Breaking into braying laughter, Ali picked up the second cage. "Welcome to your new home, little lemons. You're going to love being with us."

Sinbad groaned and stalked away. "For Allah's sake, they're lemurs, not lemons. You could at least learn what they're called as you throw away our rupees on them."

Ali perched a lemur in his lap. As a breeze stirred his hair, he spied the kohl-lined stare of his aunt on the other side of the fire. *Auntie*, he mused, *what brings you here now?*

Her rouge-stained lips pulled into a smile as she said, "My Architect has arisen."

You mean Palamedes, he thought.

The wind whispered, "Whoever said there was just one when those in Sasania Bond true?"

Several shadows crossed the space next to the fire pit. Stinging sand blurred Ali's vision and his aunt was gone. The sand stirred into Cehrazad Sasania's voice murmuring, "Once upon a time, Ali, a series of happenings led to the most wondrous of journeys."

CHAPTER 85

DESCENT OF DARKNESS

Viera had just returned to the castle after spending several days touring the Temples of the Elements. She found all of them enjoyable to visit, but Earth was by far her favourite. Even though Fire was her Element, Earth pertained to her upbringing with her Mum and Da and brother on their farm outside Iyesgarth, and she relished anything that brought back memories of her family back home. Though there was something that called to her when it came to the statues of the first Marshals, specifically those of Pembroke in the Earth Temple and Windsor in the Air Temple. At her first glimpse of them, her feet moved as if on their own to stop in front of them, her eyes drawn to their serene features. For a moment, she swore their eyes met hers and the smiles on their lips were for her. It brought a warmth in her stomach akin to when Dottsie or Mayor Senan would indulge her antics. They reminded her so of them that before she left both Temples she paid a quick visit to the statues and whispered, 'Fare thee well', feeling a sense of approval long after she returned to the castle.

On the other hand, the bitter cold within the Ice Temple was a far cry from the temperature in the abandoned stable. She'd jump at the chance for another tour of the Ice Temple if it meant escaping the oppressive heat in this decrepit structure, not helped by the humidity that hung thick and heavy in the dusty air because of a recent rain.

Sweat stung Viera's eyes, and she wiped her shirtsleeve over her forehead. Choking, she blinked past the heat rising from the dirt floor and bringing more dust with it. *Dear Evermore, why did it have to rain earlier? It's so damned muggy in here!*

Viera tossed a scrap of wood aside, finding pleasure in the thunk it made on some broken boards that were scattered against a wall. A burgundy stain flickered in a ray of sunlight that burst through a hole in the roof. "Ugh. Who knew a little bunny would bleed so much?" she said to herself, only cheered over Bedwyr housing the rabbit and her kits in his chamber.

Viera bent backwards and stretched her muscles. She settled her gaze on the splintered planks that made up the steps to the loft in the old structure, the perilous incline emblematic of the entire building's condition, which should have been razed long ago.

Viera cursed Bedwyr for not canceling when Palamedes and Maerna had been summoned for Air lessons and grammar lessons respectively. One "victim" was all he needed to satisfy him, though he'd penned the other two in for later. Bloody sadist.

Luo Shu diagrams and magic squares were tossed on the dirt floor and spread out on Bedwyr's lap, and the soft snores coming from where he reclined in a ratty chair more than hinted at his lack of interest. She arched an eyebrow at him, chewing on her lip as she pondered sneaking off. Palamedes had attempted it once, and it surprised her at how fast Bedwyr awakened and pulled the boy back to the stall he'd been cleaning—the Saracen receiving extra duty because of his failed escape.

Knocking startled her as Constantine and Ewain stood in the doorway. "It's noon," Ewain said, "We're grabbing some lunch with Bercylac and Galahad and thought we'd bring yours."

Viera jutted her thumb at Bedwyr. "I'll eat whatever he's eating."

"Rice and laverbread then."

She shuddered. "Whatever you're having."

Ewain laughed. "Fair enough. We'll be back."

After they left, Viera explored a nearby stall. She came to a section of stalls with the walls between them removed to create a large storage area. Next to some old rusted bridles, bits, and cracked leather harnesses, she spied a black rune partially covered by a rotted wooden plank. Viera tugged on it, assuming by its appearance that the board would easily break apart or come free, but she couldn't shatter it or dislodge it. She cleaned it off with her hands and discovered a small piece of wood—covered with dirt and moss—wedged against the plank and helping to hold it in place.

A sharp yank pulled it loose, and she ran her fingers over a symbol on the wedge. It was like a sigil she'd seen, but she couldn't remember where. The wood's finish was shiny except for black flakes of caked-on dirt that obscured some of the image's design.

Viera whetted her fingers with her tongue and rubbed the symbol. This made it worse, the grime becoming soft and slick and viscid. She tried to scratch through it, but her bitten-down fingernails made this a lost cause.

Frustrated, she rapidly rubbed her palm back and forth over the board, only to screech when a long splinter buried itself deep into her soft flesh. Through her tears, Viera plucked out the knifelike shard and gasped as her blood made large splotches as it dripped on a piece of wood next to her leg.

She made a fist and blood pooled in her hand. A shudder swept through her. This was no minor cut, and she would need a Healer. Keeping her arm elevated didn't seem to help, as there was so much blood flowing that she could squish it with her fingers. She started to wrap her hand in the hem of her tunic when she noticed sigils from all The Seven Elements sliding from her palm, flickering over her wrist, and levitating.

As soon as they reconstituted themselves in the air, they merged into black arrays. Low mutterings she couldn't make out rose in volume until her ears popped from the pressure building inside them. As her blood covered the sigil on the wood, it began to pulse and form a symbol Viera recognized as the same one carved into Bedwyr's shoulder.

Viera threw the board at the wall, but it stopped midflight and joined the glittering pulses of the other Elemental patterns. Together, all the arrays flew into the rafters, the stench of scorched flesh saturating the air along with the gagging smell of rotted meat.

Viera stood paralyzed as the arrays spilled blackened blood down the walls. The wood throbbed—growing darker with each pulsation—the walls drawing in and flaring out like the steady heave of lungs in a giant animal.

"What have you done?" Bedwyr yelled as he rushed into the storage room, his arm shaking as he held the hilt of his katana. "Hells, Viera! What did you do?"

The metallic taste of blood filled the air. Like a curtain of cascading water, crimson rivulets flowed over the wood. Viera scrambled to Bedwyr. "I cut myself on a board. What is this? What's happening?"

Bedwyr threw her toward the doorway. "Fomoiri."

She stumbled. "Those aren't real."

He dragged her upright and shoved her toward the front entrance. "Wrong."

The boards in front of them lit up, a subtle growl hissing into a loud screech. The door banged back-and-forth, and pitch-black streaks poured from an array carved into the wall. Viera was thrown backwards, but Bedwyr broke her fall and shoved her behind him. Black tendrils lashed out, and the appendages wrapped around her arm. "Let me go!" Viera screamed as she was pulled toward total darkness in the middle of the room.

Bedwyr slashed his hand and drew his blood into several crosses over her limbs and forehead. A harrowing squeal erupted from the dark, and the tendrils dissolved into their own shadows. He sketched another cross on his own forehead.

The old wood creaked as the walls dripped more blood and sucked in air. Ebony fire erupted from the center of the room and lines of soot swept outward and onto the dirt floor.

Viera grabbed Bedwyr's hand. "What's happening?"

"It's here."

Viera jerked upward, inhaling freezing air as a figure materialized from a pitch-black cloud. Black bones and horns split from the creature's skull, twisting above its head like dead tree branches. Piercing red orbs glowed and seemed to swim in the depths of the eye sockets. A jagged smile twisted across its face, and its sharp teeth looked as though they could slice through metal.

It made a step toward Viera, when a vision flashed in front of it, her view of the creature blocked as burgundy and gray robes snapped around it. The dirt floor began to crack like ice breaking apart on a lake, blocks of the hard soil glistening as if frost-coated.

Viera caught a glimpse of the back of a man with chestnut hair. The sight of the other quickly vanished, the creature taking his place and appearing more vibrant than ever.

Bedwyr pulled Viera behind him and shouted, "Hamyll, what's going on?"

The creature flicked out its hand and black nails morphed into sickle-sized talons. Through a raspy voice, it said, "Get her out of here, Bedwyr. Protect what's mine."

"I'm protecting her, but not because of what you think might be yours, oh Great Lord Fire Marshal." Bedwyr added an exaggerated bow and shoved Viera up the steps.

"Are we safe now?" Viera asked, shaking all over.

"Far from it. But Fomoiri don't like Constantine's religion. Draw crosses."

Vibrations threatened to shake the old stable apart. She spied Hamyll slashing at a shadow darting into the bloody wall. Clawed hands burst from the center of another array, and a squealing rat was dragged into the abyss. Bones crunched and earsplitting shrieks had Viera covering her ears. As Hamyll lunged from the center of the array, another creature bounded out and slammed him into a support.

Wood exploded, and a startled Viera fell to the ground. She froze as a pair of broken garden shears flew toward her. Bedwyr gripped her ankle and yanked her backwards, pressing her sharply down into the stairs and under his body.

Twang. She stared at the steel blades as they reverberated in the exact place where her head had been seconds earlier.

Bedwyr dragged her upright. "Don't stop drawing crosses."

Wrenching the shears from the wall, Viera bolted the rest of the way to the loft. Her hands shook as she used the blades to etch a cross into the walls.

A long scream sent her heart hammering against her chest.

Spinning on her heels, she shrieked. Bedwyr was prone on the floor and black talons pierced his leg. Dark blood seeped around the clawed hand; the arrays carved into his skin lit up. Trying anything, he dug his heels into the wooden slats to stop from being pulled down the stairs, but any relief from being yanked down was short-lived.

Bedwyr canted his chin toward the open loft doors. "Jump."

Viera pushed up her sleeves and screamed, "Tilly, come!"

A small sparrow circled above her, quickly transforming into a flurry of black and purple multicolored feathery flames. Diving, the phoenix brushed the length of Bedwyr's body and attacked the offending Fomoiri.

Boom! Two skeletal figures clashed below. Liquid bubbled and sprayed in the wake of talons penetrating the carapace of one of the creatures and tossed the second into a wall. The winning beast fixed its red stare swimming with blue on Viera, and said, "I'm one of them. Run, Princess."

Viera whined her protest, instinct urging her to help him.

The Fomoiri flashed his white teeth. "It can't hurt me. We'll meet again."

"Not anytime soon," said Bedwyr as he scrambled to his feet, limping as he drew the last crosses. "She's not yours yet, Hamyll. You promised."

"You can't stop Fate."

Bedwyr leaned out the open loft. "That's what you think."

Viera's pulse pounded in her throat as Bedwyr slid his arm under her knees. He hefted her into a bridal carry and cradled her against him.

When he brought his face closer, shivers slid through her. *Oh, Evermore, you're not going to kiss me! I should have let the shadows take you!*

His breath warmed her cheek, but he did nothing except to thrust her into the sunlight as clean air whistled in her ears and the wind whipped her hair. Bedwyr said, "Tuck and roll," and gravity took hold as Viera plummeted into a pair of arms covered in black cloth. Constantine carried her away before gently lowering her to the grass. Ewain, Bercylac, and Galahad rushed past them to the stable, their Water and Ice flowing ahead of them. Bedwyr lunged out the window with Tilly shooting over him, twin geysers slowing his descent as he hit the ground with a sharp crack and rolled head over heels.

Bercylac asked Viera if she was hurt, and she showed him her ripped palm. He applied balm and a bandage, and as soon as he finished, she tore away from him and went to Bedwyr. As her knees slammed the turf, she wrapped her arms around him. Pulling him into a fierce embrace, she squealed, "You feckin' idiot!"

With sobs racking her body, she buried her face in his robes and tightened her fingers around his cowl. Bedwyr gripped her shoulders, and she blubbered, "Don't you dare!"

He squeezed her tight against him. "You're safe, Suzume."

He called me Suzume, and the Hamyll creature called me Princess. They're both crazy!

"We need to check you over," Ewain said to Bedwyr as he probed the Knight's injured leg. "I heard a crack."

Ewain busied himself healing the claw marks, his eyes narrowing as he gingerly ran his fingers over them. "Aunt Saris, will need to examine these," he said, digging through his pockets and producing a tincture that had Bedwyr wincing and twisting away from it when it was applied. "Perhaps, Lady Blanche or—" gulping Ewain screwed the lid back on at the black oozing from the wounds— "Lady Foxbury or Lady Yuliya Blumenthal..."

Bedwyr sneered, "Cause they're more cunning than you are?"

Ewain thinned his lips and said lowly, "In this, they are."

The two exchanged a long look before Bedwyr faced away and grumbled, "If there's a break, you can at least heal that, right?"

Viera pressed her shoulder against Bedwyr. "Lucky bastard," Ewain said, after green light washed over Bedwyr's ankle. "It's a sprain."

Tilly trilled, and the grass whiffled from her wings as she flew just near enough to singe it yellow.

Bedwyr snorted. "Blackened Chicken." Tilly landed on his shoulder and fanned her flickering tail feathers over his back.

"Of course," Bercylac said, "you would mock the greatest of creatures."

Constantine crouched in front of Viera. Tilting her chin up, he tapped the dried blood on her forehead. "Crucifix?"

"We really should tighten our borders against foreign invaders," Bedwyr deadpanned. "Strange how they show up out of nowhere."

Constantine pushed aside a long patch of Bedwyr's unruly hair to reveal a crucifix drawn on his forehead. "It breeds like a bunny, doesn't it, Usagi-kun?"

"Tsk." Bedwyr wrenched back from the priest's hand. "Fomoiri don't like your God. A cross seemed like a good idea at the time."

"Bless your heart," Constantine said, rising and marching toward the stable.

Galahad scrambled after the priest. "Don't, Father. The Fomoiri might take you."

"Not today." Crimson arrays swarmed around Constantine.

Fire shot from the arrays and boards sparked. Dry wood crackled until flames spread as if through kindling. Ewain and Bercylac joined the others watching the plumes of smoke shooting from the stable. Screeches rang and ebony figures contorted as the structure blazed away.

Ice squeezed Viera's heart and she pushed herself to her feet. "No! Hamyll!"

Bedwyr grabbed her arm, forcing her to kneel. He coaxed her forehead against his shoulder. "Hamyll is fine," he murmured. "He's long gone from that stable. Of course, that was after he finished with the Fomoiri."

Viera retreated enough to peer at his face. "What did he do to the Fomoiri?"

Flashing his teeth into a smile that mimicked Hamyll's, Bedwyr met her eyes. "What we do with all livestock. He ate it."

CHAPTER 86

NEW HOMES

A loud bang echoed in the new stable that replaced the one Constantine had incinerated. Bedwyr rolled his gaze upward and inhaled the scent of fresh-cut timber infusing the air in the structure. Not a board from the old stable remained. Even the soil around it was saturated with purified water sanctified by Runemasters and Ancients. Guinevere had placed Bedwyr in charge, following her awareness that Arthwyr had sneakily tried to punish Bedwyr with chaperoning duty. To add insult to burn, the Foxburys were placed under his purview after they added some additions to a certain painting.

Gavyn and Garyth grumbled, and Bedwyr focused on Gaheris, who said little and kept his distance from his brothers. Most curious and Bedwyr wagered he was up to something.

"Feck!" Gavyn hollered and jerked a saw through a board as sweat poured down his face.

Bedwyr laughed and inspected the progress on the new structure for keeping the bunnies safe from Isolde and her ilk. A growl burred from Gavyn and he set down his saw. "What's the story with this anyway?"

"This will give our Ladies-in-Waiting space for gentler livestock." Bedwyr picked up the placard on the table next to him. In children's script, *Karen's Hutch* in blue graced the sun-yellow wood. *Karen's Hutch* was a tribute to his mother, but Bedwyr wasn't going to talk about this now, as this was a happy time and not one for sorrow.

Said Gavyn, "In the arena of not-so-gentle animals, it will be interesting to see how Viera takes to the more powerful steeds. Carydoc has Daegyn teaching her better horsemanship."

Garyth laid a board atop the roof of the new rabbit house. "The active guard for the mountains will surprise her."

Bedwyr gathered some papers from the table. "It's because your family and rulers from other realms hold the northern mountains and we aren't actively poaching each other."

"It's doable because the mountain duchies are spaced enough apart from one another." Gaheris cocked his head. "If Tryfan Heights was not as far northwest of Murphy's Hold as it is, we would be at war."

Gavyn ran his fingers along the perfect arch he'd sawed. "Dynnah Loch served as a bastion of support, and those duchies never wavered."

Garyth hammered the placard to the bunny hutch. "Uther never could break the loyalty amid the Cameliards, Gorres, DuLacs, and Sagramores."

"Carydoc and Percyval need to tread lightly," Bedwyr said as he sorted his papers into piles. "That charter they and the Dyfeds have with the Sagramores might bite them in the arse someday."

Gavyn snickered. "Oh, ye of little faith."

Gaheris thumped the stall door. "The seaside duchies went through Hells when Vertigorn called in that charter between Cornwall and Cuhlwch. That's how many of the Cuhlwch girls were forcibly married into Cornwall House."

"Most, who said they were forced, only did so to avoid the executioner's axe," said Bedwyr.

"And their options were so great during the war?"

Bedwyr slapped his pile of papers against the table. "They had a choice."

Gaheris snorted and said, "Tell that to a youth witnessing Vertigorn rape a pregnant woman and her oldest daughter over a funeral pyre."

Gavyn's face took on an ashen tinge. "Hells, Vertigorn cut the babe from his sister-in-law's womb and lit it on fire. Scorch marks remain to this day in the Cornwall courtyard. His niece watched her mother burn as Vertigorn spared her to a worst Hell as his wife."

Garyth made a small sound in his throat. "Kael Cornwall has tried to make amends when and where he can, but he's inherited a broken family. They fight him every step of the way."

Huffing, Gaheris said, "Donella Cornwall goes starkers whenever she sees her young son, Staunis. She tries to maim and kill him." He sighed and shook his head. "I've gone so far as to talk with Kael and Yuliya about taking Staunis into Foxbury."

Gavyn spun around to Gaheris. "He's about eight seasonals, right? Us taking him in at that age might be a bit much for him."

With his hands shoved into his trouser pockets, Gaheris shuffled toward Gavyn. "It's better than being dead. He's not safe in Cornwall. Kael fears that the ongoing abuse will either send him to an early Twilight or turn him into the next Vertigorn."

Gavyn was silent before saying to Gaheris, "As long as Uncle Kael and Aunt Yuliya, as Heads of House Cornwall, are in agreement, we'll take him in as a cousin."

"I would like to take it one step further," Gaheris said. "I want to adopt him as mine."

Gavyn stared, open-mouthed, at his brother. "Are you sure that's what you want?"

Gaheris stiffened his shoulders. "You know that fathering children is beyond me."

"Fine." Gavyn tacked a piece of lattice above the arch. "Then I support you."

"Ignoring Staunis potentially repeats history, which we definitely don't want to happen," Garyth said as he nodded to Gaheris. "The boy deserves to be spared of that, so you have my support in this matter, as well."

Gaheris let out a big sigh of relief. "Good, because—"

A loud shuffling of boots drew everyone's attention to Eryck Rheged as he rushed into the new stable. Out of breath, he managed, "I'm hoping you've cleared the air, Gaheris." Eryck looked over his shoulder. "Your Aunt and Uncle should be here soon."

Gaheris's two brothers gave him looks that were somewhere between awe and high dudgeon as he whistled and shrugged until they rolled their gazes elsewhere.

A grumbling hiss drew Bedwyr's attention to a raven on Eryck's shoulder. "All right, did Palamedes or Daegyn get paint on it?"

Eryck rubbed his fingers over the gurgling bird's white neck. "She's an Alkebulan raven. Elyan and I convinced Morien and Bors to breed theirs with our ravens." Eryck whistled and looked around the stable. "We're hoping to hybridize bigger and smarter birds."

As Bedwyr tucked his master rune key pendant under his robes, the raven followed the move with her beady black stare.

Eryck swayed between the threshold of the stable. "Though, we've got a problem on where to house the breeding pairs and chicks."

Bedwyr rubbed his jaw, considering the open window frames in the back wall. The stable building plans were blended with the new window for the Queen's parlor. It would be a ruddy nightmare to fix. Pointing at the window frames, he asked, "What about here?"

Eryck signaled the bunny hutch. "You have that. Messenger birds will see it as a buffet."

"Not if they're properly cordoned off and secured." Gavyn hooked his thumb toward the back. "We can create a wall here, cutting off their access with a pocket door."

Noises came from outside and Eryck made room for four hooded figures.

Kael Cornwall was one of them. He glanced around the new stable, the sunlight catching the silver in his black hair and casting a halo over him. "Good eve, nephews. We've brought Staunis and we must hurry."

Yuliya Blumenthal lowered her hood and clutched the smallest figure of the four against her. "Aye, our time is indeed limited. I fear that others in Cornwall are already onto us. If they get hold of a magistrate, we'll be stopped cold."

The third tall figure approached the table next to Bedwyr and dumped out the contents of a satchel he carried. Shoving back his hood, Alistair Kelliweg organized a Runemaster's paraphernalia. When Bedwyr glimpsed brand ink in an inkwell, he swallowed and scratched at the numeral he wore on his arm that formally designated him as his father's heir.

Alistair mixed the ink in a small bowl and said, "Baudwyn drew up the documents. Once I brand the boy, that will force Cornwall to recognize the adoption. No one will be able to contest the brand marking Staunis as a Foxbury."

"It's none of my business, but are you certain this is the right way to go about this?" Bedwyr asked, sounding genuinely concerned.

Yuliya stepped forward. "We can't guarantee Staunis's life, even for one more day, if this claim is prevented." She removed the lad's cloak. "Some in House Cornwall nearly killed him recently. If something isn't done, I'm afraid it shan't be long lest they try it again."

Bedwyr saw Vertigorn's same yellow gaze in Staunis's eyes as the child hung back and tucked himself against Yuliya.

She knelt, cupping the child's face. "You're fine, Staunis. No one here bears you ill will."

Gaheris also knelt next to the boy, gently wiping away his tears. "Allo, Staunis. Remember me?"

Staunis inched closer and flinched as if fearing a boot to his side. He caught himself and said, "Aye, Sir. You sat with me in the Infirmary after my cousins and uncles hurt me."

Kael joined Gaheris and said to the boy, "I'm sorry. Life's not fair—and even less so when your own blood harm you."

"Is your wanting him in your House out of spite?" Alistair asked, throwing a glance at all three Foxburys.

Gavyn scoffed, "I make no illusion of not being a spiteful arsehole, and if this means taking the boy from Cornwall, I'll do it a hundredfold." He winked at Staunis. "If your family doesn't want you, you can be one of ours, kit." He turned to Alistair. "Are you absolutely certain there won't be any question as to the validity of our claim for the boy?"

Alistair stroked his chin. "It will hold up, but I won't be able to erase the Cornwall brand marking him a first son. He'll always bear the brand of a Cornwall contender."

Gavyn snapped his fingers. "Lift your sleeve, Garyth. The boy's numeral two should be a Foxbury brand instead of a Cornwall brand. We keep the Fox of Druir and Sionnach in ours, sometimes blatant and other times hidden."

Garyth displayed the tattoo of a tribal fox in a numeral two on his upper arm. Alistair compared it to what was on Staunis's arm and nodded his agreement.

Gavyn came over to Staunis and crouched in front of the lad. "Did you know that my mother was a Blumenthal, just like Auntie Yuliya?" When the boy didn't react, Gavyn asked, "Do you know the history of House Blumenthal?"

Staunis sniffled and replied, "They're on the Bluffs and scholars."

"To a certain degree, aye." Garyth shooed Kael away. "The truth is, the Blumenthals were pirates first."

Yuliya yanked off her slipper and gave Garyth a good-natured rap on the head. "We don't talk about that."

Bedwyr shifted over when Eryck leaned his hip against the chair. "Lady, your ancestors were the Highwaymen of the Seas."

Grumbling, Yuliya lifted her nose in the air and ambled off, taking a seat on a box. For the supposed epitome of the scholarly side of House Blumenthal, Bedwyr thought that she swaggered across the stable like a pirate. All she needed was Budgie and a cutlass.

Garyth pinched Staunis's cheek, "Our blood has pirates and Dwarves in it. Perhaps a little something else, too, and we're always looking to expand our crew."

Staunis grinned at the Foxbury triplets. "So, I'll be like a cousin?"

"No, you most certainly will not." Gavyn tore the Cornwall emblems from the boy's sleeves and nodded toward his brothers, who each removed a Foxbury symbol from their sleeves and secured them to the sides of Staunis's tunic with tiny pins until they could be formally sewn in place. Gaheris pinned his over the front of Staunis' tunic in the only time a House symbol other than Pendragon or a Marshal's would be on another's chest.

Clearing his throat, Alistair approached with the ink, a rune-knife, and an artist's brush. He ordered, "Roll up his sleeves," and he selected the arm without the numeral on it. "Still want his arm to bear a two?" he asked Gaheris.

Gaheris maneuvered Staunis onto his lap. "Aye."

Staunis glanced toward the ink. "Will it hurt?"

"Just for a very little while," Alistair said, passing the rune-knife to Gaheris.

Gaheris asked, "How much blood do you need?"

"Four drops from each of you, as well as the child." Alistair held out the bowl of ink to them.

Gaheris completed his requirement and held Staunis tight as the boy's thumb was nicked. He let out a short squeal but seemed much more concerned with Alistair and the artist's brush, as if he knew what was coming. And he would have good reason for his anxiety. As Alistair painted the runes onto the boy's upper arm, whenever the tip of the tiny brush met his skin, the acrid smell of burning flesh filled the air.

Staunis's steady whimpers twisted through the stable until Alistair finished. Light flared from the rune and the boy let out a loud yelp, twisting from Alistair and burrowing against Gaheris's chest.

Combing his fingers through Staunis's long brown hair, Gaheris kissed the top of the boy's head. "You're my son now. Mine alone. You are forever to be known as Staunis Graham Foxbury."

After Alistair finished and gathered his tools, Kael unfurled the parchment sanctioning the adoption and offered it to Eryck and Bedwyr to sign as witnesses. Prior to signing, Bedwyr and Eryck inspected the word "Graham" beneath the branded number two. Harlan's middle name was Graham. It was a tradition in Foxbury for immediate heirs to bear the same middle name. The triplets and Tippy all shared Quinn as theirs.

Turning to the Foxbury Lords, Bedwyr asked, "Did you make him an heir?"

Gaheris beamed. "Argh, matey. He'll make a wonderful pirate, won't he?"

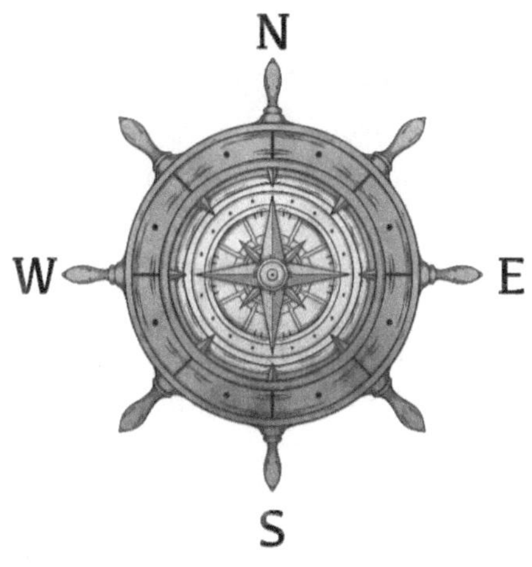

CHAPTER 87

POWDER AND ROUGE BY ANY OTHER NAME

In the parlor of the Queen's Court, Viera found the gathering rather peculiar, as beads clicking loudly countered the tap of Guinevere's manicured nails over a glass-topped table she sat behind. Viera sneaked peeks past Constantine and Aglovale to Lady Imogen Blumenthal, who certainly didn't look like nobility—with a cutlass on her hip, a smattering of holes adorning the men's trousers she wore, and a tight green leather corset that rivaled what Eerie flounced around in without concern for what others might think.

Imogen's jaunty black hat, with silver piping, sat lopsided atop blond hair with beads and feathers stuck within its braids. Whenever she moved, a broad belt—slung low over her hips—provided a glimpse of a tattoo portraying greyhounds racing across the small of her back.

Nay, Imogen didn't come close to painting a picture of respectability. This was reinforced by the Elemental breaker around her wrist—and that everyone was standing a discreet distance from her. Her large lizard, harnessed today, hissed away on her shoulder and eyeballed the nearest men as if they were dinner; the only man not given such attention was Beddoe standing next to Dinadan. Amusement glowed in his indigo eyes. Beddoe had a few Sagramore, Cuhlwch, and Cornwall men sneering down their noses at him and their hands straying to their weapon hilts whenever he was in the vicinity. Bercylac and most of the Elven delegates were respectful of the Air Elemental of twenty-three Winters and Springs, but some outright fixed him with hostility, indicating there was bad blood between them.

The Queen, clearing her throat, motioned toward Imogen. "Lady Imogen, I'm sure your cousin, Lord Gavyn, had some involvement in recent events, but alas, he has covered his tracks well enough to not incur a penalty. As most assuredly has another in the *shadows*." She paused, giving Beddoe a weighty stare that elicited a lazy smirk from him. "However, it most certainly falls to you, and as your punishment for encouraging that vile creature on your shoulder to attack Tremayne Cornwall, you are hereby banned from Court for a full year, starting today. Lord Kelliweg, please see that she makes it onto the very next transport back to the Bluffs."

Alistair bowed and beckoned for Imogen to follow him.

Affecting a mocking curtsey, Imogen doffed her hat. "Aye, aye, Your Majesty."

Fearing that Imogen would indeed receive a severe penalty for what she'd done to Tremayne, Brynn and Dinadan had accompanied her. Imogen pinched Brynn on the cheek and said, "If ever you find yourself in need of a good first mate, Brynny, you know who to whistle for to help you out. Sailfins are always better than any Knight. The worst one will put Bedwyr to shame."

Her comments brought a smirk to Dinadan's timeworn features that he smoothed out into a more neutral expression. "Your Majesty, with your permission, I shall accompany my niece until her unfortunate departure. Every moment with her is such a treasure." He performed the lowest bow his ancient body allowed, the movement seeming to strain every muscle in his body.

Guinevere gave him a slow nod. "Of course, my venerable Knight. But do make certain that your niece doesn't take a side trip to reignite past history with Xavier Cuhlwch. I fear the shame of his being left at the Bonding altar is punishment enough for his—shortcomings."

With a chuckle, Dinadan said, "My Most Esteemed Dear Lady, you have my word, there will be no such endeavour."

As Brynn reached the door, she glanced over her shoulder and waggled her fingers back at Viera. Hiding a grin, Viera counted down the seconds to feigning the need to use the latrine. A few nights giggling in the Blumenthal apartments as Imogen regaled them with lusty tales of the high seas was certainly not enough time to cement a new friendship, but Viera found the woman fascinating.

Viera's brief daydream ended as air whiffled and a prim merlin flew through an open window and settled upon a gleaming white perch. Soft fabric swished when the Queen rose and strode to the bird. She took the missive from its leather pouch and read its contents. Viera spied the Queen folding the letter and beckoned Eryck to join her.

"I've just learned that the new stable is complete—and has been for a while—and that our merlins are being nested there." Guinevere tapped her fingers on the edge of the letter. "When were you last in the new stable, Lord Rheged?"

Eryck bowed to the Queen, appearing to totter a bit as he bent over. "Ah… two days ago, Your Highness."

Setting the letter on her desk, Guinevere rewarded the merlin with a treat, the bird delicate in taking it. In the sunlight, the Cameliard seal gleamed on the bird's thin collar.

"You may wish to relocate your birds," Guinevere said to Eryck. "I wager that will be your first order of business when you leave this room."

He straightened. "I serve you first, Your Majesty."

"Wise answer, but I can see that the eagerness in your mien is not quite up to your words. I don't want any of our birds *accidentally* dining on the rabbits." She looked around the rest of the room. "That's all our business for today. You may all adjourn to your chambers."

Viera was going to try to catch up with Brynn, but her escape was for naught when Guinevere said, "Lady Tillwith, stay behind."

Aglovale wrapped his fingers over her shoulder. "Time for you to learn another way to wage war." He jiggled the domino case at Constantine. "Fancy playing a more spirited game of dominoes with a bored old man, son?"

After the room emptied, Viera performed a low curtsey. "Your Majesty."

"Come." Guinevere led Viera toward her private dressing room. "I'm going to show you how to apply makeup." She paused. "I bet you don't know that makeup is a dangerous thing?"

Viera didn't answer, cringing inwardly as she walked behind the Queen. *Ugh. Makeup. Rather than put it on my face, I'd prefer cleaning the entire stable with Bedwyr mocking me.*

At the Queen's urging, Viera sank into a velvet-cushioned rosewood chair, the mate to a vanity inlaid with leaves, flowers, birds, and woodland animals, all in silver. The furniture in the rest of the room was made from a dark wood that gleamed from fresh varnish, and it also carried the same designs and inlays as the vanity.

Feeling she had to say something, Viera remarked, "It's very pretty, Your Highness."

"My father was good with his hands. If not a noble, he would have likely been an ironsmith or a woodcarver." Guinevere brushed her fingers over a delicate deer carving on a nearby chest. "He made two of these for my wedding trousseau. Arthwyr has the other in his bedchamber. The idea was that the two of these made a whole."

"I'm sure you miss him." Viera paused to consider what she'd just said and blurted, "Your father, I mean. I know how it is for me, not being with my Da."

"There isn't a day that passes where I do not miss him. It's harder for girls to let go of their fathers. Though, it's as heartbreaking to lose one's mother."

Viera chewed her lip. "My parents didn't play favourites. If I did something wrong, I got it from whichever one found out about it first." A beat passed. "My Da used to tell the best stories in the inn after I did something bad. And his stories got better with each telling." Viera laughed, as did the Queen.

"You're hardly the only daughter who ever got in trouble with her parents. When I was a little girl, my father had me scrubbing the Dining Hall after I remodeled it into a winter wonderland when the King's Progress arrived." Guinevere sighed and wiped her eyes. "He never let me live it down."

The Queen motioned toward the mirror. Viera stared at her face. *I'm never going to be a noblewoman. Too many freckles, a grin too quick to pull at my lips, and wild hair despite the best efforts of a servant helping me.*

Guinevere flicked her delicate fingers between Viera and the mirror. "Do you know the difference between you and Jocelyn?"

Viera sulked at having to say, "Sure, class. She was born into a noble family, and she has always been given training on how to be a Lady. I was born a peasant. These things can never change, no matter how much anyone teaches me." It was Viera's turn to wipe her eyes.

The Queen took Viera's hand. "Yes, you were born a peasant, but you have something that Jocelyn nor any of the other noble daughters will ever have. Another time for that, though. I brought you here today to have you learn the value of makeup, and don't fool yourself, it has a unique importance to a Lady."

"I don't see myself ever liking it." Again, Viera considered too late what she'd just uttered. "I'm sorry, Your Majesty, I should not have said that."

"Don't apologize, but let me help you, and I'm going back to Jocelyn, which I know pleases you." Viera grimaced and the Queen squeezed her hand. "She understands that in wearing makeup she'll be putting on a show. She uses it to direct attention to what naturally draws the focus of men. She uses makeup to create interest in her while diminishing her negative attributes."

"Do not men figure this out, Your Majesty?"

"You constantly impress me with how quick you are." The Queen rubbed cream on Viera's face. "Jocelyn showed her cards much too early for the likes of Galahad and Bedwyr. They know how a real Lady presents herself." Viera started to speak but the Queen put up her hand. "It would be inappropriate for me to tell you my true feelings about certain Maids, and Eerie is an entirely separate subject, but you are smart enough to figure out most things for yourself. Just know that I have to play a role I don't often like to maintain harmony with the Houses in the realm."

Viera was intrigued by the way the Queen's hands seemed to float by themselves in front of the mirror. She wondered, with practice in front of a mirror of her own, if she could emulate Guinevere's rhythmic movements. She soon dismissed this as a silly fantasy. It would take a lot of time to be at Her Majesty's level—and Viera was hardly a queen.

As Guinevere applied what she called a "foundation," it surprised Viera in that it did make her freckles less noticeable. She said, "Your Majesty, you said that makeup was dangerous. What is so dangerous about a Lady and makeup?"

The Queen leaned against the vanity. "You have to understand the real purpose behind makeup." Her lips parted sensuously. "A woman doesn't put on makeup to be a perfect doll like a figurine in a merchant's stall. Makeup has another purpose." She turned to the mirror, and in a voice as soft as oiled steel rustling within a velvet-lined scabbard, the Queen finished by saying, "It's our war paint. No woman has ever applied it with the simple goal of using it to accentuate fluttering her lashes. We wear it to hunt. We wear it to fight. But, foremost, we wear it to win."

CHAPTER 88

SECRETS BEYOND THE VEIL

Straw rustled and the rabbit hopped around the edge of the small hutch. Nose quivering, the small buck sniffed and rose on his hind legs. Bedwyr pared a sliver of carrot and held it out. The rabbit edged forward and began nibbling. Bedwyr continued hand-feeding the bunny, ignoring a shuffling sound coming from behind him.

Viera cleared her throat but Bedwyr remained unmoved. After a few more "ahumphs" failed to motivate the Knight to look her way, she spoke in a loud voice: "Lord Wallach, I have a few questions, if I may?"

"What's with the formality? You sound like one of the Maids. Or is that the idea?"

"Sorry. The Queen told me to work on talking 'gracefully,' as she called it. Guess I got carried away."

"Practice with somebody else." Her defeated look caused him to add, "So what brought you here?"

"How did you know about the Fomoiri?"

He gave his friend another slice of carrot and turned to Viera. "I've had the displeasure of prior acquaintance with them. Is that formal enough for you?"

"Are you one of them?"

That got his attention, and he snapped, "One of what?"

"Fomoiri."

Bedwyr laughed so hard he thought he might burst. He tossed the remainder of the carrot in the hutch and said, "I'm many things, but that isn't one of them. How much have those fools told you about the final battle? And I'm positive you know what I'm referring to."

"Myrddin told me you're called a *lladdwyr perthynas*, or something like that, because of helping to kill your father." Creases deepened over Viera's forehead. "Although, as it was explained to me by Constantine, he said that it was Shiori who led the way to Uther's end."

"How very self-serving to all involved."

"How is that?"

"Because half of it is wrong."

Viera bristled, "Myrddin nor Constantine ever lied to me before."

"You have much to learn about the fine art of half-truths and omissions." Bedwyr stood. "The truth is freeing. Don't give me that look. You know exactly what I mean."

In a stance of defiance, Viera folded her arms across her chest. "I still don't believe they would lie to me."

"Do you have the courage to face the facts?"

"Aye, of course."

"Then follow me."

As Bedwyr led her past the Eastern Purity Pools, it pleased him that the chatter normally associated with her remained mercifully silent. He hesitated in front of a stone wall covered by tall hedges. He counted the stones from left to right, and when satisfied he was in the correct location, he pushed through one section of the hedgerow and dragged Viera behind him.

Bedwyr rested his palm on a stone. "Not a word to anyone, lass. If I find out you've discussed this with another, I'll ensure you meet Twilight far sooner than you're due."

Viera swallowed. "I promise I won't say a word to anyone."

Bedwyr tapped several stones and released his tainted Element into the iron within the stone. The wall swung inward and he shoved her into a passage, hissing at her, "Use your Fire so we can see."

Shaking, she summoned a flame above her palm. It became a fireball, which revealed a lumistone at Bedwyr's shoulder. He activated the mineral, bathing them in violet light.

When Viera was able to focus her eyes, she saw roughhewn steps in front of them. "What is this place?"

Bedwyr mounted the first step. "There are hidden passages throughout the older parts of the castle. If we are ever under siege, they provide a means of escape for the Royal Pair."

She placed her foot on the step. "I take it that not many people know about this?"

"And you would be right." Bedwyr pressed his palm over the cold wall. "A previous Royal Pair always lets their future successors know, but only when they think they're toward the end of their reign."

"I hope you don't mind me asking, how is it that you know about this?"

He leaned into her. "As the last living descendant of The Seven Houses, it's my duty to secure the realm in times of discord."

Viera flattened herself against the wall, Bedwyr inches from her. "Uther's death ended the Duels, right?" Bedwyr nodded. "If what I've been told is a lie, how did this really happen?"

Bedwyr allowed the tension to rise and said, "Dagonet provided the distraction. He was the Spymaster, after all. The Ravas unleashed some golems. Constantine set the main stable afire. All the loyal help performed little acts of mutiny in the name of performing their jobs."

"What did you do?"

Bedwyr snickered. "I snuck Lance in through these passages. Then he let in the Golden King so he could ride in on his white horse and be the hero everyone prayed for. All the dark King's men and their horses couldn't put Uther and his reign back together again."

"Then you're the real hero. You opened the door, so to speak."

"I'm no hero, lass. My involvement was not free. I had my price, and I was paid handsomely for my services."

"And what price would you have?"

"My father and Uther—and a few others. I chased my father through the castle. He ran and he ran. He had no public execution. His was mine."

Viera shuddered. "So, you are a *lladdwyr perthynas*?"

"Aye, that part is correct. The tale Myrddin told you about me killing my father was the truth." Bedwyr flicked an errant tendril of her hair over her shoulder. "I reveled in it." Brushing the lumistone next to her head, he activated an azure light. "And now you know."

"And now I know." She poked at the lumistone. "How are you doing that? I thought only Metal and Earth Elementals should be able to manipulate lumistones."

He stepped back and internally swore over slipping up. Half-truth it was. "My blood is keyed specifically into this castle. You'll never be able to manipulate the lumistones here. Only those of Wallach blood can ever hold such sway." He loomed over her, but the wide set of her eyes and tremor of her chin doused his irritation at her ignorance and he continued: "You only use this passage if the Hearth burns. Should that ever happen, take this one and run to the King's stables and get to The Ridge." He spun from her and ascended the steps. "If you make it that far, stay clear of the well-traveled routes. Take the animal paths, and keep away from the clearings by the rivers in the daytime."

The muscles where the Fomoiri snagged his leg started to spasm. Pain shot through him but curiosity urged him onward. Viera had once described Shiori and his mother to perfection. There was no reason she should know either. How much does she truly see? What better way to find out than to open a door for her?

Viera tightened her arms to stave off the cold and present the image of strength. But her best attempts failed her. The frigid air in the passage nestled so deep in her bones, if someone asked, she would swear that the marrow had frozen. The damp algae clinging to the walls added another layer of scent to the neck of her tunic, which she had pulled over her face. She fumed at the gray robe rustling in front of her, "Are we there yet?"

"Need a bubby?" Bedwyr asked.

Viera groaned. "You're the worst."

Moldy green sludge dribbled down the stone, causing her to shudder. The dire state of the passages competed with the bleakness of the dungeons.

The tips of her ears stung from the chill. She pulled on Bedwyr's robe and asked, "Where are we?"

Bedwyr stopped. "We're exactly where I expected we'd be about now."

She shut her mouth when a flicker of light caught her attention. A moment later, Shiori stood in front of them, the slick gleam of her hair pulled into an elaborate chignon. Shiori pressed her finger against her petal-shaped mouth and uttered: *Shish. Shish.*

Cold fingers from out of nowhere dug into Viera's shoulder. Another voice warbled as if beneath water and slid away. Shadows bled into red-and-gold eyeshadow lining Shiori's stare. Turning away from Viera, Shiori climbed onto some steps, and a weaving outline wavered behind her silvery robes.

As if in a trance, Viera followed, slipping past a dark specter in front of her.

Shiori stopped on a large step, faced a wall, thrust out her hand, and disappeared into the stone.

Except Shiori didn't. She slid into a dark entrance.

A haunting cry startled Viera into flinching and stumbling backwards. She jerked around and met Bedwyr's intense stare. But when she blinked, he was gone.

Murmurs sent tremors through her. The hair crept along her neck as she returned to where she'd last seen Shiori. Viera found Constantine standing on a ledge, and his presence calmed her. She soon discovered that this was not the man she had known.

His hair seemed glued to his forehead, and the waxy circlet on his cheek stood out livider than ever, as if displaying its own level of anger. He gasped and uttered prayers in shaky hitches, the top part of his gold crucifix poking out from the fist he'd placed around it.

The wind whined and screams echoed beyond the walls. Viera had to decide to proceed or go back. Aye, there was only one choice. She had come too far to turn around, so she lunged forward, cleared the last few stairs, and twisted around to run into the wall. Stumbling, she raced into a cavernous chamber and drew up short as she ran full tilt into a throne. Viera banged her knee into a massive claymore and it clattered over the floor. She slinked behind the mammoth chair and used the back of it to steady herself and to observe.

Constantine swayed in the entranceway and moaned; his stare fixed on the gleaming claymore a few yards from him while runes crept like vines of ivy downward from the engraving of the tree nearest the hilt. When they reached the tip, the runes faded into the metal. Viera bent to trace her fingers over the glowing runes, and upon touching the frigid metal, a hiss filled her ears.

Her vision spiraled to a field of wheat with a man painted in the shadows of a solar eclipse. The burn of the sun's reddened light forced her to squint to make out his threadbare homespun and the rough, whittled branch comprising the shaft of a warped spade in his hand. The fluttering memory revealed a young lass no older than fourteen seasonals with pink hair to rival a paint bomb as she hugged the peasant.

He ushered the lass into the waiting arms of two men and a hulking bear of a woman swathed in shadows. The farmer hoarsely ordered, "Take her, lest all shall be lost evermore."

The shadows receded and the trio reminded Viera so of the bedraggled highwaymen that predominantly featured in her nightmares. One of the men resembled the statue of Cymry Pendragon overlooking Elden's Hearth from the castle, while the woman hinted toward the large statue of Pembroke at the Earth Temple. If that wasn't shocking on its own, the passing similarity of Errol Luxley to the last man was a punch to her sternum. Wind caught over the tall grasses of the field, and the lass and trio snuffed out like candlelight as a black figure stalked toward the peasant. A fox skittered from the barn and along the fence. Obscured by smoke, green light glowed behind the creature and revealed a woman with red hair before she melted into the same fox that circled the pair and cackled.

Viera could've sworn she heard the same voice whisper, "No matter how it pains and ends me, nevermore shall you plague those of my heart while my blood blooms, withers, and blossoms forevermore."

"Foolish, Soul Link. Your purpose is to feed me. As for you, Sionnach, you fox-bitch of a Witch, you've cackled your last. No more shall the Fae hold dominion over Shadows, Light, and Twilight. Bend for your King of All, Lugh," the void rumbled, as it morphed into the impression of a towering Fomoiri with horns twisting above its fearsome head into a wicked crown.

The moon blotted out the sun, bathing the valley as if in twilight. Viera flinched as the farmer turned, and a gaze like a sunset locked as if onto hers. "Nay, Grandfather. I'm the targe for the next Fae rulers," the peasant directed at the Fomoiri, the unfurling shadows of black wings protruding raggedly from his shoulders. "Balor, you are the blight of many, but in my sacrifice, I'll be the Aegis of All. The newest Fae Royal will ascend, where here you shall fall evermore to the blood of those meant to be one."

The Fomoiri bellowed and charged the farmer, who launched himself forward with the spade whipping back over his shoulder in preparation of meeting Balor. Sickle-like talons slashed down and caught across the blade of the spade, releasing an earsplitting squeal and sparks tanging the air. Viera flinched and kicked the claymore away from her. It rang as if in protest and skidded the last few yards to thud against Constantine's boot as the vision faded.

A squall reverberated through Viera's bones and she slid around the throne. Darkness and muted light shrouded the Throne Room. In front of her, the scene solidified and a shriek bubbled past her throat.

On the lower level, chains secured Galahad, Guinevere, and an older man constrained in a kneeling position on the stone floor. The old man screamed and rattled his restraints; his gaze locked on the stairs where Viera stood. As she took in her new surroundings, blood dripped and pooled in thick puddles everywhere. Soldiers and men in noble robes lay in various stages of mutilation—and if they were lucky, Twilight.

Boom! Boom! The double doors to the chamber creaked at the intensity of what had crashed against them. "Open the damned doors! Surrender! You have no choice. I command you, dammit. Open these doors!"

Off to the side and near the bottom of the staircase, Talia lay still as her blood stained the floor and her abdomen.

Linny pressed a crimson rag to Talia's midsection. "Please hold on."

A blurry shadow raced toward Viera and grabbed her arm. The figure faded away immediately, leaving her gasping and shaking. In the snap of a finger, chainmail clinked and Uther Pendragon stormed past her, his face cold and graying despite the madness darkening his chiseled features. He kept rubbing at his shoulder.

Glancing toward the nearest doorway, Viera tried to run toward it, but was stopped by what she saw. Charred marks and ruptured flesh and Elemental arrays stretched over pale skin. Blood covered familiar gray robes while a bristling white fox braced its limbs over Bedwyr, who lay sprawled out on the stairs. With gore staining its fur in multicolored splotches, the fox snarled and its ears pressed flat against its head.

Uther knelt, grabbed the fox's neck, and tossed it from Bedwyr. The animal's slim body crashed into a pillar. Bones cracked and the creature stilled, one side grotesquely punched in from the impact. Its sharp yapping ended, and the rattle coming from deep within betrayed the thread of life the fox clung to, the whine striking a chord in Viera, as she'd never heard a sound so sad.

The Mad King slammed his boot into Bedwyr's abdomen and rolled him down the flight of stairs. Blood gushed from Bedwyr's mouth, rewetting the darker patches over his tunic as a weak whisper slid past him. Uther stood over the crumpled mass on the stairs. As he straddled

Bedwyr, he summoned up two shards of long metal. He pierced the floor with one blade, steel kissing the side of Bedwyr's face.

Uther flipped the other shard in the air. Viera brushed away tears as shadows filled the stairway and Twilight beckoned. An acrid scent filled the air and Fire robes whisked past. Her initial thoughts turned to Hamyll and his rising from the ashes like an avenging phoenix. He would fix everything.

But, no! Not him! It can't be!

The wet smack of metal cleaving skin and bone preceded a head thumping down the stairs and between Guinevere and Galahad. When the decapitated body rolled down the steps, as if trying to follow its head, blood spurted from the neck and sprayed the duo tethered to the floor.

Viera fell to her knees as tears warmed her cheeks. She covered her mouth to stifle hysterical squeals. As Uther's decapitated head lolled on the floor, his hard eyes blinked before stilling and staring back at her.

Tearing her gaze from the dead Mad King, she prayed Hamyll would materialize as the killer. But she knew better, as no amount of blinking erased Constantine as he stood over the dead King, the claymore in the priest's hand and his face splattered with Uther's blood.

"It-wa-was-ya-you," she stuttered.

Constantine's Fire robes morphed into his cassock; the light garment no longer splattered with the blood that ended a war. She shuddered, hoping her stern gaze at the priest conveyed her disgust with the half-truth she'd been told. *Nay, it wasn't half of anything; it was the deliberate blurring of the truth in all of its entirety.*

Viera shook hard enough that she feared falling apart on the stairs. Her vision contorted into misshapen shards of the past spilling into the room. Bedwyr set a bracing hand on her shoulder as he stood at her side. Her sight righted itself, and she half wished it would spin about to align into a different reality.

There was no such fortune to be had. Bedwyr's touch drove her to the chilling revelation of what whispered in the drafty halls of the castle. Twilight had descended during the Battle of the Hearth, and there was not a clean hand amid any of those involved in the execution of that blood-laden blip in the fall and rise of kings and reigns.

"Why didn't you tell me the truth?" Viera challenged Constantine even though she knew she wouldn't get a reply.

"He couldn't," Bedwyr said, as Constantine dropped the blade in his hand on the throne. "Not with that sword being made from the mad

Jabberwock King, Rallorc. The Dragon King, Leinnet, championed Evermore and put down Rallorc with a common spade somewhere in the Valley. To this day, where remains a mystery."

She whipped her head toward Bedwyr, trying to make sense of Lugh and Balor as Leinnet and Rallorc. Perhaps their true names were lost over time and from the bardic tales of generations ago... Or all that arose from those fields that looked so like the valleys of home was a hysterical dream that battered its way to the forefront of her mind.

Her misgivings derailed as Bedwyr added, "*Vorpal* chooses the Aegis of Evermore only when our people need a defender. That person is meant to be a secret, but there are occasions when people, events, and Fate demand otherwise."

"Aegis?" she whispered, her gaze settling on the blade.

"Evermore's Targe or Shield. Usually it's the King of Evermore, but sometimes—" Bedwyr shrugged— "*Vorpal* defies its master and chooses another to defend Evermore. Despite what many believe, shields are the backbone of protecting the people. The day the Hearth fell, *Vorpal* chose Constantine to shield us. When anyone else puts it down, it returns to the current Aegis or someone leading to the next Aegis."

Viera gulped. "What does that mean?"

The sword faded from sight to only return tucked between Constantine's cummerbund and cassock. "*Vorpal* won't leave Constantine until it recognizes another or feels it is time to seek out its next Aegis. When it does, runes will glow on the blade," Bedwyr said. "It'll settle for a Pendragon or Marshal if it must, but when its time has come, *Vorpal* will move on."

Viera stared at the priest hunching his shoulders. "Why?" she asked him.

Constantine's face portrayed deep remorse, but this faded as he peered past her to Bedwyr and recited: "*Domine benedic et protégé familiam meam.*"

Bedwyr narrowed his eyes. "You said that when the nobility tried to execute me."

"And I meant every word of 'Lord bless and protect my family.'" The priest lifted his hands, then crossed himself. "Forgiveness comes in many forms. As does love and acceptance. Regret, though? A life of regrets is far heavier than one built stone by stone on the first three. I loved the family I made too much to let them become my greatest loss."

CHAPTER 89

FAE HOPE

Dydd Mawrth, or the Wednesday, after Constantine's reveal, Viera followed Galahad to the East Stable for a morning ride with Bercylac. She had to sidestep Constantine on the way, as she was avoiding him, unable to reconcile his part in killing Uther and allowing the act to be attributed to another. Not even Arthwyr explaining the need to hide Constantine's involvement in Uther's death from the Sagramores, Cornwalls, and Cuhlwchs eased her anguish. Recognizing her discomfort around him, the priest respected her enough to temporarily withdraw from Court.

Stable hands and grooms flitted about the courtyard as Bercylac readied his reindeer for the day. Two figures appeared in the doorway of the stable, Percyval leading a large destrier into the sunlight. Viera had gotten to know the older noble over the course of a few days following Gavyn entering the Infirmary shaken and haggard a few nights ago. Whispers about Court dissected how someone so happy could be so broken deep down. Viera suspected it had to do with Gavyn no longer able to handle his losses. Regardless, she joined Percyval in keeping vigil over his former student.

As the older noble stopped next to Viera, he asked her, "How ya doing, lass?"

"Fine," she said, "How's Gavyn?"

"He'll be fine. Constantine is with him."

Doubt crept into her voice as she asked, "How is he helping?"

"Sometimes we find resolution through different counsel." Percyval pulled a silver star on a chain from his tunic. "Gavyn has suffered since he lost his father. After my son's loss, I found relief with the Ravas. In Constantine, Gavyn might discover his." He tucked away the pendant and added, "Punishments we inflict upon ourselves ripple outward like waves. Those closest to us tread the same troubled waters."

"Aye, Sir," Viera whispered, "I'll mind your counsel."

"On that note," he said, swinging up onto his horse, "I'll leave you to it."

Bercylac led a reindeer from the stable with Bedwyr's horse, Olwen, following behind the lighter-colored animal. Gereant followed on a short stubby dark dun Shetland pony. The two Ancients sent Galahad on and the Elven King motioned for Viera to approach.

Bercylac said, "You're riding with me on Blixem. Bedwyr gave us permission to take Olwen out for a run."

Handing Viera some sugar cubes, the Elven King showed her how to give them to the reindeer. As the reindeer chased the sugar over her palm, his dark expressive eyes met her stare. When Blixem licked her fingers cleaner than they had ever been, he snorted and shifted toward her so she could easily mount him from the ground.

Bercylac seated her securely on Blixem and joined her in the saddle. Once they crossed the Lockinge, he guided the reindeer toward a path leading to the grassier fields outside the Hearth, an area also familiar to Viera. Coolness whispered across her skin and she looked back gratefully to Bercylac.

When they reached the fields, Bercylac halted Blixem. He and Gereant released the mounts. Olwen took off into the fields, and Viera panicked at losing the mare.

Gereant snorted. "Don't worry, lass. She'll be back. Bedwyr trained her to find familiar grounds. Most in his stables are the same. Even the ones he sold off to downsize his herd will return either to a Wallach stable or wherever the homing ritual has based them."

"Why downsize his herd?" Viera asked.

Bercylac said, "Bedwyr refuses to overly support a King's military ever again. He also retains the right to step aside if it benefits the realm."

The Dwarven King pointed at a break in the grass and they followed the path toward a rivulet. When they reached the stream, Viera said to Bercylac, "You wanted to discuss Ancient business?"

Gereant grunted, "Arthwyr requested we give you time."

They stepped onto a sandy embankment and stopped near some calm water. Bercylac skipped a few stones and said, "When we've spoken to you in the past, it had been concerning general issues or because Myrddin had sought our counsel. Arthwyr finally gave us permission to discuss a few finer points on Ancients."

Gereant dropped onto a boulder. "So, ask your questions, lass." He beckoned to the sky. "It would help us along if ya'd summon your darker phoenix."

At Viera's whistle, Tilly crackled into sight with a flash of light over the river. The phoenix settled on Viera's bare shoulder and trilled the haunting notes of Homage to the Ancestors.

The memory of Bedwyr when he brushed his fingers over the phoenix's cheek was the first thing she wanted to discuss. She said, "No one has ever touched a phoenix of mine without being burned except me. Why was Bedwyr able to touch it and not get fried?"

Gereant lowered his chin, his hooded brows and helmet veiling his eyes. "Strange how Bedwyr is what we wanted to talk to ya about as well."

Viera stroked Tilly's tail feathers, black and blue flames dancing harmlessly over her skin. She repeated her question, "So how could Bedwyr do this and not get burned?"

Bercylac settled on the boulder and draped his arms over his knees. "There are only two ways one can touch your phoenix. The first being if the person is the strongest of Fae."

With so little known about the Fae, the slightest crumb of information was valuable. Perhaps she was not as alone in possessing Fae blood. Her voice came out breathless and imploring: "So Bedwyr is like me? He's a Fae too?"

Bercylac guffawed. "He's so far removed from the Fae, they would be incompatible."

So much for finding another like her. She picked at a blade of grass, bending it until it drooped like the current cant of her face. "He's something dark, though, right?" She yanked a few more blades, longer this time, and braided them into a Valley bracelet. "I doubt he's Elven or Dwarven."

Gereant rumbled a low scoff. "Your instincts serve ya right. But that wasn't so hard to figure, was it, lass?" She said nothing. "Let's see if you're as smart as they all say. Why do ya think Bedwyr can touch that Firebird? Ya think about it now before ya speak."

She scoured her mind for any Ancient lore she remembered. *Was Bedwyr part Hells Hound?* His black hair could shift into black fur, and when he was enraged, his eyes went from cinnamon to blood red in an instant. Viera crinkled her nose. Cuchulain often called Bedwyr a mad dog. He was barking mad, but he didn't smell like a dog unless he marinated himself in alcohol.

Maybe he's a kelpie. They lured their victims next to water, which is also where they feasted on them. He was a Water Elemental and always threatening to kill people and bury the bodies where no one could find them. *What better place than the soft ground around a lake? Bedwyr was a Kelpie. Sure, that was it. Hells, this is stupid.*

Dejected, Viera sighed and admitted, "I have no idea why Bedwyr can touch a phoenix and not get singed to the bone."

Both Kings looked at one another and Bercylac said, "Tywyll cannot burn one who has already embraced Final Night."

Her ears pounded as she met Bercylac's cyan and pink gaze. "What?" she croaked.

"Bedwyr found Twilight after his father, Uther, and Vertigorn finished that dark ritual." Bercylac lowered his voice. "He breathed his last at the Witching Hour of Alban Hefin. His heart stilled. When Shiori found us in the woods, she had him with her and he had no pulse. Aye, he was dead."

Viera came close to the Elven King and said, "But Bedwyr has a pulse. I felt it when I painted him on Mala."

Gereant patted his tunic and dug out a pouch with a black pendant in it. "He has Eerie to thank for that. The lass kissed him, and it activated their Bond and reset his heart."

The burn in Viera's chest threatened to rupture her skin. There was a certain ease in the way the Ancients tore her beliefs to shreds.

Bercylac circled her knee with his thumb, soothing the jittery jump of her leg. "Tywyll embraced Bedwyr once. She took him home as she brings all who slide into Twilight."

Viera wiped away the threat of tears. "Bedwyr is here, though."

"Aye, the rituals called Bedwyr back. The blood of his mother and of his last surviving sister anchored him to life. He was born anew, like the phoenixes you summon."

"So, he's an Ancient—a phoenix?"

Said Gereant, "Bedwyr is not a true Ancient. At least, not a recognized one." The Dwarf held up the black medallion. "He's the birth of an Ancient but not a phoenix. Bedwyr will die, but his new nature won't allow it to be so soon." He made a guttural laugh. "Hells, he might outlive us all."

Viera pressed her lips together and groaned. "So, what is he?"

Bercylac surprised Viera when he answered: "We aren't sure. Bedwyr is the first we know of who is born of blood, shadows, and a crimson moon. When he rose again, he did not return through a path of Light. Nay, he was reborn as one of Twilight."

The Dwarf scrubbed his hands through his beard. "Don't get us wrong. We have our suspicions about Bedwyr. Problem is, whoever brought him back wasn't able to return him to Light."

Bercylac reached into a sachet on his belt and pulled out a white crescent pendant that, except for the color, looked much like the one Gereant was holding.

"So, who do your *suspicions* tell you might have returned Bedwyr?" Viera asked as she scrutinized the second pendant.

Gereant looked at Bercylac, who nodded. "We suspect the Unseelie Queen. But there's no way to prove it."

The clinking of chains had Viera looking from one pendant to the other. "What's with the medallions?"

Gereant chuckled. "We weren't honest with Myrddin concerning the Seelie King and the Unseelie Queen. Neither one vanished into thin air without having a final say."

Bercylac lowered the pendant as Gereant lifted his. The crescents snapped together and Gereant held the conjoined result. Gray light flared from the seams, fading into the familiar carving of a tree that showed no breaks whatsoever, the bottom half of the pendant black with a silver moon and the top half white with a gold sun.

"Before the Unseelie Queen disappeared, she approached Gereant and me privately and gave us hope." Bercylac nodded and Gereant handed the unified pendant to Viera. "One day, Balance will bring our people together and turn other natural enemies into the staunchest of allies."

Viera accepted the pendant, and both warmth and a chill seeped into her fingers.

"It was the last anyone in our Council ever saw her." Gereant thumped Viera's leg. "In time, the Seelie King sought us with the same message. They entrusted us with these pendants until two of their heirs emerged. We've seen potentials—none who made it to their Blooding. You're the only one possessing the Unseelie Queen's and the Seelie King's combined heritage."

Tilly cooed and, with a flare of her tail feathers, winged toward the castle. When she blurred from sight, Viera focused on the Ancients. "Thank you for this—" tucking the necklace against her chest— "and for everything you both shared with me."

Gereant grunted and turned toward the fields. "You're the Seelie and Unseelie legacy, child, but even more so—you're our hope."

Trilling dragged Bedwyr from his desk. He stalked toward his balcony, determined to shoo away the nuisance. Striding into the sunlight, the harsh bark of his voice died in his throat.

Orbs swimming with dark flames returned Bedwyr's stare. Wholly unimpressed, the phoenix shook out her plumage, and a loose feather settled against his boots. Flame-like tongues wavered over it. Winnowing coos urged him to collect the gift.

Bedwyr reached down and picked up the feather, straightened, and met the phoenix's gaze. As the phoenix bobbed on the guardrail, Bedwyr scratched her head and chuckled at her clucking.

"Fine. Have it your way, you overgrown chicken." He tapped his finger against her beak. "But he has to come to me first."

The phoenix cackled loudly, as if she really was a chicken.

The banging on his door was more than providence. Bedwyr crossed his chamber and dropped the feather in the last *Book of Water* and snapped the cover shut. Whatever had been imbued in the Marshals' books allowed them to touch and contain a phoenix's feather amid their hallowed pages, and this held true for even the Twilight Phoenix. Bedwyr slid the tome back into the relative obscurity provided by his bookshelf. No one else need know of his hypocrisy.

Hesitation was not even a consideration as he raised the latch. Bedwyr would not balk from his responsibility and oath to Evermore.

He pulled open the door and addressed his visitor: "About damned time, you useless Dragon Lord. I've been expecting you."

CHAPTER 90

NEW RISES AND BEGINNINGS

Viera had made a point of visiting Gavyn in the Infirmary when Constantine was occupied elsewhere. A week later, Gavyn had been released and seemed haler, though no less fragile as he eked through finding counsel in Constantine. Now regret edged Viera's approach as she joined the pair in the Chamber of the Eclipse. As she cleared her throat for their attention, Constantine stepped aside.

"Viera," Gavyn said, tucking a cross beneath his robes, "I trust you are well."

"Aye. You?" She smiled, fractious and uncertain. "No more sneaking bara brith into the Infirmary for you, eh?"

"I'm getting there. One step at a time." Gavyn chuckled before sobering. "But I'm not the only one you're meaning to talk to."

With a wink, Gavyn sauntered away and Viera closed her fingers over Constantine's arm. "Regret might be heavier," she said, shaking him, "but forgiveness, acceptance, and love last far longer."

He pulled her into a hug. "Aye, and it took a few years for me to understand that. You grasped it far quicker than I did."

Her attention returned to Gavyn standing over diagrams spread in front of Dagonet and Kae. Arthwyr sat across from the trio, relief in his smile as Balin added insight on Uriah's work. Skittering around the table,

Dagonet flopped into the vacant chair next to Arthwyr. The half-brothers pointed and pored over a diagram.

After a while, Arthwyr stood and those standing settled into their seats. Viera and her friends took chairs that had been set up for them to observe Eryck's induction into the Knights.

"As some are aware, our ranks need new blood and perspective." Arthwyr ruffled Palamedes' hair on his way past. "Our youngest students have not had the opportunity or pleasure to experience an induction into the Eclipse."

Arthwyr called out, "Come, Eryck. You've waited long enough."

Eryck rose, halted in front of Arthwyr, and bowed as Lance approached.

"This way, son." Lance directed Eryck to the hearth. "You will bow and the oath is—"

Arthwyr returned to the younger nobles. "We train students under the expectation that if they serve well, they might one day assume one of our posts. Knights are members for life."

Myrddin joined Arthwyr. "A lordship does not mean you will become a Knight."

Percyval shoved his chair under the table and ordered, "Hold up. There is something I promised Lowen." He waved for Eryck to join him. "Your father would be proud of the man you have become. For that reason, I won't allow you to become a Knight."

Arthwyr twitched and several around the table murmured.

"Not without giving you what Lowen wanted most for you. Your grandmother and I discussed this at length." Percyval removed his family signet ring for the House of Rheged. "This is yours, Eryck."

Percyval slid his signet ring onto Eryck's finger. "Now, Arthwyr can Knight you into the Eclipse." He pinched Arthwyr's arm and returned to his seat. "All yours, Arth. Try not to do anything to his face. I still hope to marry him off one of these days."

Viera frowned and asked, "What happens to Elyan now?"

Myrddin patted her head. "Elyan is Percyval's second oldest. Lowen inherited Rheged, and in fathering Eryck, secured the line. Elyan will one day be the Head of Pellinore."

"But he's a Rheged."

Arthwyr thumped his knuckles over the table. "Flexibility flushes new life into the nobility. My mother came from the Kyner line and they included peasants from Kyner Craggs in marriage."

She turned in her seat to the man next to her.

Arthwyr chuckled and waved his hand at Bedwyr. "Which brings us to Bedwyr. There is no one left in Wallach to depose him. He dispatched all who would and despite being twenty-one winters, answers to no one."

Myrddin snorted. "Most of the time he doesn't even answer to you, Arth."

"Why is there such an allowance?" Viera asked.

Arthwyr rounded the table. "The Wallachs are the one family that won't hesitate to eradicate a ruler if the survival of the realm requires it. They have leave to prune the refuse when the Kingship becomes corrupted."

Hunger swam in Bedwyr's eyes as he straightened in his seat. "If you fail your vows and responsibility, it's my oath to bring the realm from the shadows."

Arthwyr clasped Viera's shoulder. "No matter how he feels over our friendship and brotherhood, or any for that matter, Evermore is his first priority." He sidestepped Viera and stood over Bedwyr. "Stand aside. Stand beside. Whatever you do, don't stand between him as the divide."

The King pushed aside the empty chair reserved for the Marshal. "Fight me, Bedwyr. Question me. Defy me. Make me earn your fealty and the trust of the people the Pendragons forsook long ago."

Bedwyr replied. "As you wish, Your Highness."

Arthwyr mussed Bedwyr's hair and faced Viera. "That is our personal charter. One day he'll swear fealty to one most deserving of his fidelity. Until then, his current disloyalty ensures Evermore will become Balanced once more."

After Eryck's Knighting, Viera observed Maryck, Ulrich, and Harlan standing with their new Masters following another ceremony for them. Lance had won the right to be their Master. Morien was Maryck's secondary Master as Trystan had claimed Ulrich as his student. On the other side of the table, Harlan clustered with his uncles and Baudwyn. Balin would be Harlan's Master with Eryck as a secondary Master.

Viera glanced at the map on the table, pondering her future, when a low chuckle had her looking up to find Arthwyr standing beside her. She laughed when he, as King, asked if he might take the empty seat next to her.

Arthwyr settled into the chair. "Have a good chat with our Ancients, did you?"

Viera inched her fingers toward the pendant she wore around her neck. "Aye, Sire."

He leant forward and tugged at the two chains she had braided together, and he gently pulled up the medallion so he could see it. "They showed me those pendants, when they were separate." He paused to study the tree. "I have no idea what it means or how our Fates will turn out. What I do know is that events tend to repeat themselves when necessity calls for it."

Viera massaged the tree on the pendant. "Your Highness, do you know anything about this necklace that you *can* tell me? The Kings were forthright in every regard, but they made it clear that they still know very little."

Arthwyr removed his sword from his scabbard and set it in on the table. "Viera, I can only tell you that there was a similar necklace a long time ago on a painting my mother and maternal grandmother, Aelwyn, once owned. My sister, Morgaine, took it with her when she Bonded, and it has since been lost." His thumb brushed the hilt, and a tree exactly like the one on her pendant formed on the metal. It glowed and disappeared as fast as it had appeared. "There's a lot of significance in symbols. They seem to always hold dual meanings, and their real truths aren't realized until the right person comes along."

Viera gave a reluctant shake of her head. "As it involves me, Your Highness, I think it's all coincidence."

Arthwyr gave her a gentle scoff. "All I can say to that is, 'We'll find out, won't we?' Do you want to know who was in my mother's painting?"

"Of course, Sire."

"Llewelyn, the first Fire Marshal, and Cymry Pendragon, the first King of Evermore. Cymry was ever close to Fire, and for this reason the Element has always been tied to the Pendragons. I don't know if that pendant in the painting was an artist's fanciful rendition, but I've learned that too many coincidences are folly to ignore."

Viera wrapped her fingers around the medallion. "Why would Llewelyn have such a pendant?"

Arthwyr shook his head. "I'm not sure. It's fun to speculate. Her origins were rather mystifying."

She slid the pendant beneath her robes. As she did, a bluish gleam passed over Arthwyr's arming sword. She stretched her fingers toward the blade and stilled atop the metal.

Said Arthwyr, "His name is *Clarent*, the sword that is. My father-in-law designed and smelted him. He's the male half of the Royal Pair for *Excalibur*."

She caressed the hilt, and she felt a vibration against her skin that was more like a hum. "He sings," she said as she examined the sigils engraved on the base of the blade. "Do all swords with these symbols react like this?"

Arthwyr jerked up. "Aha, there is indeed a great power within you. My gamble at taking you within our Inner Circle will pay off. Only Uriah, Dagonet, and Kae have been able to induce a metal weapon to sing for them." He patted her on the back. "You will do great things for the realm; of this I am confident."

"I wouldn't count on that, Sire." Viera made a clownish face. "I mess up a lot."

Myrddin appeared next to them and leaned against the table. "I couldn't help but hear. Child, we all make mistakes when we first start out. Arthwyr and I firmly believe that the day will come when you will be a force in this kingdom. Maybe not soon, but in time it will happen."

The creepy sensation of someone watching her preceded Bedwyr as he walked up to her. "You have the honor of accompanying me to move that warren of rabbits from my chamber."

The King nodded and Viera stood.

"What about Palamedes and Maerna?" she grumbled.

"Palamedes has a training session with Eerie, and Maerna has a grammar lesson," Myrddin said as he pulled Viera aside and gave her a huge hug. "I promised your parents I would do well by you, and I want to fulfill that pledge." He held Viera so tight that she didn't know what to think. He continued, "I'm not going to ruin the surprise. Just know that Bedwyr is going to say something to you that requires a decision on your part."

She whispered in his ear, "Can't you tell me what it is now? Or at least a hint?"

"Nay. I don't want to influence you. Just know that whatever you decide, I'll stand by you." He kissed the crown of her head. "Go now with Bedwyr, and I'll see you at our evening meal. Nimue has the staff preparing a special dinner."

Viera bowed to Arthwyr, who winked at her and jabbed his finger into Myrddin's shoulder. The words "So mote it be, whatever it might be," drifted back to her.

CHAPTER 91

THE OFFER

Viera's carping floated through the room as Bedwyr flipped through a book.

"Please… just… oh, feck… stop hopping, will you!" Viera begged the rabbits.

Looking up from his fifth pass over the same paragraph, Bedwyr tracked her efforts. He rested his chin on his palm as Viera struggled to put two grayish-brown fluff balls into the small wire cage at once. She no sooner shoved one in when the other squirmed free and escaped her grasp. When she recaptured it, the first one bounded off.

Viera gave up and sat back against the enclosure, her hair puffed around her and wild strands drooping everywhere. A bunny sniffed at her legs. She lunged, grabbed it, and pushed it through the mesh door. "Are we taking these to the new stable?"

He propped his legs on the edge of his desk. "We are."

"Oh, Great Knight, I don't see much of *we* in this."

She chased after a rabbit, but it scampered under a chair. "I thought these things stayed pretty much in one place. But, nay, not these. They're like—"

"Quit complaining. Think of it as a test."

"Can I ask you something?" Bedwyr nodded and she continued, "Do you think… do you think my family is proud of me?"

"Who cares?"

"I just hope they care."

"They won't be there for your successes—or failures." Bedwyr jammed a desk drawer closed and yanked open another. He pulled out a small black box and turned to Viera. "You don't ever say goodbye to them, nor they to you. Just fare thee well until another time. But you're always with each other, no different from how I am with Shiori."

A bunny jumped into Viera's lap, breaking her concentration. "Does it get easier to say fare thee well?"

"Nay." He traced his fingers over the mother-of-pearl design of a sparrow inlaid upon the slick ebony surface of the lacquer case, which he placed on his desk. "Each time we leave the ones we care about carries its own separate sorrow. That never changes—for any of us."

He rose from his chair, and one thought echoed in his head. *Yours will always be hardest, Suzume.*

He stepped around his desk, his fingers pressing the box as he dragged it over the surface. It took a monumental feat not to toss the box back in the drawer. "What did Myrddin give you when he first accepted you as his Apprentice?"

"I… I was supposed to get a gift or something?"

Bedwyr stared at her as if she had no more sense than the animal in her lap. "How the Hells are you so… Did you take a holiday when you signed your contract?"

She lifted her hands, palms upward and level to her shoulders.

"Well, you're supposed to get something—and give a gift in return."

Her face lit up like Yule had arrived early. "What am I supposed to get? Oh! Oh! Can I have a cat like Galahad's Moggy?"

"Nay, you can't have a damned cat."

"No Moggy. Then how about my own horsey? I'm riding better than ever, you have to admit."

He tapped the box against his shoulder. "Are you done?"

She protruded her lower lip. "I guess."

"What Myrddin gives you is up to him. He might be waiting for it." Bedwyr motioned for her to rise. "Knowing him, he forgot."

Viera climbed to her feet. Setting the bunny in the cage was easy this time.

Bedwyr held out the box for her, and she hesitantly took it from him. "What's this for?"

"Choosing an Apprentice."

"You're choosing an Apprentice of your own?"

Bedwyr snorted. "I've already chosen one."

Viera tried to open it, but the top didn't budge and there was no latch. "Let me guess. Your Apprentice is the unfortunate soul who figures out how to open this box?"

The corners of his mouth formed a brief grin. "Something like that."

Viera shook the box close to her ear. "You might fit an Iyesgarth friendship gift in here. I'll help you give it to Jocelyn, if that's who you're going for. She'll love it."

"I wouldn't dream of it."

The lid clicked when Viera put pressure on one side. In neat Evermorean script, the name *Viera* was written on cream vellum. Beneath this, in Nihongo, was *Suzume*.

"I could not formally offer you an apprenticeship in front of the others—" he leaned forward, catching all of her wide-eyed emerald stare— "Not with how I rejected Maryck and Ulrich. Nor can I with the charter of my House. The Wallachs don't give out House symbols. Not unless the person becomes a Wallach, or if I support that person's rise to the Kingship."

Viera secreted the paper into her robes. There were two fans inside the box. Silver lined the panes and rich dark wood shone in the room's sunlight, as well as on the Sakura engravings inlaid on the fans' guards. She lifted one and opened the folds. "It's beautiful."

"Beautiful, but Tessen are very deadly." Bedwyr pointed at the fan. "That isn't the traditional Evermorean exchange for an apprenticeship. Aye, far more personal."

"I take it that another was meant to wield them?" Bedwyr didn't respond, so she closed the fan and laid it in the box and pressed her concern: "I guess you're telling me that I'm the second choice?"

"Don't be offended. My mother promised Olwen she would be Shiori's Apprentice. Those fans were to be the gift Shiori gave Olwen when my sister started her training."

Viera snagged another wayward bunny and deposited it in the cage. "I'm missing something in all this."

"My father's gift to Olwen for reaching thirteen summers was to kill her." Bedwyr swallowed and returned to his chair. "But that's all in the past. If you accept my apprenticeship, I vow to train you to stand equal to anyone in this or any other realm. You will fear no one. Not me. Not our King. Not any King."

Bedwyr settled back in his seat and his chair creaked. He opened the inkwell on his desk to pen a letter to his equerry in Tryfan Heights. As loath as he was to visit the dreary holdings, he needed to prepare for his autumnal visit. He dipped his quill into the ink and scratched the tip of his quill over the vellum.

Dear Dante,

Expect my arrival on the—

Chains clinked and fabric brushed his arm, drawing his attention from the parchment.

Both Tessen fans hung from Viera's belt. She pointed at the empty case. "Is the box part of my gift, or do I have to give it back?"

Bedwyr stared at her.

"I'm asking this because I want to know just how much I have to give you in return." Viera shook the box at him. Her effect made it clear that whatever it was, it wouldn't come easy. She stomped her foot. "So, what do you want from me? Let's hear it?"

He ground his teeth. "How about silence?"

"Oh, I know!" She flailed as though attempting to fly. "An Iyesgarth welcome gift. The Queen has chipmunks in the arbor. You just gotta taxidermize the tail right for optimal scratch."

Bedwyr set his chin on his palm and stared at Viera. *What's the standard return policy on Apprentices again?* Warmth filled his stomach and he sighed. *Nay. It was too late the second I saw you.*

CHAPTER 92

THE MARSHAL'S REVEAL

No better painting had graced Elden's Hearth until Arthwyr's birthday present debuted one fine Agosti afternoon as Viera had witnessed the momentous occasion. The painting portrayed all of the Knights of the Eclipse in poses indicative of their positions. The big moment saw the Court and servants assembled in the atrium to the grand entrance of the castle.

The curtain had fallen away, and an ethereal screech from their Queen made the gathered throng flinch. Guinevere spun on her heels and pointed one at a time at the three redheaded Foxbury Knights, and screamed, "You! You! You! Each of you will pay dearly!" She snatched a broom from a servant and brandished the "weapon" as well as any Knight might his broadsword.

Her features contorted and she charged. Gavyn took the first blow, rapped firmly across the top of his skull. Garyth and Gaheris tripped over each other in their haste to make it out of the main archway. Guinevere, not to be dissuaded by their hasty departure, tore after them, waving the broom wildly as The Seven Sisters, Talia, and Linny clattered in her wake with an accompaniment of feather dusters, dustpans, mops, and war cries of, "Down and out with the rubbish!"

Displaying their roguish charm at its finest, the Foxbury triplets had "touched up" the painting the previous night. The vaunted birthday present was removed from the wall and now hung in the Memorial Hall where Viera and her friends examined it in greater detail.

Viera muffled her laughs as Brynn pointed to a fox drooling over Gereant's leg. "It's their best work ever," the Blumenthal Maid said. "A shame it shan't go in a more public place than here."

"Not with the Queen frothing at the mouth to have it destroyed," Maerna said. "A wonder Arthwyr got it from her grasp."

Palamedes ran his fingers over the image of a hookah painted between his brothers. "Dagonet, a few Foxes, and a falconer might have assisted. Eerie helped a little and Bedwyr is safeguarding others in his room. They're going to Tryfan Heights to be duplicated and refurbished."

Viera, Brynn, Delilah, and Maerna continued down the width of the painting, when they stopped at the section where bunny ears had been drawn on Bedwyr's head. "May the Foxes' vandalism go on in infamy," Brynn said, smoothing the new baldrics on her sleeves designating her as Lamorac's and Ewain's new Apprentice Healer. "Though, they could never come close to beating out Bedwyr in this arena."

Viera shrugged. "What makes you say that?"

It was Brynn's turn to shrug. "Bedwyr either destroys or tosses out what he doesn't like. He's responsible for getting rid of many royal artifacts after the Duels."

Delilah giggled. "He was pretty bad. He gave away many of the vases in the castle to the peasantry, saying they were chamber pots."

As they made it down the painting, a gong rang through the hall for lunch. They cut between two statues and rounded the bend to a hallway that opened into the main corridor for the grand entrance. Castle staff and House personnel were in the throes of packing.

Viera and her friends entered the dining hall. They walked to the far wall where a large painting of the various Knights hung with Arthwyr front and center and Lance and Myrddin flanking him.

"Why are your brothers not on here, Palamedes?" Viera asked. "I don't see the Ancients, Morien, or Bors either."

Said Maerna, "This picture portrays only the original Knights inducted into the Eclipse. Twenty-nine in total, including some names you wouldn't know who have met Twilight."

Viera scanned the remarkably good likeness of Lord Kelliweg. "Baudwyn was one of the first?"

"Aye. During the Duels, Baudwyn funneled money to Arthwyr, straight from the Treasury. He also came up with a way to increase the demand for black wool, and to offset the costs for dying it."

Viera creased her brow. "Black wool?"

Maerna bent toward Viera. "This was all Uther. He wanted only black wool. But he paid out the arse for white wool too."

Viera peeked over her shoulder at the Treasurer sitting between Garyth and Tippy at the feast hall table. "How was Uther paying for white wool if he wouldn't accept it?"

"The white wool went through Wyllt Way. My father soaked it in charcoal and steeped it in black ink. Simple process with Ewain and Tippy involved." Maerna smiled broadly. "By buying this wool, Uther helped pay for our war efforts against him. There's a reason Baudwyn is called the Treasurer of Evermore."

Viera asked, "Is it a real title, like the Marshal?"

Delilah flicked her hair over her shoulder and pointed to the picture as she spoke. "The first Knights held various positions during the Duels. Some are familial titles. Others were codenames, such as the Spymaster for Dagonet and the Falconer for Trystan."

"If you look closely, he had the name of the Knight and his designator put on this painting." Maerna tapped the bottom of Constantine's image. "See here? Constantine is called the Shepherd of Evermore."

Viera traced the two lines with her fingers and said, "Aye, the Shepherd. It suits him." She matched the men with the ones she knew, stopping on a dark-haired man with light-green eyes and a rounded face. "Is this Eryck's father?"

"Aye, Lowen Rheged," Brynn said, thumbing the wooden indulgence Eryck had given her and was ever tucked into her cummerbund. "The Dragoon of Evermore. His was the first memorial erected after the Duels of the Draigs."

Viera continued down the painting until she came upon a trio of redheads sitting next to Renard Foxbury. She doubled back to look at anyone she'd missed in the painting, and one name stood out by its absence. "Why is Hamyll not included in this picture?" she asked. "He's a Knight of the Eclipse, right?"

"My uncle wanted no recognition toward his efforts." Maerna lowered her chin and her hair curtained her like a black mourning veil. "He insisted that any paintings of him be destroyed and none commissioned. My father and Arthwyr respected his wishes."

Grief swelled within Viera. Hamyll appeared as a shade—and only in the most distressing of times. *Guess he was Fated that way, but why him?*

Viera concentrated on the painting further. A gray-haired man stood next to the penultimate Knight in the entire picture: Uriah Cameliard. He was the old man in the abandoned Throne Room—and another ghost from her scattered glimpse of Evermore's past was brought to light via this work of art. He was the one who went to Bedwyr's side and saved his life. She beamed at the image and mouthed, "Thank you."

Her attention shifted to the last figure. Even here, Bedwyr scowled. Uriah had his arm extended to him, and he bore a light smile. His hand was above Bedwyr's shoulder as he reached across the distance the younger Knight put between himself and the other Knights.

Viera bent closer to see what Bedwyr was designated as, and she gasped at the deep gouge in the canvas that had eliminated any recognition. She picked at the scraps and tried to reassemble the name, but the damage was too severe. She stilled at an extra carving above Bedwyr's name.

Viera seethed, "Those ruddy bastards!" She reeled toward where the Sagramores sat at the table. "Wait 'til I give them a piece of my mind."

Maerna locked Viera into place. "The Lord of Metal and Gray himself."

Viera stared at the vandalism. "Truly?"

"Bedwyr was eighteen winters and angry at the world. Arthwyr Knighted him first, believing that the one who lost the most deserved the honor more than any other."

With curiosity brimming in Palamedes' eyes, he edged closer to Maerna and asked, "Knighthood is a great honor. Why in Hells would he do this?"

Maerna took a deep breath. "Bedwyr didn't want to be a Knight. When he received his summons to Court, he sent Shiori back with a message for Arthwyr to go feck himself."

"What changed his mind?" Viera asked, returning Palamedes' vigorous nod. "It had to be something really special."

"It was Guinevere's father." Maerna's head shifted to the man next to Bedwyr. "Uriah, Dagonet, and Guinevere knew how deeply Bedwyr mourned the loss of his mother and his siblings."

Delilah slid her fingers over Viera's. "Uriah was the only one who could convince Bedwyr to become a Knight, and he did. Arthwyr made some promises and formal concessions, and Bedwyr was Knighted in the gardens. Few saw the ceremony but most know the history." Maerna waved at the painting. "Guinevere was less than thrilled with this one and wanted another one made. But Arthwyr laughed at the 'touch-ups,' and it became his favourite."

Viera brushed some letters carved into the canvas. "Let me guess. Bedwyr's addition to the rendition?"

"Aye," Brynn said. "He was the first. It was only fair he held the ultimate title for the Knights."

Viera stared at the carved letters, familiar enough to read *The Eclipse* as the one Bedwyr chose to carve as his designator. She turned to the brooding figure of Bedwyr seated at the table behind them. Dagonet draped his arm over Bedwyr's shoulders. Despite prodding at the offending arm, Bedwyr leaned into the touch.

Viera said to Maerna. "What was Bedwyr's original designation?"

Swiveling her head from Palamedes and the other two girls, Maerna scuffed her boot over a cleft in the stone floor. "Father made me and others promise to keep this among ourselves until you were ready."

Viera's stomach tightened as she looked each of her friends in the eye and received cautious nods from them. "Ready for what?" she asked.

Maerna clasped Viera's wrists with both her hands. Time froze as Maerna's soft voice became the loudest Viera had ever heard:

"Ready to learn that Bedwyr is The Marshal of Evermore."

The Beginning

Appendices

Knights of the Eclipse

Aglovale Pellinore: Lord of Pellinore Falls. Long white hair and beard. Blue eyes. 6'6". 70 Winters. Fire Elemental. The Scholar of Evermore.

Arthwyr Pendragon: King of Evermore and Elden's Hearth. Blond hair and beard. Blue eyes. 6'4". 48 Autumns. Metal Elemental.

Balin Cameliard: Lord of Spitsbergen. Cornstalk yellowish hair and beard. Pale blue eyes. Metal Elemental. 6'1". 30 Summers. The Chamberlain of Evermore.

Baudwyn Kelliweg: Treasurer. Short, spiky gray hair. White eyes. 5'11". 35 Winters. The Treasurer of Evermore.

Bedwyr Wallach: Lord of Tryfan Heights. Black hair. Reddish brown eyes that shift between cinnamon to blood red. 5'8". 21 Winters. Water Elemental.

Bercylac Bredbeddle: Elven King of Ribeena. Light green skin. Long emerald, rose, orange, and turquoise hair; glimmer of gold teased and laced with effervescent strands. Eyes glow with catlike pupils. Pink surrounds his pupils before the outer color shifts into cyan. Pointed ears. 5'10". 382 Summers. Ice Elemental.

Bors Numidia: Future Mercenary King. Alkebulan and Muslim. Black skin. Short black hair. Dark brown eyes. 5'10". 18 Winters. Metal Elemental.

Carydoc Ynyr: Lord of Gwent. Short black hair peppered with gray and white. Blue eyes. 6'0". 53 Autumns. Earth Elemental. Steward of Evermore.

Constantine: Catholic Priest from Viteliu. Born in Milan. Black hair. Honey-gold eyes. 29 Autumns. 6'2". Fire Elemental. The Shepherd of Evermore.

Dagonet Vagary: Orange hair, goatee, and mustache. Teal eyes. 39 Springs. 6'1". Metal Elemental and Alchemist. The Spymaster of Evermore.

Dinadan Blumenthal: Lord of Blumenthal Bluffs. White hair and beard. Greyish-green eyes. 5'11". 84 Winters. Master Scribe. Earth Elemental. The Scribe of Evermore.

Ector Kyner: Lord of Kyner Craggs. Shaved himself bald when he started to lose his hair. Keeps a beard and handlebar mustache. Has blue and black sigils tattooed on his head, arms, and legs. Brownish-green eyes. 6'3". 62 Summers. Earth Elemental. The Grandmaster of Evermore.

Elyan Rheged: Future Lord of Pellinore Falls. Auburn hair. Green eyes. 6'3". 25 Springs. Wood Elemental. The Archer of Evermore.

Ewain Gorre: Lord of Gorre Retreat. Blond hair. Green left eye and violet right eye. 5'10". 31 Springs. Water Elemental. Healer. Healer of Evermore.

Gaheris Foxbury: Lord of Murphy's Hold. Red hair. Blue eyes. 6'0". 31 Autumns. Wood Elemental. The Balancer of Evermore.

Galahad DuLac: Future Lord of DuLac. Dark curly brown hair. Blue eyes. 5'6". 21 Springs. Water Elemental. The Herald of Evermore.

Garyth Foxbury: Lord of Murphy's Hold. Red hair. Blue eyes. 6'0". 31 Autumns. Wood Elemental. The Marauder of Evermore.

Gavyn Foxbury: Lord of Murphy's Hold. Red hair. Blue eyes. 6'0". 31 Autumns. Wood Elemental. The Tactician of Evermore.

Gereant Dumnonia: Dwarven King of Dumnonia. Red hair and long beard. Blue eyes. 4'5". 547 Autumns. Metal Elemental.

Kae Kyner: Future Lord of Kyner Craggs. Blond hair. Brownish-green eyes. Tanned. 5'11". 29 Winters. Metal Elemental. Master of Metal Work and Weaponry. The Seneschal of Evermore.

Lamorac Pellinore: Future Lord of Pellinore Falls. Hickory brown hair. Violet eyes. 5'11". Born at the Witching Hour between Summer and Autumn (30). Healer. The Constable of Evermore.

Lance DuLac: Lord of DuLac Pines. Dark brown hair. Sea green eyes. 5'11". 38 Winters. Earth Elemental. Originally Lance Ward. The Ebony Knight of Evermore.

Lionel Rava: Russkan. Fire Elemental. Master Treasurer. Brown hair. Dark brown eyes. 5'9". 36 Winters. The Messenger of Evermore.

Morien Ziyad: Lord of Kindah. Future King of Marrakesh. Short-cropped curly black hair. Black-skinned. Black eyes. 6'8". 35 Summers. Earth Elemental.

Myrddin Emrys: Lord of Wyllt Way. Black hair and beard. Gray eyes. 6'6". 47 Winters. Fire Elemental. The Mage of Evermore.

Percyval Rheged: Born Percyval Pellinore and became the Lord of Rheged. Auburn with white twining through his hair. Green eyes. 6'4". 65 Autumns. Wood Elemental. The Chancellor of Evermore.

Safir Dariush Sasania: Former future Emperor of Saraceni. Black hair. Black eyes. 6'4". 28 Summers. Fire Elemental.

Segwarides Emad Sasania: Dark-brown. Light almond skin. Hazel eyes. 6'4". 28 Summers. Fire Elemental.

Trystan Kurjeris: Eastern gypsy and thief from Lietuva area. Wilds Master. Dirty, silvery blond hair with tribal beads. Hazel eyes. Age uncertain but assumed to be 27 Summers. 6'0". Wood Elemental. The Falconer of Evermore.

LADIES AND MAIDS OF EVERMORE

Anya Pendragon: Queen of Bach Haus. Blond hair. Brown eyes. 32 Springs. 5'7" Metal Elemental.

Blanche Rheged: Lady of Rheged and Seventh Sister of Earth. Dyed black hair. Green eyes. 5'11". 62 Summers. Earth Elemental.

Brynn Blumenthal: Honey-blond hair. Forest green eyes. 5'1". 15 Springs. Earth Elemental.

Constance Cornwall: Mousy-brown hair. Yellowish-green eyes. 5'6". 15 Springs. Earth Elemental.

Delilah Cuhlwch: Streaked brown and silver hair. Amethyst eyes. 5'3". 15 Autumns. Air Elemental.

Eerie Chia: White hair. Magenta eyes. 5'6". 18 Winters. Air Elemental and born with an Oracle's Sight.

Felicia Cornwall: Blonde. Brown eyes. Bucked teeth as a child. 5'2". 16 Autumns. Water Elemental.

Guinevere Cameliard: Queen of Evermore. Catholic. Platinum blond hair. Glacial Blue eyes. 5'9". 38 Winters. Ice Elemental.

Imogen Blumenthal: Blond braids with beads and feathers. 5'7". 28 Summers. Green eyes. Wood Elemental.

Jocelyn Sagramore: Platinum blond hair. Cobalt blue eyes. 5'4". 15 Springs. Water Elemental.

Kazue Abe: Youngest daughter of Naboru Abe and Rosen Llyr. Black hair. Hazel eyes. 5'7". 22 Winters. Metal Elemental.

Linny Rava: Russkan. Brown curly hair. Hazel eyes. 5'2". 34 Autumns. Non-Elemental.

Maerna Emrys: Heiress and future Lady Emrys. Black hair. Gray eyes. 5'3". 15 Winters. Fire Elemental.

Morgaine Pendragon: Queen of Suthseaxe. Black hair. Blue eyes. 32 Springs. 5'9". Metal Elemental.

Reese Kelliweg: Blond hair. Gray eyes. 5'8". 23 Autumns. Earth Elemental.

Saris Gorre: Matriarch of Gorre House, Retired Healer, and Seventh Sister of Water. Gray hair. Blue eyes. 5'8". 63 Winters. Water Elemental.

Sachiko Abe: Lady of Abe Bay. Wife of Haruki Abe. Black hair. Hazelnut brown eyes. 5'7". 45 Autumns. Water Elemental.

Tavrina Cuhlwch: Dark-brown hair. Wears spectacles and has muddy grayish-brown eyes. 5'3". 16 Winters. Wood Elemental.

Tippy Kyner (nee Foxbury): Lady of Kyner Craggs, Midwife, and Seventh Sister of Wood. Red hair and blue eyes. 5'7". 29 Springs. Wood Elemental.

Viera Tillwith: Pumpkin farmer. Chestnut brown hair. Green eyes with brown flecks. 4'11". 14 Summers. Fire Elemental.

Yuliya Blumenthal: Lady of Cornwall Shores and Seventh Sister of Air. Brown hair. Blue Eyes. 5'9". 42 Summers. Air Elemental.

Noblemen of West Evermore

Alistair Kelliweg: Treasurer and Runemaster. Silver blond hair. Gray and brown splotched eyes. 5'10". 27 Winters. Wood Elemental.

Cuchulain Sagramore: Lord of Sagramore Halls. Straw-colored hair and beard. Cobalt blue eyes. 6'3". 60 Springs. Water Elemental.

Daegyn Dyfed: Future Lord of Dyfed Landing. Brown hair that shifts to green. Brown eyes with green flecks. 5'6". 14 Summers. Earth Elemental.

Daisuki Abe: Youngest son of Naboru Abe and Rosen Llyr. Dark brown hair. Green eyes. 5'10". Wood Elemental. 24 Springs.

Eryck Rheged: Future and heir of Rheged. Black hair. Mint green eyes. 6'0". 18 Autumns. Wood Elemental.

Greshit DuLac: Wheat-blond hair. Ice blue eyes. 5'11". 24 Autumns. Water Elemental.

Hamyll Emrys: Fire Marshal under Uther Pendragon's reign. Brown hair. Blue eyes. 6'1". 21 Summers. Fire Elemental.

Harlan Foxbury: Future Lord of Foxbury. Castle: Murphy's Hold. Red hair. Blue eyes. 5'7". 15 Autumns. Wood Elemental.

Harris Sagramore: Future Lord of Sagramore Halls. Straw-colored hair. Cobalt blue eyes. 25 Summers. 6'3". Water Elemental.

Haruki Abe: Lord of Abe Bay. Eldest son of Naboru Abe and Rosen Llyr. Brother of Nimue, Daisuki, and Kazue Abe. Husband of Sachiko. Black hair. Dark brown-nearly black eyes. 6'0". 49 Summers. Metal Elemental.

Kael Cornwall: Lord of Cornwall Shores. Greenish-yellow eyes. Black and silver hair. 6'1". 40 Winters. Air Elemental.

Maryck Pendragon: Crown Prince of Evermore. Dirty blond hair. Blue eyes. 5'6". 16 Autumns. Metal Elemental.

Palamedes Rasim Sasania: Black hair. Hazel eyes. Light almond skin. 5'4". 15 Springs. Air Elemental.

Staunis Cornwall: Brown hair. Yellow eyes. 9 Autumns. No Elemental Presentation yet.

Tremayne Cornwall: Black and white streaked hair. Yellowish-green eyes. 6'0". 25 Winters. Metal Elemental.

Ulrich Pendragon: Second in line to the Throne. Silvery blond hair. Blue eyes. 5'9". 15 Summers. Metal Elemental.

Xavier Cuhlwch: Blue eyes. Grayish-blond hair. 6'2". 26 Summers. Fire Elemental.

ORACLES

Aisling Chia: Medium blond hair with gray. Dark brown eyes. 5'6". 46 Summers. Former Air Elemental.

Lubaba Cuhlwch (nee Cornwall): White streaked brown hair. Hazel eyes. 5'7". 47 Springs. Former Water Elemental.

Nimue Abe: Lady Abe. High Oracle of the Oracle's Guild. Dark brown nearly black hair. Blue eyes. 5'10". 44 Autumns. Former Fire Elemental.

Zabrina: Gray hair. One gold and black iris. Former Metal Elemental. 5'9". 19 Winters.

HANDS OF THE KEEP

Jarvis Ward: Master Brewer and Curer of Meats. Kitchen servant. Blond hair and beard. Blue eyes. 6'2". 38 Winters. Earth Elemental.

Florian: Royal Tailor.

Micah Vagary: Brown hair. Green eyes. 5'8". 40 Springs. Water Elemental.

Primula Fiori: From Viteliu originally. White-streaked black hair. Blue eyes. 5'9". 69 Springs. Earth Elemental.

Shiori Murasaki: Black hair. Black eyes. 5'7". Age Unknown. Water Elemental.

Talia Ward: Ghanaian. Ananse Mistress. Hazel eyes. 5'4". 38 Summers. Water Elemental.

Foreign Allies

Benedict Medici: Catholic Priest and mentor to Constantine. Gray hair and gray hair. 5'8". 70 Summers at Twilight. Fire Elemental.

Francis Borja: Catholic Bishop and mentor of Constantine. Dark ochre eyes. Gray and white patched hair and beard. 5'10". 70 Winters. Fire Elemental.

Lorenzo Sforza: Black hair. Golden eyes. 6'4". 40 Springs. Fire Elemental.

Wilhelm Auraboralis: Future King of Auraboralis. Dark brown hair. Icy blue eyes. 5'4". 15 Winters. Ice Elemental.

Peasants

Beddoe: Quartermaster and Pirate. Black hair. Purple eyes. Blumenthal vassal. 5'10". Born at the Witching Hour between Winter and Spring (23). Air Elemental.

Cletus: Cabbage and carrot farming neighbor of the Tillwiths. Blond hair. Blue eyes. 6'0". 28 Summers.

Dalinger Weiss: Chief with Evermore's Watch. White hair. Blue eyes. 6'2". 68 Winters. Air Elemental.

Dante: Bearded eunuch. Short black hair. Black eyes. 6'1". Unknown age. Earth Elemental.

Darna Eynon: Black hair. Brown eyes. 34 Autumns. 5'10". Master Healer. Air Elemental.

Dottsie: Iyesgarth's blind Healer and Seer. White hair and milky eyes. 5'5". Age Unknown. Earth Elemental.

Garrett Tillwith: Pumpkin farmer. Black hair. Dark brown eyes. 5'6". 16 Springs. Earth Elemental.

Lincoln Limawit: Pompous mayor. Beady green eyes. 5'0". 39 Winters. Earth Elemental.

Noeman: Ancient merchant from the Isles Seas. Brown eyes and thinning dark hair. 6'0". Age unknown.

Peter Decole: Mason Master. Graying brown hair. Blue eyes. 57 Winters. Earth Elemental.

Rhoshlyn Tillwith (nee Aessidhe): Black hair. Green eyes. 5'7". 40 Winters. Earth Elemental.

Sully Tillwith: Auburn hair. Black eyes. 6'2". 43 Summers. Earth Elemental.

Ursula: Former brothel slave. Mordred's mother. Black hair. Grayish-brown eyes. Water Elemental. 5'7". Age unknown.

SARACENS

Alibaba 'Ali' Sasania: Black hair. Hazel eyes. 5'8". 19 Summers. Air Elemental.

Dunyazad Sasania: White hair. Black eyes. 5'4". 50 Autumns. Air Elemental. Nicknames: Mâmân, Auntie, or Dunya.

Janus: Juggler. Dark brown, nearly black skin. Vitiligo on his forearms and face. Short black hair with white patches and brown eyes. 5'8". 19 Winters. Non-Elemental.

Marjanah: Black hair. Violet eyes. 5'5". 15 Springs. Water Elemental.

Sinbad 'Sindhi' Sasania: Dark brown skin. Bald and black eyes. 6'1". 24 Winters. Fire Elemental.

EAST EVERMOREANS

Agravaine Vulgate: Lord of Vulgate's Vault. Black hair. Orange eyes. 6'3". 32 Winters. Fire Elemental.

Armand Jotnar: Black hair. Blue eyes. 24 Springs. 5'8". Ice Elemental.

Carmryn Foel: Lady of Foel's Loch. Long black hair. Burgundy eyes. 41 Autumns. 5'11". Water Elemental.

Ceridwyn Foel: Lady of Foel's Loch. Long black hair. Burgundy eyes. 41 Autumns. 5'11". Water Elemental.

Dain Foel: Youngest triplet son of Carmryn Foel. Brown hair. Burgundy eyes. 6'0". 26 Springs. Earth Elemental

Dother Foel: Middle triplet son of Carmryn Foel. Brown hair. Burgundy eyes. 6'0". 26 Springs. Earth Elemental.

Dub Foel: Oldest triplet son of Carmryn Foel. Brown hair. Burgundy eyes. 6'1". 26 Springs. Earth Elemental.

Errol Luxley: Runemaster and Runebreaker. King of Thieves. Sandy hair and beard. Muddy brownish-green eyes. 5'10". 35 Springs. Air Elemental.

Henri Vulgate: Gray hair. Orange eyes. 5'10". 25 Summers. Air Elemental.

Isaac Minkrune: Blond. Blue eyes. 5'10". 25 Winters. Fire Elemental.

Kenneth Minkrune: Lord of Minkrune Manor. Short blond hair. Grayish-blue eyes. 5'9". 47 Summers. Fire Elemental.

Lilwy Foel: Auburn hair. Gray eyes; one splotched with light brown. 5'4". 15 Autumns. Wood Elemental.

Mordred Pendragon: Wavy black hair. Steely blue eyes. 6'0". 23 Springs. Metal Elemental.

Sluagh: Highwayman. Greasy hair. Yellow teeth. 5'8". Age unknown. Air Elemental.

Ymir Jotnar: Lord of Jotnar's Tomb. Gray hair. Blue eyes. 6'2". 42 Autumns. Earth Elemental.

HONORABLE MENTIONS

Abe Naboru: Lord of Abe Bay and Llyr Lighthouse, husband of Rosen Llyr, and father of Haruki, Nimue, Daisuki, and Kazue. Onmyouji Shinto Priest. Black hair. Black eyes. 6'2". 92 Winters at Twilight. Metal Elemental.

Anya Pendragon: Queen of Bach Haus. Blond hair. Brown eyes. 31 Springs. 5'7". Metal Elemental.

Archibald Windsor: Former Air Marshal. Sandy blond hair. Brown eyes. 5'9". 79 Summers at Twilight. Air Elemental.

Balor: Fomoiri King.

Boran "Cehrazad" Sasania: Former Empress of Saraceni. Sister of Dunyazad. Widow of Shahryar Sasania. Wife of Aglovale Pellinore. Mother of Safir, Segwarides, and Palamedes Sasania. The Architect. Nicknames: Cehrazad and Badgir. 5'9". 49 Springs at Twilight. Air Elemental.

Bres the Blighter: a Fomoiri King that possessed Rallorc the last known Jabberwock King.

Cymry Pendraig (Pendragon): 1st King of Evermore. Blond hair. Blue eyes. 6'0". 96 Autumns at Twilight. Metal Elemental.

Darren Dyfed: Black hair. Green eyes. 6'1". 26 Autumns at Twilight. Earth Elemental. Dragoon of Evermore.

Dernion Pendragon: King of Evermore during the period when the Air and Ice Marshals reportedly died out due to a curse that affected both families. 5'9". 82 Winters at Twilight. Metal Elemental.

Elaine DuLac: Oldest of the DuLac daughters and heiress of DuLac Pines. Soul Bond and wife of Lance DuLac. Mother of Galahad DuLac. Black hair. Blue eyes. 5'6". 39 Springs at Twilight. Water Elemental.

Elden Pendraig (Pendragon): 1st Queen of Evermore. 1st High Oracle. 5'8". 94 Winters at Twilight. Fire Elemental.

Holger Danuske: King and Lord of Suthseaxe. Long blond hair and beard. Scar down the left side of his face and blind in left eye. One green eye. Imprint of horse hoof on the side of his head. 6'3". 38 Summers. Metal Elemental.

Igraine Kyner: Late Queen of Evermore. Mother to Arthwyr, Morgaine, and Anya. Black hair. Brown eyes. 5'5". 46 Autumns at Twilight. Water Elemental.

Jormund Wallach: Former Lord of Wallach and Tryfan Heights. Last Metal Elemental Lord of the Lord of Gray and Metal. Dark brown hair. Cinnamon brown eyes. 6'0". 41 Autumns at Twilight. Metal Elemental.

Karen Wallach: Black hair. Green eyes. Cousin of Ewain Gorre. Of Uesugi blood. Mistress of Shiori Murasaki. 39 Springs at Twilight. Water Elemental.

Kef: Kitchen Master during the civil war. Short dark hair. Brown eyes. 5'10". 62 Summers at Twilight.

Keyne Senan: Deceased Mayor of Iyesgarth. Blue eyes and fair hair. 5'11". Age Unknown. Air Elemental.

Lowen Rheged: Black hair. Green eyes. 6'2". 29 at Twilight. Wood Elemental. The Dragoon of Evermore.

Lucan Cornwall: Late and Exiled Lord of Cornwall Shores during the civil war. Older brother of Vertigorn. Water Master for Galahad DuLac and Bedwyr Wallach. Gray hair. Blue eyes. 5'10". 44 Springs at Twilight. The Bodyguard of Evermore.

Lugh Bheara: Fomoiri Prince and grandson of Balor, who created and Fae/Fomoiri blessed a spade and sent Balor back to the Hells while sacrificing himself. Father of Finneas Bheara. 5'11". Age Unknown. Metal Elemental.

Mabily Bheara: Lover of Lugh and mother of Finneas Bheara. Previous Unseelie Queen. 5'7". Age Unknown. Fire Elemental.

Melinda Mathonwy Dyfed: Lady of Dyfed, mother of Daegyn, wife of Darren. Partially Fae. The Equerry of Dyfed Landing. Earth Elemental. Brown hair. Brown eyes. 5'6". 23 Summers at Twilight. Earth Elemental.

Morgaine Pendragon: Queen of Suthseaxe. Black hair. Blue eyes. 31 Springs. 5'9". Metal Elemental.

Orion: Mordred's best friend, fellow fisherman, and bastard. 5'8". Died on a fishing charter when he and Mordred were 15. Water Elemental.

Renard Foxbury: Late Lord of Foxbury House and Murphy's Hold. Red hair. Blue eyes. 6'2". 51 Autumns at Twilight. Wood Elemental. The Warden of Evermore.

Reveryn Waskinsyn: Solicitor of Tegid Foel. Former Hood of Locksey and secret Secondary Master to Dain Foel. 5'9". 53 Winters at Twilight. Grayish-white hair. Brown eyes. Non-Elemental.

Rosen Llyr-Abe: Lady of Llyr Lighthouse and Abe Bay. Wife of Abe Naboru and mother of Haruki, Nimue, Daisuki, and Kazue. Brown hair. Blue eyes. Oracle. 5'8". 96 Springs at Twilight. Fire Elemental.

Talisen Bach: King and Lord of Bach Haus. Shoulder length pale gold hair. Amber eyes. 5'10". 36 Winters. Wood Elemental.

Tegid Foel: Lilwy's father and the late Lord of Foel's Loch. Graying red hair. Mottled brown and gray eyes. 6'2" but stooped from enchantment to 5'11". 53 Autumns at Twilight. Wood Elemental.

Tobias Esau: Last Water Marshal and Lord of Esau Islet. Gray hair. Blue eyes. 6'1". 89 Summers at Twilight. Water Elemental.

Tor Cuhlwch: Black hair. Brown eyes. 5'11". 41 Summers at Twilight. Water Elemental. The Guardian of Evermore.

Vertigorn Cornwall: Younger brother of Lucan Cornwall and late Lord of Cornwall Shores. Greasy yellow hair. Yellowish-green eyes. 5'8". 37 Summers at Twilight. Earth Elemental.

The Wallach Children: Water Elementals. Daughters: Seren, Iona, Olwen, Wysteria, Rowena, and Daphne. Son: Halwyn (renamed by Bedwyr as Raito).

Uriah Cameliard: Catholic. Lord of Spitsbergen. Master Weapon Forger and Alchemist. Gray hair. Ice blue eyes. 5'10". 64 Winters at Twilight. Metal Elemental. The Artisan of Evermore.

Uther Pendragon: Former King of Evermore. Father of Arthwyr Pendragon and Dagonet Vagary. Husband of Igraine Kyner. Blond hair and beard. Steely blue eyes. 6'4". 62 Springs at Twilight. Metal Elemental.

Zelda Sagramore: Mother of Eryck Rheged and wife of Lowen Rheged. Blonde hair. 5'6". 28 Winters at Twilight. Water Elemental.

ANIMALS

Adur: Segwarides' camel.

Badgir: The golem Palamedes, Viera, and Maerna create.

Blixem: Bercylac's reindeer.

Budgie: Alkebulan gray parrot. Shared between Trystan, Constantine, and Gavyn.

Camie: Galahad's mare.

Donder: Wilhelm's reindeer.

Gales: Lamorac's stallion.

Golly (or Golau): Viera's male sparrow

Gringolet (Gringo): Gavyn's stallion.

Hengroen: Arthwyr's stallion.

Ibil: Bors' Bactrian camel.

Isolde: Trystan's merlin.

Lailo and Ken: Myrddin's mare and stallion.

Lluagor: Carydoc's mare.

Lunete: Ewain's mare.

Morgan: Gaheris's mare.

Moggy: Galahad's cat.

Olwen: Bedwyr's mare named after his sister.

Sid: Viera's Cú Sídhe (Fire Wolf).

Smeeg: Imogen's sailfin lizard.

Tadas: Trystan's stallion.

Tilly (or Tywyll): Viera's female sparrow.

Tivrus: Percyval's stallion.

Troyes: Lance's stallion.

Zephyr: Safir's mare.

Elements and Elemental Colors

Air: Blue, White, Orange

Earth: Brown, Green, Cream

Fire: Red, Black, Yellow

Ice: Gray, White, Blue

Metal: Black, Gray/Silver, Gold

Water: Blue, Green, Purple

Wood: Green, Brown, Yellow

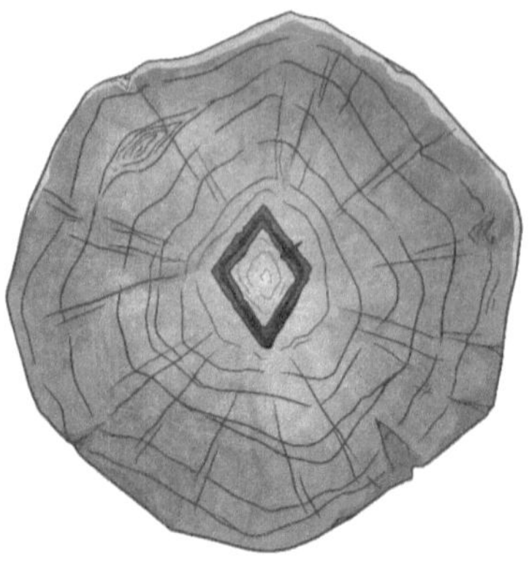

Oracles: Gray robes

Healers: Blue and triskele symbol

Treasurers: Brown and yellow robes

Scribes: Yellow robes with black runes and passages in lines over their robes

ELEMENTAL FIGHTING STYLES

Air: Awyr

Earth: Gweryd

Fire: Tan

Ice: Ia

Metal: Metel

Water: Dwr

Wood: Pren

ELEMENTAL KATAS

Katas for Elements	1	2	3	4	5	6	7	8	9	10
Metal	Eins	Zwei	Drei	Vier	Funf	Sechs	Sieben	Acht	Neun	Zehn
Fire	En	To	Tre	Fire	Fem	Seks	Sju	Atte	Ni	Ti
Water	Hitotsu	Futatsu	Mittsu	Yottsu	Itsutsu	Muttsu	Nanatsu	Yattsu	Kokonotsu	To
Earth	Moja	Mbili	Tatu	Nne	Tano	Sita	Saba	Nane	Tisa	Kumi
Air	Ek	Dui	Tin	Char	Panch	Cha	Sat	At	Nau	Das
Wood	Nane	Jees	Tree	Kiore	Queig	Shey	Shiaght	Hoght	Nuy	Jeih
Ice	Ohta	Kyehti	Kulma	Nelji	Vitta	Kutta	Ciccam	Kaavci	Oovce	Love

FOUR SUITS

There are 52 cards in the game. They are divided into suits. The suits are shuffled up in their individual stacks.

Four dice are used; one for each suit. Each dice has their respective suit carved into them: Diamonds, Spades, Hearts, and Clubs. A player rolls the dice. Whichever suit has the highest number, the player picks the top card from that suit's stack. If the player's highest suit equals another, the two respective dice are rolled until one comes out higher than the other. Then, the player picks the top card from that suit.

The value of the card determines the winner, regardless of suit. The only time that changes is if two players draw the same number from their respective suits. Then, the suit value comes to play. Diamonds are the highest card when two of the same number is pulled. Following that is Clubs, Hearts, and Spades.

Realm's Currency

Currency of Evermore	Value	Type of Metal	Symbol Engraved
Shinnies	0.01	Copper	Spade
Shillings	0.05	Copper	Spade
Ingots	0.25	Copper	Spade
Drams	0.5	Electrum	Heart
Shekels	0.75	Electrum	Heart
Krones	1	Electrum	Heart
Quids	5	Silver	Club
Crore	10	Silver	Club
Liras	20	Silver	Club
Ducat	50	Gold	Diamond
Lakh	100	Gold	Diamond

House Symbols, Guild Symbols, and Elemental Sigils

Prior to the mass misappropriation of cultural and historical symbols, the various symbols in this volume were researched and incorporated based upon their original symbolism and context. This work and the author do not condone weaponizing and corrupting symbols to inspire fear, prejudice, or discrimination against any other person or group of people.

Guilds/Occupations

Evermore (Country): Seven Elemental and Oracle runes surrounding a silver crown.

The Ebony Knight sigil: a targe showcasing all of the lunar phases. The original appeared to mirror phases of the sun in certain light.

Evermore's Watch: Silver suits (Diamond, Club, Spade, and Heart respectively) on two-by-two checkerboard black and white pattern. Similar to the Treasurer's symbol.

Former Brothel crest: A heart with an upside-down heart over it. An S on the crest stands for Siren (foreign sex slave) while an N stands for Nymph (native sex slave).

Healers: Blue triple spiral symbol with evenly spaced arms curved to the right (Triskele).

Maritime/Navy of Evermore: A ship's helm wheel with a compass in the middle.

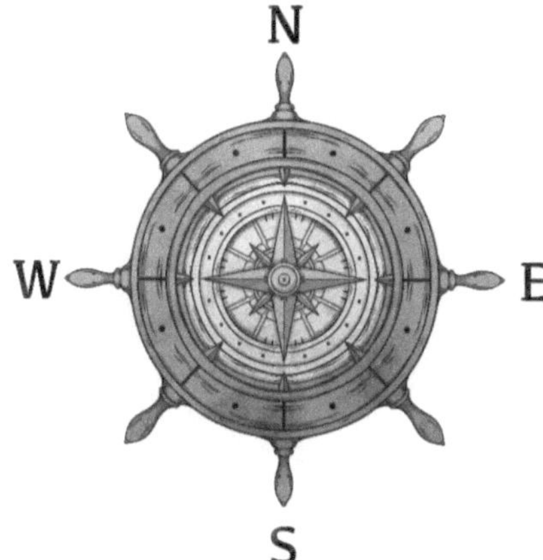

Oracles: Two palms cupping a gray circular orb (scribing ball) with *Ansuz* in the middle.

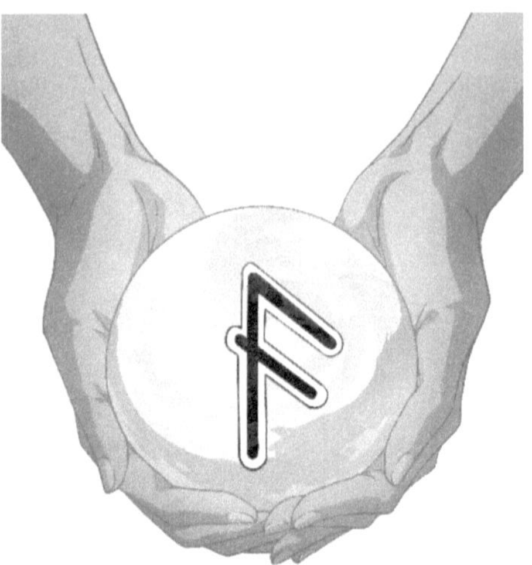

Runemasters: Seven runes of the Elements (*Kaunaz, Jera, Laguz, Hagalaz, Algiz, Ingwaz,* and *Isa)* pointing outward around a circle with chinks in a torque surrounding the runes.

Runebreakers: Gray and black circle closing in the seven runes of the Elements; symbolic of a breaker cutting off an element.

Scribes: Open book with the sun rising from the pages.

Slaves: Had heated irons wrapped around their ankles, forearms, wrists, and necks to produce chained brands. Wards received the marks on their forearms.

Treasurers: Gold suits (Diamond, Club, Spade, and Heart respectively) on two-by-two checkerboard black and white pattern. Similar to the Evermore's Watch symbol.

SEVEN HOUSES OF EVERMORE

The Seven Houses: Shield-shaped emblem with a heart encircled by the gold crown of the Kingship of Evermore. A black dagger through the top of the heart. Four drops of blood drip from the bottom of the organ in the perpetual sign of sacrifice for the realm.

Original Seven Houses of Evermore							
Element	Metal	Water	Fire	Air	Earth	Ice	Wood
House Color	Gray	Blue	Red	Orange	Brown	White	Green
Family Name	Wallach	Esau	Llywelyns	Windsors	Pembrokes	Cadogans	Druirs

THE SEVEN ELEMENTAL SYMBOLS

Air: Orange circle with three blue lines with arrows going from the bottom left quadrant to the top right quadrant. Three white lines with arrows going from the top left quadrant to the bottom right quadrant.

Earth: Three triangles depicting a cream-topped mountain range. The outer shapes are a dark evergreen and central shape a rich umber.

Fire: A hearth with a fire. Colors are red, black, and yellow.

Ice: Gray, white, and blue snowflake.

Metal: Two silver swords with gold hilts superimposed on a black circlet.

Water: S-shaped purple line separating bright blue from forest green. A droplet of blue appeared on the upper right field of evergreen with an opposing droplet on the lower left of the blue part of the emblem.

Wood: Green, brown, and yellow circles in the shape of growth rings.

Western Nobility

Abe: White lined pentagram.

Abe-Llyr: Became a white pentagram with the blends of a white raven profile for certain occasions such as Bonding, births, and deaths.

Llyr: White raven splayed like a star. Head top of star, wings spread like arms of star, talons stretched like legs of star and tail fanned outward like bottom of star.

Blumenthal: A crossed quill and sword.

Cameliard: White Unicorn bowing its head to a gold cross on a silver heart-shaped emblem.

Cornwall: Black downward pointing triangle encompassing fifteen gold circles. Five of the spheres comprise the first row of bezants. The circles spilled down with four in the next row, three in the third, and so forth in the descending lines.

Cuhlwch: Two boars (Twrch Trwyth (black tusked) and Ysgithyrwyn (white tusked)) charging each other.

DuLac: Shield with the Water symbol rising from a chalice. S-shaped dark purple line separating navy blue and forest green for Water symbol. Water symbol = Yin and Yang sign.

Dyfed: Spring green shield and profile of a brown rearing horse with white mane.

Emrys: Twin obsidian dragons squared off against each other with red flames shooting from their mouths on a gray backdrop.

Foxbury: Snarling fox on a yellow shield.

Gorre: A circlet of blue with two silvery lions and their locked paws over a dead serpent. Beneath the body of the snake, gold threading formed the words *Virtue*, *Love*, and *Justice*.

Gwent (Ynyr): A shield divided in half with the left side in blue and right side in black. Three gold fleurs-de-lis: two on the top and one on the bottom in the middle.

Kelliweg: Gold diamond bordering an oak with green leaves and brown roots.

Kyner: Octagon emblem of a gray Griffin on a field of sky blue.

Numidia: Horse with a palm tree on a circular yellow shield.

Pellinore: The profile of a yellow lion stretching its far paw out in defense upon a purple backdrop.

Pendragon: Silver Dragon gripping a gold chalice and sword in its front claws.

Rheged: Black inverted chevron and three ravens on a gray shield banner. Two of the birds are at the top of the emblem; the last raven resting beneath the interior angle of the chevron. The bottom raven flies toward where the lines of the chevron met.

Sagramore: Shield displaying a field of bright red and a square of white on the upper left corner. A lone black star was sewn into the ivory. The final two shapes of gold stars made up the bottom and top right portion of the red background.

Vagary: The diamond-shaped emblem of common theater and marionette masks. The gold one's teeth bear a feral grin. The silver mask's mouth dips and three tear droplets dotted its' cheek.

Ziyad: A green circular emblem with two lions on their hindlegs reaching for a crown upon a pedestal.

Viera's combined Abe-Emrys symbol: Twin obsidian dragons squared off against each other amidst a backdrop of gray. The white lines of the Abe pentagram centered amid the red flames erupting from their mouths.

Eastern Nobility

Bach: White circlet with bard's harp in the center, two silhouetted and sitting wolves facing each other as the arms of the harp and their head ascend back as they howl at a centered silver moon.

Danuske: Two tribal wolves bordering a gray circle (one chases the moon on the bottom part of the circle and the other wolf chases the sun on the top part). In the center of the symbol, Fenris holding the handle of Mjolnir in his jaws and the split symbol of the sun and moon combined on his forehead.

Foel: Robin with orange chest, brown back, and white bottom encased in a black star.

Grendel: Ouroboros encircling a golden sun.

Jotnar: Silver and ruby Valknut (interlocked triple triangle) symbolic of the Jotnar Giants.

Minkrune: Flame-red banner displaying a black adder (ruby eyed) with cross sections of gold diamonds on a teardrop-shaped shield.

Luxley: Field of green displaying two white goats with horns locked and forehooves pressed together while balancing on their back legs.

Vulgate: Two-headed golden eagle displayed (beaked and membered gules) over a purple fess vert shield with a green bar horizontally crossing the middle of the eagle.

FOREIGN HOUSES

Auraboralis: Reindeer in the middle of a lope with its head pulled back. Behind the black silhouette, the silver, blue, and white of the geometric snowflake symbol.

Borja: Square emblem with a bright red border surrounding bright yellow. Red bull in the center over a field of grass. Eight bursts of flame on the border evenly spaced.

Dumnonia: Green triangular symbol of a Warhammer crossed with a shepherd's hook.

Medici: Yellow shield of five red bezants framing the bottom and sides. Centered in the top is a blue circle with three yellow fleurs-de-lis (two on the top and one beneath them).

Mizuno: Upright three-leaf arrowhead plant or Tachi Omodaka with two wavy water lines at the bottom of the stalk.

Murasaki: Similar to the 'family' they herald from, Murasaki is a pseudonym following the Heian Court manners where to refer to someone by personal or family name was vulgar and too familiar. Those claiming the Murasaki name in this series claim a pseudonym family. There is no symbol for them.

Bredbeddle (Ribeena): A circlet of interlaced holly. Three battle axes at different crossed angles superimposed upon the wreath. Beneath the battle axes in Elvish script, "As each one we are all."

Sasania: a black simurgh (Persian mythical bird like a peacock with the head of a dog and claws like a lion) with copper wings. Red plume of fire comes from its mouth.

Sforza: Basilisk devouring a child. Opposite the serpent, a black imperial eagle, tongue hanging from its beak, had its wings spread in flight.

Uesugi: Two sparrows in flight within a stalk of bamboo.

Visconti: Basilisk eating a child (after marrying into Sforza; Sforza adopted this part of the Visconti symbol into their own shield.)

HEAD OF HOUSE SYMBOLS

WESTERN HEAD OF HOUSE SYMBOLS

Abe-Llyr: Blended kanmuri hat with Llyr headband/diadem white raven/splayed as star for the male Head of House and Llyr headband diadem blended with white star and raven kanazashi hair ornaments.

Blumenthal: Compass Pendant Necklaces

Cameliard Chaplets: with white diamonds/mother-of-pearl, topaz, silver and pewter.

Cornwall Collars: made of Blue John Fluorite, Diamonds, jet stone, and imbedded in gold.

Cuhlwch Circlets: black and white crown made with jet stone and mother-of-pearl.

DuLac Diadems: with silver, sapphires, pearls, and aquamarines.

Dyfed: Horse Arm Bracers and Laurel

Emrys: Twin Black Zirconium Dragon Ear Cuffs.

Foxbury: Pebble Penannular brooches made with gold, agate stones, amber, and fashioned into a Celtic Fox tribal design.

Gorre Lariats: made of silver and Blue John Fluorite.

Kyner Crests: melded crown of Griffin, human bone, and iron with Griffin engraving at the center.

Pendragon: Crowns with Seven Elemental and Oracle runes bordering the sides and Dragon in the center.

Pellinore Plastrons: made with gold and amethysts.

Rheged Coronets: Crown made of silver with emeralds and diamonds

Sagramore Sautoirs & Chaplets: Gold necklace and matching gold crown embedded with white and red jasper, carnelian, and quartz.

Wallach: Master rune key for the Marshal/Head of the House.

Ynyr: Sapphire, onyx, and ivory plaited sash with gold fleur-de-lis worked into the plaiting.

EASTERN HEAD OF HOUSE SYMBOLS

Bach: Iron crowns engraved with lupine shapes and removable sea glass wolf pendants.

Danuske: Iron arm rings with twin wolf heads on the ends, the sun and moon engraved over the back and the wolves' tails twined about the Mjolnir in the middle.

Foel Robin Broaches: the gold robin broach with an enameled red breast in a mother-of-pearl setting. The Head Witch of Foel would undergo a ritual where a Robin was emblazoned on their skin marking them as the Leader of the Foel Coven.

Grendel: Gold Ouroboros headdresses.

Jotnar Cavern Crowns: Made with silver, rubies, and diamonds.

Minkrune Snake Torques: Gold snake torque with ruby eyes.

Vulgate: Violet Flame Opals and obsidian in iron wrought crowns.

DEFINITIONS

Light: In Evermorean, it is a concept meaning life. Staying in the light means staying alive or being safe.

Twilight: It is the Evermorean concept of death. Embracing Twilight, is a way of alluding to passing away or dying.

Shadows: The space between Twilight and Light.

Algiz: rune for Metal.

Ansuz: rune for the Oracles.

Atakebune: large wooden Nihongo ship.

Atmokinesis: the ability to manipulate and command the weather.

Bairn: another name for child.

Baka: Nihongo for idiot or stupid.

Bakayarou: Nihongo for stupid arsehole.

Bara brith: speckled bread with dried/candied fruits and steeped in tea.

Brined kippers: type of brined/pickled fish.

Ceffyl Dŵr: a type of kelpie that can take on a human form.

-chan: Nihongo honorific usually used for female children or teens. Sometimes used by people of a senior status to a junior status.

Claymore: a type of sword.

Cú Sídhe: a canine manifestation or summoning usually by a girl or woman. Takes the form of a wolf, fox, dog, jackal, etc. based on the strength and/or ability of the summoner.

Daimyo: one of the great samurai lords who were vassals of a Nihongo shogun. Also refers to the land of the family.

-dono: Nihongo honorific reserved for a lord or master, but doesn't necessarily mean an individual is a noble. It translates as 'Milord' or 'Milady'.

Drills: Nickname for Drill Masters or Drill Instructors.

Duels of Arthwyr's Red and Uther's White Draigs: The civil war between Arthwyr and Uther Pendragon. Also, called the Duels of the Draigs or the Draigs' Duels. Arthwyr was called the Red Dragon (Draig) while Uther carried the White Dragon (Draig) name.

Elemental breaker: metal collar, bracer, bracelet used to nullify an Elemental's element.

Fan-sister: a relationship fostered between two girls in Han or Goryeo where the girls learn social customs and grow into their adult lives. They exchange letters through silk or paper fans.

Feckenza: Yiddish term for fans.

Fomoiri: Evil powerful and much feared sentient creatures that feed on and devour souls in Twilight.

Golem Mactep: Golem Master

Hagalaz: rune for Air.

Igo: Far Eastern board game with black and white stones.

Inari: the Nihongo fox goddess.

Ingwaz: rune for Wood.

Isa: rune for Ice.

Jera: rune for Earth.

Kami: Nihongo word for a God or Goddess.

Kaunaz: rune for Fire.

Kitsune: Fox-shifter.

Knarr: type of boat.

-kun: Nihongo honorific usually used for a male children or teens. Sometimes used by people of a senior status to a junior status.

Kunai: small daggers typically used to scale walls.

Lagaz: rune for Water.

Llamhigyn y Dŵr: Water Leaper. Frog-like reptile with bat or bird wings that allow for it to fly coupled with a barbed stinger at the end of its tail.

Lumistone: type of mineral used as a light source. Only activated by Earth and Metal Elementals.

Modified elemental breaker: a breaker that has been intentionally damaged to no longer work with its original rune key and/or synched to another rune key.

Nenju: Nihongo wooden bead necklace, bracelet, or rosary used in Shinto and Buddhism.

Nikah: part of the Saracen wedding ceremony where the couple exchange vows and sign their marriage contract/promises.

Nunchaku: Wooden or metal rods attached together by a chain.

Ofuda: a Nihongo paper talisman used for Shinto.

Oilliphéist: sea-serpent type monster that can take on a human form.

Sai: Nihongo three-pronged dagger.

Sake: rice wine.

-sama: Nihongo honorific used for people of higher status.

-san: Nihongo honorific used between equals of any age. Similar to Mr., Mrs., Miss, or Ms.

Scrying ball: smooth crystal ball used for Divinations.

Shuriken: pieces of metal used as throwing knives. Sometimes made out of Nihongo coins.

Tanuki: Racoon dog shifter.

Tessen: Nihongo fans used for martial arts.

Usagi: Nihongo word for rabbit.

DAYS OF THE WEEK

Monday	Tuesday	Wednesday	Thursday	Friday	Saturday	Sunday
dydd Sul	dydd Llun	dydd Mawrth	dydd Mercher	dydd Iau	dydd Gwener	dydd Sadwrn
Water	Metal	Wood	Ice	Air	Earth	Fire

COUNTRIES

Country/Continent	Fantasy Name	Nationality	Language
Africa	Alkebulan	Alkebulan	Alkebulan
China	Han	Hanyu	Hanyu
France	Gallia	Gallian	Gallian
Germany	Allemani	Allemanian	Allemanian
Ghana	Ghana	Ghanaian	Ghanaian
Italy	Viteliu	Viteliuian	Viteliuian
Japan	Nihon	Nihongo	Nihongo
Korea	Goryeo	Hangul	Hangul
Lithuania	Lietuva	Lietuvan	Lietuvan
Morrocco	Marrakesh	Marrakeshan	Marrakeshan
Russia	Russka	Russkan	Russkan
Saraceni	Saraceni	Saracen	Saracen

Seasons/Months

Seasons	Months	Name of Month	Holidays	Date	Type of Festival
Spring	March	Mawrth	Alban Eilir	March 1st	Light of the Earth
	April	Ebrill	Bubble Festival	April 1st	Spring Cleaning
	May	Mai	Beltane	May 1st	Bright Fire or Fertility
Summer	June	Juni	Alban Hefin	June 21st	Light of the Summer or Shore
	July	Julai	Mala	July 14th	Paint Festival
	August	Agosti	Lughnasadh	August 1st	First Part of Harvest/Close of Summer
Autumn	September	Septamber	Alban Elfed	September 21st	Second Part of Harvest
	October	Oktober	Autumn Moon Festival	October 14th	Moon
	November	Novamber	Samhain	November 1st	Last Collection of Harvest
Winter	December	Nollaig	Yule	December 21st	Yule
	January	Eanair	Homage to the Dead Week	January 14th–January 21st	Memory of Ancestors
	February	Feabhra	Imbolc	February 1st	First Shoots/Sign of Spring

FAMILY TREES

ABE

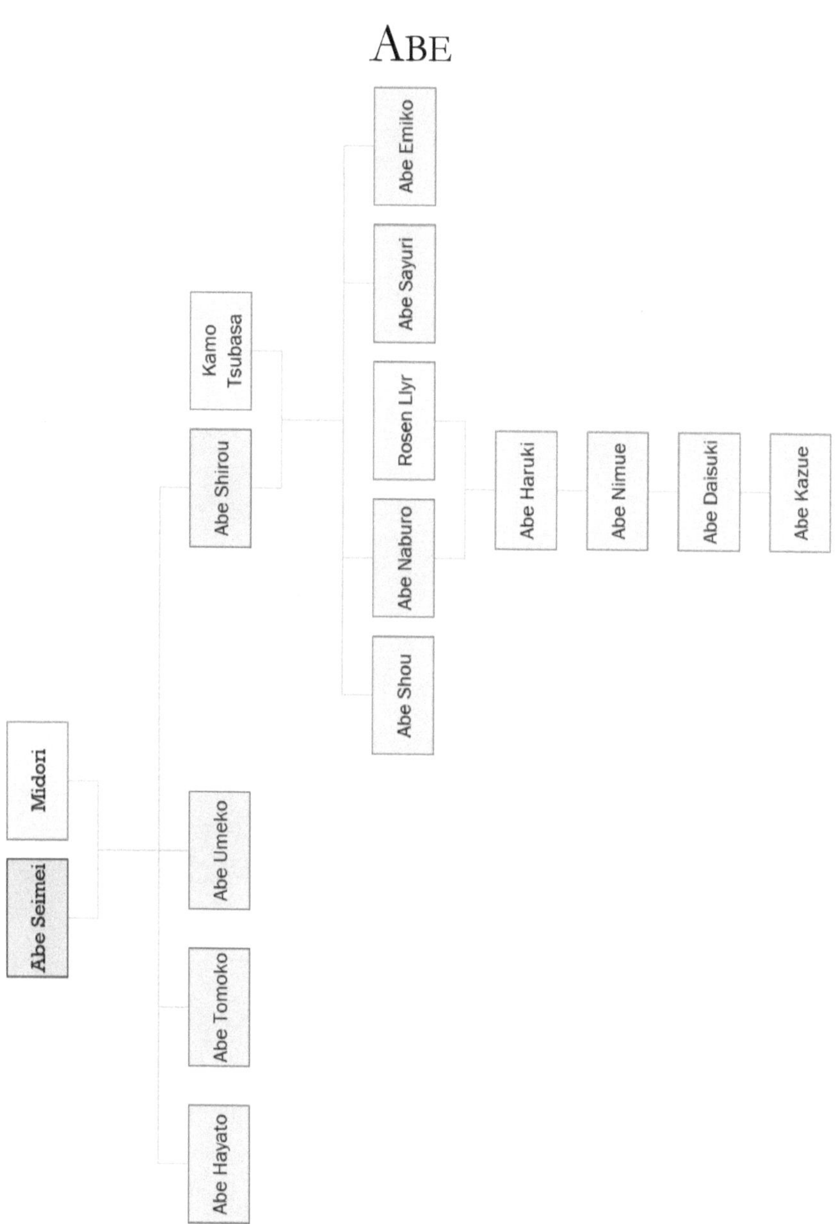

ABE-LLYR

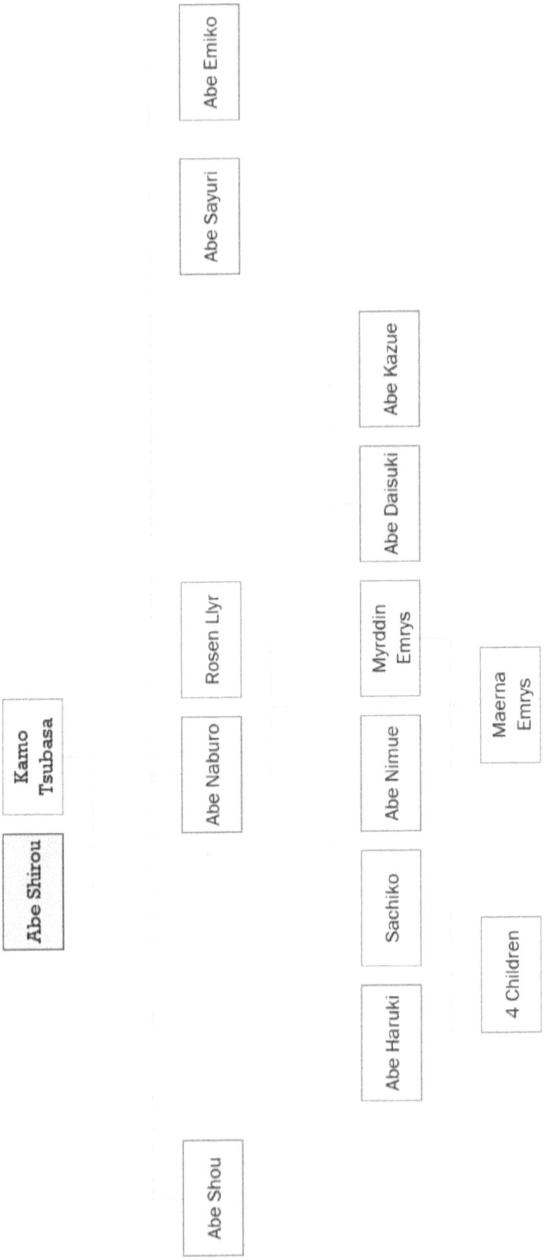

Abe Emiko

Abe Sayuri

Abe Kazue

Abe Daisuki

Rosen Llyr

Myrddin Emrys

Maerna Emrys

Kamo Tsubasa

Abe Shirou

Abe Naburo

Abe Nimue

Sachiko

4 Children

Abe Haruki

Abe Shou

AURABORALIS-EMRYS

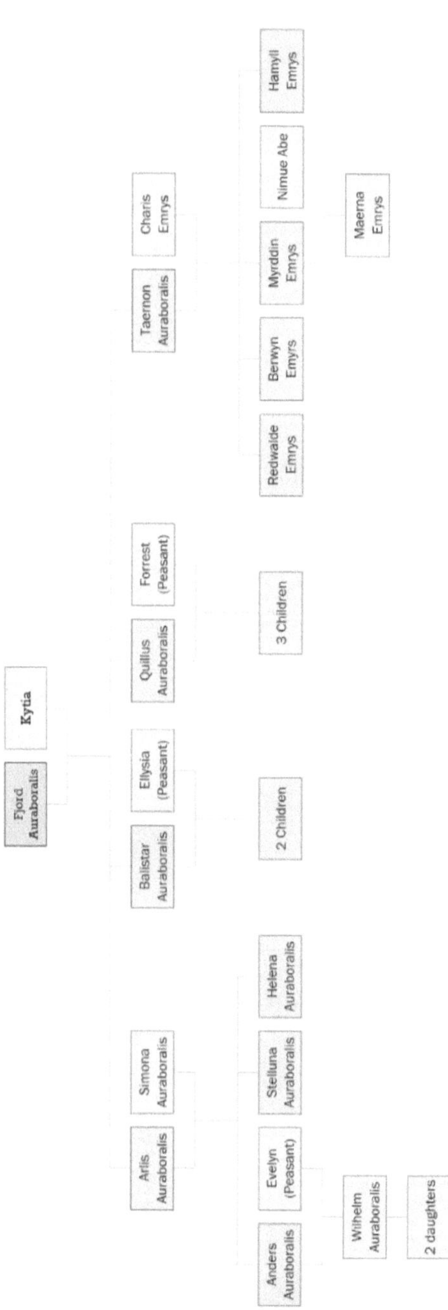

BACH

Osian Minkrune
Runa Bach
4 Children
Ylva Bach
Freya
6 Children
Ragnar Bach
Anya Pendragon
Talisen Bach
4 Children
Embla
Vidar Bach
Frode Danuske
Gunhilde Bach
Morgaine Pendragon
2 Children
Holger Danuske
7 Children
5 Children

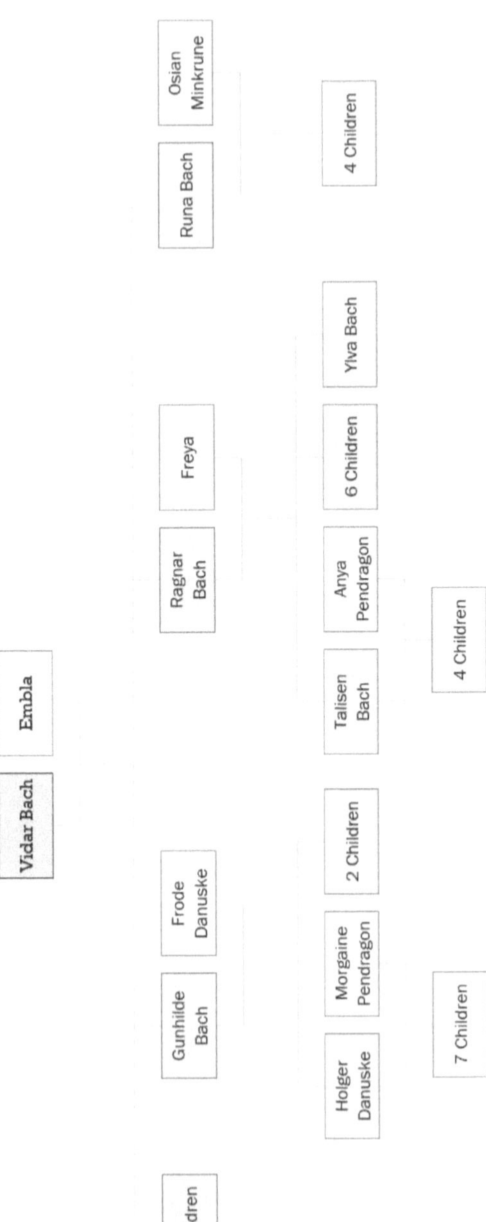

BLUMENTHAL

Pierrs Blumenthal
Bonny Anne
Dinadan Blumenthal
Mariely Cornwall
Keely Blumenthal
Renard Foxbury
Yuliya Blumenthal
Kael Cornwall
Rori Blumenthal
Calyco Rackham
Imogen Blumenthal
Siobhan Cornwall
Graden Cornwall
Kalen Cornwall
Gavyn Foxbury
Collette Sagramore
Garyth Foxbury
Baudwyn Keilliveg
Gatheris Foxbury
Tippy Foxbury
Kae Kyner
Harlan Foxbury
11 Children
Minerva Blumenthal
Dawson Fischer
8 Daughters
Brynn Blumenthal
Jalone Blumenthal
Dinid Blumenthal
Artemis Blumenthal

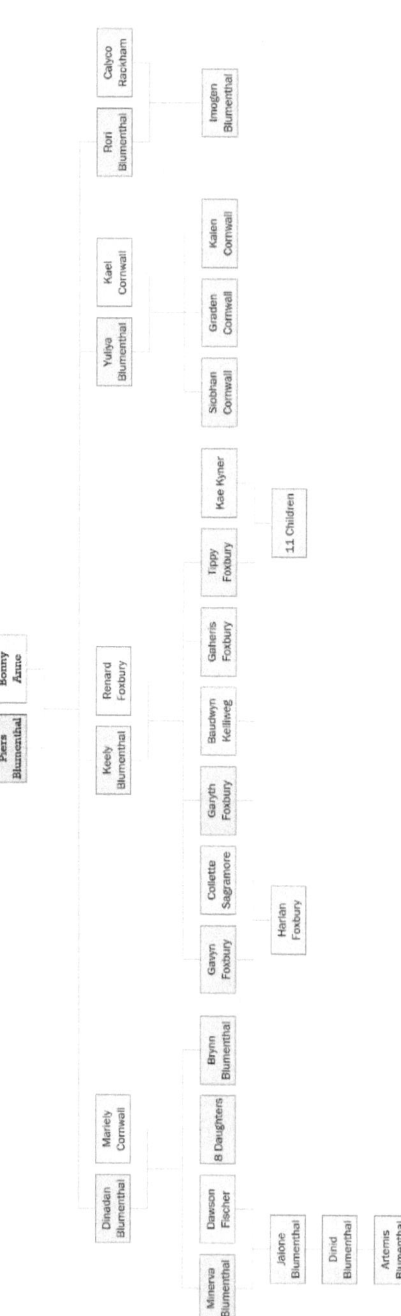

CAMELIARD

Alistair Cameliard — Enys

Uriah Cameliard — Camille Montblanc

2 Daughters

Guinevere Cameliard

Arthwyr Pendragon — Balin Cameliard — Edwina Brechwell

Maryck Pendragon

Ulrich Pendragon

Sistrina Brechwell

Cedric Brechwell

Tobian Cameliard

Cornwall

Raygren Cornwall
Engrid Cornwall
Lucan Cornwall
Reilynn (Peasant)
Mariely Cornwall
Dinadan Blumenthal
Dresmene Cornwall
Algar Sagramore
Vertigorn Cornwall
Donella Cornwall
Selena Cornwall
Kael Cornwall
Yuliya Blumenthal
3 Children
Constance Cornwall
Felicia Cornwall
Tremayne Cornwall
Brynn Blumenthal
8 Daughters
Dawson (Fisher)
Minerva Blumenthal
2 Daughters
Vertigorn Cornwall
Donella Cornwall
Stauns Cornwall
3 Children

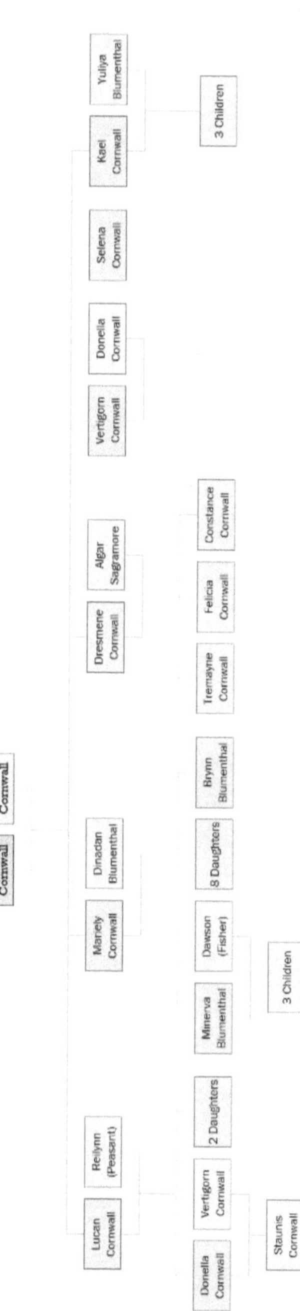

CUHLWCH

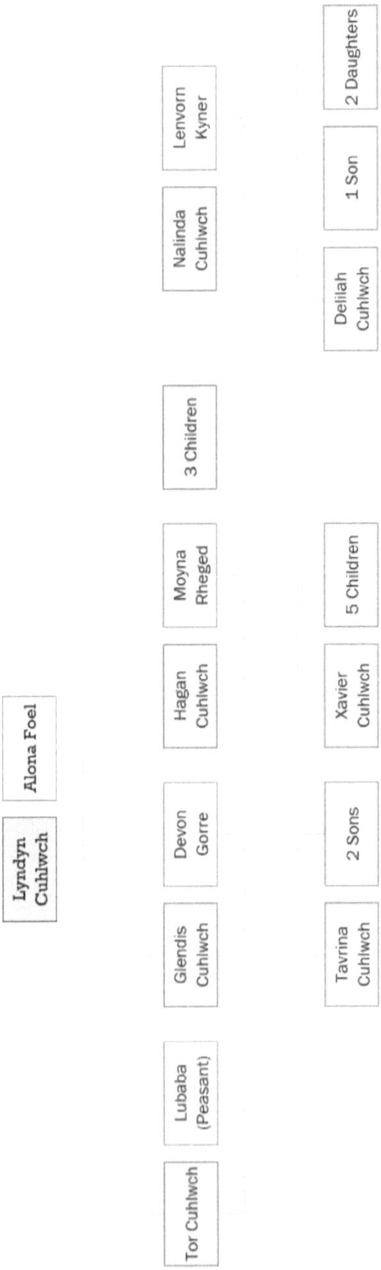

Tor Cuhlwch

Lubaba (Peasant)

Lyndyn Cuhlwch — Alona Foel

Glendis Cuhlwch

Devon Gorre

Hagan Cuhlwch

Moyna Rheged

3 Children

Nalinda Cuhlwch

Lenvorn Kyner

Tavrina Cuhlwch

2 Sons

Xavier Cuhlwch

5 Children

Delilah Cuhlwch

1 Son

2 Daughters

Danuske

Harald
Danuske
Sigrid
Thyra
Danuske
Svend
Frode
Danuske
Gunhilde
Bach
Monife
Colburn
Danuske
Adara
Minkrune
2 Children
4 Children
Holger
Danuske
Morgaine
Pendragon
2 Children
Oya
Danuske
6 Children
7 Children

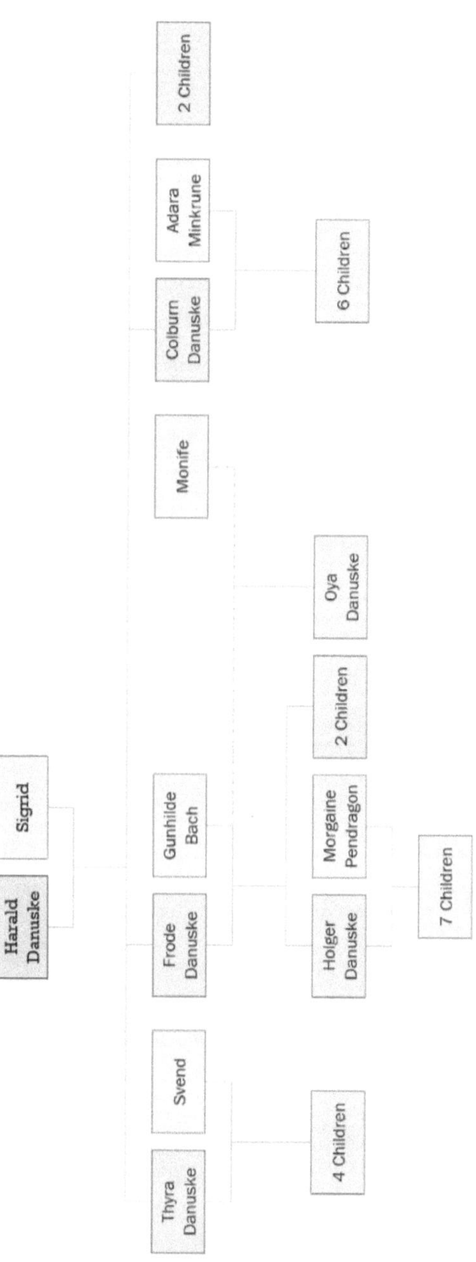

DuLac

Grayson DuLac — Cordelia Esau

Darwyn DuLac — Irene (Peasant)

Faris DuLac — Stanton Cuhlwch

Cienna Gorre

Yale DuLac

Brayley DuLac — Ashleya Gorre

Rayka DuLac — Enders Sagramore

3 Children

Malaya DuLac — Edmund (Foreign Noble)

Estella Gorre — Kenneth Minkrune

4 Children

Aerona Minkrune

Cordelia Minkrune

Brigid Minkrune

Dilys Minkrune

2 sons

Isaac Minkrune

7 Children

Elaine DuLac

Nora DuLac

Lucille DuLac

Odette DuLac

Torina DuLac

DuLac

Yale DuLac
Cienna Gorre
Elaine DuLac
Lance Ward
Nora DuLac
Tamor Cuhlwch
Lucille DuLac
Odette DuLac
Torina DuLac
Braylon Vulgate
Galahad DuLac
Cybella DuLac
Greshit DuLac
4 Daughters
Siarl Vulgate
Julie Vulgate
4 Children

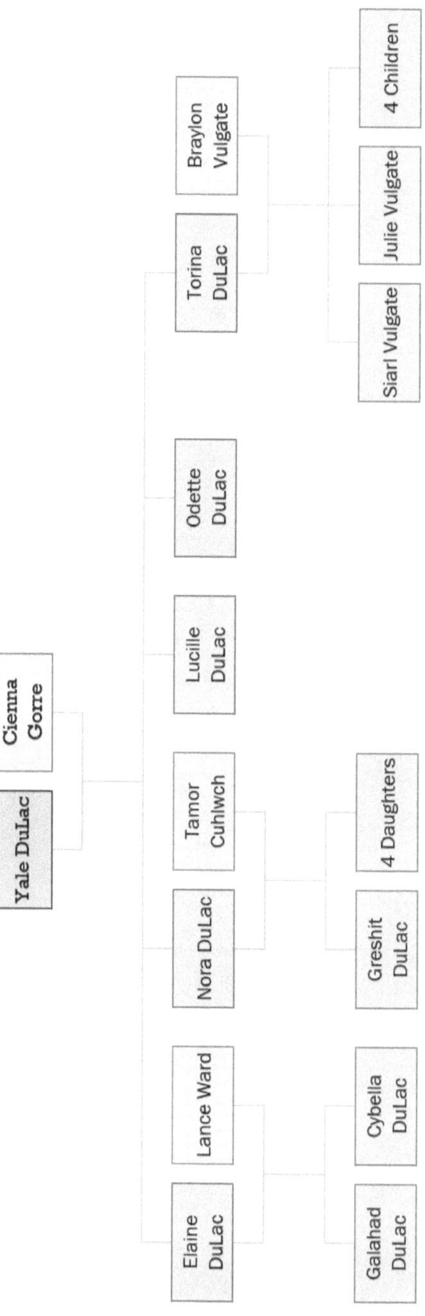

DYFED

Pwyll Dyfed
Rhiannon
Pryderi Dyfed
Cigfa
Alys Dyfed
Cassian Llyr
Sioned Dyfed
Rhys Ynyr
Nia Dyfed
Osian Rheged
3 Children
2 Children
Gildforde Dyfed
Rohan Dyfed
Tyrone Dyfed
Oileala Dyfed

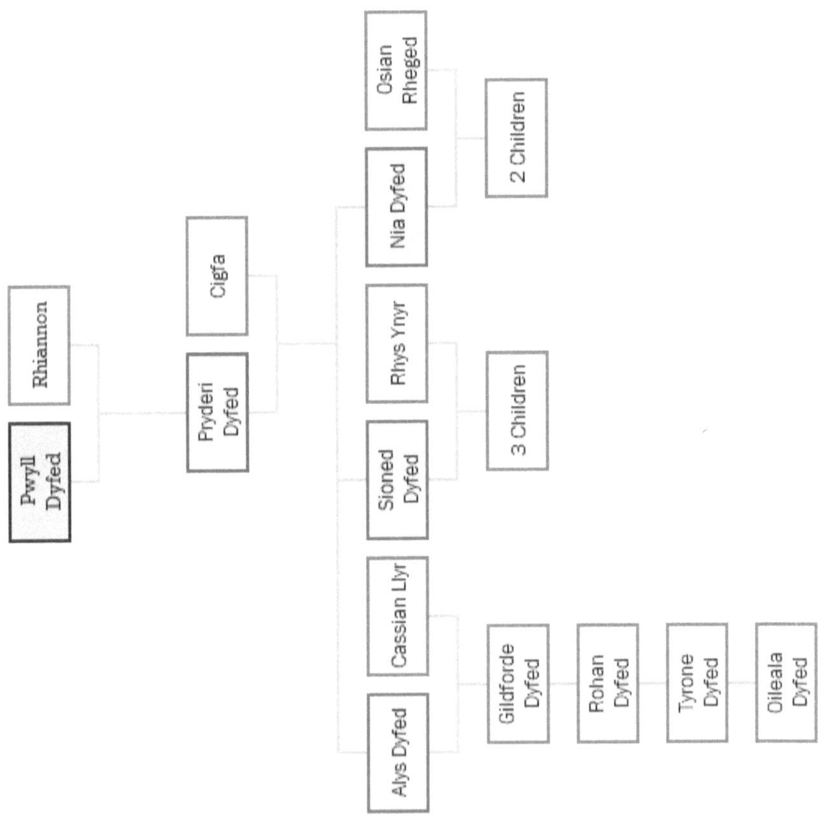

DYFED

Gilforde Dyfed
Cydell Ynyr
Darren Dyfed
Shayla Dyfed
Odele Dyfed
Sherwin Dyfed
Gesselyn Dyfed
Melinda Mathonwy
Galen Rheged
Brianne Auroraboralis
Devon Ynyr
Daegyn Dyfed
2 Children
3 Children

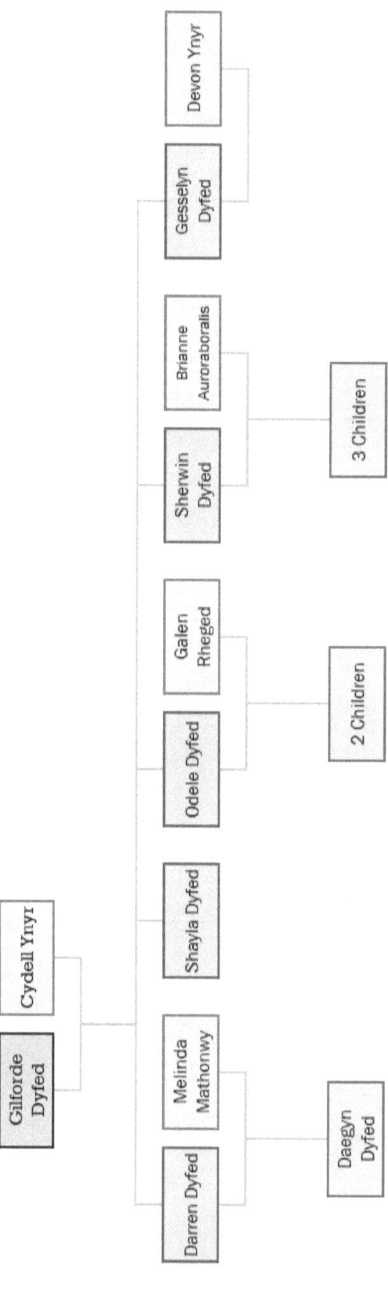

EMRYS

3 Daughters
Blaise
Dinas Emrys
Taernon Emrys
Charis Emrys
Hamyll Emrys
Nimue Abe
Myrddin Emrys
Berwyn Emrys
Redwalde Emrys
Maerna Emrys
Viera (Adopted)

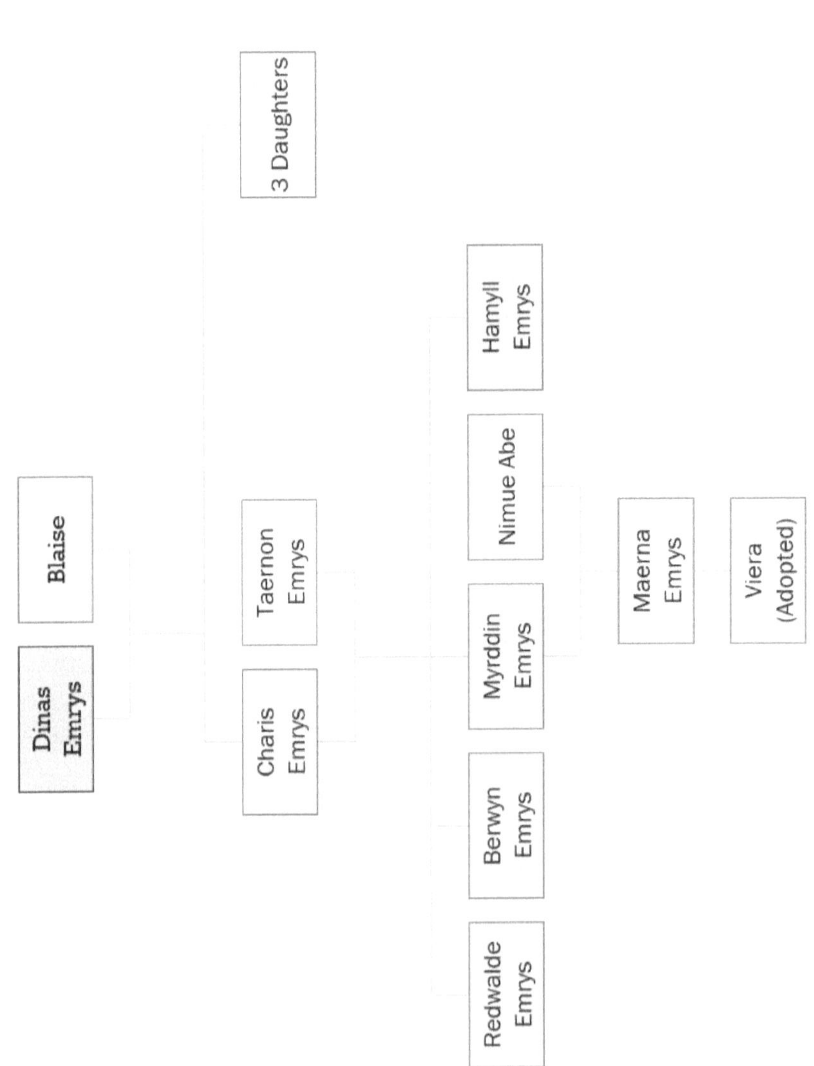

ESAU

Alun Esau
Kendra Foel
Tobias Esau
Bellame Vulgate
Timund Esau
Grissa (Peasant)
Cordelia Esau
Grayson DuLac
Charlus Esau
Petunia Gorre
Darwyn DuLac
Irene (Peasant)
Brayley DuLac
Ashleya Gorre
Rayka DuLac
Enders Sagramore
Iris Gorre
Saris Gorre
Daniel Gorre
Edgaren Gorre
Yale DuLac
Faris DuLac
Malaya DuLac
Estella Gorre
4 Children
3 Children

FOEL

Baldur Foel
Gyda Danuske
Rhion Foel
Catrin Bach
Inkeri Foel
Enzo Visconti
Halstein Foel
Nia (Peasant)
Alys Foel
Jeshua (Peasant)
Strom Foel
Effyn Blumenthal
2 Children
2 Children
3 Children
2 Children
Dylan Foel
Beatrice Visconti
Tegid Foel
Torsten Foel
Bethany Foel
Carmryn Foel
Ceridwyn Foel

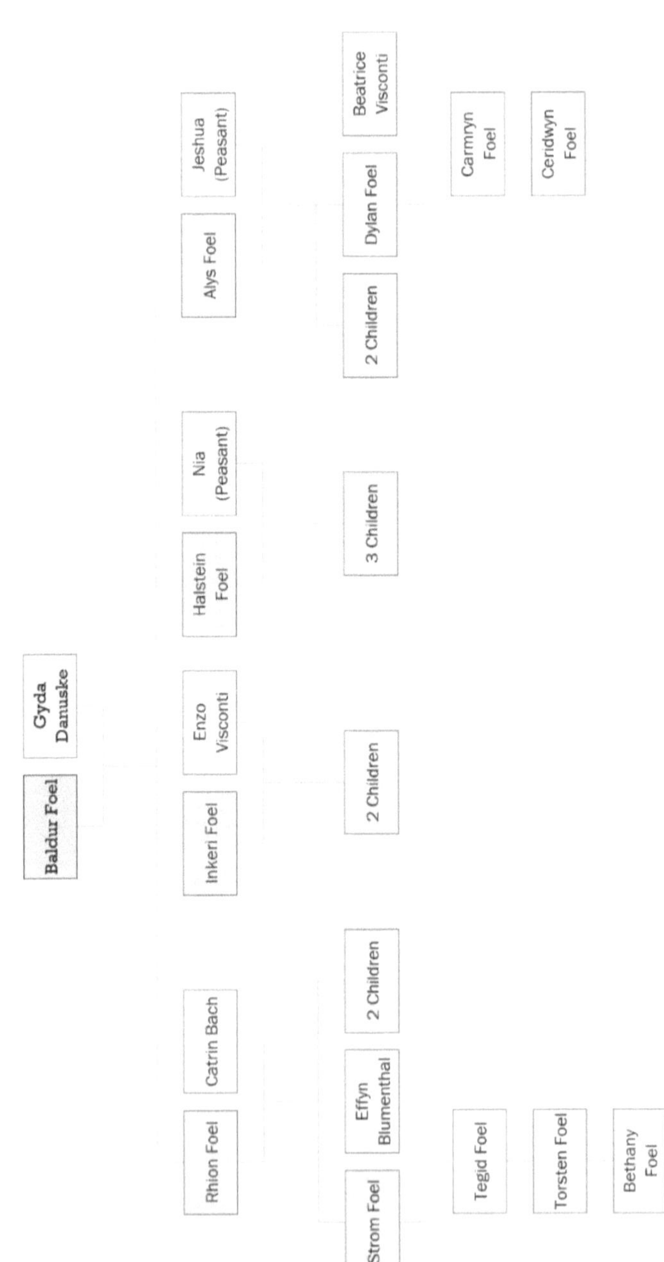

FOEL

Strom Foel
Effyn Blumenthal
Tegid Foel
Ceridwyn Foel
Torsten Foel
Yurika Vulgate
Bethany Foel
Lilwy Foel
Mordred Pendragon
Morphran Foel
Carian Foel
Alistair Foel
Reese Kelliweg
Shae Kelliweg

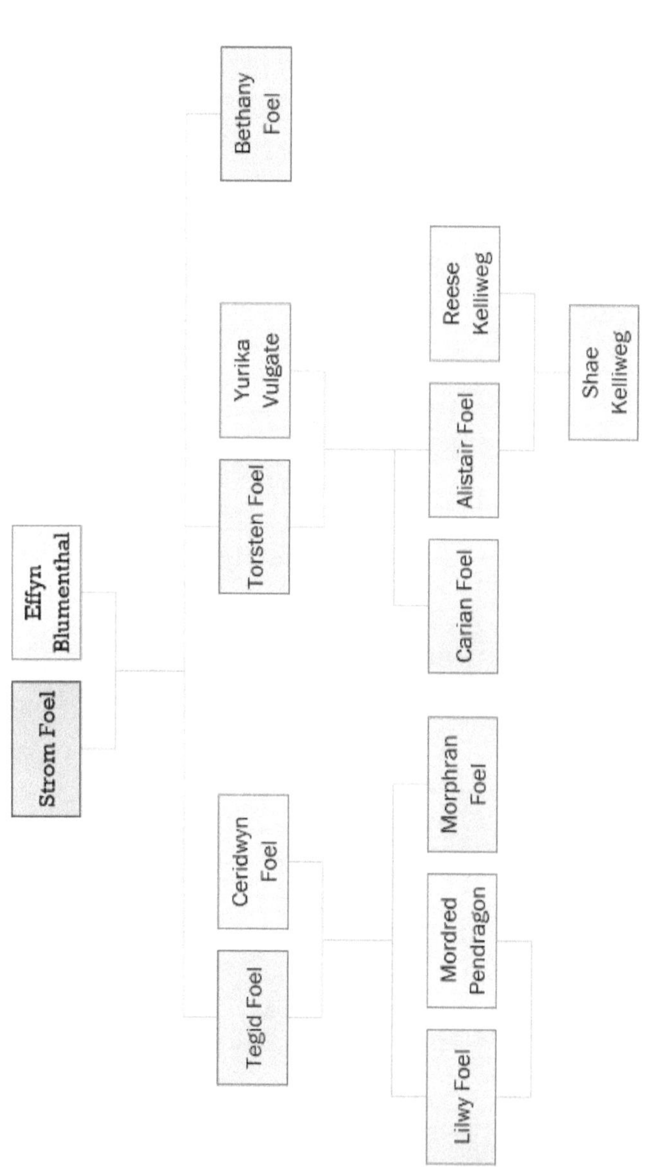

FOXBURY

Chandler Foxbury
Phyana (Peasant)

Darvon Foxbury
Yaletha (Peasant)

Cahir Foxbury
Dacy Foxbury
Thelia (Peasant)

Amonica Foxbury

Kesara Foxbury
Lounder Foxbury
Henley (Peasant)

Slade Foxbury

Renard Foxbury
Keely Blumenthal

Sydney Foxbury
Alcott Foxbury

Gavyn Foxbury

Garyth Foxbury

Gaheris Foxbury

Tippy Foxbury

FOXBURY

Renard Foxbury
Keely Blumenthal
Gavyn Foxbury
Collette Sagramore
Garyth Foxbury
Baudwyn Kelliweg
Gaheris Foxbury
No Spouse
Tippy Foxbury
Kae Kyner
Harlan Foxbury
Staunis Cornwall
10 Children
Rory Kyner

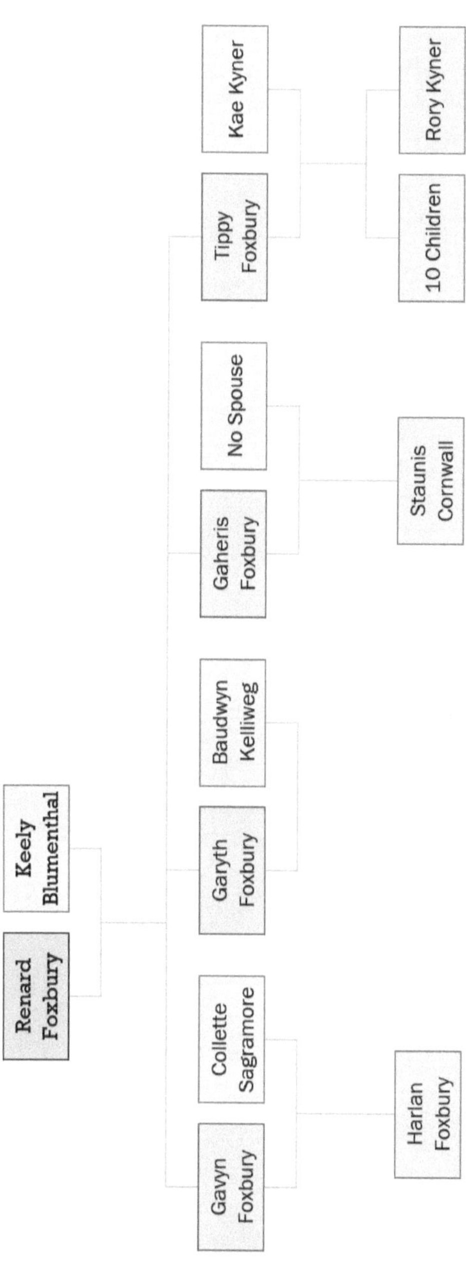

GORRE

Petunia Gorre
Charlus Esau
Iris Gorre
Uesugi Keisuke
Saris Gorre
Talon (Peasant)
Daniel Gorre
Marian (Peasant)
Edgaren Gorre
Amelia Ynyr
Jormund Wallach
3 Daughters
9 Children
Ewain Gorre
Lamorac Pellinore
3 Daughters
Devon Gorre
Glendis Cuhlwch
2 Children
Tavrina Cuhlwch
Kevyn Cuhlwch
Karen Gorre
Seren Wallach
Bedwyr Wallach
Iona Wallach
Olwen Wallach
Wysteria Wallach
Rowena Wallach
Daphne Wallach
Raito Wallach

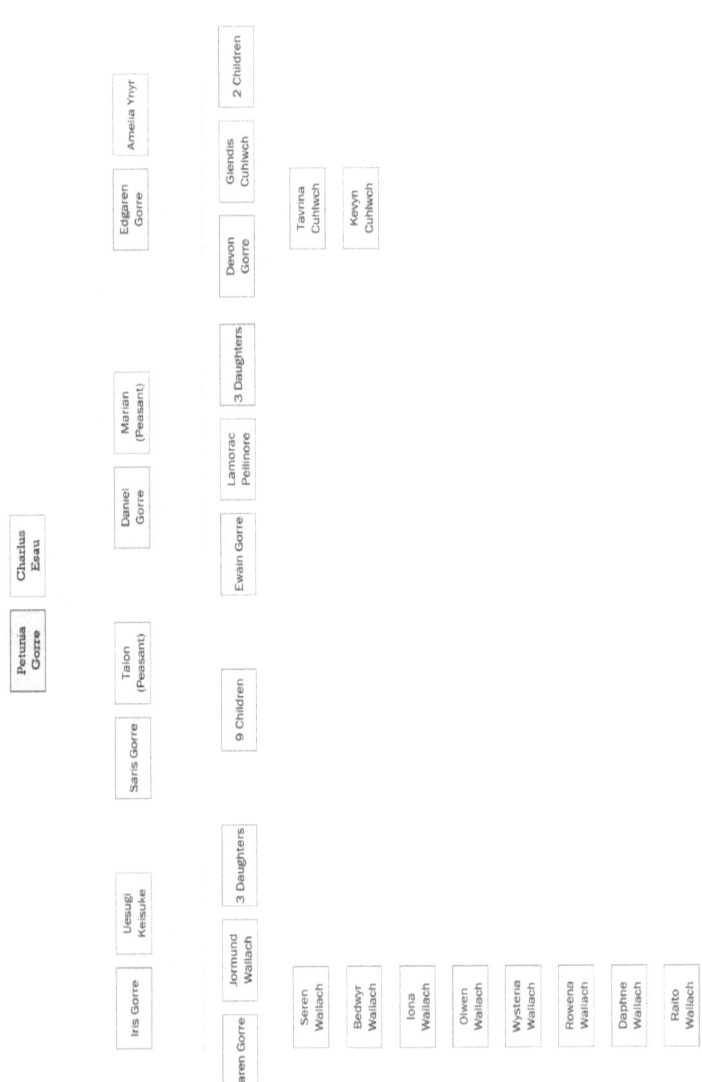

GRENDEL

Tedar Grendel
Sulynn
Cyrtrin Grendel
Jiranty Grendel
Stone
Glynn Grendel
Nobomi
Xola Grendel

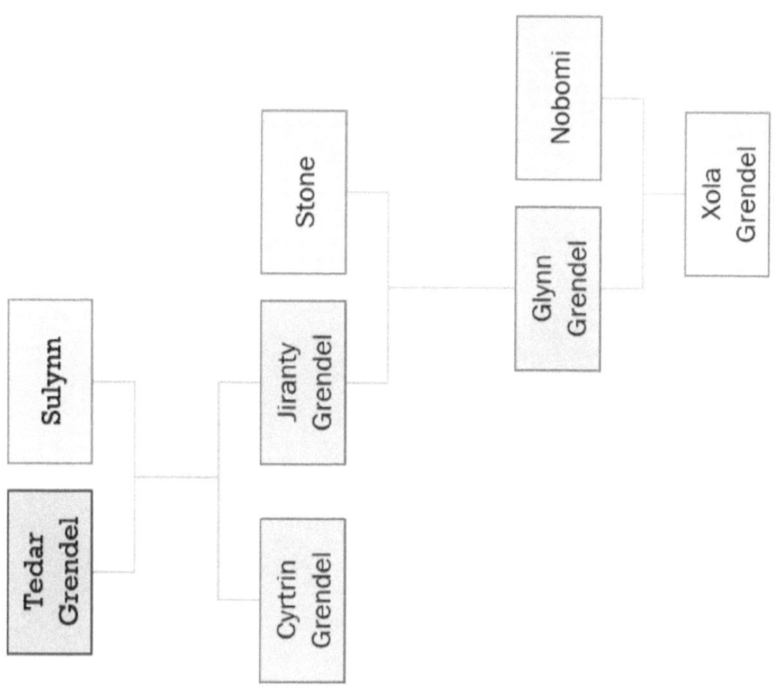

JOTNAR

Ivar Jotnar
Cristyn Cornwall
Ymir Jotnar
Carmryn Foel
Eydis Jotnar
Wilton Minkrune
Aren Jotnar
Reigna Foel
Harek Jotnar
Seirian Vulgate
Dub Foel
Dother Foel
Dain Foel
Brigid Minkrune
4 Children
Kalus Jotnar
5 Children
3 Children
Armand Jotnar

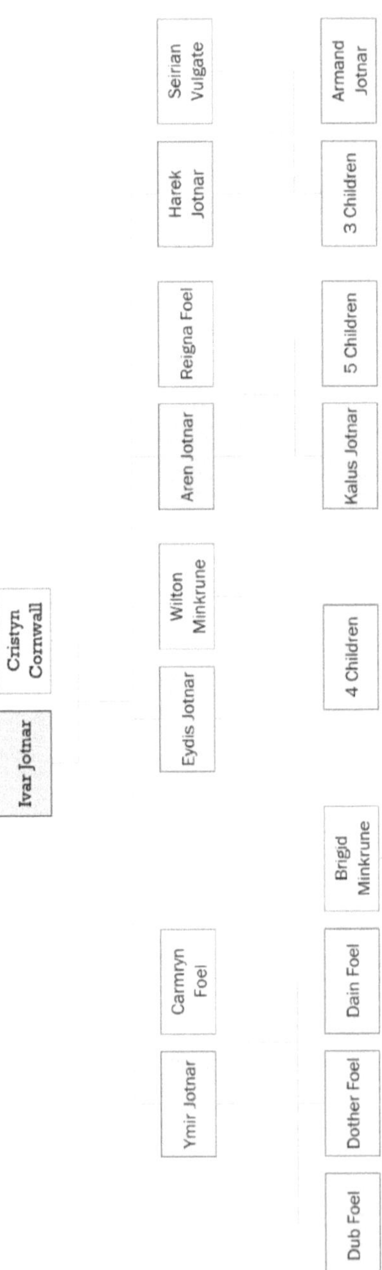

KELLIWEG

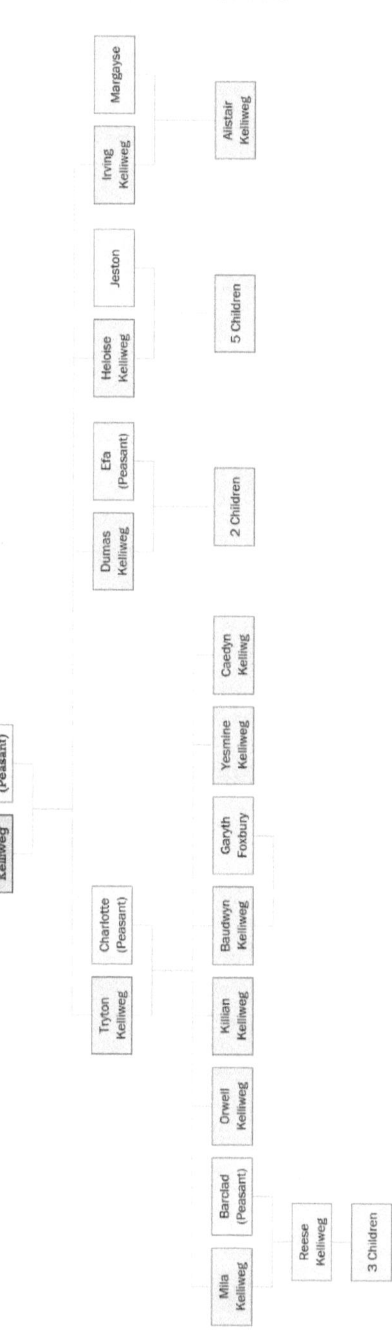

Byron Kelliweg
Mila (Peasant)
Tryton Kelliweg
Charlotte (Peasant)
Dumas Kelliweg
Efa (Peasant)
Heloise Kelliweg
Jeston
Irving Kelliweg
Margayse
Barclad (Peasant)
Orwell Kelliweg
Killian Kelliweg
Baudwyn Kelliweg
Garyth Foxbury
Yesmine Kelliweg
Caedyn Kelliweg
2 Children
5 Children
Alistair Kelliweg
Mila Kelliweg
Reese Kelliweg
3 Children

KYNER

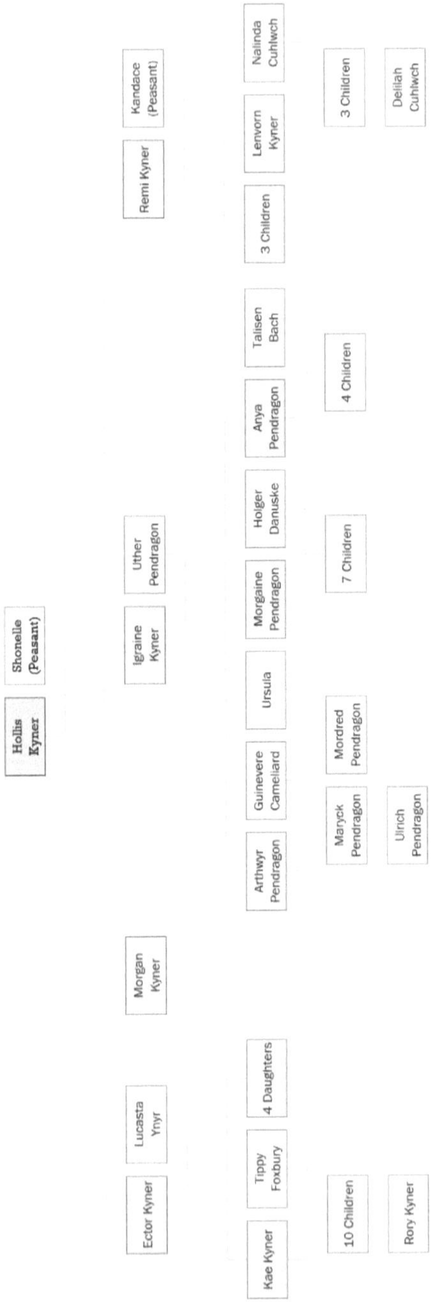

Hollis Kyner — Shonelle (Peasant)

Remi Kyner — Kandace (Peasant)

Igraine Kyner — Uther Pendragon

Morgan Kyner

Ector Kyner — Lucasta Ynyr

Arthwyr Pendragon — Guinevere Cameliard

Ursula — Morgaine Pendragon — Holger Danuske

Anya Pendragon — Talissen Bach

3 Children

Lenvorn Kyner — Nalinda Cuhlwch

3 Children

Delilah Cuhlwch

4 Children

7 Children

Maryck Pendragon — Mordred Pendragon

Ulrich Pendragon

Kae Kyner — Tippy Foxbury

4 Daughters

10 Children

Rory Kyner

MINKRUNE

Keigan Minkrune
Bedelia
Hansa Minkrune
Cuchulain Sagramore
Adara Minkrune
Colbum Danuske
Kenneth Minkrune
Estella Gorre
Cassadee Minkrune
Solon (Foreign Noble)
Osian Minkrune
Runa Bach
Harris Sagramore
Sowena Cornwail
4 Children
Jocelyn Sagramore
6 Children
2 Sons
Isaac Minkrune
Brigid Minkrune
Dain Foel
Aerona Minkrune
Kalus Jotnar
Cordelia Minkrune
Dilys Minkrune
Cyran Minkrune
4 Children

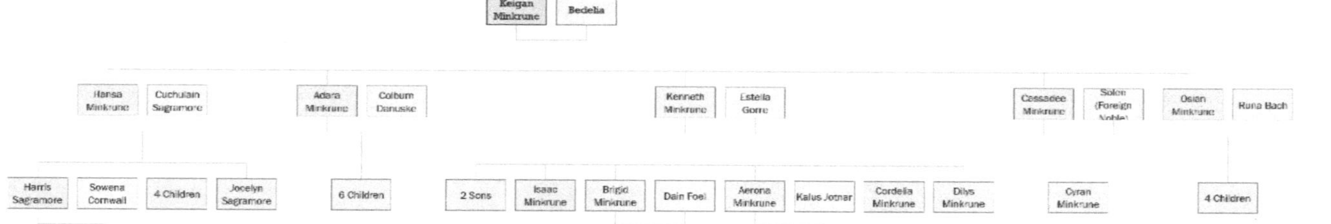

Pellinore

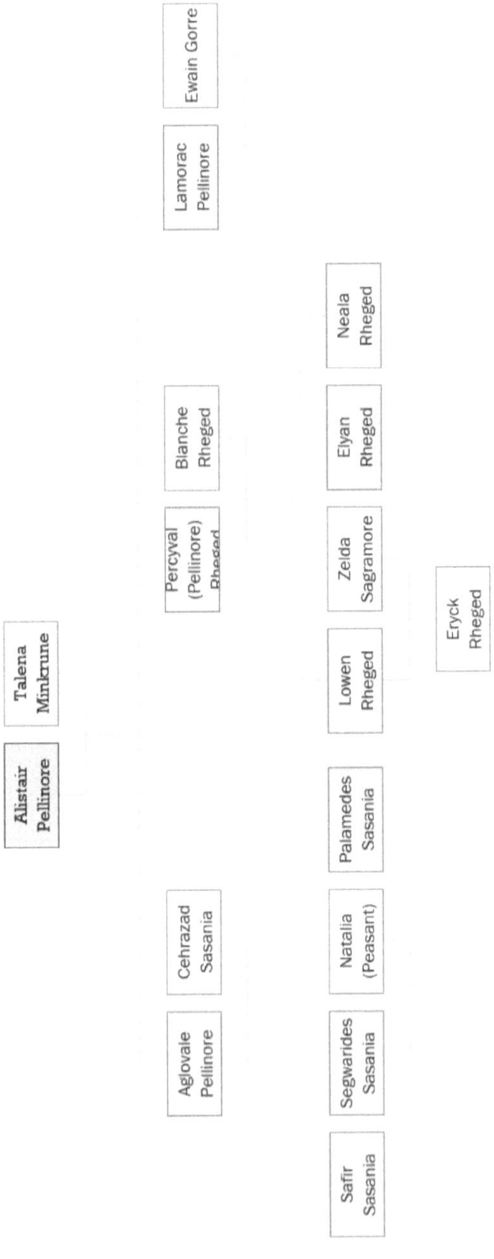

Alistair Pellinore — Talena Minkrune

Aglovale Pellinore — Cehrazad Sasania

Percyval (Pellinore) Rheged — Blanche Rheged

Lamorac Pellinore — Ewain Gorre

Safir Sasania

Segwarides Sasania

Natalia (Peasant)

Palamedes Sasania

Lowen Rheged

Zelda Sagramore

Elyan Rheged

Neala Rheged

Eryck Rheged

PEMBROKE

Terran Pembroke
Elenis Ynyr
Hadley Pembroke
Everest Pembroke
Nia Dyfed
Chantel Pembroke
Clevon Pembroke
Craig Pembroke
Wrenley Rheged
Glenys Pembroke
Landon Pembroke

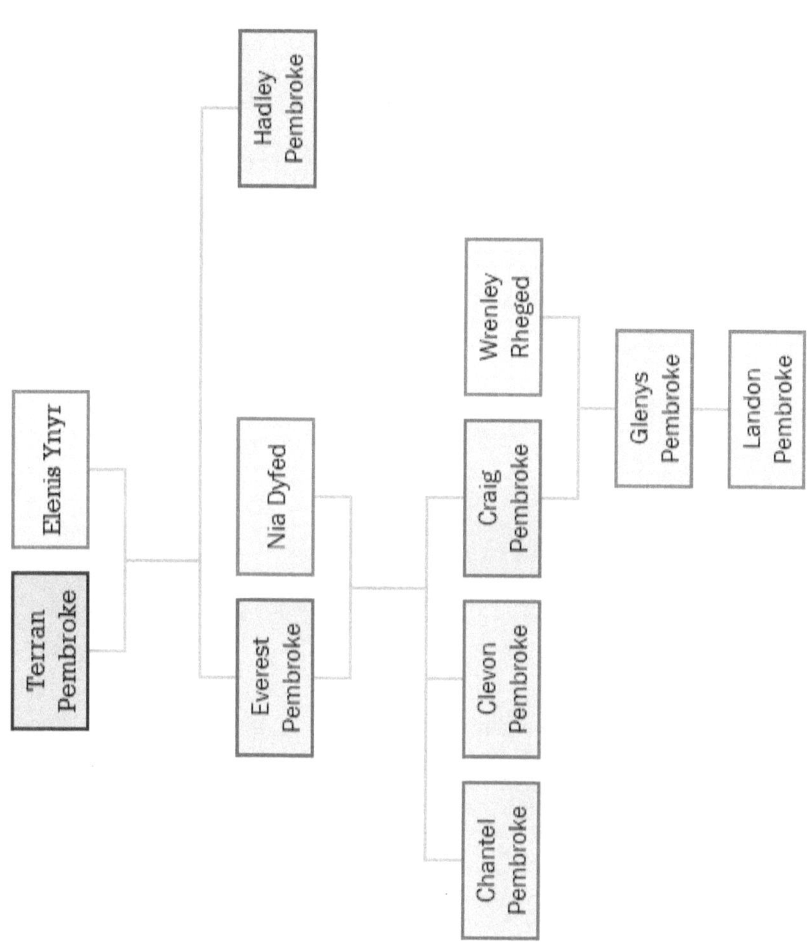

PENDRAGON

Celeste Tallut
Micah Vagary
Dagonet Vagary
Talisen Bach
Anya Pendragon
3 Children
Holger Danuske
Morgaine Pendragon
4 Children
Ursula
Igraine Kyner
Guinevere Cameliard
Mordred Pendragon
Aelwyn
Uther Pendragon
Arthwyr Pendragon
Maryck Pendragon
Ulrich Pendragon
Constans Pendragon

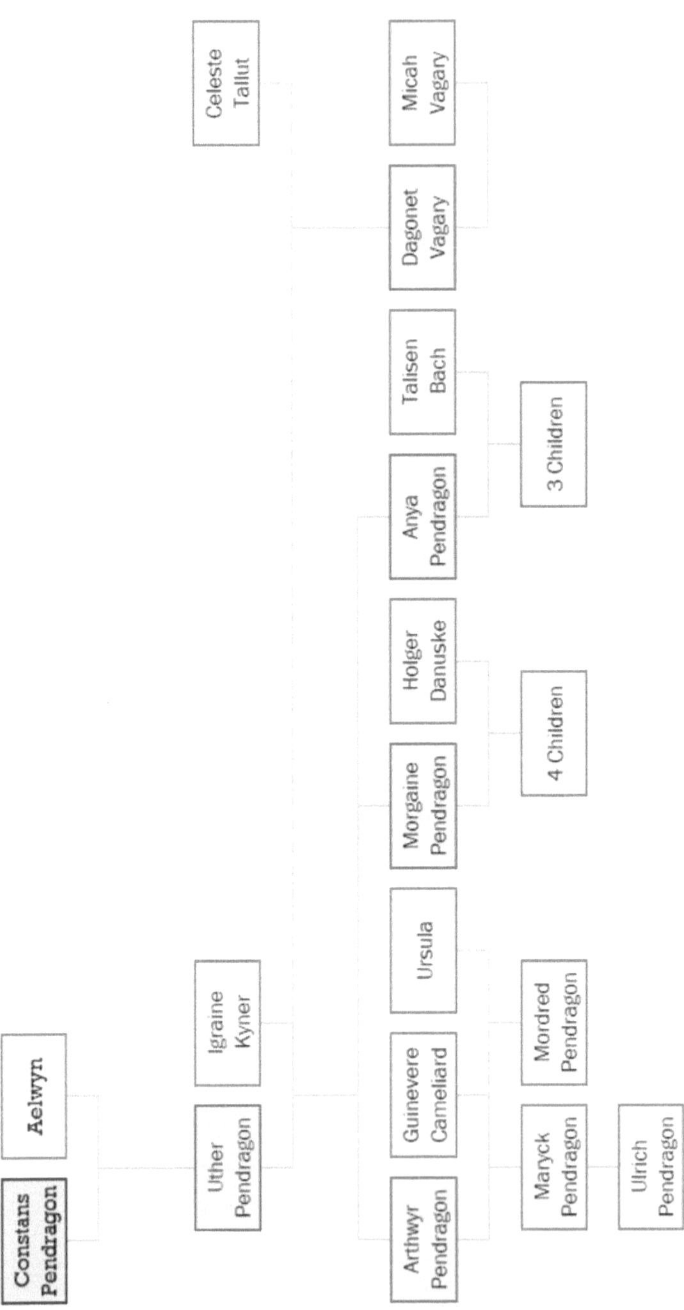

Rheged

Bran Rheged
Glenys Pembroke
Ronne Rheged
Adele Camelliard
Reddrom Rheged
Rhia Rheged
Raylynn Rheged
Lynette Ynyr
Bevan Rheged
Sian Cornwall
Korvyn Rheged
Blanche Rheged
Fianna Rheged
Keana Rheged
Moyna Rheged
Trudy Rheged

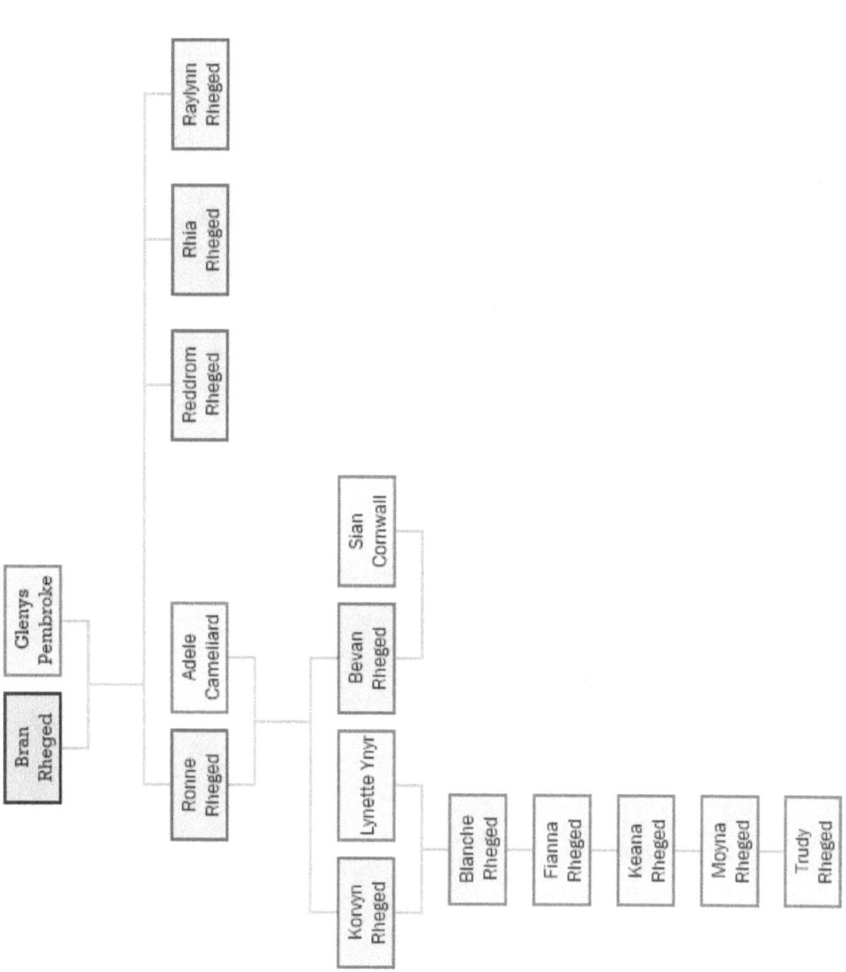

RHEGED

Korvyn Rheged
Lynette Ynyr
Blanche Rheged
Percyval Pellinore
Fianna Rheged
Keana Rheged
Moyna Rheged
Hagan Cuhlwch
Trudy Rheged
Xavier Cuhlwch
Lowen Rheged
Zelda Sagramore
Neala Rheged
Elyan Rheged
Eryck Rheged

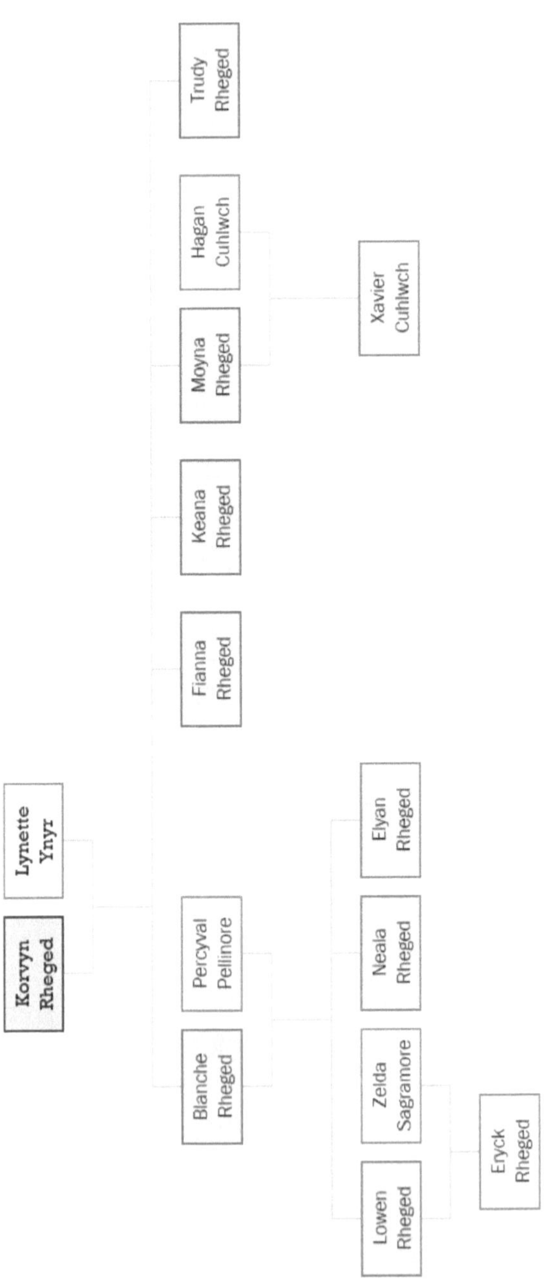

SAGRAMORE

Wyndel Sagramore
Corla
Elven Noble
Cuchulain Sagramore
Hansa Minkrune
2 Children
Zelda Sagramore
Lowen Rheged
Coillette Sagramore
Gavyn Foxbury
Eryck Rheged
Harlan Foxbury
Renee Foxbury
Harris Sagramore
Sowena Cornwall
4 Children
Jocelyn Sagramore
Algar Sagramore
Dresmene Cornwall
4+ Children
Tremayne Cornwall
Felicia Cornwall
Constance Cornwall

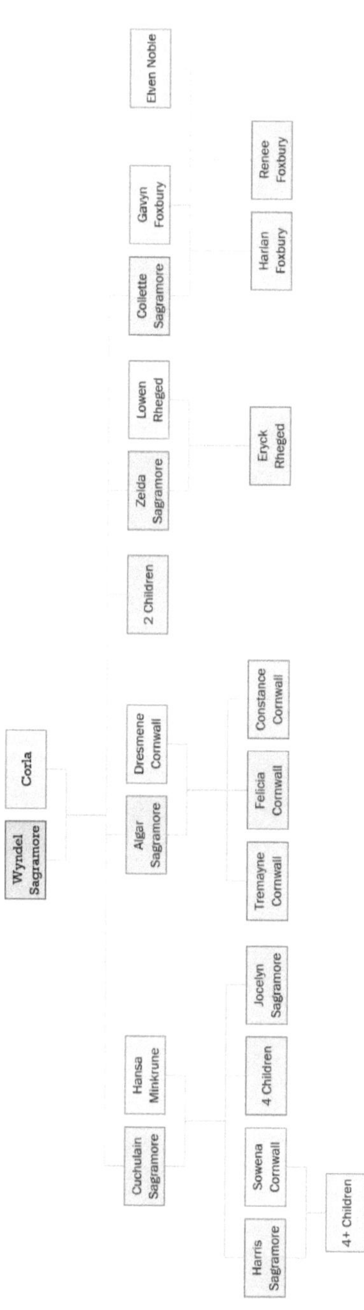

SASANIA

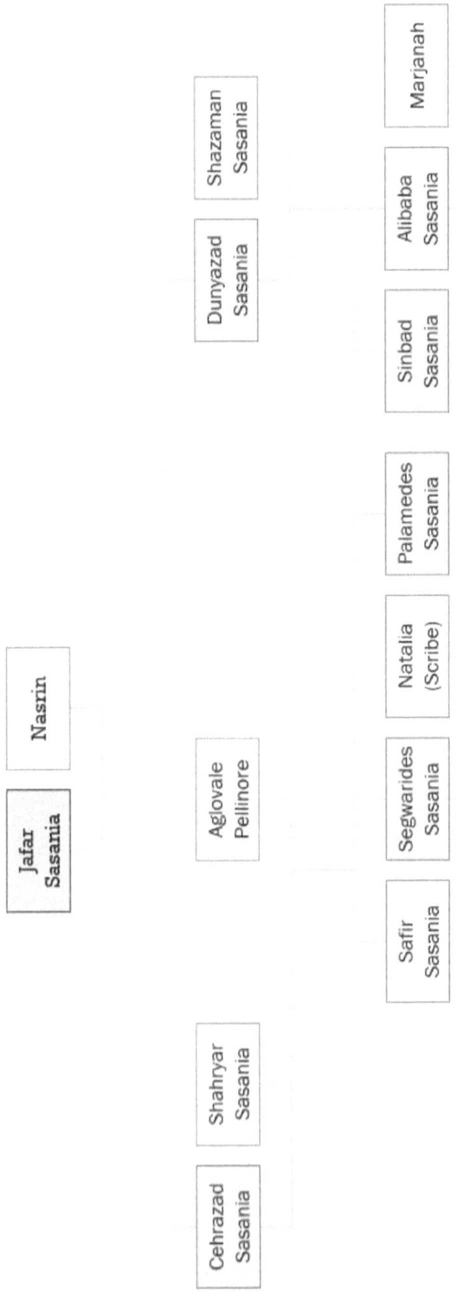

Jafar Sasania — Nasrin

Shahryar Sasania

Cehrazad Sasania

Aglovale Pellinore

Dunyazad Sasania

Shazaman Sasania

Safir Sasania

Segwarides Sasania

Natalia (Scribe)

Palamedes Sasania

Sinbad Sasania

Alibaba Sasania

Marjanah

Sforza

Giovanni Attendolo
Elisa Petraccini
Muzio Attendolo Sforza
Antonia
3 Mistresses
Lucia Marsciano
8 Children
Bosio Sforza
Cecilia Aldobrandeschi
Griselda Sforza
Francesco Sforza
Bianca Maria Visconti
Gregorio Alessandro Sforza
Costanza Varano
3 Children
Francesco Sforza
12 Children
Costanzo Sforza
3 Children

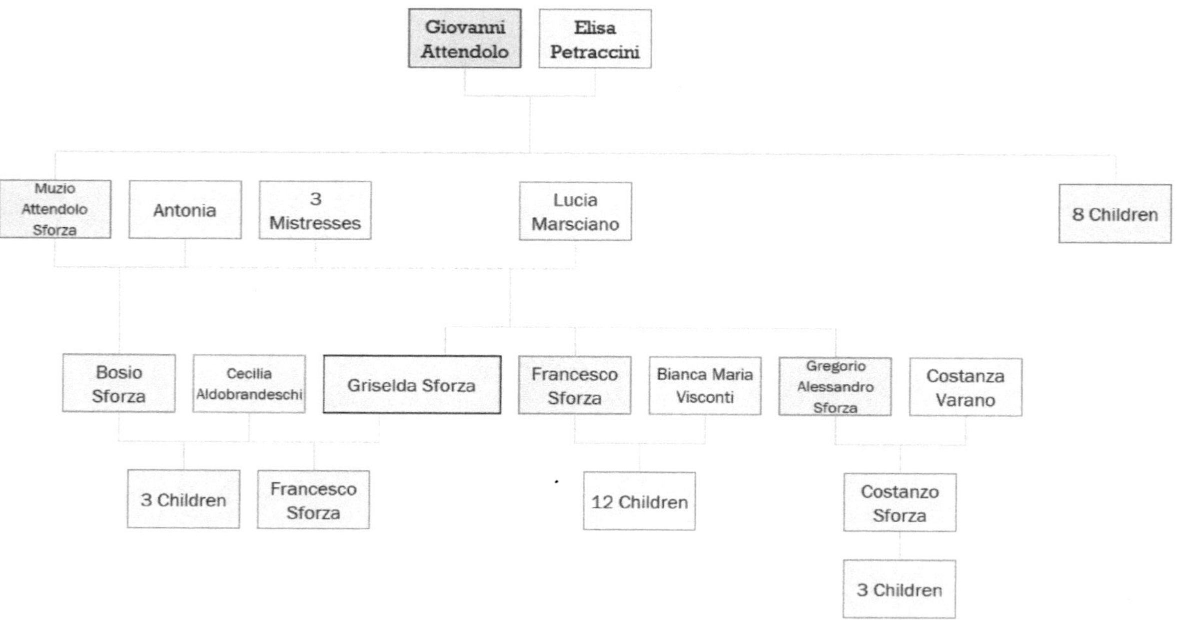

SFORZA

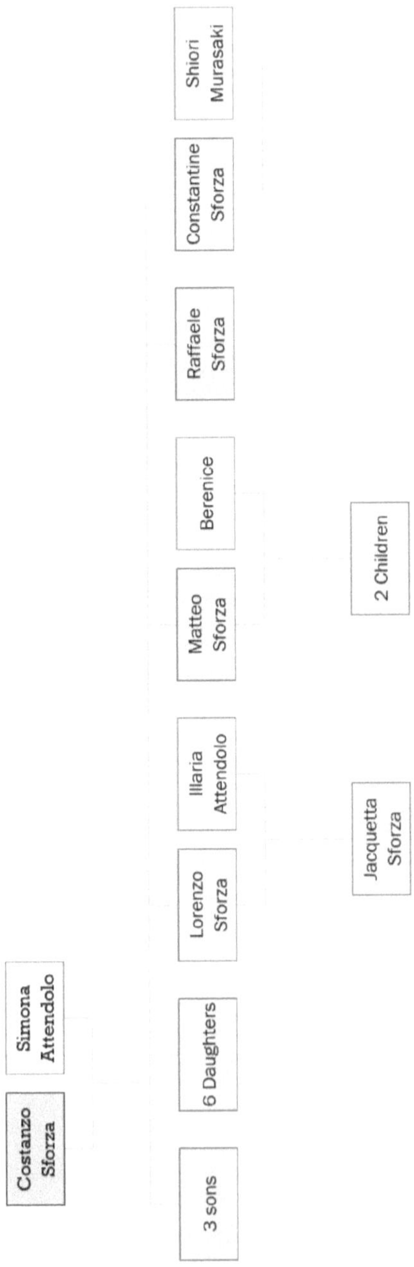

Costanzo Sforza

Simona Attendolo

Lorenzo Sforza

Illaria Attendolo

Matteo Sforza

Berenice

Raffaele Sforza

Constantine Sforza

Shiori Murasaki

3 sons

6 Daughters

Jacquetta Sforza

2 Children

VISCONTI-FOEL

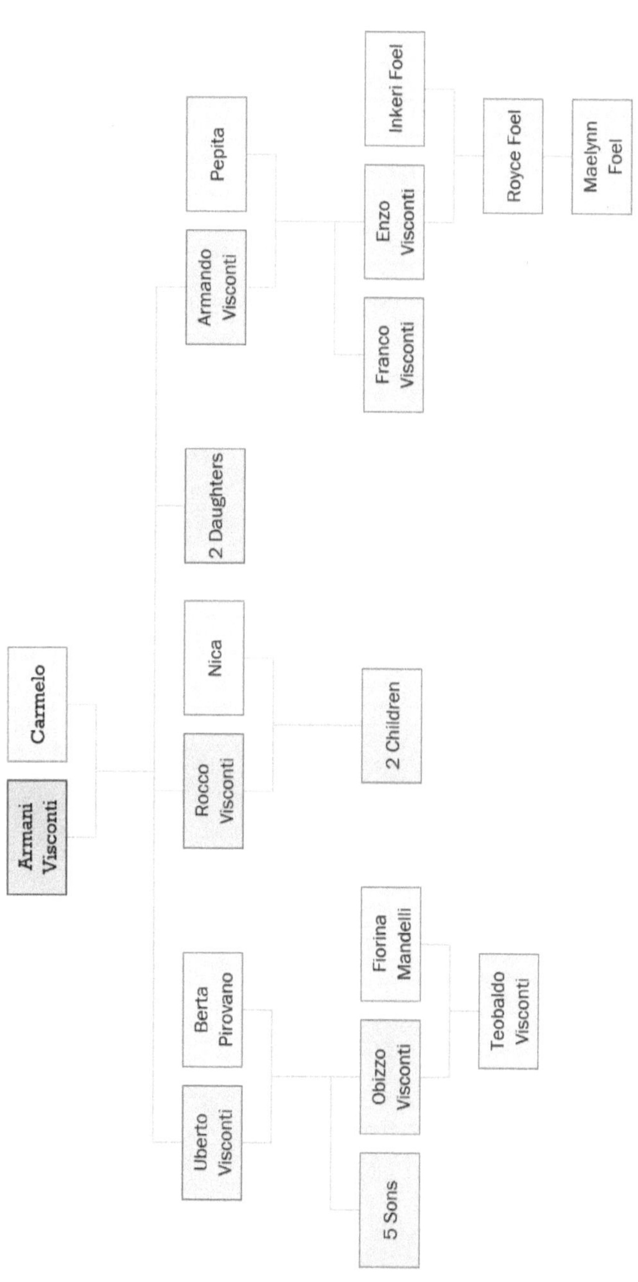

VISCONTI

Teobaldo Visconti = Anastasia Pirovano

Matteo Visconti = Bonacossa Borri

Galeazzo Visconti = Beatrice d'Este

Giovanni Visconti

Luchino Visconti

Stefano Visconti = Valentina Doria

Azzone Visconti

Matteo Visconti II

Bernabo Visconti

Galeazzo Visconti

VISCONTI

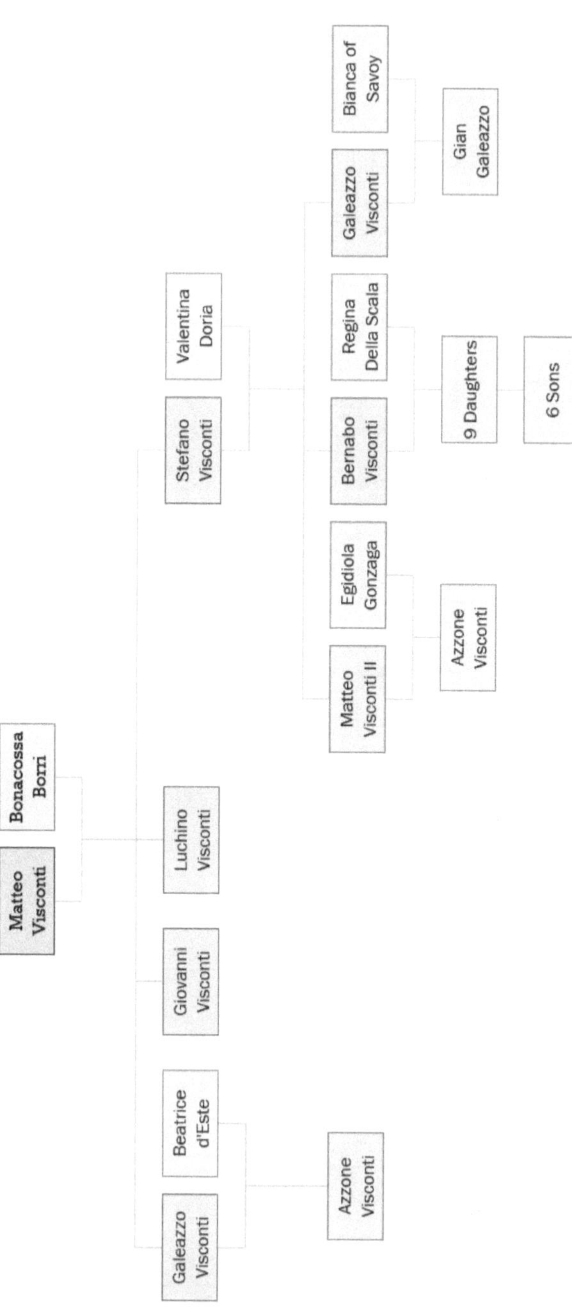

VISCONTI-SFORZA

VULGATE

Lorian Vulgate
Ingrid von Allemani
Medraut Vulgate
Delwys Bach
Kynan Vulgate
Elvinia
Enwen Vulgate
Bedraynt Wallach
Mercedes de la Gallia
Yurika Vulgate
Torsten Foel
Aeron Vulgate
Bristol
4 Children
Braylon Vulgate
Torina DuLac
Jormund Wallach
Karen Gorre
Llewdwyn Vulgate
Marhaus Vulgate
2 Sons
Agravaine Vulgate
3 Daughters
Carian Foel
Alistair Foel
Henri Vulgate
Siarl Vulgate
Julie Vulgate
4 Children
7 Children
Bedwyr Wallach

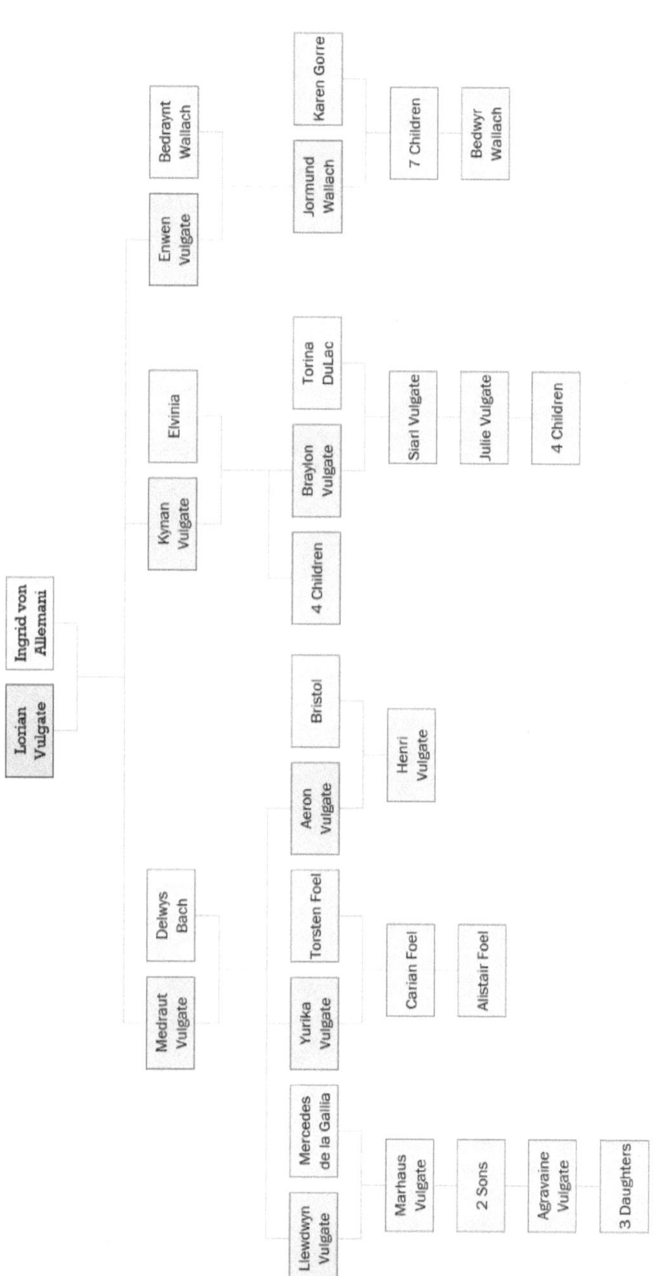

WALLACH

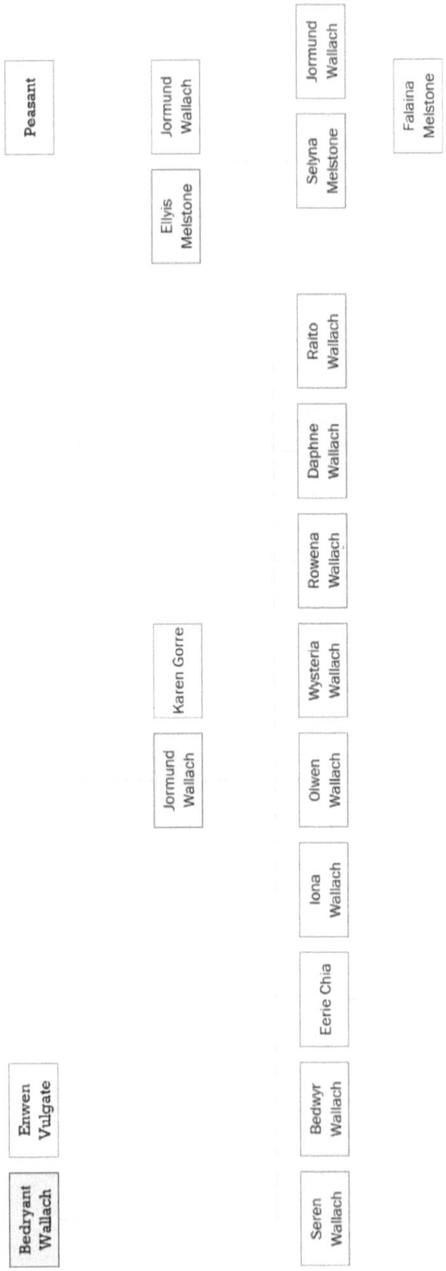

Peasant

Jormund Wallach

Ellyis Melstone

Jormund Wallach

Selyna Melstone

Falaina Melstone

Raito Wallach

Daphne Wallach

Rowena Wallach

Karen Gorre

Wysteria Wallach

Jormund Wallach

Olwen Wallach

Iona Wallach

Eerie Chia

Bedwyr Wallach

Seren Wallach

Enwen Vulgate

Bedryant Wallach

Huzzah!

Thank you kindly for embarking upon this quest. The next epic adventure with West and East Evermore arrives for *Chronicles of Evermore: Rise of the East* next year.

You can Follow me on social media at:

Twitter: ChroniclesofEvermore (@Graham_Rivers1) / X

Facebook: www.facebook.com/chroniclesofevermore

Instagram: www.instagram.com/chroniclesofevermore/

Website: www.ChroniclesOfEvermore.com/

If you enjoyed this chapter in the saga, please review at your favourite haunts like Amazon, Barnes and Noble, or Goodreads.